ARBOR
VITAE

SUSAN X MEAGHER

ARBOR VITAE

ISBN 0-9770885-0-2

THIS TRADE PAPERBACK ORIGINAL IS PUBLISHED BY BRISK PRESS, NEW YORK, NY 10011

FIRST PRINTING: FEBRUARY 2006

—

Acknowledgements

Thanks to my partner for her help, support and patience, which is nearly endless. Without her I wouldn't have the time or energy to write about life, love and relationships.

Thanks to Daylene, Anne, Melanie, Cindy, Kat, Karen and Lori for reading this story at various stages of its life. I know the story is better because of their help and encouragement.

Other books by Susan X Meagher

I Found My Heart in San Francisco

Awakenings

Beginnings

Coalescence

Disclosures

Anthologies

Undercover Tales

The Milk of Human Kindness

Infinite Pleasures

Telltale Kisses

At First Blush

For further information visit the author's website

www.sxmeagher.com

CHAPTER ONE

One word came to mind when Clancy O'Connor pulled her truck up to the address she'd been searching for. *Wow.*

Not normally one at a loss for words, the young woman had come upon a place that seemed to have that effect on her. She checked her clipboard carefully to make sure and then hopped out of the pickup. Self-consciously, she dusted off her spruce-green cotton shirt and smoothed out some of the wrinkles in her khaki cargo shorts.

Casting a quick glance down, she noticed that she had chosen gray socks, which now peeked out of the tops of her dark brown, ankle-length work boots, and was thankful that she had chosen a sedate pair. Her bright yellow ones with green cows might not be appreciated.

Leaning over so she could see her reflection in the large side-view mirror, she bent from the waist and tried to remove some of the white dust that had settled in her hair. She knew it would do little good, and she reminded herself to try to schedule client meetings first thing in the morning...especially when a trip to the quarry was on the agenda.

When she had herself looking as presentable as she could manage, she checked her pocket watch, which hung from a stainless-steel carabiner on her wide leather belt, and noted she was right on time. Looking into the mirror again, she tried out her most confident, professional, yet friendly smile and decided she was ready.

Her heart was beating a little quickly, and she wiped her damp hands on her shorts before taking a calming breath and ringing the buzzer on the gate. She rocked back and forth on her heels, trying to bleed off some of her nervous energy, and jumped noticeably when a buzzer rang out harshly.

Guessing correctly, she pushed open the pedestrian gate and stood stock-still for a moment, enraptured by the magnificent home. It was her favorite style, an authentic Craftsman. Clad in weather-darkened brown shingles, its exposed rafter ends and knee braces under the long, low eaves gave the home a distinctive and distinguished look. A broad, deep porch ran the width of the house, the overhanging roof supported by massive river-rock columns. The river rock also covered the chimney and foundation, aesthetically tying the large, rambling home together.

She knew the homeowner would be waiting, so she stopped staring and started walking. Her boots crunched over the leaves littering the macadam, and the profusion of flowers and shrubs calmed her a little, as beautiful plants always did. The drive was long and curving, and she was so mesmerized by the great variety and the uniqueness of the plants she encountered that she nearly collided with the woman standing on the top step of the porch. Clancy stumbled backward, her foot missed the bottom step, and she was dumped unceremoniously onto her seat.

"Are you all right?" The woman's worried gaze searched Clancy from head to toe. Then a pair of strong, sure hands reached for her and slid down from her shoulders to grasp her elbows lightly.

Biting back a curse at her clumsiness, Clancy nodded and tried to get to her feet, but the strong hands held her right where she was. "Are you sure you're all right? You shouldn't move until you're certain."

Her heart was still racing from adrenaline, and Clancy consciously tried to calm herself. "I'm fine. Clumsy and distracted, but fine."

The hands left her arms, and the woman stood, revealing her impressive stature. She looked at least eight feet tall, but Clancy realized that her perspective was skewed by the fact that she was still sitting on her ass. Once the landscaper was standing, the women's heights were significantly equalized, and Clancy realized that her prospective client was only a couple of inches taller than she.

"Abby Graham," the client said in a smooth voice. "That first step is a doozy."

"Clancy O'Connor." She shook Abby's hand firmly. "I wish it was the steps. It's the stepper. I was looking at your flowers and forgot where I was. Who does your landscaping?"

"Oh, I use a nice young man—Refugio Lopez."

Clancy's eyebrows shot up. "I know Refugio, and he is a nice guy, but he's a 'mow, blow, and go' guy. This was done by an artist."

Abby shrugged, looking surprisingly shy. "Oh, I thought you wanted to know who cut the grass. I, uhm…I suppose that I did the design."

"You did this?" Clancy turned and extended her hands, pointing at the lush garden. "And you're calling *me* for help with your landscape?"

With a laugh that was nearly musical, Abby inclined her head. "Do you really like it?"

"I love it! It's got everything that most landscape designs lack!"

"Such as?" Abby asked, not so subtly fishing for a compliment.

Warming even more to her subject, Clancy took a few steps and got down on her knees. She lovingly caressed a border of perennial shrubs, annual flowers, and a few bulbs—all clustered together. "Just in this one little patch you've got four seasons of color, six different shades of green, and five heights. There's enough visual interest in just this patch to attract and hold my attention for a good ten minutes! And this is just a tiny, tiny part of the border." She got up and gazed at Abby with a wide smile. "You've got a real talent here, and I'm being completely honest when I wonder what you could possibly need me for."

Abby beamed. The smile lit up her whole face, highlighting merrily dancing eyes. "You have no idea how much I needed that little boost today. Thank you."

Clancy cocked her head and took a long look at the woman, noting that she was quite attractive. But lurking right behind the bright eyes and wide smile was a pall of sadness. Clancy was surprised when she felt an urge to boost the woman's spirits. "I do suck up to clients," she revealed, her voice dropping to a conspiratorial whisper, "but in this case, I don't have to."

Still grinning, Abby said, "I'm gonna take that on faith and believe every word. Come on inside, and we can talk. She turned and opened the door, waiting for Clancy to enter. "I was surprised you didn't pull into the drive."

Clancy took a few more steps, debating how honest to be. "I'm not used to working on homes this nice," she admitted, a slightly sheepish look on her face. "I've never been to a home with a gated entrance, and I didn't know what I was supposed to do."

"I think the gate is a little ostentatious, to tell you the truth. But it does keep door-to-door salespeople from waking me up on a Saturday morning."

They reached the kitchen, and Abby said, "Tell me all about yourself. I'd love to hear about your background."

"There's not much to tell," Clancy said, taking a stool at the breakfast bar. "I've had my license for two years and I've been busy the whole time, but most of my jobs have been fairly small." She nodded when Abby produced a pitcher of lemonade. "Honestly, I'm surprised that you found me. Where did you get my number?"

Abby smiled and set a frosty glass in front of her. "From the Gay and Lesbian Yellow Pages."

The glass was nearly to her lips, and Clancy thanked the heavens that she hadn't taken a sip. Spitting a mouthful of lemonade on a new client was never a good idea. She was so flummoxed by the fact that Abby was gay that she couldn't even attempt a response.

Abby continued, "I make it a rule to support women professionals if I can." Her nose wrinkled in a grin as she added, "You were the only landscape architect in the book. By the way, I loved the little rainbow-colored tree in your ad. That's a very cute touch."

"Thanks. I don't use it in all of my ads, since most straight people wouldn't understand the connection. That's my special gay-people ad."

"Well, it really caught my eye." Abby winked and added, "But again, you *were* the only architect."

Clancy barked out a laugh and said, "That's true, but there're a few landscapers and garden designers listed. Did you consider them?"

"No. I wanted an architect. The job I want to have done is complex. The person I hire has to have the proper training and credentials."

Clancy looked at the woman carefully, letting her mind settle around the information she was learning about Abby. The tall, thin woman looked fit and healthy, and Clancy guessed that she participated in some regular form of exercise. Her hair was short and colored an attractive salt and pepper, with pepper predominating. It was tough to guess her age, but Clancy had a feeling that her gray hair was premature.

An unlined, tanned face with a strong jaw and deep-set blue eyes made for a terrifically attractive package, and Clancy felt her heartbeat pick up again as she wondered whether the woman was partnered. Deciding to go for broke, she tried to frame the question without being too obvious. "So do you live alone?" she asked, nearly biting her tongue as the words tumbled out.

Another flash of pain washed across Abby's face, and Clancy mentally kicked herself once again. The strong chin tilted down, and Abby's eyes stared blankly toward the floor for just a moment. "Yes, I suppose I do live alone," she said quietly. She shook her head briefly, and Clancy was stunned to see a few tears slide down her cheek. Abby wiped at them angrily, muttering, "I'm sorry. I've had a very tough weekend."

"I'm really sorry to hear that," Clancy said. She continued to gaze at Abby, trying to show her interest and concern.

Abby looked at her briefly and then continued. "Yesterday was my birthday, and I'd been fantasizing that my daughter would come home and surprise me." She shook her head and muttered, "Silly."

"Where does she live?" Clancy asked gently.

"The poor thing is a freshman at UC Santa Cruz. She has finals soon, and I would've been upset with her if she'd spent the whole weekend traveling down here." Giving Clancy a slightly embarrassed glance, she said, "I set myself and my daughter up in a no-win situation. She wanted to come home, but I told her not to. She really pressed me, but I held firm. But then I kept imagining that she'd come anyway." She bit her lip as if trying to keep her emotions under control. "I've never been alone on my birthday. It was…much harder than I thought it'd be."

Clancy spared a quick look at Abby's ring finger. The left hand was bare of adornment, and the landscaper tentatively asked, "Are you…single?"

With a sad smile, Abby nodded. "My husband died five years ago…this week. Every year, on the anniversary of his death, I've focused on the fact that it would be easier the next year. I thought that I'd be free of the grief by now." She shook her head slightly and said, "I'm not."

"Were you together long?" Clancy asked, forcing herself to ignore her mild disappointment that the woman obviously wasn't a lesbian.

"Twenty years. We had twenty wonderful years together, and I have two fabulous children who constantly remind me of the love we shared." She looked away again and whispered hoarsely, "Sometimes all of that just isn't enough."

"I can't imagine," Clancy said. "It must be wonderful to have loved someone so much—but so hard to go on alone."

"It is. I wouldn't trade the years we had together for anything on earth, but the devastation is greater than I could've imagined." She sighed deeply and leaned over to wipe her eyes with her hands. When her body shifted, Clancy saw a simple gold band on a thin gold chain fall from her yellow-and-blue print blouse. Abby tucked it back in and tried, rather unsuccessfully, to smile. "You probably think that I'm unstable, but I swear you're the first complete stranger I've ever unburdened myself to. There's something about you that makes me babble away. Do you have this effect on everyone?"

Clancy returned the smile. "I like talking to people. Always have. I used to spend my weekends in my mom's floral shop, chatting away with the customers."

"Ah. Is that where you developed your love of flowers?"

"Yeah. I suppose so. Little did I know that all of those weekends would pay off someday."

"I'd be happy to sit in the kitchen and gab all day," Abby said, "but I'm sure you have other appointments. Shall we take a look at the project I'm thinking of?"

"Sure. I blocked out three hours, so we're doing fine on time."

Abby shot her a warm grin and said, "You *must* like to talk if you block your time so generously."

"Well, the first meeting is the most important one, so I like to spend as much time as possible to get to know both the project and the client. If you like me and think I can do the work, that's half the battle."

"Then a quarter of the battle is over," Abby said, and Clancy grinned with genuine pleasure at the thought that this lovely woman already liked her.

When Abby opened the double French doors in the rear of the kitchen, a pair of dogs raced into the room like twin bolts of lightning. Ignoring their owner, they made their way to Clancy, tails wagging so quickly that they were mere blurs. Clancy immediately sank to the floor, exclaiming in delight, "What do we have here?"

"These," Abby said, "are the result of a suggestion my grief counselor made. She thought that bringing some new life into the house would help us get through the rough patches. We picked them up three years ago—also this week," she added. "My counselor thought it would give us a boost to get through the anniversary." Speaking in an excited voice, she said, "We've got to have a celebration, girls! It's the anniversary of your adoption."

At the sound of her voice, the dogs started jumping and then spinning around in tight circles. Both women laughed at their exuberance, and when the pups heard Clancy's laugh, they set upon her with a vengeance.

"What kind of dogs are they?" Clancy asked, giggling as her face was licked in a mad frenzy.

"They're Portuguese Water Dogs," Abby said. "I can make them stop, if you mind."

"Not a bit. I love dogs." Clancy looked at the pair, saw some vague similarity, and wondered aloud, "Are they related?"

"They're from the same litter," Abby said. "Artemis here is a black-and-white particolor with a wavy coat, and Athena is a black-and-white with a curly coat."

"Cute names," Clancy said. "Are you the goddess of the Amazons, puppy?" She tickled Artemis under the chin and laughed when Athena pushed her way past her sister to get some special attention.

"My daughter had a brief fascination with mythology," Abby said. "I put my foot down at Aphrodite for this one." She indicated the curlier dog. "I knew it would devolve into a nickname, and there was no way I was going to call the poor thing Aphro. Besides, I think Athena suits her better."

"They're adorable," Clancy said, sputtering as Athena gave her a wet lick right on the lips. "Friendly, too!"

"Yes," Abby said, chuckling softly. "They're Portuguese dogs, but they love to French-kiss."

"I've been out with women who weren't as skilled," Clancy said, getting to her feet with some difficulty. She heard the words come out of her mouth and visibly cringed. "Sorry," she mumbled. "That was…"

"Nonsense," Abby said. "I assumed you were gay when I called you, Clancy. It certainly doesn't bother me to have you refer to being with women." She saw the dogs begin to get too rambunctious, and she said in a firm voice, "Girls, leave Clancy alone for a moment. Down!" Both dogs gave her a quick look to ascertain her sincerity, and when they saw she meant business, they sat down right at Clancy's feet, waiting for permission to nibble on her again.

"Okay," Clancy said, looking slightly uncomfortable. To shift attention away from herself, she bent to give each dog a pat on the head. "Well-mannered dogs."

"You have to have a firm hand with Porties, or they'll run the house. Oh…I hope you don't mind if I call you Clancy," she added. "I didn't even think to ask."

"Of course not. Do you mind if I call you Abby?"

"All of my friends do," Abby said.

Clancy's smile was bright and happy. "Okay, Abby. Let's take a look at this project."

They walked outside, and Abby pointed to a steeply rising slope and an old, faded stockade fence running along the property line. "I want to have that fence taken down and put up a stucco wall."

"Okay, that's not too big a job," the architect said. "I'll just climb up and take a look." The hill was so steep that Clancy had to hold on to a few sturdy trees to get to the top. Then she walked along the property line for a few minutes, getting a feel for the space.

When she came back down, Abby looked up at the fence and said wistfully, "I'd love to be able to put up a nice, short wooden fence, just tall enough to keep the dogs in. But a young family has moved in up there, and their kids stand at the fence and drive the dogs absolutely mad. It didn't bother me too much at first, since they hear them barking more than I do, but I saw a little hand sticking through a gap in the fence the other day, feeding the dogs God-knows-what, and I decided I had to do something."

"Have you talked to the parents?"

"No," Abby said, shaking her head. "I want to have good relations with them, so I'd rather just eliminate the problem."

They spent a solid hour discussing what Abby thought she needed, and Clancy took notes the entire time, scribbling drawings and short sentences in a large, rubber-covered notepad. Clancy saw Abby's curious glance and patted the neon orange book. "I work in the rain a lot. This keeps everything nice and dry."

"Looking at the way you dress and the tools you carry makes me have confidence in you," Abby said.

Grinning broadly, Clancy said, "I take my work very seriously, Abby. I haven't had any big commissions yet, but I will. I treat each project like it's my own house— I care."

"I can see that. You have a very open face. I bet it's hard for you to get away with lying."

"No one's ever mentioned that," Clancy said, stone-faced.

"My God, you're horrible!" Abby laughed hard, and Clancy joined her. Immediately, the dogs started running around the yard, playfully biting each other and then running up and down the hill in a mad dash.

Wiping the tears from her eyes, Clancy asked, "Do they do that every time you laugh?"

"Only if I laugh…and it has to be a bellylaugh. I guess it's their way of joining in the fun." She watched the dogs for a moment as they calmed down and lay on the grass, their legs stretched out so the cool ground touched their bellies. "They haven't done that in a while. I guess it's my responsibility to laugh more so they can have fun, too."

"It's good for the whole family," Clancy said, happy to see three contented faces smiling at one another.

❧

The architect spent the next half-hour taking careful measurements with Abby, who eventually offered to help by taking notes for her. When she was finished, Clancy dusted herself off and said, "I'll work up a plan and get back to you by the end of next week. Does that sound good?"

"Perfect."

They walked out through the house, and when they got to the front porch, Clancy stood and stared out at the landscape, trying to take it all in. "If I lived here, I'd never get a thing done. I'd sit right on one of these comfy-looking chairs and let the world roll by while I watched my flowers grow."

"You know," Abby said, "that's exactly what I did on my birthday. I sat here most of the day, reflecting and letting the plants remind me of the cyclical nature of living things."

"Don't you have any other family, Abby? Any friends you could have spent the day with?"

Abby nodded. "Oh, sure, I have a lot of friends. And I could have spent the whole day with them. I did agree to have dinner with several of my buddies, but I wanted some time alone."

"To think?"

"Exactly," she said. "I didn't use to be so introspective, but since my husband died, I spend more time than I probably should thinking about life…and death."

Giving the woman a smile, Clancy found herself saying, "It's good to spend time thinking about life, 'cause we have a lot of power to make our lives better. But don't spend too much time thinking about death. It'll take care of itself."

Looking at the young woman for a few moments, Abby cocked her head and asked, "How are we doing on time?"

Taking a peek at her pocket watch, Clancy said, "I've got over an hour until my next appointment. Why?"

"How about joining me for lunch? We could sit out here and enjoy the plants."

"Lunch? Really?"

"Yeah. I'd love to spend some time with someone who appreciates the work I've done here. Most people just look at it and say, 'Nice lawn.'"

"You're on," Clancy said. "I could easily spend an hour talking about the fabulous drift of delphiniums you have on the little rise over by that beautiful ficus." She narrowed her eyes and said, "You created that rise, didn't you? Nice touch. I love to contour a flat expanse of lawn. It makes all the difference in the world."

"You're my kinda woman," Abby said. Her face lit up in a smile that erased ten years. "Have a seat while I go make up a fruit-and-cheese platter." She paused and asked, "You do eat cheese, don't you?"

"Any kind, any time," Clancy said, settling down to take in the setting.

❧

The hour passed far too quickly, and Clancy stood and brushed some crumbs from her shirt. "That was one of the nicest lunch hours I've had since I started working. I normally stop for a taco or a hamburger—if I have time to stop at all."

"Call me the next time you're in the neighborhood," Abby said. "I'd love the company."

Laughing, Clancy said, "I'm not in the neighborhood very often, but I'd gladly go out of my way to do this again."

Abby stood and started to walk Clancy to her truck, both dogs trotting along companionably as they walked down the long drive. "Now, next time, pull up to the gate and give a honk. I've got a closed-circuit camera so I can see who's waiting."

As they approached the truck, Abby chuckled slightly and added, "I think I'll be able to recognize you. You're the only person I know with a screaming-yellow truck."

"She's my baby." Placing her hand lovingly on the top rail of the bed, Clancy said, "My first big purchase."

"It's lovely," Abby said. "And it was even lovelier meeting you, Clancy. I look forward to working together."

Clancy knew she was grinning like an idiot, but she couldn't stop herself. "I'm psyched! This is gonna be fun!"

"I've never had fun having construction done at my house, but if it can be fun I bet you're the woman to do it."

"You betcha," Clancy said, practically vibrating with excitement as she got into her truck.

Clancy was sitting at her drafting table, chewing on the end of a drawing pencil, graph paper stuck to every horizontal surface. Her roommate, Michael, came up behind her and placed a hand on her shoulder, making her jump several inches. "Shit! I hate it when you scare me like that!"

"I swear that I don't try to sneak up on you," the man protested. "You just concentrate so hard that you don't hear me come in."

"What are you doing home this early anyway?" she asked absently, her attention already split between him and her drawings.

"It's eight-fifteen," he said. "That's not early."

She grabbed her watch and tilted it so she could see the face. "You're shitting me!"

"Nope. What are you working on, anyway? You've been tied to that chair every night this week."

"I'm doing the plans for that woman who lives on the Arroyo," she mumbled, a little embarrassed to have spent as much time on the plans as she had.

"You're working hard enough to relandscape the Rose Bowl," he said. "What's up with this job?"

She sighed, and rubbed her weary eyes with the back of a hand. "This is the biggest job I've ever had, Michael. This woman's obviously wealthy, and I bet she's got a lot of connections. There are a lot of people out there who'd probably love to hire me if they knew about me. I just haven't had a way to get a toehold with the movers and shakers. This woman might help me get there."

"I hope it works for you, baby," he said, ruffling his hand through her short hair.

"Thanks," she said, placing her hand atop his and giving it a pat. "I know you're my biggest fan."

"Is this mover and shaker…available?" Michael asked.

"Yes…kinda…and she's just my type."

"Oh, Lord, don't tell me," he said, rolling his eyes. "Does she have all of her own teeth?"

She slapped at him playfully. "I don't like them old! She's mature," she sniffed.

"She's old," he decided. "Come on, how old is she?"

"I'm not sure, but she's got a daughter in college." She shrugged at Michael's raised eyebrow and said, "I know you think it's a neurosis, but I happen to prefer women who've seen the world and know what they want from it."

"You," he teased, tweaking her nose, "prefer women who've seen the Second World War. But I still love you."

"I love you too, Michael. And I think Abby might have seen the Vietnam War, but that's as far as I'll go. She might be…oh, thirty-nine or forty. I'm sure she's younger than my parents."

"Oh, that's reassuring," he said, laughing. "Now take your nose out of those drawings and join me for a quick dinner."

She rubbed her empty stomach and said, "I didn't have lunch today. Good thing I've got a few spare pounds to carry me over."

He looked at her critically. "You've got a few spare muscles, but other than that, you can't afford to lose an ounce." He started to walk into the kitchen and then stopped. "You said she was 'kinda' available. What's that mean?"

"She probably thinks she's straight," Clancy said, wrinkling up her nose. "But she's a widow, so she's clearly available."

"Oh, God," he moaned. "Why don't you make things tough, Clance? Turning an old widow into a lesbian who's hot for you is just too easy!"

❧

A week after they'd met, Clancy sat at Abby's circular kitchen table, nervously smoothing out her plans. She had the drawings facing herself, not yet ready to share them with Abby. Clearing her throat, she began. "I've drawn a few different ideas, and I've written up an estimate for each of them. Ready to take a look?"

"I am," Abby said, her excitement obvious. "Let's see what you've got."

Clancy turned the first drawing around and showed Abby the wall just as the homeowner had envisioned it. "Here's the stucco wall," she said. "Nothing fancy, but very functional."

"This looks just fine," Abby said. "I can add some climbing plants, and in a few years, it won't look so stark. What's the estimate?"

"I could do this for around $17,500—painted, of course."

Raising an eyebrow, Abby paused for a moment and then nodded. "Okay, what else do you have?"

"Even though you said you wanted a plain wall, I thought a big expanse of white stucco could look awfully harsh. So I added this ceramic tile cap. Every ten feet, I put in a window of four glass blocks," she noted. "That way, the kids and the dogs can see each other but not touch each other."

Abby was staring at the design, studying it intently. "Well, first off, let me compliment you on the drawing. It's so lifelike, I could believe it was a photograph."

Adroitly twirling a pencil in her fingers, Clancy said, "I like to draw. I considered art school, but one day I realized that the only things I ever drew were trees and plants. Being a landscape architect allows me to merge all of my interests." She gave Abby an endearing grin and added, "Well, not all of them—but most of them." Slightly embarrassed by the double entendre, Clancy cleared her throat and tapped her pencil on the drawing. "What do you think of the design?"

"Inspired," Abby said. "The details you've added prevent it from looking like a big monolith."

"That's the idea," Clancy said, her excitement growing. "You have a lot of property here, and a stucco wall this large could look a little like a fortress."

Abby shuddered. "That's the last thing I want. How much would this cost?"

"With all of the details, this would run you about $20,000 if you don't go crazy on the tiles." She held her breath, hoping that the price wasn't more than Abby was willing to spend.

"Are you quite sure of that, Clancy?" Abby gazed into the architect's eyes with a curious look on her face.

"Uhm…yeah, I'm pretty sure. But I could look at it again and see if I can get the price down."

Abby held up a hand to stop her. "Either you're seriously underbidding, or the other architect I consulted was very overpriced. He gave me a quote of $25,000, and that was for plain stucco—unpainted."

Clancy's face flushed, and she felt herself searching for words. "I…I…"

"Clancy," Abby said, her voice low and quiet, "how much profit did you factor into your quote?"

"I wasn't gonna make much on the job," she admitted. Looking into Abby's eyes, she told her everything. "Making a profit isn't the most important thing to me on this job. Doing such good work that you'll tell all of your friends about me is what matters. I need more jobs like this, and I hope that you'll help me get them."

Abby nodded briefly, accepting the explanation for the moment. "Show me what else you have hidden there."

With a definite gleam in her eyes, Clancy pulled out the next design. "This one occurred to me when I spent some time considering the entire property. You didn't happen to notice me hanging out by the gate earlier in the week, did you?" she asked, grinning impishly.

"No, but I'm miffed that you didn't tell me you were coming. I would've loved to have had lunch with you again."

"It was about six. I wanted to see your yard when the dew was still on the grass. That's my favorite time of day, and it's when everything looks the softest."

"Something else we have in common," Abby said. "I usually sit on the back patio in the morning. Listening to the birds perks up my whole day."

Clancy realized she was giving the woman a very goofy grin, and she forced herself to get back to business. "I really like this design, but it's a much more expensive option." She turned the drawing around, pointing out the neat river-rock pattern. "This mirrors the columns you have coming up the front stairs, and the short wall in the front yard," she said. "It ties the entire property together—and softens the line of demarcation between the front and the back."

"Nice," Abby said, trailing the tip of her finger lightly over the various elements of the drawing. "Very nice," she added when she met Clancy's eyes.

"This one will almost double the price," Clancy added, wincing a little as she made the statement.

Abby nodded and grasped the edge of the paper, lifting it just an inch. "I see more under there. If you're saving it for last, it must be your favorite."

"This is a pipe dream," Clancy said, "but I couldn't resist drawing it. I was thinking about what you said about the kids and how the dogs went a little nuts with them. Then I figured that the noise of the kids alone might be more than you wanted to hear."

"I've tried to keep my 'Old Lady Graham' image well hidden," Abby admitted, "but there're times I want to stand on the back patio and scream, '*Shut up, you little monsters!*'"

Clancy laughed at the image of the elegant, refined woman doing just that. "Would you have a rolling pin in your hand?"

"Or a broom," Abby said, joining in with her laugh.

"Well, this last idea would drown out the sounds of the pitter-patter of little feet," Clancy said. She unveiled the drawing, smiling when she heard a delighted purr come from Abby's lips.

"Oh, Clancy," she moaned, "this is fabulous." In the drawing, the river-rock wall gave way to a number of large boulders piled atop one another. The boulders eventually leveled out to create a small pool about halfway down the hill. The overflow from the small pond cascaded down the rest of the way to pour into the swimming pool. Abby seemed mesmerized by the drawing, her eyes lingering on the stream of blue water that splashed into the pool, creating a series of ripples that skimmed across the glassy surface. "I've always wanted to live by the water," she sighed. "It never dawned on me that I could have the water come to me."

She made eye contact with the young landscaper and said, "This is the one I want. How much will it cost me?"

Clancy swallowed and said, "The absolute best I can do is $75,000."

Abby nodded, her lower lip sticking out for a moment. "How long will it take you?"

"Hard to say. Probably most of the summer. I wouldn't count on much privacy this season."

"I wouldn't mind that, but I know that Hayley—my daughter—is planning on lying by the pool all summer. I hate to take that away from her."

"Well, if you're not in a hurry, we could really take our time," Clancy said. "We could wait until we had all of the boulders picked out and make sure we were ready to go before we broke ground."

"That could work," Abby said. "I could clear out a space on the side of the house, and we could store everything there. Then we could start work closer to the end of the summer."

"That'd be great for me," Clancy said. "I'm much busier in the summer than I am in the fall."

Abby fixed her with her steady gaze again and asked, "How much profit for you in this job?"

"None," she mumbled, staring down at the table.

"We have a deal," Abby said, "as long as you add in your usual fee for your services."

"What?"

"You heard me," Abby said. "I want you to be personally involved, and you won't be able to do that if you're scrounging for cash. I promise I'll give you as many recommendations as you can handle, but I won't be able to live with myself if you're out there working for nothing. That's my final offer."

Clancy let out a very relieved breath and extended her hand. With a smile as wide as her lips could handle, she said, "You've got a deal."

As soon as Abby returned to the house, she picked up the phone and dialed, unconsciously humming a tune.

"Hello?"

"It's me," Abby said. "And I just hired myself a contractor."

"Super! Did you pick Wayne?"

"Ahh…no, Ellen, I didn't. I picked the young woman I told you about."

Abby could hear her friend sigh, and it gave her a tiny bit of pleasure to hear that Ellen had been invested in who she hired. "Why go asking for trouble? Wayne's been working for us and dozens of our friends for years. He's a known quantity."

"I know," Abby said. "But he doesn't need the work. He didn't even come to bid on the job. He sent some kid over who gave me an estimate, and then Wayne called to schedule. I felt… I don't know…I guess I felt like he assumed I'd hire him, and he didn't have to try to impress me."

"It's just a wall," Ellen said drolly. "What's to impress?"

"The girl I hired spent a lot of time on the idea. She came up with four options, and I wound up choosing something that hadn't occurred to me."

"She suckered you, didn't she?" Ellen asked, laughing. "You're the easiest touch in town, Abby, and she probably sensed she could make you overspend."

"I'm not overspending, whatever that means," Abby said. "And she's going to do the job for a lot less than Wayne would charge for the same thing."

"You know what they say about going with the cheapest bid…"

"I do," Abby said. "But we really clicked. We have the same aesthetic, and I trust her to do a fantastic job."

"How can you click in the time it takes to run a tape measure around your property?"

"We spent a lot of time together," Abby said. "We had lunch together the first day she came over, and we had another long talk today. This is going to work out."

"Well, I'm sure you know what you're doing, but enthusiasm and inexperience aren't always the best pairing."

"Neither are disinterest and lack of inspiration," Abby said, smiling while acknowledging that she'd won the point. "This kid lit up my whole house with her ideas, and that type of enthusiasm should be rewarded."

"You're right," Ellen said. "I forget that we were young once. You can't get experience if people won't give you a chance. And it is nice to be able to hire a woman."

"A lesbian, no less."

"Really? You two *did* talk."

"I didn't *ask* her," Abby said. "She just looked like a lesbian. She had that platinum-blonde hair with dark roots that's popular right now, and it sticks up all over her head. Very trendy."

"I don't know any lesbians with platinum-blonde hair," Ellen said.

"Oh, it was more than that. I just got a vibe from her." She waited a second and then added, "Plus I used the Gay and Lesbian Yellow Pages to find her."

Ellen laughed, and Abby joined her.

"Vibe, my ass," Ellen said. "Cheater!" As soon as the word was out, she hung up, resorting to their game of having the last word. Abby looked at the phone for a moment, considering calling her friend back and trumping her. But she decided to go outside and look at the hill for a minute.

The dogs followed her and sat at her feet at she tried to imagine what the new landscape would look like. She wasn't very successful, not having the eye for such things, but she knew that it would be wonderful.

She reflected that she hadn't told Ellen the entire reason for choosing Clancy. But she hadn't wanted to offend her oldest friend. And Ellen would definitely be offended if Abby had told her that Clancy was the best listener she'd found in ages. She was still a little shocked that she'd opened up to a total stranger, but somehow, it didn't feel odd. It felt strangely natural when she'd done it, and she was pleased to see that Clancy had been just as open and friendly and bright when she'd visited today—none of that "have to tread carefully around the fragile widow" stuff that so many people in her social circle still did.

Even though she knew she was taking a chance on a relatively inexperienced person, Abby didn't have a shred of doubt that the person was worth the risk.

Chapter Two

Abby wanted to get moving on the project immediately, even though they weren't going to break ground for three months. By mid-May, she and Clancy had spent three more afternoons together, plotting out details, and after they had gone over everything for the fifth time, Abby sighed and said, "We're going to have to redo the pool deck. With the rustic look of the stones, the smooth concrete doesn't cut it. I think we need to finish it with large, flat stones that'll mirror the wall."

Clancy gave her a worried look, but Abby shrugged it off. "I was going to redo it next year anyway."

Clancy dragged the toe of her boot along the weathered concrete. "How long have you had this surface?"

"Since we put the pool in. That's been…gosh, I guess it's been ten years."

"Really? You were pretty forward-thinking to put in such a naturally shaped pool ten years ago. Quite a trend setter there, Ms. Graham."

"That's me," she said, smirking at the description. "Actually, we had a forward-thinking pool designer. I'm glad we went with this look, though, especially now that we're going to have such a natural look with the wall."

Clancy looked up at the hill and shielded her eyes as she squinted into the late-afternoon sun. "It's gonna look great when the waterfall is finished. It'll look like a natural spring flowing down that hill and splashing into a cold blue pool."

"You can see it, can't you?" Abby asked.

The architect looked a little sheepish and then nodded. "Yeah, I can. Once I draw something—I can see it. I'm just waiting for the details to be filled in."

Her enthusiasm seemed to be contagious. "I can't wait to see it, either," Abby nearly squealed. "When do we pick the materials for the deck? I'm ready to go!"

Clancy held up a hand. "Whoa! I don't do pools."

"Oh," Abby said some of the air leaving her sails. "Do you know someone who does?"

"Yeah, the same guy who's going to do the waterfall. My dad."

"Your dad?"

"Yep. I'm subcontracting the plumbing for the waterfall to my dad. He can do the pool deck, too."

"Nepotism?" Abby asked, her tone teasing.

"Yeah, but only because he does great work, and I'm sure you'll like him."

"I'm sure I will," Abby said. "I know you wouldn't use someone whose work wasn't at least as good as yours. Could you have him work up a quote for me?"

Clancy reached into her notebook. "I already did. I had a feeling you might want to do this."

Abby shook her head. "Your thoroughness is very impressive, Ms. O'Connor." She scanned the page, noting each component and the estimated time to completion. "This looks fine. Let's add it to the job."

"You're gonna keep the whole family busy this fall. Do you need a good florist?"

"You know, I just might. You'd better give me your mom's card."

🌿

They spent the following Friday driving out to a quarry in Irwindale to take their first look at boulders. Neither woman was impressed with the selection, so Clancy decided they'd have to head farther out to find what they needed. It was a warm, smoggy afternoon, and the air conditioning in the truck was cranked as high as it could go. "Do you have anything else scheduled for today?" Abby asked.

Clancy spared a look at the clock on the dash and said, "Nothing major. I assumed we'd be here all afternoon."

"How about this evening?" Abby persisted. "Are you free for dinner?"

"Dinner? You want to have dinner?"

Clearly embarrassed, Abby jumped in and tried to backtrack. "It's no big deal. I thought—"

"I'd love to," Clancy interrupted. "I was just surprised, because I don't have many clients who treat me like a real person—who eats."

"You seem like a very real person," Abby assured her. "And I'd really like to pick your brain, if you don't mind."

"About?"

"Well…" Abby hemmed a little and finally looked away. "Would you be averse to talking about…sex?"

Clancy was only too happy to talk about sex—but she was sorely disappointed when she learned that Abby wanted to talk about her daughter's sex life. Still, she was very pleased that Abby trusted her enough to think of her as a confidant rather than strictly as an employee.

🌿

They stopped at the local gourmet grocery store in South Pasadena and walked around the expansive place, trying to decide what to have. Abby insisted on buying the food, but she let Clancy purchase a nice, fruity zinfandel, which she suggested would go well with the swordfish they had selected.

Back at the house, Abby fired up the grill while Clancy opened the wine and set it to chill. Then they sat on the shaded patio under the bougainvillea-covered pergola. Clancy had worked hard all week, and she felt a little stress leave her body now that the workweek was over. "Tell me about your daughter."

Abby smiled the warm, love-filled smile that was always present when she spoke of her children. "She's a delightful girl," she began, "and we've always been close. She didn't go through any of that adolescent rebellion that most girls torture their parents with."

Clancy grinned and said, "Don't remind my mom. She's still mad at me for things I did fifteen years ago."

Abby cast a doubtful glance at the young woman and said, "She's angry about things you did when you were, what—eight?"

"I know I look like I'm twelve, but I'm going to hit the big 'three-o' this December."

Blinking in surprise, Abby said, "I mean this as a compliment, Clancy, but you could easily pass for twenty."

"I know, I know. I still get carded."

"You'll be glad for that in a few years," Abby reminded her.

Waiting a beat, Clancy asked, "How old are you?"

"I just turned forty-five," she said. "Put your eyes back in your head. You don't have to be nice. I know. I look every day of it."

"No! Not at all," Clancy insisted. "You look much younger than that. Your face doesn't have a line on it. I thought you were around forty, but that's only because you told me you had a daughter in college."

"Thanks," Abby said, running a hand through her thick hair. "I think I look my age, but I could look younger if I dyed my hair. Most women start as soon as they see the first speck of gray." She shrugged and added, "I'm not most women."

"Their loss," Clancy said, smiling warmly.

Abby's smile was one that seemed to have been developed to brush off compliments and take the focus off herself. "I'd rather spend the evening chatting about anything except what's been bothering me, but I should be an adult. Are you still willing to give me some advice about Hayley?"

"Sure. What's the issue?"

"I suppose this is the dark side of being close to your kids. She tells me absolutely everything," Abby said.

"That's bad?"

"It can be," Abby said, her expression contemplative. "There are a lot of things I don't want to know about."

"Oh! She tells you *everything*," Clancy said. "Including the things most of us spend hours trying to make sure our parents don't find out about."

"Precisely. And now she's been talking about her sex life in a way that's beginning to worry me."

"Worry you?"

"Yes. Hayley's always had the normal supply of boyfriends—none of them very serious. But now that she's in college, she's starting to show a bit of a wild streak, and I'm not sure how to react to it."

"Nose rings? Full-body tattoos?"

"No," Abby said. "But you could give me advice on the tattoo front."

"I only have one," Clancy assured her, sneaking a look at the armband of needlepoint ivy that ringed her bicep.

"It's nice," Abby said. "But no, it's nothing like that." She paused for a moment. "She told me that she thinks it's time to start having sex. I was so flustered that I didn't know how to react."

Clancy cocked her head. "I'm not sure what you mean. Start having sex…?"

Abby paused, obviously organizing her thoughts. "This is one of the many times I miss my husband. He was so good with Hayley. He knew exactly how to reach her without her thinking he was telling her what to do."

Clancy listened attentively as Abby continued her tale. "I think I've mentioned that Will and I had two kids. Trevor is finishing up his master's degree in urban planning at MIT. Hayley is a freshman at UC Santa Cruz, majoring in something different every time I talk to her. She's young to be in college. Her sixth birthday was a day or two before school started, so she was the youngest in her class. She's gifted, though, and we allowed her to skip third grade because she was so bored. In retrospect, that might have been a mistake. She's always tried to be as mature as her classmates—even when she wasn't. One year doesn't seem like a lot, but it can be a big difference at some critical ages. I'm afraid that the transition to college might be one of them."

"Mmm…that makes sense. I was one of the youngest in my class, too. I always felt like I had to struggle a little to keep up."

"Hayley's a great kid, as I said, but socially, she's always been a follower," Abby said. "I've done my best to try to build her self-confidence, but it's been slow to come. I'm afraid that she wants to experiment with sex because everyone else does."

Clancy eyed Abby for a moment, an uncertain smile playing at her lips. "Isn't that part of the reason you did it?"

"No," Abby said, "not at all. I did it because I fell in love."

"Oh. *Oh!* I get it. You're upset because Hayley hasn't said she's in love!"

"Exactly. She's not even seeing anyone! She's simply decided that she wants to have sex, and she doesn't seem to care who she has it with! That's so unlike her, it's really worrying me."

"Yeah. I see that," Clancy said. "What did you say to her?"

"I don't think I was coherent!" Abby said, starting to laugh. "I made some noises about love and commitment, but she told me that sex wasn't like that anymore. Now it was just another thing to do…like going to a movie or having dinner."

"Wow," Clancy murmured. "It was a big deal the first time I had sex. I guess things could have changed a lot since I was seventeen, but I think it's more likely that Hayley's trying to test you—you know—to see what your reaction will be. I did *that* a lot at seventeen."

"I suppose you could be right," Abby said. "I hope that I can have a more rational talk with her before she grabs the first boy she sees and makes his day. That's not how I want her to experience sex."

"No, I'm sure it's not, but it's hard to have much control when they're out of the house, isn't it?"

"Damn, I wish she were a scientific prodigy. Then she would have wanted to go to Cal Tech, and I'd have been able to watch her every move."

"I lived at home when I started having sex, Abby, and I'm sure my parents didn't know."

"Another theory down the drain," Abby said, shaking her head as she got up and started for the kitchen.

🌱

It was such a nice night that Abby prevailed upon Clancy to accept a suit and go for a swim.

Clancy changed in the bathroom by the laundry room, and by the time Abby returned from her bedroom Clancy was already in the pool, kicking the length of it while resting on her back.

Abby jumped in noisily to let Clancy know she was there. Then they spent a few minutes slicing through the warm water, both doing a languid backstroke.

After a while, Abby hopped out and poured a glass of wine for each of them, padding back and extending the plastic wineglass to Clancy. "Cheers," she said, slipping back into the water with barely a splash.

Clancy hung onto the deck by her arms, kicking her legs out behind her.

Abby smiled furtively at the dark golden tan that marked Clancy's neck and arms, contrasting with the relatively pale skin on her shoulders and back. Her tattoo encircled her arm right at the bulge of her bicep, and Abby wondered how much time Clancy had spent flexing her muscle before deciding where to put the design. Given the way Clancy seemed to organize her life, Abby was sure that both the design and the placement were intentional.

They chatted about this and that, just relaxing after a long day and a nice dinner. Abby wasn't sure why she was so fascinated, but her eyes kept darting back to Clancy's body. She thought she'd seen women of every shape and description during her many years of visiting health clubs, pools, and country clubs, but she'd never seen a woman built quite like Clancy.

She looked like an average young woman in her clothes, but her body was lean and muscular...much more muscular than Abby would have suspected. Her body was clearly built from hard work, and her uneven tan highlighted the fact that she didn't spend her days at the pool. There was something honest and well earned about her body, and Abby found that she enjoyed watching the swells and dips of Clancy's back and shoulder muscles when she moved in the water.

"You in there?" Clancy asked, moving her hand in front of Abby's face.

"Oh! Sure! I...was just daydreaming."

Clancy laughed softly. "I don't know what you were thinking about, but you looked like you were enjoying yourself."

"Ha!" Abby realized how forced and unnatural her laugh sounded, but she couldn't begin to explain what had been going through her head. As was her habit, she dismissed the stray thoughts and brushed them away, clearing her mind as she concentrated on entertaining her guest.

"Where are you off to today?" Michael asked. Clancy had gotten dressed and ready to go at seven, and was now anxiously looking out the window.

"Abby and I have an appointment to look at some rocks way the hell out to City of Industry. She wanted to drive, so she's gonna come pick me up."

"She's not one of those old ladies who gets into the fast lane to go thirty-five, is she?"

"You know," Clancy said, gazing at her longtime friend, "for that, I'm going to make you stay until she gets here. I want you to take a gander at this old lady."

"Happy to," he said. "Now that I know she's straight, I can size her up for sugar-mama potential."

"Oh, charming," Clancy said. "Very charming. I'm sure she'll jump into your arms and ask if she can support you."

Abby's knock interrupted their banter. "Ready to go?" she asked brightly when Clancy opened the door.

"Sure am, but come in and meet my roommate first."

Abby came into the room, and Michael smiled in his normal, friendly manner. "Michael Hamlin," he said, extending his hand. "Clancy's been raving about your project for weeks now. It's nice to finally meet you."

"Abby Graham. It's very nice to meet you, Michael. You'll have to come to the party we're going to have when we're finished."

"I'd love to. I never get to see Clancy's finished projects." He ran a hand through Clancy's close-cropped hair and said, "Don't forget we have a project tonight. Time for a shoeshine."

"Right. I'll be home by the time you are." Clancy kissed her roommate on the cheek, and they said their goodbyes.

They were halfway down the path to Abby's car when she turned her head and asked, "Why do you make plans to have your friend shine your shoes?"

"What?...Oh!" Clancy laughed heartily at the image of Michael taking a brush to her worn boots. "That's what the thing he does to my hair is called. Michael's a hairstylist."

Abby glanced at the coloring. "You know, it really becomes you. It's a little out of the ordinary...and somehow very lesbian-looking."

Clancy brushed her hand across her spiky white-blonde hair. "It looks lesbian? Really?"

"Uhm...a little bit. Yeah."

Smiling, Clancy nodded. "Cool. It's just about played out stylewise. I guess I'll have to something different if I wanna be cutting-edge. But if it looks dykey, it's still serving a purpose."

"I think it's cute. But I still don't know why on earth you call it shoeshining."

"Well, he puts a thick peroxide solution onto a long piece of cardboard and then kinda buffs my head with it. It actually looks a little like he's giving me a shoeshine—on my head, of course."

"I think you should stick with it until something else strikes you. It gives you a certain *je ne sais quoi*. Besides, blonde works really well with your skin tone."

"Thanks. I think I'll probably stay blonde. But don't you go getting any ideas. You should stay like you are. I think the silver in your hair is absolutely fantastic."

"Do you really?" Abby asked, sounding uncharacteristically tentative.

"Oh, yeah! It looks great against your tanned skin, and it's perfect with your eyes. I wouldn't change it for the world."

Clancy noticed that Abby sneaked a glance at herself in the rearview mirror when they got into the car. It could have been that she was checking the positioning of the mirror, but Clancy had a feeling that her friend was taking a look at her graying hair...and she hoped that Abby would learn to appreciate just how lovely it was.

🍂

After a quick stop for coffee and scones, they set off. Clancy hadn't been sure what to expect, but the car Abby drove caught her a little by surprise. "How long have you had this beauty?"

Abby patted the dashboard of her brand-new, bright-red Lexus convertible. "I admit it," she said. "It was a midlife-crisis birthday gift. I've been feeling so stuck lately that I thought it might perk me up. I guess I was also trying to lure men by shamelessly exploiting one of their known weaknesses."

"It's a gorgeous car," Clancy said. "Has your plan worked?"

Abby sported a wry grin. "Not really. I'm still striking out with regularity."

Leaning back against the door in the small interior, Clancy let out a light chuckle. "I can believe a lot of things, Abby, but I can't believe that you don't have your pick of men."

Abby's tanned skin flushed a little at the compliment. "I wish I were lying." She spared a moment to look at her friend, and Clancy could see how discouraged she seemed. "I thought I felt old when I found myself a widow the same week I turned forty. But that was nothing compared to how it feels to be unable to get a second date with a decent man."

Bridging the distance between their seats, Clancy placed her hand on Abby's shoulder. "You're serious."

"Yes, I'm completely serious. It's something that I'd never considered, Clancy. I mean, I don't think I'm among the world's most beautiful women, but I'll admit to coasting through my youth on my looks. I was always popular with boys, and I fended off more men than you would believe when Will and I were first together."

"I don't doubt it," Clancy said. "And don't be too quick to take yourself out of the running for the world's most beautiful women, either."

Abby gave her a quick look and then laughed softly. "You catch me by surprise, Ms. O'Connor. I'm never quite prepared for some of your comments."

"I'm telling it like I see it."

"Well." Abby's color was a little high, and she quickly glossed over Clancy's comment. "I guess it didn't occur to me that my success with men would evaporate. I mean—in many ways, I'm a better catch now than I was when I was thirty, but that doesn't seem to matter." She blew out a frustrated breath. "Every one of my friends has already introduced me to her 'A list' of eligible men. I'd guess that I've been on twenty dates in the past year. There wasn't one man—who I liked—who has called me for a second date."

"But why?"

"My best friend finally told me the truth last night. A week ago, I went out with her favorite bachelor, and we seemed to hit it off. He didn't call—so I finally cornered her and insisted that she tell me what was going on." Her expression was so hurt that Clancy felt herself wince. "Ellen admitted that Jeff told her he couldn't date someone who looked as old as he did."

"But you don't look old!" Clancy said. "You don't have a wrinkle on your entire face! And you act so young and vibrant! Jesus, Abby, you're such a catch, a guy would have to be insane not to want to go out with you!"

Abby patted her friend on the leg. "You're very good for my ego. Can I hire you to call me once a day and cheer me up?"

"No, but I'll do it for free," Clancy said, beaming at her.

Abby's smile was quick, but it faded just as quickly. "I really don't blame the men. It's just a sign of our youth-worshiping culture. These are professional, power-broker guys, and that quest for the best extends to women. Why choose a forty-five-year-old if you can get a twenty-five- or thirty-year-old? It's the survival of the fittest in the dating game."

"Sure it is," Clancy agreed, "but everyone has a different notion about what qualities he finds most desirable. You haven't met a guy who's looking for quality. God, I don't like to date twenty-five-year-old women, and I'm not even thirty. I like a woman who has some depth, some experience."

"Mmm," Abby murmured. "I wish your philosophy would rub off on the men I've been dating. I'm afraid I'm going to have to start despoiling retirement homes."

Clancy's laugh turned into a choke when her scone decided to ignore her esophagus and head straight for the trachea. But the image of Abby going door to door at the local retirement home was worth the discomfort.

❧

They drove along in silence for a while, both women lost in their thoughts. Clancy finally broke the silence when she asked, "Are you sure you're ready to start dating? Maybe you're not giving off the right vibes."

"Meaning?"

"Well, I don't mean to pry, but are you still grieving for your husband?"

Abby nodded slightly. "In a way, yes. I don't think I'll ever get over losing Will. But I honestly think I'm ready to love again."

"I thought that you might not be showing that you're into dating yet. 'Cause if you really acted interested, a quality guy wouldn't notice your hair color. Not every man wants a trophy."

"Hmm…you might be onto something. I *have* been down lately, and maybe that comes through."

"Why are you down?" Clancy asked, barely stopping herself from stroking Abby's thigh to soothe her.

Abby's hands gripped the wheel a little tighter, and Clancy could see a well-defined muscle flex in her forearm. "I'm feeling like I might never get another chance at love. I have friends—good friends. They keep me interested and involved in life. My kids make me very happy, and they visit as often as they can. But I miss the closeness that you can only find with a lover. I miss the intimacy…I miss being held at night…and of course, I miss sex. But most of all, I miss headrubs." She sighed wistfully. "Will always stayed up later than I did, and most nights, he would read for a while. He always rubbed my head."

She looked decidedly uncomfortable, but she continued. "I don't know why, but that's the thing I miss the most. That slow, rhythmic headrub put me to sleep most nights for twenty years." Just a quick glance let Clancy see the flash of pain in her expressive eyes. "How do you get over losing that?"

"I don't know," Clancy murmured, a little overcome by the desolation she saw in her friend's gaze. "Maybe you don't. Maybe you can't. But that's no reason not to try again. There has to be someone out there who can give a woman a nice, soothing headrub…or maybe something else that would give you that same feeling of connectedness."

Abby gave her a resigned smile and said, "Thank God Will left me with enough money to live well. I could always hire someone to rub my head. Lord knows there are stranger job descriptions out there."

"You'll find someone," Clancy insisted. "Someone who can soothe all of your stress away with the touch of his hand. I'm sure of it."

"You're going to have to have enough confidence for both of us. Mine's just about shot."

"I can do that," Clancy assured her. "I'm all about confidence."

❧

This boulder-hunting trip had been even less successful than the last, and on the way home, Clancy delivered the bad news. "We're gonna have to get more creative with the boulders. I think we're unhappy with them because the ones we've seen are so round and smooth. They almost look manufactured."

"That's it exactly," Abby said. "They look more like concrete than stone."

"I don't think we're gonna find anything in Southern California; we're gonna have to go to the source. How do you feel about a road trip?"

"Road trip, huh?" Abby said with a grin crinkling her mouth. "That might be the ticket for chasing the blues away. Let me know when and where."

❧

"You know," Abby said as they made their way back to the freeway, "I find that I talk about myself constantly when we're together. But I really don't know much about you. Tell me about the important milestones in your life."

"Okay. What do you want to know?"

"Tell me your coming-out story," Abby said.

Clancy laughed. "You know the lingo, don't ya?"

"Oh, my God, was I being too forward? I only wanted—"

"Abby, I'm teasing. Really. That's the kind of thing that lesbians usually get out of the way the first time they meet, and I think it's cool that you're not afraid to ask."

"I feel very comfortable with you, and I'm interested in learning more about you. For most of my gay friends, coming out has been a very big deal."

"I think that's true for many people," Clancy agreed. "But it wasn't for me. I realized I was gay when I was in high school, but the only person I told was Michael."

"You've known him that long?"

"Oh, yeah. We met when we were freshmen in high school. He's been my best buddy ever since. Anyway, I knew in high school, but I didn't have anyone to practice with. Near as I could tell, I was the only lesbian in the entire school."

"Oh, you poor thing!"

"It was hard, as a matter of fact, but I met someone when I was working with my dad, and we had a fairly brief but very intense affair. It was a decent way to come out."

"You worked with your father?"

"Yeah. My parents didn't have the money to send me to college, and I didn't wanna be stuck with student loans my whole life, so I worked for my dad for four years. It was hard work, but I learned a lot, and it helped me decide that I couldn't stand to work at a trade. Being a woman in construction is a constant struggle," she said. "It's so much easier now that I'm the person who hires and fires."

"I can imagine," Abby said. "So have you had the great love of your life yet?"

"God, I hope not! I've dated some nice people, slept with a few, liked a few of them well enough. But I've never felt the way I want to feel about a woman."

"How's that?"

"Like we help complete each other," Clancy decided. "Like we're better together than we would be apart."

"I had that with Will," Abby said softly. "It's worth whatever you have to do to find it."

"That goes for both of us. I need to experience it for the first time, and you need to experience it again."

"No arguments." She looked at Clancy. "How did your parents take the news that you were gay?"

"It was hard for my mom," she said thoughtfully. "Very hard, as a matter of fact. Our relationship didn't suffer, but she struggled for years to be even moderately comfortable with it. She's fine with it now, I think. I mean, it's not something we discuss very much, but she seems to want me to find a partner."

"What about your dad?"

Grinning, Clancy said, "My dad's one of those guys who thinks his kid can do no wrong. I really can't imagine him giving me a hard time about anything. He's very cool with it. We even check out girls together."

"It must be nice to know that your father will support you, no matter what. I don't think my kids feel that way about me," Abby mused. "But I'd have to say that Will was like that—particularly with Hayley. It was so hard for her to lose her daddy."

Clancy gave her a look filled with empathy and said, "If she felt anything like I do about my dad, I can't imagine how hard it was for her. My dad's like my North Star—he's a constant guiding presence in my life."

Abby wiped away the tears that had started to fall and murmured, "She was thirteen when Will died. I thank God every day that we've only gotten closer because of his death."

"What did he die of, Abby? Was it sudden?"

She nodded and shifted in her seat. Clancy saw her swallow. "I kissed him goodbye at eight on April 29th. He was pronounced dead at nine." She met Clancy's gaze and added, "Massive coronary."

"Did he have a history of heart trouble?"

"No. He was in fantastic shape. He'd been an athlete his whole life, had low cholesterol and a very low pulse. He was Mr. Health Food," she said, some of the inflection coming back to her voice. "But he had a congenital heart defect that hadn't been detected during his medical exams. It could have been fixed if they had known about it—but they didn't," she finished quietly.

Clancy gave her friend a quick look to make sure she was okay to continue to talk about the issue. Abby looked composed and open, so she said, "I've always wondered what would be worse—to lose someone quickly or to have to see someone die slowly. My grandfather died a slow, lingering, painful death, and it was really awful to watch him fade away."

Abby gave her a look and shook her head. "I don't know which would be worse, to be honest. I've done it the quick way, and I've gotta tell you, it sucks, too."

🌱

They were close to home when Clancy said, "Let's not let this day be a waste. Wanna have lunch together?"

"Sure." Abby smiled. "Where would you like to go?"

"Let's stop somewhere and pick up some salads or sandwiches. I wanna dine alfresco."

After picking up a pair of fruit salads, they went to Clancy's favorite outdoor dining spot. "I hate to admit this," Abby said, "but I honestly don't remember the last time I visited Descanso Gardens. This was a great idea."

"Well, we're both plant junkies," Clancy reminded her. "What better place to soothe the soul a little bit?"

They found an empty picnic table and sat down to enjoy their meal. "I brought my children here when they were small," Abby said. "They always liked the tulips, for some reason."

Clancy took a bite of her salad and nodded, her mouth too full to speak. When she swallowed, she said, "I do, too. I was up here at least four times in February. I guess I like them because so few people around here bother to put them into their landscapes."

"I usually put in a couple of hundred—running them down both sides of the drive," Abby said. "But I didn't do it this year. I let a lot of things slide once Hayley left for school."

"You don't seem to have let many things slide," Clancy said. "Your schedule is busier than mine, and you don't have a full-time job."

"I need to stay busy. I play golf three times a week, tennis twice, and I'm very involved in a few charities. My hobbies are what've kept me sane. The sports keep the adrenaline pumping, and the charity work helps remind me of how wonderful my life really is."

"Tell me about your charities. You've never mentioned them before."

"Well, I have a few that I'm passionate about, but lately, one is taking up all of my time. I'm in charge of the entertainment for the Children Living with Cancer Carnival. It's our major fund-raiser for the year, and every year it becomes a bigger production."

"I've heard about the carnival," Clancy said. "Isn't that the one all the Hollywood celebrities go to?"

"That's the one. Luckily, I'm not on the committee that secures the 'talent' to participate. I do the nitty-gritty work—getting the booths set up, hiring the food concessionaires, the clowns and jugglers and face painters. It's very unglamorous, but I enjoy it."

"When's the event?"

"It's next Sunday, and I'm getting to the panic stage."

"Need an assistant? I'm very good at following directions."

Abby looked at her friend for a moment. "Are you serious?"

"Completely. I know that a million things can go wrong at a big event. I'd love to help out."

"I'd be thrilled to have the help. It's incredibly generous of you to offer."

Making a dismissive gesture, Clancy said, "No big deal. I'm guessing that Saturday is the worst day for you, right?"

"Yeah. Setup is the worst. Something always goes wrong."

"I'm free on Saturday, so I'm your woman. What time do we start?"

❦

Saturday morning quickly turned into Saturday afternoon, and the vendor who'd been hired to set up the booths was nowhere to be found. Abby had been calling and paging the company frantically, but they were obviously ignoring her calls. Clancy got on the phone and tried to find another vendor, but they both knew the chances of finding someone to put up fifty booths on a moment's notice was nil. Finally, at nearly three o'clock, the truck arrived. The vendor had sent only four men, and from Clancy's experienced perspective, it seemed he'd picked up the first four guys he'd seen hanging out on the corner of one of the home centers, looking for day labor.

Taking a look at Abby, who seemed to be nearly faint with worry, Clancy said, "Leave this to me. By the end of the day, the booths will all be up."

"But Clancy—!"

"I know what I'm doing. There must be a million things you have to do. You take care of them, and let the master work." She gave her friend a very confident, very engaging smile, and Abby's expression cleared, her worried frown disappearing.

"Are you sure you can do this? I don't want to doubt you, but without those booths, we're in deep trouble."

"I give you my word," Clancy said, gazing directly into Abby's eyes.

"That's good enough for me." Abby threw her arms around Clancy, pressing her into a cozy hug. "I'll stay out of your way."

You can stay right here if you'll throw in a few more of those hugs, the landscaper thought wistfully before she focused her attention on the massive job that lay before her.

Luckily, the lighting crew had finished by the time night fell, and the portable towers provided plenty of light for the construction crew to continue working into the night. At eleven o'clock, Abby found Clancy perched upon a sturdy yellow ladder that read "O'Connor Landscaping." "Hi," she said, trying to stifle a yawn. "I bet you haven't had a thing to eat, have you?"

"Nope." Clancy smiled down at her. "But I'm on number forty-nine. When I hit fifty, I'm gonna be at McDonald's faster than you can say 'Big Mac.'"

Abby looked behind the architect and saw a large generator; then she noticed that Clancy was using a nail gun. "Did you bring those things with you?"

"No. I called my guys and had them bring some tools up. I sent those useless idiots from the booth company home. Make sure you deduct a substantial amount from the bill."

"Clancy! You brought your crew up here?"

"Sure. They know what they're doing, and they're trustworthy. Why not?"

"Damn, I don't know what I would have done without you. No one on my committee has any experience with this type of thing."

"Well, we're about done, so find your wallet. You owe me dinner, Ms. Graham, and I'm gonna hold out for the super-size!"

Abby went back to the portable trailer she'd set up as an on-site office and started to gather her things. By the time she was ready to leave, Clancy was, too. Approaching the architect from behind, Abby saw the young woman reach into her wallet and take out every bill she had. She divided her money among the men, laughing and speaking quietly. The men all shook her hand and got back into the truck they'd come in, calling out goodbyes as they drove away.

"How much did today cost you?" Abby asked, approaching quietly.

"Oops!" The landscaper turned and shrugged. "Not too much. I haven't been able to spare much for charity until now. But now that I'm making a little more money, I'm happy to make a donation—and give my guys a little extra money for the week."

"Let me pay you back," Abby said, "I have a budget for this, Clancy."

"No, no, I'd really like to do this for the organization. They do good work."

"Are you sure? I've imposed on you so much already."

"You haven't imposed on me one bit. I did this because I wanted to. I feel good about it," she said, looking around at the perfectly constructed booths.

Abby sidled up and put her arm around her shoulders, sharing her view. "I've always maintained that you get so much more than you give when you help others."

"I agree completely. Now let's get out of here so you can have the satisfaction of buying me dinner."

"It's a deal. But friends don't let friends eat fast food. We'll go someplace where we can use utensils and cloth napkins."

"You're teaching me a whole new way of life." She grinned rakishly and said, "I think I like it."

The event was over at six o'clock on Sunday night, and by the time the last guest had gone, both Abby and Clancy were ready for bed. Clancy stood up and stretched, almost able to touch the ceiling of the small trailer. "Well, I guess it's time to start dismantling everything, huh?"

"God, no! We have a crew to take care of the organization's things, and the vendors are responsible for their own takedown."

"Those jerks in charge of the booths probably won't show up!"

"Oh, yes, they will. You'd be amazed at how good people are about getting their equipment back…when they were completely inept at getting it set up on time."

"Eh, I know that type of business, too. I used to work with a nursery that had wonderful plants but terrible delivery guys. They'd snap a sapling in half and then try to tell me it'd be fine. Idiots."

"I'll come up to supervise the idiots tomorrow, but it shouldn't be a tough day. We're basically finished."

"We're really done for the day?" Clancy asked, her body aching from constant activity.

"Yep. Well, as soon as we have dinner, that is. How about a big pizza, a cold beer, and a hot tub?"

"That's a lesbian dream date!"

"Then grab your things," Abby said. "'Cause you've got a date."

I wish I did, Clancy thought, her crush on Abby growing stronger with each passing day.

Chapter Three

Early on a Monday morning, Abby double-knotted the laces on her running shoes, grabbed the retractable leash, and called to the dogs, "Walkies, walkies!" The pair came scampering through the house and slid across the entry floor to come to rest right in front of their mistress. "I'll never know how you manage that," she mused aloud.

They started off, heading for the Rose Bowl—which the dogs loved because it was a popular place for pooches to gather, giving them many sniffing opportunities.

They were about halfway there when she heard a familiar voice calling out to her. "Will you three slow down?"

She did, lengthening her stride and slowing her pace. Her friend Ellen Chenoweth finally came up alongside her, and the dogs immediately started to frantically lick the salt and sweat from her bare legs. The woman gazed at the pair fondly and petted each fluffy head. "It's a little odd," she said, "but there's something nice about having another living creature act like you're the most delicious taste treat in the world."

"You mean Neil doesn't do the same?"

Ellen laughed and fell into place beside Abby as they started off again. "We're about twenty-five years past that 'even your sweat tastes good' period."

Neil and Will had been law partners, and the foursome had been friends since before Will and Abby were married. The Chenoweths lived just three blocks away, and their two sons had been fixtures in the Graham home when Abby's son, Trevor, was in school. "When are the boys coming home?" Abby asked. "Trevor won't be home long, but I know he'd like to see them."

"I'm still not sure what their plans are," Ellen said. "All I know is that they'll delay buying plane tickets until they have to pay full fare."

Abby shook her head and laughed, knowing that her friend's observation would prove to be accurate. "Kids are always a challenge, aren't they?"

"They are indeed. So what's up with your two?"

"Hayley gets home before Trev, since he's going to spend some time with my parents. She doesn't have any plans—other than staying out late and lying by the pool, of course."

Ellen glanced at her friend and asked, "Does it bother her that Trevor's found such a wonderful summer project? I mean, going to Venice to work with an international group of urban planners is a very big deal!"

Abby smiled. "I know it and you know it, but Hayley still thinks of him as a much older person. If he figures out how to make Venice the leading city in Italy, she won't be surprised or jealous."

"You're lucky you didn't have two boys," Ellen said. "Mine have never been supportive of each other."

Abby didn't respond, privately thinking that her kids would support each other no matter their sex. They ran in silence for a few minutes, all four of them managing to keep a steady pace. "I was just thinking about how proud Will would have been of Trev," Ellen said.

"Yeah, I think about that every day. I wish he were here to see what a fine young man we've raised."

"Trevor's always been a gem. Will wouldn't be a bit surprised at how well he's doing. You've done a great job with both of the kids, Abby. I know it hasn't been easy without Will."

"No, it's never easy raising kids, and doing it alone for the past five years has been hard. But it's paying off, Ellen. I'm confident that both of the kids have gotten through the worst part of their grief. I think I'm about ready to sit on the sidelines and let them care for their aged mom."

Ellen gave her friend a wry grin and tossed off a challenge. "Race you to the rose garden!" She took off at a sprint and was dusted in a matter of seconds; the competitive spirit was never far beneath the surface of Abby's calm demeanor. "Aged, my ass!" she called to the fleet form.

Late that afternoon, Clancy was sitting at Abby's kitchen table, the pair going over the plans for the permanent plants that would bracket the new stream. They'd been working for over an hour and were just about to wrap up when Clancy's cell phone rang. "Do you mind?" she asked Abby before she answered.

"No, please do."

Clancy pressed the talk button. "Hello."

"Hey, Clance, it's Michael. How mad would you be if I canceled for tonight?"

"How mad would I be? Let's see…this is my favorite activity of the whole week, and if you don't go, I won't go alone. So…I'd say that I wouldn't be mad, but I'd be disappointed. Why? What's up?"

"Oh, it's no big deal. One of the girls at work wants me to go on a double date with her and her boyfriend and a friend of theirs. I'll just tell her I can't make it. No biggie."

"Level with me, Michael. What do you want to do?"

"Well, I like going dancing with you, but this girl is supposed to be really hot, and…"

"Go ahead and go," Clancy said, chuckling. "You haven't been out in weeks. You're gonna forget you're straight."

"No chance of that, blondie-blonde. Sure you don't mind? I hate to disappoint you."

"You don't do it very often, Mickey. It's okay."

"Cool. I'll tell you all about it later tonight—or even better, tomorrow if I get lucky."

"Have fun, bud. Talk to you later."

She put her phone back on her belt, smiling to herself.

"Michael?" Abby asked.

"Yeah. We go dancing on Monday nights, but he has a chance to go out on a real date, so I excused him."

"Dancing?" Abby asked wistfully. "I love to dance. I'm one of the few women who was lucky enough to marry a man who loved to dance, and he had to go and die on me. Where's the justice?"

"Actually, we're only taking lessons. I'm pretty good, but Michael's a rank beginner."

"Really? What kind of dancing are we talking about?"

"Country and Western," Clancy said, giving her friend a slightly embarrassed smile.

"Country and Western?" Abby asked. "Like square dancing?"

"No, more like line dancing. It's very '80s, but a lot of gay people are still into it." She laughed and said, "Well, a lot of people are into it, gay and straight, but it's pretty dated here in LA."

"It sounds like fun," Abby said. She paused a moment and asked, "Why don't I go with you?"

"You?"

Clancy's expression was so incredulous that Abby was a little wounded. "It was just a suggestion."

"No, no," Clancy said, seeing the hurt. "I'd love to have you go, but we take the lessons at a gay bar. Would you be comfortable going to a place like that?"

"Clancy, my best friend in college used to drag me to a leather bar on Sunday afternoons for a beer bust. I've probably been to more gay bars than you have."

Her face beginning to light up, Clancy asked, "Are you sure? I'd love to take you."

"What do I wear, and when will you pick me up?"

❦

Clancy returned to Abby's at seven o'clock, rang the bell, and stared openmouthed at the person on the other side of the door.

Abby was even taller than normal, wearing scuffed black boots with decorative bits of metal on the toes. The boots poked out from beneath the hems of a very faded pair of boot-cut jeans that fit her like a second skin, making Abby look more like a working cowgirl than a poseur. A thin, sleeveless chambray shirt, tucked neatly into the jeans, clung to Abby's lean torso.

Abby raised her fingers and snapped them in Clancy's face. "Are you in there?"

"Wha...? Oh! Damn, I zoned out for a minute," Clancy said, her cheeks coloring. "I...I...uhm...must be more tired than I thought."

"Are you sure you want to go? We could do this another night."

"And have you waste this outfit? No way. Besides, I'll get my second wind once we start dancing."

"Do I really look all right? I tried to follow your advice and dress so I'll stay cool, but I haven't worn this since the last time we went riding, and I'm a little uncomfortable."

"You look great!" Clancy exclaimed. "Really great. Do you ride locally?"

"Oh, no. Will and I used to take the kids to a ranch in Colorado for a week or so in the summer. We went for almost eight years. It was a great way for the family to bond—no TV, no phones, no radio. We loved it."

"Well, you'll certainly fit in tonight," Clancy said.

"You look like a native yourself." Clancy was wearing black jeans, a lavender tank top, and a pair of dark purple cowboy boots. She carried a cream-colored straw hat in her hand, and she settled it onto her head at Abby's comment. "Very nice," Abby said.

They walked into the kitchen, and Abby grabbed a black felt cowboy hat, brushed off a spot of dust, and bowed graciously to her friend. "Shall we?" she asked, "I'm ready to kick up my heels, pardner."

They arrived at the bar at seven-thirty, and the crowd was still very light. They each paid the $5 cover, but Clancy insisted on buying the first round. "What'll it be?" she asked as they made their way to the bar at the back of the large room.

"What are you having?" Abby asked.

"Whiskey, water back," Clancy said. "Makes me feel like a cowboy."

"Make it two," Abby said, settling the black hat on the back of her head.

They took their drinks and sat on stools at a small round table. "It's not fancy, but it's pretty comfortable," Clancy said.

"It's very nice," Abby said. "Much nicer than the places I used to go with Steven, my friend at UCLA. This place is friendly, too. I used to get the nastiest looks when I went to some of his favorite spots. In the '70s, most gay men didn't like to socialize with women."

"There are still a few places in West Hollywood that are like that," Clancy said. "But most of the places here in the San Gabriel Valley are just fine."

Abby looked around and noticed some couples already on the dance floor. "Boy, some of these people are good."

"Yeah, there's a group of people who come all the time, and lots of them have been dancing for fifteen or twenty years. I look like I've got two left feet compared to most of them, but I still enjoy it."

"I think this will be fun," Abby decided. She took her shot of whiskey, drained it in one gulp, and then took a sip of water. "Smooth," she said, grinning and wiping her mouth with the back of her hand just like a cowpoke. "Another?"

"Uhm…sure," Clancy said, draining her own glass. "I dance much better when I lose some of my inhibitions."

"I do, too. Although there's a fine line between losing my inhibitions and losing my mind. You'll stop me before I start dancing on the bar, won't you?"

"I'm not sure I'm the one you should rely on," Clancy said, laughing. "That's kinda like asking the fox to watch the henhouse. Michael always says I'm absolutely fine and then absolutely drunk—with no warning whatsoever."

"I haven't been drunk in years. I'm not even sure I'd recognize the warning signs."

"I usually know a few people here," Clancy said, giving her friend a grin. "I'll ask an unbiased observer to keep an eye on us."

They got through the instruction for the first dance without difficulty—but that was with the music playing at half speed. As the music picked up, Abby struggled a little, but by watching her more proficient accomplice, they were able to do a fairly decent job. "You're good," she said, grinning at her friend.

"Thanks. We've been doing this since Christmas, and it's starting to sink in. I can tell you're a dancer, by the way. You catch on really quick."

"Years of ballet," Abby said, rolling her eyes.

The instructor let them use the same step for three consecutive songs, and by the last one, they were both doing quite well, even at full speed. The dance was a fairly energetic one, and by the time it was over, they were both panting.

"Damn, I need a breather," Clancy said. "How about another round?"

"Okay, but get me two glasses of water this time. I'm parched."

Clancy was gone for nearly ten minutes, and when she returned, Abby looked over the shoulder of the dark-haired woman who'd taken Clancy's seat, making contact with Clancy's narrowed eyes.

Striding over to the pair, Clancy set the drinks down, giving the woman occupying her seat a level stare. "Sorry, but I didn't bring one for you."

"I'm not thirsty," the dark-haired, tough-looking woman said, turning her attention back to Abby.

Clancy tapped the woman on the shoulder and said, "You're in my seat, and you're chatting up my date. This is a big bar, and there's a big crowd. Now go find your own seat and your own woman." Folding her muscular arms over her chest, she added, "Now would be a good time."

"I told you I wasn't alone," Abby said, shrugging at the interloper.

"She was gone forever," the woman said, addressing only Abby. "Anyone who leaves a good-looking woman like you alone for that long can't be too interested."

Clancy settled her hat on her head, put her hand around the woman's bicep, and started to squeeze. After just a few seconds, the intruder hopped off the chair, wincing noticeably. "Thanks for being so cooperative," Clancy said with a fake smile. "Don't come again, now, ya hear?"

As the woman skulked away, rubbing her arm, Clancy tipped her hat back, exposing a bit of blonde hair, and said, "Sometimes a woman's gotta do what a woman's gotta do."

Abby had been quietly laughing, and she placed her hand on Clancy's arm. "That was so much fun!"

Giving her a curious smile, Clancy asked, "Fun? Really? I was afraid that would make you uncomfortable."

"No, not at all! That's the most interest anyone's shown in me in five years! I was just about to leave with her, but I didn't want to be rude. Mama always said to dance with the one that brung ya."

The look on Clancy's face nearly caused Abby to fall on the floor in hysterics. "I'm kidding, Clancy," she gasped. "Kidding!"

"Jesus Christ," Clancy said, dropping her head into her hands. "I was sure you were serious!"

"Nah. I prefer blondes." Abby took her drink and threw her head back to drain it. She looked at the incredulous expression on Clancy's face; then she stuck out her hand and grasped Clancy's. "Let's dance!"

During their next round of instruction, the women got separated when the dancers formed into long rows to execute the moves. Abby was right in the middle of the first row, and Clancy was near the end of the third. The dance was one of the slowest, sexiest ones that Clancy knew, and she was just about to go up and give the instructor a big kiss for choosing this particular night to feature it.

Watching Abby much more than her own feet, Clancy closely observed her friend as she hooked her thumbs into her belt loops and swayed her hips to the beat, doing a slow, sexy bump and grind. She had her hat pulled down low, and her gray-flecked hair showed just a bit under the black felt, providing a very attractive contrast. With the toe of her boot, Abby drew a long, wide line across the floor, then stomped her boot sharply and executed a full turn. Clancy was so mesmerized that she was the very last person to turn—almost allowing Abby to catch her staring. *Good God, she's got a sweet ass! What in the hell is wrong with the men in this town? There aren't enough twenty-five-year-old actress-model-whatevers to go around, fellas. Wake up and see the hot women waiting for you, you fools!*

After another half-hour of nonstop dancing, Abby caught Clancy's eye and nodded toward the bar. They met up at the edge of the dance floor, and Abby loosely draped her arm around her friend. "How about a little whiskey and a lot of water?"

"Let's do it," Clancy said. "My turn to buy."

"Are you sure? I thought it was my turn."

"I have no idea. But I've got ten bucks in my pocket, and it wants to get spent. Have a seat, pardner."

While they were trying to rehydrate, the instructor thanked everyone for coming and jumped down off the small stage. "Is that it?" Abby asked.

Smiling at the disappointed look on her friend's face, Clancy said, "You've got a hell of a lot of energy stored up there, doncha?"

"This is fun!" Abby said, her excitement obvious. "I really do love to dance, and this is more energetic than most dancing. It's like taking an exercise class as well as a dance class."

"Yeah, you can really work up a sweat."

"Are you having fun?"

"I'm having a blast! I think I'm gonna give Michael his walking papers and bring you every week."

"Oh, I don't want to break up a good partnership," Abby said, giving Clancy a quick pat. The next song began, and Abby watched the dancers start to move. "Oh! A two-step. Do you know how?"

"Sure do. Shall we?"

They made their way to the dance floor, but just as they reached the edge, Abby put her hand on Clancy's arm. "Uhm…I've never danced this way with a woman."

"Oh! Well, we can…we don't have to dance together. We'll wait for another line dance."

Abby blinked at her and then broke out in a laugh. "No, no, I just wondered— how we decide who leads?"

Clancy put her hand on the small of the taller woman's back and urged her forward. "That's easy—I lead. I *always* lead," she added with a rakish wink.

🌱

The women seemed a little stiff with each other as they aligned themselves properly. Even though the two-step position was casual, Clancy felt her heart rate pick up when Abby drew close and lightly gripped the landscaper's bicep. "Ready?" Clancy asked, her mouth a little dry as she looked up and met Abby's eyes.

"Lead me."

They started to glide around the edge of the floor, with Clancy holding her head up high, leading Abby with a sure, confident style. They moved well together, their thighs brushing lightly during their long, graceful strides. After moving around the floor several times, Clancy raised an eyebrow and asked, "Wanna get wild?"

"Wild is my middle name," Abby said, chuckling. "Give me your best shot."

Ooh, would I ever love to, Clancy thought, nearly swooning. "Up for a little change of pace?"

"Yep. What'll it be?"

"How about a quick, quick, quick, quick, slow? Get your heart pumping a little."

"Lead the way, pardner."

Clancy did, and they started to move quickly around the floor, using the far outside of the circle to avoid running into the slower dancers. *Ooo, baby, if she can follow my lead this well, I'd love to see her moving under me in bed. I bet she's fan-fucking-tastic!*

"Is that all you've got?" Abby asked, obviously taunting her partner.

"Far from it. Know this one?" Clancy moved Abby off the floor to explain the step. Abby wasn't familiar with it, but she was a good student, and after a few slow run-throughs, they were back at it.

At a slightly slower pace, they moved against each other, lightly trailing their hands over each other's bellies. Then Clancy turned to face in the same direction as Abby, both of them stepping backward while they held hands. Clancy spun her partner once; then they pivoted away from each other, with Abby spinning another one-and-a-half times. They both faced forward, and Clancy spun her again, so that they ended up in their starting positions. "Damn, you're good," Abby murmured.

"That's what all the ladies say," Clancy said, showing her most winning grin.

"I don't doubt it," Abby said, laughing heartily. "I don't doubt that for one minute."

They danced so long that both women were completely sober by the time Abby looked at her watch and said, "Good Lord, Clancy, it's almost midnight! You have to work in the morning."

"Yeah, I do, but I'm having so much fun, I don't care."

Draping an arm around her shoulders, Abby said, "Well, I care about you. You work hard, and you need your rest. Let's hit the trail."

"Oh, all right, but only if you promise to come with me again."

"I might be here by myself the next time you come," Abby said. "The dancing's great, the whiskey's good, and the girls are sweet on me!"

Chapter Four

The following Tuesday, Clancy gave her friend a call around midmorning. "Hi there; it's Clancy."

"Oh, I know your voice by now. You're the one who always sounds happy."

"That's me. Hey, you told me once that if I was ever in the neighborhood, I should drop by for lunch. Does the offer hold?"

"Of course it does. Can you come today?"

"Yep. I'm going to a nursery in South Pas, so I could stop at the market and pick something up. Will that work for you?"

"Absolutely. I don't have a thing scheduled until three. Come whenever you can. Oh, and Clancy? Will you pick out something for the spot where I dug up the spring bulbs? I need some yellows and oranges."

"You've got it. I know the spot you mean."

"Wow, my life is in great shape. I know a doctor who makes house calls, and now I have a landscaper who does, too. All I need is a dentist, and I'm set."

When Clancy arrived, she saw that the house was in an unusual state of disarray, with CDs, books, and articles of clothing strewn around the kitchen. Suddenly, it hit her, and she asked, "Hayley's home, isn't she?"

"How did you guess?" Abby asked, staring pointedly at the mess. "One day, and the house looks like we had an earthquake. But I'm glad to have her, no matter how messy she is."

They took their lunch outdoors and started to eat, both of them gazing out at the plants for a few minutes. "Have you had a chance to talk to Hayley about her, uhm...dabblings?"

Abby nodded, waiting to speak until she had swallowed a sweet bit of cantaloupe. "I followed your advice and let her talk. She spouted some dogma about how women have to claim their own sexuality. A woman can't wait for a man to make the first move." Abby rolled her eyes and added, "I bit my tongue, even though I wanted to tell her that I heard that same rhetoric at UCLA when I was her age. It was a load of BS then, and it still is."

"So, you weren't carried away on the 'Sisterhood is powerful' bandwagon?" Clancy joked.

Abby gave her a considered look and raised one dark eyebrow. "Has someone been reading her history books?"

Clancy nodded and said, "I was a women's studies minor in school. I've done a lot of reading about the women's movement."

"Mmm…I wasn't in the forefront of the movement, since I was in grade school when it began, but I was, and still am, very much a feminist. The only part of Hayley's message that I reject is that you can base your sexual response on a political agenda." She fixed Clancy with an intense gaze and said, "I've always thought that was wrong. To me, feminism is about being able to reach your true potential—no matter what it might be."

Abby shook her head, her expression pensive. "I can still recall late nights in my dorm room, smoking grass with one particular woman who was a campus leader. She was one of those people whom everyone is drawn to. Do you know the type?"

"I do."

"Anyway, we spent endless nights discussing sexuality. Sex was a very, very political issue at UCLA at the time. Her position was unshakable—you could only really know what true sisterhood was if you experienced what it was like to love another woman physically." She looked at Clancy with a half-smile, some of her thick hair falling onto her forehead.

Clancy's heart began to beat more quickly. She'd been part of many discussions like this, all ending with the other woman saying, "I'm a lesbian." It was tough, but she managed to toss off a comment. "Let me guess. She was willing to be your tour guide?"

"That was part of the plan," Abby said, smirking. "You know, if she hadn't put the hard sell on me, I might have given lesbianism a try. All of my friends slept with other women at least once. But I hated to be told that I *had* to do anything—so I turned her down."

Clancy's heartbeat slowed, and the adrenaline stopped pumping. "Ever regret it?" she asked, hoping against hope.

"No. Not at all. I'm sure there were many, many people I could have slept with who could have pleased me sexually, but I've always been the type who has to be in love to share my body. That requirement has worked well for me, and I have no regrets."

"Sounds like Hayley doesn't feel the same way. Are you disappointed in her for wanting to skip the love part?"

"No, not really," Abby said thoughtfully. "She's a very different girl than I was. When she was just sixteen, she started to…well, things have changed since I was young. I don't feel comfortable talking about specifics, but she's done more than I had when I was her age. I tried to talk her out of doing too much too soon, because I knew she wasn't mature enough. Regrettably, she admitted later that she didn't enjoy it much—that the boy she was seeing wasn't very concerned with her pleasure."

"What makes her think things will be different now?"

"Oh, I don't know. I suppose she thinks that having intercourse will make a big difference. It won't," Abby said, smirking. "But I don't know how to convince her of that. If a young man doesn't give you pleasure before you start having intercourse, he's not likely to learn how just by penetrating you."

"Wow! Do you two really talk this frankly?"

"Yeah. We always have."

"Damn, I can't imagine talking to my mom about kissing, much less anything really racy."

"Our openness has its benefits," Abby said, "but it's really hard for me sometimes. I want her to make her own choices in life, but I desperately want to shield her from as much pain as I can. I hope that I can convince her that sex doesn't have to be merely another way to spend an hour—if it even takes that long! I don't want her to believe that crap! Besides, she'll get her heart broken that way."

Clancy reached across the table and patted Abby, letting her fingers trail across the smooth, cool skin on the back of her hand. "Hearts can mend. They get stronger by healing the little breaks."

"Has your heart been broken?"

Shaking her head, Clancy said, "I've had a few little nicks taken out of it, but it's never been fractured. I'm pretty careful with it."

Abby nodded. "Don't be too careful. You've got to risk to love."

"I think I know that, but I won't give my heart away unless I know the woman I choose is deserving of it. It's the only one I have."

Giving her hand a return pat, Abby said, "That's going to be one lucky woman." She looked at the flat of plants Clancy had placed on the corner of the steps. "And I'm a lucky woman for having a friend with such good taste in plants!"

"Not to mention a trade discount," Clancy said, smiling.

On Thursday afternoon, Clancy stopped by Abby's house with some rock samples. She briefly wished she had a wheelbarrow in the back of her truck when she tried to wrangle the rocks around to the back yard. Abby came out to help her, and the pair managed to get all of the samples unloaded, even with the always-helpful dogs licking at Clancy's sweaty legs. "I get the definite impression that my popularity would plummet if I started to wear long pants."

"Do you ever wear long pants when you work?"

"Nope. I got used to wearing shorts when I worked with my dad. I can't imagine feeling comfortable any other way."

"It's your signature," Abby decided. "That and your colorful socks, that is."

"Oh, these." Clancy held her foot out, as if she needed to remind herself of her little quirk. "Well, since all of my shorts and my shirts fall along some point of the khaki palette, I decided I needed a little color so I didn't bore myself to death. My casual clothes are really bright," she added. "All khaki was a little hard to get used to."

"I think your style suits you to a T," Abby assured her. "It's very—you."

"I'll take that as a compliment, even though I think it's code for 'You're pretty odd, Clance.'"

Abby gazed at her for a moment and pursed her lips. "Mmm. You are a little quirky, but in my book, that's a very, very positive characteristic. I meet too many people who aren't happy unless they look exactly like all of their friends. They're always afraid to step out of the box."

Clancy laughed. "I'm out of the box…I'm out of the closet…I'm just plain out."

"You wear it well," Abby said. "Say, Hayley should be home soon. Wanna stay and say hello?"

"You probably want to spend the evening together. You can call me with your—"

"No, no," Abby said. "I'd like for you to meet Hayley—and Trevor, too. She went to pick him up at the airport." She glanced at her watch. "They should be home soon."

"Are you sure?"

"I wouldn't say so if I weren't."

"Then I'd love to meet them."

The younger Grahams arrived home just as Clancy and Abby started to discuss the attributes of the river-rock samples. Abby's face lit up so brightly when she heard the garage door open that Clancy was unable to stop smiling just from observing her friend's joy. The dogs caught the rising level of excitement and began to run through the house, barking wildly. Abby gave her young friend a wry look and asked, "See why it's so hard to get used to living alone? This place has been a madhouse since Trevor was a baby."

The laundry-room door burst open, and a tall, handsome young man entered, his grin matching his mother's. Right on his heels, a much younger copy of Abby struggled in, carrying two suitcases.

Abby threw her arms around her son and gave him a hug that looked as though it would squeeze all of the air out of his lungs. He hugged her back with equal gusto, closing his eyes against the emotion that flowed between them. "God, I've missed you," she whispered, just loud enough for Clancy to hear.

The young woman dropped the suitcases and gave Clancy a shrug. "I barely get a nod when I come in."

"That is such a lie!" Abby dived for her and wrapped her in a bear hug from behind, cuddling her close to her body. She looked at Clancy from over her daughter's shoulder. "This is my most precious daughter, Hayley. Hayley, this is Clancy O'Connor."

Hayley tried to extend her hand for a shake, but Abby was holding her so tightly that she couldn't get free. "Mom," she whined, struggling for release.

As she let her go, Abby slapped her sharply on the butt. "I don't ever want you to feel unloved."

"Stifled, crushed, smothered…" the young woman teased.

"Those are fine," Abby agreed. "Just not unloved."

After quietly watching the interplay between his mother and sister, the young man stepped forward and offered his hand to Clancy. "I'm Trevor," he said in a rich baritone.

"Good to meet you, Trevor. Your mom's been telling me about the project you're going to be working on. It sounds fantastic. You don't need any landscape architects, do you?"

He smiled at his mother, who was beaming at him. "Mom seems to think Venice will rise or fall based on my input. It's really a simple project to keep a bunch of unemployed urban planners off the streets over the summer. Kinda like summer camp."

"He's being modest," Abby insisted. "He's brilliant, and I'm confident that Venice will remain vital if the government only follows his suggestions."

Trevor gave her a look that was filled with affection. "No matter what, I know I'll always have one fan in my corner."

"I'm in your corner, too," Hayley reminded him. Giving him her best little-sister look, she added, "As long as you don't piss me off."

"Hey! Watch your language!" Abby chided, sounding very much like a mom.

"We're in college," Hayley said. "We can say 'piss.'"

"I'm forty-five, and I manage to get through the day without being vulgar."

"True, but then, you're perfect," Hayley joked, sticking her tongue out at her.

"I've got to set a very high standard for you two to aspire to," Abby said, wrinkling up her nose at her daughter.

Hayley leaned over and kissed her mother on the cheek, and Clancy was struck by the warm familiarity that all three of the Grahams exhibited. She stood up and said, "Well, I'll let you all get settled. How long will you be home, Trevor?"

"A week. I've got to be in Venice on Sunday."

Abby looked at her and explained, "Hayley and I went to Boston for Trev's graduation, but she had to go right back to school to finish her exams. I came home alone while Trevor went to spend some time with his grandparents."

"Your parents?" Clancy asked.

"Yes. Pasadena is their home, but they spend most of the spring and all of the summer in Maine. Since Trev was close, he's visited them for a couple of weeks every year that he's been at MIT. Since he'll have such a short time here, I hated to let him go this year, but it's important that he spend time with his grandparents, too."

"I'm going to Maine at the end of the summer," Hayley volunteered. "Grams and Gramps needed a little break to recover from Trev."

Giving her daughter a playful scowl, Abby commented, "We always thought it was important that each child have some time alone with my mom and dad. I'm surprised it's continued this long, but they both seem to enjoy it."

Clancy headed for the door. "I sure wouldn't mind a couple of weeks in Maine. But duty calls. Give me a buzz when you've made a decision about the rock, Abby."

Hayley gazed at Clancy for a moment and then turned to her mom. "Why don't we have Clancy stay for dinner, Mom? I really want to hear about your project."

Abby gave her a slightly surprised look but quickly said, "Any interest, Clancy? We're having Trevor's favorite dish—steak fajitas, cooked on the grill."

Clancy's eyes lit up, and she offered only a token protest. "I'm all dusty and grimy."

"You're perfectly fine," Abby scoffed. "I think you should stay, but if you have other plans…"

"No, no plans. If you don't mind a slightly grungy landscaper at your table, I'd love to stay."

❧

Trevor was in charge of the grill, Abby handled the rice and refried beans, and Hayley was in charge of making the homemade flour tortillas. Clancy was surprised not only to see people making their own tortillas, but also by how companionably mother and daughter worked together.

"I take it you've done this before?" she asked Hayley.

"Yeah. We've always all cooked together." Her eyes clouded a little as she corrected herself. "Well, Trev didn't do much before, but he's taken over for Dad now."

Clancy nodded and leaned back on her stool, observing the young woman. She wasn't an exact copy of her mother, Clancy realized now that she had time to study her. While her face was strikingly similar, her body was much slighter, almost willowy. Hayley was also shorter than her mom—Clancy guessed she and Hayley were about the same height. Though there were some differences, Clancy found the girl fascinating. It was, in some ways, like looking at a living, breathing version of a very young Abby, and that pleased the architect no end. *I love Abby's graying hair, but the jet-black is stunning with that skin color and those eyes. Damn, these people got in line more than once when they were handing out good looks!*

She let her mind drift to imagining Abby as a young woman, and although she wouldn't have minded having Abby's current personality pasted onto this young copy, she had to admit honestly that she'd rather have the original. The young woman was definitely pretty and more than a little sexy—but Abby had such depth, such seasoning. That couldn't be substituted for, in Clancy's considered opinion.

Trevor brought in the skirt steaks he had grilled, looking quite proud of himself. His mother took a peek and gave him a kiss on the cheek for a job well done. He gave Clancy a slightly embarrassed look as Abby added a hug that lasted nearly a minute.

He had many similarities with Abby, too, although his features were the masculine version. The main differences were that his eyes looked more gray than blue, and his body was almost bulky. He was tall, about six foot two, and he had to weigh over two hundred pounds. He wasn't overweight by any means, but he looked like he could hold his own with a jackhammer, and Clancy briefly wished he were going to be around for the summer. She could always use another pair of hands—especially big, strong ones.

Over dinner, Clancy swore repeatedly that she'd never be able to buy tortillas again—that Hayley had ruined her for the commercial version. The young woman beamed at her, and Abby smiled so brightly through dinner that her cheeks must have hurt.

"So Hayley, your mom tells me that your plan is to lie on a raft and not get out of the pool all summer. Any truth to the rumor?" Clancy asked.

The young woman smiled and rolled her eyes briefly at her mother. "I really wanted to get a job, but my school year runs a little longer than everyone else's. Then I'll have to leave to go to Maine for a few weeks." She shrugged her shoulders. "That doesn't leave much time."

"She's omitted the fact that she's never worked a day in her life," Trevor interjected.

Clancy raised an eyebrow, and Hayley nodded. "That's true, but it doesn't mean I don't want to work. It just hasn't worked out."

"Yeah, employers aren't going door to door looking for help much any more," Trevor said, winking at Clancy.

"Why don't you see if Clancy needs another laborer?" Abby asked, ineffectively hiding a teasing smile.

Hayley's vivid blue eyes settled onto Clancy, and she asked, "*Do* you need any help?"

Clancy sized the girl up and decided to tell the truth. "To be honest, I could use some help—but I think Trevor would be more suited to the help I need." She smiled at him and admitted, "I was licking my chops as soon as you walked in the door. A sturdy guy like you could really come in handy."

"I wish I were going to be here. I love to work outside. Hayley, on the other hand, likes to lie in a lounge chair and ask anyone passing by to bring her a cool drink."

"I'm not like that!" the young woman huffed. "Come on, Clancy, isn't there something I could do? You could help me show these two that I can hold my own."

"Honey, you're putting Clancy on the spot," Abby interrupted. "This is very strenuous work, and besides, we've decided to put the project off until you leave for school. I don't want a bunch of workmen ogling you while you work on your tan." She gave Clancy a light slap on the back and said, "Sorry to impugn your employees, but she looks too darned good in a swimsuit."

"Oh, they love to ogle," Clancy admitted agreeably. "But I can't point the finger at them; I do it myself." She suddenly realized what she had said and blushed three different shades of red. "I mean—I sometimes look at—well, not—I didn't mean—I certainly wouldn't look at you—uhm…"

She was floundering so badly that Abby immediately came to her rescue. "We all look when we see a particularly fine example of whatever sex appeals to us. I've been known to drool a little when I see those California Highway Patrol officers."

"Oh, God! Mom and her uniform fetish!" Hayley moaned.

"It's hardly a fetish, honey," Abby said. "And I'm sure I'm not the only woman who loves a man in a uniform."

"I'm certain that's true." Clancy smiled at her, grateful for the rescue.

Abby gazed thoughtfully at her daughter and said, "If you don't mind, I'd love to start the project now, Hayley. I was only holding off because of you."

"What do you think, Clancy? I'm a good worker—I think," she added tentatively.

Clancy gave the girl a long look, seeing the hopeful expression. "I'll tell you what. I've got about two weeks' worth of work clearing the hill where the new wall and waterfall will go. It's certainly not easy work, but if you want to do it, it'll free up one of my guys to work on another project. I pay my unskilled laborers $12 an hour. That's not a lot—and I'm sure your mom could get you something that pays as well for a lot less work—but if you want to do it, you're hired."

Hayley extended her hand and shook Clancy's. "We've got a deal."

"After the preliminary work is finished, we'll reassess and see if you want to continue. The next phase of the project is a lot tougher, but if you like it, I'm sure I could find something for you."

"I'm sure I'll like it," Hayley decided with the brash confidence of youth. Giving her brother a haughty look, Hayley said, "You won't ever again be able to say I've never worked, big guy."

The younger Grahams decided to go for an after-dinner swim, and after Abby bit her tongue to stop herself from warning them to be careful swimming on full stomachs, she and Clancy started to clean the kitchen. "I really enjoyed myself tonight," Clancy said. "Your kids are delightful."

"It's funny," Abby said thoughtfully. "I'd always dreamed of having kids—but I pictured them as kids, you know? Rather than adults, that is."

Clancy nodded agreeably.

"But I've found that I enjoy them even more now that they're becoming their own people. If Will were here, I'm sure this would be the best time of my life."

Clancy placed a hand on Abby's shoulder and gave it a squeeze. "I wish he were here for you, too. I can see how much you miss him."

Unexpectedly, Abby turned and buried her face in Clancy's shoulder. "It's so hard sometimes when the kids are here. They remind me of him with every gesture, every look. Hayley inherited so many of his expressions," she sobbed. "And Trevor looks exactly like him from behind. I see him standing outside by the grill, and my heart catches in my throat. I could swear it was Will." She cried so hard that she was gasping for breath. "It breaks my heart."

"I'm so sorry, Abby," Clancy soothed. "I'm so sorry for your loss."

Weakly, Abby straightened and tried to compose herself. "I hate to let them see me cry. I know they've largely gotten over it, and I hate that I haven't."

"You had the bigger loss," Clancy insisted. "They lost their father, but you lost your husband, your lover, your friend."

Abby nodded while wiping her eyes with a tissue. She gazed at her friend for a moment and then said, "You really understand, don't you?"

"A little bit," she said. "My grandfather died a few years ago, and my grandmother and I are very close. She talks to me about her grief. Even though she's much older than you are, I imagine the experience is about the same. Grief is grief."

"Would you like to see Will's picture?" Abby asked in a rough voice.

"Yes."

Abby placed her hand on Clancy's shoulder and guided her into the living room. Clancy had never been in the space, and Abby watched her eyes dart from detail to detail.

"Wow," Clancy said. "This room is perfect. Just perfect."

"Are you a fan of the period?"

"Oh, yeah," Clancy said, her gray eyes sparkling with interest. "I wavered for a long time deciding between being a residential architect and sticking with landscapes. If I could have worked on houses like this, I would have made the other choice." Her gaze wandered slowly around the room. "Is this all original?"

"Yes. We didn't do anything to this room. We're just the third owners, so we didn't have to correct any mistakes that a multitude of residents would probably have made through the years."

"Thank God no one screwed around with your stained glass," Clancy said. "So many people break one and take out the others."

"No, we were lucky." Clancy was standing next to one of the stained-glass panels that bracketed the picture window, and the last rays of the sun were streaming into the room, painting it in pale blues, purples, and grass-greens. A shaft of light caught her hair and made it nearly glow with a rich amber hue.

"Why would you use the rest of the house if you could be in here?" Clancy said, almost to herself. "The exposed redwood beams, the gorgeous fireplace, this wonderful window seat."

Abby was surprised to find herself touching Clancy's shoulder. She felt happy to have someone appreciate the very things that make her love the house so dearly. "It is special, isn't it?"

"Stunning. One of the best examples I've seen—except for the Gamble house, of course."

"I'm not sure you know it, but this house was built by a man who'd worked for the Greene brothers," Abby said, naming the preeminent designers of the California Craftsman style.

Clancy dropped to her knees, crossing herself ostentatiously. "I'm adding to the design of an almost-Greene and Greene?"

"You sure are," Abby said, smiling down at her, "and I know you're the woman for the job."

Clancy got to her feet, looking a little woozy from the information she'd received. "I hope you're confident enough for both of us," she gulped.

"I thought you were all about confidence."

"I'm confident about you," Clancy clarified. "Big difference."

"You'll do a fine job." Abby gave her a squeeze and led her over to the bookcases that flanked the beautiful windows. "I have dozens and dozens of pictures, but I put most of them away. The room had started to remind me of a mausoleum." She picked up a framed portrait of the entire family. "This was our last Christmas together," she said. "We were all so busy that year, we almost skipped it. I'm so glad we didn't."

Abby watched Clancy study the picture, getting pleasure from the way the intent gray eyes darted from face to face. It was hard for Abby to look at the picture, recalling the day the photographer came to the house and posed them. She and Will were sitting on the sofa in their living room, and the kids were standing behind them, Trevor behind her and Hayley behind Will. She and Will were holding hands, and it made her smile to see how natural the pose was. She didn't recall having the photographer ask them to do that; Will just took her hand whenever he had the chance. She was happy that the portrait was very informal. Everyone was laughing— not smiling; laughing. They had all been enjoying themselves. She leaned toward Will, her head resting on his shoulder, and her eyes were nearly closed as she tried to control herself. Will looked impish—a little like he'd been caught doing something that he shouldn't have been.

Clancy looked up and asked, "Private joke?"

"No. I don't even remember what he said, but Will cracked us all up right before the shutter clicked. There were a lot of shots from the session that were more posed—more traditional—but this one captured us perfectly."

Blinking back tears, Clancy extended her hand, and Abby's immediately fell into it. "I've never seen a family portrait that captured the real people. This is precious." She squeezed the hand, released it, and then looked into her friend's eyes. "Thanks for sharing it."

Abby put the photo back on the shelf and walked to the next case. She removed another photo and smiled as she considered it. "I keep this one to remind myself I was once young." They looked at the picture together, Abby smiling wistfully as she looked at her younger self sitting on Will's lap, her arms draped around his neck. He was looking at her with undisguised interest, but she was staring right into the camera, a wide smile lighting up her face. She smiled when she noted how much Hayley looked like her at this age.

"Will's mother took this not long after we started dating," she said, gazing at the photo fondly. "You can't tell from this angle, but he'd grabbed a handful of my ass and was giving it such a hard squeeze that I was ready to scream. He knew I wouldn't say a thing since his mother was there. He was such a tease!"

Clancy looked a little stunned. "Damn, Abby, you should have been a model!"

"I had a few offers," she admitted. "There were always talent scouts hovering around UCLA in the '70s." She put the picture back in its spot. "I had no interest. My parents are both professionals, and I'd always assumed that I'd make a living with my brain, not my body." She looked thoughtful for a bit and said, "In a way, I didn't fulfill my dreams, but I don't have a regret in the world. I would never have trusted a stranger to raise my babies, and with Will's schedule, I wanted to be home whenever he was. It worked out."

"I can see how happy you are with your decisions," Clancy said, "and I can see what a great mom you are. Your kids are very, very lucky."

"I hope so. But I think we've been on the memory-lane detour long enough. Let's go grab a cold drink and sit outside with the kids."

"What about the dishes?"

"They'll still be there tomorrow. One thing Will's death did was show me that my time with the kids is precious. I don't want to waste a minute."

They sat by the pool until Trevor announced that he was going to bed. Abby walked Clancy out to her truck, and the pair paused by the door for a few minutes. "I had the best time tonight," Clancy said.

"I had fun, too. You really seemed to hit it off with the kids, and I want to thank you for going out of your way to compliment each of them so generously."

"I didn't go out of my way," Clancy maintained. "Your whole family is very complimentable." She wrinkled up her nose and said, "I don't think that's a real word, but you know what I mean."

"I do," Abby said, her laughter making Clancy grin in response. They were quiet for a moment, Abby giving her friend a long look. "I'd love to meet your parents. They did such a good job with you—I'd like a few pointers."

"Well, I don't know about that, but you'll meet my dad soon. He wants to talk to you about your thoughts for the pool deck."

"Great. Let's make plans to meet soon. Maybe both of your parents could come for dinner?"

Clancy laughed, her expression revealing a little disbelief. "You're going to spoil me for normal clients, you know. Not only do you feed me with regularity, now you're feeding my parents."

"Do you still think of me as a client?" Abby asked, furrowing her brow slightly.

"Yes," Clancy said. "I think of you as a client I've been lucky enough to turn into a friend."

"The clients who don't get to be your friend don't know what they're missing," Abby said, smiling.

Clancy looked down at the ground, shyly kicking some stones with the toe of her boot. "Hey, I have a question," she said. "In the picture of you and Will, you were on this porch, but you said you were only dating."

"Oh, didn't I tell you? This is the house that Will grew up in. His parents were ready to retire when we got married. They moved to Palm Springs and gave the house to us as the world's best wedding present."

"Wow! I had no idea!" She looked up at the distinctive pitch of the roofline. "To get an almost-Greene and Greene—without a mortgage!"

"Yes, it was an awfully nice way to start out. Sometimes I wish they hadn't moved away, since they didn't get to spend much time with the kids, but I think they were happy in the desert."

"Past tense?"

Abby nodded. "They both died when the kids were still young. Trevor has some good memories, but Hayley was still a baby when Will's father died, and his mother died just a year later."

"That's a shame," Clancy said. "Grandparents are awfully important."

"Yeah, they are." She laughed softly. "While Will's parents were alive, I always felt like we were living in their house. But once they died, we both felt a little more free to do what we wanted with it."

"You made changes?"

"Yeah. Quite a few. The house had six bedrooms originally, but they were all rather small. We took the three rooms at the end of the hall and had them turned into a large master suite with a big attached bathroom. Then we had the kitchen redone about ten years ago." She made a face and said, "Don't ever let anyone talk you into remodeling a kitchen when you're living in the house."

"Thanks for the advice," Clancy said, smiling. "This is the nicest house I've ever been in, and I'm so grateful that you're letting me make my mark on the landscape. It means more to me than I can say."

"I'm the lucky one," Abby insisted. "Someday, people will say, 'That's a Clancy O'Connor landscape, you know.'"

"I doubt that, but it's nice to dream."

"You're gonna do a marvelous job. I'm really lucking out here. I'm gonna get a great design and a great friend in the bargain."

Clancy impulsively threw her arms around Abby and gave her a heartfelt hug. "Thanks for having confidence in me."

Abby patted her soothingly while holding on for as long as she could. The warmth of Clancy's body and the genuine emotion that radiated from her filled Abby's soul in a way that nearly brought her to her knees. But she took a breath, cleared her mind, and said, "That's what friends do."

"Well, this is a surprise." Margaret O'Connor emerged from the back of her floral shop and beamed at her daughter. "A pleasant surprise, I might add." She walked around the counter and gave her only child a generous hug. "What are you doing in my neighborhood?"

"I had to go check out some plants at a nursery in Cucamonga. I hate to be in the 'hood and not say hello to my dear mother."

"What do you need?" Margaret asked suspiciously, kidding gently.

"Not a darned thing. Everything is fine. I'm working hard; I'm getting paid."

"Good for you!" Margaret ran her fingers through her daughter's close-cropped hair. "It took me a while, but I've really gotten used to your being a blonde. You wouldn't even look like yourself with brown hair again."

Clancy walked around the counter and stuck her head into the huge walk-in chiller. "Nice roses," she commented. "I like the coral ones a lot."

"Thanks," her mother said, still a little suspicious of the visit. Clancy was a very loving, devoted daughter, but she wasn't the sort to drive to Sierra Madre for no reason.

"How's Gramma?"

"She's good," Margaret said. "You're coming to the barbecue on Sunday, aren't you?"

"Huh?" The young woman was obviously distracted, but she nodded. "Oh, sure. Of course I'm coming. I might bring Michael."

"He's always welcome."

"Cool." Clancy sat on the stool behind the counter and rocked back and forth, just as she had when she was a child. "Got any orders to fill?"

"Sure. Why?"

"Can I help?"

"Clancy." Margaret put her hands on her hips and stared at her daughter. "You don't come out to Sierra Madre in the middle of a working day to help me fill orders. Now, what's up with you?"

"Nothing," she said, a touch of irritation in her voice. "I'm not busy, and I thought it would be fun to spend the afternoon with you. If you don't want me here…"

Margaret went to her daughter and grasped her firmly, holding her against her ample breasts. "Of course I want you here. You'd still be living at home if I had my choice." She released her and placed a hand on the small of her back to lead her into the workroom. "I have an order for a big twenty-fifth-anniversary party. Wanna do the arrangement for the head table?"

❧

"Something is definitely up with Clancy," her mother said after she and her husband had gotten into bed that night.

"I think it's nice that she came up to spend some time with you. Do you have to second-guess her all the time?"

"Second-guess! When have I ever second-guessed her?" Margaret sat up and glared at her husband, daring him to contradict her.

He merely gave her a fond look and a pat on the side. "Let's see…you tried to talk her out of being gay. As I recall, that period lasted for several years. Then there was the tattoo, and the—"

"Fine! You laugh all you want, John. Something is bothering her, but she's not able to talk about it."

He gave her a patient smile and said, "When she's ready, she'll talk about it. She always does, Margaret."

She grabbed her pillow and tossed it at him. "You're as bad as she is!"

Chuckling, he pushed the pillow away from his face and said, "I take that as a compliment." His face crinkled up in a grin as he reminded his wife, "So would she."

"Rub it in. Go ahead and rub it in."

Since Clancy's birth, the O'Connors had had a running joke concerning which of them the child was closer to. For many years, the clear winner had been John, and he was loath to discontinue their game now that he was winning.

"Hey, she came to you this time," he reminded his wife. "Did you try to draw her out?"

"Yes! I asked her at least five times, and each time she told me there was nothing wrong!"

"Oh, Margaret, have you learned nothing from the master?" He was clearly rubbing it in, but his wife wanted information badly enough to allow him to torture her.

"Go on," she said wearily. "Lecture me again."

He puffed out his chest, pleased to be in this position. "Okay. The key to Clancy is never to ask her a direct question. She only talks if she doesn't realize she's revealing anything. You have to work around the question, Margaret. You can't hit the kid head-on."

"You know that's not my style," the chronically blunt woman grumbled, blowing out a frustrated breath.

"I know, sweetheart. You leave the girl to me. I'll get it out of her at the barbecue."

"No! I want her to confide in me for a change!"

"Okay," John said patiently. "Give me your best guess as to what's bothering her."

She thought for a minute. "It's her love life. Or her lack of one." He gave her an encouraging look, and she continued. "There was something there, John. Something's…God, I hope she's finally getting serious about someone."

He chuckled at her expression. "This from the woman who tried for years to convince her that she wasn't gay."

"Honey, it's been twelve years since she told us. I'd be happy if she brought a well-mannered goat home to meet us."

Laughing at her exaggeration, he said, "I agree it's high time she found someone, but you can't rush her, sweetie."

"She's going to be thirty this year, John. Having a relationship that lasts longer than a month is not rushing!"

"Well," he admitted, "I would like to at least meet one of her girlfriends. Maybe she's discovered that she's really straight, but she's afraid to admit it since she made such a big deal about being gay."

"I don't think you should hold your breath on that one, honey," Margaret said. "I don't know the first thing about lesbians, and even I would tag her as one. She's got the look."

"Oh, since when did you develop a sense of lesbian style?"

"Well, I don't have one, but she reminds me a little bit of that Ryan girl. You know the one."

"Ryan?"

"Yes, honey, the girl from the talk show. And that cute movie where she had the orgasm."

"Orgasm? They made a movie about orgasms?"

"No, no, that was a little part of the movie. She had that funny orgasm in the deli."

John gave her a wide-eyed look. Then, slowly, recognition dawned. "Meg Ryan? Are you talking about Meg Ryan?"

"Yes! Clancy reminds me of her a little bit. Clancy says she has a talk show now."

"Honey, I think you're talking about Ellen DeGeneres. Those are two different women."

"Oh, right. Well, since Clancy dyed her hair, she looks like the Ryan girl, and…well, I guess she looks like the DeGeneres girl because they're both…lesbians."

John O'Connor buried his head under his pillow. His wife barely heard his muffled, "Don't you ever say that to her face."

Chapter Five

The barbecue was winding down, and John O'Connor realized he'd have to admit defeat. He'd unobtrusively cornered his daughter at every opportunity, offered up plenty of leading questions, and even resorted to a direct one—all to no avail. He decided he had to resort to his secret source and called Michael over to the grill. "Anything going on with Clancy lately?" he asked bluntly. "She seems distant—like something's on her mind, but she won't talk about it. Her mom is under the impression that she might be seeing someone."

"Well, I can put that rumor to rest," Michael said. "She's not seeing a soul. All she's been doing is working and reworking those plans for that house in the Arroyo. That job means an awful lot to her."

"Is she worried about it?" John asked.

"Yeah, she must be," Michael said. "She's over there all the time—and she's been all over Southern California looking for the perfect materials. There's no way she's gonna make a dime on the job with all of the hours she's putting in."

"That could do it," John said. "She's always withdrawn when she's worried about something." He clapped the young man on the back. "Thanks for the info, Michael. It pays to have an insider who's not opposed to leaking secrets."

"I only leak things that are for her own good," Michael said. "I don't tell you the really sordid stuff."

John backhanded him in the gut, and the hairstylist reminded himself never to tease the brawny contractor about his precious daughter.

❦

Armed, as it were, with a new pair of boots, a pair of pigskin gloves, and a bandanna to keep the sun off her neck, Hayley climbed the steep hill alongside Clancy early on Monday morning. "We'll probably build some temporary steps to avoid fatigue and make it easier to bring supplies up here, but for now, I think this is the most direct path," Clancy said.

Hayley nodded and looked at the ground carefully, as though she were making a mental note to go up the hill the same way next time. They reached the top, and Clancy walked along the uneven slope like a mountain goat, her determined stride not faltering a bit. When they reached the far edge of the property, she stood with her hands on her hips and surveyed the fence line.

"We're going to come out about two feet," Clancy instructed, holding her hands out to give Hayley an idea of the distance. "We're gonna leave this ivy on most of the hill 'cause it's a good ground cover, but we have to get rid of it along the line of the new wall. This stuff can have roots that go down eighteen inches, and it can be thick enough to dull the blades on the trencher, so we have to do it by hand. What I want you to do is clear every scrap of vegetation from the fence to two feet out. If you find any significant roots, I want you to mark them with one of these little flags."

She held up a foot-long piece of stiff wire with a two-inch square of red plastic attached to the end. "That way, we'll know where to dig them out."

"I could do that, too," Hayley volunteered.

"You're gonna have your hands full; trust me," Clancy assured her. "Now, this is a little unconventional, but it works great." She took out a dozen plastic grocery bags and handed them to Hayley. "Fill these up with the ivy that you dig up. When one is full, tie it off and throw it to the bottom of the hill. That way, we can get rid of the stuff without lugging it down at the end of the day."

"Cool," Hayley agreed. "You're pretty smart."

"Trial and error. I've made a lot of errors."

"What are you going to be doing?"

"Well, I'm going to be supervising you. Maybe I'll sit in the shade and drink lemonade." At Hayley's raised eyebrow, Clancy chuckled and said, "Your mom makes that same face."

"She stole it from me."

"I'm sure." Clancy looked at the list of tasks she wanted to accomplish by the end of the day and decided. "I think I'll work with you. I want you to get a feel for the easiest way to do this."

"Great! Let's get started!"

It was just the two of them in the enclosed, private yard. Abby and Trevor had left before seven to play golf with Ellen and her son, Sam, leaving the two laborers to their task. The day was really heating up, and at around eleven, Clancy went down the hill to grab a pick-mattock. The heavy, worn tool had a sharp pick on one end and a squared-off cutting tool on the other. Clancy pulled a small diamond file from her back pocket and spent a few minutes properly sharpening the mattock. Hayley glanced at her. "What in the hell is that?"

"It's a mattock. It cuts through about anything—including feet, so stay clear of it. I decided I might as well get rid of the roots as you find 'em." She'd been standing still for a few minutes but was still extraordinarily hot. "You don't mind if I take my shirt off, do you? I don't normally work in my sports bra, but it's scary hot today."

"No. Go right ahead. I got used to being naked around other girls at school this year."

"Mmm…that's tempting in this heat, but I think the shirt is enough." Clancy shrugged out of her wet shirt, wiped her brow with it, and then hung it on the stockade fence. She stood in her gray sports bra and spruce-green shorts, and took a long pull off the liter bottle of water she had brought up with her. Sighing deeply when she thought of the effort she'd have to expend, she started to work, swinging the heavy tool from over her shoulder down to the roots—time and time and time again. The sweat was running off her body in rivulets, leaving a noticeable patch of mud where it landed on the ground. Her face was so flushed that it looked like she'd been burned, and after nearly a half-hour of constant work, she stopped for another drink.

Hayley was staring at her slack-jawed. "I've never seen anyone work that hard!"

"Sure you have," Clancy said. "They're just not people you know. You see people in this neighborhood every day working this hard—or harder. You see gardeners and maids and construction workers and roofers working their butts off. They're invisible to you."

"I guess you're right. But it seems different when it's someone you know."

Clancy took off her cap and doused it with the remaining water, now warm. She plopped it back onto her head and started up again, not stopping until high noon. Now her shorts were as wet as her hat, and she looked like she was about to pass out.

"You don't look so good," Hayley ventured.

"Oh, if you mean my red face, that's perfectly normal for me. It'll go away as soon as I rest for a bit."

"We get to rest?"

"Yep. Time for lunch." Clancy strode down the hill and over to her backpack, taking out an enormous Tupperware bowl filled with fruit salad. Glancing at Hayley, she suggested, "Don't eat anything too heavy, or you'll be sick."

The young woman nodded and took off for the house, removing her boots and socks before entering. She emerged a few minutes later with a bagel smothered in cream cheese. They sat together under the pergola, the sun deflected from their heads. "How long do you usually break?"

Clancy swallowed and said, "Depends. If it's raining or really cold, we like to keep going. But when it's hot like this, it's really best if we take at least an hour. Most of my guys grew up on farms in Mexico, and they're used to taking a little nap after lunch. It's really not a bad idea."

"If I slept now, I might not get up until tomorrow," Hayley moaned. "I don't know how you do this every day!"

"Well, to be honest, I don't. I usually let my guys do the installations, but they're all busy this week. I didn't want to wait to get started, so I figured I'd pitch in."

"Do you like your work, Clancy? It seems so hard."

"It is, but I love it. I was on the fence about being a regular architect or doing this. I'm really happy with my choice."

"Hey, if we're gonna take a long break, why not jump in the pool? I'm sure it'd feel great."

"Oh, I don't know. I've never done anything like that on a job."

"Have you ever had the daughter of the owner on your work crew?"

"Ha! No, I haven't, come to think of it. Does that give me carte blanche with the pool?"

"It does if you're with me. Come on and ditch those filthy boots. Let's cool off!" Hayley hopped to her feet and went into the house. She emerged a few minutes later, wearing a faded red swimsuit and carrying another in her hand. "I think this'll fit you," she said. "It's one of my mom's."

"I hope it's not too stretchy," Clancy said. "Your mom's longer than I am."

Hayley laughed, the sound so much like Abby's melodic laugh that Clancy couldn't help grinning at the girl. "My dad used to call her his long drink of water. I never knew what that meant, but he said it all the time."

Clancy unlaced her boots, leaving a substantial deposit of dirt and mud on the patio. She had to nearly pry her socks off, but she doffed them and wiped as much of the dirt off her legs as she could. "Be right back," she said. She went into the bathroom by the laundry and quickly put on the long suit. She didn't care how it looked as long as it stayed on. She was so excited about the beckoning water that she ran across the patio, dived into the deep end, and came up sputtering. "Damn! That feels great!"

"The pool has never felt so good," Hayley agreed enthusiastically.

They floated limply for a while, neither having the energy to do much else. It was tremendously refreshing, and Clancy thanked her new laborer several times for the generous offer.

A portion of the deep end was in shade, and both women stayed in that section to keep the sun off their bodies as much as possible. "I like your tattoo," Hayley said, looking intently at the band of green ink.

"Oh, thanks. I had it done when I was in college. It's aged pretty well," she commented. "I was afraid it would fade."

"How long ago was that?" Hayley asked.

"Mmm...I graduated in 1998," she said.

"That's about what I thought,"

"Don't try to guess my age that way," Clancy warned. "I worked for four years before I went to school." She could see the teenager trying to work the numbers and saved her the trouble. "I'll be thirty in December."

"You're kidding!"

"Nope. I'm planning on having a huge party. You're officially invited if you're still gonna be in town."

"Cool! I'd love to come." She looked at the tattoo again and asked, "Did it hurt a lot?"

"No, not really. It felt more like an irritation than real pain. It hurt the worst on the underside of my arm. The skin's pretty sensitive there."

"What hurt worse—the nipple ring or the tattoo?" Hayley asked with studied casualness.

Damn! Shoulda taken that out today! "The nipple ring," Clancy said, hoping the subject was closed.

"I was thinking of getting something pierced," Hayley said, and Clancy had a feeling she didn't mean her ears.

"Well, I don't regret it, but I was a lot older than you are when I had it done."

"I think I'm the only girl on my floor who doesn't have a tattoo or a piercing. This summer's gonna be a waste if I don't get one or the other before I go back to school."

"Is that really the best barometer?" Clancy asked. "There has to be something else that could save the summer for you—other than marking up your skin permanently."

"Why's it okay for you? I'm an adult, too."

"Hayley, you're seventeen. I'm almost thirty. That's a big difference."

"Damn! You sound like my mom! I thought you'd be cooler!"

Clancy blinked at the young woman, and Hayley noticed her startled expression.

"Oh, shit. Did that upset you?" Hayley asked, giving Clancy a very earnest look. "I didn't mean to."

"Nah. I don't get upset easily. I guess I was being a little parental. I'll try to act less like your mom and more like your boss." She gave the girl a smile that was immediately returned.

"Is it okay to ask the boss a personal question?"

"I guess it depends on the question."

"I was wondering if you were in a relationship."

"No," Clancy said, laughing. "The boss will entertain a few personal questions. I'm single right now. I've been working too hard to go out much this year, so I haven't been meeting people."

Hayley looked at her for a moment, then asked, "You're queer, right?"

Clancy gave her a crooked smile. "Yep. Doesn't bother you, does it?"

"I go to Santa Cruz!" Hayley said, as though that fact made her shockproof.

"Right," Clancy said, nodding. "How about you? Seeing anyone?"

"No. I'm not really into that," Hayley said. "Relationships are so limiting. Casual sex makes more sense. I don't see why having sex means you have to spend all of your time with one guy."

"It doesn't mean that," Clancy agreed, "but you'll probably change your mind one day."

With a tiny furrow between her eyebrows, Hayley tilted her dark head and asked, "You think I'm a dumb kid, don't you?"

"Nah, not at all, but I think that you'll change your mind about what you want from sex a couple of dozen times by the time you're my age. When I was eighteen, I wanted to be consumed by a lover—but I learned that I need a lot of autonomy. You change your mind as you get more experience."

"Maybe," Hayley said, "but I think I'll always want my freedom. That 'till death do us part' stuff is so over."

"Not for me. I'd love to sleep with one woman every night for the rest of my life. But I haven't found one I can stand for more than a couple of months—so I've got my work cut out for me." She inclined her head toward the hill. "Speaking of work…"

"Okay, boss. Back to the rock pile."

❧

Regrettably, the weather turned hotter, and by Wednesday, Clancy had decided that she needed to start even earlier to avoid sunstroke. Abby was helping all she could, bringing them lots of water and a few small snacks throughout the day, but the only way to make the day bearable was to start at dawn's first light.

It was almost eleven when Hayley asked, "Remember what you said about your guys taking a long nap in the middle of the day?"

"Yeah, I remember," Clancy panted, clearly exhausted from the heat.

"Why don't we do that today? The sun is off this part of the hill by two. We could start up again then and work until six."

Clancy wiped some of the sweat from her eyes and nodded blankly. "I don't normally do that, but I'm feeling awfully sick to my stomach. This could be dangerous."

"Great!" Hayley said with as much enthusiasm as she had left. "Let's hit the pool."

Clancy followed her down the hill, nearly salivating at the thought of swimming, when Abby stepped out onto the patio. "Ready for some lunch?"

"No, thanks," Clancy said immediately. "My stomach's upset."

"She's overheated," Hayley said, and when Abby got a good look at the architect, she agreed with the assessment.

"I'll get you a swimsuit," she said decisively. "You need to cool off." She went into the house, with Clancy following after she took off her boots. The dogs happily licked the dirt, sweat, and mud from her legs, while Clancy giggled hysterically. She took the proffered suit and then ran into the bath by the laundry room to change, saving herself from the flailing tongues in the process. Her tan was comical, and Abby had to force herself not to giggle when she saw it. Clancy had been using the strongest possible sunblock, but she had managed to get even darker, which drew even more attention to her pale skin. She saw Abby's expression and took a look down her body—pasty white feet and ankles, pale skin from the edge of the navy blue suit to midthigh, and slightly tan shoulders bracketed by very tan forearms and lower legs. "I'm thinking of contacting Playboy about a centerfold," she said.

"You have a great body," Abby said, giving her a long, assessing look. "Maybe you could be in the 'Girls in the Construction Trade' issue."

"Some guys probably find farmer tans sexy," Clancy insisted. "It could be a big seller."

"No doubt. Now get out there and jump in that pool before I have to take you to the hospital."

"Aren't you going to come too?"

"Well, I thought I'd make lunch first."

"Come on," Clancy urged. "For a little while?"

Abby flashed her a smile and gave in. "Okay. Until you two are up to eating a little."

Hayley walked barefoot into the kitchen, having wrestled off her boots and socks.

"Hurry up and change, and get back outside," Clancy said. "It's not good to go into an air-conditioned room when you're as hot as we are."

"Then get outside," Hayley said, giving her boss a faux scowl. She looked at her mother and said, "We're gonna take a long nap and then get started again at two."

"Really?" Abby gave Clancy a questioning look, and the architect nodded.

"It's a little dangerous today, with the heat and the smog. I was having trouble breathing. By two, the hill will be in shade, and it should be safe to work then."

"Maybe we should call this off until it cools down," Abby said.

"Well, I've got my guys scheduled to start here the week after next," Clancy explained. "I'll have a huge hole in my schedule if we don't get going then."

"But I'm worried about you," Abby said, gazing at Clancy with round eyes.

"One of the hazards," Clancy assured her. "A bad tan, calloused hands, and the possibility of heatstroke. You don't have to worry about us, Abby. We're used to it, and we know how to protect ourselves."

"Hayley doesn't," she insisted.

"I'm fine, Mom. It's Clancy who's doing the hard work."

Abby looked at her friend, her concern showing in her eyes. "I'm honestly worried about you, Clancy. You look completely exhausted."

"That nap does sound pretty good," she admitted. "I think I'll grab a raft and take a nap in the pool."

"I'm gonna take a shower and a nap," Hayley said. "Wouldn't you be more comfortable in the guest room?"

"No, I really do hate to be in air conditioning during the day. It makes it seem that much hotter when I go back outside."

"I'm willing to risk it," the girl said. She started to head for her room. "I'm willing to risk anything."

Clancy and Abby laughed at her dramatic attitude and went back outside. Clancy dived in, grabbed the nearest raft, and kicked until she was in the corner of the pool that was fully shaded. Hopping onto the soft surface, she sighed in satisfaction and paddled over to Abby. "This is gonna feel *so* good."

Abby smiled at her and said, "I'll go in and prepare a light snack for when you both wake up."

Clancy was asleep by the time her head finished nodding, and when Abby finished in the kitchen, she looked out to find that her friend's raft had drifted into the sun. *How do I fix that?* She changed into a suit and grabbed the book she'd been reading. She steadied one of the upright floating lounge chairs, got in, and kicked until she reached the landscaper. Gently pushing the raft, she maneuvered it into the shady corner and then settled down to read.

Well over an hour had passed when Trevor came home from his visit to the Federal Building to get his passport updated. He looked around the house, trying to find some sign of life. He knew his mother had to be home; he had her car. Walking into the kitchen, he glanced outside and saw his mom, her book on her lap, her foot pressing Clancy's raft into the corner. Clancy was lying on her stomach, her head turned to the side, both arms dangling in the water. Abby's gaze had settled onto her face, and Trevor couldn't help but notice the affection that seemed to flow from his mother toward her.

He wasn't sure why, but something about the tableau was unsettling, and he turned away, trying to put the scene out of his mind.

※

By six o'clock, a substantial portion of the work Clancy had hoped to accomplish was finished, and she was feeling much, much better. It was still hot, but with the sun off their bodies, the heat was bearable. They hadn't eaten after their nap—Clancy's stomach was still a little balky, and Hayley didn't have an appetite either—so now they were both ravenous.

Abby came out at six on the button and said, "Dinner will be ready in a half-hour. That's enough time for you both to shower." Clancy gave her a puzzled look, but Abby placed her hands on her hips and stated in her most motherly voice, "I don't want any arguments out of you, Clancy O'Connor. You've used up five thousand calories today and haven't replenished them. You need a good dinner—and that's what you're going to get."

"Yes, Mom," she mumbled, drawing a snicker from Hayley.

Abby's retreating form answered. "I heard that."

※

For the rest of the week, they followed the same schedule. Clancy brought her own swimsuit and a long-sleeved, oversize T-shirt to wear over it, extra protection to keep the sun off her body while she napped. She also remembered to bring a long strip of elastic tubing, and she tied one end to an ankle and the other to a heavy chair, effectively holding her in place in the shady end of the pool.

She ate dinner with the Grahams every night and spent the remainder of each evening playing in the pool. The whole family liked to enjoy the pool during the warm evenings, and Clancy found herself eagerly joining in on the family tradition.

※

Trevor had to leave for Italy on Saturday, and like every other time since Hayley had gotten her license, she drove him to the airport. That way, Abby got to cry in private, and Trevor and Hayley got to spend a little time decompressing and critiquing the visit.

They hadn't gone very far when Trevor asked, "So how do you think Mom's doing?"

"I think she's pretty good," Hayley said thoughtfully. "I'm glad that she hasn't had any dates since we've been home. She's been going out a lot, you know."

"Uhm…I didn't know it was a lot," Trevor said, giving his sister a nervous look. "I'm not ready for this, Hayley. I can't think of her with another guy."

"Well, I don't know a heck of a lot, but from the little she's said, she's not having much luck."

"What? Mom's so cool! What guy wouldn't want to date her?"

"Make up your mind, Trev," Hayley said, laughing heartily.

"I don't know, Hayley. I mean, I want her to be happy, but—"

"Don't you think she's happy? I think she's much better than she was at spring break."

"You know, she does seem better," he said. He was really trying to get a handle on something niggling that was hovering at the edge of his brain, but he wasn't having much success.

"She's so hot for this project, Trev. You know how wild she is for the yard. Having something like this to concentrate on is probably helping her mood."

"Yeah," he said, smiling as he thought of his mother. "It must be the project."

Then, suddenly, Trevor felt his stomach lurch when he considered the shy glances that he saw Clancy give his mother, the look on his mom's face when she was watching Clancy sleep in the pool, the way she sang to herself while making dinner—as she had when his father was alive—the constant care she lavished on the architect to make sure she wasn't working too hard. All of a sudden, it made sense to him. His mom was definitely happier than she'd been in a long while, but it wasn't the landscape that was putting a smile on her face—it was the landscaper.

Thoughts flew around in his head, the image of his mother and another woman making him intensely uncomfortable. Trying to compose himself, he caught a glimpse of his sister's calm face and said, "I think you're right. The project is probably keeping her happy."

"Hey, Trev? We'll never get so old that a few boulders and a little stream will make our whole summer, will we?"

"Nah, not us, Hayley." He gave his sister a forced smile, hoping that his suspicions were only that.

❧

Both of the Graham women were sad to have Trevor gone, and they picked feebly at their dinner. The silence was companionable, but Abby finally broke it. "We might as well admit how much we're gonna miss Trevor and get it over with."

Hayley looked at her for a moment; then Abby watched her daughter's face transform as her eyes closed and her lower lip started to tremble. "I hardly got to see him at all." She wiped her eyes with her napkin, angry with herself for crying so easily.

Abby reached out, covered her hand, and slipped her fingers around her daughter's. "I know it's hard, honey. I feel the same way when you leave. God," she sighed, "I was a basket case when you left for school last September. Pam and Maria and Ellen each called me every day for two weeks. I think they were afraid I was gonna hang myself."

The young woman stared at her mother. "Is that true? Was it that hard for you?"

Laughing softly, Abby said, "I wasn't suicidal, honey. There's no way I'd put as much work into raising you two as I have and not stick around to see the results."

"But you were sad?"

"Of course I was sad!" Abby looked at her daughter as though she'd asked whether the dogs could talk. "I cried every day for at least a month! I can't count the number of times I lay on your bed and cried—knowing you wouldn't be coming home that night. It was rough."

"Damn, Mom, why didn't you tell me?"

Abby squeezed her hand and shook her head briefly. "That's one of the pains of parenthood, baby. You don't burden your kids with your problems. I want you to have your own life, and going away to college is the best way I can think of to start. I would never want you to be worried about me. I know you had your own problems adjusting."

"I feel like such a jerk!" Hayley said. She pulled her hand away and stood to clear the table. "I was on the phone every other day complaining about some stupid little thing! I never would have done that if I'd known you were sad."

Abby got up as well and caught Hayley at the sink. She wrapped her arms around her waist and rested her chin on her shoulder. "I loved that you called me so often. It didn't matter what we talked about. I was happy that you trusted me to help you work out some of your problems."

"I do trust you, Mom. I don't think I knew how lucky I was until this year. Some of the women I've met have horror stories about their mothers that you wouldn't believe!"

"Sure I would," Abby said. "I've met some dreadful parents. Especially when you were in high school. Some of those parents should have been investigated by the state!"

"I never noticed," Hayley said. She leaned back a little and put her head on her mother's shoulder. "I wasn't aware of a lot of things in high school. I feel like I'm waking up and seeing the world now that I'm in college."

Abby tilted her head and kissed Hayley's cheek. "I hope you always know that I'm here for you, baby. No matter what, I'm on your side."

Hayley slipped from her mother's embrace and began to clear the remainder of the dishes. She made a comment that sounded like it was tossed off casually, but Abby heard the implied question. "You're not always on my side, Mom. You wouldn't like it if I started bringing guys home to stay overnight."

"No, I wouldn't like it," Abby said. She leaned against the counter and crossed her legs at the ankle, her arms crossed over her chest. "I not only wouldn't like it, I also wouldn't allow it. But that doesn't mean I'm not on your side. I love you when I have to say no as well as yes."

"I like the yeses better," Hayley said, grinning slyly. "And I'm not so sure you'd stop me from bringing a date home."

"Then you'd better not try me," Abby said. "Because you'd be very embarrassed. I'm not kidding around about this, Hayley. No overnights until you're very serious about a boy—preferably engaged."

The girl stopped and stared at her mother. "That's not gonna happen, Mom. Marriage might have worked in earlier times, but it doesn't work in the twenty-first century. Haven't you read the statistics? Over half of all marriages end in divorce! People don't think of marriage as a permanent thing anymore. It's dating...until you're sick of each other."

"Statistics can be misleading, Hayley. A lot of people believe in marriage. I do; your father did. All of our close friends are still with their spouses or partners."

"But you're from the previous generation," Hayley explained. "You were at the tail end of the trend."

Abby laughed, trying to force her eyes not to roll. "It's not a trend, honey. It's a way to have deep meaning in your life. There's nothing more satisfying than having someone in your life whom you trust completely, who's your friend and lover and playmate all rolled into one. Being married gave me security and a structure that I loved."

"Yeah? Where did all of that security and meaning get you? Dad's gone, and you haven't had any of that stuff for five years! Don't you miss it?"

"Is that a rhetorical question?" Abby asked. She went to the table and sat down, looking at her daughter in puzzlement. "How can you even ask that? I miss your father more than I could ever begin to tell."

"No, not Dad. I know how much you miss him," the girl said. "But you could have some of the things you had with Dad if you'd loosen up."

"Loosen up?"

"Yeah. You told me you've been dating. Where are those guys?"

Abby let out a wry laugh. "I haven't clicked with anyone. I've liked a few of them, but they didn't like me enough to call me again."

Hayley looked suspicious. "Come on, that can't be true."

"Thanks for the vote of confidence, honey, but it is true."

"Something's wrong here." Hayley sat down, looked at her mother for a moment, and then asked, "What do you tell these guys?"

Thinking about the question for a minute, Abby said, "I tell them about your dad, and I tell them about you and Trevor. I tell them about the things I'm involved in and the sports I like. The usual stuff." She smiled. "I don't know if you've noticed this, but on first dates, men like to do most of the talking."

"Yeah, I've noticed," Hayley said, chuckling. "But think about it, Mom, why should a guy call you again? Maybe men weren't this way when you were young, but nowadays, they like to get laid. If one of the guys you liked drove you home, and you asked him in for sex, you'd at least fill some of the void."

"Void?" Abby managed to get out. "What void?"

"The void in your life since Daddy died. Wouldn't you be happier if you were having good sex?"

"Oh, Hayley." Abby rested her forehead on her open hand and tried to think of where to start. "I don't know who has convinced you that most women like no-attachments sex. It's not true, honey. It takes a while to know someone well enough to mesh with him sexually. God, what would you do on the date? Tell him what positions you like? How you like to be touched? What you will or won't do? Why not have a card printed up with your requirements?"

"That's not a bad idea, Mom. It's more honest that way. If you like him enough to go out with him, and you get along well on the date, why not have sex and see if it works?"

Abby's voice started to gain volume. "Because you'd walk away from some great guys! Sex isn't like fitting gears into a machine! It's nuanced and subtle, honey. Every time is different! When you're with someone you love, you learn how to read his signals. Sometimes you want tenderness, and sometimes you want to..." She stopped and shook her head. "This is getting far too specific. I don't want to know the details of your sexual life, and I certainly don't want to talk about mine."

"That's so hypocritical!"

"How's that?"

"You want me to tell you things, but you won't tell me stuff that you do. That's not fair."

"Fair or not, I'm not talking about your father and my sex life. It's too personal. Children shouldn't be subjected to that."

"I'm not a child, Mom. I know you and Dad had sex. It's no big deal."

"Yes, it is," Abby said. "It is a *very* big deal. It was one of the ways we communicated, Hayley. One of the ways we showed how much we loved one another. One of the things that gave us both joy. It was a very big deal, and pulling one of the guys I've been out with into my bed would never, ever come close to replicating what I had with your father."

"You don't know that," Hayley said, unwilling to give up. "You haven't tried it. How many guys did you have sex with before Daddy?"

"Seventy-eight," Abby said, gazing at her daughter calmly.

"Seventy-eight! Jesus, Mom! What the hell was going on with you?"

"Nothing," Abby said. "That was merely a little trick to show you why I won't tell you. There isn't a number I could say that couldn't be manipulated to fit whatever point you're trying to make. I told you earlier that my sex life is my own business, honey—before, during, and after my marriage."

"Then mine should be, too," Hayley said.

"I agree! I never have and I never would ask you specifics! You're the one who announced that you were going to stop looking for a boyfriend and start having sex for sex's sake."

"I'm sorry I brought it up. Real sorry."

"I am, too, but only because it lets me see that I haven't impressed upon you how wonderful it is to be in a good relationship."

Hayley looked at her mother for a moment. Then she said quietly, "You're not in one now, Mom, and you haven't been in one for five years. If you wanted one, I think you'd have one by now."

Abby stared at her daughter for a moment. Then she got up and went outside, both dogs trailing her. She sat down and stared at the pool, looking at the tiny ripples that skimmed across the surface. The wind was freshening, as it always did in the early evening. The cool ocean breeze had finally made it up the arroyo, and she calmed her racing thoughts as the light wind tossed a few locks of her hair about her head.

She was feeling numb, and she hated the way she and Hayley were interacting. She knew the girl was growing up and trying to find her own way, but she didn't like this new, confrontational style Hayley was developing. Knowing that Hayley was mimicking some of her friends from college, Abby reminded herself that Hayley had a very good foundation and would probably seem more like her old self in a year or two. But that didn't make things settle well now. She'd never avoided having a talk with Hayley, but now she was almost hesitant to make time for them to be alone.

As the minutes passed, Hayley's words kept coming back, and she began to think about them in depth, eventually seeing her recent choices with a different slant. In her heart, she had to admit that she hadn't been showing her true self to the men she'd been seeing. All they saw was a once strikingly beautiful, now very attractive middle-aged woman who spent the evening talking about her dead husband and her two kids. *Why do I do that? Am I ready to have a relationship, or am I only trying to act like I am?*

Chapter Six

Abby invited the O'Connors for a kind of working dinner, thinking she'd kill the proverbial two birds. After the meal, they made their way to the patio to continue the discussion. Abby, Clancy and John got right down to business, with John pulling out some design suggestions for the pool deck. Hayley looked at Margaret and asked, "Would you like to see the rest of the house? We didn't have time for a tour before dinner."

Noticeably thankful, the older woman agreed. "I'd love to. This technical talk goes right over my head."

They examined the house in some detail, Margaret's innate sense of design leading her to exclaim over many details of the house. Like her daughter, she was drawn to the living room, and she and Hayley sat down on the matching leather-covered sofas to soak up some of the ambiance. The pair spent a good long time together, chatting about nothing in particular.

"This is so nice for me," Margaret said. "I don't get to see Clancy in her work environment very often, and it's very reassuring to know she's spending her days with such nice people."

Hayley smiled and said, "It's not only her days, Mrs. O'Connor. We have dinner together almost every night."

Margaret blinked in surprise. "You do?"

"Sure. We changed our schedule around so that we take a three-hour break in the middle of the day. It's hot then, so we swim or nap and then have some lunch. We don't finish until six or seven—until my mom makes us come in for dinner."

Margaret did her best not to gape. *Naps? They take naps together? Dear Lord, don't tell me this girl is what's keeping Clancy so busy! She's remarkably attractive, but she can't be twenty years old!* As the girl continued to speak, Margaret had to admit that except for her age, Hayley was exactly the kind of person she could picture Clancy with. She was poised, well spoken, very friendly and outgoing. Her mind seemed quick and agile, and her enthusiasm for nearly everything was contagious. *I don't care if she's the perfect match! Clancy can't start dating a girl who probably can't even vote! It's bad enough that she wants a woman! I have to talk to John about this. He'll know how to talk some sense into her.*

John O'Connor sat at the table, proudly watching his daughter explain her series of beautifully rendered drawings. He'd consulted with her before, but he'd never seen her interact with a client on a social level, and he was impressed. *She seems so comfortable*, he thought. *I feel like a big lug when I'm at a client meeting, but Clancy acts like she was born into this kind of money.* He sneaked another look at Abby, thinking, *'Course, having a client like this one would sure make me wanna spend a long time meeting. She's one fine-looking woman. And she's so nice to Clance!*

He was pulled from his thoughts when Clancy started explaining how she was going to have the hill drain. He looked at her elevation drawing, glad to find it so well thought out. "I think you did a very smart thing to have the water collect into a French drain at the bottom of the slope." He tapped the paper, indicating the expanse of lawn next to the hill. "Good idea to loosen up this soil, too."

"Yeah," Clancy said. "In a bad storm, the French drain could be overwhelmed. I thought that putting a healthy depth of pea gravel under the lawn would take care of any overflow."

"I didn't know you were going to remove the sod," Abby said, looking concerned.

Clancy reached over and touched her hand, and John watched as Abby stared into his daughter's gray eyes, hanging on every word. "It's impossible to bring in the kind of equipment we're gonna need and not make a mess of your lawn. As long as we have to resod, we might as well do it right." She gave her a smile and said, "Don't worry. It's all included in my estimate."

Abby smiled back at her and said, "Oh, like I'd worry about that." She leaned over and nudged Clancy with her shoulder, grinning at John. "I have to force her to bill me for everything. This is the first time I've hired someone who *I* feel like I'm taking advantage of."

John looked from one woman to the other, wondering what in the hell was going on. He'd been in the business for a long time, and he'd never had a client touch him and tease him like Abby was doing. *Not that I'd mind*, he thought to himself. *But there's something more than business going on here, and if I know my girl, she's got her eye on Abby. But why does it seem like Abby has her eye on my girl?*

As soon as they were in the car, John gave his wife his most superior smile and said, "Well, that's one mystery solved."

"Not so fast," she said, not wanting him to get the jump on her again. "I figured this one out, too."

"Oh, did you now?"

"I certainly did, John O'Connor. And I'm nearly sick over it!"

"Oh, Margaret, give the kid a break."

"Break nothing! It's not normal, and if she doesn't snap out of it, you're gonna have to set her straight!"

"Normal?" He blinked at her. "I don't think we're talking about the same thing."

She took out a piece of paper and jotted a few words down. Handing her husband a similar scrap, she said, "I know exactly what's going on. Maybe you're the one who's missing the boat."

"No chance," he said, his confidence showing in his eyes.

"Okay, Mr. Know-It-All, write down what you think is going on." He smirked at her but did it. She folded both pieces of paper, initialed and dated his, and had him do the same to hers. "I'm gonna put these away and wait for the mystery to be revealed. I'll bet you twenty bucks that I'm right."

"You're on, big spender. I can already count the money!"

❧

On Friday afternoon, Clancy paid her young laborer, giving her cash so she didn't have to go to the bank. "You did a very good job clearing the hill, Hayley. If you're interested, I'll find something else for you to do."

"You're on," Hayley said. "I've gotta go—I'm going out with my friends tonight. But I'll be ready on Monday morning!" They shook hands, and the girl took off, negotiating the steep hill easily after two weeks of practice.

Abby got home just as Clancy was packing her truck. "Hi," the landscaper said. "Have a nice day?"

"I did not," Abby said, her tone surprisingly snappish. "My retractable roof wouldn't come up, and I had to drive home from Beverly Hills in this heat with the sun baking down on my head."

"Your new car!" Clancy walked over and took a look. "This is a pretty complex system. Having the roof slide into the trunk is no easy feat." She stuck her hand down on the side of the cowl and rooted around for a moment. With a grunt, she pulled her hand out, revealing a jewel case. "Nelly Furtado," she said. "Must be Hayley's."

Abby ground her teeth together. "Where is she?"

"Luckily for her, one of her friends picked her up a few minutes ago."

"Lucky, indeed. I have a headache that would kill a lesser woman. My dear girl also managed to make off with my sunglasses the last time she drove the car. All the glare sure didn't help this headache."

"Damn, Abby, you'd better go put your suit on and float in the pool after you take some aspirin."

"Sounds good, but only if you'll join me."

"You're on, boss. I can't think of a better way to end the week."

❧

Client and architect floated along on their rafts in a drowsy silence until Abby said, "So tell me how my baby did during the last two weeks. Was she any help at all?"

"Oh, yeah, absolutely. She's a great kid, Abby. You should be proud of her."

"I am," she sighed. "As much as I complain, I love everything about her. She's like a little tornado around the house—but she's the cutest little tornado in the whole world."

"She's a lot of fun to be around," Clancy agreed. "We talk a lot on our breaks. It reminds me of just how young a seventeen-year-old is."

"Her birthday is in July. I'm sure she'll be happy to finally be eighteen. It sounds much older, doesn't it?"

"Yeah, I guess it does. She *is* in a hurry to grow up, but I guess I was, too."

Abby slipped off her raft. "I need to swim a bit. Do you mind?"

"No, not at all. Have at it."

Clancy's idea of a swim was to lie in one spot and let the water cool her fevered body. Abby, however, meant that she wanted to exercise. She staked out her half of the pool and started to churn out laps, slicing through the water with a smooth economy of motion. She was obviously used to swimming regularly, and Clancy wondered whether she'd been a competitive swimmer when she was younger.

The architect lay on her raft, watching Abby's body glide through the water, her strokes never hesitating, each one identical, measured, rhythmic, and smooth. Clancy had been keeping a rough count, but she eventually lost track and just watched, mesmerized—her eyes drifting time and again to Abby's round ass, which just peeked out of the water as she moved.

She could tell when Abby was nearly finished because her pace slowed. Then, gradually, she stopped. Turning onto her back, Abby kicked through a pair of laps and floated over to Clancy.

"I have a feeling this isn't your first time in a pool," the landscaper said.

"No. If I'm not playing golf or running, I usually go up to the aquatics center at the Rose Bowl and peel off fifty or so laps. It clears my head."

"It keeps you in great shape, too," Clancy said, unable to keep her eyes off the sleek body that floated next to her.

"Yeah, I do all right for an old lady."

"Uh-huh. That act might work on some people, but I'm not buying it."

Abby grabbed a raft and hoisted herself onto it. She lay down, her chest moving noticeably from her exertion. She still had a small frown on her face, and Clancy asked, "Headache still there?"

"No. I feel all right now. Why?"

"You look like something's bothering you. Are you mad at Hayley for screwing up your car?"

"Oh, God, no!" She laughed. "If I got mad at her every time she or her friends did something thoughtless…" She slipped off her raft and started to tread water so she could stay upright and face Clancy. "I'm not angry, but I'm frustrated with her. We've talked a lot in the last two weeks, and she seems to have missed some of the most important lessons that Will and I tried to impart."

"Commitment?" Clancy asked.

"Yes, commitment is part of it, but I thought we modeled how rewarding it can be to find a partner and work on your relationship. She seems to think that sex is fulfilling with or without love—or even deep attraction! I don't know where she got that idea!"

"That's probably what she sees at school and on TV. Her peers are more influential than you are right now."

"I know, I know," Abby said, clearly frustrated. "That's been true for years. I just thought that my influence would have gotten in by now."

"Now you know how my mom felt," Clancy said, making a face.

Abby looked at her for a moment and then shook her head. "Because of your lesbianism?" Clancy nodded, and Abby said, "That's not the same thing at all. I'd much rather have Hayley fall in love with a woman than have indiscriminate sex with a man."

Mouth gaping open, Clancy finally said, "I'm stunned. Do you really feel that way?"

Looking mildly surprised, Abby said, "Of course. There's nothing wrong with lesbianism."

"Boy, I wish my mom felt that way. She still thinks it's unnatural."

Abby nodded. "Maybe I feel this way because I understand the attraction." She stared up at the hill while Clancy impatiently waited for her to continue. "There's something very…organic about loving someone of your own sex. I mean, I don't think of my friends sexually, but I can see how easy it might be to breach the friend barrier and love a woman—given the right circumstances."

Clancy smiled at her friend, her heart beating rapidly as she considered how open Abby seemed to the idea of making love to another woman. "Wow."

"That surprises you?" Abby looked pleased.

"Yeah. Very much. The way you talk about Will…"

"I loved Will with my whole heart, but if things had been different back at UCLA, I could have wound up with a woman. Circumstances can make a huge difference in a life."

Clancy nodded, still tingling all over. "I don't think I had much choice in the matter. Really, my mom wasn't paying attention."

"Your mom?"

"Yeah. I acted like a baby dyke from the time I was a little girl. I dressed like my dad; I imitated everything he did. Heck, I had a little metal shovel when I was three! I used to go with him to job sites and dig little holes while he was excavating for a pool." She laughed, thinking back to those pleasant memories.

"I was a little tomboy myself," Abby told her. "That doesn't make you gay."

"No, of course it doesn't, but my tomboy period never ended. I was dreaming about other little girls as early as I can remember, and I've never stopped. I wasn't very forthcoming with my thoughts, but my mom should have noticed something when I never had a boyfriend. I think she was trying to ignore the signals."

"You could be right," Abby said. "It's hard to face things about your children that make you uncomfortable."

"Hayley'll come around. I predict she goes through a lot of phases before she figures out who she is."

After they'd floated a while longer, Clancy saw Abby repeatedly press against her temples with her fingertips. "Now your headache's back, isn't it?"

"Yeah. Must be the glare. I think I'll take a nap—that usually helps."

Clancy looked at her friend and saw the lines of tension around her eyes and the tight, drawn set of her mouth. She wasn't sure why she offered, but something told her that Abby didn't want to be alone. "You know, Michael sometimes gets a lot of tension in his neck and shoulders. He's taught me how to give a great shoulder massage. How about it?"

A tiny sparkle flickered to life, and Clancy saw the longing in Abby's eyes. "I would be eternally grateful for that. Are you sure you don't mind?"

"I wouldn't offer if I did."

They got out of the pool and dried off. It was such a beautiful afternoon, now that the sun had cleared the back of the house, that Clancy suggested they stay outside. She knew that nothing filled Abby's soul as much as sitting on her patio, listening to the birds chirp, so she made a simple request. "I can't bear to put those grimy, wet clothes back on, but it might get cool soon. Could I borrow one of Hayley's T-shirts?"

"Sure. I'll get you one." Abby came back with a T-shirt for Clancy and a sky-blue tank top for herself. She also had a bottle of vanilla-scented massage lotion in her hand. "I'm ready for you," she said, smiling tentatively.

Clancy sat on one of the cushioned lounge chairs and scooted around until she was snug against the back. She dropped her feet to the ground and motioned for Abby to sit between her legs. "Come on down."

Abby did, sitting rather stiffly until Clancy began to knead her shoulders. "Oh, my God," she moaned after just a few minutes. "Those hands are lethal weapons."

Clancy chuckled. "Manual labor gives you nice, strong hands. This isn't too hard, is it?"

"Ooh, right on the edge of pain," Abby sighed. "Just perfect."

They were both quiet for a few minutes, with Clancy's powerful hands digging deep into the tense muscles. After a while, Abby's head began to move with the pressure, and soon after that, it began to loll back and forth. "Someone's starting to relax," Clancy murmured softly.

"I'm nearly unconscious."

Clancy stopped her massage. "Let me get up for a sec."

Abby leaned forward and watched as Clancy extracted herself from the lounge chair and then brought another one to face in the opposite direction. She scooted it next to Abby's chair and sat down, facing her friend. Stretching her legs out, she patted her thigh and urged, "Come rest your head on my lap. I've got a good nap waiting for you right here."

Abby's eyes lit up in surprise, and Clancy could see that she was hesitant to accept. "Really?"

"Sure. You look like you need a little loving care. Let me help." She patted her lap again and gave her friend a warm smile.

Abby turned around, moved her torso onto Clancy's chair, and then settled her head onto her lap. Her body was stiff, but as soon as Clancy's hand moved through her hair, the tense body relaxed noticeably. Row after row of the short strands stood up straight and then fell gently. "Do you like to feel my nails?" Clancy asked softly.

"Yes," Abby hissed, sending a wave of sensation surging through Clancy's body. "Good Lord!"

Forcing her voice into its normal register, Clancy said, "Feels nice, doesn't it?"

"Mmm…you have no idea."

But Clancy did have an idea of how wonderful it felt to have someone you were beginning to care for deeply trust you enough to rest, uninhibited, in your care.

Clancy said a few words and asked a question or two, but her calm, soothing voice sounded like it was miles away after a few minutes. Abby felt herself sink into the half-conscious state that a good headrub carried her to. She was awake enough to feel the strong, defined muscles in Clancy's thighs; to detect her clean, chlorine smell; to feel the warmth of her skin against her cheek, but she was too blissful to comment on any of it. Neither was she able to thank her friend for the nicest gift she could remember receiving in quite a while.

As her body relaxed further, a surprising thought came unbidden to the very edge of her conscious mind. *Mmm…was I lying before, or do I think of my friends in a sexual way?* She snapped out of her tranquil state, unable to push the thought aside. *I don't know where this is coming from, but I feel like I could jump the friendship barrier with Clancy. Something about her touch is so soothing—but so stimulating.* Pressing her thighs together, Abby acknowledged, *She's stimulating a lot more than my emotions, too. Damn, no one has made me throb like this in five years!*

She tried to control her physical response—to reassure herself that having someone, anyone, touch her in such a gentle way would arouse her. But she was unable to disabuse herself of the surprising depth of her feelings for the woman who caressed her so lovingly. *Will you stop worrying? You're not a dog! You don't have to give in to every passing impulse—and that's what this is. Just relax and enjoy it. You might not get another headrub for five more years! She's a friendly, open woman, and she's just rubbing your head, not asking for your hand in marriage!*

It took a few minutes, but Abby was finally able to soothe her mind and sink back into her previously tranquil state. She managed this mainly by using her exquisitely honed powers of denial and her equally sharp hedonistic urges that allowed her to feel…rather than think.

Clancy had a hard time telling whether Abby was awake or asleep. Her breathing was slow and rhythmic, but her eyes were moving under her lids, and her face bore some faint lines of tension. Clancy kept up the gentle rub, mixing in delicate little scalp scratches, never letting her hands still. Finally, after a very long time, she heard Abby's breathing grow deeper and saw her jaw drop open just a little, and she knew she was asleep.

She spent the next two hours merely observing the sleeping woman, relishing the closeness and the feel of the head in her lap. It was more moving than thrilling—Clancy having bundled away her romantic feelings for the afternoon. She had banished all such thoughts, caring only that she could provide some comfort for a friend who needed a little support.

Even though she had her lust firmly in check, Clancy couldn't hide her love for the gentle creature that she held. Her heart swelled with affection and warmth for the lovely woman, made even lovelier by sleep. When she was fully asleep, Abby's face softened, and the years melted away. She actually looked a good ten years younger, and though part of Abby's appeal was her age, Clancy liked seeing some of the youthful charm back on the beautiful face—if only to remind her that it was still there, just waiting to be tapped.

The blue eyes, now tightly shuttered, moved quickly beneath their lids; Abby was obviously deep in a dream. The sun had nearly set, and though both women were dry, the evening breeze was a little cool on Clancy's bare skin. Thinking that Abby might be cold too, she reached as far as she could and just managed to snag a dry towel. She shook it out and laid it lengthwise along Abby's long body, now curled up tight on the chair next to her. Running her hands down the cool skin of the sleeping woman's arm, Clancy let herself enjoy the sensation of being able to calm and soothe her friend, and she decided right then that if this was all they were ever able to share, she would consider herself very lucky. Abby was such a generous, loving soul that Clancy was determined to accept whatever she was able to give—and be completely grateful for it.

By the time Abby stirred, Artemis was lying on the end of her lounge chair, curled up against her legs and providing needed warmth. Athena was lying on Clancy's chair, providing the same for her. Abby let out a small groan and wiped lazily at her eyes. Her eyes shot open after a moment, and she gasped, "Why is it dark?"

"Uhm…science wasn't my best subject, but I think it's because the sun's on the other side of the earth for half of every day."

Summoning all the energy she could, Abby slapped weakly at Clancy's bare thigh. Her hand lingered there for a moment. Then she rotated her head and met the architect's eyes. "You're freezing!"

"No, I'm not. I've got your nice warm head on my lap and Athena's nice warm body against my shins. There's about six inches of cold skin; your hand just happened to land on it."

Abby rolled over and said, "I don't really believe you, but I'm going to act like I do." She directed a grateful look at her friend. "Thank you for this. I haven't felt this cared-for in years."

Clancy was still idly playing with the short, stiff hair at the back of Abby's head. "I'm surprised you and Hayley don't trade headrubs."

Shaking her head gently, Abby said, "No, we don't. I still rub her head or give her a backrub when she's having trouble relaxing, but I don't ever ask for one for myself." She looked at Clancy and said, "I'm always cognizant that I'm her mother—I'm here to provide for her, not to ask her to do the same."

"Don't you think that changes over time? Didn't it change with your mom?"

Abby stretched languidly, getting out the kinks that her position had created. "Yes, I suppose it started to change when I was in my thirties and has gotten much more pronounced in the last few years. I feel more like my mother's friend now. But that comes at a price, too. I would never ask her for a headrub, even though I'm sure she would happily give me one. Our dynamic has changed, and I think we've lost that physical connection for good."

"I guess things have just started to change with my mom and me. I suppose Hayley is a little young to think of you as a friend."

"She is. She's gonna need a mom for quite a few more years." She groaned and said, "I hope she realizes that." She sat up slowly; then she reached down and patted Clancy's warm, sleep-creased thigh. "Thank you again for this. It really helped."

"You're welcome. I know it can be hard being a mom, Abby. I know my mom was at the end of her rope with me many, many times."

"Really? You seem so level-headed."

"Well, I am now, but my mom and I had many tests of will."

"Like?"

"Well, my tattoo is a good example," Clancy said, reflexively rubbing her arm. "I was going to get a nice laurel wreath around my ankle, but my mother forbade me to. So of course, I had to get a much bigger tattoo in a much more visible place. Thank God I like it, or I'd be kicking myself every time I wore a sleeveless shirt."

Abby reached out and traced one of the small ivy leaves. "I like it, too. It suits you."

Now that Abby was fully awake and exhibiting her more playful side, Clancy allowed her libido to return in full force. Her skin felt hot as the cool digit traced along it—like Abby's finger was a red-hot branding iron. She shivered from the sensation, and Abby read the shiver but misinterpreted it. "You're getting chilled. Let's go inside."

Following meekly along, Clancy stood in the kitchen feeling a little uncomfortable. She was still in her swimsuit, and the T-shirt didn't quite cover her. The air conditioner had been on, and the house was very cool, making Clancy's nipples pop out. Abby gave her a quick glance and said, "Let me get you something to put on. We can put your clothes into the washer so you can bear to put them on again."

"Are you sure? I don't want to put you out."

"How is doing a tiny load of laundry going to put me out? Now hand 'em over."

"I just thought you might have something you'd rather do this evening."

"If you weren't here, I'd probably lie on the couch and watch TV. Having company is much preferable." She gazed at her for a second and quickly added, "But if you're ready to go home…"

"No. I'd much rather stay here with you. I really enjoy your company."

"I do, too." Abby smiled warmly. "Now give me your clothes, and we can have a nice evening doing laundry together."

The pair watched a DVD while Clancy's clothes were in the washer. Neither woman talked much, but Clancy was hyper-alert for any more clues as to how Abby felt about her. She didn't learn much, to her displeasure, because Abby was her usual self—upbeat, witty, polite, and hospitable.

When the clothes were in the dryer, Clancy snapped her fingers and said, "I almost forgot to tell you something. I got a good lead on some well-worn boulders and rocks not far from the Merced River. It'll take about four hours to get there, but driving is the only way to go, since it's three hours from the closest airport. Do you still want to take a road trip?"

"What's your feeling about this? I don't mind going, but I really don't want to waste that long in the car if these aren't what we're looking for."

Giving her a long look, Clancy said, "I think we'll like them, but I can't be sure until I see 'em. Tell you what—I'll drive up this Saturday. If I like 'em, I'll take some pictures. Then you can decide."

"No, no, we decided to make this into a little getaway. I still want to do that. Would we go up and back in the same day?"

"Well, we could. How do you feel about eight hours in the car?"

"Not very good. Are there any nice places to stay?"

"Nice? I doubt it. Rustic, bucolic, pastoral—I might be able to arrange."

"Rustic, huh?" Abby asked speculatively. "Oh, what the hell. It's not like my social calendar is so full. Could we go next Saturday morning?"

"Yeah. That could work out great. I'll make the arrangements."

"Find us someplace nice if possible," Abby said. "A roaring fire, a big, redwood hot tub. We might as well mix as much fun in as we can, right?"

Clancy almost had to pinch herself to stop her mind's eye from dwelling on an image of Abby, completely naked, playing footsie with her in a big, bubbling hot tub, a sky full of twinkling stars forming a canopy over their heads. "Right," she said. "Fun is definitely on the agenda."

Chapter Seven

The first day of work with the full crew went better than Clancy had expected. She'd been worried that her attention would be too fragmented for her to keep an eye on Hayley and make sure she wasn't asking the girl to do too much, and she was pleased when that wasn't the case. She ate lunch outside under a tree with her crew while Hayley went inside to make herself something. The young woman had been gone for a few minutes when Ramon, the crew chief, walked over and sat down next to Clancy. "The girl...why's she here?"

Ramon always cut to the chase, and Clancy knew it would be a waste of time to lie to him. "I like this family. We've been having dinner together and hanging around. Hayley wanted to help, and she's an extra pair of hands."

"She's worth $7, no more. She can't dig, she can't climb, she has no muscles."

Clancy nodded. "You're probably right, but she can still help out. Let's treat her like we treat Armando's son when he helps."

"Armando's son is thirteen years old," Ramon said. "All he does is carry branches and rocks away. And you pay him $7."

"I know that," Clancy said. "And that's probably what Hayley will be doing. So feel free to give her orders. Just don't ask her to do anything too hard. I don't want her to hurt herself."

While they were talking, Hayley emerged from the house. She looked around and found Clancy, and a beautiful smile bloomed. She was carrying two Popsicles—one obviously for Clancy.

Ramon stood and made a clucking sound with his tongue. "Ah, I think I see why the girl is here. Why do you try to hide things from me, *jefa?*"

"I'm not hiding anything, Ramon. She's seventeen years old!"

"My mother had two children by that age," Ramon said, laughing to himself as he took up a place near the rest of the men.

Hayley approached and held out a cherry Popsicle. "Thought you might like something cold," she said.

"Thanks, Hayley." Clancy accepted the confection and smiled when she put it into her mouth. "It's been a long time since I've had one of these. It's just the thing on a warm afternoon."

Hayley nodded, working to keep the melting treat from running onto her hand. She had a decidedly sensual way of licking the Popsicle, and Clancy wondered whether it was unintentional. Hayley hadn't given her any vibes and had spoken exclusively of guys when they'd chatted, but something seemed a little different today, and Clancy was fairly certain that she wasn't imagining it.

As soon as she was finished with her Popsicle, Clancy stood up, the stick still in her mouth. She brushed off her pants and walked along the hill, making sure that everything was being done perfectly. Although she was working closely with the crew, she was no longer acting as a laborer. Now she was really doing her job—directing, supervising, and troubleshooting. It was still tiring, but it wasn't as physically exhausting as her two weeks of pick-and-shovel work had been. The weather had also cooled off a bit—temperatures were now in the eighties, a welcome change from the heat.

Abby came home around four, having been in and out since Clancy and the crew had arrived. She had joined her usual foursome for a round of golf, mostly to keep herself busy and out of the way.

She stood at the sliding glass door and allowed herself the guilty pleasure of observing clandestinely for a few minutes. Seeing Clancy, she smiled warmly at how completely adorable she looked in what Abby thought of as her uniform. Today's sock selection was a wild one—bright purple with a red-and-gold print, and her baseball cap echoed the purple color. *She is so damned cute*, Abby thought, seeing just a few locks of white-blonde hair sticking out of the back of the cap.

Clancy was standing on the side of the hill, her clipboard thrust against her hip, checking off items while she conversed with Ramon. She pointed with her pen, gesturing all around the yard while he nodded at her. A substantial-sounding engine was rumbling, and Abby couldn't put a damper on her curiosity any longer. She walked out onto the patio and discovered one of the men using a rather large contraption along the lot line. Clancy was speaking loudly, to be heard over the noise, and when the machine shut off abruptly, Abby could hear Clancy speaking in a very natural-sounding Spanish.

Ramon barked out a few orders, also in Spanish. Then Clancy nodded, said, "*Bueno*," and headed down the hill. Abby smiled at the graceful, unconcerned way the architect navigated the steep slope, looking as though she'd been doing so her whole life. Clancy was about halfway down when she glanced up and smiled like she'd spotted a long-lost friend. Abby's heart skipped a beat at the decadent pleasure of having someone's face light up just because of her, and her smile echoed her happiness.

"You speak Spanish so well," Abby said. "I hope you're not saying anything that Hayley needs to hear, though. It's all she can do to order dinner in a Mexican restaurant."

"No, both Ramon and I speak English," Clancy said, smiling. "We've got Hayley busier than a one-armed paperhanger." She pointed to the far end of the hill, where Hayley was putting rocks into a wheelbarrow. "We're trenching to get ready to put in the posts for the wall. The trencher kicks out the bigger rocks, and we've got Hayley picking them up. Doesn't make sense to leave them on the hill."

"Is she capable of doing that?" The hill looked higher from this vantage point, and Abby could easily envision her daughter falling down it.

"Oh, yeah. I told her to only fill it half-full and then take it down to the dumpster. I can guarantee one thing," Clancy said. "She'll never work harder for twelve bucks an hour."

"I think it's good for her. I'm a little worried that she'll hurt herself, but I guess she'll recover from a few scrapes and blisters."

"I've been doing this since I was a kid, and I can count my scars on the fingers of one hand."

"There's something we can do in Merced," Abby said, giggling. "We can sit in the hot tub and show each other our war wounds."

Clancy met Abby's eyes and looked like she was going to speak. But then she just smiled rather vacantly and stood there, the sun glinting off her teeth, as she privately reflected upon something that obviously pleased her.

By the middle of the week, the posts for the wall were in, and the men had set the first course of concrete block. Now Hayley was mixing mortar and carting it up the hill, having learned the art of a proper mix from Clancy.

The architect had been impressed with how intent Hayley was on doing the job right. She listened to the instructions like Moses before the burning bush, and she was so serious about it that Clancy tried to joke to relax her. "Nobody's gonna die if you do this wrong once or twice. If it's too runny, just add some more Quikset. If it's too stiff, add more water. No biggie."

"But I want to do it right," she said earnestly. "I don't want to disappoint you. I know you're counting on me."

"Yeah, I am, but you've been great so far. Don't sweat it."

"I see how much it means to you to do a good job. So it means that much to me, too."

Clancy gave her a slightly puzzled look, patted her on the back, and said, "A good work ethic will serve you well." As she walked away, she wasn't sure, but she had a feeling that Hayley was staring at her. Her suspicions were confirmed when she met Ramon at the top of the hill. "Either your shorts are on fire, or the girl likes to watch you walk away, *jefa*."

The architect yanked off her baseball cap and wiped her forehead dry. "My mother's in Sierra Madre, Ramon. She's the only one I need."

On Friday afternoon, Hayley hung around while the crew was cleaning off their tools. "Have any plans tonight?" she asked Clancy, with forced casualness.

"No. I'm beat by Friday. I usually go home, get into the tub, and read a book until I fall asleep. I'm almost always in bed by ten."

"Clancy! You're wasting your life! Let's go do something tonight. I'm full of energy!"

"I can tell," Clancy said, watching Hayley bounce around. "But I'm full of lethargy. Why don't you go out with your friends?"

The young woman looked momentarily disappointed but rallied quickly. "I will. I just thought it might be fun to mix things up a little. I like you."

Clancy smiled at her, pleased that Hayley liked her enough to want to hang out. "I like you, too. But I'm too old to keep up with you. I need to veg."

"Okay, but you might have more stamina if you partied more."

Laughing, Clancy said, "Try that when you're thirty, and see if it works."

"I'll do that," Hayley said, full of youthful braggadocio.

Hayley turned and walked into the house, making Clancy sigh with relief. From over her shoulder she heard a soft voice ask, "Why do you not go with the girl? She'll make you feel young again."

All Ramon earned for his remarks was a glare.

❦

Abby got home as Ramon was driving away with the crew. She waved at the men and pulled up next to Clancy, who was getting into her truck. "Ready to go?"

"Yep. I love Friday nights," Clancy said, giving her friend a wan smile.

"Big plans?"

A Mercedes SUV pulled up next to Abby, and an attractive young blonde woman lowered the window. "Hi, Mrs. Graham. Is Hayley ready?"

"I didn't know you were going out together, Kerry. Go ahead and honk."

The young woman did, and seconds later, Hayley ran out of the house. She looked like she'd had a relaxing day at the beach, and Clancy realized how long it had been since she was seventeen. Hayley winked at Clancy, saying quietly, "Last chance."

Clancy shook her head and waved. "Have a good time."

"Be home by one or call me," Abby said.

"I'm staying over, Mom," Hayley said. "I'll be home tomorrow afternoon."

"Have fun," Abby called out as Hayley got in the car.

They pulled away, and Abby said, "Do you ever wish you were in college again?"

"Nope."

"Me either," Abby said, laughing. "Once was enough. Oh! You were telling me about your big plans."

"I plan on going through the drive-through window at Taco Bell, taking a long bath, and being in bed by ten."

"You're a wild one."

"What about you?"

"Oh, I'll make myself dinner. I thought Hayley would be home, so I've got far too much." She cocked her head and asked, "Would you like her swordfish? I have some mango-papaya salsa for it, and I was going to oil-roast some little potatoes and squash."

"Gosh, Abby. I don't know if I can give up my Burrito Supreme."

"Come on. Let's go put our suits on and sit in the Jacuzzi while the barbecue grill warms up."

"There isn't a word that's come out of your mouth that isn't absolutely fantastic," Clancy said, smiling at the mere thought of the evening to come.

After relaxing in the Jacuzzi, Clancy swam a few laps to cool off while Abby cooked dinner. They ate outdoors, the warm night perfect for dining in wet swimming suits. After they'd finished, they both took showers to rinse off the chlorine, and by eight-thirty, they were in the family room, relaxing on the huge sectional that covered two walls.

Abby had on a pair of well-worn pink flannel boxers and a roomy, lightweight, sky-blue sweatshirt. Because Clancy's clothes were filthy, Abby had loaned the landscaper an outfit—a pair of green-and-gold silk paisley boxers, courtesy of Hayley. A gold T-shirt strained across her shoulders, Hayley being the same height but significantly narrower through the shoulders than the muscular landscaper.

They had raided the refrigerator for dessert, but the only thing that appealed to either of them was a quart of fresh strawberries that had caught Clancy's attention as soon as they entered the kitchen. Abby saw her eyeing the fruit and suggested, "Wanna experience one of my favorite munchie-slaying snacks?"

"Why, Mrs. Graham, I believe you're referring to being baked. Do you still partake of the evil weed?"

"No," Abby said, laughing lightly. "I stopped after college. It's so tiring having kids that the last thing you want is to intentionally make yourself more tired."

"That makes sense. It doesn't make me tired, but it makes me want to get horizontal—with a partner. Since there's nothing worse than being massively horny and all alone, I don't do it very often, either."

"This is more fun, anyway," Abby decided. "We can have the munchies without the sexual side effect."

I've already got that one, Clancy moaned to herself. *In those snug little boxers, you look good enough to eat.*

They sat next to each other with a tray filled with plump red strawberries, chunks of sliced banana, a saucer full of brown sugar, and another filled with sour cream. Abby showed her friend a few of her favorite variations, and Clancy quickly decided that she was a fan of the taste treat. They had eaten over half of the berries when Clancy said, "The only thing we need is a dish of melted chocolate. Then I'd be in heaven."

"Get ready to meet St. Peter," Abby said. As she got up to walk into the kitchen, Clancy followed the slow twitch of her hips, unconsciously licking her lips at the sight of Abby's firm, round ass. She had seen her friend in shorts, slacks, a swimsuit, and even tight jeans, but nothing else she'd worn had ever shown off her shapely ass as much as the slightly snug boxers.

I've gotta get a grip here, Clancy thought, trying to slow her rapidly beating heart.

Abby reappeared a few moments later and handed Clancy a bottle of champagne. "Will you open this for me? Nothing goes better with chocolate than champagne."

"What are we celebrating?"

Thinking for a moment, Abby said, "We're celebrating the fact that it's Friday and we have a bottle of champagne in the refrigerator." She turned and Clancy laughed along with her, managing another long look at her departing form.

Abby came back with two champagne flutes and said, "I'm out of the chocolate I like best. I called the market, and they're going to bring some over."

"You ordered chocolate? Just chocolate?"

"No," Abby said, smiling. "I also ordered some more of these strawberries and another bottle of champagne." She shrugged and said, "We might not need it, but I like to be prepared."

"I had no idea the market delivered."

"Well, they have a minimum order. The wine helped meet it."

"I'm not even gonna ask. I never spend more than twenty bucks at a time there."

"It was a little more than that," Abby said, smiling enigmatically. She sat next to Clancy and held out her glass. "It's a nice champagne that I was saving for a special occasion. I think this counts." She clinked her glass against Clancy's and said, "To Fridays."

"To Fridays. Mmm…I know nothing about wine, but this is very, very nice."

"That's all you have to know. Stick with what appeals to you, and you'll always make the right choice."

Clancy scooted back to lean against the arm of the sectional, sticking her legs out. She gave Abby a thoughtful look, took another sip of her wine, and asked, "What appeals to you? I know you haven't been able to find the person you're looking for, but I don't really know what's on your list."

Giving her a sly smile, Abby closed an eye and tilted her glass in Clancy's direction. "I'll give you my list, if you'll give me yours."

"Done. Let's start with the most obvious element. What type appeals to you?"

"Type? Physical type?" Clancy nodded, and Abby furrowed her brow. "I don't have an answer for that. I loved the way Will looked—he was big and kinda bulky. He had broad shoulders and powerful arms, like a bigger version of Trevor. It was so nice to lie in his arms and feel him engulf me with his body." She sipped her wine and said, "But I've dated guys who couldn't snap a pencil in half. So I'd say that the physical package isn't that big a deal. How about you?"

"Mmm…well," Clancy said, shifting nervously, "I guess I'm pretty flexible, too."

"I detect a little prevarication," Abby said, narrowing her eyes. "Have a little more truth serum, and give that question another try."

Smirking, Clancy drained her glass and held it out for more. "Okay," she said, taking a breath. "I've dated a wide range of physical types, but all of my relationships have been with dark-haired women. I like tall, lanky types, too." She cleared her throat and added, "I've never had any success in landing the type of woman I'm most attracted to, though."

"Really? That surprises me. I'd think you could have your choice of women."

Clancy focused on everything but her friend's eyes. "No, that hasn't been true. I think part of the reason I strike out is because I look so young."

"What does that have to do with it?"

"Uhm…physically, I'm most attracted to older women. I really like the contrast of graying hair with a tanned face. There's something…I don't even know what it is, but I've always liked that look. But most older women think I'm a kid, and they won't give me the time of day."

"Huh," Abby said, not commenting further. She picked up the wine bottle, and Clancy detected a slight tremor when she poured. "Okay!" she said, a little too brightly. "You have a preference for type, and I'm pretty flexible. What's next?"

"Well," Clancy said, grateful that Abby had not followed up on her comment, "what kind of personality appeals to you?"

"Oh, that's easy. I'd love to find someone like Will. He was serious about his work—very professional and competent. But he was a kid at heart. He saw the humor in everything, and he could make me laugh without even trying. I have to have someone who can make me laugh. I won't settle for less."

"Mmm…that's important to me, too. Life's too short to be serious all the time."

"Good answer." Smiling warmly at her friend, Abby said, "You know, I have to thank you for something that's very important to me. You've helped me learn how to laugh again. I'd started to forget how."

"You haven't had much to laugh about for quite a few years, but if I've helped in any way, I'm very glad of that."

"You've definitely helped," Abby said, grabbing Clancy's bare foot and giving it a tug. "Some of my friends have been very, very supportive over the past few years, but they treat me so gingerly—like they're afraid to laugh or tease me. You treat me like I'm my old self."

"I didn't know you when you were in your deepest grief. It's probably easier for me."

"Perhaps," Abby agreed. She reached out with her hand and started to trace idle patterns on the sole of Clancy's foot, making Clancy squirm with desire crossed with confusion. "You look a little squished there." Taking hold of Clancy's big toe, she pulled the leg onto her lap and then pulled the other foot over as well. "Better?"

Clancy shifted a little, knowing she hadn't answered Abby's question but not sure she could speak coherently.

Abby took a generous drink of her wine and looked at her friend through the crystal. "What else do you want to know, buddy?"

Uhm…why are you playing with my feet? Not that I want you to stop, of course. Just as she considered this, Abby removed her hand. Involuntarily, Clancy wiggled her toes, longing for more contact. Without a word, Abby's hand drifted back, and their eyes met, warm smiles echoing between them.

Forcing herself back to the conversation which was scattered at best, Clancy managed to ask, "Are you looking for a professional? Someone like Will?"

"No, not necessarily. The problem is that most of the people I meet *are* professionals—doctors and lawyers and the like—but that's not important to me. I'm looking for a quality person—not a person who makes a lot of money. I want someone who wants to take it slow and enjoy me and enjoy life. I'm not interested in some high-powered guy who spends all of his time advancing his career. I need someone who gets pleasure from sitting on my front porch and watching the flowers grow."

Clancy heard the words and tried to convince herself that one of their favorite activities was not sitting on the porch and watching the flowers grow. Stunned at the direction the conversation was taking she was unable to comment or react in any way. Quickly, Abby filled her glass again and took three deep gulps, draining her glass in a moment.

Unsure how she should react, Clancy tried to clarify where Abby was heading, "Finding someone who shares my interests and hobbies is important to me, too. I think there are people like that out there for both of us. Heck, maybe I should try my hand at fixing you up. Maybe one of the nurserymen I know would be right for you."

Giving her a grateful look, Abby said, "We'll get right on that as soon as things settle down around here."

"Good idea." Clancy sipped her wine, occasionally gazing at her friend. "Maybe you can introduce me to some of your single women friends," she said, chuckling softly.

"I don't have many single friends, but I know a few married women who might want to explore a little." After a slight pause, Abby asked, "Interested?"

Now even further confused, Clancy said, "No. No interest. I take marriage vows very seriously—even if the person who made them doesn't."

"That's an admirable quality," Abby said, smiling in a way that looked relieved. "That's another thing for my list. I would only seriously date someone who shared my moral code—or at least came close. Some people think the Ten Commandments might not be relevant any longer, but if you follow them, I guarantee you'll have a peaceful life."

"I can't disagree. If you don't lie, don't cheat, don't steal, and don't take advantage of other people, you might lose out to someone who doesn't have scruples, but you'll sleep well at night. That's gotta be more important than money."

Abby took another sip of her champagne and looked across the room, staring at nothing in particular. Her hand started to travel a little bit, tickling all the way up to Clancy's knee. "Is it just me, or do our lists match incredibly well?"

"No," Clancy said, clearing her throat, "it's not just you, but that isn't surprising. I think we're a lot alike."

"I don't know if that's true." Abby fixed Clancy with an intent gaze and said, "Honestly, you remind me of Will. More than anyone I've ever known."

Clancy felt her shoulders shrug. "Huh. Go figure." *That was smooth. Something is happening here, you dolt! Don't act like you're oblivious to it! Maybe she needs a little encouragement!*

The doorbell rang, and when Abby went to answer, Clancy tried to get her breathing under control. *What in the hell is going on here? Is she flirting with me? It seems like it, but I'm sure as hell not gonna make a move if she's not! Fuck, fuck, fuck! This is why it's so hard to lust after a straight woman!*

"Be back in a minute," Abby said, poking her head into the room.

Shortly after the microwave dinged, she returned with a ramekin filled with rich, dark, melted bittersweet chocolate, the scent wafting up to Clancy's sensitive nose. "Good God, that smells fabulous."

Snaring a berry by its dark green stem, Abby dipped it into the luscious chocolate and leaned down to hold it to Clancy's lips. Nonplussed, Clancy opened her mouth mechanically and bit down when instructed. "Do you like it?" Abby asked softly, her eyes never leaving Clancy's.

Unable to concentrate with Abby's eyes boring into her, Clancy had to close her eyes to be able to answer. "Heavenly," she said, her voice sounding high to her own ears.

Abby dipped the large berry once again and pressed it to Clancy's lips. "Open wide," she said, her voice dropping almost to a whisper.

This time Clancy's eyes remained open, and she felt the warmth that radiated between them. Abby held her position for just a moment longer and then looked away as if afraid of what she saw when their eyes met.

She resumed her seat, and over the next several minutes, they quietly devoured the entire supply of berries. There was not a word spoken between them, but Clancy could feel a pull toward Abby that felt like being drawn in by a powerful magnet. Their connection felt like a living, pulsing reality, and she could feel it grow as the moments passed.

When the berries were gone, they moved onto the bananas, their taste improved dramatically by the addition of melted chocolate. Still silent, they alternated dipping the sliced bananas into the ramekin, growing a little more playful as each tried to grab the final piece.

"Last bite," Clancy declared. She held up the chunk and positioned it a foot higher than her mouth, letting a few fat drops of chocolate drip lazily onto her tongue.

"Dibs!" Abby said impishly and graced Clancy with a sweet, affectionate smile.

Clancy's body shifted, and her arm came up to settle onto the back of the sofa. "You want this?" she asked tauntingly, holding the morsel over Abby's open mouth.

"Yes. I do."

Clancy stared at the glint of excitement in her friend's eyes. Abby's mouth was curled up into a sexy pout, and suddenly, her hand was on Clancy's bare thigh. Cool, soft fingers started to climb slowly, and when the fingers reached the edge of the boxers, Abby slipped one elegant finger just far enough inside to let Clancy know that she was inviting her to make a move.

Dropping her voice down to its most sensual timbre, Clancy asked, "Are you sure you want it?" Her eyes roamed over her friend, searching for any sign of hesitation.

Abby didn't respond immediately. Her head was tilted back against the sofa, and she rolled it just enough to be able to look directly into Clancy's eyes. "I want it," she whispered, her hand tenderly stroking the warm skin. "I'm surprised, I'm scared, I'm amazed—but I'm sure."

Clancy dropped the tidbit back onto the tray and closed the scant distance that separated their bodies. She was poised just above her friend and hesitated for a moment, knowing that there was no turning back once she leaped the chasm.

Abby closed her eyes and gently touched Clancy's shoulder, exerting a slight pressure as she pulled her closer. When they were inches apart, Clancy paused again, just long enough for Abby's blue eyes to flutter open. A small, gentle smile settled onto her lips, and she slipped her hand behind Clancy's neck. She licked her lips and pulled until their mouths were nearly touching.

Clancy could feel Abby's breath on her face and the heat that radiated from her. She desperately needed to kiss her, but the moment seemed so perfect that she had to savor it—if only for a few seconds. She finally leaned in, brushing her lips tenderly across Abby's. She could feel a slight tremor and heard a soft sigh leave her parted lips. Then that determined hand was cradling the back of her head again, holding her in place.

"Kiss me again," Abby whispered.

Her voice was so thrillingly seductive that Clancy pressed herself close and let her mouth eagerly explore the wealth of sensations that Abby's body presented. The sweet smell of her skin, the warmth of her body, the incredible softness of her lips, the way her mouth opened to welcome Clancy's searching tongue—all combined to make the landscaper nearly swoon. Her heart was racing, the blood pounding in her veins as she pressed forward, feeling Abby's body begin to yield to her.

Slowly, Abby reclined onto the seat of the sofa, and she looked up at Clancy with a mixture of wanton desire and stark fear in the depths of her beautiful eyes.

Clancy was shaking noticeably, her entire body coiled with tension. Abby straightened out her legs, and Clancy felt herself being pulled tightly against her body. She let her eyes close languidly when she felt the firm breasts press against her own. Abby's hand reached out; her fingers slipped between their bodies to find the substantial ring piercing Clancy's right nipple.

The move took Clancy by surprise, and her head lifted as a startled gasp left her lips. "Oh, yes," she hissed, eyes closed, head thrown back.

Both elegantly shaped hands went to Clancy's head, pulling her down forcefully. Abby's mouth opened slightly, and Clancy's lips immediately joined hers, crushing their mouths together in a frantic, passion-filled kiss.

Their kisses continued with reckless abandon, the fire between them rapidly growing out of either woman's control. Clancy fought with herself, reminding her conscience that it was wrong to push Abby if her friend had the slightest doubt. With every bit of discipline she possessed, she lifted her head and paused just above

Abby's red, slightly swollen lips. "Yes?" she asked, holding her breath to await the answer.

Abby gazed at her for a full minute, her eyes wandering up and down Clancy's face, looking like she was searching for an answer. But her voice was clear and confident when she finally said, "Yes. Definitely yes."

Clancy's mouth claimed hers once again, and the architect's muscular body began to gently rub against Abby, creating a slow friction that made her heart race. A warm, soft hand crept under the leg of her boxers, and the moment Abby's fingers grazed Clancy's curls, they both began to shake.

Abby's inexperience didn't show. She toyed with Clancy, touching her just enough to make her mad with desire, even though she was merely grazing the top of her thigh. While her fingers played, she leaned in and started to kiss the full, pink lips, her moans making Clancy pulse with desire. They held each other tightly, pressing their breasts into one another. They kissed until both were out of breath; then Clancy shifted her head so that she could look into Abby's eyes, desire radiating from the blue orbs. Immediately they fell into another embrace, kissing and sucking on each other's lips with rapidly escalating intensity.

"I'm getting a little dizzy," Abby said, blinking slowly. "I don't know if it's from your kisses or the champagne."

"Maybe it's both." Clancy pulled her close and kissed her with renewed passion, making Abby moan and squirm. The next time their oxygen-starved lungs forced them to pull apart, Clancy looked at the taller woman and whispered, "I have to touch you. Everywhere. Will you sleep with me?" She was speaking directly into Abby's ear, gently nibbling on her earlobe.

"Yes." She sighed deeply. "Yes, I will."

One last time, Clancy pulled back and looked into her friend's eyes. "Are you sure? I don't want you to ever regret this."

Her head nodded, then Abby kissed Clancy, her touch firm and steady. "I'm completely sure."

They stood, Clancy took her hand, and they walked toward the stairs. She stopped abruptly to ask, "What about Hayley? Any chance she'll come home?"

"None," Abby said. "She almost always stays with a friend on the weekends. She's never come home unexpectedly."

Clancy nodded. Then her eyes shot wide open again. "What about the dogs?"

"They're fine," Abby assured her, patting her gently on the side. "But you're a doll to think of them. I'll put the chocolate away so they don't eat it or knock it over." Clancy watched her move, her mouth going dry when she saw the sensual, feline grace that her friend exhibited when she was aroused. Joining Clancy on the stairs, Abby draped her arm around the smaller woman's shoulders. "They can sleep alone for one night. I choose you," she said, dropping a kiss onto the soft skin of Clancy's neck.

"Poor dogs." Then her face creased into a wide grin as she added, "Lucky me."

They reached the top of the stairs, and Abby seemed to hesitate for a moment. Clancy's heart tripped, hoping desperately that she hadn't changed her mind. But a moment later, the brunette turned to the left and guided Clancy into an attractive but sparsely appointed room. The space surprised Clancy, mainly because the rest of the house was filled with personal mementos and photos of the family. This room, while nicely decorated, was devoid of any such adornment.

Abby looked around the space and asked, "Is this all right? It's…the guest room."

"Fine. It's fine."

Abby was standing just inside the door, her body shaking, all of her confidence gone. They were standing close to each other, and Clancy guided Abby's arms to drape around her neck. Then she put her hands on Abby's hips, smiling gently when she felt the womanly curves under her hands. "Are you okay?"

"Yes," she said thinly. "I'm a little…uncertain. This is my first time—"

"No, it's not," Clancy interrupted. "I'm sure you've made love more than I have. It's not much different from what you're used to. All that's important is that we express how we feel." She gave her a confident smile and said, "I'm sure you're an expert in how to do that."

The small pep talk seemed to reassure her significantly, and Abby grasped Clancy's hand and led her to the bed. Clancy sat and gazed up at her friend, her heart hammering in her chest. Abby looked down at her, her hands resting on broad shoulders. She bent to kiss her, keeping her touch light and delicate while their bodies became accustomed to this level of intimate contact.

Clancy's hands slipped from Abby's waist down to her hips, and she pulled her close. Leaning over farther and farther, with Clancy pulling gently, Abby eventually straddled Clancy, greedily sucking at her lips and tongue with the skills of a master. Clancy felt like her head would explode, having her long-felt desire finally becoming a reality. The passion was building quickly, and Clancy took a breath in surprise when Abby started to take control.

Abby sat up slightly and yanked her sweatshirt over her head; then she slid from Clancy's hips and tugged on her, trying to move her. Clancy's feet were still on the floor, and she wasn't sure where Abby wanted her. But when Abby whispered, "Come up here," she scrambled onto the bed and sat facing Abby. Abby grasped Clancy's T-shirt and removed it, stopping abruptly when her eyes settled on the shining nipple ring. She gazed at it for a moment, clearly mesmerized. Her hand moved tentatively toward it, and Clancy gently reassured her, "Go on. Touch it. Any way you want."

Her eyes shifted and locked onto Clancy's, and she asked, "Doesn't it hurt?"

Clancy smiled gently and shook her head. "No, no. Not at all. It feels great. That's why I got it. To make my nipples even more sensitive." She took Abby's hand and moved it to her breast, silently encouraging her to explore. Abby did, watching Clancy's face as she touched the ring lightly.

Clancy tried to smile to encourage her, but she could feel her eyes rolling back in her head. Having Abby gingerly touch her breast gave her more sensation than she could ever recall having, and she struggled to remain upright. Slowly, carefully, Abby started to explore a little more enthusiastically. When she gently turned the heavy ring, Clancy felt her eyes narrow, and she nearly growled.

Clancy's clit began to throb when Abby bent and took the decorated nipple into her mouth, sucking gently while her tongue moved the ring up and down and pulled on it slightly. Her eyes never left Clancy's, and it took more strength than Clancy could have imagined to refrain from throwing Abby onto her back and diving between her legs. But she was determined to let Abby proceed at her own pace. Even if it killed her.

"That feels so good," Clancy said, her words poor vehicles for expressing how Abby made her feel. Abby switched to the other breast and sucked at it deeply, making Clancy's back arch while she groaned and clawed at the bedspread.

Even though they were shaking, Clancy's hands explored Abby's body while her breasts were being fondled so deliciously. She touched her everywhere she could reach, grinning in delight when her touch created a rash of goosebumps all along the soft skin. Abby was moaning throatily with each lusty suck, and she lifted her head abruptly to lock eyes with Clancy. Without a word, she stuck her thumbs into her shorts, pushed them off, and then tossed them aside and lay on her back. Clancy clambered over her with a questioning look, and Abby grabbed her and pulled her down, smiling when their eyes met.

"I need…" she started to say. Then she grasped Clancy's hand and guided it between her legs, sucking in a shaky breath when the supple fingers slid into her wetness. "Touch me. Touch me…inside."

Clancy slid one arm around her shoulders and drew her close while she entered her with agonizing slowness. Abby's breathing was harsh and shaky, and when Clancy's fingers had traveled the length of her, Abby grasped the muscular arm and held her still, panting gently as she felt her flesh conform to the fullness. "Kiss me," she breathed, her eyes closed tightly.

Clancy dipped her head and lavished a shower of kisses on the soft lips. Her hand started to move slowly, and Abby's hips began to thrust to meet her. They kept up the smooth, slow, rhythmic pace, their tongues dancing against one another's the whole while.

Abby's legs spread even wider, seemingly trying to increase the depth of penetration. Clancy sensed her need and rotated her wrist, her fingers sliding along the floor of her vagina. She let her fingers curl a bit to follow the contours of the slippery flesh, smiling through the kisses when Abby gasped in pleasure and clutched at Clancy roughly. "Oh, God," she groaned. "So good."

Holding her just a little tighter, Clancy slid another finger in and smiled broadly as Abby purred with pleasure. Their mouths joined again, Abby sucking voraciously on Clancy's tongue. Both of Abby's hands slid down, and she grasped Clancy's powerful arm firmly, taking control. Slowly but steadily, she guided her, increasing the pace inexorably, urging Clancy to thrust a little harder.

Abby's mouth opened, and her jaw moved, but not a sound emerged. She gasped for air, and Clancy could feel the flesh tighten around her fingers. Gripping hard,

Abby held her still, her hands wrapped tightly around Clancy's forearm, her entire body rigid—on the edge of the precipice. Keeping her fingers still, Clancy gathered a dollop of lubrication onto Abby's clit and started to gently rub her thumb over it. The wet flesh that enveloped her fingers began to pulse and throb, and she lightened her touch even more, barely skimming across the ultrasensitive skin. Abby's grip grew stronger, and her body coiled. Her breath caught in her throat just seconds before she blew it out in a great rush as she exploded into paroxysms of sensation, washing through her body like a raging torrent of feeling.

Clancy watched her mouth open, but no sound came out. Her eyes were half-closed, her breathing rapid and harsh…but she was utterly silent. But even though not a sound left her lips, her shuddering body provided a stunning commentary on the pleasure that buffeted her.

Slowly, her muscles began to relax, and she loosened her grip on Clancy's arm. Her muscles must have been cramping, because she whimpered slightly when she tried to stretch out. Clancy planted a few soft kisses on her face and then gently wiped at the beads of perspiration on her brow. Abby draped her arms around her neck and pulled her close once again, kissing her lazily. "How could you possibly know my body so well?" she murmured after a few minutes.

Clancy grinned rakishly. "Seen one, seen 'em all?"

"Uh-unh." She kissed her again and then spent a few moments looking into her eyes, clearly trying to see what Clancy was feeling. Finally, she smiled and said, "You're a fantastic lover. That's all there is to it."

"Like I'm gonna argue with that?" Clancy started to run a hand along Abby's moist skin. "Let's say that we inspired each other." Abby gave her a curious look, and Clancy said, "You showed me what you needed. It's easy to be a good lover if your partner shows you what she likes."

"So…that was okay? Guiding you like that? I didn't want to seem too…pushy."

Clancy kissed her again, lingering on her particularly succulent lower lip. "Of course it was. There's nothing worse than making love to someone and having her lie there, making you guess." She shuddered and said, "I've had that experience once. And once was more than enough."

Abby brushed at the damp hair along Clancy's temple and placed a kiss there. "Have you had many lovers?" Her eyes suddenly lit up, and she immediately tried to retract her question. "I don't know why I asked that! You don't have to tell me."

"I don't mind," Clancy soothed. "You're my fifth." She gave the matter some thought and specified. "My first time was when I was eighteen. Then I met a woman the next year and thought we had a chance to make something happen. But she was too closeted for me. My standards are pretty high, and I had a dry spell for a couple of years," she said, chuckling. "Next, I dated Julie, and we were on and off for a couple of years. My last was three years ago. That was a very brief, very unsatisfying rebound fling that I shouldn't even count," she said. "So if I toss her out, you're number four." She rolled onto her side and grinned playfully. "I shouldn't have to count someone who didn't like plants, didn't laugh at my jokes, and didn't manage to give me an orgasm, should I?"

"How do you know that *I* can?" Abby asked with a slightly frightened look.

"Oh, you'll do just fine," Clancy said as she patted her side. "I was about ten seconds away when you came. If you can turn me on that much without even touching me, we won't have a bit of trouble."

Abby gave her a shy look. "Is that true? Were you really close?"

"Oh, yeah." She started to kiss Abby again, moving her lips softly along her jaw and then down her throat. "You turn me on more than anyone I've ever been with. There's something about you that I find absolutely irresistible."

"I bet you say that to all the girls."

Clancy looked at her carefully, seeing her uncertainty. "No, I don't. I've enjoyed being with almost all of my lovers, but I never felt that elusive spark. I can't name it—all I know is that I feel it with you."

Abby looked at her for a moment and then swallowed and said, "I want to make you feel it now." Her hands roamed up from the waistband of Clancy's shorts to glide over her breasts. "Will you tell me what you like?" She met her eyes and admitted, "I'm really nervous."

Enfolding her in her arms, Clancy nodded, rubbing her chin against the top of Abby's head. "I'll give you a running commentary if you want. I can be like those announcers on the golf tour, where they whisper in the background."

Abby pulled back and smiled. "I'll let you know if it's too much, but I'd really like it if you erred on the side of full disclosure."

"It's a deal." She hugged her tightly again and said, "There's one thing I'd really like."

"What's that?"

"I'd like for you to spend some time getting to know my body. Don't think about orgasms. Explore and enjoy yourself. It'll help you feel more comfortable—guaranteed."

Abby nodded and explained, "You feel so different from a man. It's a little hard to get used to."

"My body's like yours," Clancy whispered conspiratorially into her ear. "I know you touch yourself."

Abby looked up at her, earlobes tinted pink. "You know that?"

"Uh-huh. I can tell."

"How?" Abby asked, her eyes wide.

"'Cause your body's *so* hot. If my body were as hot as yours, I'd be stroking myself all day."

Rolling her eyes, Abby kissed Clancy's head. "You had me thinking I looked like…God, I don't know what I thought." She pushed against Clancy. "You're very open about sex, aren't you?"

"Yeah, I am. Does it bother you?"

"No, no, it'll just take some getting used to. I act more than I talk…about sex, that is." She looked at Clancy again and said, "Of course I masturbate. I could count the times on one hand during my marriage, but since then…" She shrugged. "My sex drive started to come back about three years ago—and since I didn't have any other outlets…"

Clancy rolled onto her back and spread her arms wide. "You do now," she teased gently.

"I guess I'd better take full advantage," Abby said, her expression sober. "You never know when the opportunity will arise again."

Gazing at her thoughtfully, Clancy wondered where the hell that comment had come from. But she didn't want to act like it was a foregone conclusion that they would continue their intimacies—especially if Abby didn't think they would. The last thing she wanted to do was push her, so she bit her tongue and smiled up at her, trying to send the silent message that she hoped this was only the first of thousands of times they'd make love.

Abby sat cross-legged on the bed and let her eyes roam up and down Clancy's body. She seemed nervous again, but Clancy thought she'd better just stay quiet and let Abby get her bearings.

"It's a little like performing before an audience," she said, her voice shaking.

Clancy moved around and sat against the headboard, pulling Abby with her. She held Abby in her arms, rubbing her gently for a few minutes. "Wanna go to sleep? It's okay if you do."

"No." Her head shook quickly, the short hairs at the base of her head tickling Clancy's chest. "I've lost the mood a little, and now I feel uncomfortable. It's like the difference between returning a serve in tennis and teeing off in golf. It's much easier if you only have to react."

"Well, why didn't you say so? As you've said, I'm a stupendous lover, so I know how to fix that."

"Uhm…I believe I said fantastic," Abby jokingly corrected.

"Either way, I've got the answer. We're gonna play Follow the Leader," she said, grinning when she saw the look on Abby's face. "I'm gonna show you what I like—by doing it to you." She punctuated the sentence by touching Abby's nose at the last word. "You'll learn what I like, and you won't be teeing off. You'll be returning my serve."

A grin settled on Abby's face. "Will this work?"

"Oh, yeah. Like a charm." Clancy smiled and said, "The first thing that you have to know is that I like a lot of kissing. A whole lot of kissing. You can never have too much kissing." She placed a gentle, meaningful kiss on Abby's soft lips, and her eyelids fluttered closed. Pulling away slightly, she waited just a breath and then said, "Your turn."

Abby's smile crinkled the corners of her mouth, and she leaned in and returned the kiss with equal fervor. "Like that?"

"Perfect," Clancy sighed. "Let's do a few more so we're clear, okay?"

"Practice, practice, practice."

They kissed gently, tenderly, expressing the affection they felt for each other. Clancy was softly panting when they broke apart, and she said, "You catch on quick."

"Thanks. I've taken that class before. It's the advanced-placement courses that have me worried."

"You're doing great—just great," Clancy assured her. She placed Abby on her back and leaned over her. "Let's move on. Now," she said, her eyes roving all over Abby's bare body, "I love to have my lips kissed, but that's not the only place I like a good kiss. A little sucking, a little nibbling—even a gentle bite or two are all very nice." She demonstrated her point to perfection, painting a warm, wet path from Abby's chin to her toes.

As soon as she paused, Abby flipped her over, pinned her to the mattress, and returned the favor, making Clancy moan with pleasure.

She had to blink to focus, but Clancy gathered herself to instruct, "Don't forget the rear view." Rolling Clancy over, Abby followed no path this time, alternating a wet, sloppy kiss to the back of her knee with a bite on the neck, a slow suckle of a little pink toe with long, luxurious licks along her spine. Clancy was shivering from the sensations, unable to keep her body from twitching roughly.

Abby moaned insensibly while her mouth and tongue and teeth marked Clancy's smooth, soft body. Panting roughly, she turned Clancy over and gazed into her eyes with wanton desire. "I'm ready—I'm so ready, Clancy."

"So am I," she whispered, moving down Abby's body like a leopard stalking its prey. She settled down, draped one long leg over her shoulder, and dipped her head between Abby's thighs. She gently spread her lips, delighting when she felt the shudder run down Abby's entire body. Keeping her eyes on her partner's, she pressed her face against Abby and gave her a deep, wet kiss, letting her tongue just peek out of her parted lips.

"Oh, God," Abby moaned, twitching her hips sensually.

"Mmm-hmm," Clancy purred, her mouth beginning to water from the burst of sensations that suffused her senses. Abby's sweet/salt taste; her delicate, musky scent; the throb of her pulse, almost visible through the swollen flesh—all combined in a delightful mélange of pleasure. She gathered her thoughts and tried to focus, beginning to gently nibble on the puffy outer lips, running her tongue along every inch of skin, Abby's guttural moans providing the rewarding accompaniment. Drawing a thin inner lip into her mouth, she lightly suckled it, her toes curling when she heard Abby cry out.

She was completely taken aback when she felt her whole world turn, and she found herself on her back—Abby hurriedly pulling the boxer shorts off. Beautiful blue eyes were narrowed with desire when Abby panted huskily, "I have to...touch you...taste you...something!"

She looked desperate—so desperate that Clancy couldn't help but laugh a little. "Come here," she said, raising her arm. "Nestle up here and relax a little. You look like you're about to faint."

Her smile was shy and a little embarrassed. "I feel so needy," Abby said. She lay next to Clancy and rested her head on her chest. "It's been so long since anyone has touched me. I feel like I'm going to combust!"

"We've got all night. No need to rush. Just breathe deeply and let your body relax." She rubbed Abby's side, and matched her breathing, pleased when Abby's grew deeper. "That's it. Just slow down and enjoy the ride. We've got a long way to go."

"We do?" Abby asked, her voice sounding tentative.

"We do if you want to." Their eyes met briefly. "Do you want to?"

"Oh, God, yes, Clancy. I want to. I truly want to." She nestled back into Clancy's embrace. "What do we do next?"

"Whatever you want. Whenever you want."

"I want to touch you. All of you."

Clancy arched her back, lifting her body. "Take 'em off," she said, chuckling. "I love to be naked."

Abby reached for the waistband on the boxers and slowly slid them down. Clancy dropped back onto the bed; Abby removed the shorts and tossed them aside. "Now what?"

"Whatever you want. Touch me, kiss me, read me a story. Whatever makes you happy."

"Reading hasn't crossed my mind for quite some time. But my hands itch at the thought of touching your skin." Her hand hovered over Clancy's belly, trembling slightly, and then gently settled. With long, smooth strokes, she touched her, gliding from torso to midthigh, pausing to explore a little as she went. "Nice. So nice." Her voice was sweeter than honey, and Clancy's eyes closed as she wound herself around Abby, needing to feel her body.

Their hands moved slowly over each other's bodies, touching and being touched for a long while. Abby's hand stroked up Clancy's inner thigh, and a muscular leg stretched out while Clancy murmured, "Yeah…that's nice."

Abby's palm was clammy, but Clancy knew the only way to get over her nervousness was to keep going. So she spread her legs out and waited for Abby to take the next step. She didn't have long to wait. Like a spider, delicate fingers crawled up her leg; then all five fingers paused, hovering over her vulva. Clancy shifted her hips, raising herself up to meet Abby's hand. She sighed when Abby stroked her like a cat, running her hand over her short, dark hair like a pelt.

Inquiring fingers tickled the apex of her thighs, and Clancy opened her legs, inviting Abby in. When one lone finger slipped past her lips, Clancy thrust up to meet her, unabashedly showing her desire.

She usually concentrated on the sensations, but Clancy knew it was vital to let Abby know what she was feeling. So she diverted her attention just enough to be able to speak while Abby's fingers grazed her clitoris. "Ooo!" she hummed. "Like a shock!"

"Too much? Too hard?"

"No. No. Shocks are good. Very good. Anything you want. Touch me anywhere…everywhere."

Abby shifted out of Clancy's loose embrace and moved down, resting her head on Clancy's thigh. "I want to look at you."

Clancy moved her leg a little, giving Abby better access. Again, Abby touched her, this time starting lower and working her way up. As her finger moved, Clancy's voice rose until she was squealing with delight.

"This is so interesting," Abby said. "Truly fascinating. It never dawned on me…how I must look."

"Take your time," Clancy said, even though she was about to slip her hand between her legs and give herself some relief.

"You look so aroused," Abby purred, her voice so sexy that Clancy nearly came.

"Yeah…yeah. Aroused."

"You're so wet…" She reached down, caught a trickle of moisture, and then rubbed it between her fingers. "It feels just like my own."

"Mmm." Clancy was interested in Abby's observations; she just wished they'd come later—preferably after an explosive orgasm.

"I like to cover my clit with moisture and rub it very…very delicately," Abby whispered. "Like this."

"Fuck!" Clancy cried, her body flying into a climax that took her—and Abby—completely by surprise. She hadn't had a second to allow the buildup she normally experienced; just a single touch set her off like a rocket. She had grabbed Abby's shoulders at the touch and was now trying to relax her grip while her body stopped spasming. "That…damn," she muttered, embarrassed. "I've never been so…unprepared."

Abby smiled up at her, looking tremendously pleased. "Did I do that?"

"Hell, yes, you did that!" Clancy laughed, throwing her head back and letting her joy flow from her body. "I think I might have died if you'd put your fingers inside of me. I need a few more drinks before I can work up to that!"

"Aww…" Abby climbed up next to her and wrapped her arms around her. "You're teasing me."

"No, I'm not!" She grasped Abby's hand and looked at it carefully. "Sure you don't have a live wire hidden somewhere?"

Abby put her arm around Clancy's waist. "Was that fun for you…satisfying?"

"It was a fantastic start," Clancy said, turning Abby's head so she could kiss her hungrily. "Now, just let me catch my breath and we'll keep testing our limits. One at a time."

❦

It had only been a few minutes, but Abby was itching with longing. "I…I want to taste you," she said. "When your tongue touched me…God…it was otherworldly. I wanna do that to you."

"Anything for you," Clancy said, smiling. "Not that you're asking for much of a sacrifice." She relaxed onto the bed, spreading her legs wide at Abby's urgings. Abby tried to nestle into the warm space but couldn't get comfortable. Tossing a pillow onto the floor, she got onto her knees and tugged Clancy toward the edge of the bed, smiling when Clancy carefully placed her feet on her shoulders and lay back.

Abby wasn't sure what to expect, and she dipped her head rather tentatively. Hovering above Clancy for just a moment, she felt her heart calm as she regarded her—so open and vulnerable. The gift that Clancy was offering was one she took very seriously. Abby leaned into her and returned the passion-filled kiss that Clancy had previously graced her with.

The sensations burst upon her tongue—indescribable, unique, and yet deeply familiar, reminding her of her own scent—one that she'd tasted on Will's lips so many times. She breathed in and let Clancy's fragrance fill her senses; then she began to explore. With her tongue and her lips, she moved over every bit of flesh both hidden and openly revealed. Clancy moaned continually, her hands clutching Abby's hair, sometimes pulling a little too firmly. Whenever Clancy would yank hard, Abby would back off, wait a moment, and then move on to another less-sensitive spot. But as soon as Clancy's body relaxed, she'd dive in again, grinning to herself when she drew another gasp from her.

Her hands were resting atop Clancy's thighs, and as she continued to nuzzle her, Clancy reached down and directed one hand toward her opening. "Come inside me. I need to feel you."

With her mouth never ceasing its gentle sucking, Abby slid into Clancy's warmth, a small groan leaving her when she felt how deliciously slick and hot Clancy was inside.

She was so enraptured by the experience that she almost failed to hear Clancy pant out, "Hold…still…hold still, and let me move against you."

Abby stilled her tongue and her fingers, but Clancy grabbed her hand and pushed it into herself, urging Abby to continue penetrating her. Her hands went to Abby's head, and she pulled almost completely away from her touch, Abby observing in rapt fascination. When her swollen flesh was barely touching Abby's soft tongue, she pumped her hips, letting herself glide against Abby for just a few moments. She whimpered softly and then stilled completely, and after just a heartbeat, Abby felt her begin to pulse and twitch deep inside. After a few powerful contractions, Clancy grasped her lover's head tightly and panted out through gritted teeth, "Soften your tongue and lick me everywhere. Gently…gently," she urged, her voice rising in a full-throated moan as Abby followed her instructions precisely.

Slowly, Clancy released her grip and let her legs drop from Abby's shoulders to fall along the mattress. Abby climbed onto the bed and wrapped her arms around Clancy's trembling body, holding her gently until her wildly beating heart slowly calmed. Clancy finally summoned the energy to look at Abby, giving her a wan smile as she said, "I didn't explode…but it was close."

When Clancy could string together a few coherent sentences, she nuzzled her face against Abby's breasts and said, "That was worth waiting for." She turned her head a little and pulled a perky nipple into her mouth, giving it a quick suck. "Your turn."

"Again?" Abby asked, showing her white teeth. "I get to go again?"

"You can go again and again and again. I can keep going until you've had your fill." She waggled her eyebrows rakishly and said, "Some of the few benefits of youth—appetite and stamina."

"I might take you to your limits. I've got five years of pent-up desire lurking right underneath this placid surface."

"We'll see who gives out first." Clancy gave her a toothy grin and added a little growl. "Now, where were we when you zoomed ahead of me in the game?" Abby lay flat on her back and spread her legs, a shy smile covering her face. Clancy smiled back at her and said, "Ahh…that's right. I was partying right around…here." She scooted down so that her head was nestled between Abby's legs and shot her a grin. "That's right, isn't it?"

Abby didn't even attempt to respond. She merely ran her fingers through the short hairs at the back of Clancy's head and pushed her gently toward the target.

"Mmm," Clancy purred when she tasted Abby's essence once again. "Delightful." She settled down comfortably and nuzzled her face in close, using just the tip of her tongue to trace lightly over all of the surfaces.

Abby tried to press against her, but Clancy wasn't about to be hurried. She was going to take Abby on a nice, slow, sensual ride, and she knew exactly where she wanted to go. Pressing her hands against Abby's hips, she lightened her touch even more, giving her partner the clear message that she was in control.

After a moment of struggle, Abby's body stilled; she sighed and said, "You're the boss."

Clancy's head lifted enough to make eye contact. She winked playfully. "You've got that right," she said. Then she dropped her head and let her desires lead her. She decided that nothing would please her more than simply to savor the sensual delights of Abby's body. She languidly explored the sights, the sounds, the tastes and aromas that her senses virtually drowned in. She was nuzzling softly against the wet, warm flesh, determined to taste every bit of the skin that throbbed against her tongue. Abby started to moan a little louder, jerking her hips more forcefully, so Clancy eased off again, smiling when she heard Abby let out a frustrated grunt.

Clancy came up onto her elbows and breathed a stream of cool air across Abby's heated skin. "Trust me," she murmured softly. "I'll take you there. Relax and let me love you."

Reaching out blindly, Abby grasped one of Clancy's hands and brought it to her mouth, kissing across her knuckles and then pressing the warm palm against her face. "I do trust you, Clancy. I do."

Even though they'd been sleeping for only an hour or so, Clancy woke just after seven. A bright, full smile settled onto her face when she felt Abby shift in her sleep and cuddle up even tighter. The architect let her hand drift down and stroke Abby's back, soothing her in her sleep. As she caressed her, Abby's breathing deepened, and she shifted and then stilled. *God, she's a beautiful woman. And can she ever make love!* Her eyes rolled in her head as she recalled a few images of their passion-filled coupling. She'd held a sneaking suspicion that Abby would be very free and loving in bed, but the reality had exceeded her expectations—by a mile.

She heard one soft whimper and then another, and she quickly realized that it wasn't Abby making the sounds but the dogs. She gently moved Abby's head from her own chest and placed it on a pillow. "Sleep tight," she whispered and then padded across the room to find her discarded boxers and T-shirt. Putting the wrinkled clothing on, she silently opened the door, shushed the dogs, and then sank to a crouch and allowed them to give her a very warm greeting. "The whole family has talented tongues," she commented to the pups as she led them downstairs.

Taking a peek into the laundry room, she pulled her shorts, panties, and shirt from the dryer. Abby had obviously done her share of laundry, because Clancy's dirty red socks still sat on the floor, along with her sports bra. "Somebody's learned her lesson about red wool socks," she commented to the dogs. "And she knew that I don't like my bras put in the washer. We've already proved we're compatible."

After giving the dogs breakfast, Clancy figured out how to use the coffeemaker and went outside to wait for the coffee to brew. She curled up on one of the loungers, and both dogs climbed onto the surface with her, their warm, soft bodies lulling her into a deep sleep.

❧

Abby woke slowly, her body a little stiff and a little sore from the thorough loving she had received. Even though it was a completely unique experience, she felt remarkably comfortable, to her surprise, with the realization that she and Clancy had thoroughly breached the friend barrier. The scent of the young woman lingered, and she smiled, a little amazed and more than a little pleased with herself. *I don't know if I surprised Clancy, but I shocked the hell out of myself.* She and Will had enjoyed a very fulfilling sex life, and he had always complimented her on her willingness to experiment and express herself. But she was surprised that she had done so with a new partner—and a woman, no less. *Maybe I'm not getting older,* she thought with a smirk. *Maybe I'm getting better.*

She assumed that Clancy was in the bath, but when she didn't hear a sound for a few moments, her heart started to beat rapidly. "Clancy?" she called. When she got no answer, she got up and peered out the window, but the yellow truck wasn't in its usual spot. Going to the door of the guest room, she opened it and called out again. "Clancy?" The only response was two eager dogs, running up the stairs quickly, licking her bare body enthusiastically. Her heart sank, and she began to feel a little sick to her stomach. *She left me? We made love all night long, and she got up and left?* She called out again, knowing that she was wasting her time. If Clancy were anywhere in the house, the dogs would be with her. *She must have left. Maybe her closing the door is what woke me.*

She fell onto the bed and lay completely still for a few minutes, her heart thudding in her chest. *Did this mean nothing to her? Was this just sex for her?* The minutes ticked by, and the dogs climbed onto the bed with her, Athena laying her head on Abby's belly.

108

What could have made her leave? This doesn't make sense—unless she didn't have as wonderful a time as I did. She felt sick to her stomach again, thinking of the intimacies she had shared with Clancy and of how willingly she had offered herself to the young woman. She got up slowly, feeling more like an eighty-year-old than herself. *Maybe she's not the type to stay over after she has sex.* She went to the stairway and leaned on the railing, thinking of how wonderful it had felt to walk up the stairs the night before, filled with anticipation. *Well, I'm not the type of woman who wants a drive-by sexual encounter. I guess I didn't know her as well as I thought I did. That's one mistake I won't make again. I swear I'll never sleep with another person unless I'm sure about her...or him.*

She squeezed her eyes shut, feeling like the orderly foundations of her world had been shaken. She shook her head as she padded into the bathroom to wash the scent of their lovemaking from her body. *Things I wish I'd decided yesterday.*

❧

When Abby got into the shower, the dogs ran back downstairs to see Clancy. They were pretty sure they weren't due for a bath, but a dog could never tell, so it was safer to be on a different floor when the shower started. They leapt onto the chaise, waking the architect from a sound sleep. "Hey, give a woman a little peace, huh?" she growled at them. Even though they'd woken her before she was ready, she couldn't stay mad at them. She was nearly giddy with happiness—her dreams of being with Abby not only coming true, but also coming true in a spectacular way.

She stretched, went into the kitchen, and heard the shower running. "Hey, she's up," she commented to the dogs. Then she wondered why she always conversed with them, because they were never able to keep up their side of the discussion. "How should I play this, guys? Does she like to have breakfast in bed?" she asked, only to get the silent treatment again. She decided to let Abby dictate the tone for their interactions. *Just in case—I won't put my real clothes back on. She might be taking a shower so she's nice and fresh for another roll in the hay.*

A silly grin settled onto her face, and she started to whistle. She took out a tray and poured a cup of coffee, adding a little half-and-half, just the way Abby liked it. Then she added a glass of juice and a bowl of granola, slicing a banana on the granola to make sure Abby got her vitamins. While she was preparing breakfast, the phone rang, and she heard a woman leave a message on the answering machine confirming plans to play tennis at ten o'clock. *Damn! It's already nine-thirty.* She sulked mildly and groused, *I guess we won't be going back to bed.* She heard Abby walking around upstairs, and she grabbed a vase and filled it with water. Then she took some shears and went outside to cut some flowers to add to the tray.

Abby came downstairs a moment later and stopped in surprise when she saw the neatly prepared breakfast. "Clancy?" she tried one more time. The coffee was hot, so she knew the young woman was close by, and her heart started to beat faster. She poked her head out the door and found the landscaper walking across the patio in her bare feet, last night's boxers and T-shirt covering her body. They made eye contact, and Abby immediately burst into tears, crying helplessly as Clancy ran the rest of the way, nearly dropping the vase in her eagerness to set it down.

"What's wrong?" Clancy asked softly. "Tell me."

"I…I…I thought you'd left," she gasped out. "I thought you slept with me and then walked out."

"Abby! I've never done that in my life." She held her at arm's length and gazed at her seriously. "You wouldn't be the woman I'd start that with."

Resting her head on Clancy's shoulder, Abby cried piteously, letting out all of the hurt and abandonment she'd felt when she'd woken up alone. "I'm sorry," she sniffled several minutes later. "This is so new for me—I don't really know how to behave."

"Hey, all you have to do is be yourself. You can never go wrong expressing how you feel."

"I feel better now that I know you're here. Much better."

"I feel better now that you're up." Clancy held the vase up in front of Abby and said, "I brought you flowers. Well, technically, I brought your flowers to you."

"Thank you," Abby whispered. "They're beautiful."

Clancy led her to the breakfast bar and urged her to sit. "You've got a tennis date in a few minutes. You'd better eat quickly."

Abby moaned and sat down to gulp down the food Clancy had provided for her. "I like bananas on my cereal," she said with an uncertain smile.

"I do, too," Clancy said, ruffling her hair gently. "Oh, thanks for not putting my socks in the washer. I forgot to tell you that they still bleed."

"No problem," Abby said, finding herself looking up shyly to meet Clancy's eyes.

Clancy went into the bathroom by the laundry to get dressed, and she came out a few minutes later, a little wrinkled but mostly clean. Abby was finishing her meal, and Clancy came up behind her and wrapped her in a hug. Abby grasped the arms that encircled her and gave them a squeeze. "I had one of the most remarkable nights of my life last night," Clancy whispered, tickling her ear. "It meant a lot to me, Abby, and I hope it meant something to you, too. I…I don't want to press you about the future, but I wanted you to know that." She leaned around just enough to reach Abby's lips and give them a lingering kiss. "Have a nice day playing tennis with your friends."

Abby nodded and watched the young woman walk toward the front door. Abruptly, Clancy turned and scampered back into the laundry room. She picked up her unwashed bra, sheepishly tucked it into one of the pockets of her cargo shorts, and blew Abby a kiss.

Abby watched her leave, feeling her heart sink when Clancy closed the door. *How can I miss her already?*

When she returned home from her tennis match, Abby desperately wanted to see Clancy, but something held her back. She put her hand on the phone and removed it three times before she shivered slightly and walked away, hugging herself. She found herself wandering aimlessly around the house, looking for something to occupy her mind. Restless and twitchy, unable to fix on anything for long, she scratched at the skin on her arms. Her body was fatigued…as tired as she'd felt in ages. She and Clancy had slept for only an hour or two, and three sets of tennis with her friends had served to deplete the small amount of energy she had. But her mind wasn't listening to her body.

The dogs were as restless as she, always tracking her mood. She looked at two pairs of brown eyes and said, "I'm going to go lie down, girls. Wanna join me?"

They wagged their tails excitedly, though they had no idea of where they were going. Together, they went upstairs, and the dogs ran into the master bedroom when Abby opened the door. She smiled at them, always comforted by their happy faces.

Kicking off her shoes, Abby walked slowly around the room, looking at it with new eyes. *Oh, baby, I know you wouldn't like this, but I've turned our room into a museum!* She touched the bronzed baby shoes, Will's first pair, and then picked up the photo of him being held by his parents at his baptism. She stroked the silver frame gently, put it down, and surveyed the rest of the room. It had taken her two years, but she'd managed to give nearly all of Will's clothing to a homeless shelter. She'd taken the boxes of mementos they'd saved after his parents' deaths, though, and put the majority of them on display in their room.

A ragged teddy bear, a particularly adorable picture of Will on a merry-go-round, his grade-school graduation picture, and a few other keepsakes from his youth dotted her dresser and the bookcases. These had joined the family pictures already adorning the walls when Will died—pictures from the time they started to date up to a few months before his death, chronicling their two decades together.

I can't leave it this way, honey. I can't. She sank to the bed, reaching out blindly to stroke the dogs, her constant allies in her fight against depression. *I know you'd want me to go on, and I can't go on when I'm surrounded by all of these things…* She gestured helplessly, looking at the items that cluttered her furniture. *I've got to put some of these things away.*

She got up and took the old, threadbare stuffed animal and dropped back onto the bed. For a long time, she cried…helplessly…just as she'd cried for the first months after Will had died. It felt like another piece of him was dying now, and she was sick with grief. The dogs licked her face and her head, trying to calm her down. But they weren't able to help her today. She was losing another small piece of Will, and this time, she was doing it by her own hand.

Chapter Eight

{ t took a long time to calm herself, but after a long nap Abby was feeling like a good facsimile of her usual self. She called Clancy, her heart beating like it had when she called Will for the first time. Clancy answered on the third ring, sounding a little muddled. "H'lo?"

"Oh, did I wake you?"

There was a long yawn, then the landscaper said, "I won't even try to lie. If I didn't know better, I'd think I'd been with four women last night."

Abby's heart clenched, but then she recalled what Clancy had said about her sexual history. "That's a joke, right?"

Laughing, Clancy said, "Yeah. I've been with four women, but that's over a ten-year span." She paused for a second. "Do I tease you too much? I thought it was pretty clear I was joking."

Embarrassed, Abby said, "It was clear…to a normal person. I'm just feeling…pretty shaky today. Last night was wonderful, but it was a very big step for me. I need to…I don't know…sit with it or get used to it or something."

"Wanna talk about it? I'll come over."

"No, that's not a good idea. Hayley will be home soon, I think. I'm not sure what her schedule is, but I can't risk it."

"Oh. Ahh…right. That's important."

"It's vital, Clancy. My kids have to come first."

"Yeah…yeah, I know that. I guess I'm kinda…I guess I'm feeling weird, too. Last night was a big jump."

"Really, really big."

"Maybe we'll feel like ourselves tomorrow, huh?"

"Uhm…maybe. But we're having some friends over tomorrow for a barbecue. I won't have any spare time."

"Right. Right. No problem. I'll see you on Monday. Maybe we can chat or have dinner or something."

"Sure. And…thanks for understanding my…uhm…situation. That means a lot to me."

"Doing my best. So…see you on Monday. And if you change your mind or just wanna talk—about anything—give me a call."

"I will." Abby hung up, knowing the call had been stilted and strangely formal. But she hadn't been sure how forthcoming to be and hadn't even known how to say goodbye. She knew she had strong feelings for Clancy, but she wasn't sure what her feelings meant. Was it love…desire…need? Thinking about feelings and the complications that Clancy would bring to her life was making her head hurt, so she went back upstairs for another extended nap, the dogs following obediently—even though they would rather have gone for a run.

❧

The last place Clancy wanted to be on Monday morning was on a hill with Hayley Graham when the fantastically attractive Abigail Graham was just a few dozen feet away, but that was where she found herself. Hayley had fallen behind on rock detail, and Ramon suggested that Clancy could take a full wheelbarrow down the hill much easier than Hayley could. So they worked together, with Hayley on her knees picking up rocks as quickly as she could, handing the bigger ones to Clancy and tossing the small ones right into the wheelbarrow. When the barrow was full, Clancy would muscle it down the hill, take it out to the dumpster, walk it up the ramp they'd built, and turn it onto its side, flinching when the harsh clatter hit her ears. By the time she got back, Hayley had a mound ready for her, and she bent over and tossed them all in.

It wasn't particularly hard work, especially for Hayley. She was able to carry on a mostly one-sided conversation while she collected the omnipresent rocks. "Did you have a good weekend?"

"Uh-huh."

"Do anything exciting?"

A dozen shocking responses went through Clancy's head, but she decided to stick with "No."

"Me either. I was doing some thinking about stuff we've talked about, though. Like being in relationships."

"Hmm?"

"You know. You told me that you liked being in relationships. I was thinking about that, and I decided you might be right."

Clancy didn't say a word. She just looked at the girl, trying to figure out where she was going.

"I was talking to Kerry. She's my friend you saw on Friday night. She's in love with a guy at Cal, and when we talked about it, it started to make sense…you know…like how it just happens, even when you weren't planning on it."

"Uh-huh," Clancy said, not sure where they were headed but feeling like she might not want to go.

"If you meet someone who you're really, really attracted to, why wouldn't you want to stick with them? I mean, it seems kinda stupid to meet someone you like and then leave them. Doesn't it?"

Clancy was more than a little dismayed to note Hayley's intentional omission of the pronouns *he* and *him*. She'd heard enough young women try to get through a story by using only *they* or *them* to have it catch her attention. "Yeah. That does seem kinda stupid. Of course, the hard part is finding someone you like and having them like you as much. That can take quite a few tries. I'm still looking."

"Well, maybe you've been looking in the wrong places." Hayley looked up and gave her a dazzling smile, so much like Abby's that the landscaper nearly fell to her knees and kissed her. But the Graham woman she wanted was in the house, and she was desperate to see her…talk to her…touch her…anything to know that Abby hadn't freaked out and made a pledge of perpetual celibacy.

That night, Abby called Clancy not long after the landscaper returned home for the night. "Hi," she said. "Was today as hard for you as it was for me?"

"I don't know," Clancy said. "But it was hard. Real hard." Clancy had no idea what was going through Abby's mind, so she tried to say the minimum while being positive.

"What was the hardest part for you?"

"Mmm…not seeing you. Not knowing how you were feeling."

"Know what I felt like?"

"Not a clue."

"I felt like grabbing you and going someplace quiet…like my bedroom."

"Wow!" The sun shone, and the sky turned bright blue in Clancy's world. "What a wonderful thought."

"But…that's not possible."

Clouds began to gather on the horizon. "Right. Sure. So…what's going through your mind?"

"I think…no, I know that I need some time. I have to think about all of the ramifications of…this. And I need to be with you to think some of this through."

"How about this weekend?" Clancy knew she sounded like she was asking for a very big Christmas present, but she couldn't help herself. "We can still go look at rocks and talk while we're there."

Abby wasn't feeling very lighthearted, but she let out a laugh. "Being with you…alone…in a motel would seal the deal. I can hardly stop myself from going up on the hill and kissing you until you're cross-eyed."

"That's a good instinct. Instincts are good."

There was a pause, then Abby said, "I want to give in, but I can't. At least, not yet. I can't act like this doesn't affect my family, Clancy. It does."

"I know that. And I'll try not to pressure you. Just…just remember that you deserve to be happy, too."

"I'll try," Abby said. "I'm used to putting my needs last, but I can't do that forever. My kids are almost grown now."

"They're grown," Clancy said. "As soon as Hayley's eighteen, she could get married or join the navy."

"According to her, she'd probably prefer the navy," Abby said, chuckling. "She swears she's not interested in a lasting relationship. A different sex partner in every port."

Clancy knew there'd been a recent change in that view, but she didn't mention it. She wasn't going to serve as the go-between for mother and daughter—especially when her messages might serve to ruin her chances with Abby.

🌿

The women agreed not to see each other during the week, both sure that they were sending enough vibes out to alert the neighbors as to how attracted they were to one another. On Wednesday, Hayley went into the house for lunch and asked her mother if she could invite Clancy for dinner. Abby's stomach clenched, but she felt like she had to agree. Later, Hayley went up to her boss and proposed the idea. "Mom's making steak enchiladas for dinner tonight. Wanna stay?"

Fortuitously, Clancy didn't have to invent an excuse. "Oh, thanks, but I can't. I'm going bowling with some friends."

"Bowling?"

"Yeah. We go to a place in Chatsworth."

Hayley made a face that she immediately tried to hide. "That sounds like fun. Maybe I'll tell my friends about it. We like to do different kinds of things."

"That could be fun, but you can't go on Wednesdays. It's all leagues. You have to be on a team to get a lane."

Not one to give up easily, Hayley said, "Well, maybe we'll come and watch you. We could have a few drinks. It'd be fun."

"You're not old enough to drink!"

Hayley laughed. "Do you honestly think there's a person in the San Gabriel Valley who doesn't have a good fake ID?"

"Oh. Right." Clancy thought for a minute and then said, "There's a very big fine for a bar owner letting underage people in. The owner's a friend of mine, Hayley. I'd have to tell him if I saw you there."

She looked absolutely indignant. "You'd tell?"

"Yeah, I would. It's just a fun night out for you guys, but he could lose his business. You have to think about how the things you do affect other people, you know. That's part of being mature."

"Yeah, right," the girl said. "You're my boss at work, but not in my personal life." She turned and walked over to Ramon, ready for her next task.

🌿

Hayley was cool to Clancy the rest of the day, and she hadn't thawed out by Thursday morning. Clancy hoped that the incipient crush had gone the way of most fleeting attractions, but Hayley was friendly again by Thursday afternoon.

That night, Abby called Clancy, and the pair talked for a long time—just as they had every night that week. "The thought of being alone with you this weekend is driving me crazy," Abby said. "Hayley's gonna wonder why we can't go up and back in a day, but we've got to stay over."

Clancy thought for a minute and then said, "You're the one who suggested we stay overnight. And that was before we even kissed."

"Shouldn't take a lot of thought to figure that one out," Abby said, laughing. "I've obviously been wanting you longer than I've been willing to admit."

"Why, Mrs. Graham! You are always a surprise!"

"The first day you showed up at my door, I remember walking behind you and thinking what a nice ass you had. I think I had a crush on you the first time I looked into those gray eyes."

"Come on, Saturday," Clancy said, trying not to sound like she was begging. "We need to be alone. And to kiss."

"I…I hope this doesn't sound idiotic, but I might want to slow down…sexually."

"Slow down…?"

"I've got a lot to think about, Clancy, and I can't let my libido make my decisions. We have to talk this weekend…not just moan."

"Kissing?"

Clancy could almost hear Abby's smile. "I don't think I could resist kissing you. Actually, I'm sure I couldn't."

"Kissing you is enough to satisfy any woman. Honestly, just being with you is enough."

"I'll be at your house on Saturday morning at around eight."

"I can't wait," Clancy said.

Laughing a little, Abby said, "Don't forget to bring your lips."

❧

Her smile disappeared as soon as she hung up the phone. Unable to quiet it, Abby closed her eyes and let her conscience have its voice. Every difficult lesson she'd ever learned flashed through her head. She knew without a doubt that she should put a stop to this right now. But she couldn't. She needed this so much that she couldn't turn back, even though she knew this would be hard for her kids and her parents and her friends. But for once in her adult life she consciously decided to think of herself first.

Taking in a cleansing breath, she went to her room, stripped naked, and lay in bed. For nearly an hour she touched her skin, letting her mind focus on the way she'd felt when Clancy had touched her. She purred with pleasure as she recalled the sensations that had washed over her body. Touching herself was a very poor substitute for Clancy's masterful hands, but dwelling on the memories of their time together let her experience the evening all over again…slowly and decadently.

❧

The work week was finished, and Clancy was paying Hayley on Friday night when Hayley asked, "Have any plans for tonight?"

"Yeah. To get a good night's sleep before we drive up to Merced tomorrow."

"Can I go with you? I want to make sure the rocks are right, too, you know."

"Ahh…no, you can't. We're taking your mom's car. Only two seats."

An annoyed expression settled on Hayley's face. "Why couldn't she buy an SUV like everybody else?"

Clancy laughed. "You know, most girls would be happy to drive a Lexus coupe. When I was your age, I had to drive my mother's floral-delivery van."

"Yeah, but you could make out in the back, couldn't you?"

Hayley had her on that one, and Clancy spent a moment thinking about her first lover and how they'd roll around in the back of the van, then have to brush the dirt and flower petals off each other before they went home. "I never kiss and tell. Besides, my mom might still ground me."

Smiling, Hayley said, "I like a woman who can keep a secret. You know, I was thinking that we could go get something to eat. Even you have to eat dinner."

"No, I'm good. I've got something at home."

Hayley looked at her for a minute. Then she finally locked eyes with her and said, "This isn't about food. I'm asking you out."

Clancy's eyes widened. *Damn, why weren't girls this forward when I was seventeen!* But she wasn't interested in this particular girl, and she had to think of a way to tell her without upsetting her. "Uhm...that's not a good idea, Hayley. I'm working for your mom, and I'm sure she wouldn't like it if she thought I was hitting on you."

"I'd tell her the truth." She gave Clancy a very sexy smile and added, "I'm hitting on *you*."

"Ahh...yeah, I guess you are. But she still wouldn't like it."

"My mom's cool about things like this. She has lesbian friends. She won't flip."

"Hayley, I hate to be so rigid, but I can't go out with a client's daughter. It's not right."

It was obvious that Hayley was starting to get perturbed, and Clancy could see her blue eyes darken. "Is that really the reason?"

"Yeah. It is."

"Fine. I'll ask my mom if she'd mind." She was clearly calling Clancy's bluff, and the blonde cursed herself for having told such a flimsy lie.

Clancy looked at the girl, seeing how resolved she was. "There's...more. I...I don't date women who have to ask their moms if they can go out. You're a great girl, Hayley, and if I'd known you when I was your age, I would have been in heaven. But I'm almost thirty years old. We're at different places in our lives."

"I'm not asking to marry you, Clancy," she said, obviously angry and embarrassed. "I'm asking you to go out to dinner."

Clancy wouldn't yield. "No, I can't. It doesn't make sense to have a date if I don't see this going anywhere. And I don't." The girl closed her eyes for a moment, and Clancy knew she was on the verge of tears. "Look, Hayley, I think it's great that you had the nerve to ask me. I really do. But you'd be happier with someone your own age. I swear you would."

"I don't like people my own age," she said, her voice husky. "I like older...people. That's why I've never gone out with anyone for long. They're too immature."

"Hayley, there have to be older people at Santa Cruz. Look for a grad student or a teaching assistant or something."

"I don't need dating advice," she said coldly. "I asked you out. You turned me down. End of story." She turned and walked toward the house, and by the time she got there, Clancy could see her shoulders shaking.

❧

Clancy went home and waited until seven o'clock, figuring that Hayley would probably be out with her friends by then. She dialed Abby, happy to have her answer on the second ring. "Hi, it's me. Are you alone?"

"Yes, I am. I was just thinking about calling to ask you out to dinner."

"Would you mind if I came over? I need to talk to you about something."

"What is it?"

"It's…let me come over," Clancy said. "I want to see you."

"All right," Abby said warily, "but I wish you'd tell me what you want to talk about."

"I'll be there in ten minutes," Clancy said, hanging up before Abby could ask another question.

As promised, she arrived in just a few minutes. They hugged each other but didn't kiss, both of them feeling unsettled—Clancy because of what had happened with Hayley and Abby because she didn't know what was bothering Clancy. Abby offered a beer, which Clancy gladly accepted. They went outside and sat down. Then Clancy steeled her nerves and said, "We have to talk about Hayley."

Immediately, Abby straightened. "Hayley?"

"Yeah." Clancy took a sip of her beer and tried to decide where to start. "I've been getting some…vibes from her. I think she has a crush on me."

Abby's head jerked noticeably. "What? Hayley has a crush on *you?*"

Smiling, Clancy said, "It's not *that* hard to believe, is it?"

"No, no, of course not. I mean, *I* have one." She absently stroked Clancy's thigh. "I never imagined…"

"To be honest, I think this is pretty new for Hayley. I was only certain of it when she asked me to go out with her tonight."

"Go out with her? Out…like hanging out? Maybe she thinks of you as a friend. She certainly wouldn't think of it as a date if Kerry was going along."

"No, Abby. Kerry wasn't going to go along. She wanted to go out with me…alone. She wanted to go on a date. I'm sure of it."

"Oh, God, why didn't you tell me this before?" She held her face in her hands, mumbling something to herself.

"I wasn't sure until tonight. I've been so fixated on you that I missed the little clues she's been giving me."

Abby lifted her head and looked at Clancy for a few seconds, her eyes slightly narrowed. "How long has she been giving you clues?"

Flustered, Clancy said, "I don't know. She...asked me to hang out with her once...no, twice before. I thought it might be a crush, but it seemed really harmless. Kinda like you have on a teacher at school."

Abby's gaze didn't falter. "If you'd told me before, I wouldn't have considered getting involved with you. This is hard enough for me without thinking I'm poaching on my daughter's territory."

"I'm *not* Hayley's territory! I'm nobody's territory." She stood up, walked a few steps, and then turned and put her hands on the back of her chair. "I told you as soon as I thought Hayley was serious. I'm not the type to tell you every thing that happens between us. She deserves privacy, too."

"Oh, shit, Clancy, I didn't mean it that way." Abby stood and walked over to Clancy, gently trailing her fingers back and forth across her shoulders. "I shouldn't have snapped at you. I know you wouldn't do anything that would hurt Hayley...or me."

"I wouldn't," she said, gazing unflinchingly at Abby.

"I'm sorry." Abby's voice was a whisper. "I spoke before I thought."

Clancy's shoulders slumped. "'S okay. I'm just...I'm just pissed that this happened. Damn it, Abby, I've had a crush on you since the day we met. I can't believe that I finally got to make love with you. And then Hayley has to gum up the works with this silly fantasy."

"Silly? Why is it silly?"

"Because I'd never be attracted to a teenager. I haven't given her any indication that I'm into her. This is all in her mind. It's what kids do."

"What do adults do?" Abby asked, giving Clancy a look she couldn't decipher.

"Do you mean us?"

"Yeah. What happened with us?"

"I think we've been giving each other signals...for a while now. Don't you?"

Abby nodded, looking a little embarrassed. "I wasn't sure if you could tell. In a way, I didn't want you to." She looked Clancy in the eye and said, "But in another way, I desperately wanted you to notice. I'm...I'm very, very attracted to you. It scares the hell out of me, but I can't stop thinking about you. I feel lost when you're not here."

Clancy put her hands on Abby's waist. "I've been nuts about you since the first, and the more I know you, the more I want you."

Leaning forward just a little bit, Abby draped her arms around Clancy's neck and kissed her. She took her time, kissing her just the way she'd fantasized. She nibbled on her lips and then sucked each one into her mouth, teasing the tender skin with her teeth. Then she pulled her tightly against herself and began to probe her mouth with her tongue, keeping up her sensual investigation until Clancy felt limp and powerless in her arms. When she finally let her go, Clancy stumbled a little as she tried to steady herself.

"I...I..." Clancy gave up trying to talk. She let out a breath and brought her hands up to scrub at her face, shaking her head in amazement. "I've never been kissed like that before." She looked into Abby's eyes and said, "Please do it again."

Abby put her arms around Clancy and pulled her head down to rest on her breast. "I want to," she said, "but I'm so confused." Clancy could feel the heavy sigh that filled her friend's lungs. "I don't know what to do. I want you. I want you so badly. But this is hard for me—so much harder if Hayley's feelings are involved. Can you understand that?"

"Yeah, yeah, of course I understand that. That's why I told you. She just has a crush, but I thought it might—"

Abby shook her head, cutting her off. "No, it's hard for me even without bringing Hayley into this. I'm…a straight woman."

Clancy moved and dropped into her chair, staring up at Abby.

"That's what my label has always been," Abby said, her voice nearly pleading. "I was open-minded about sex and could have slept with a woman, but I always assumed I'd get married and have kids. But am I straight? I don't even know. How…how can I not know something so basic about myself?"

Clancy shook her head, clearly at a loss.

"Do straight women lust after other women? After we went dancing, I lay in bed and touched myself while thinking of what it would be like to taste you." Tears came to her eyes. "Do straight women do that?"

"I don't know. I just don't know. I guess some straight women have lesbian fantasies—"

"But this is a fantasy that I want to make happen. This is a fantasy that *is* happening. And every part of me except the rational part wants to take you upstairs and make love to you again."

"I don't have a rational part," Clancy said, smiling gently. "So all of me wants to take you up on that offer."

Abby bent and kissed her on the head. Then she stretched, moving her arms across her chest, and shook her hands out at her sides. "One of the detriments of motherhood. There's always a rational part." She held her hand out and helped Clancy to her feet. "You're a handful," she said, finally smiling.

"Yeah. I probably outweigh you, and you're a couple of inches taller than I am."

Abby let out a massive breath and then trailed her fingers down both of Clancy's shoulders and arms, stopping to trace the triceps. "I'd love to see those muscles that make you so sturdy. I love muscles. I loved kissing the little dips on your arms the other night."

Clancy couldn't help herself. She stuck her right arm out and turned it to make the tricep pop. "Never been in a gym in my life," she said. "These are from moving mounds of dirt from one place to another."

"I…" Abby's smile faded. "I have so much I want to say to you. So many things I want to do with you." She brushed her fingers across Clancy's lips. "But I don't know what to do right now. Do you understand?"

"I don't think I do, Abby. I…I want to, but I don't know what it's like to be a mother, and I don't know what it's like to have feelings for a woman after spending my whole life thinking I was straight."

Giving her a sad smile, Abby said, "Don't forget the part where mother and daughter both have a crush on the same woman."

Clancy took in a breath and prepared herself to tell Abby that she cared about her enough to get beyond any obstacle. But something stopped her. She was sure of her feelings, but she wasn't sure enough of Abby's to tell her what was in her heart. Instead, she put her arms around Abby's waist and held her, neither of them speaking.

After a long time, Abby said, "You should go. If Hayley's upset, she might not stay out long. She doesn't follow her predictable patterns when she's angry."

Clancy smiled a little and put her hand on Abby's shoulder, giving it a squeeze. "It's been a tough night for both of us. Maybe we both need a good night's sleep."

Abby nodded, unable to read a thing from Clancy's thin smile. "I guess I'll see you…"

Clancy took her hand and started to move away. As she did, their arms extended and then dropped to their sides. She turned and left the yard, missing the tears that immediately formed in Abby's eyes.

❧

Later that night, after letting the dogs out, Abby went upstairs, relieved when she heard Hayley enter a short time later. She still couldn't sleep, but at least there was one less thing to worry about. The dogs left her bed, heading downstairs to keep Hayley company.

Abby lay there for a very long time, the jumble of thoughts in her head impossible to sort out. She was incredibly attracted to Clancy, and her sexual desire wasn't even the biggest part of her attraction. It was the whole package—her personality, her kindness, her sincerity, her…self. She was frightened to admit it, and she thought there was very little chance of the relationship's ever getting off the ground, but she knew she was falling in love. With a woman…fifteen years younger than she…who was solidly situated in a blue-collar lifestyle…and whom her daughter had a crush on. *Well, at least we both speak the same language,* she thought before thumping her pillow with a fist and trying once more to get comfortable.

❧

Clancy was having just as difficult a time at her apartment. She'd had a beer and then another, but she was anxious and wide awake. So she turned on the TV, lay down on the sofa, and watched old movies until she eventually fell asleep.

At dawn the sun hit her right in the eyes, and she stumbled to her feet, finding her way to her bedroom. She flopped down on her futon, fully clothed, hoping to sleep until Abby was less confused and Hayley was back to chasing boys.

❧

At eight-thirty, Abby knocked gently on the door of Clancy's apartment. Michael answered immediately; he was dressed and looked like he was on his way to work. Abby was relieved—not only that he was up, but also that he would probably be leaving, giving her some time alone with Clancy.

"Hi, Abby," he said. "Are you and Clance going rock hunting again?"

"Yes. We're going up to Merced. Uhm...isn't she up?"

"I don't think so. But it's not like her to sleep late. I'll go check on her."

"Oh! No, don't do that. I'll call her later."

"Don't be silly. She might be in bed reading or something. Sometimes she hangs out in her room."

Before she could stop him, he walked into the hallway that separated the bedrooms and knocked softly. When he didn't hear a response, he poked his head in. "Clance?"

She turned her head a little, her face still partially covered by the pillow. "What?"

"Abby's here. Aren't you supposed to be up?"

She was on her feet in a snap. "Abby's here?" She was a little unsteady, and Michael reached out for her.

"Hey, are you okay? You hung over?"

"I'm fine. Just tired. Thanks for waking me."

She walked into the living room with Michael, who said his goodbyes and left for work. Clancy was still trying to appear awake, but her sleep-creased face didn't help matters. "Hi," she said, her voice cracking. "Sorry I'm such a mess."

"Oh, Clancy, I didn't want to wake you up. I mean, I did, but I didn't."

The landscaper shook her head, trying to make the circuits start firing, but she knew that only caffeine and a shower would do that. "I see Michael made some coffee," she said, indicating the pot. "Why don't you pour us both a cup while I take a quick shower?"

"If you're sure..."

Clancy put her hands up and lowered them slowly, asking for quiet. "You wouldn't have come over here at this time of the morning if you didn't need to see me. Now just chill for a minute, and let me get my brain working." With that, she walked into the bathroom, closing the door quietly.

Abby didn't know what to do. She'd expected a much warmer welcome, and she debated leaving. But she knew that would only make matters worse. She sat down at the kitchen table, and her eyes drifted to a note that Michael had obviously left.

> *Julie called—again!*
> *She obviously wants what you've got, girl.*
> *Put her out of her misery, but make sure I'm home to join you*
> *when you do it.*
>
> *Michael*

Abby felt her stomach begin to churn. *What kind of person have I gotten myself mixed up with? I thought I knew her!*

She was still sitting at the table when Clancy came out of her room, dressed in a pair of jeans and a blue-and-white print shirt. Clancy smiled at her guest and said, "I'll bet you didn't know I had long pants."

"Oh. Right." Abby gave her a weak smile. "I'm sorry I didn't pour coffee. I didn't feel like having any."

Clancy stood a little awkwardly. "Are you all right? You look…kinda pissed."

"It's nothing. I was just a little put off by how grouchy you were when I first got here."

"Grouchy? I…I didn't realize…but I'm sorry if I was. I had about two hours of sleep, and my head hurts. I had too much to drink. I…apologize if I upset you."

"I said it's all right," Abby said tersely. "I'm sorry I bothered you. I thought we had plans, but—"

"Oh, fuck! We're going to Merced! I just thought we'd…I don't know…cancel because of this stuff with Hayley!"

"You could have said so," Abby said, feeling humiliated.

"Damn, damn, damn! I'm so sorry, Abby. Really, I am."

"It's nothing." Abby shifted, looking uncomfortable. "Maybe you're right. Maybe we should let things rest for a while and see what happens. We're not in a rush to buy those rocks." She stood and said, "Why don't you go back to bed? As a matter of fact, I should do the same. I think I'll go back to bed and start the day over."

"Hey, hey, hey," Clancy said. She walked over and stood close to Abby. Her hand moved, retreated twice, and then fell to her side. "Are you sure you want to leave? You must have wanted to go to Merced."

"I don't know why I came. I think I should have stayed in bed." She turned and walked to the door, saying over her shoulder, "I'll talk to you later."

Clancy went to the door and watched Abby walk down the path. When Abby was out of sight, she dropped her clothes right where she stood and then went back into her room and fell onto the futon, bruising her shoulder when she hit the wooden frame.

❦

Clancy slept until eleven and then lay in bed for a while, trying to figure out what had gone wrong. She was completely at a loss, feeling that she'd done as well as she could, given the circumstances. *Hell, I didn't have any obligation to tell her about Hayley. I stepped up and told her something that I knew would screw my chances with her. Shouldn't I get a little credit for that?*

She got up and took another shower, a longer one this time. By the time she went into the kitchen and made a new pot of coffee, she was feeling a little more like herself. She was still naked, but Michael wasn't due home until at least six. When the coffee was ready, she sat down at the kitchen table to read the paper. But a note written on one of her artist's pads caught her eye. She was halfway through the message when she spat her coffee all over the paper. "Holy fuck! What in the hell is wrong with you, Michael?"

Dashing across the room, she grabbed her clothes and started to get into them, trying to put her shirt on while she shimmied into her pants. Her buttons were askew, her shoes were untied, and she wasn't wearing a bra, but she grabbed her wallet and her keys and then ran out of the house.

Pulling up in front of Abby's house a few minutes later, she breathed a sigh of relief when she saw her working on one of her flower borders. Making her feel even better were the facts that the garage door was open and the car was missing—meaning Hayley was in it and gone. Clancy walked up to the gate and called, "Abby! Will you let me in?"

The dogs reacted first, running to the gate in a blur. Abby's head swung around, and she caught sight of Clancy. For the first time since they'd met, the taller woman didn't smile. In fact, Clancy could see her shoulders rise and fall in a gesture that looked suspiciously like indifference. She got up and walked to the gate, her face bearing an utterly blank expression. "What's up?" she asked, lifting an eyebrow.

"Can I come in? I think I know why you're upset, and I can explain what happened."

Abby leaned against the wrought-iron fence, shaking her head. "Maybe it's best for everyone if we stop this right now. This is all too, too complicated for me." The dogs were looking at their owner and then at Clancy, whining softly when the landscaper didn't enter.

Clancy stood at her full height and stuck out her chin. "No," she said, her eyes boring into Abby's. "No way. Either let me in, or I'll stand out here and explain myself. But everybody who walks by is gonna hear me."

"I can't be involved in this kind of thing," Abby said, sounding tired and defeated. "I don't need or want drama in my life."

"You think I do?" Clancy asked, her voice louder than it had to be. "You wanted to make love to me last Friday. *You* wanted it. But today, you don't wanna be involved in 'this kind of thing.' What the fuck does that mean? You don't want a woman? You don't want a gardener? Where don't I measure up?"

"Please be quiet!" Abby whispered harshly. "I have neighbors!"

"Your neighbors can kiss my ass! Now let me in, or they'll all know what happened!"

Muttering, Abby snapped. "I obviously had the wrong impression about you."

"God damn it! Listen to me!" Clancy was nearly at full voice, and she grasped the metal bars of the gate so firmly that Abby was afraid she'd bend them. "You know me! Don't let some stupid note from Michael change how you feel!"

"You're scaring me," Abby said quietly. "I don't like to be yelled at."

All of the fire went out of her, and Clancy leaned heavily against the gate. Her voice was filled with tears when she said, "God damn it, Abby. Don't treat me this way. I don't deserve it."

The first sign of tears sent Abby scurrying to the gate, and she flung it open. "Let's go into the back yard and talk."

The dogs darted out of the open gate and jumped all over Clancy, looking like they'd gotten their long-lost friend back. She petted both of the girls, enormously glad that at least two of the members of the family were happy to see her.

As soon as they sat down, Clancy explained the note. "Julie is my ex. The one I had the on-and-off relationship with. Every once in a while, she calls me. I never encourage her, and I rarely speak to her. When I see her, I'm polite—nothing more."

"The note sounded like this woman is more than an ex," Abby said, looking at the ground.

"She's an *ex*," Clancy said. "I'll admit that she's not over me, but I'm over her. I was over her a couple of years ago, but she still thinks I'll give her another chance. I won't."

"But the note—"

"Is a product of Michael's perverse sense of humor. He thinks it's funny that she's still hung up on me. He's always teasing me about how irresistible I am. It's a joke. A stupid joke."

Abby was still staring at the ground, and when she spoke, her voice was soft and tentative. "He said something about his being home when…"

Clancy ran her hand through her hair, cursing under her breath. "He's been teasing me about that since we were in high school, always joking about wanting to watch. But it's only funny because it's never gonna happen. Michael has never seen me kiss a woman, much less have sex with one. I'm very, very private about things like that, and he knows it."

"Really?" Abby's lower lip was trembling, and Clancy could see the wall coming down.

"Really. I'm very serious about love." Clancy got up, stood beside Abby, and then started to run her fingers through her hair. "I don't fall in love easily, and when I do, I do everything I can to make it work."

Abby started to cry, her face scrunching up like a small child's. "That's what I thought," she sobbed. "I was so hurt when I felt like I didn't know you. I was so scared," she said, crying harder.

Clancy knelt in front of her and wrapped her arms around the shaking shoulders. "Shh…shh…it's okay. Everything's all right. You *do* know me. You know me very, very well. I am who you think I am. I swear."

"I was so hurt," she said again, her voice still shaking.

"I know, I know." She tilted her head and started to kiss every spot her lips could reach. Finally, she slid her hands through Abby's hair and pushed her head back to look into her eyes. Abby looked hurt and vulnerable, but there was a spark of desire in her eyes. Suddenly, surprisingly strong arms enveloped Clancy, and the women began to kiss—tenderly, tentatively at first, but quickly growing into heated, passionate kisses.

Abby was quivering with desire, her body shaking with pent-up need. It was crazy to be kissing right on the back patio, but neither woman could stop herself. They kissed and kissed, rubbing their bodies against each other, making themselves weak with desire. Regretfully, Clancy started to pull away, peppering Abby's lips with soft kisses as she did. "I can't…" she gasped, nearly breathless. "I'm not gonna be able to stop." Her eyes were glassy and wide, and her cheeks flushed even through her tan. She was shaking, and Abby drew her into an embrace, holding on tight.

Clancy could feel Abby's heart racing, her chest rising and falling in a quick cadence. Her shirt was damp with perspiration, and a drop fell from Abby's cheek and landed on Clancy's. The architect pulled away and wiped her friend's forehead with her thumbs. "What are we gonna do?" Clancy asked. "I can't let you go, but I don't wanna hurt Hayley." She blew out a breath and added, "I don't want anyone to get hurt."

Abby didn't answer for a long time. She had one hand resting on Clancy's shoulder while the other played with her hair, her fingers running through the white-blonde mane, captivated by the short, stiff locks that jumped back up when her hand passed over them. "I think it's too late for that. Someone *will* get hurt."

The women sat on a lounge chair, not touching, barely looking at each other. After a long while of inattentively looking at the landscape-in-progress, Clancy said, "Why don't we go to Merced? I feel like I'm sitting on Death Row, waiting for the warden to come to my cell."

"What?"

"Hayley's gonna come home at some point, and things are probably gonna get ugly. She was really, really angry with me."

"Oh." Abby looked up at the sky and then shook her head briefly. "She didn't mention a word to me when she went out this morning. Actually, she seemed completely normal."

"Maybe that's a good sign. I might have blown this all out of proportion."

Abby looked at her for a second and then said, "That's not what you do. If you thought she was upset, she was upset. She might just not want me to know. She's very proud. She hates to be embarrassed…and she rarely tells me when she feels foolish."

Clancy stood. "I'm gonna drive up to Merced. I can't just sit here all day. I'm no…I don't…I'm not the most patient woman you'll ever meet."

"Oh, what the hell? We might as well both go. Whatever's waiting for us will still be here tomorrow."

"Pack a bag, and let's get out of here. If you don't mind going in my truck, that is."

"It's fine." Abby stood close and put her hand on Clancy's side, giving her flesh a brief squeeze. "I'm not sure I'll be good company. I've got a lot on my mind."

"'S okay. I just need to do something. Driving is something."

When they reached the quaint little motor court, they went in together, and Clancy had to clear her throat to find her voice, because it hadn't been used for over three hours. Abby had been true to her word—she hadn't been very good company. She'd stared out the window for the whole ride, leaving Clancy to stew silently, not having any idea of what was going through Abby's mind.

When they approached the desk, the proprietor looked up and asked, "Help you?"

"Yeah. I made reservations earlier in the week. O'Connor."

"Oh, yes. Here we are. Two rooms, right?"

Sparing a quick glance at Abby, who was staring straight ahead, Clancy shrugged and said, "Uhm…right." After the tense, silent trip, she had no idea whether Abby wanted to share a room with her, so she decided not to press the issue. *You should have cleared this up before you got inside, you dope!* She extracted her wallet from her jeans and pushed her credit card toward the woman, not stopping when Abby tried to interrupt. "I'll get the rooms," she said. Looking at the desk clerk, she asked, "Where's the best place in town to have dinner?"

"How fancy do you want to get?" the woman asked.

"Very," Clancy said.

"That'd be the Hitching Post. Take the main road north about three miles. You can't miss it."

"Thanks," Clancy said when the woman handed over the keys.

When they walked back into the bright sun, Abby said, "I didn't bring much to wear to a fancy restaurant."

Clancy was relieved just to hear her voice again. "Up here, 'fancy' means the bar is in a separate room from the restaurant. You look fantastic just the way you are."

Abby looked away, looking like the compliment had made her uncomfortable. "Thanks." She gave Clancy a smile—her first of the trip—and said, "You look nice today. I'm sorry I didn't comment earlier."

The architect was wearing a very bright print campshirt in shades of orange and yellow. Faded, form-fitting jeans and black Birkenstock sandals finished off her outfit, making her look taller and a little older.

"Well, now you've seen almost my entire wardrobe. I keep telling myself that I've got to buy a few nice things, but I never get around to it."

"I like your little uniform," Abby said, but Clancy noted that her smile faded as soon as she finished the sentence. "Let me freshen up, and then we can go have dinner, okay?"

Clancy nodded and handed her a key to one of the bungalows. Each room was a stand-alone unit with a bath and a bedroom, and Clancy was pleased to find that they were neat, clean, and relatively updated. There was a big television in the room and a queen-size bed, and she looked at it briefly, hoping against hope that Abby would share the bed with her.

During dinner, they steered clear of any upsetting topics and focused on the landscaping plans. Clancy had been tweaking them in every spare moment she had, and she excitedly regaled Abby with every new bit of minutia she could recall.

Abby picked up the check after a brief argument; then they headed back to the motel. The night was cool and dry, and a soft breeze whistled through the massive pine trees that the cabins were nestled into. "Wanna stay outside and enjoy the evening?" Clancy asked.

Abby nodded and sat in the rough-hewn swing that graced the porch of her cabin. It was the only seating available, so Clancy squeezed in next to her, their thighs touching all along their length. Fortunately, Abby didn't move her leg, and Clancy was slightly heartened.

Screwing up her courage, Clancy asked, "Wanna talk about it?"

Abby shook her head gently and said, "Not really. I'm not the kind of woman who can process my feelings quickly. I need to let things percolate for a while." She looked at Clancy and added, "Give me time, okay?"

"Of course." She wanted to touch her so badly that she could taste it, but Clancy kept her hands firmly atop her own knees. "I don't want to rush you. I know this has been a very, very emotional time for you. I'll do my best to back off."

Looking at her curiously, Abby asked, "Would you like to talk? Just because I need some time to reflect doesn't mean that you do, too."

"Uhm...I don't have a lot to say." Summoning all of the affection she could muster into her gaze she said, "All I want is to make sure that you know how much I care for you. My feelings for you run very, very deep, and I very much want a chance to work this out."

A long, delicate hand reached out and landed on Clancy's thigh. Abby's voice was soft and held a heavy note of curiosity. "Is that true?"

"Is what true? That I have feelings for you or that I want the opportunity to build a relationship?"

"Uhm...either, I guess," she said. "I'm not sure I know where you think this is going."

"What? I thought I'd made it clear that I want to have a relationship with you."

"You've never said that in so many words," Abby said, staring at her.

"Give me a break! We haven't been able to see each other all week! Damn, I'd say a million things if I could be with you!"

Eyes downcast, Abby said, "I'm sorry. But you give me mixed signals. I thought you'd at least ask me if I wanted to share a room. It...made me feel like you didn't want to be too close."

Clancy slid off the swing and got to her knees, grasping Abby's hands. "I was upset about what had happened with Hayley. I thought...I thought that Hayley's asking me out might make you change your mind."

"It should," she said, looking over Clancy's head to stare into the pines. "My children have always...always come first." She looked down and met Clancy's eyes. "I know that this is going to have serious—maybe even disastrous—repercussions for my family." The smallest of smiles touched her lips, and she reached out and stroked Clancy's cheek. "But I want you so badly." She closed her eyes and shivered, her head shaking slowly. "I've never been this torn about anything in my life."

"We can work it out. We'll be very, very discreet."

With a sad, resigned expression, Abby said, "We can't be discreet for long. I can't juggle lies to my kids, my parents, my friends, my neighbors. This will come out, and it will probably come out soon. That's why I have to know that you're serious about this." She put her hands on Clancy's shoulders and said, "I'm begging you. Level with me. I have to know how you feel about me."

Closing her eyes, Clancy planted soft kisses all over Abby's hands. "I know it's early, but I think you're the one. *The* one," she reiterated. "I'm falling in love with you, Abby."

"You want to be in a committed, exclusive relationship with me?"

Giving her a very puzzled look, Clancy said, "Yes, of course!"

"I don't mean to doubt you," Abby said. "But the note from Michael really threw me."

"Damn, *please* put that out of your mind. I am totally, thoroughly single. I have no interest in any woman in the world—except you. I'm very old-fashioned about relationships—even though I'm fairly adventurous when I'm in one. I'd love to show you exactly how adventurous I can be," she added, leaning forward just enough to be able to detect a hint of Abby's perfume.

Abby closed the distance between them and placed a delicate kiss on Clancy's warm lips. "Will you sleep with me tonight?" She waited for a second and added, "I'm…I don't think I'm ready to have sex again, but I'd love to hold you. Is that okay?"

"Of course. You can hold me tonight, tomorrow…as many nights as you'll have me," Clancy replied, her voice catching a little.

Abby got up and extended a hand, and Clancy gladly took it. "Let's take this one day at a time, okay?"

"That works, too." Clancy smiled broadly and took her hand to lead her into the cabin.

❦

Clancy stood just inside the door of the small room, looking around awkwardly while she tried to decide what to do. Abby looked more than a little nervous, too, and she gave Clancy a tentative smile and inclined her head towards the bath. "I'll just brush my teeth…"

"Oh! Uhm…maybe I'll go do the same. Be right back." *This is too weird*, she thought, leaning against the door of her room. *We act like we're total strangers.* She brushed, flossed, and brushed again, mumbling to herself the whole time. Deciding that she was feeling a little grungy from the drive, Clancy took a quick shower, giving herself a good talking-to while she scrubbed herself. *The only way to make Abby feel comfortable is to tell her how you're feeling—and encourage her to do the same when she's able. Just be honest with her.*

Freshly scrubbed and feeling a little better, Clancy put on some never-worn flannel pajamas that she'd found at the bottom of her dresser.

She'd been gone longer than she'd planned, and Abby was already in bed when she entered. Abby gave her a relieved glance and said, "I thought you might have changed your mind."

Clancy quickly crossed the room and perched on the edge of the bed. Reaching out, she ran her hand down Abby's face, lingering over her features with her thumb. "What's up? You act as though you're expecting me to be a real asshole, and you know me better than that."

"I don't know. This whole thing has me so mixed up. I don't feel like I can trust my instincts right now. I honestly feel like I'm in a fog."

Her thumb kept stroking, and Clancy lowered her voice and softened it. "Anything I can do to help? Wanna talk about it?"

Abby shook her head, once again avoiding Clancy's gaze. "Too much. I just need to sleep."

When she stood, Abby's eyes followed her. Clancy walked around to the other side of the bed and tossed the covers back. As she slid in, she smiled and said, "I know how to distract you, and relax you, and make you sleep like a baby."

Abby's eyes widened in surprise, staring at Clancy warily.

Perturbed at her expression, Clancy said, "I'm not going to pounce on you." She sat up against the headboard and pulled Abby's head onto her lap. "I only wanted to rub your head."

Abby's chin quivered for a second before tears began to slide down her cheeks. "I'm sorry. I'm sorry about everything. But please…please don't be angry with me."

"It's all right," Clancy said, trying to sound reassuring. "Don't think about a thing. Just feel my touch."

Abby's body felt a little stiff and unyielding, and Clancy gently soothed, "Come on now; relax for me. Concentrate on your breathing…that's it…that's the way." She smiled down at Abby as she felt her muscles start to relax and her body mold itself along her length. Abby's arm draped across Clancy's thighs, and her hand tangled in the generous folds of her pajamas.

Clancy gazed down when she heard Abby's soft voice murmur, "Perfect. Just perfect. This was exactly what I needed."

Giving her hair an affectionate ruffle, Clancy said, "I'll do my best to always give you what you need, Abby. I promise that."

"I promise to try to believe you. That's the best I can do right now."

On the way back to Los Angeles, Clancy commented, "I'm not sure if this was the best day to look at boulders. Every one was beautiful…perfect and smooth. Just like your skin."

Abby's hand playfully covered her mouth as she chided her, "You're going to have to behave when we get back home, you know. You may as well get into practice right now."

Clancy nodded, her eyes still dancing. "I'll be good. I'm just so completely happy, Abby. Everything seems perfect today."

Abby was driving, but she diverted her attention long enough to grasp Clancy's hand and give it a gentle kiss. "It seems perfect to me, too. Being away from home was a wonderful break. I feel rested and calm."

"I feel very connected to you. Holding you made me very, very happy."

"Me, too." She placed Clancy's hand on her thigh, and the pair lapsed into a comfortable silence, both of them ruminating about the events of the weekend.

Clancy noticed that Abby's body grew stiff as they drew near Los Angeles. "You seem pretty tense. Worried about going home?"

"Yes. Very."

Clancy was quickly learning that Abby became almost monosyllabic when she was worried about something, but she wasn't willing to let this issue slide. "We should talk about it. We need to make a decision about how we're going to play this."

"We can't let Hayley know…no matter what," she said, her face a mask of worry.

"Okay, we can do that. But I hope you mean that we can't tell her right now…"

"Yes. Oh, yes! Of course that's what I mean. She'll get over her hurt feelings soon. And she'll be going to Maine in a month—then right to school from there."

Clancy felt a little sick to her stomach at the thought of waiting for a month, but she nodded. "I don't need to tell another soul. We'll keep this between us until you're ready to go public."

"No, no. That's not necessary. I know you're close to your parents, Clancy; they'll pick up on this. So will Michael. I don't want you to lie to them."

"If it comes up, I'll be honest. But I'm not going to go out of my way to tell people until you're ready."

Abby gave her a relieved glance and blew her a kiss. "I should have known you'd be understanding about this. I don't know why I was worried about talking to you about it."

"'Cause it's all new to you. You're not used to having to hide a part of your life." She gripped her thigh with gentle pressure and said, "We'll work this out. I promise."

"I trust you," she whispered.

🌶

A few miles later Abby said, "I wonder how surprised people will be about this? I can't help thinking that someone hasn't picked up on the connection that's been building between us."

Running her hand up and down Abby's thigh, Clancy asked gently, "Do you honestly think you've had a crush on me for a while?"

"I don't remember the last time I sat around in my pajamas playing 'eat the strawberries from my fingers' with any of my other contractors," she said thoughtfully, adding a wry glance at Clancy.

"You know I meant before last Friday night," Clancy said, giving her a pinch.

"I didn't recognize it at first, but in retrospect, I've been sexually attracted to you for a while; I just forced the conscious thoughts down."

"Tell me how you've been feeling," Clancy said. "Don't be afraid."

"I'm not afraid…exactly," Abby said, smiling again. "But this isn't what I do best." She took in a breath and squared her shoulders. "I've been feeling very close to you for weeks now. But I didn't read it right. It wasn't something that I expected, so I didn't know how to classify my feelings."

"What have they been?" Clancy persisted.

"Mmm…at first, I thought I was feeling maternal toward you," Abby said. "But that didn't last very long. You didn't give off any 'daughter' feelings toward me, so my maternal feelings died pretty quickly. I guess I just thought we were becoming friends," she said.

"Uh-huh," Clancy said, her hand stroking lightly across Abby's thigh. "Then what?"

Frowning slightly, Abby said, "You're not going to let me get away with avoiding the question, are you?"

"You don't have to answer," Clancy said, "but no, I'm not going to let you sidestep it."

"You're as bad as Will," Abby said, her mouth creasing into a grin. "He always wanted me to talk before I was ready…maybe because I would have put him off for weeks." Clancy just smiled at her, waiting her out. "Okay, I already told you about the night we went dancing."

"Yeah. That was a good one," Clancy said, wiggling her eyebrows. "But I've been thinking about that, and I wondered how you weren't freaked out by having that fantasy."

"Umm…that's not how I am. I'm…sexual. I've had thoughts about men and women, and women with women, and men with men. I've had fantasies about having a motorcycle cop pull me over and…well, let's just say that I wouldn't want to act that one out. But it still turns me on."

"Okay, okay, I've had fantasies I wouldn't want to act out, too, but…somehow, it seems like having lesbian fantasies would freak most straight women out."

"Says you."

Clancy laughed, realizing how weak her argument was. "Yeah, I'm the authority."

"I've had the odd fantasy about girls and women since I started feeling sexual. But men were always my primary focus. I felt straight."

"But now?"

"Mmm…this might sound strange, but my sexuality has always felt a little like citizenship."

"Yep. It sounds strange."

"Hush," Abby said, narrowing her eyes playfully. "This makes sense…to me. I'm an American. Not because of anything inside me, though. Just because that's where I was when I was born."

"And because your parents are American."

"Exactly!" Abby grinned at her. "You're getting it!"

"The hell I am!"

"Damn, I thought you were with me." She winked at Clancy and tried again. "My parents were American; my friends were American. It wasn't a big deal. But when I went to college, I saw there were other countries. I could have moved to one of them and changed my citizenship. But I didn't. I stayed right where I'd been…but I fantasized about living in France or Canada. That didn't make me feel unpatriotic. Just international."

Clancy nodded. "Interesting. Odd, but interesting. What made you want to cross the border?"

"You did, of course. I was reacting to what I could feel—from you," she said, coloring pink.

"Arghh!" Clancy dropped her head into her hands, finally peeking out from between two fingers. "You knew?"

"Ahh…yeah. I've known for a while. I think I've known since the first time we went swimming together."

"You saw me checking you out, didn't you?" Clancy asked, her head dropping back against the seat.

"Uhm…yeah. But it was fine with me, Clancy, really," she said earnestly. "I was…complimented."

"Complimented? Not freaked out?"

"Why would it freak me out to have such an attractive, engaging person find *me* attractive?" Abby asked, her expression one of puzzlement. "No one had given me that kind of attention in a long while. It was great for my ego."

Looking at Abby for a few moments, Clancy finally said, "Damn, but you're evolved. Most women would have thrown me out and locked the door."

"Well, now, wouldn't that have been stupid?" Abby asked, chuckling softly. "We've had some wickedly wonderful adventures, and I never would have known those pleasures if I'd been offended."

"You don't think you would have been receptive to another woman?" Clancy asked, still baffled by Abby's easygoing attitude about sexual orientation.

"I haven't been up until now," Abby said, shrugging. "I think you're just incredibly special." She placed her hand on Clancy's leg and said, "I mean that sincerely."

"I feel the same. I'm eternally grateful that you gave me a clear signal that you were interested. I never would have made the first move."

"Never?"

"No, never. I wouldn't put someone I cared for in that position. I wanted your friendship more than that."

"It would be wonderful if we could keep the friendship…*and* the other, wouldn't it?"

"That's my goal. And I'm a very persistent woman when I have a goal."

🌾

They were blocks from Abby's street when she took a turn and headed for the Rose Bowl. Clancy looked at her quizzically, but Abby just stared straight ahead until she reached the parking lots. She guided the car to the farthest section, turned off the engine, and turned to Clancy. "I need to kiss you."

Clancy smiled warmly and melted into her arms. They savored each other for a long while, kissing and touching gently until the sun set. "That wasn't nearly enough," Abby breathed into Clancy's ear, sending shivers up her spine. "I'd love to have my hands all over you right now. The thought of your body makes my mouth water."

"I need to either go home or get out and make love to you on the asphalt," Clancy moaned. "I'm so turned on I could scream."

"Do you want me to…?" Abby asked hesitantly, running a fingernail up the seam of Clancy's jeans.

Shaking roughly, astounded by Abby's boldness, she said, "No. I mean, yes, I want you to—desperately—but no, I don't want to do it here. I want sex to be special. I can wait until we're ready to be together again…I've waited thirty years for you."

"Every time will be special," Abby vowed. "How could it not be with a romantic like you?"

"Do you have plans for tonight?"

"Yes. I have dinner plans. Uhm…I don't quite know where to go from here. I…I'm really not good at this."

"No problem. I'll drop you off at home, and I'll see you tomorrow morning. We've got a big day planned."

"Thanks for being so understanding and so patient."

"I'm a woman who makes long-term plans. I can be very, very patient…when I have to be."

❧

Michael came home at around eight, and Clancy struggled out of bed to greet him. "Hey, buddy," she mumbled.

He took a long look at her and said, "You look wiped. You feeling okay?"

"Yeah." She yawned noisily and said, "I was already in bed, but I thought I'd better get up and share a little something with you." She looked uncharacteristically ungainly as she stood there in her tank top and baggy pajama bottoms, and he walked over to her and offered a hug.

"Are you sure you're all right? You look funny."

"I'm fine," she insisted, patting him on the waist. "I'm actually totally great but worried sick."

"Odd combo," he said slowly. "Wanna explain?" Because they were close to her room, they walked inside, and soon, both were sprawled across the futon.

"I uhm…Abby and I…we…"

"You didn't!" he cried, slapping her on the rump.

"Oh, I did." She sighed and rolled fully onto her back. "It was blissful."

"So she figured out the lesbian-sex part, huh?" His eyes were dancing with interest.

"No comment," Clancy said. "Next question?"

"I'll assume you had great sex," he decided, "and that explains the 'totally great' part. Now, where does the 'worried sick' part come in?"

"There are a few…problems," she said. "Her daughter has a crush on me, and I've been trying to convince her I'm not interested."

"Well, well, well. Aren't we the hot commodity? Any other girls in the family you can hook?"

"Not funny, Michael. I really care about Abby, and I want this to work."

"Sounds like a strange family," Michael said. "Actually it sounds like a great porn movie. A lesbian mom-and-daughter combo would be a big seller!"

"Do you want to be serious about this or make fun of me?"

"I'm sorry, Clance." He put his hand on the small of her back and rubbed it gently. "This is just pretty wild stuff for you. It's not common for you to be in the middle of a lesbian soap opera."

"And I don't wanna be now! I really care for Abby, but I'm afraid Hayley will screw things up!"

"I assume Abby knows her daughter's gay, right?"

"No." Clancy shook her head slowly. "Neither of them has ever been with a woman."

Michael sat and stared at his friend for a moment. "You convinced two straight women to turn? That's not fair! There aren't gonna be any straight women left in Pasadena!"

"I didn't turn anyone into anything! I don't know if Hayley's serious or not. She might just be trying to be adventurous. You know how kids are."

"I never tried to be gay—just for the fun of it," Michael said. "Doesn't seem like much fun to me at all."

"It's different for girls," Clancy said, giving him a scowl. "They're more flexible about sex."

"Now, that's good news," he said, giving her a winning grin.

"None of this is good news. Except the fact that Abby wants me."

"That is good news, babe. Do you think you have a chance to be a couple?"

"I have no idea! We didn't resolve anything, Mikey! We made love last weekend, and it's been a roller coaster ever since. I'm not sure whether we have even a remote chance of having a lasting relationship. I'd marry her tomorrow, but she might not be able to continue with this. I'm totally freaked!"

"Oh, poor baby." He scooted closer and started to massage her head and shoulders, making her sigh as some of the tension started to leave her body. "I've known you for sixteen years now, and I've never heard you come close to saying that you wanted to marry someone. Are you sure about this…about her, Clancy?"

"Yes. She's the one, Michael. She's the first woman I've ever felt like this about—and if I can't have her, I don't know what I'll do."

"Shh. Don't worry about all of the bad things that could happen, Clance. Think about the good things. Even if it doesn't work out, why not have a little time where you believe that it will?"

"You're right. I'll lie here and remember how it felt to hold her. That might calm me down enough to let me sleep."

"This can work out," he promised, kissing her head. "If she's the woman you believe she is, I'm sure she's not jerking you around."

"She'd never do that," Clancy said. "She's concerned about Hayley. Well, I guess that's the main thing she's concerned about. She's one of those people who can't talk about the things that bother her the most."

"Danger! Danger!" Michael cried, laughing. "This will never work out! You can't *stop* talking about what's on your mind!"

"I know, I know. But maybe it's best not to have both of us be chatterboxes. Having two people who talk about their feelings constantly could be totally obnoxious."

"Well, you certainly yak enough for any two women, so I guess it can all equalize. Now get some sleep, and take a night off from worrying, okay?"

"Okay. I love you, Michael."

"I love you too, Clance. Sleep tight, and dream about a happy future."

❦

Clancy was lying in bed, dreaming of the pleasure of being in Abby's arms, when the phone rang. She reached for it and sighed softly when she heard her voice. "I miss you," Abby whispered.

"Oh, I miss you, too," Clancy drawled sexily. "Wanna come over and warm my bed?"

"I'd give anything. But since I can't do that, I wanted to call and say goodnight."

"G'night. I wish I could kiss you goodnight, but that'll have to wait. But in my dreams, I'm holding you in my arms and kissing you so tenderly. It makes me feel warm all over to even think about."

"If it's real, it'll feel just as good—or better, if we wait to be together until things settle down."

"It couldn't feel better," Clancy said softly. "It's been a week, and I'm still tingling."

"Me, too. I lie in bed at night and think about how you made me feel. It's like watching the sexiest movie ever made."

"I don't know if it'll help me sleep, but I'm gonna do that right now. If I can't have you, I can dream about you."

"I hope our dreams become reality…soon."

Chapter Nine

When Clancy arrived at the Graham house on Monday morning, she was filled with as much apprehension as she had been the day she'd originally taken her plans over for Abby's approval. She was the first to arrive, but Ramon and his men pulled up before she'd had the chance to leave her truck. They all chatted for a moment and then started to unload their tools. Everything seemed normal, but Clancy knew that the seemingly normal atmosphere was an illusion.

Her instinct was confirmed when Hayley didn't bound out of the house as she usually did. The back doors were closed, and the shades were down—another unusual occurrence.

When they were ready to work, Ramon asked, "Is Hayley coming? I need her."

"I'm not sure," Clancy said. "I guess I'll have to fill in."

Ramon smiled, looking a little too happy to Clancy's eye. "It's gonna be a long day, *jefa*. Time to mix mortar."

Grumbling to herself, Clancy got to work. She didn't mind the labor, but it meant that she couldn't inspect the work with the same care she normally did. And if anyone needed her help, she'd be leaving Ramon without the mortar he needed to set the concrete blocks in place. If she'd known Hayley wasn't going to work, she would have hired an additional man for the week or had Armando bring his son, Jesus.

She wasn't sure, but she thought she heard voices coming from the house. At one point, a door slammed, and Ramon looked at her with a quizzical expression. Not knowing what was going on and not wanting to tell Ramon any of the details of the previous weekend, she shrugged.

After about half an hour, Hayley came out—having obviously been crying. Clancy was up on the hill, but she walked down and met her on the lawn. Hayley was trying to look nonchalant, but it wasn't working. She looked like a little girl who'd been punished and now had to apologize—against her will. She wouldn't look Clancy in the eye, and her voice was tense and angry. "I came to tell you I quit. I'll stay for two weeks if I have to, but I don't want to."

Clancy waited for a second and then spoke her mind. "If you don't want to be here, I don't want you. This isn't the type of work you can do if you're not concentrating."

"Yeah. This is really complex stuff," the girl said, sounding bitter and spiteful.

Her attitude hit Clancy in exactly the wrong place. She stared at the girl for a moment, but Hayley never lifted her chin. "Even manual laborers have feelings. This work was good enough for you last week."

Hayley looked up and fixed Clancy with her intense blue eyes. "I have feelings, too!"

"Yeah. And when they're hurt, you blame other people. You've got a lot of growing up to do, Hayley. Do the working-class women of the world a favor—don't try to date us if we don't measure up to your normally high standards." She turned and went back up the hill, leaving Hayley standing on the lawn, looking stunned. After a moment, the girl went back into the house, slamming the sliding glass door so hard that it almost jumped its track.

After a few minutes, Clancy saw the Lexus drive away. She wasn't sure whether mother or daughter was driving, but she hoped that it was Hayley and that she was going far, far away.

Shortly after the Lexus left, another car pulled up to the house and honked briefly. Clancy saw Abby walk down the drive, clad in a sleeveless polo shirt and a pair of khaki shorts. She saw her turn and scan the hill just before she got into the car, and Clancy smiled when Abby saw her and gave a tentative wave.

It was nearly quitting time when the back door opened and Abby emerged, with both dogs straining at their leashes. She took them to the far side of the property to relieve themselves, catching Clancy's eye when they went back toward the house. Abby gestured to Clancy, and the landscaper walked down the hill.

"Can I get you something to drink? I just went to the grocery."

"Sure. I'll wait out here so I don't get the floor dirty."

Abby gave her a chiding glance and said, "Take those boots off, and come in the kitchen. I miss your lips." She turned and headed in, leaving Clancy to swallow to get the moisture back into her mouth.

The dogs were overjoyed to see her, and she let them lick her on the face and mouth before she stood and reached for Abby.

"That's a very gentle soap by the sink. I'll get you a towel."

"They're your dogs!"

"Yes, and you'll note that I don't allow them to lick *my* mouth. I know where those tongues have been—it's not pretty."

Clancy looked at the girls and idly thought aloud, "I've always wondered what it would be like to be able to lick…" She stopped midsentence when Abby gave her a stern look. "Boy, you've got that mom look down!" She turned and started to wash her face and hands, and kept going when she saw how dirty her arms were. Abby handed her the towel and placed her hands on the architect's hips while Clancy dried off.

"I don't mean to treat you like a kid. That's not how I think of you."

"Joking." Clancy smiled and then added, "I have a feeling you had to play tough-cop mom this morning. Wanna talk about it?"

Abby sat down at the kitchen table and gestured for Clancy to do the same. "I'm so disappointed in her," she said. "Maybe this is making her crazy because she's never been turned down by anyone she was interested in, but that's no excuse. She's acting like a spoiled brat, and I have to say, that's one of my least favorite species on the planet."

Clancy let out a relieved breath. "I'm glad you don't let her act like a brat. I saw too many of them while I worked for my dad."

"I try not to. But I only have so much control. Nature has a role, too."

"Speaking of nature…you haven't said a word about how you feel about Hayley being interested in a woman…any woman."

Abby looked at her for a moment and then started to laugh softly. "I'd probably feel different if I wasn't falling in love with you at the same time. I've hardly given it a thought."

"You should," Clancy said, not wanting to make matters worse but also not wanting to have it hit Abby later.

"We talked about it a little this morning," Abby said. "Nothing too intense, since we were arguing about whether or not she had to go out and talk to you."

"That must have been fun."

"Yeah. It was a blast," Abby said, her voice flat. "I went into her room this morning to wake her up, and she said she'd quit. When she admitted she hadn't told you, we started to argue. It came out that she was angry because you'd turned her down."

Clancy took Abby's hand and chafed it gently between her own. "That must have been a very weird conversation for you to have."

Smiling tentatively, Abby nodded. "'Weird' is a good word. She must think I'm a remarkably open-minded mother, since I barely blinked when she told me. I suppose it helps to know ahead of time."

Still stroking her hand, Clancy said, "She actually told me you're open-minded. She said you have lesbian friends, and you wouldn't care that she was interested in a woman."

Abby nodded. "That's probably true, but it would still take me a while to get used to the idea. If she's serious about this." She looked at Clancy, then a small frown settled on her face. "Do you think she's serious?"

"I have no idea. I didn't get any vibes from her at first. I think she might just be trying to…" She pulled off her cap and scratched her head. "I'm clueless."

"She acted like she was telling me she was dating a boy with red hair," Abby said. "She tossed off the comment like it was nothing at all. I raised her to be open-minded, but I'm not sure I'm comfortable with her being *this* open-minded."

Now Clancy was frowning. "So…you *would* be upset if she was attracted to women?"

"Just because I'm a mother doesn't mean I'm a hypocrite," Abby said, smiling. "All I'm saying is that it would take me a little time to get used to it. And…" She thought for a minute. "I'd like to think that she had to think about it, too."

"Why?"

"Why?" Abby gave her a puzzled look. "Why?"

"Yeah. Why? If you have lesbian friends, and you're attracted to a woman, why do you think Hayley has to be cautious about this?"

Abby gave her a blank look. "I'm not sure. It just doesn't seem like the kind of thing you should do on a whim."

"Because…?"

"I don't know, Clancy. It just seems like something a girl should think about before she jumps into it!"

"But you were in college when you considered moving to another country. Why's it different for Hayley?"

"It's not! I thought about it…and decided to stay in America. I just want her to think about the things she does, Clancy. I want her to be more…thoughtful."

Clancy removed her hand from Abby's and leaned back in her chair. She took a sip of her drink and then asked, "Does talking about this upset you? You seem pretty frustrated."

Abby nodded. "Yeah, I am. I don't do well at talking about things if I'm not prepared."

"Then maybe you'd better think about this a little more," Clancy said. "Maybe you'd better think about how you feel about lesbianism. It's not just a concept anymore, Abby. This is my reality, and if you wanna be involved with me, it's gonna be your reality, too."

Abby sat completely still for a moment. Then she looked at Clancy and said, "You might be right. I need to talk to Hayley a little more and then think about what I'm doing. Right now, I'm letting my sexual feelings take over."

"I love your sexual feelings," Clancy said, smiling at her, "but this is much more than sex. Like I told you on the weekend, I don't want a fling; I want love. Loving a woman is a big decision, and it seems like you've stepped away from the possibility before. I think we should cool things until you've thought about that."

Abby crossed her arms over her chest and gave Clancy a look that the architect couldn't read. She didn't look angry or puzzled, but her eyes were slightly narrowed, and her lips were pursed. After a moment, she said, "You're right. I don't want you to be right, but you are."

Clancy got up and kissed her friend on the top of the head. "Call me if you wanna talk. I'm always available."

"I…" Abby began to say, but stopped when Clancy didn't break her stride.

When Clancy got home, she took off her clothes and took a long shower. After she was dry, she debated what to do with her evening. Watching television didn't interest her, and she didn't feel like reading. What she wanted to do was go to Abby's house and shake her until she starting talking. Clancy had never been with a woman who was so guarded or so reticent to talk about her emotions while she was in the middle of them, and it was starting to drive her mad. But she didn't have any idea how to make the process go any quicker. She knew that she had to accept that Abby was different than she was and to learn to live with that difference—or end the relationship before it got any more involved.

Unable and unwilling to think about it anymore, she went into her room and lay on her bed, deciding that she was too depressed to do anything more demanding.

❧

Abby didn't call that night or the next, and just before Clancy went to bed on Wednesday, Michael stopped by her room. "Any word from Abby?"

"No, nothing. She didn't even come outside today. I don't know her well enough to know if she's thinking or ignoring me."

"Give her the benefit of the doubt," he said. "What could it hurt?"

She gave him a half-smile. "I suppose you're right. I'll try to assume she's sorting things out. But if she ignores me for long, I'm gonna hide after work until she thinks I'm gone, then jump out from behind a tree and tackle her when she lets the dogs out."

"Good idea. Glad to hear that you're thinking clearly as usual."

❧

On Thursday night, Abby broke the silence by calling Clancy less than an hour after the architect had left the property. "Hi. Wanna go out for dinner?"

"Dinner? Uhm…sure. I guess. Where do you wanna go?" Her heart was hammering in her chest, and she was sure her teeth were chattering audibly. But Abby sounded like she always did, and that reassured Clancy—a little.

"Someplace where we can talk privately."

"How about the Continental?"

"The Continental? I don't think I know it."

"Are you kidding me? You've lived in Pasadena all your life! Everyone knows the Continental!"

"Well, I don't. Where is it?"

"Close to you, but parking is a bitch. So I'll jump in the shower while you drive over here. One car will be easier than two."

"Deal. I'll be there in half an hour."

"Oh, Abby? We'll probably be outside, so bring a sweater."

"Great. I love to eat outside."

An hour later, they arrived at the Lake Street address. There was a long line, and Abby was a little disappointed that this was obviously a regular hamburger joint. But when they got to the counter, she saw that she could order nearly anything. The menu was truly humongous. "Is this a Greek restaurant?"

"Kinda," Clancy said. "And those are my favorite things. The shish kebabs are great."

"Interesting."

A smiling man came up to them and embraced Clancy. "Where have you been? I haven't seen you or Michael for weeks!"

"Oh, it's nothing personal," Clancy said, smiling. "I've been working like a dog."

"Who's this?" he asked, giving Abby the once-over.

"This is my friend Abby. Abby, this is Mike, one of the owners. Michael and I have been coming here since we were in high school."

"They're my best customers," Mike said, but Abby doubted him, given that Mike hugged nearly everyone in line.

"Any chance we can sit outside, Mike?" Clancy asked. "Abby and I have some business to discuss, and we need privacy."

"It is done," he said immediately. "Find Ricardo, and tell him to set you up."

She smiled at him and nodded. "Will do. Thanks, Mike."

"You don't have to wait in line," he said. "Shish kebabs?"

Abby nodded mutely, and Clancy winked. "We'll go get our table."

They walked to the front of the line, and Clancy paid for two orders of shish kebabs and a liter of Roditis wine. Then she took Abby by the hand and led her through rooms that seemed to have no connection to one another. They finally reached a lovely, quiet patio that was nestled up against a grocery-store parking lot. The place was oddly tranquil, and Abby was very happy that they were able to be outdoors. Clancy found Ricardo, and after she'd hugged him, too, he led them to the quietest corner of the place. There was no table, but in a moment, Ricardo had one brought over. He put two chairs next to it and then draped it with a red-and-white-checked oilcloth. A server came over and delivered their wine and some bread before they'd had a chance to sit down.

"Well," Abby said, looking around the dark, intimate nook, "I love the little Italian lights. Very cute."

"This isn't the world's finest dining," Clancy said, "but it feels like home. And it's as cheap as they come." She laughed nervously for a moment and then smiled when Abby took her hand. "I've missed you."

"I've missed you, too," Abby said. "More than I could have imagined."

Before they'd taken a sip of their wine, Mike appeared with their entrees. "Here you go," he said. "You can stay all night, if you want. I told Luz to ignore you if you don't ask for help."

"Thanks, Mike. This is perfect," Clancy said. With a small bow, Mike was off.

Abby was smiling fondly at her friend. "Does everyone like you?"

Clancy blushed at the compliment. "Uhm…most people do. I'm a good customer. I don't ask for much, I'm polite, I always leave a good tip, and I'm faithful."

"That's part of the reason I like you," Abby said. "Although you've never tipped me."

"Play your cards right," Clancy said, giving her a sexy smile.

Abby touched the corner of Clancy's mouth. "That's another reason. You, Ms. O'Connor, are a very sexy woman."

"Sometimes. So what's been going on in the Graham household? Are things calming down?"

Abby took a bite of her food and nodded her approval. "A little. Hayley and I have talked about her new interest, and I'm still not sure if she's truly interested in dating women in general. She's a tough one to figure out."

"How about her mom? Is she interested?"

"I don't know if I'm interested in general," Abby said, "but I'm very interested in you."

Clancy ate some of her rice pilaf and smiled. "Interested enough to tell your family and friends? Interested enough to put up with the shit you'll get from some of the people in your life?"

"Yes, I am," Abby said. "I know it'll be hard, but I don't think I can turn back now. I'd feel like a coward."

"A coward?"

"Yeah. I'm very, very attracted to you, Clancy. It wouldn't take much for me to fall hopelessly in love with you. If I didn't act on this, it would only be because I was frightened, and that's not how I like to live my life."

Clancy's smile grew. She took another sip of her wine and then touched Abby's glass with her own. "I love a woman with guts." She put her drink down and asked, "Have you thought about why you said Hayley should give some thought to this before she went out with a woman?"

"Yes, I have," Abby said. "I think it's exactly the same way I felt when she started to date boys. I wanted her to think about it, decide what she wanted in a boy, how far she was willing to go sexually, how much of her time she wanted to devote to dating. You know, what was most important—her friends, her time with the family, or dating."

"Huh. I never spent time thinking about that," Clancy said. "Maybe because I could never get a date."

"That's changed," Abby said, smiling. "An entire household is ready to take you on."

Clancy ignored the comment and pressed Abby a little. "So you don't think that being in a lesbian relationship is a bad thing? Or that Hayley is doing something…abnormal?"

Abby looked shocked. "No! Of course not! I just surprised myself the other day when I was unable to put this into words. I've told you, I don't think well on my feet. That's why I was a history major. I take the long view on almost everything."

"Hmm. I'm careful, but I can always explain why I do something or like something. Will that drive you crazy?"

"Not if my way doesn't drive you crazy."

"Oh, you drive me crazy, all right." Clancy was staring at Abby's lips, and finally, Abby couldn't resist her for another second. They leaned into each other and kissed, their meals forgotten once they'd tasted each other's lips.

❦

The following Monday, Abby watched Clancy and the men put their tools away. Then she made a scramble for the front door, trying to look like as if it were happenstance that she'd chosen that moment to get her mail. "Oh, hi, Clancy, Ramon."

Ramon gave her a gleaming smile, his white teeth contrasting with his sun-darkened skin. "Good evening, Mrs. Graham."

"Hi, Abby," Clancy said. "Wanna see what we've accomplished in the last few days?"

"Sure. Is now a good time?"

"Perfect. We're all packed up." She patted Ramon on the back and said, "See you tomorrow." He got into the truck and started it, the radio playing loudly as soon as the engine kicked over.

When he pulled away, Clancy made a face. "I tell him he's gonna ruin his hearing, but he never listens to me."

"You're so cute," Abby said. They were standing just inside the gate—not a very private place. Abby gave Clancy a look that was filled with longing. "I've been thinking about you all day and remembering how your mouth tasted last night. I barely remember what we had for dinner, but I'll never forget how delicious you were. I wish I could kiss you right here."

"And you're the woman who couldn't get a second date, huh?" Clancy asked, smirking a little. "The better I know you, the more certain I am that you weren't trying, Mrs. Graham. You're as hot as a cheap pistol, and you could get any man in town if you looked at him like that."

"You're the only person I want, Clancy, so only you get the look."

Forcing herself not to take Abby's hand, Clancy asked, "Hayley home?"

"No. I dropped her off at a friend's house a little while ago. A group of her friends are going to a concert at the Hollywood Bowl and then staying overnight together. I'm all alone."

Her comment was loaded with innuendo, and Clancy gave her a racy smile. "Know what would be fun to do?"

Abby nodded and then started to run, with Clancy following in hot pursuit. They reached the front door, both dogs going wild when Clancy stopped at the door to take off her boots and socks. The women were laughing, the dogs were jumping, and the whole house seemed alive. "This is just like when the kids are both home," Abby said. Almost immediately, her smile faded, and she said, "I hope that didn't sound like I think of you as a kid."

Clancy gave her a wide smile. "You don't treat me like a kid. Not ever."

"Still…"

Clancy smoothed the lines between her eyebrows with the tip of her finger. "Abby," she soothed, her voice dropping into a sexy timbre, "I don't think maternal thoughts when I do this." She slid her hands around her lover's hips, drew her close, and then tilted her head to kiss her gently, teasing her lips open with her tongue.

Abby responded enthusiastically, opening her mouth to suckle on the tip of the pink, wet tongue.

With a lusty growl, Clancy backed her up against the kitchen counter and pressed her hips into her, straddling her legs. She grasped her head and kissed her hungrily, not stopping until she felt Abby's surprise give way to a keen response. They were grinding against each other furiously, with Clancy trying to get her hand between their bodies to palm Abby's breast. Abby joined in the quest, helping her lover unbutton her shirt—her need for her irresistible.

Neither heard the heavy footsteps approach the back door, and when John O'Connor peered in, he practically fainted dead away. He turned to leave, but Athena picked her head up and started to growl, causing Abby to turn her startled gaze to the door.

"Oh, shit," she muttered, pushing Clancy away. "Your father's here."

Clancy whirled and faced the thoroughly embarrassed man. Then she turned Abby around hurriedly to help her button her shirt and tuck it into her shorts. With as much dignity as she could gather, she strode over to shush the dogs and let him in.

"Uhm…hi, Dad," she said, her cheeks flushed with embarrassment. "Guess what?"

He tried to make light of the situation, giving Abby a grin as he said, "I've gotta start picking friendlier clients. Mine pay me by check."

Clancy slapped him in the gut but found that his attempt at humor had been successful. Abby actually looked relieved, and she approached him and said, "I'm so sorry, John. We shouldn't have been doing that."

"Why not? It's your house," he said. "You're both adults, and you didn't know I was coming over. I should be the one to apologize. I saw Ramon outside, and he let me in. Said you were back here looking at the work. I just assumed it was okay to…"

"It's fine," Clancy said. "We should have more self-control." Looking at him tentatively, she asked, "Are you okay with this?"

"Well, I don't see any reason not to be." He gave Abby a quick look and then turned back to his child. "She certainly isn't after your money. She probably doesn't have a criminal record or a drug problem." He looked at Abby and asked, "You don't, do you?"

"No," she said. "I don't drink to excess, either."

"Well, that's actually a bad mark in my book, but I won't hold it against you." He chuckled at his own joke and shrugged. "As long as you don't break my little girl's heart, I don't have a problem with you."

"I would never do that intentionally," Abby said softly, her eyes meeting Clancy's. "She deserves nothing but the best."

"Then we're agreed. Now, does anyone care to stop smooching and take a look at some of the samples I brought with me?"

Clancy gave her father a warm hug. "Thanks," she said. "It feels great to know you're on my side."

"I am. Wouldn't place bets on your mother, though. I think you two ought to come to the house this week and make nice with her."

Giving Abby a sheepish look, Clancy asked, "Are you willing to do that?"

"Of course. Any night is just fine."

"How about Saturday?" John suggested. "Then I can have a few drinks and not have to worry about getting up early."

"Since when has that stopped you?" Clancy asked.

"Never has. I just don't like to worry about it."

John left at around six, and as soon as he did, Clancy went in to grab a pair of beers. Abby was already sitting on the loveseat, and she patted the other cushion when Clancy came back out. "That was…interesting," she said, rolling her eyes. "It's been twenty-five years since Will's mother caught us groping each other. I'm out of practice."

Clancy took a long pull on her beer and leaned her head back, letting some of the tension go. "I knew people would find out—I just thought they'd find out by my telling them." She gave Abby a smile and said, "That's the first time my dad has ever seen me with a girl."

Abby blinked at her. "You mean *with* a girl? Or with a *girl*?"

"Both. Either. Your choice." Clancy gave her a long look and said, "I've never taken anyone home to meet my parents."

"In how long?"

"Twelve years," she said. "I never had anyone I cared for enough."

"But you said you said you dated someone for quite a while. I assume that was Julie."

"It was," Clancy confirmed. "I went out with her for nearly a year."

"And yet…?"

"And yet," Clancy said, "I didn't take her to meet my parents." She looked down at the ground for a minute and then stared into space as she continued. "Things were never smooth and easy between us. I say that we went out for a year, and that's technically accurate, but it took us eighteen months to be together for twelve."

"Huh?"

"In eighteen months, we weren't speaking for at least six. We'd fight, vow to never see each other again, wait a few weeks, get back together, and go through the whole cycle again. I think we liked the drama as much as we liked each other."

"But if you cared enough for her to keep getting back together, why didn't you want to share her with your parents?"

"It's not just because of how I felt about Julie," Clancy admitted. "My mom wants me to be in a relationship—and if I bring someone home, that's going to send a very clear signal to her that I'm serious. I haven't wanted her to start supervising me—and watching to make sure I don't screw it up."

"Oh, Clancy, I'm sorry I accepted your father's invitation. I didn't know you felt like that about it."

Clancy's eyes widened and she said, "I don't feel that way about *you*, Abby. I want them to know you."

"You do? Are you sure?"

"Abby," she said softly, her eyes locked onto her friend's, "I told you the other night that I was falling in love with you." She placed a soft kiss on her lips and added, "I meant it. You're not just some woman I want to sleep with."

Leaning her head on Clancy's shoulder, Abby brought her hand up to rest on her abdomen. "I'm very glad to hear that. You're not someone I'm wasting my time with, either. Every moment is precious."

"But you're not ready to think about the 'L' word, are you?"

"Uhm…does that means lesbian or love?"

"Love," Clancy said. "That's the important 'L' word."

"No," Abby said, shaking her head, "I've got too many things to sort through first."

"But that doesn't mean that you won't love me someday, right?"

"No, it definitely doesn't mean that. Are you hungry?"

"Not starving. Why?"

Abby's fingers dug between the folds of Clancy's shirt to tickle her washboard abs. "You need to eat better. You've lost some weight that you can't afford to lose."

"We can eat later," Clancy murmured, bending to kiss Abby's neck. "Much later."

"Hey," Abby said. "It's Monday. Don't you have your dance class?"

"Oh, right! Wanna go with me? Or would you rather stay home and neck?"

"I'd rather stay home and neck, but since I was ready to have you on the floor of the kitchen, I think we'd better go out if we're gonna take this slow. You had me half undressed, Ms. O'Connor!"

Clancy blinked, then her eyes widened. "I didn't even realize what I was doing, but I had to feel your skin!" She leaned back and said, "We'd better go out!" She started to stand and then asked, "How would you have answered the question if I'd been asking if you were a lesbian?"

"I don't think I can be a lesbian, given how much I enjoyed having sex with my husband. And I think it's perfectly normal for straight women to have all sorts of fantasies. But straight women don't want to act on their lesbian fantasies," she said, wrinkling her nose. "I think that makes me a bisexual, don't you?"

"Whatever feels right for you," Clancy said. "I don't care what you call yourself as long as you want to kiss me."

❦

When John O'Connor arrived home, he spent a few minutes sitting in his truck, trying to decide how much of his afternoon adventure to share with his wife.

Realizing that he didn't normally have much success in keeping things from Margaret, he went and greeted her in his normal fashion. "How's the prettiest girl in Sierra Madre?" he asked, coming up behind her to kiss her neck.

"Not bad," she said, patting him gently. "How's the biggest bull thrower in town?"

"Good. Had a good day. We dropped a fiberglass pool into a yard in less than three hours."

"That's nice, honey." She was stirring something on the stove and suddenly recalled something. "Did you go by Abby's today? I'm dying to hear how Clancy's doing with her big job."

"Yeah, I dropped by," he said, as neutrally as he could manage. "It looks like they've made good progress. Clancy seems happy."

"Oh, good. I think I'll call her after dinner to wish her well. I know this is awfully important to her. If she does a good job, she's hoping that Abby will give her some recommendations, you know."

"Yeah. I know."

He went to the refrigerator to get a beer. Margaret fixed him with a look and asked, "Was everything all right, John? You're acting a little funny."

For a moment, John thought about what had happened. Then he decided that Clancy likely found the whole thing funny. If that were the case, the odds were good that she'd tell the story on herself—and Margaret would learn that he'd been holding out on her. With a sigh, he shrugged and said, "I think I win the bet we made, honey."

"What? How do you know?"

"Get out the papers," he said.

Margaret went to her purse and pulled out the slips of paper. She opened hers and read, "Clancy and Hayley are falling in love."

John shook his head. "Now read mine."

She opened his and read, "Clancy's got a crush on Abby." She blinked and then blinked again. "Abby? She's old enough to be Clancy's mother!"

He sipped his beer. "It's the truth, Margaret. They admitted that they're involved."

"You went over there for a meeting, and they looked at you and announced that they were dating." Her raised eyebrow and deep frown showed that she was not buying the story.

"No, it was a little more embarrassing than that." He looked at her and wrinkled his nose just like his daughter often did. "I caught them kissing."

"Oh, for goodness' sake! Don't tell me Clancy was doing that in front of her crew!"

"No, Margaret. They were in the kitchen. I saw Ramon come down the hill right when I was coming up. We stopped and chatted for a minute, and he told me Clancy was in the back with Abby. I went around to the back, and when I didn't see them, I assumed they'd gone inside, so I went to the door and looked in." He gave his wife a smile and said, "We were all embarrassed, but we got over it. I asked them over for dinner on Saturday. I think we need to get to know this woman, Margaret. I think she's gonna be around for a while."

She sat down heavily on one of the chairs that bracketed the kitchen table. "John, that woman has to be as old as I am! It's not right!"

"Margaret, Clancy's almost thirty. It's long past the time we could tell her who to date."

"Nobody knows that better than I do, John. Even when she was younger, I never got anywhere telling her what to do. I just want to make sure she's thought this through." She shook her head. "I can't imagine why she'd choose someone so much older."

"She's always been interested in older women, Margaret. Hell, when she was eighteen, she'd only turn her head for a woman over thirty."

Margaret stood and put her hands on her hips. "And how do you know that?"

Uh-oh. I had to open my big mouth. "Well...we talk about things. You know that."

"You talk about women that you find attractive?" Her wide eyes and pink face told him she was not a fan of this practice.

"She was on my crew," he explained, as though that would make it clear.

"How does that make any difference? She's your daughter! You don't ogle girls together."

"Who says we ogled?" he asked defensively. "Yes, she's my little girl, but she's also my buddy. I treat her like I treat my friends—and I've got to tell you, that's part of the reason we're so close."

"Fine," she huffed. "It's unseemly, and you know it, but I'm obviously not going to convince you otherwise." She had her arms crossed over her chest, and after a minute she looked at him curiously. "She's always been like this?"

"Always," he nodded soberly.

"But why? Doesn't that mean there's something...wrong with her?"

"Wrong?"

"Yes, wrong! You know what they say about people with a...mother fixation."

Her mouth was curled up into a look of pure distaste, but John put his arms around her and gave her a gentle hug. "There's nothing wrong with her, Margaret. Some people like blondes...some like brunettes...some like skinny girls...some like girls who remind them of their mothers."

Gasping in pain, he once again reminded himself not to taunt his wife when he was in the middle of hugging her.

❧

Abby was dressed in her cowgirl gear when they drove to Clancy's house. Michael was home, and he smiled at the women when they entered. "Howdy," he said to Abby. "Hear you're takin' my spot at the hoedown."

"As long as you don't mind," Abby said. "I don't want to step on any toes."

"I don't mind," Michael said. "I stand up all day, so it's nice to sit down and put my feet up at the end of a long day."

Clancy went to change, and Abby sat down next to Michael. There was a brief, uncomfortable silence. Then he said, "I'd give up my spot anytime to see Clancy with you. She's happier than I've seen her in years."

Abby blushed slightly. "She makes me happy, too, Michael. I'll do almost anything to make this work."

He nodded, letting her words sink in. *Damn, I wish she hadn't added that "almost."*

❧

The women had an even better time dancing now that they weren't shy about touching each other. Clancy's heart was beating hard, and she wasn't sure whether it was from the workout or how close she was holding her partner. During a timeout to have a glass of water, Abby asked, "Is it really okay with Michael to give up his dancing lesson?"

"Sure. We're buddies—we don't spend a lot of time apologizing for little things. He backs out if he has something better to do, and so do I."

"How long have you lived together?"

"Three years now," Clancy said. "I moved into his building when I graduated from school. We got a two-bedroom in the place where he had a one-bedroom."

"You were at home before that?"

"Yep. I stayed at home until I was through with school. It was the only way I could manage it financially."

"How was that for you? I'm not at all sure that my kids would want to live with me during college."

"It was fine," Clancy said, tipping her head back to take such a big drink of water that her hat almost fell off. "Since I went to work for my dad as soon as I graduated from high school, our roles changed a bit. I wasn't just a daughter—I was also an employee and a co-worker. He and I grew closer, and my mom started to let go—more and more as time went on. After I came out to them, things changed even more. After a while, they didn't even complain when I stayed out all night. Since they treated me like an adult, I didn't mind being there."

"Maybe that's my problem," Abby decided. "Maybe I haven't made that transition yet."

"It's different in your situation," Clancy reminded her. "They're home for such a short time, it's hard to set up a system that works for all of you."

"I suppose. It's hard to think that they'll never live here again, but I guess that's the way of the world."

"What about your mother?" Clancy asked. "Has she let go of you?"

"Of me? Clancy, I'm forty-five!"

"I know that. But what about us?" She took another drink and looked around nervously. "I mean…if there is an us when you're…I mean, if you decide to…"

Abby placed a hand on Clancy's arm and patted her reassuringly, "I want there to be an us, too. I really want that, okay?"

Clancy nodded quickly, looking chagrined. "Sorry. I know we already decided that. I just can't help wondering about the future."

"Well, let me tell you this. You'll find that my mother is a delightful woman—without a judgmental bone in her body. My dad's a little more traditional, but he's a good man and only wants me to be happy. I'm confident they won't have any long-term issues with us." She chuckled and said, "My mom's basically adopted some of my gay friends. She threw a huge party for my friend Maria's fortieth birthday—without even consulting me first!"

"Do you have many gay friends?"

"Oh, sure. My friend Ellen and I play doubles with Maria and Pam every Saturday morning. I'm their daughter Alyssa's godmother. And I told you about my friend Stephen, who I went to UCLA with, didn't I?"

"You mentioned a friend that you went to bars with."

"Oh, God," Abby said. "I can't believe I haven't told you all about him! He was as close as a brother, and when he died of AIDS, it was absolutely devastating for my parents as well as me. Through him, I got involved with the AIDS Service Center here in Pasadena, and eventually, I served two terms on the board of directors. I made dozens of good friends through that. I gave my friend Spencer away when he married his boyfriend last year—"

"Damn, you've got as many gay friends as I do!" Clancy said, laughing heartily. "So will you tell any of your friends about us...if there is an us?" she added with an impish smile.

"Of course I will," Abby said, grabbing Clancy's nose and giving it a tug. "And just for the record, Ms. O'Connor, there already is an us." Running a hand up and down Clancy's arm, Abby looked at her and said, "If things don't work out between us, I'm going to be a wreck. I'll need my friends to pull me through it—so I'm going to tell them soon."

Clancy scooted her chair over until it was nestled between Abby's spread legs. "If things don't work out between us, it'll be because you can't make the commitment. I'm already in."

Abby nodded. Then she laced her hands behind Clancy's neck and kissed her tenderly. "I think I am too. I'm just...cautious, remember?"

"Thinking is highly overrated. I'm a woman who likes to dance...and kiss. Which one do you want to do first?"

Abby smiled seductively and took off her hat.

Chapter Ten

The next day, Hayley came home from her overnight and took a long nap. She got up while the crew was taking its lunch break and sat in the kitchen, staring outside with a scowl on her face.

"What's going on inside that frown?" Abby asked, ruffling her hair on the way to the laundry room.

"I hate having them here. We should have waited until fall. I can't even use the pool."

"You have friends who have pools," Abby reminded her. "And you can always go to the Rose Bowl to swim."

"I don't have my own car," Hayley whined. It was her mother's least favorite tone of voice.

"You can use Trevor's old bike, and you can use my car when I don't need it, honey. You can drive me to the golf course on the mornings I play. I can get a ride home."

"I don't wanna get up at seven just to give you a ride. And nobody rides a bike for transportation once she's in college."

Abby realized this was one of the times that her daughter didn't want to brainstorm to figure out a solution to her problem. She wanted to gripe. And because Abby didn't like to hear griping, she started to go back upstairs to give herself a timeout. She was almost out of the kitchen when Hayley said, "I think I'll go to Maine now. There's nothing much going on for the next two weeks."

"But I already bought your ticket. I'm not sure we can change it."

Hayley gave her a puzzled look and said, "You can change it. You might have to pay a fee, but that's no big deal."

Abby looked at her for a moment and then cocked her head. "Why would I have to pay a fee? I didn't change *my* mind at the last minute."

"Oh, please!" Hayley got up and put her cereal bowl in the sink. "You can afford a couple of hundred bucks, Mom."

"Of course I can, but I'm not going to pay for you to change your ticket."

The girl turned and stared at her mother. "I thought you understood! I can't stay here with Clancy outside! A couple of hundred dollars means nothing to you! Nothing!"

"Hayley, it's not about the money; it's about being accountable for your decisions. I paid to send you to Maine when you wanted to go. If you want to change your ticket, you'll have to use your own money. You worked for a few weeks. That's what your savings are for."

"Thanks," Hayley said, biting off the word. "Thanks for helping me out. I worked like a dog to make a little money, and now I have to spend it just to have a decent summer!" As she walked up the stairs, she was mumbling loudly enough for Abby to hear. "It wasn't about the money when I wanted a car, it wasn't about the money when I wasn't allowed to go skiing over Christmas, it wasn't about the money when I couldn't go to an out-of-state school—" Her slamming door shut off her litany of complaints.

Abby closed her eyes and counted to ten, not wanting to continue the fight. She knew she *was* helping Hayley out, but she also knew that it would be years, if ever, before her daughter realized it.

🦋

Even though Abby wasn't concerned about telling her friends or her family about her newfound affection for another woman, she was tremendously nervous about the dinner she and Clancy were to attend with the O'Connors. She changed clothes three times, tentatively deciding on a pair of cream-colored linen slacks and a sky-blue cotton sweater vest. She answered the door a few minutes later, finding Clancy in a bright red-and-white Hawaiian-print shirt, a pair of faded jeans, and her Birkenstocks. "Pretty dressed up for the O'Connors," Clancy teased. Taking a look at Abby's scrunched-up brow, she asked, "Are you weirded out about this?"

"Yes! I want them to like me. I really want to make a good impression."

"How could you not?" She put her arms around Abby's waist and hugged her close. "Anyone with a brain would like you—and my parents both have functioning brains. My gramma will be crazy about you, too. Just relax and be yourself."

"All right," she grumbled, heading for the back door to let the dogs out one last time.

🦋

Abby took a few calming breaths as they walked up the drive of the O'Connor home. "You're sure this is okay?" she asked again, tugging her sweater into place. "I don't want to look too much older than you, but I'd feel silly going to your parents' house in jeans."

Clancy stopped. "Abby, you look lovely. This is what you're comfortable in. You don't need to put on an act. You are who you are, and I don't want you to change a thing. You believe me, don't you?"

"I do. I'm just so nervous."

"Let me calm you down a little." Clancy slipped her arms around Abby's waist to give her a warm, soft, lingering kiss.

The front door opened, and John O'Connor stepped out, smiling when he saw their embrace. "Will you two give it a rest? Gramma's got a weak heart, ya know."

Abby flushed deeply, only partially relieved when Clancy said, "Her heart's stronger than yours, Dad, and the last time she needed babying was in about 1925." When they reached the door, Clancy gave her father a hug and kissed his cheek. "You'd better be the one who starts behaving. If you scare Abby off, I'm gonna hurt ya."

"You don't scare off that easy, do you, Abby?"

"No, I'm pretty hardy, John. I'm not used to a lot of teasing, though, so you might have to bear with me for a while."

"I can do that. Now come on in. I'm famished."

They walked into the modest frame bungalow and were immediately greeted by Margaret. "Getting Clancy home for a Saturday-night dinner is quite a feat," she said, shaking Abby's hand. "Thanks for your help."

"It wasn't my doing," Abby said. "Clancy really wanted to come."

"Come on in and meet my mother," Margaret said. She led them into the kitchen where a small-boned, fleshy, redheaded woman stood at the sink, shucking corn. "Mom, Clancy and her friend are here."

The woman turned and gave her granddaughter a wide smile. "Turn off the damned TV so an old lady can hear, will ya, Bitsy?" Clancy did as requested and gave the elderly woman a hug and a kiss.

"Gramma, this is my friend Abby. Abby, this is my grandmother, Eileen Donovan."

"Pleased to meet you, Ms. Donovan," Abby said. "Call me Eileen." She looked from one woman to the other and twitched her head. "So this is your new girlfriend, eh, Bitsy?"

"Something like that, Gramma," Clancy said, slipping her arm around her grandmother's waist. "We're not engaged or anything, but I think of her as my girlfriend. Pretty, isn't she?"

Abby gave her a mostly outraged look, but Eileen agreed immediately. "Oh, she's pretty, all right. But why are you lettin' your hair turn gray, honey? Havin' color in her hair makes a gal feel young."

Deciding to play the game, Abby said, "Having Clancy around makes me feel young, and she likes it this way."

"I do," Clancy agreed, smiling at Abby with a toothy grin. "I think her hair and every other part of her is beautiful."

"Well, I guess that's all that matters," Eileen agreed. She gave Abby another long look, squinting in the poor fluorescent light. "What color was it when you were young?"

"Gramma!" Clancy cried. "Abby's still young!"

"That's okay," Abby said, seemingly not bothered by Eileen's bluntness. "My hair was jet black. That's part of the reason I don't dye it. I really loved the color, but jet-black hair on an older woman really looks dyed."

"Eh, who cares if it looks dyed? My hair was a mousy brown when I was a girl, and now I'm thinking about going blonde like my little Bits here. People will think we're sisters." She threw her head back and laughed heartily, and Abby was struck by the similarities between Clancy and her grandmother. "Time to get busy, girls. We've got chicken to barbecue. Who's gonna do it?"

"I will," John said, walking over to the sink and giving his mother-in-law a friendly pat on the back. "I've been doing the barbecuing for over thirty years, Eileen. Get used to it."

"You never know," she said, shrugging. "Things change." Giving the younger women a cheerful look, she said, "Well, you two can make a salad, then. I've done my share. Nobody eats for free around here."

Abby blinked at her, extremely unaccustomed to the ultracasual attitude of the O'Connor/Donovan household. But when Clancy started to wash her hands before getting to work, Abby joined right in and helped her make a large green salad, including cucumbers, tomatoes, and carrots from John's extensive backyard garden.

When they were finished, Margaret took over and prepared corn on the cob and some steamed broccoli, the latter also from the garden. By the time she was finished, John was coming in the back door with the chicken, a deep red sauce dripping from the succulent-looking pieces.

They ate at the kitchen table, a breeze coming in the back door, bringing in the sweet scent of a magnolia tree.

"Everything is absolutely delicious," Abby said, complimenting all of the various cooks. "And the vegetables are amazing, John. So fresh and sweet."

"We'll have you back when the corn comes in," he promised. "If you can get it into a pot of boiling water within five minutes of picking it, you won't recognize it as the same stuff you buy at the grocery."

Abby lifted the cob she was working on. "This seems pretty darned delicious to me."

"He's not kidding, Abby," Clancy said. "Fresh-picked is a whole different experience." Looking at her father, she asked, "Middle of July, Dad?"

"Maybe even a week early. Don't worry; we won't forget you."

Eileen cocked her head after assessing Abby for a few minutes. "So what's your story, Abby? You from around here?"

"Oh, yes. Born and raised in Pasadena. I still live there."

"In the nicest house I've ever been in," Clancy added. "A beautiful Craftsman, Gramma. You know how much I like them."

"I do," she said, smiling warmly at her granddaughter. "So what else? We want details, honey. This ain't just a social call. We're trying to figure out if we like you."

Abby was momentarily taken aback, but the sparkle in Eileen's pale, sky-blue eyes assured her that she was mostly kidding.

"Okay, I'll do my best to impress. Born here, went to school here. Graduated from UCLA with a history degree—"

"Oh, when did you graduate?" Margaret asked.

Abby recognized her hidden question and said, "I'm forty-five, Margaret."

"Oh! Well, that's not why I..." she started to say, but a pointed look from her daughter forced her to capitulate. "Well, I did wonder..."

"It's fine," Abby said. "I'm not embarrassed about my age." She cleared her throat and took a sip of iced tea. "I was married after my freshman year and was pregnant by January. I gave birth to our son and went back to school after taking a semester off. I stayed at UCLA to earn a master's degree in history. I didn't think I'd ever use it, but I wanted to have something to fall back on in case I ever had to support myself."

"That's a smart move," Eileen said. "You can't ever rely on anyone else to take care of you."

Abby smiled at her, liking her feistiness, which reminded her of Clancy. "My husband was an attorney at O'Reilly and Monroe, and he died of a heart attack five years ago in May."

Eileen reached out and grasped Abby's hand, startling her a bit. "I lost my husband three years ago," she said, her eyes watery. "It's horrible, isn't it?"

"It was," Abby said, seeing the frank understanding that only someone who had gone through the experience could share. "It still is—but it gets easier as the days pass. I don't think I'll ever be entirely over it, though."

Giving her a small smile, Eileen shook her head and released Abby's hand. "No, I don't think so, either. My time's just about up, but you've got your whole life ahead of you, honey. Forty-five is nothing these days. I say it's time to kick up your heels a little."

"Oh, I think I've done that," Abby said, giving Clancy a shy smile. "Let's see...I told you about Trevor, who recently got his master's degree in urban planning at MIT, and there's also our second child, Hayley, who just finished her freshman year at UC Santa Cruz. I've never worked outside of the home, but I stay very busy. I play golf and tennis, and I swim, and I work with a few charities. My parents are both alive, and they live in Pasadena also, although they spend their summers in Maine. Oh, and I have two dogs, both of whom love Clancy, and that's about it."

"Forgive me for asking," Margaret said, getting right to the heart of the matter, "but is this your...first time with a...in a...lesbian..."

Abby almost said that Clancy was the first lesbian she'd been in, but she didn't think Margaret would appreciate the joke. "I've never dated a woman before, Margaret. I was very happily married, and I assumed that I'd eventually meet another man." She turned and smiled at Clancy, very aware of the hand on her knee. "But I met Clancy, and something clicked between us." Turning back to the others, she asked, "Who can explain attraction?"

"That seems very...I've never heard of that happening before," Margaret said.

"Well, it's not very common in my experience either," Abby admitted. "It took me completely by surprise."

"It doesn't matter if other people do it, Mom," Clancy said. "Abby feels comfortable with this, and that's all that matters."

"Oh, of course, that's true," Margaret said, still looking unsettled. "And I certainly didn't mean to question your decision, Abby. I'm just not very knowledgeable about these things."

"We have a lot of things to work out," Clancy said, her gaze sweeping across all of the members of her family. "We're just dating right now, okay?"

"No problem," John said. "We won't put your name on the Christmas card yet, Abby."

"You don't even put my name on the Christmas card," Clancy said.

"I would if you chipped in for half," John said. "Nobody gets a free ride, ya know."

"Yeah, yeah," Clancy said. She got up and started to clear the table, waving Abby off when she tried to help. "What did you make for dessert, Mom?"

"How do you know I made dessert?" Margaret asked, raising an eyebrow.

"'Cause you always do when we have company. You're the best baker in the Valley, and you know it." She leaned over and kissed her mother on the top of the head, and Abby smiled at the affection that Clancy showed her family.

"I don't know about the 'best baker' title, but I did whip up a lemon meringue pie," she said. "With fresh lemons from our tree," she added for Abby's benefit.

"Ooh, my favorite," Abby said. "I could eat lemon meringue pie any time, anywhere."

"You're in luck, because Mom makes a fabulous one," Clancy said.

Abby looked at Margaret and said, "I'd love your secret. I've tried many times, but the meringue never sets right."

"I'll give you a few pointers. It's Clancy's favorite, too, so you'd better learn how to make it." Abby felt her heart skip a beat at the multilayered look that the slightly older woman gave her. She wasn't able to read it all, but something about her tone indicated that Margaret was giving her tacit approval to the pairing, and Abby fervently hoped she understood the signals properly—because she very much wanted these people not only to tolerate her, but also to approve of her.

"Did you have fun?" Clancy asked after they had said their goodbyes and were settled in the truck.

"Fun? Was it fun?" Abby asked, narrowing her eyes as though she were deep in thought. "Well, once dinner and the inquisition were over, I started to have fun, but before that I was a nervous wreck!"

"That's so cute!" Clancy pulled Abby close and kissed her enthusiastically. "You were absolutely fantastic tonight. Thanks for trying so hard."

"I know your family means a lot to you. Of course I'd be worried about making a good impression." She batted her eyelashes, trying to look ingenuous. "Do you think they liked me?"

"Of course they did! Everyone likes you, Abby. You're one of the most likeable people I've ever met." She gave her another few kisses and said, "When Dad was giving you a tour of the garden, Gramma pulled me aside and told me that you were a keeper." Placing a kiss on the tip of Abby's nose, she added, "That's high praise."

"She's a pistol," Abby said. "I see a lot of her in you, you know."

Clancy's face grew serious and she said, "I hope that's true. She means the world to me, Abby. She's always been there for me—without question."

"Did she always live with you?"

"No. We lived with my grandparents until I was five or so. My dad was struggling to get his business started, and my parents didn't have enough money for a down payment on a house. We stayed with them until we bought our current house. Then about…I'd guess it's been seven or eight years…my grampa's health started to fail, and they moved in with us so we could all help care for him. So we've lived together often, but not constantly."

"It's obvious how fond she is of you. I particularly like the nickname she has for you."

Clancy covered her eyes briefly and shook her head. "'Bitsy' is one of the better ones. You'll be amazed at how many embarrassing names she has for me."

"Well, I think it's cute. I can just imagine you as an itsy-bitsy little thing."

"Better watch it there, Abby. I'm going to meet your parents someday, and I'm sure I'll learn a few embarrassing things about your youth. Tread carefully."

"Okay, Bitsy. I'll mind my manners." She snuck her hand up around Clancy's neck and pulled her closer; then she went for her lips, kissing her with a rapidly rising fever.

"Being happy makes me hot," Clancy whispered, "and I'm very, very happy." She set upon Abby's lips with a vengeance, pressing her against the door of the truck. Jumping when she heard a soft knock on the windshield, Clancy sat up and looked out the open driver's door window. "Oh, Jesus!"

"Your, uhm, your mom wanted you to take the rest of the pie," John said, looking slightly less embarrassed than he had the first time he'd caught them.

"We actually talk and eat and do all sorts of things together, Dad," Clancy said, scooting over to accept the pie. "We're not always making out."

"Fine with me if that's all you do," he said, chuckling. "If ya wanna build up a little nest egg, put a buck in a piggy bank every time you have sex during the first year you're together, then take a buck out every time you have sex for the rest of your lives. If ya live to be a hundred, you'll still have money left. Hell, if we'd done that, we coulda sent you to college!" He laughed heartily, then reached into the truck to give Clancy a playful punch on the shoulder. "I don't blame you a bit, Clance. She's a fine-lookin' woman. Looks like she knows how to kiss, too."

"Does anyone know if it's possible to die of embarrassment?" Abby asked.

"Nah," Clancy assured her. "We'd all have been gone long ago. Embarrassing each other is the O'Connor family birthright."

Chapter Eleven

H aving paid the penalty fee with her own money, Hayley packed up for her vacation on Friday. She didn't have to leave for an hour, and when Abby emerged from the shower, the girl was lying across her mother's bed, idly petting the dogs which flanked her.

Abby went to her closet, spending a moment to choose an outfit. "Communing with the dogs before you leave?" She pulled an unstructured cotton dress from her closet and slipped it over her head.

"No. I came to talk to you."

Abby walked over to the bed and sat down. She touched her child's cheek and asked, "Is something wrong?"

"Yeah." Surprisingly, Hayley scooted over and put her head in her mother's lap while she encircled her waist in a hug. She was snuggled against her so tightly that Abby automatically began to stroke her head.

"What is it, baby? Tell me."

Hayley started to cry, her face morphing into a facsimile of the same expression she'd made ever since she was a little girl and had skinned her knee. "I'm sorry I was such a jerk about changing my ticket."

Abby ran her thumbs across her cheeks, catching the tears when they overflowed her lids. "Oh, honey, that's okay. I'm not angry with you."

"I can't...I can't go away when I know you're mad," she sobbed. "I might never see you again."

"Hayley!" Abby reached down and grasped the girl, moving her so she could look into her eyes. "What brought this on?"

"I...I think about...stuff like that when I fly or go on a trip," she said, still crying hard. "Daddy didn't know he'd never come back when he left the house that day."

Abby pulled her daughter close and hugged her with all her might. "Oh, sweetheart, you'll come home, and I'll be waiting for you. Try not to think about such sad things."

"But I do," she insisted, unable to be consoled. "I don't want your last memory of me to be my whining about some stupid ticket!"

"Hayley." Abby rubbed Hayley's warm skin, trying to calm her. "I would never let some silly thing like that color how I feel about you." She pulled back and looked into her eyes. "Your father and I had countless arguments, honey, but I don't remember any of them off the top of my head. That's not what lasts. It's the love we feel for each other that remains. I promise you that, baby." She hugged her again and asked, "Isn't that how you feel about your dad? Do you remember the fights you had with him?"

"No," Hayley admitted, her voice still shaking. "I don't remember fighting with him."

"You did," Abby said, laughing just a little. "Every child has arguments and disagreements with her parents. It's one of the ways we grow up. But they're forgotten quickly, honey. I promise you."

Hayley looked at her mother, her eyes so filled with pain that Abby's heart clenched. "Do you love me, Mom?"

Abby held her to her chest and whispered, "I love you and Trevor more than I'll ever be able to tell you. You mean the world to me, Hayley. I love you with all my heart."

❦

The pair sat together on the bed for a long time. They didn't say much; in fact, Abby thought her daughter had fallen asleep. Hayley's head rested on Abby's lap while she tenderly drew her fingertips through her daughter's long black hair. Hayley could rarely resist the slow, soothing massage and invariably fell asleep, just as she had when she was a baby and Abby would scratch her back. But this time the girl wasn't sleeping—she was thinking. She stretched and rolled onto her back, leaving her head pillowed on her mother's lap. "Would you be cool with it if I turn out to be queer?"

With her heart going from a slow, steady beat to a full-on gallop, Abby forced herself to take a slow, deep breath, trying to make her racing thoughts settle down so that she could answer. Not for the first time, she wished that her daughter would give her some vague warning before she threw a bomb at her, but she was sure that wouldn't happen in the near future.

"Do you think you are?" Abby asked, trying to find out what Hayley was really asking—and why—before she got in too deep.

"I dunno."

Great. She never makes things easy. "Why ask the question?"

"I was just thinking about it. You didn't have much reaction one way or the other when I told you about Clancy." The girl shifted a little and turned her head so she could look into her mother's eyes. "Why?"

"Why?" *Because I had a warning. Clancy told me you were interested in her after we made love for the first time. No, that won't fly. Think of a good answer. She always knows when you're not being honest.* "I guess I didn't react much because it didn't seem like a big deal."

"It was a big deal to me!" Blue eyes immediately blazed with indignation.

"No, no," Abby soothed, stroking Hayley's cheek. "I know you were upset with Clancy, but you didn't act like you were heartbroken. You acted like she'd hurt your feelings and embarrassed you, not like you were so crazy about her that you couldn't go on."

Hayley's mouth slid into a small smile. "I guess that's true. She really pissed me off. She wouldn't even consider going out with me. Made me feel stupid."

"Haven't you ever turned anyone down flat?"

"Yeah, but nobody cute!" There was a momentary pause; then Hayley started to laugh, with Abby following right along.

"Pretty confident there, aren't ya?"

"No, not really. You know what I mean, don't ya?"

"I'm not sure. Tell me."

"I don't hang around with a guy unless I'm a little interested in him. Clancy treated me like she liked me, and I know she's single. All I wanted to do was have dinner with her, but she acted like she'd rather stab herself!"

"Oh, honey, I'm sure it wasn't that."

Hayley looked right into her mother's eyes and asked, "Did she tell you about what happened?"

"Yeah, she did," Abby said, her heart beating so hard that she was sure Hayley would be able to feel the blood pounding in her thighs.

"Did she tell you why she wouldn't go out with me?"

"Uh-huh." Abby had never tried so hard to sound casual, and she found it much harder than she would have guessed. "She didn't think it was right to go out with you because of her position. It's not a good idea to go out with a member of a client's family. Clancy's very careful about things like that."

"She goes out with you," Hayley said, one of her dark eyebrows rising a bit. "You went out to dinner last night."

"Right," Abby said, wondering whether Hayley knew CPR in case her heart stopped, "but I'm the client. You're my precious daughter. What if you'd gone out and you fell for her, but she didn't feel the same? She couldn't afford to have me take your side. She's a professional, honey. Not just someone you met on your own."

Hayley gave her mother one last look, which Abby couldn't read. Then she moved again and settled down with her head in her mother's lap. "I guess she was right," the girl said. "All she did was refuse a date, and I threw a fit."

"I think she was right," Abby said, "but I hate having your feelings hurt—even though Clancy did the proper thing."

"I'm over it," Hayley admitted. "Pretty much."

Scratching her scalp again, Abby asked, "Do you think you're gay?"

"I don't know." Hayley sighed dramatically. "I don't know what I am. I've never met a guy who really clicked; I thought I'd try a girl."

"I guess that is the other option," Abby said, trying to sound lighthearted.

"It's frustrating, Mom. Do you know that I've never had an orgasm with a guy? Never! I thought a woman might care enough to at least try!"

Oh, God, why does she have to tell me things like this? "Hayley, anyone who cares about you will try to satisfy you. Not all men are clueless."

"All the ones I've fooled around with have been."

"Then you need to shop better. I could always tell if a guy was interested in me long before we got romantic. I bet you can tell, too."

"They all seem interested in me. By the end of the first date, they're all over me!"

Abby tried not to laugh. "That's not how a guy shows he's interested in you as a person. That's how he shows he's interested in your body. There's a huge difference!"

"What's the difference, Mom?" She'd turned her head and gazed into Abby's eyes, looking guileless and innocent.

"When a man's really interested in you, he uses the date to get to know you—not just as time to kill before he can start pawing you. If he's interested in you, and you're interested in him, you'll feel it. I promise."

"I'm not sure you're right. Nobody really dates at school. You just hang out."

"Really?"

"Yeah. I'll go to a party with my friends, and there are always guys there. Eventually one of them starts talking to me…and…you know."

Now Abby was interested in some details. "No, I really don't. What do you mean?"

"You start talking and have a couple of beers…then you hook up a little."

"And that's a date?"

"Pretty much. Guys don't buy you dinner or anything anymore. That's over."

A thousand thoughts went through Abby's head, but she knew the only thing that mattered to Hayley at this point of her life was the behavior of her peers. "Let's say that you have fun hooking up a little. Then what?"

Hayley shifted on the bed, nuzzling against her mother until she felt comfortable. "Then you meet at another party or something on campus, like a basketball game."

"Still no dinner, huh?"

"Nope."

"And your friends are with you?"

"Uh-huh. It's not like really dating. It's a group of people hanging out…then some of them hook up."

"I'm glad I was born when I was," Abby said, laughing. "I got taken to movies and dinner and dances. And I was usually alone with the guy. It was pretty easy to get to know him."

"Is that how it was with Daddy?"

"Yes. That's exactly how it was. He asked me out to dinner. I spent hours getting ready." She laughed at the memory. "My friends were all giving me advice on what to wear. I think I ended up borrowing everything but my underwear."

"Did ya have fun?"

"Oh, yes," Abby said. Her eyes fluttered closed, and she spent a moment reliving the moment she first got into Will's car. "By the time dinner was over, I knew he was special. And I could tell he was interested in me. He called me the next day, and I think I would have gone crazy if he hadn't."

"Did you sleep with him?"

"Of course I did," Abby said, watching her daughter's eyes grow wide. "Where do you think you and Trevor came from?"

❧

On the way to the airport, Abby began to feel melancholy about having her baby leave the nest once again. "I hope you have a great time in Maine," she said, "even though I'm gonna miss you like crazy."

"I doubt that. You're probably sick of me by now. I know I get on your nerves, Mom."

Stunned, Abby said, "Hayley, I'm never sick of you! Why would you ever think that?"

Hayley stared out the window blankly, not even looking at the variety of buildings on the USC campus as the car crawled through the slow traffic on the 110 freeway. Traffic was moving slowly enough for Abby to look at her daughter's profile for long moments. The young woman looked very depressed, much more than she usually did after a small disappointment. "Sweetheart, what's going on? I'm very glad that you came home, and I'm sad to see you go. If anyone seems upset about your stay, it's you."

Hayley nodded slightly. "Maybe you're right. Maybe I should have gone to Italy with Trevor. Of course, you probably wouldn't have let me go. I couldn't go last Christmas."

Abby sighed, wondering how many times that topic would be brought up. "I would have been happy to send you to Europe with Trevor. I even suggested it at one point. You know very well why I wouldn't let you go at Christmas."

"Yeah, yeah, I know. We need to stay together on the holidays."

"That wasn't my main reason, and you know it. I wasn't going to let my daughter go skiing in Gstaad without any adult supervision. I know your friends have a lot of money, and they're used to having a lot of freedom—but that's not how you and Trevor were raised. My job is to protect you until I feel you're old enough to make mature decisions. And when you're with Kerry and Dana and Maya, you get carried away."

"I do not," she grumbled.

Abby was tempted to recount instances when Hayley had, in fact, gotten carried away when she was with her friends, but she thought it best to drop the matter. She reached over and caressed Hayley's hair, running her fingers through the thick black strands. "No matter what you might think, I'm going to miss you. I love you—plain and simple. And I always try to make decisions that are in your long-term best interests. Even though you think I treat you like a child, I honestly try not to."

Hayley turned and gave her mother a half-smile. "I know you love me, Mom. It's not your fault I'm having a shitty summer. Maybe things will be better by the time I get back from Maine."

"I hope so. I know summers are important, especially since you only have three more before you have to start supporting yourself." She smiled at the stunned expression on her daughter's face, reminded once again how very young Hayley often seemed.

❧

Abby watched the minutes tick by like hours, feeling as though Clancy would never finish for the day. When the crew finally knocked off at six, the landscaper walked down to the house and knocked on the door. "Hi," she said, obviously being a little more businesslike because Ramon was nearby. "We've finished as much as we can right now. Wanna take a look?"

Outside, Abby smiled at Ramon. "You've done a wonderful job so far. I'm very, very impressed."

"Thank you, Mrs. Graham. We have a good crew."

Abby went to the edge of the pool, looking up at the hill to take in the stark concrete-block structure. It's going to look great when it's finished," she said. Turning to Clancy, she said, "I need one more thing added to the project."

"Sure. We love to add things, don't we, Ramon?"

"It depends on the thing," he said, his mouth curling up in a smile.

"This one is simple," Abby said. "I talked to my new neighbors and offered to paint the side of the wall that faces their property. They're going to choose the color soon. Is that okay?"

"You don't have to do that, Abby," Clancy said. "The wall is entirely on your side of the property line."

"I know I don't have to, but the gray concrete block is pretty stark. My side will look lovely, but theirs…well, I wouldn't want to have them put up a wall that I'd have to finish off."

"You're a good neighbor," Clancy said.

"We love to paint," Ramon said. "No heavy lifting."

"Great! I'll get their color choice and let you know."

Ramon gave her a slight bow and said, "The crew is in a hurry to get home. There's a big *fútbol* game tonight."

Abby looked puzzled, but said, "Have a good weekend, Ramon. We'll see you back here soon."

As the man walked away, Abby said, "It seems early for football."

"He's talking about soccer," Clancy said. "All of the guys are from Mexico, and there's a bar they go to in Los Feliz to watch the Mexican national team on satellite."

"That sounds like fun," Abby said. "Maybe we should join them."

Clancy gave her a hungry look and asked, "Did Hayley leave?"

Abby removed Clancy's cap and intently played with her hair, acting unconcerned. "Uh-huh. We're all alone."

"Then we probably should go to Los Feliz. There won't be anything fun for just the two of us to do."

Abby grabbed onto the architect's khaki shirt and playfully tossed her around. "I have a couple of things in mind, and the first one is going for a swim. Care to join me?"

"Well, it's not soccer, but it'll have to do," Clancy said, giving her a toothy grin.

After a long, relaxing swim, Abby brought out plastic glasses filled with cold beer. The pair sat in the Jacuzzi and let the warm water soothe away the stress of the week. "I'm so relaxed, I could fall asleep right here," Clancy said.

"No dinner?" Abby moved closer and put her arm around Clancy.

"Well, maybe a little dinner."

Kissing a wet path up the tanned, muscular arm, Abby said, "How about a few kisses? Does that interest you enough to stay awake?"

"I guess I could stay up for a few...but then it's right to bed," Clancy said, smiling.

"Bed it is."

Abby met her eyes and gave Clancy such a stupendously sexy look that Clancy nearly slipped off the bench in the tub. Smiling to herself, Abby got out and turned to walk toward the kitchen. Clancy watched her long, lean body, realizing that she wasn't tired anymore. In fact, she was tingling all over and couldn't wait for dinner to be finished.

When Clancy got to the back door, Abby handed her a towel, a T-shirt, and a pair of boxers. "I put your clothes in the washer. They looked like you'd been buried in mud!"

"This was a dirty day. Mind if I wash my hair?"

"No, go right ahead. I'll have dinner ready by the time you're finished."

Clancy batted her eyelashes and said, "Those are the words I've longed to hear."

Giving her a pat on the seat, Abby said, "Get going now. You don't want your dinner to get cold."

Clancy walked into the bathroom, whistling a happy tune as she did.

After dinner, they cleaned the kitchen together, chatting about the project. Abby kissed Clancy on the head and said, "Why don't you go into the den? I'll toss your things in the dryer and be right in."

Clancy did as she was directed, but she wasn't sure how to turn the TV on, so she sat down with the dogs, all three expectantly waiting. Abby laughed when she walked into the room a few moments later. Clancy was sitting on the couch, flanked by Athena and Artemis, all three of them upright and alert. "What are you all waiting for?"

"Our favorite person."

Abby smiled, but it faded immediately. "I've been...I don't know how to ask this..."

"What is it? Is something wrong?"

"No, not wrong, but…" She let out a breath and said, "I'm worried about your truck."

"My truck?" The look on Clancy's face was one of total confusion. "What about my truck?"

"If we…if you decide to…stay over…" Abby began, her voice catching on nearly every word.

Clancy stood and went to her. Putting a hand on her shoulder, she said, "Don't worry about that. I'll move it a few blocks away. No one will see it."

Abby closed her eyes. "I feel like a fool for worrying about this, but I know all of my neighbors, and one of Hayley's friends lives just down the street."

"It's not a problem. I'll move it right now."

"Let me drive behind you so you don't have to walk."

"That's not necessary. Really. But you can make me a nice cold drink for when I get back."

"What would you like?"

"Surprise me," Clancy said. She blew Abby a kiss and then went out the back door to get her boots.

Clancy returned a few minutes later, smiling when Abby opened the pedestrian door in the gate. "I forgot about getting back in," she said. "I could have been out here all night!"

They walked into the house together, the dogs rejoicing at Clancy's return. In the den, there were two large glasses of lemonade sitting on the coffee table. "Mmm…I love lemonade," Clancy said. She sat down, picked up a glass, and took a large drink before Abby could say a word. Abby did hold up a hand and try to signal, but she was too late. Clancy nearly spat the mouthful across the room. She slapped her hand over her mouth and managed to get it down; then she looked at Abby like she'd tried to poison her. "What in the hell is in this?"

"I thought you might like something a little stronger than regular lemonade," she said, looking sheepish. "Trevor clued me in on this. I swear I tried to warn you…"

Clancy picked up the glass, sniffed it tentatively, took a more moderate sip, and then said, "You know, it's good…now that I'm prepared for it." She smacked her lips and added, "Actually, it's very good. How do you make it?"

"It's pretty easy. Take a can of frozen lemonade, and add a can of vodka, along with two cans of water. Voilà!"

"Wow. This is the kind of cocktail my friends would like."

"Feel free to share," Abby said. She took a drink and relaxed into the corner of the sectional sofa. "I don't know what you like to drink, other than beer. I just took a guess that you'd like vodka."

"I usually drink beer, but I can drink just about anything except rum. Got sick on that once. Never again."

"I'm…I guess I'm a little nervous. How about you?"

Clancy linked her hands around a knee and rocked back and forth for a moment. "Little bit. Sometimes the second time is just as nerve-wracking as the first."

"It's been a really long while since I've had a second time. A really, really long while."

"You know," Clancy said, "even though I haven't done this in a while, I have learned one thing in my dating career."

"What's that?"

Clancy took a drink and then said, "Don't rush it. You can't plan on when the right time will strike you. Doing things on a schedule guarantees a bad experience."

Looking at her with affection, Abby asked, "Have you had many bad experiences?"

"Yeah, I've had my share. Things were hard when I was young. We'd have to have sex because we had a place—rather than a burning desire."

"Mmm…makes sense. But things seem so much easier when you're young, don't they?" Abby sipped her drink as she looked at Clancy contemplatively. "As you get older, you think more." She laughed softly. "Thinking gets you in trouble."

"Yeah, there was a simple beauty to being able to think only about the present. Gets harder every year." She smiled at Abby and said, "Now I think about today, tomorrow, next year, the rest of my life."

"Do you think of me when you think about the rest of your life?"

Clancy nodded. "Definitely." She put her drink down and turned so she was facing Abby. "Every time. You're in my plans…my dreams."

"That makes my heart race." Her eyes fluttered closed. "It's been such a long time since someone's cared about me like that."

"I care about you. Very, very much."

"I care about you, too. It astounds me how much."

"Still nervous?"

Abby smiled wryly, "More than ever."

"Let's go sit outside. It's a lovely night."

"Okay. Will I be warm enough?"

Clancy looked at her outfit—a roomy sweatshirt the color of lime sherbet and a pair of pink oxford-cloth boxer shorts. "You might be a little chilly, but I can help keep you warm."

They went outdoors, the dogs following them as usual. "It's perfect out," Abby said, "but you can still keep me warm."

Clancy sat down on the thick pad of the loveseat and put her arm around Abby. "I feel a little like a teenager at a movie. Should I have tried the fake yawn before I inconspicuously draped my arm across your shoulders?"

Abby laid her head on Clancy's shoulder. "No, I think we can skip ahead a little bit. Let's act like we're in college—at least."

"I can do that." Clancy leaned back, able to spot a few stars through the ambient light of metropolitan Los Angeles. "It's so nice out here. I can smell the magnolias and the night-blooming jasmine."

"Yeah. There's something about jasmine…"

Clancy's voice dropped into a lower register. "Mmm-hmm. Something about it smells sexy…seductive."

Abby sat up and placed her finger just below Clancy's ear. Slowly, she slid it down her neck, past her shoulder, running it all the way to her hand. A riot of goosebumps followed in her wake, and she saw Clancy shiver. "I love it when your voice gets low and sexy."

"Something about you makes it that way. When we're together, I immediately find myself wanting to hold you. It's all I can do to stop myself from hugging you when you come outside to bring water to us."

"Maybe your men would just think you were very, very thankful."

"No, they're a pretty savvy bunch. Ramon picked up on Hayley's crush on me before I did."

"Oh." Abby, suddenly and obviously uneasy, looked at her. "Do you think he knows about us?"

"If he does, he hasn't said anything," Clancy said. "He's pretty up front, so I'd expect him to ask me if he thought something was going on."

Abby shook her head, looking like she was trying to dislodge a thought. "I don't know why it bothers me. It shouldn't."

"Doesn't matter if it should or not. You can't order your feelings around. If you want, I'll brush Ramon off if he asks."

"No, don't do that. We'll figure out what to do when the time comes."

Clancy sat quietly, taking in the small night sounds of the neighborhood. An occasional car would drive by, but their privacy wasn't disturbed by headlights any longer now that the concrete blocks were up. The only clue that they were surrounded by other people was the muted sound of an engine straining up the steep hill. This was the quietest, most tranquil yard she'd ever been in, and merely sitting outside made her feel rejuvenated.

They sat that way longer than either realized, and Abby got up when they'd finished their drinks, bringing out refills. Clancy accepted, even though she was starting to feel the effects of the alcohol. She didn't normally drink on a work night, but she usually had a few drinks on Friday night to relax after a long week.

After another few minutes had passed, Abby cuddled up closer and put her hand on Clancy's stomach. "You have the hardest little belly I think I've ever felt. Is this a six-pack?"

"Yeah," Clancy said, laughing a little. "As long as I stay at around a hundred and twenty pounds, they're visible. But they're the first things to go when I put on a little weight. The muscles are still there, but you can't see 'em."

Abby was quiet for a moment and then asked, "You can see them?" Her voice sounded both sexy and curious, and Clancy decided to tease her a little.

"Uh-huh. We should have left the lights on when we made love."

"So…I could see them…now?"

"Yep. But you've got to take my shirt off."

Abby put her hand on the dark green T-shirt she'd given Clancy, tentatively stroking from her shoulder down to her elbow. "I love the way you fill out a shirt. I can feel the material straining here at the seam. I've never touched a woman who felt like you do."

Chuckling, Clancy asked, "How many women have you felt?"

"A few," Abby said, smiling when Clancy did a little comic take.

"A few...like your daughter and her friends when you're putting sunblock on their backs? Or a few...like..." She stared and said, "I don't even know what I'm asking."

"The latter," Abby said, nodding mysteriously.

"I thought you'd resisted all attempts to make you a feminist lesbian."

"I did. But I didn't know what I was resisting until I'd had a little taste. You know I'm a curious person."

Clancy turned in her seat, her head cocked at a severe angle. "Spill it. Now."

Abby laughed. "There isn't a lot to tell. I went to school during a very turbulent time. Young women were questioning everything they'd ever been taught. I didn't realize it at first, but most of my friends were starting to pair off and sleep together. Most of them weren't exclusively lesbian, but they weren't opposed to an occasional woman lover."

"Damn, now you've got me wondering if my mom ever did that!" Clancy's voice warbled a bit in alarm.

"Did your mom go to college?"

"No. She married my dad not long after graduating from high school. Why? Do you need a degree to experiment?"

"No, of course not." Abby laughed. "But that was the right environment for being around women who were trying things like that. We had segregated dorms, lots of marijuana, four women to a room..." She smiled. "Things happened that wouldn't have happened to a young woman who still lived at home. Besides," she said, "why does it bother you so much to think of your mother having sex with another woman?"

"I'm barely comfortable with her having sex with my dad! Quit freaking me out!"

Abby put an arm around her and gave her a comforting hug. "Calm down, baby, I'm sure your mother and father only had sex once. And that was probably an accident that happened while they were asleep. I'm sure neither one of them felt a thing."

Clancy poked her in the ribs and pulled away. "Think about your mom getting sweaty with another woman, and see how it feels!"

"Point well taken," Abby said, showing an exaggerated look of distaste.

"Besides, I think you're just trying to throw me off the trail. I wanna know what *you* did in college, not what my mom didn't do."

"I didn't do much. A few kisses; some backrubs. Lots and lots of stiff muscles at UCLA," she added, chuckling.

"Tell me about these kisses," Clancy said, drawing closer. "Give me an example."

Abby looked at her, a quizzical expression on her face. "You're really interested, aren't you?"

"Hell, yes! I had no idea you'd ever kissed another woman!"

"Well, I don't know if you've ever kissed a man."

"I haven't. Now tell me about this!"

"Okay, okay," Abby said, giggling a little. "I didn't know a few kisses would be this big a deal."

"They are," Clancy said, staring at her intently. "Spill it."

"All right." Abby sat back. She thought for a few moments and then said, "The woman I told you about—Katie—the campus leader who tried to convince me that feminism equaled lesbianism."

Clancy nodded and then sat back too. Even though she was sitting quietly, she was more alert than Abby had ever seen her, intent on every word.

"We'd only been friends for a short time," Abby said. "I was a freshman, and she was a senior. We met while working on a project for some cause...I don't even remember what it was. I was very impressed with her and probably had one of those adolescent crushes on her."

"My mom didn't have crushes on girls," Clancy said, her tone making it clear that this wasn't up for discussion.

"Right. Well, we got to be friendly, and we'd go to her room to talk or smoke a joint. I thought I was pretty cool to be hanging around with a senior, and I was probably a little starstruck. Katie was always giving a speech or championing some great cause." She laughed at the memory. "It all seemed very important at the time. Anyway, she started to talk to me about women loving women. I hadn't given the topic much thought before, but it didn't particularly shock me. It seemed...pretty natural."

"Natural? Were you attracted to girls when you were younger?"

"Yeah, a little bit," Abby said. "I had crushes on a couple of teachers and thought some of the older girls in my school were about the coolest things ever created. But I'd never associated sexual feelings with those crushes. I just thought those girls were...divine," she said, laughing again.

"So what happened with Katie?"

"Well, she rubbed my back one night while I was very stoned, and I wouldn't have minded if she'd turned me over and touched me wherever she wanted."

"You wouldn't have minded? *Minded?*"

"Yeah. It felt very sensual and erotic...but it didn't make me want to jump on her. It would have felt very natural to have her touch me, but I wasn't craving it. It's hard to explain."

Clancy blinked. "I guess it is, 'cause I'm clueless!"

"It's not that big a deal. Not long after that, she was in my room one afternoon. I lived in a dorm close to where the football team practiced. It was a warm fall day, and I had the windows open. I remember hearing an occasional shout from a coach and the thud that a football makes when you kick it. I felt like such a college girl." She smiled again, thinking of herself at that age. "Katie was sitting on my bed, and the afternoon sun hit her, making all sorts of gold and red highlights in her hair. I sat down next to her, and she put her hand on my thigh. We sat there for a few minutes, looking into each other's eyes. Then I put my hand on her cheek and pulled her closer. We smiled at each other, and I found myself kissing her."

"Wow," Clancy said, nearly slack-jawed. "*You* kissed *her!*"

"Yeah, I certainly did. She kissed me back, and that felt awfully good, so we started to make out."

"You said a few kisses!"

Abby smiled. "So math's not my best subject. I don't know how many kisses we shared. But it felt great, and I could easily have kept going—if my roommate hadn't come in."

Clancy slapped herself in the forehead. "Damn that roommate!"

Running her hand up and down Clancy's leg, she asked, "Why do you want me to have had sex with a woman? What difference does it make?"

"A lot!"

"Why?"

"I don't know. I'd just feel better if this was a long-standing desire. It sounds like you could take it or leave it. That's…not how it was for me. At all."

"Hey, just because Katie and I didn't have sex has no bearing on us. I'm very, very attracted to you, Clancy. And I know who I am now. I'm not afraid of this."

"Is that why you didn't have sex with Katie? Were you afraid?"

"Not…afraid, no. But I liked it better when I was making the first move. Kissing her that day felt good to me. But the next time I saw her, she was only interested in having sex. She kept trying to talk me into it. That never works with me. I don't respond well to pressure."

"Sounds like she was a lesbian," Clancy said, looking a little ill. "God knows I would have been on you like a bodysuit."

"You're not like that. You've been very understanding."

"I'm more understanding now than I would have been then. You might have had to call security."

"I refuse to believe that. You're a gentle woman. I love that about you."

"I'll keep reminding myself of that," Clancy said. "I don't wanna make Katie's mistake."

"Hey, I was eighteen at the time, and I wasn't in love with Katie. I was infatuated with her. It seemed…adult…dangerous…illicit…to kiss a woman."

"None of this is helping my confidence. Are you sure now? I…I can't even believe I'm saying this, but if you think this is a phase, I'd rather stop now. Making love with you takes too much of my heart. I'd…break if you changed your mind after I was hopelessly in love with you."

"I've grown up," Abby said. "I'm not trying to make myself feel like an adult. I'm not trying to impress anyone. I'm falling in love with you, Clancy, and I'm ready to move forward."

"You've grown up nicely," Clancy said, closing her eyes and resting her head on Abby's shoulder. "Very nicely."

"Don't be afraid," Abby said. "Don't be shy."

Clancy put one arm around Abby's back, the other behind her knees, and slid her right onto her lap. "You don't mind if I make the first move, do you?"

Giving her a delectably sexy kiss, Abby whispered, "I prefer it." She tilted her head and started to nibble on Clancy's ear. "So responsive," she murmured, letting her hand brush over the nipple that had hardened in moments. She draped both arms around her neck and hugged her close. "I like this," Abby said. "A lot."

"I like it, too," Clancy agreed, staring intently at her partner's lips. "Perfect for kissing."

They stayed just that way, kissing each other until they were mad with desire. They finally managed to stumble into the house and make it upstairs, where they made love to each other until they were fast asleep in each other's arms.

Chapter Twelve

The next morning, Abby ran around the house in a panic, late for her tennis match and so tired she was giddy. Clancy kissed her on the way out the door, waving goodbye as Abby insistently signaled that she should close the door from the garage—because she was wearing nothing but a love-filled smile.

❦

Abby called Clancy when she got home from her tennis match. The architect answered on the fourth ring, sounding a little slow. "H'llo?"

"Ohh…did I wake you?"

"Little," Clancy admitted. "I started working on some plans and then woke up to find my head on my desk. I took that as a clue that I might need a nap."

Laughing softly, Abby said, "I could use a nap, too. I'm not used to staying up so late."

"Wanna nap together?"

Clancy sounded adorably hopeful, but Abby wasn't as enthusiastic. "I'd love to, but I have a dinner to go to tonight. If I had you in my bed, I wouldn't feel like napping. Do you mind?"

"Hell, yeah, I mind," Clancy said, chuckling. "I wanna be on you like aphids on roses."

"Aww…a flower simile. I want that, too, but I have to be alert tonight. I'm on the committee that puts this dinner together, and I'm going to have to run around like mad." She thought for a second and then asked, "How about coming over to meet me when I get home?"

"Sure. What time?"

"Come whenever you want," Abby said. "The dogs would love to have some company. You could use the Jacuzzi, take a swim."

"I'll be there before you leave if you don't stop tempting me," Clancy said. "Hey, would it be okay if I brought Michael over?"

"Of course! There's only one rule—no glass in the pool or Jacuzzi. You know where the towels are, right?"

"We can bring our own towels, Abby. We don't have to act like we're going to a spa."

"Don't bother. Really. We have plenty, and I wash a load of towels nearly every day. It's no trouble."

"We'll see," Clancy said, making Abby laugh at her attempt to sound like a parent. "I'll see you when you get home."

"I can't think of a better thing to make me wrap up my business as soon as possible. See you then. Oh! I'll leave the pedestrian gate unlocked and put a key in the barbecue. You'll have to open the door to let the dogs out, or they'll go mad."

"Great. I'll have Michael drive so the neighbors don't see my truck in front of your house on a Saturday night."

Abby was quiet for a moment. Then she said, "Thanks for thinking of little things like that. Every little thing you do makes me love you a little more."

"I only think of the little things because I'm always thinking about you. So I guess we're in luck."

"God knows I am. Incredibly lucky."

Clancy and Michael played in the pool like a couple of kids. Clancy had brought out all of the pool toys—the volleyball, the squirt guns, the Frisbees, and a big ball filled with some kind of material that made it sink like a stone. She'd caught Michael unaware when she tossed that one at him, and the weighted ball hit him smack in the chest. But for payback, he'd made her dive to the bottom to retrieve it.

Clancy was very glad that Abby didn't mind Michael's knowing about their relationship, and she'd kept him up to date on everything that had happened. He was supportive, as always, but she could tell that he was worried things wouldn't work out for her.

"So tell me again where this daughter is?" he asked, while they were throwing the weighted ball at each other.

"She's in Maine, visiting Abby's parents. She'll be back in two weeks."

"And then what? Is Abby gonna tell her about you?"

"Ahh…I don't know. We haven't talked a lot about the future, Michael. This whole thing is hard for her, and she gets a little freaked out when she thinks about everything that could happen."

He cradled the ball under his arm for a moment, giving the dogs—who had been chasing each throw—a rest. They swam to the steps and put their front paws on the top step, each panting while turning her head to keep an eye on the ball. "Just because she doesn't think about things doesn't stop them from happening," Michael said. "What if her daughter demands that she stop seeing you? Would she?"

Clancy had been patting the water with the flat of her hands, making tiny ripples. She didn't look up to answer the question. "I don't know. I honestly have no idea."

In a voice filled with kindness, Michael said, "Don't you think you'd better find out before you get in too deep? I can tell how crazy you are about this woman, Clance. I'd hate to see you get your heart broken."

"I…I don't think she'd do that to me. I mean…I know she wouldn't do it unless she absolutely had no other choice."

He nodded, looking like he was going to say something else, but instead, he looked at the dogs and said, "Break's over, girls. Time to get back to work." As soon as he launched the ball at Clancy, the dogs dived back in, swimming from one person to the other, always just a second too late.

🌱

Abby arrived home at around midnight, finding Michael and Clancy sitting on the loveseat on the patio, each of them covered by a breathing black-and-white lap blanket. Michael was dressed, but Clancy was still in her suit. "This looks like a very happy group," Abby said, smiling at the foursome. The dogs sat up when they heard her voice, and both tails began to wag, but neither left her perch. "Is that the best you two can do? No kiss?"

Clancy patted Athena on the butt, and the dog reluctantly jumped to the ground. She walked over to Abby and gave her a quick kiss, smiling when she pulled away. "I have more than a kiss for you," she said. "Given how you look…" She waggled her eyebrows suggestively, making Abby giggle like a schoolgirl. "You look fantastic. I've never seen you in a dress before; I didn't know what I'd been missing."

Abby wanted to fold herself into Clancy's arms and have the blonde lavish her with compliments, but she minded her manners and greeted her guest. She extended her hand, and she and Michael shook. "It's good to see you again. Did you find everything you needed?"

"Yeah, we had a great time," Michael said, his white teeth contrasting with his dark coloring. "I haven't played in a pool in a long time."

"I love to see people enjoy the pool. You're welcome any time, Michael."

"You might regret that invitation," he said, giving her his most engaging smile.

Abby spent a moment looking at him, struck by how very attractive he was. His hair was thick, black, and perfectly cut, and his dark eyes were kind and playful. He had a boyish look about him, yet he looked very mature. It was a nice disparity and added to his style. It puzzled Abby that she hadn't previously noticed how attractive he was, but then it dawned on her that she'd only had eyes for Clancy—even at the beginning.

She realized that it was her turn to talk and said, "I doubt that. I love to have people over." She put her arm around Clancy and gave her a gentle hug. "One person in particular."

Michael started to get up, trying to dislodge a very reluctant Artemis. "Don't leave yet," Abby said. "Stay and have another drink."

"Thanks, but I should get going. I worked a full day today, and it's catching up with me. I only stayed this late to keep Clance company."

"And I appreciate it," Clancy said, putting her arms around him for a rough hug. She kissed his cheek, and he rubbed the top of her head, their affection for each other very much like that of siblings. "I'll be home sometime tomorrow, okay?"

"Sure. Call if you're gonna stay over again. You know I'm in charge of you when your dad's not around."

Clancy laughed, knowing that Michael was only partially kidding. Her father had often told Michael that he was expected to keep an eye on Clancy, something he would have done anyway. "I'll call. I always do."

Another hug for his roommate and a half-handshake/half-hug for Abby, and he left, both dogs whining a little at losing him.

Abby started to turn and happily discovered a pair of arms wrapped around her waist. She faced Clancy and placed a gentle kiss on her lips. "Miss me?"

"Like air. Now, let me get a good look at this dress, 'cause I want you to wear it at least once a week." She stepped back and did a slow circle around her partner, nodding her approval as her eyes narrowed in thought. "That's one damn fine dress."

"I'm glad you like it. It's really quite simple."

"Yeah, it is. But that's what makes it so sexy." She ran her hand down her partner's side, rubbing her fingers together to feel the fabric. "Silk?"

"Yes," Abby said. "And a little something else to give it body. Probably rayon."

Clancy circled behind her and nibbled on her neck, fully exposed by the scoop neckline. "That's what I like about it. The body." She placed her hands low on Abby's hips, running them languidly across the expanse of black fabric clinging to her shapely ass. "The body's very, very nice." She moved to the side and started to kiss a path from the strap down the bare arm and all the way to Abby's wrist, pushing aside a pair of gold bracelets with her tongue. "Have I mentioned that I like the body?" she asked, looking up into Abby's eyes.

"Come up here and kiss me." Abby grasped the straps of her swimsuit and tugged. "You can only tease a woman so long."

"What's your limit?"

"Whatever it is, I'm sure you'll push me past it," Abby predicted, wrapping her arms around Clancy for a hug and a long, lush kiss.

❦

By the time they'd made sure the dogs had gone to the bathroom, turned off all the lights, set the alarm, and gotten ready for bed themselves, nearly half an hour had passed. Clancy walked out of the bath to find Abby half-asleep, lying across the bed clad in only a T-shirt.

"Come on, baby," she cooed. "Time to get under the covers."

Abby protested weakly. "No…no…time to make love."

"We can make love tomorrow. You're too tired to enjoy it tonight. Come on." She was pulling the covers down as she spoke, and Abby found herself effortlessly rolled over and then put back onto the cool sheet.

"I can wake up," she said, her eyes closed.

"I know you can, but you don't need to. We can lie in bed tomorrow and play with each other all day. Doesn't that sound nice?"

"Uhm…nice," Abby agreed. She nestled her body against Clancy's, sighed heavily, and was asleep before her partner could say a word.

"G'night," Clancy murmured to the sleeping woman. "I love you."

Clancy woke with a start, her hand reflexively grasping her breast. Her eyes flew open, her head jerked up, and she gasped—her fight-or-flight response kicking in immediately. But her body relaxed a moment later, and a giddy laugh bubbled up from her chest.

One impish blue eye had rotated in her direction, a half-smile exposing even, white teeth that tugged at the steel ring hidden beneath Clancy's tank top. "You know," the blonde muttered sleepily, her hand dropping to lace through Abby's hair, "an impartial observer might say that it wouldn't be pleasurable to be awakened by someone tugging on her nipple." Her lips split into a grin as she decided, "They'd be wrong."

Abby's head lifted, and she asked, "Is this…okay?"

"Yeah. It's very okay." Clancy pressed lightly on the back of her head, and Abby nipped at the ring again. Petting her gently, Clancy said, "You seem fond of it."

"Umm-hmm. I'm very fond of it. It's…hot."

"It makes me hot to hear you say that," Clancy murmured. "Wanna nibble on the real thing?"

"Yeah." Abby grasped the hem of the shirt and tugged it off when Clancy raised her arms. Her mouth dropped to the shiny, heavy ring, and she poked the tip of her tongue through it.

Clancy growled, the sound rumbling through her chest. Her hips shifted as her legs spread, and she wrapped them around Abby's waist. She let out a satisfied sigh and rocked her hips a few times, her eyes tightly closed. "Nice. So nice."

Abby sat up and pulled her T-shirt off; then she placed her forearms on either side of Clancy's head and started to rub her breasts lightly over her partner's, catching her turgid nipple on the ring time and again. The most adorable sounds were coming from Abby's open lips—tiny grunts, soft sighs, and sexy growls as she worked over her.

Clancy's legs dropped to the bed; then her hands drifted down to cup Abby's ass. Her hands moved all over the smoothly muscled surface, making Abby sigh with pleasure. She could feel her partner's thighs compressing rhythmically, seeking satisfaction, so she guided her to straddle her leg to provide a little relief.

Abby's head tilted up, and the surprised look on her face quickly turned to one of intense satisfaction as she felt the strong thigh pressed firmly against her. Without thought, she began to pump her hips, her eyes closing tightly as she did. Clancy's hands went to Abby's breasts and began to squeeze and compress the flesh, keeping time with her rough movements.

Testing, seeking ways to increase the sensation, Abby placed her hands on Clancy's shoulders and locked her arms, gliding back and forth on the slippery leg as her mouth dropped open, grunting out her pleasure.

Clancy strained to nip at the tempting breasts that bounced just above her face, but Abby's iron grip didn't allow for any upward movement. That didn't stop her hands from grasping them, though, and she pinched and tugged on Abby's nipples, taking Abby just to the edge of pain.

Abby was close, her eyes glazing over as she felt the sensation building deep in her belly. The feeling was so intense that it felt like a strong cramp that began to radiate out from her abdomen, eventually growing to a warm, satisfying pulsing that eased the cramp and suffused her entire body with wave after wave of pleasure.

She wasn't aware of making a sound, but as the muscles in her arms started to shake and finally give way, she tried to speak but realized that her throat was slightly raw. "Was I shouting?" she asked dully, her mouth pressed against the pillow.

"Oh, yeah. If we had close neighbors, they'd be banging on the walls." Clancy murmured into the soft hair that tickled her chin. "It was incredibly sexy."

Abby rolled off Clancy's wet body and draped an arm over her eyes. "That was a completely unique experience."

Clancy braced her head on her hand, looking at her curiously. "What was?"

"I've never…done anything like that."

"'S nice, isn't it?"

"Yeah. It felt instinctive," she mused. "I wonder why I never had that instinct when I was…well, before."

Clancy tugged Abby's arm away from her face and stroked her cheek gently. "It's okay to talk about Will…to talk about your life…your experiences. It's part of you that I want to get to know."

"I don't want to…I don't know…upset you."

"Learning about you can only help us to grow closer. I wanna be closer—much closer."

Abby nodded and took a quick breath, forcing herself to tell the story without losing her nerve. "I was just thinking about what it would have been like to try that with Will. His legs were so hairy, I would have had friction burns. I was thinking that I was glad the desire didn't strike me until I was astride a nice, smooth thigh."

"Really, really personal question?" Clancy asked tentatively.

"Sure. We've been pretty personal recently. A question shouldn't throw me over the edge."

"I…uhm…assume I'm the first person you've been with…since Will?"

Abby nodded. "You are."

"Don't take this the wrong way, but I thought this would be harder for you," she said, searching Abby's eyes.

Blinking in surprise, Abby asked, "How much harder could this be? I don't know if I'm coming or going! We've been walking a tightrope for weeks!"

Clancy nodded energetically, her hands gesturing. "No, no. I'm talking about sex. If I found myself in bed with a man, I'd be stunned; then I'd try to figure out what the hell was going on! But you don't seem like you're doing that, Abby. You're acting like you've been doing this all your life, and it stuns me!"

Abby propped herself up just enough to place a warm kiss on Clancy's lips. "I haven't done that today," she said, a girlish grin lifting a corner of her mouth. Clancy returned the favor, pressing her lips gently upon Abby's. When she pulled back, Abby gathered her thoughts and said, "I'm not explaining myself well. I don't always know how I'm feeling. I mean…I know if I'm comfortable or uncomfortable…but I don't always know why. I'm comfortable having sex with you, Clancy, but I'm not sure why. Maybe it's you…maybe it's me. I honestly don't know."

"I guess I just assumed this would be hard for you. But you seem very relaxed."

"Sometimes I am; sometimes I'm not. But I don't necessarily talk about it much. That's not how I am. I work things out on my own most of the time. I sit down and write during the day. I cry a lot," she said. "But I cry when I'm alone. I'm private." She reached out and ran her thumb along Clancy's bottom lip, moaning softly when the landscaper pulled it into her mouth and sucked gently. "I can't stop touching you." She lay atop Clancy and began to kiss her, probing her warm mouth with her tongue. "This feels so right."

Clancy blew out a breath, her need growing stronger with each kiss. "It does feel right. We can make it work, Abby. We'll take it slow so you can stay comfortable. We'll do this right so that you feel nice and safe."

"We're doing fine," Abby said. "We don't need to change a thing. I just need time on my own to think…and feel."

"Take as much time as you need," Clancy said. "I won't rush you. When you're ready, we'll take the next step."

"I want this to work," Abby said. "You have no idea how much."

They lay together for a long while, touching each other gently, soothingly. Clancy's thrumming body calmed down after a bit, and she was very pleased when Abby started to talk.

"Can I tell you a few things?"

"Sure. Anything."

"I told you I worked with a grief counselor." Clancy nodded. "Well, I had a lot of things to get through before I could start dating. It was hard to imagine that I'd ever want to be sexual with another man. I felt so horribly guilty—even though I knew I shouldn't." She gave Clancy a thin smile and said, "One thing helped a lot."

"What's that?"

"Will and I had a little joke that we'd been making since we were newlyweds," she said, her eyes fixed on a point near Clancy's collarbone. "Every time the topic came up, he'd make me promise that I'd start dating soon after he died."

Clancy's hand stilled, and she looked at her questioningly. "Really? Why?"

"Will was ten years older than I was," Abby said. Clancy blinked at this information, and her lover gave her a knowing smile. "I was just like you. Always attracted to older men."

"Technically, that's not *just* like me," Clancy playfully reminded her.

"Right. Pronouns are important." The brunette kissed her partner and continued, "Will didn't come from a very long-lived family. I think I told you that both of his parents died before our kids had time to get to know them well. He was certain he'd die before me, and he gave me a consistent message during our entire marriage. He used to say that nothing would make him happier than to look down from heaven and see that I was taking a date to his funeral."

"Macabre, but sweet."

"It was a little macabre, but it was important to him. He used to tell me that I was so full of love that he couldn't bear the thought of my pining away for him. He wanted me to share my love again."

Clancy cleared her throat and looked at Abby tentatively. "How do you think he would have felt about your being with a woman?"

Abby laughed. "He would have been tremendously upset—that he wasn't able to join in. It was one of his little fantasies."

"You didn't ever…?"

"Lord, no! We had a very fulfilling, very traditional sex life. Our love for each other was plenty to keep the excitement going."

"I like traditional sex, too." She took Abby's hand and placed it on her breast. "As a matter of fact, I'd love some right now."

"Well, lesbian sex is a little untraditional for me, but I've always been a good student." Abby leaned over and kissed Clancy hungrily, revealing the depths of her desire. "And I think you're going to be my favorite teacher."

❦

After a long, lazy day of lying in the pool, napping, kissing, and kissing some more, Clancy looked at her watch and let out a regret-filled sigh. "I've gotta get to sleep. I'm gonna need all my wits tomorrow when my dad and his crew show up."

"Are you going home?" Abby asked, looking puzzled.

"I don't want to, but I have my tools in my truck. You'd have to get up and drive me to my apartment so I could be back by the time the guys get here."

"Damn. Ellen's going to meet me at the Rose Bowl at six-thirty to run. How do you feel about getting up at five-thirty?"

"Not great. How about you?"

"I'd do it…just to be close to you." She saw the indecision in Clancy's eyes and changed her mind. "That's too early. You've got a big day tomorrow, and you need some sleep. I'll take you home."

"We'll figure this out someday…right?"

"Oh! Of course we will! It's going to take a little time, but if I handle this right, everything will work out. Don't worry about it. Really." She lovingly stroked Clancy's cheek, gazing deeply into her eyes. "It'll work out."

"Okay." She put on a smile and kissed Abby tenderly, turning up the heat just enough to let Abby know what she was missing. "Let's go."

Abby held onto her for a long time, finally releasing her so they could walk to the car.

❦

Clancy slept surprisingly well, having been reassured by Abby's confident declaration that they would eventually work things out. But Abby put off going to bed as long as she could. She was so tired that she eventually gave in—but the bed seemed so brutally large and empty that she couldn't even close her eyes. She lay there thinking of how wonderful it had felt to sleep in Clancy's arms—how she hadn't slept that well since the day Will had died—how merely getting horizontal with Clancy had made her feel both incredibly relaxed and stimulated at the same time.

She rolled over onto the other side of the bed and tried to find a hint of Clancy's scent on the pillow or the sheets, but nothing remained. Knowing she would never be able to relax, she went downstairs and lay on the sofa, eventually having to turn the television on to have enough background noise to ultimately drift off.

❧

When Abby woke, the dogs were sitting on the floor, staring at her with what looked like outraged expressions. "What?" she mumbled, brushing the hair from her eyes. "What's wrong?" She looked at her watch and saw that it was already seven. "Oh, shit! The crew's gonna be here, and I haven't let you two out yet!"

They stared at her, tails wagging, clearly saying, "That's what we just told you."

She was still wearing her sleepwear and knew she couldn't appear in the back yard like that. So she opened up the front door, letting the dogs have a little treat. The front yard was planted with so many delicate flowers that she usually didn't let the dogs use it for their bathroom, but she didn't have many options.

While the pair galloped around the large space, Abby went into the kitchen and turned on her coffeemaker. She was out of sorts and headachy, partially from lack of sleep and partially from the poor quality of sleep she'd gotten on the sofa. Her mood didn't improve when she realized she'd forgotten about her date to meet Ellen. A quick call to Ellen's house, apologizing for her absentmindedness, didn't make her feel better.

She heard some loud noises coming from the back yard, so she pulled up the curtain over the kitchen window and watched a different group of men scaling her hill. John O'Connor was standing on the lawn, chatting with Clancy, and just seeing her lover made Abby's spirits improve.

By the time her coffee was ready, the dogs had finished their jaunt and were ready for breakfast. They'd tracked their muddy paws through the entryway, but she knew that was entirely her fault, so she didn't complain to the culprits.

After all three had breakfast, Abby cleaned the entryway floor and went upstairs to take a shower. The dogs were puzzled once again, not having gotten their morning exercise. But their ability to complain was fairly limited, so they went back into the den and climbed onto the sofa to sleep.

By the time Abby came back downstairs, she was feeling a little more like herself, but she was still unsettled. Spending two nights with Clancy and then having her gone was more than a little disturbing, and Abby was determined to figure a way out of their dilemma.

At eight, she went outside to see how things were going. The crew was poised to start digging the course for the waterfall, and Clancy was standing on the top of the hill, bending over to peer into what looked like a surveyor's scope. "Good morning, John," Abby said.

"Hi, there," he replied, giving her a big grin. "My girl's doing the picky work right now."

"What is she doing?"

"Oh, she's using a laser level to check elevations. She wants to make sure the water flows down the hill properly. You know—so it follows the curve of the hill and doesn't spill out."

"She looks like she knows what she's doing." Clancy was signaling one of the men to move a little to his right and hammer in a stake with a bit of red plastic tied to the top.

"Oh, she knows what she's doing," John agreed, looking proud of his daughter. "She's a whiz at the math involved." He laughed softly. "Never was my strong point."

"How about a cup of coffee?"

"Thanks. That'd be great." He let out a shrill whistle, and Clancy looked up. She waved at Abby and then gave her father her attention. "Going inside for a cup of coffee. Don't screw up!"

"Thanks," she said, giving him a wry grin. "Always appreciate a vote of confidence."

The dogs were happy to see John, giving him the joyous welcome they reserved for people they'd met at least once. He laughed at their antics, saying, "We never let Clancy have a dog, but a pair like this wouldn't have been so bad."

"Oh, I love them. They've been life-savers for me the past few years. It's nice to have a pair of puppies who are always home when you need them, who never ask for much, and are always overjoyed when they see you."

"You sure don't get that from humans," he agreed, laughing at his own joke.

He stood at the window above the sink, watching his daughter work. "She's done a good job so far, Abby, and I'm not just saying that 'cause she's my kid. She's the best I've worked with, and I've worked with some jackasses who charge three times what she does."

"I've been very impressed, and I'm not just saying that because she's my…" She stopped abruptly, not knowing what term to use and not wanting to be too graphic.

He looked her right in the eye. "What is she to you?" he asked, obviously comfortable with the direct approach.

"What is she, or what would I like her to be?" she replied, surprising herself with the question.

"Either," he said. "Well, both, but you can start with either one."

She smiled at him and said, "Right now, we're…dating, I guess. We have a lot of things to work out—mostly my things. But I'd give anything to have her for my spouse."

She'd said the last words so wistfully that he felt bad for her. It was clear that Abby wasn't sure what she'd be capable of, but it was just as clear that she wasn't toying with Clancy's heart. "Sorry I asked," he said. "I can be pretty snoopy. But I hope you two can work things out. You're exactly the kind of woman she's always wanted, Abby. Exactly."

Abby beamed at him and put her hand on his arm. "I had no idea that I wanted a woman like Clancy," she admitted, "but I want her more than I can express."

John looked at the woman for a moment, seeing every quality that had attracted his daughter—Abby's obvious beauty, her gentle nature, her quick mind, the way she immediately put a person at ease, and her sweet sincerity. "You two'll be fine," he said reassuringly. "I'd bet on it."

After he'd made sure the job was well in hand, John left for a few hours to bid on another job. Today's project was sheer manual labor, and he'd given much of that up years before. Even though her crew had moved on to another job while the plumbing was being installed, Clancy still needed to be on site, because the digging was all according to her specifications. Though she needed to be around, she wasn't terribly busy, and after a while, she started thinking about picking up a shovel and lending a hand. But she knew that wouldn't be right, so she walked around the yard, taking a good long look at the trees.

Abby must have sensed her edginess, because she walked into the yard a few moments later. "Clancy," she called, "can I see you?"

The blonde walked over to her and smiled. "Any time," she drawled.

"I didn't really want anything, but I saw you looking at the trees. Is anything wrong with them?"

"No. They look fine. But I think you should thin out that California sycamore before the rains come. You don't want the crown to bear too much weight when it's on an incline like this. She's a beauty, and the last thing you want is to lose her."

"I've never heard anyone refer to trees in the feminine gender. It's cute."

Clancy swept her hat off with one hand and scratched her head with the other. "I didn't realize I did that, but they do seem feminine to me. I'm not sure why."

Abby looked at the tree in question and nodded. "I suppose you're right about her. I usually call Arbor Culture."

Making a face, Clancy said, "The San Gabriel Valley chainsaw killers!"

"They're bad?"

"Well, they're not the worst, but I've seen some of their crews go in and do nothing but top a tree. I'd like to personally wring the necks of everyone who's ever done that."

"But they say that they prune selectively."

"That's what they say, and if you watch them and insist that an arborist be here, they'll probably do that. But if they can get away with it, they go up top and give 'em a crewcut. It's disgusting," she said, making such a face that Abby had to laugh.

"Well, I don't want to disgust you."

"Don't worry about it. I'll take care of it for you."

Abby wanted to dip her head and kiss her, but she knew she couldn't. Instead, she said, "You know you can come in if you want to."

"No, I'd better not. I'll let you know when I need you."

"Okay." Abby went inside to catch up on some e-mail. She was working at her laptop, which she had set up on the kitchen table, when she heard a faint click. The dogs jumped up and ran to the sliding glass door, ears and tails up. Abby glanced outside but didn't see anything, so she went back to work. After a minute, she heard another click, this one a little louder. As soon as she got up, the dogs started to bark, sure the house was under attack. She opened the door and heard "Hey, give me a hand here, will ya?"

Abby stepped out onto the patio and saw that a massive number of small branches lay on the ground around the sycamore she and Clancy had just discussed, and as her eyes scanned up the tree, they landed on one familiar-looking tree surgeon—perched upon a sturdy branch that loomed a good twenty feet above the ground.

Before she could censor herself, she shouted, "Clancy! Get down from there this instant!" Without waiting for a reply, she took off, running across the lawn to stare up at her lover.

As Abby stood next to the tree, peering up into the sun, a calm voice said, "I know you didn't mean to use that tone of voice with me."

Abby had been too horror-struck to even think of moving, but Clancy's words allowed her to come to her senses. She looked up at the landscaper, panicked at her distance. "Clancy, you could kill yourself up there. Please get down!"

"Abby," she said, her voice still calm and unemotional, "this is what I do for a living. I've trimmed hundreds of trees, and I know what I'm doing. Besides, I wouldn't kill myself if I fell. A broken leg or two at worst."

"That's not making me feel better."

"Don't make me climb down; I'll just have to climb right back up. I need you to help me. Will you?"

"All right," she said, trying to tamp down her fear. "What do you need?"

"I'm gonna have to take this big branch down. I hate to do it, but it's not gonna make it if we have a bad storm. If it rips off, the whole tree will probably die."

"But…" Abby looked up at her in shock. "That's half of the tree!"

"I know," Clancy said. "The tree should never have been pruned this way. See how the two main branches come off the trunk?"

"Yeah."

"That's not good. Somebody pruned the tree when it was too young. Screwed it up," she said, shaking her head. "We should cut her down and plant a new one or take this whole side off." She could see how stunned Abby looked, and she gentled her voice. "We can save it," she said. "I'm sure we can."

Tears shone in Abby's eyes, and she put her hand on the trunk. "This was the only tree we ever planted. The kids wanted to plant a tree for Arbor Day. We…all went to the nursery together, and they picked this one," she sniffled, then rubbed her eyes with the back of her hand. "I can't bear to lose it."

"Then we have to do this," Clancy said, sure and calm. "It'll be a different-looking tree, but it'll live."

"Are you sure? I could call someone for a second opinion…"

"I'm sure," Clancy said, "and I wouldn't say that if there was a doubt in my mind."

Abby nodded. "Do what you have to do," she said. Then she turned and dashed for the house, obviously in tears.

Clancy was up in the tree for a long time, making quick, careful cuts, slowly working her way back to the sturdy branches. It had been a fairly dangerous and very strenuous job, and she was covered in sweat, dirt, and sap when she was finished.

Abby had obviously been watching from the kitchen, because just before Clancy started to climb down, she was at the base of the tree. "Oh, my God! Clancy, please, please be careful!"

Shaking her head, Clancy started to descend, her sure-footed movements nearly causing Abby's heart to stop. In moments, she was on the wide bottom branch, and she took off her saw and tossed it quite a distance from the tree. Then she jumped, bending her knees to absorb the impact as she landed.

Abby grabbed her and held onto her with a death-grip. "You scared me half to death," she whispered.

"Hey, hey," Clancy soothed as she felt Abby's body shake. Then she shot a glance at her father's crew, knowing they'd all been staring. "What's up with this? You know I do this kind of thing."

"No, I didn't," she insisted, her eyes wide. "I had no idea you climbed trees."

"Well, I do. It's one of my favorite parts of my job, as a matter of fact. I love trees, and I love being able to take proper care of them. I got certified as an arborist last year."

"But it's so dangerous!"

"It has the potential to be dangerous, but it's like anything else. If you're careful and prudent and take precautions, you should be fine."

"Going up in my tree without me out here watching you wasn't prudent. That was foolish."

"No, it wasn't," Clancy said. "I didn't have to use a chainsaw."

"You use a chainsaw?"

"Not very often. I don't often do tree removal, 'cause my time is worth too much for that. I usually just make a few critical cuts to keep a well-cared-for tree in good shape."

"I don't know how I'll stop worrying about you. This frightens me to death!"

"Hey, I never go up without someone close by. The guys on my dad's crew were right here if I needed 'em. I've been climbing trees since I was three, Abby, and over the years, I've learned how to fall. I promise you that I take all of the proper safety precautions." She put her hand on Abby's back and guided her into the house.

Once they were away from the others, Clancy wrapped her arms around her lover and held her for a long time. Abby could smell the strong scent of freshly sawn wood on her body, but it only reminded her of how frightened she'd been. Clancy continued, "I've got a lot to live for, and I'm not about to have my life cut short just to trim someone's tree. Please try not to worry."

Now that she was holding Clancy, Abby's heart started to slow its wild beat. "You always have your phone, don't you?"

"Uh-huh. Always."

"Will you promise that you'll call me before you climb any big trees and then call me when you're finished?"

She made a face, looking dismayed. "Oh, Abby, is that really necessary? It'll just worry you."

"Please, Clancy? Just until I get used to this." She hugged her even tighter and said, "I can't bear the thought of losing you."

"Okay. I'll let you know whenever I'm going to climb. I don't want you to worry about this though, okay? I promise I won't climb without telling you—but you have to promise not to worry."

"I'll do my best," Abby vowed, doubting her ability to comply completely but willing to try.

♣

When the crew was done for the day, Clancy and John went into the house and gave Abby an update. Then John looked at his daughter and said, "I'm going home, champ. How about you?"

"I think I'll hang around," she said, walking over to Abby and sliding an arm around her waist. "I think the homeowner needs a little more of my time."

John smiled at the pair and walked out, mumbling, "Twenty-five years in the business, and I'm still waiting for a kiss."

"He's so cute," Abby said, laughing. "Just like you."

"He wishes," Clancy said. "So…what does my homeowner want? Separate bedrooms again?"

"No!" Abby looked shocked at the suggestion. "I hardly slept at all!" Waiting a beat, she asked, "Did you sleep well?"

Clancy, thinking quickly, answered, "Not as well as I do when I'm with you."

"Then we're gonna take to take a few risks. Do you mind parking your truck a couple of blocks away?"

"No, I don't. I'll move it around so no one sees me more than once."

Abby sighed heavily. "I hate to make this seem so cloak-and-dagger, but I can't think of a better idea. Can you?"

"It's no big deal. All that matters is that we're together." They sat down after Clancy made sure she didn't have any pitch or sap on the seat of her shorts. They both tried to ignore the gaping hole in the landscape where the other half of the tree had been, but it wasn't possible. "I'm really sorry about your tree. I wish I could have trimmed it enough to make sure it could hold rain."

Abby had a sad, wistful look on her face. "It just looks so…" She trailed off, not able to put into words how misshapen and lopsided the formerly stately tree looked.

"It's a real loss. I hate to do things like that." She was quiet for a few moments and then said, "A family up in La Canada had planted a tree for each of their kids when they were born. They had five kids, but they'd only had room close to the house for two trees. Of course, they planted them too close, and they wanted me to make them stop growing or something!" She looked frustrated and a little angry. "It wasn't my fault they didn't know how to plant trees! They were totally pissed when I told 'em how much it would cost to move both of 'em and how they'd probably die anyway. So I cut them down and planted two new ones properly…and they stiffed me."

"They stiffed you?" Abby asked, amazed.

"Yep. Wouldn't pay. I could have taken a lien out on their house, but I decided not to. They were really upset that the older kids' trees were gone, and they took it out on me."

"That's ridiculous!" Abby fumed.

"Happens. People are very attached to their trees. Like you were."

"It wasn't just the tree, although that's part of it. It's having a family keepsake…"

"Amputated," Clancy said quietly. "I know it looks bad, but I was as conservative as I could be."

Abby patted her gently. "It's not your fault. I just have to remind myself that nothing's permanent. No matter how much we want it to be."

"Over the years we'll even it up. It'll be leggy…but that's not so bad. It won't be as good as it could have been if it'd been trimmed properly from the start…but it won't look ungainly. I promise."

"Over the years?"

"Yeah. I'm sorry it can't happen faster."

Abby kissed her cheek. "I just got chills when you said that like there wasn't a doubt you'd be here to do the trimming. I love how sure you seem."

Clancy stuck her feet out in front of herself and laced her hands behind her head. "Hey, it's easy to be confident when you have a big saw."

❧

Late that night, Clancy was snoozing lightly, her head pillowed on Abby's thigh. A long-fingered hand was sliding through her hair, relaxing her so thoroughly that she wasn't sure whether she was awake or asleep. Abby's free thigh was raised, and a biography of John Adams rested on it, the book pressing against her stomach so she could read one-handed, the pages turning quietly every few minutes, her calming massage never varying. One of the dogs hopped onto the bed, rousing Clancy, and she lifted her head to stare into sad-looking blue eyes gazing at her wistfully. Voice thick with sleep, Clancy rolled onto her back, asking, "What are you thinking about?"

"You," Abby said. She trailed her fingers through the soft blonde hair and said, "I wish I had a way to keep you, and every other person I love, safe from harm."

"Life sucks sometimes, doesn't it?"

"It does. I can usually relax and enjoy it—but then something happens to remind me of how fleeting it all is and how easily it can disappear." She kissed her fingers and pressed them to Clancy's full lips. "I'll be fine. I just need to remind myself that you know what you're doing and that there are millions of ways for you to get hurt. Focusing on one of them isn't productive."

"Abby, I can't promise that I'll live to be a hundred, but I'm sure gonna try. I know how hard Will's death was for you, and I promise that I'll never knowingly put myself at risk. I promise you that," she repeated.

Clancy sat up and leaned over to turn off the bedside lamp. Lying on her back, she patted her thighs, urging Abby to rest her head on them. "Come on. Time for a nice headrub." Abby scooted down on the bed and rested on Clancy, whimpering with delight when the strong, sure fingers began to slip through her hair.

"We're both whole and healthy and perfectly safe," Clancy whispered. "We can't know what tomorrow will bring. All we can do is live every moment of today. We have today, and that's all we need."

Chapter Thirteen

They were able to pull off the hidden-truck trick for two days, but on Wednesday, Abby held Clancy prisoner in bed. Clancy didn't fight too hard to get free, but their playing made her late, and she consequently ran the risk of having someone in the neighborhood see her hiking down the street. She finally extricated herself and ran for the shower, Abby scampering in right behind her.

By the time Clancy saw her truck in the distance, it was almost eight o'clock. She heard a car behind her slow. Then a voice called out, "Car trouble, *jefa?*"

Clancy turned to see Ramon's smirking visage. "No, I'm fine, Ramon. You'd better get going. Mrs. Markowitz doesn't like it when we're late."

"Just checking," he said. "This is a very dangerous neighborhood."

Clancy gave him a semiperturbed look, waiting for him to get to the punch line. "I heard there's a woman who's been sneaking into homes and kissing young girls," he said, laughing at his joke.

"I'm not a young…" she started to say and then realized that he thought she was dating Hayley. Stunned, she merely stood there, looking bewildered.

"No, you're not so young," he said, laughing. "You're old enough to go to jail!"

"You truly don't know what you're talking about, Ramon. But I can tell you that I have no interest in younger women. I'm here on business."

"Oh, *sí,*" he said. "Funny business."

When she arrived back at Abby's, she went in to tell her that Ramon was wise to them—with a twist. For some reason, this bothered Abby even more. "I don't want your men to think you'd date a young girl—especially since you'd probably be doing it behind my back! I hate that!"

"It's okay. I don't care what the guys think."

"I do." Abby sat down at the kitchen table and cradled her head in her hands. "I'm sorry I was so childish this morning. You would never have run into him if I hadn't been acting like a fool."

Clancy crouched down in front of her and gazed into her eyes. "Don't ever apologize for that. Having fun and being playful is part of what I love about being with you. I don't ever want you to change."

Abby let out a breath. "I hate to say it, but we're gonna have to sleep apart. This is making me too nervous. If Ramon saw you, I'm sure some of my neighbors have, too."

Clancy's shoulders slumped. "Could we squeeze both cars into the garage?"

"No, the house was built long before people had two cars. I suppose you could use the garage, but you couldn't take your truck out during the day…"

"No, that won't work. I have to be able to go check on my crew. We're taking down a big tree just a few blocks from here. I have to go over and see how it's going during my lunch break."

"You could use my car."

Clancy made a face. "I don't think you'd want me to load all of my tools into your tiny trunk. Plus my crew would wonder when I'd won the lottery."

Abby sighed in resignation. "I guess it won't work."

"No, I don't think so. But we can still spend our evenings together, can't we?"

Abby smiled at her, delighted by the hopeful tone in Clancy's voice. "Of course we can."

The work day went smoothly, and Clancy didn't have to involve herself much at all. But standing around watching her father's crew solder copper pipe together wasn't very stimulating. Her dad was at another site, so she needed to be present to answer questions or deal with problems. She could have gone into the house, but she knew that wasn't a great idea. The guys on the crew tended to take things into their own hands if someone in authority wasn't there, and she didn't want anything—even the smallest problem—to come up on this job. The only stimulating part of her day was the mad dash she made to the Markowitz house to check on the tree removal.

By four o'clock, she was nearly mad with longing to see Abby, but her lover wasn't home. Clancy wasn't sure where she'd gone, but she'd seen her leave right before their lunch break, making the afternoon drag even more.

She knew she should get into her truck and go home, but she didn't want to leave without having dinner together or at least kissing Abby goodbye. So she dawdled while her father's crew packed up, telling them goodnight while she was still inside the locked gate. Knowing that the dogs were missing their yard, she put them on their leashes and let them drag her up the hill to see what was happening to their playground. The girls spent a long time sniffing around, getting their noses unbelievably muddy. When they came back down, the pups wanted to go for a swim, and Clancy dutifully rinsed them off first, leaving a glop of mud on the lawn. When she unhooked their leashes, they both dived into the pool, looking like a couple of especially furry members of the swim team.

All three of them heard Abby drive up. The dogs stopped their play and treaded water for a second; then they put their ears back and scampered out of the pool, heading for the side gate, barking their heads off just in case someone else was driving Abby's car into the garage. They were sitting by the back door, dripping wet, when Abby entered the kitchen. "I have on nice slacks, girls. Let me put on my suit before I come outside." She waited a beat and then asked, "Does anyone else out there want a suit?"

"Sure," Clancy said. "I'm always up for a swim."

Abby emerged a few minutes later, surprisingly successful in her attempts to get the dogs to stay on the ground. "Paws," she said sternly. They whined a little and wagged their tails in frustration, but they managed to keep all four on the floor. To reward them, Abby threw one of their floating toys, and they both flew for it, creating a great splash when they did. "How about you?" Abby asked her lover. She stood close to Clancy and kissed her delicately. "How can I make you jump for joy?"

Clancy moved a little closer and then kissed Abby's neck, staying in the neighborhood while she slowly slid one of the straps of her suit down. She moved to the other side of her neck, kissing it lightly, lowering that strap, too. She started to kiss a line from Abby's throat down between her breasts, pulling the suit down inch by inch, revealing more skin.

By this time, Abby's fingers were working at the buttons on Clancy's shirt. Their lips met while they undressed each other, Clancy waiting a few beats for Abby to catch up. Once they were both naked, the blonde took Abby's hand and pulled her along while she ran for the deep end. They both jumped into the pool, making huge splashes and compelling the dogs to race to them to make sure they were safe.

Each dog swam from Abby to Clancy and back again, forming a tiny circle of lifeguards. "Why do they do that?" Clancy laughed when Athena put her muzzle right next to her mouth.

"I'm not certain. But someone who knows Newfoundlands told me that water dogs can smell certain chemicals on your breath that indicate if you're exhausted or afraid. So don't look too tired, 'cause I'm not sure what they'd do next!"

"Yeah, without a swimsuit, I don't think I'd want them to drag me to safety. They might grab this handy ring." She put a finger through her nipple ring and made a face.

"That's mine!" Abby swam over and dunked her head under the water to latch onto the ring playfully, making Clancy giggle.

Clancy put her arms and legs around her lover and then rested her head against her neck. "I like it here," she said, smiling when she saw how furiously Abby had to tread water to keep them both afloat. "Let's stay in the pool all night long."

❦

They stayed in until they were both wrinkled, but hunger finally compelled them to emerge from their aquatic playground. They had a simple dinner of French bread, some aged and fresh cheeses that Abby had picked up at the market, a bunch of sweet grapes, and a little galia melon—so sweet it was intoxicating. They each had a glass of wine, and when they'd finished, their hunger for food was sated, but they were both craving another form of satisfaction.

Abby was sitting on Clancy's lap, sweet suckling sounds coming from their passion-filled kisses. It was getting dark, and Clancy knew she had to leave then—or not at all. She put her hand on the back of Abby's head and patted it gently, making the brunette lift it and gaze at her with smoky eyes. "Make love to me," Abby said, her voice thick and slow. "Right here. Right now."

"Oooh, baby, I want to, but we decided I should go home. Your neighbors..." She trailed off helplessly.

"I don't care," Abby said. She grabbed the blonde and held her so tight it hurt. "I can't let you go. I can't."

"I...I feel like I have to say no," Clancy said. "I'm worried you'll be upset tomorrow morning when my truck's here."

Abby closed her eyes and let her head drop to Clancy's shoulder. She didn't say anything for a minute, and Clancy was worried that she was angry. But she eventually asked, "Where are your keys?"

"In my shorts. Why?"

"Don't move. I'll be back in a few minutes." She got up and grabbed Clancy's shorts, rooted through the pockets, and found the keys, dangling them for a moment to show she'd retrieved them. Clancy saw her go into the house but couldn't tell what else was happening.

Abby grabbed a pair of shorts and a shirt, buttoning it while the garage door lifted. She pushed the release button located just inside the garage and started to walk toward the opening gate. She was almost at the truck when her neighbor called out, "Hey, Abby!"

"*Shit!*" she muttered. "Hi, Steve." She kept walking, crossing to stand on the edge of his driveway. "How are things?"

"Good. Nothing to complain of. The bigger question is, how are things with you? We're all waiting to get back there and see what's going on in your yard."

Oh, wouldn't that be fun! "I'll invite the whole block over when we're finished."

He gave her a puzzled look and asked, "Have your plans changed? I see your architect over there all of the time."

Before Abby could reply, they both spotted a figure laboring up the road. "Oh, boy," Steve said, "here comes Marjorie. Can you fake a sudden illness?"

"I'm gonna turn tail and run," Abby said, but she hadn't gotten two steps away when the shrill tone of her downhill neighbor called out, "Oh, Abby! You're just the woman I've been looking for."

Making a face that only Steve could see, she said, "Hi, Marjorie. What's up?"

"What's up with you? We're all dying to know what's going on over there." She looked longingly at the open garage door. "Why don't you give us a peek?"

"No, no, now isn't a good time," Abby said, wracking her brain to think of a reason why it wasn't. "I just came out to get something for my architect. She's on the clock, you know. I'm always looking to save a few dollars."

Still looking at the door, Marjorie said, "Oh, you couldn't care too much about cost. Your architect's truck is in front of your house every day. We used an architect to put up our gazebo, and I don't think we saw him twice! Are you changing your plans every other day?"

"No, not really. She's just very hands-on," Abby said, glad for the darkness so her neighbors couldn't see her blush.

"You must be spending a fortune!" Marjorie said. She lowered her voice a little and said, "If you don't mind my asking, how much is this all costing you?"

Mentally hitting Marjorie on the head with a shovel, Abby gave her a tight smile and said, "I don't have the final figure yet, but I'm sure we'll come in within budget."

"I still think you made a mistake to hire that woman…I mean, girl," Marjorie said. "She doesn't look old enough to be out of college, much less have any experience. She's probably using your project as on-the-job-training."

"No, she's not," Abby said, her tone growing chilly. "I'm very happy with her. And she's not always working when she's here. She's a lot of fun to be around. We've become friends."

"Oh, Abby, this is the first thing you've done on your own. Don't mix business with pleasure. It's just not smart to fraternize with contractors."

Abby put her hand on Marjorie's arm and fixed her with an insincere smile. "I'm pretty good at picking my friends. Don't spend another minute worrying about me." She turned and started to walk back to her own home, adding a wave delivered over her shoulder. "Night, all."

As soon as she crossed the threshold, she closed the gate and lowered the door, mumbling to herself as she went back outside. She looked massively disappointed, and Clancy asked, "What's going on?"

"You're going home," she said, flopping down onto a chair. "My neighbors ganged up on me. I was gonna move your truck, but I couldn't! Steve from across the street called me over and asked what was going on that my landscaper was at my house so late."

Clancy put her hand over her eyes. "What did you say?"

"What could I say? He must think we're re-creating the Los Angeles aqueduct system back here!"

"Ooh, that sounds uncomfortable."

"It got worse. The neighborhood gossip saw us talking and made a beeline for us. She tried to weasel her way into the garage to take a peek."

"Shit! She would have gotten an eyeful!"

"Yeah, she sure would have. And the entire neighborhood would know about us by tomorrow afternoon."

"Really? Are you sure?"

"Positive. She started a Neighborhood Watch program just so she could have an excuse to know everyone's business. She broke up a functioning marriage when she told a man down the street that the electrician came by his house every Friday morning."

"God damn! That's hard to believe!"

"Honey, she's the reason I'm so paranoid! She's probably talked to Hayley's friend's mother once or twice already."

Clancy's eyes closed, and she sat down heavily. "Damn!" She put her head in her hands for a moment and then looked up at Abby. "But I'm kinda glad to know you had a good reason for being so paranoid."

Abby sat on her lap and touched her chin, moving her head so their eyes met. "I told you why I was being so careful. I distinctly recall telling you that one of Hayley's best friends lives just up the street."

Clancy nodded. "Yeah, I know, but I didn't think a kid would pay much attention one way or the other. I just thought that..." She trailed off, looking embarrassed.

"You thought what, honey? Tell me."

"I thought you were embarrassed. Embarrassed to have people know we were friends."

Abby wrapped her arms around her lover and kissed her on the head. "You know a lot about me, but there are some things you're just not getting." Clancy looked up and felt herself being pulled into Abby's eyes, dark and serious in the dim light. "I will never...ever...be embarrassed about you. I only care about Hayley or Trevor finding out before I can tell them. That's my only concern." She held Clancy's chin again and repeated, "My *only* concern."

Clancy put her head on Abby's shoulder, able to feel her pulse beating in her throat. "I feel stupid."

"You have no reason to feel stupid. We're just getting to know each other. I'm sure there are thousands of things I don't know about you."

Gazing at her, Clancy asked, "You know how much I want to be with you, don't you?"

Abby smiled at her. "I do. And I haven't lost my need for you. Can we go to your house?"

Brightening, Clancy said, "Sure! But it's really hot, and it's supposed to stay hot all night. I don't have air conditioning."

Abby gave her a surprised look. "You don't?"

"Huh-uh. I've got a little fan, but that's it."

Making a face, Abby said, "I can live with the heat. But I don't like to leave the dogs here alone. They get anxious when no one's home all night."

Laughing, Clancy said, "I don't think I wanna know how you found that out."

"Let me just say that I used to have a pair of leather moccasins that I loved."

"Okay," Clancy said, addressing the girls. "We're going to rough it, puppies. I'll show you how doggies in the working-class neighborhoods live."

Michael wasn't home, so all four of them went into Clancy's room as soon as they got to the apartment. Clancy brought a bowl of water with her and closed the door. The dogs looked confused, but they jumped up on the couch when Clancy sat down. "Do you have a bed?" Abby asked, looking around discreetly.

"Yeah. This is a futon," Clancy said. "It's not as nice as your bed, but I'm used to it." The room was hot—very hot—and she got up, turned on the pint-size fan, and then opened the window to let in some hot, dry air. "I'll open the bed so we can take off our clothes and hope to cool down." She shooed the dogs and then lowered the back of the couch, making a simple adjustment to turn it into a full-size bed.

"This is nice," Abby said, looking around the room. "It looks like you." There were a couple of framed pictures of flowers on the walls, both by Robert Mapplethorpe, one of Abby's favorite photographers. "I love your pictures. He was so gifted."

Clancy smiled. "He knew a sexy calla lily when he saw one." She grasped Abby's hand and pulled her close. "Wanna undress each other again?"

"Yes, but let's do it quicker this time. Now it's a life-saving measure."

"Maybe we'll feel better if we act like we're in my luxurious sauna."

"Oh, a little heat shouldn't stop us. We make a lot of our own."

"That's what I'm worried about." Clancy quickly helped her lover out of her clothes, noticing that Abby's chest was flushed pink. "We'll feel better when we lie down and have the fan directly on us."

Abby lay down and blew out a breath. The air that moved up and down her body was almost worse than no air at all. It was as dry as dust and smelled of pollution.

"Bad day for a Santa Ana, huh?" Clancy asked rhetorically.

"Yep. I've gotten so used to the wind blowing from the sea to the mountains that it takes me by surprise when it turns around and blows from the desert to the sea. And I'd like to complain to whoever's in charge. Santa Anas aren't supposed to happen in the summer."

"I'm with you," Clancy said. "It was a tough day today. I got a nosebleed from the air being so dry."

Abby put her hand on Clancy's belly, feeling the heat that rose from her. "Are you all right?"

"Oh, sure. My sinuses don't like dry air. I should probably live in Florida."

Abby's eyes opened wide. "Don't you dare think about moving!"

"I live exactly where I want to. Florida would be my...mmm...forty-eighth choice if I had to pick a state."

"What are forty-nine and fifty?"

"Arizona and Alaska. Arizona's dryer than California, and the growing season's too short in Alaska."

"Florida has a long growing season," Abby reminded her.

"Yeah, it does, but I hate humidity worse than dry weather. I'd just be a little wet spot on the ground if I worked in Florida."

"I feel like that might happen tonight." The dogs were lying on their sides, both of them on the wooden floor. They were panting heavily, but Abby knew they'd be fine. She wasn't so sure about her own body, however. "I guess I'm more used to air conditioning than I thought."

Clancy leaned up on one elbow and gazed at her thoughtfully. "I can't give you air conditioning, but I have a temporary solution. Wait right here." She was gone for no more than a minute, and when she returned, she carried a large bowl filled with ice cubes. "When I'm really hot, I cool my neck and wrists down. It helps."

Abby sat up and held her arms out. "I'll take anything you've got."

Clancy turned off the light and then kneeled behind her. "The first one's gonna feel pretty cold," she warned.

Abby flinched when the cube touched her neck, but it felt absolutely marvelous. "Ohh, baby, keep 'em coming." Clancy took the cube and ran it across her shoulders and then down her spine, watching it slip into the spaces between the vertebrae. Abby murmured encouragement, moving her body an inch or two to get the ice in the right spot.

Something about the way she was twitching on the bed started to heat Clancy up in a particular location, and she began to get a little more creative. She popped a cube in her mouth and started to place cold, wet kisses across Abby's shoulders. Those were met with a sexy moan as Abby pressed back against her. Soon, each hand held a piece of ice, and both hands were making abstract patterns on Abby's chest.

Before Clancy could blink, she was lying on her back with Abby rubbing a cube across her nipple ring and then down her belly. She let out a startled mew when Abby fiendishly slipped the ice between her legs, letting it melt as it slowly slid lower and lower.

Soon, they were rolling around on the futon like a pair of kids, ice everywhere. They were both laughing so helplessly that the dogs pried themselves from the floor to take a look. But when they saw there was nothing for them to eat, and no one looked like she needed help, they flopped back down.

Abby tried to wrestle Clancy onto her back again, and she was doing well until Clancy decided she wanted to be on top. Effortlessly, she flipped Abby over and then pounced on top of her, growling with satisfaction when Abby wrapped her legs around her waist. With her face a mere inch from Abby's, Clancy put another ice cube in her mouth and started to kiss her. They passed the melting cube back and forth for a long while, with Abby gently pressing her hips against Clancy's body while she gazed into her eyes.

It didn't take long for Clancy to yearn to move down, and she did, with one of the last cubes in her mouth and an impish expression on her face. Abby mewed when Clancy's cold lips touched her and then whimpered when the ice hit her clit. She twitched and tried to shift her hips, but Clancy held her tight, forcing her to stay right where she was. In a few seconds, she didn't want to get away, and Clancy felt a pair of hands clasp the back of her head—preventing her from pulling away. But the blonde had no intention of leaving her little nest, and they spent a good, long time learning how to cool off and heat up simultaneously.

Abby woke up a few minutes before the dawn broke. She spent a moment trying to orient herself, knowing that Clancy's head was on her chest and that a muscular thigh was holding her in place. But she couldn't figure out why she was so unbearably hot or why the bed felt so clammy. She opened her eyes and saw that they were in Clancy's room, and the evening came back to her. *Oh, you're a little devil, Ms. O'Connor,* she thought, recalling the way they'd played with each other deep into the night. *I had a ball, but now that the ice has melted, I'm miserable!*

She gently tickled Clancy's knee, causing her to mumble something and roll over, freeing Abby. She placed a foot on the floor and started to get up—only to fall right back down, her back screaming for mercy. She pulled her knees to her chest, and the spasm started to pass. Slowly, carefully, she rolled into an upright position and then scooted over so her feet could touch the floor. It took her another three or four minutes, but she finally stood up—or as far up as she could get. *Please don't wake up before I'm able to stand!* she pleaded silently. *Your gramma probably doesn't have this much trouble getting out of bed!*

Bent over, and stiffer than she'd been after running the LA Marathon, Abby put on Clancy's T-shirt and went to the bathroom. When she returned, Clancy's eyes were just opening. "Hi," she said. "Sleep well?"

Abby smiled back. "Like a dream."

They were in a hurry to get showered, take the dogs out, and get back to Abby's before the crew got there, so they bathed together. As with most of their dual endeavors, this one involved a lot of giggling, pinching, playful slapping, and kissing. Abby ran back to the bedroom clad only in a towel, with Clancy chasing her. They managed to get dressed without too many more interruptions, and when they went into the kitchen, Michael was making a pot of coffee. An attractive brunette was sitting at the kitchen table, obviously wearing one of Michael's shirts. "Hi," Clancy said, stopping so abruptly that Abby nearly ran into her. "I didn't know you were home."

"We got home late," he said. "Kelly, this is my roommate, Clancy, and her friend, Abby. Abby, Clancy—Kelly."

Kelly looked very tired and underdressed, and she didn't get up. "Hi," she said, giving the other women a slightly puzzled look. The dogs ran from Michael to her, sniffing rudely. "Were you all in there together?"

"Yeah," Clancy said without elaboration. "Gotta go. See you later."

"Bye," Michael said, and Kelly waved lazily.

When they hit the walk, Clancy said, "Sorry about that," making a face.

"I think we'd better think of another way. It's been a long time since I had to meet strangers before breakfast, and I rather like it that way."

"We'll figure it out. Somehow."

When they reached the house, Abby used her opener to open not only the gate, but also the garage. "Wait right here," she said, hopping out. She got into her car and backed it out, moving it to the small, paved pad next to the house. She motioned for Clancy to put her truck in the garage, so the landscaper did. Abby closed the garage door and walked up next to the driver's window. "You're not leaving until Hayley comes home," she said. "You can put your tools on the passenger seat and tell your crew whatever you want. They'll find out soon enough anyway."

"But I don't have any clothes!"

"You don't need any," Abby said, and then turned and walked into the house.

Chapter Fourteen

Abby relented and let Clancy go home for clothes after work, but she made her take the Lexus. "I don't want to have my neighbors see your truck going in and out of my garage. They won't even register that I'm not driving the Lexus."

"Okay, if you're sure."

"I am. Now hurry back here so we can have dinner and go to sleep in air-conditioned comfort."

Later that night, Clancy stayed outside and supervised the dogs as they made their final visit of the evening to the doggie bathroom. When they'd finished, the trio went upstairs, and Clancy spotted Abby emerging from the room at the end of the hall, carrying her toothbrush. Abby stopped and stared at Clancy for a moment. "I just realized I've never shown you my room. I…uhm…"

Clancy walked down the hallway and met her, taking her into her arms. "No big deal. You don't have to share everything with me."

"I just didn't think I could relax…"

"Abby, I don't think I'd be too crazy about sleeping in the room you and Will shared, either."

Abby searched Clancy's gray eyes and asked, "Are you sure I haven't offended you? I wouldn't hurt your feelings for the world."

"If you want to show me, that's fine. But if you don't, that's fine, too."

"Come on." Abby grasped her hand and led her back down the hallway. She opened the door, smiling when the dogs raced past her and leaped onto the bed, waiting for her to join them. "They think it's their room."

Clancy looked around the large, warm, inviting space and smiled at Abby. "Now, *this* looks like you." She noticed the plethora of framed photos, mementos of trips, and a number of dog toys lying on the floor next to a very large, seemingly brand-new dog bed. "It's nice in here." She gazed at the pictures of Abby and Will, an abbreviated chronicle of their entire married life. One picture in particular caught her eye. A significantly darker-haired Abby had her hands laced behind Will's neck, and his hands were on her waist. They were kissing, and both were smiling widely while their lips touched. Abby was elegantly dressed in a sexy black sequined dress, and Will looked dashing in a well-tailored tuxedo. They looked very happy to be in each other's arms and very comfortable with each other physically.

"That was our tenth anniversary," Abby said. "My parents threw a lovely party for us. Our twentieth would've been the next big one, but we weren't going to make a big deal out of it. We thought we'd have a real blowout for our twenty-fifth." She let out a wistful sigh that said more than any further comment could have.

Clancy ran her finger around the edge of the frame, contemplating the picture for a few moments. "I'm so glad that you had this. It makes me feel warm all over to know that you were so in love for such a long time."

"I was," she said, her voice very soft. She stared, unblinking, at the picture that Clancy held in her hands. Clancy stood very still, watching the emotions flicker across her lover's face.

Finally, Abby's eyes closed, and she said, "I'm still in love with him. His death didn't change my feelings. Our relationship will always be the same. And he'll always be exactly as he was the day he died." She gazed at Clancy with watery eyes and said, "I'll catch him and pass him—he'll always be forty-nine—still grousing about the big fiftieth birthday party I was planning for him."

She wrapped her arms around Clancy and cried softly, her body shuddering as the smaller woman held her tightly. "I miss him so much," she murmured. "But it helps…it really helps more than you'll ever know that you let me talk about him and how I feel about him." She drew back, wiped her eyes, and said, "People get tired of hearing you talk about your dead husband. If you don't suck it up and act like nothing happened, they stop inviting you places. A lot of people avoid me to this day. Seeing me reminds them of Will, and they don't want to think about the fact that he's gone."

"You don't ever have to censor yourself around me. I'm very, very interested in how you feel—how you've dealt with this—how you've managed to go on." Clancy held her lover at arm's length and looked deeply into her eyes. "I mean that."

"Thanks." Abby shook her head and brushed her hair from her eyes. "I've been thinking about him so much these days. I'm sure that's partly because of…us," she added softly. "I'm sure it'll pass soon."

"I know it's hard for you, but don't feel like you have to bottle things up on my account. It's hard for me to see you in pain, but it's the only way to get it out."

"I know. Lord, I know. My grief counselor told me that so many times that I have it imprinted on my brain. I guess I thought that over time, I'd get the feelings out, and they wouldn't jump up and bite me at the most inopportune moments."

"Give it time. This'll settle down." She looked at Abby contemplatively for a moment and said, "Why don't I keep my things in the guest room and use that bathroom? You keep your toothbrush here. That way, we can both have a little space. I don't want you to change your routine."

"Okay. That would be really nice."

Clancy tucked an arm around Abby's trim waist and said, "Let's go to bed." As they left the room, the dogs blew past them, and Clancy closed the door firmly, hoping to leave the memories behind them—for at least one night.

Abby sat on the bed, smiling as she watched Clancy put her clothes into the empty dresser. "Do you get a discount when you buy six pairs of the same shorts?"

"These," Clancy said, shaking a pair at her, "are the world's most perfect shorts. Six pockets, wide belt loops, rubber buttons on the fly, quick-drying nylon/cotton blend, roomy in the crotch. And they come in five colors."

"Clancy, those are five very slight variations on the same color."

"No way. These are radically different colors. I've got brown, tan, green, beige, and chalk."

Abby shook her head and walked over to the dresser. "You've got khaki times five. Luckily, they look adorable on you."

"I make up for my monochromatic wardrobe by having very, very colorful socks and underwear. Wanna see?"

Abby peeked into the drawer where Clancy had neatly laid out her things. "Well, that is certainly a riot of color." Clancy, indeed, had some of the most colorful panties that Abby had ever seen. No two were alike, and each one was louder than the next. Stripes, polka dots, plaids, zigzag, tie-dyed, and animal prints vied for supremacy in the drawer. Abby's eyes moved from the panties to the wild socks, and she commented, "I'm going to have to put on my sunglasses to do your laundry."

Clancy looked up at her and gave her a gentle hug. "You don't have to do my laundry. I'm very self-sufficient."

"I want to. You work hard all day. When you're finished, I don't want you to have to worry about anything. Let me take care of you for a little while. Please?"

"I would've thought you had someone doing that kind of thing for you. Why don't you have any help?"

"We never have." Abby lay down, letting out a tired sigh when her body relaxed against the mattress. "When we were newlyweds, we discussed how we wanted to spend our money. We'd already decided that I probably wouldn't work after I graduated—since we wanted to have children right away. Will sat down with his little spreadsheet and showed me how much it would cost to have someone clean the house every week. Then he projected that out over one year, two years, and so on. We decided that we'd rather save that money and use it for our vacation fund—so that both of us could enjoy it. That money took us to Europe three times," she said, smiling warmly. "Even later, when we could easily afford it, it seemed like a waste of money. It took me a while to learn how to cook and clean, but now I think of my household tasks as my job—and I like my job."

"If you want to add my grimy clothes to your job description, I'll gladly accept your offer."

"I do. I want to spoil you a little while you're here."

When Clancy had finished unpacking, she walked over to the closed door. "Do you normally let the dogs sleep with you?"

"Yes, but it won't kill them to sleep in the hall for a while."

"Can we let them back in? I hate to throw them out of their home."

"If that would make you happy, feel free." Clancy opened the door, and the elated pair flew into the room, sliding across the bed to bang into Abby. "Come here, you," the laughing woman called, crooking a finger at Clancy.

Impetuously, Clancy ran across the room and jumped onto the bed, sliding just as the dogs had. When she banged into her, Abby wrapped her arms around her and squeezed her tight. "You are the sweetest woman I've ever had the pleasure to know."

"Doggies need love, too."

"Yes, they do. It'll be interesting to see how they react to our being…intimate."

"They were fine at my apartment, but they were too hot to want to snuggle. If they don't behave, a little time in the hall won't kill 'em," Clancy said, chuckling softly. "Although tonight, I'd love to wrap my arms around you and go right to sleep."

"So soon?" Abby asked. "You already want to sleep instead of make love? Which one of us is fifteen years older?"

"I've been telling you that you have more energy than I do. I wasn't kidding! But cuddling can be nice too, can't it?" Clancy lay down and opened her arms. Abby gladly snuggled into her warm embrace, laying her head upon her chest.

"This is very, very nice."

"It is," Clancy said. The dogs dug and pulled at the covers for a moment; then they both settled down, Athena against Clancy's thighs, Artemis snuggled tightly against Abby's shins. "Blissful," the blonde murmured as sleep captured her.

The soft trill of an alarm woke Abby at six, and she opened her eyes just enough to try to find its source. Her eyes finally landed on the dresser, where Clancy's watch lay next to her wallet. It didn't seem like the device was going to stop on its own, so she lifted Clancy's sleep-heavy arm and leg from her body and slipped out of bed as stealthily as possible. Turning off the insistent little alarm, she turned to go back to bed for a few minutes, but when her eyes landed on Clancy's sleeping form, she stopped abruptly and gazed at her for a few long minutes.

The blonde was wearing just a goldenrod tank top, and the bright color complemented her golden skin perfectly. Her hair was attractively mussed, with several of the longer strands covering her eyes. Pink lips were slightly open, revealing just the edges of her white, even teeth. Both dogs were curled up against her back, their limbs so entwined that only their coat textures differentiated them. The trio looked sweet and peaceful, and Abby thought rather gratefully how seamlessly Clancy was able to fit into her life. *The pups are always friendly,* she thought, *but they only show this kind of trust and affection with really good people. There wouldn't be a problem in the world if it were just me and the dogs—but it's not. We have to make sure the kids can accept this.* Shaking her head to dispel the intrusive thoughts, Abby let Clancy's peaceful countenance soothe her for a minute, letting her eyes linger on her lovely face.

Her affectionate feelings were mingled with a sexually charged magnetic pull that demanded she stop watching her lover sleep and join her. As she slid into bed, Clancy automatically molded her body to hers, drawing her leg up to drape over Abby's hip. Abby's hand wandered down the muscular back, tracing some of the more defined muscles through the cotton and then lingering upon the bare, smooth globes of her ass. *Somebody needs to wake up*, she thought decisively, feeling an unmistakable throb between her legs. Her fingers tickled between Clancy's soft cheeks, and she felt Clancy start to move against her.

Slipping forward a few inches, she flicked her fingers back and forth, drawing a gentle purr from Clancy's waking body. Suddenly, a warm, wet mouth was attached to her neck, and the purr grew louder. *Oh, it's gonna be a good day*, Abby thought as a tingle of sensation skittered down her spine.

After her very pleasant wake-up call, Clancy haphazardly maneuvered Abby into the shower, banging into walls and doors as they kissed hungrily. She spent as much time washing all of Abby's nooks and crannies as she did performing her own ablutions, but she wasn't complaining in the least. She had her pressed up against the tile, Abby's cheek resting on the warm surface while Clancy rubbed up against her slick back. "I think someone is definitely a morning person," Clancy whispered into her ear.

"Mmm-hmm," Abby moaned sensually. "It's my favorite time." She turned, draped her arms around Clancy's neck, and said, "We got into the habit when the kids were little. We were always too tired at the end of the day to even think about being sexual—but if we got up early enough, the kids never disturbed us. Believe me, that's a requirement for good sex. Nothing ruins a mood faster than hearing 'Mommy! Mommy!' when your partner is sucking on your nipples. Do you like mornings, too?" She dipped her head and offered Clancy a slow, probing kiss.

"Uhm...what was the question?"

"Never mind," Abby grinned, bending to suck a rigid nipple into her mouth. "You've already answered my question once, and you're about to answer it again."

Clancy poked her head into the house in the late afternoon to ask Abby to come out and see what they'd accomplished. "The guys are just packing up for the week. Let's go sit outside so I can impress you with all of the details of our accomplishments."

She pointed at the refrigerator, and Abby took her cue and pulled out a beer for her, smiling at Clancy's nod. After a few minutes of the detailed description of nearly every shovel of earth that had been turned, they sat down on the teak settee and enjoyed the late-afternoon breeze. "So Dad's crew is finished for the time being. My guys will come back on Monday—or as soon as the boulders are delivered. We'll get them in and fill all the soil back into the trenches. Then we can test the system. We're really moving now."

Clancy put her arm along the settee's back, and Abby wrinkled her nose and sniffed a few times. "I like the way you smell when you've been working all day."

Clancy sniffed herself ostentatiously and looked at Abby skeptically. "You're joking, right?"

"No. Not at all. I'm used to how men smell when they sweat, and I've got to tell you—*you* are a very welcome change. You have a definite scent, but it's earthy and musky—not unpleasant in the least."

"Well, thanks. I'm very attracted to the way you smell, too. Maybe that's part of the chemistry, huh?"

"Perhaps. Did you have a good day? I mean, I'm impressed with what you've accomplished, of course, but did you enjoy yourself?"

"I did. Things went well all around today." Reaching for Abby's hand, she ran her thumb all around the soft skin of her palm. "Are things settling down a little for you now? You seem pretty happy." She was looking at her tentatively, and Abby squeezed her hand and nodded.

"I'm feeling great. Really content."

"Uhm...I know you're not crazy about talking about things until they've jelled in your mind, but I keep thinking that the other shoe is about to drop, and it's scaring me."

"Other shoe?" Abby stared at her blankly. "I don't have a clue what you're talking about."

Clancy shook her head in frustration, knowing that she wasn't expressing herself very well. "Okay. Here's the deal. When we're together—like now—things seem totally natural between us...like we've known each other for years."

Abby nodded, encouraging her to continue.

"But sometimes, I'm out here working, and I get struck by a real sense of panic." She gazed at Abby thoughtfully and said, "I'm afraid that it's going to hit you, and you're going to freak—ya know?"

"Freak?"

"Yes. Freak." Clancy was further frustrated, and her furrowed brow showed it. "About everything! All of my friends have always warned me about falling in love with a straight woman. It never dawned on me that having lesbian sex would seem like a nonissue for you. Actually, that's the only thing that isn't in flux!"

"Well, how should I react?" she asked. "I've never been in this position before."

"That's my point! I don't know anyone who's ever done something like this. I don't think you do, either. There are so many issues—your kids, your parents, your friends, your nosy neighbors. Those people matter! And they're gonna have opinions about me. Some of 'em aren't gonna be enthusiastic about us being together. I know that as clearly as I know anything."

"Oh, Clancy," she murmured, taking the smaller woman in her arms. "Don't spend your time worrying about things like that." Pulling away, she placed soft kisses all over Clancy's face, grimacing when she pulled away. "Dirt," she said, wiping at her tongue.

"Always a hazard with me."

Abby ruffled her hair a little and said, "Small price to pay. Now let me tell you a few things—about me and about my circumstances." She took in a breath and began. "I only have so much energy. About half of my energy is just trying to keep up…do you know what I mean?"

Clancy nodded and patted her gently. "I assumed you'd have feelings like that, even though you haven't talked about them much."

"Yeah. Just because I don't talk about my feelings a lot doesn't mean I don't have 'em." She leaned over and placed a delicate kiss on Clancy's cheek. "I don't feel guilty about having sex or being sexual with a woman. But I have some guilt that's focused on the fact that I'm going on—I'm being loved and touched again—and Will's still dead. He'll never get to experience pleasure like we've been enjoying. That makes me so sad." She wiped at the tears that seemed to always lurk just underneath the surface and smiled sadly. "I wish he were here, Clancy, but then I wouldn't have this with you." She leaned forward and kissed her tenderly. "I'm so enjoying sharing this with you."

"I am, too," Clancy murmured, adding a few kisses of her own.

"We're agreed, then," Abby smiled. "Now, like I said, half of my energy is going toward dealing with those feelings and how it feels to fall in love again. The other half is focused on worrying about how my kids will handle this—especially Hayley. They're both open-minded, but having a friend who's gay is one thing…"

Clancy saw the teasing sparkle in her eyes and tenderly kissed the soft lids. "This is probably a pretty unique circumstance."

"So—half of my mind is on myself and Will and us, and the other half is on my kids. What I've decided to do is let myself have this time—without letting any of those worries ruin this for us." She scooted around a little so she was facing Clancy. "I haven't had a hell of a lot of fun in the last few years. I deserve this—and I'm going to take it. When Hayley comes home, we're going to have our plates full trying to decide what to do about this—but until then, I want to enjoy you in every way."

"I can do that," Clancy said. She was obviously trying to look confident, but her worries were still evident in the lines on her face.

"I don't mean that in a selfish way," Abby insisted. "But I guess it is selfish. I want to put those worries away, and I can do that. But if you can't…I want you to tell me."

"I…I think I can."

"You don't look very certain," Abby said, trying to ease the lines that had formed between her lover's brows.

"I'm…not," Clancy said, her shoulders falling dejectedly. "I'm worried about what's gonna happen. What if Hayley totally freaks about this? What if your parents are upset? What if your friends don't approve?"

Abby closed her eyes and sat quietly for a few moments. "I don't know how we'll deal with that. I truly don't know." Bringing Clancy's hand to her lips, she said, "But we *will* deal with it. Somehow." She touched Clancy's cheek so that they were looking into each other's eyes. "Does that reassure you?"

"A little. But I'm still worried that you're gonna regret this—even if your kids don't give you a hard time. It just seems like such a leap!"

"The lesbian thing?"

"Yes!" Clancy said, frustration showing again.

"That's really the least of our troubles, baby."

"But that's the one thing I've heard from my friends ever since I came out. Straight women will break your heart. It's the lesbian mantra!"

"We don't have to adopt anyone's mantra. Let me tell you a few things. I don't want to sound like I'm boasting, but I'm a very, very open-minded person. I don't think of people by category. I really try not to lump people together based on some characteristic, you know?"

"Yeah, I know. That's one of the things I admire about you."

"Thanks. I guess what I'm trying to say is that how people categorize their sexuality doesn't affect how I feel about them—so it doesn't affect how I feel about myself very much, either. I was completely satisfied with my sexual orientation for my whole life. I never longed for a woman's touch…although I would have been fine with being with a woman if things had turned out that way. But now that I've experienced being loved by a woman, I see how different it is and how it reaches a different part of me. It's very rewarding—and very pleasing, and I'm very glad that we're sharing this."

"So you're saying that you really don't think you'll freak?"

"No, I don't. For one thing, I'm not that kind of person. I know what tragedy is. I know what it's like to have my whole world turned upside down. I lived through that—and I still wake up most mornings happy to be alive. Worrying about the sex of the person I'm being intimate with is such a minor issue in the scheme of things. It's really too inconsequential to bother with." She gave Clancy another lingering kiss and said, "I'm really open-minded about sex. Will and I weren't bored in the least, and that was after twenty years of monogamy. I like to experiment and try new things. My habit was never to say no unless I'd tried it. This is another new experience—a very, very pleasurable experience, I might add."

"I like the way you think," Clancy said, wrapping her arms tightly around Abby's body. "One more good reason to have an experienced, mature lover."

"Hey, we've got to have some benefits."

"You have more benefits than I can count."

"Speaking of counting, I can almost count your ribs. You go shower while I make dinner; then we can talk some more, if you want to."

Clancy stood and stretched her body out. "Nope. I'm finished. You've allayed all of my fears—for a while, at least. We'll chill until Hayley comes home."

"It's a deal," Abby said, drawing Clancy to her and pulling her shirt from her pants. Several warm, lingering kisses along Clancy's abdomen made both of them forget their agenda; they stumbled into the living room and spent the next hour showering each other with affection.

Sated and happy, Abby slipped her clothes back on and sat down in the den. Dialing her parents, she waited for a moment, pleased when her daughter answered. "Hi, baby. How's everything going?"

"Hi, Mom," Hayley said brightly. "Everything's great. The weather's really warm and sunny, and I spent most of the day going on a long bike ride. Gramps has a really cool recumbent bike, and I rode the wheels off it."

"I don't even know what that is, but if your grandfather bought it, I'm sure it's very high-tech."

"Yeah. Sometimes I forget how cool Gram and Gramps are, but then I hear people at school talking about how their moms and dads don't know how to use computers! Isn't that weird?"

"A little, but some people don't like change. Luckily, your grandparents aren't like that. They're never afraid to try new things."

"Yeah. Gramps has the whole house wired for Wi-Fi. I can surf from anyplace!"

"Are you having fun, honey? Keeping busy?"

"Yeah. I'm doing good. They're both working on things, so they give me some space. I've been going to the beach every day…you know…hanging out."

"Have you met anyone to hang out with?"

"Yeah. I met a guy from California who's visiting his family this week. He works for an energy-alternatives foundation in San Francisco."

"Oh. How old is this guy?"

"I think he's about twenty-five or twenty-six. He's pretty cool, Mom. We've been hanging out with his brothers at the beach. They're a lot of fun."

"What's his name?"

"Alexander," she said, pronouncing each syllable distinctly. "Isn't that a great name? He calls himself Alex, but I think Alexander sounds cooler."

"That's a very great name," Abby said, smiling to herself. "Have you seen each other in the evening?"

"Yeah. We went out clubbing last night. His family's been coming here for years, and he knows a lot of people. It was great."

"I'm glad you're having fun, honey. Alexander sounds like a nice guy."

"Oh, he is. Really smart, funny, and sweet. And he has the most wonderful face. Strong, but sometimes he looks almost pretty." She sounded like she was talking about a Greek god, and Abby had a feeling that her little girl was smitten once again.

"Are you going to be ready to come home? I'd hate to have you miss out on the fun. I'll change your ticket for you if you want to stay longer." Abby was shocked at the words that were coming from her mouth. She realized she was trying to talk Hayley into staying away—just so she and Clancy could have more time together. She felt like hitting herself on the head with the phone, but Hayley reassured her.

"No, I'm ready. Alexander leaves on Sunday, so I'm ready to leave, too. I might stop and see him before I go back to Santa Cruz, though. If that's okay."

"We can probably work something out, since we have some time to change your reservations. How do you feel about coming home?"

"Good. Why?"

"Why? You were more than a little upset when you left here, Hayley."

"Oh. Right. I was kind of a bitch, wasn't I?"

"I wouldn't use that word, but you weren't showing your best side."

"I'll apologize to Clancy...and mean it this time. I treated her like shit, Mom. And she didn't deserve it."

"Not many people deserve that, honey. I'm sure she'd appreciate it."

"Maybe I'll work with her again. I could use some extra money."

"Mmm...I don't think that'll work out. They've mostly finished the water feature, and I think things are pretty technical right now."

"Oh! They've done that already?"

"Uh-huh. You'll be amazed at how much is finished." She waited a beat and then said, "If you'd like a job, I could ask around."

"I would," she said. "I know I'll only be home for a few more weeks, but I don't want to lie around and do nothing. Alexander was telling me that he doesn't have enough hours in the day to do all the things he has to do. I'm not living up to my potential, Mom."

Abby smirked to herself, wondering how long it would be before Hayley was urging her to trade in her Lexus for an electric car.

Chapter Fifteen

On Saturday morning, Abby extricated herself from Clancy's embrace and headed for her bathroom. She was scheduled to meet her usual partners—Ellen, Pam, and Maria—for their nine o'clock tennis match, and she knew she'd play poorly if she didn't have a decent breakfast.

After her shower, she tiptoed past the guest room, hoping to allow Clancy to sleep as long as possible. Seconds later, she was met in the kitchen by a rumpled but smiling young woman who was in the middle of toasting a bagel. "What'll it be? I could make you an omelet, or eggs any style, or cereal…"

"Aren't you just the sweetest thing," Abby said, giving her cook a warm kiss. "I thought you were still asleep."

"Nah. The girls and I want to see you off. We can go back to bed if the mood strikes us."

"You need to get your sleep when you work as hard as you do. You really should catch a few more hours when I leave."

"I might. When will you be home?"

"Mmm…depends. We usually have lunch after we play, but I don't think I want to be gone that long."

"Go ahead. Really. I know you enjoy seeing your friends. Don't rush home on my account. Actually, I could spend the morning visiting a client or two. Saturdays are the best times to catch most people at home."

"All right. We'll have lunch…same as always." She draped her arms around Clancy's neck and said, "I'd like a bagel with a little peanut butter and some granola. I need some protein before I play."

"Coming right up. I'll watch you eat, and then take a little nap and get some work done."

Abby watched her prepare the simple meal, sipping a cup of coffee as Clancy moved around the kitchen. "I really appreciate that you don't begrudge me my time with my friends. They mean a lot to me."

"I'm not that kind of person. I need time for myself, too, so I really do understand the pull."

"We're a pretty compatible pair, Ms. O'Connor," Abby said, her lips quirking into a grin.

"Couldn't agree more," Clancy said, delivering breakfast and a sweet kiss.

❦

Ellen Chenoweth wiped her face repeatedly, finally bending over the sink to splash cold water on herself. "Whose bright idea was it to switch partners?" she grumbled. "I swear you ran my legs off, Abby. Never again, sweetie! I'm on your side of the net, or I'm going home!"

"Now you see what we have to put up with," Pam said. "It's nice to get a breather."

Maria gave her lover a lethal stare, and Pam tried to extricate herself from the hole she had dug. "I didn't mean that you're an inferior player, honey; I just meant that…uhm…Abby's a little taller, and her serve comes in at a funny angle…and…"

"That's okay, Pamela," Maria said archly. "I know exactly what you meant—but since it's the truth, I can't really complain. Abby could kick our respective asses in singles. Hell, she could probably beat any two of us *as* a single!"

"Enough!" Abby didn't generally mind being complimented, and she *was* a far superior player, but she hated to have it brought up too frequently. "I play more than you guys do, and I've played longer than any of you—it stands to reason that I'd be sharper."

"Honey," Ellen drawled, "I could pitch a tent on that court and play every moment that I wasn't sleeping, and I still couldn't beat you. Face facts, Abby, you rock!"

"Somebody's kids are home from school," Abby teased. "You only use colloquialisms when you hear them from the boys."

"Yes, I revert to their ages when they're home," Ellen agreed. "And of course, they both need a car today, so I can't stay for lunch."

"That's okay. We'll catch you next week," Abby said.

"Oh! I almost forgot! I have a new man for you, Abby," Ellen said, bursting with enthusiasm. "He's a lawyer with the Federal Exchange Commission, and Neal says that he's a real find. He's just getting back on his feet after a nasty divorce, but luckily, his ex-wife is a surgeon, so she didn't suck him dry." Smiling brightly, Ellen added, "No kids, either." Dropping her voice, she said, "I think he has a low sperm count."

Be still, my heart, Abby thought. She shook her head briefly and said, "Keep him on hold, Ellen. I've… uhm…met someone…and I want to see where it goes before I accept any more blind dates."

"Tell me all about him," Ellen demanded, Maria and Pam looking on interestedly.

"Mmm…I don't want to jinx it," Abby said. "Give me a few weeks, and if we're still together, I'll tell all."

Ellen gave her a long, appraising look. "I wasn't going to say anything, but you've got a spring in your step that I haven't seen in years. This guy must be good for you."

"We'll see," Abby said, trying not to lie too much.

"One way or the other, we'll get you fixed up, Abby," Ellen said. "I won't stop until you're married again. You're too fabulous a woman to be alone when you don't want to be."

After a round of goodbyes, the remaining threesome left the locker room for the outdoor restaurant. They were seated under a large umbrella, idly observing a good singles match, when Maria said, "Ellen's right, you know, Abby. You have a spark in you that's been absent for far too long. I know you don't want to talk about this guy, but I want you to know that we both hope this works out."

Abby gave her friends a shy smile and lowered her eyes to pick at her Cobb salad for a moment. "I...uhm...would like to talk about it a little. It's kinda complicated, so I didn't want to get into it in the locker room, but if you're interested..."

"Yes, we are!" Pam said, her eyes flickering between her partner and Abby.

"Okay," Abby said slowly, trying to figure out where to start. "Uhm...like I said...it's complicated..."

"He's not married, is he?" Maria blurted out, drawing a scolding look from Pam.

"Do you do that at work, honey?" Pam asked dryly. "I can't imagine that's good for business. Aren't psychiatrists supposed to be kinda quiet?"

"I'm perfectly well behaved when I'm with a patient," she sniffed. "But I'm not with a patient now, so I can be as abrupt as I want. Right, Abby?"

"Right, Maria. I don't mind your direct style one bit—as a friend, that is. If my psychiatrist did that, I'd fire her!"

"You neither have, nor need, a psychiatrist," Maria scoffed. "You just need to get laid with some regularity by a man who can appreciate a wonderful woman."

Abby flushed deeply and cleared her throat. "Well, that's where you're off, Doc. I've been being laid quite spectacularly—but it isn't by a man."

Only the plop of the ball hitting the court could be heard for several moments as the women tried to get their minds around Abby's announcement. "You're sleeping with a...with a woman?" Pam asked, her voice an octave higher than normal.

"I am," Abby said. "I don't know quite what I was thinking of the first time, but since then, it's...she's...become quite addictive."

"What does Hayley think about this?" Maria gasped.

"Oh, I must not have mentioned that Hayley is up in Maine for her annual visit. She's going to be gone for another week. She doesn't know—and I'm not sure how, or when, to tell her."

"Well, I have an opinion," Maria said. She looked at Abby for a moment and said, "I wouldn't tell her unless you're serious about this woman. I think it's bad for Hayley to learn too much about your sex life—unless it's going to affect her in the long term. Now, if you're serious about this, and you want to have a relationship with her—then by all means, you should tell Hayley and Trevor. But not until then."

Abby nodded agreeably. "That's what I thought."

"I told you that you didn't need a psychiatrist," Maria said.

"I'm gonna need one if I don't get some details!" Pam burst out. "Who is she, how did you meet her, have I ever dated her...?"

Abby smiled at the teasing and told the tale. "She's the landscape architect who's been working on my house. Little did I know that you could obtain a perfectly delightful lesbian lover by home delivery," she said. "Now, I can't guarantee it, but I doubt that you've dated her, Pam. She's only been out for twelve years, and you've been with Maria for twenty. So if you have dated her, neither Maria nor I want to know about it."

"What's her name?" Maria asked. "We must know her if she's a professional in the San Gabriel Valley."

"Clancy O'Connor," Abby said, smiling when two blank expressions greeted the name. "I've gotten the impression she doesn't do a lot of work in the lesbian community. But I'd really like her to get some contacts. She's very talented."

"Sounds like she's talented in many areas," Pam said, grinning lasciviously.

Maria slapped at her and warned, "Get your mind out of the gutter, honey. Abby doesn't want to talk about the gory details…do you, Abby?" she asked hopefully.

"Not many of them," Abby said. "But I will say that she's a wonderful person, and she's been very patient and gentle with me. She doesn't pressure me, and she's even allowed me to clam up like I normally do when I have things on my mind."

"She sounds like a prize," Maria said. "I'm really surprised we don't know her, though. I thought we knew everyone."

"Apparently not," Abby said. "One lesbian slipped under the radar."

"How are you handling the…uhm…lesbian thing?" Pam asked. "This is a pretty big change for you."

"I don't know," Abby sighed. "I'm trying just to live for the day and worry about it tomorrow."

"I think that's a song," Maria said thoughtfully.

"I'm not above borrowing my life-changing decisions from songs," Abby said. "I'm just having a marvelous time. I feel loved and cared for and desired and lusted after for the first time in five years, and I'm going to do my best to make this work. I deserve love, damn it!"

"Hear, hear," Pam said, patting Abby on the hand. "You do deserve it, and as long as you're happy, we're happy for you."

They finished their meals with more questions about Clancy and the job she was doing for Abby. Eventually, Abby stretched and said, "I've got to get home to Clancy."

"She's at your house?" Maria asked, eyes widening.

"Yes," Abby said, somewhat defensively. "I trust her. I'm quite sure she's not stealing the good silver."

"Oh, I didn't mean that! I'm just wondering why she's staying with you—I mean—it's so soon…"

"Aren't you the people who always ask, 'What does a lesbian do on a second date?' I believe 'Rent a U-Haul' is the correct answer."

"Yes, but…"

"But nothing, Maria. Hayley is only going to be gone for two weeks. I decided that I wanted to keep Clancy as my love slave for the entire time Hayley is gone.

She's not homeless—she's not a drug addict—she's not trying to take advantage of me, so why shouldn't I have her at my house?"

"Uhm…I can't think of a reason in the world," the psychiatrist said, smiling.

🌿

Abby looked antsy to leave, so they urged her to go and stayed behind to sign the check. "So what's your diagnosis?" Pam asked.

"Hard to say. This is very impulsive behavior for Abby—but that's the only thing that worries me. It honestly doesn't surprise me that much that she'd be drawn to a woman; she's certainly not very hung-up sexually. I'm just worried about the suddenness of the whole thing. That's not like her."

"No, it isn't, but she sure seemed happy. She reminded me of how she was when we first met her."

"You know, she did," Maria mused. "I wonder who this mystery woman is? Maybe she's like Abby—coming off of a long marriage or something. That would explain why she's only been out for twelve years."

"Maybe she's not very out…you know, kinda semicloseted?"

"Yeah. That's the only reasonable explanation. If she was very out, we'd know her. We need to meet this woman. Maybe we know her but don't know her name."

"Hmm…but what if she's not out? That worries me a little," Maria said. "A woman in her late forties who's still in the closet might have some issues about being a lesbian. That might be hard for Abby to deal with—you know how open she is about things."

"Well, there's one way to find out what the story is," Pam said. "Ask them over for dinner!"

🌿

When Abby returned to the house, she was a little surprised to see Clancy's truck in the garage, and she had to smirk at herself when her heart picked up a beat. *If I start doodling 'COC loves ATG,' I'm going to voluntarily commit myself!*

The dogs didn't run out to greet her, which was also a little odd, but the whereabouts of the threesome was resolved when Abby walked into the kitchen and looked out the window. Clancy was lying on one of the pool floats, clad in just a long-sleeved T-shirt. Her arms were stretched out to the sides, each hand holding onto another float, each float occupied by a very content-looking dog. Abby started to laugh so hard that her sides ached. She slid the door open, still laughing. Three sets of eyes blinked at her, but only the gray eyes showed much enthusiasm about her arrival. "Don't just stand there; grab a float and get in here. My arms are tired!"

"How on earth did you get those beasts up on those floats? I know it wasn't easy!"

"That's an understatement," Clancy said, chuckling. "But they kept swimming out and trying to get on with me—and I didn't want those sharp claws on my bare legs. Since I got them settled, they've been blissfully happy."

Abby stripped off her clothing and surprised Clancy by diving in completely naked and swimming up to her, a beaming grin covering her face. "I wanna get on your float too." She looked as happy as Clancy had ever seen her, and Clancy immediately tried to satisfy her request. She had to let go of the dogs, but they were so relaxed that they didn't seem to mind. Clancy tugged on her partner, and their joint efforts soon resulted in Abby lying atop her, the float riding very, very low in the water but still holding them up. "Just before you came home, I was wondering if it was possible to feel any better," Clancy murmured. "There was only one thing missing before—but everything's perfect now."

"I'm happy, too," Abby said. "I was surprised but very, very pleased when I saw your truck. I thought you were going to go see some clients."

"I took your advice to relax. Besides, the dogs said they needed me."

"They talk to you more than they talk to me," Abby said, kissing Clancy again. "Guess what I did?"

"Dunno."

"I came out to Pam and Maria this morning." She lifted her head and looked into Clancy's eyes. "It went very, very well."

Clancy's mouth was gaping open at a comical width. "Did you plan on that?"

"No. But Ellen said she had yet another date planned for me, and I told her that I was seeing someone. I'm not sure why, but I didn't want to tell her about us; when she left, I told Maria and Pam."

"And they took it well?"

"Of course." She lifted her head again and asked, "Why wouldn't they?"

"Well, geez, Abby, I don't know. This is a very big change for you!"

"They're my friends. I've known them for over fifteen years, and I wouldn't expect anything less from them. Don't forget that they're lesbians, and on top of that, Maria is a psychiatrist, for goodness' sake. She's required to be supportive!"

"You're okay? No second thoughts about telling them?"

"No, not at all. It feels good to tell someone. I don't have a bit of shame about being with you, Clancy, and it feels good to show that I'm proud of what we have."

Clancy gave her a warm, wet, chlorine-infused kiss, lingering for quite a few blissful moments. "I'm proud of you."

"I'm really glad you're home. I need this."

"I need this, too," Clancy said, burrowing her head into Abby's neck. "I'm glad I was a lazy bum this morning. The bad news is that I made an appointment for later."

"Ooo…" Abby looked up and gave her lover a pout. "Do you have to?"

"Yeah. Gotta pay the bills."

"Can I pay you to stay home?"

"Nope. I'm a self-made thousandaire. But you can let me know how much you missed me when I get home."

"Consider it done. I'll think of something creative."

❧

Abby had obviously been thinking of ways to show Clancy that she was missed while she had been gone, because she backed the architect up against the counter as soon as she entered the kitchen. The dogs were scampering through the room, barking and wagging their tails, but Clancy couldn't get away to even give them a quick pet. Busy, determined fingers worked at the buttons of her shirt, and when Abby had it undone, she pushed it from Clancy's shoulders and tightened her hold on it—trapping Clancy's arms. "I've got ya now," she growled, kissing Clancy everywhere her moist lips could reach. She was pressing against the muscular young woman tightly, grinding her hips against her while she kissed her senseless.

"I've never felt more welcome."

"You're nowhere near as welcome as you're gonna get."

"I hope that was a dare," Clancy gasped. "I can never turn down a dare."

Abby twitched her shoulders, brushing her breasts against Clancy's. She stopped abruptly and cocked her head. "Did you take your ring out?"

"Mmm." Clancy thought for a moment and then nodded. "You usually can't see it under my clothes, but I switch it out when I go to see clients. Just to be safe."

"Switch it out?" Abby's fingers slid up to encircle the nipple, and her smile grew wider. "What's this?" The rigid point was nearly bursting from a tiny little ring that surrounded it. She reached behind Clancy, unhooked her bra, and then let her fingers explore thoroughly. Clancy didn't say a word; she just relaxed against the counter and let Abby's searching fingers excite her all the more. Suddenly, her shirt was tossed to the floor; then her bra fell atop the shirt, and Abby's tongue was tracing the small gold circle before Clancy could blink.

Abby's mouth went from one breast to the other, and after a moment, Clancy realized that her goal was to try to make one nipple as firm as the other. "You'll never get there, but it's okay with me if you keep trying all night," Clancy finally murmured, clutching Abby's head and drawing it closer.

Abby's eyes shifted, meeting Clancy's, and she swirled her tongue around the taut nipple a few more times, not willing to give up her goal. "Why won't it work?" she mumbled, her mouth full of the swollen flesh.

"The collar is pretty snug, and it really pumps the nipple up." Clancy's hand was in her partner's hair, urging her on, and with each particularly firm suck, she let out a little gasp, making her words hard to follow.

The dogs had been very patient with them so far, but they'd finally reached their limit. Athena marched over to the door and let out an outraged bark, glaring at both of the groping women. "Somebody's been ignored too long," Clancy decided, patting Abby's head. "Come on, let's take care of them and then go upstairs. Alone," she said, eyes twinkling.

❦

Abby joined her partner in bed and cuddled up close. As usual, her hand immediately went to the jeweled nipple. "You really do like this, don't you?" Clancy asked, smiling at her.

"Yeah. I'm not even sure why. Maybe because it's so different." She shrugged her shoulders and said, "Who knows? Maybe I have a latent nipple fetish that I never knew about." She leaned over and licked both breasts like they were pink ice cream cones. "Will didn't like to have his nipples played with." She stilled abruptly and looked up at Clancy with chagrin. "I'm sorry for saying that. I'm sure you don't want to hear things like that."

Clancy grasped her chin and tilted it up. "Of course I do. I'm interested in everything about you. You know that by now, don't you?"

"Yes, I do, but…"

"But nothing. If some little thought or reflection occurs to you, and you want to share it, I want to hear it. I really love the fact that you and Will had a good sex life, and I want to know anything that you particularly liked—so I can do it, too—or didn't like—so I can avoid it."

"You really don't mind? It felt a little like I was comparing you to him, and I don't want you to think that."

Clancy smiled. "I don't mind being compared—as long as I don't suffer in the comparison."

"You don't. You can hold your own against any opponent." She traced the ring with the tip of her finger and said, "Tell me about this."

"This particular piece of jewelry? Or the piercing?"

"Both," Abby said, her curious finger still circling the tiny gold ring.

"'Kay. I have, as you might have noticed, very sensitive nipples. I was dating Julie at the time, and she had both of hers done. It turned me on so much to see the look on her face when I played with her jewelry that I decided to have my own done."

"Didn't it hurt horribly?" Abby's face twitched into a sympathetic grimace.

"No. I told Hayley it did, though," she said. "But that was just to put her off."

"Hayley? Why were you discussing this with Hayley?"

Clancy patted her softly, saying, "I didn't bring it up, honey. I had the heavy ring in when we went swimming. She said she was thinking of having something pierced, and she asked how much it hurt."

"Oh, God," Abby sighed. "I've got to cut her allowance." She started to chuckle, shaking her head. "Lord knows what she'll look like by the time she's through her rebellious phase."

"Hey, I wasn't in a rebellious phase. Well, maybe just a tiny bit."

"Tell me about having it done," Abby said. "I can't believe it didn't hurt."

"Mmm…actually, it felt like it does when someone bites you just a little too hard. It only lasted for a second or two—not bad at all. It throbbed a bit for a day or so, and it was tender for a while—just like any healing wound. The worst part was that after about a week, I wanted to play with it, because I was really aware of it—but it wasn't healed yet. Kinda drove me nuts. It was like having an itch you couldn't scratch."

"But now you're really happy with it?"

"Very. I'm planning on having the other one done, too, but I should have had it done earlier in the year."

"Why didn't you have them both done at once?"

"You can't play roughly with them until they're fully healed. That took a few months for me." She grinned at Abby for a minute, but Abby didn't understand her point. "I didn't want to have both of them out of commission. I honestly don't know if I would enjoy sex as much if my partner couldn't play with my nipples. It was hard ignoring my little pal for all of those months." She patted her nipple fondly, cracking Abby up.

"What does it feel like now?"

"Generally, I don't notice it. I mean, if I concentrate, I can feel the weight difference when I have the heavy ring in, but it's mostly not noticeable. It's during sex that I love it. And I do *love it*. I like to have my nipples tugged on really hard, and having the heavy ring in provides an excellent handle."

"I know," Abby said. "I love your little handle. I guess I assumed it was permanent, though. I had no idea you could change it out."

"Oh, yeah. I have a lot of jewelry. Actually, nipple jewelry was the only gift that Julie ever gave me. I have quite a collection."

"I wanna see it all," Abby growled, giving the adorned bud a rough suck.

"Oh, you will. You'll see it and nibble on it all." She reached down and pressed against one side of the ring that encircled her nipple. A catch gave way, and she lifted the ring off. "This one is cool. It's really invisible—except for the fact that it makes my nipple as hard as a rock."

"I thought it was just your flesh that kept it in place. I didn't realize there was a little bar that went through your piercing."

"Yeah. Cool, huh?"

"Can you leave it out for tonight?" Abby asked, tweaking the ripe-looking berry with the tip of her finger. "I want you all natural."

"Anything for you."

"You like them treated roughly, huh?" Abby asked with a gleam in her eyes.

"Very," Clancy breathed. "I like my nipples to get a real workout, but I need tender, loving care down below."

With a rakish grin, Abby bent to her task, giving Clancy a confident look just before her lips latched on. "I can do that. With pleasure."

They lay in a tangled mess of sheets, their moist skin forcing them to nearly have to peel apart when one of them moved. "You certainly do know how to follow instructions," Clancy said. "My nipples are throbbing!"

Abby was up on one arm immediately, searching Clancy's face. "I hurt you?"

"Good hurt," Clancy said, pressing a kiss to her shoulder. "Very good hurt." Abby lay back down and snuggled close. "You seemed to enjoy torturing me a little, babe. I looked at your face at one point, and you looked…fiendishly happy."

"Mmm…that feels about right. Maybe I've been hiding a sadistic streak, too. God knows what else I'll find out about myself."

"You okay with this?" Clancy asked softly while she ran a hand along Abby's spine.

"Yeah, yeah. It's just funny learning how to love a woman. Like I've said before, the sensations are really different—and the feelings I get are really different. Both experiences are great—they're just very, very different. It's like going out for some great sushi one night and then having some fantastic Italian dish the next. I love 'em both—but they're hardly in the same category."

"Which am I?" Clancy chuckled. "Sushi or Italian?"

Abby smiled and said, "Not to revert to a stereotype, but you're definitely the sushi. A little exotic, but clean and fresh-tasting, with a delightful aftertaste." She licked her lips and let her mouth twitch into an even wider smile. "A very delightful aftertaste."

Clancy nuzzled her head between Abby's breasts and licked the soft skin. "How's it with a man?"

"I can give you my view, but this is a limited sample. Will was my only real partner."

Clancy sat up and looked at her in surprise. "You were a virgin when you married?"

"God, no!" Abby laughed. "We had sex before we married, and I played around a lot in high school and college. I didn't have intercourse before Will—but that's the only thing I didn't do."

"Why not? Guilt? Worried about pregnancy?"

Abby shook her head. "No. Neither, actually. It was a purely selfish decision."

At Clancy's puzzled look, she explained, "As I've mentioned, I have a very cool mother. She started talking to me about sex—in great detail—when I was around eleven or twelve."

Chuckling softly, Clancy said, "I'm still waiting for that talk with my mom. Maybe she'll do it on my thirtieth birthday."

"Oh, give her a break. It's a hard thing to do, and many moms opt out of it."

Clancy nodded agreeably. "In her defense, I think she was waiting until I expressed an interest in boys. I think she was afraid of talking to me before I was ready."

"Well, my mom was very proactive. We talked about it really casually—just a little bit at a time, and she did it very conversationally, usually using herself as an example."

"Like how?"

"Oh, she'd tell me about a boyfriend she'd had when she was young and talk about how he always pressured her to go further than she really wanted to. Over time, I got the correct impression that a lot of boys would want to have sex with me and that sex wouldn't necessarily mean the same to them as it did to me. She told me that you had to train a boy to please you—and that it took a long time. Her main point was that I shouldn't let a boy touch me just because *he* wanted to. She's a firm believer in women claiming their own sexual pleasure—and she believes that the only way to do that is to force men to meet your needs."

"And that made you decide to wait?"

"No, I didn't consciously decide to wait. I'd let anyone who I was interested in touch me, but I wouldn't let him go any further if he didn't show a definite interest in pleasing me. It amazed me how many guys would stick their hands into my pants for two seconds and then try to shove my head into their laps. No way!" She shared a laugh with Clancy and added, "Over time, I saw that my mom was totally right. Most of the guys weren't interested in making love; they were interested in getting off. And there was no way I was going to be merely a semen receptacle. Not me!"

"Were these guys insane? All they had to do was spend a little time making sure you got off, and they couldn't do it?"

Abby chuckled softly. "I didn't tell them the entrance requirement, Clancy. I waited to see if they were naturally interested. I assume that older guys would have been more sensitive, but eighteen-year-old guys are totally focused on their penises—at least, in my experience."

"But Will was different, right?"

"Oh, yes. Very. We slept together on our second date," Abby said, chuckling softly. "He was twenty-eight years old and had a lot of experience. He had me so hot on our first date that I would have done it right then, but I didn't want him to think I was too loose."

"And you liked it right from the start?"

"I did. I was a little nervous, but he was so patient and gentle with me—I told him that I'd never had intercourse, and he spent an incredibly long time making sure I was ready. I was so glad that I'd waited for a good lover," she sighed. "He was funny about sex. Well, he was just plain funny. But he honestly thought that one of his jobs was to make me love sex as much as he did. He was a very practical guy, and he reasoned that if I liked sex, I'd want to have it often. And if we had it often, it wouldn't be hard to stay monogamous."

She grinned at Clancy and said, "I think he was a little afraid that it would be hard to be with just one woman for the rest of his life." Her smile grew wider and turned a little wistful when she added, "It wasn't. I'm absolutely certain that he was always faithful to me." She laughed softly and said, "I made sure he got what he needed, so he'd never have the temptation to cheat on me."

"So…how is it different?" Clancy asked, her curiosity still piqued.

Abby thought for a minute and said, "Well, most of it's the same, really. He played with my entire body—just like you do. His whiskers irritated my skin sometimes, but generally, the foreplay was the same. The main difference is intercourse. I loved to be filled up by his body—it's hard to describe, but it's such a feeling of connectedness. You can feel a man throbbing inside of you when he comes; I really loved that."

"Is it very different from the feeling you get when my fingers are inside of you?"

"Yes, it is different. Not better or worse—just different. As I say, I loved feeling Will inside of me, but I love the way you touch me, too. Your fingers are more flexible than his penis was, and they can touch different parts of me. God, Clancy, when you put your finger just inside and rub my G-spot, I nearly see stars!"

Clancy gave her a kiss and added a tickle between her legs. "You look like you're seeing stars," she murmured. "It nearly makes me come to see the look on your face."

"That's part of the difference!" Abby said, Clancy's comments bringing another detail to mind. "Seeing the look on your lover's face when he comes while he's inside of you is part of the difference between making love to a man versus a woman. It's very bonding, very intimate. There's a built-in tension there, too—you never know when the man's going to come, and sometimes you're racing the clock, trying to get there first. So it's great to feel him inside of you—great to know he's feeling such pleasure, too, but not so great when he comes a minute or two before you do, and you just lose it. That's one of the benefits of being with you; I know you're concentrating on me and that you're not going to get distracted by your own needs."

"It won't be exactly the same, but we can re-create some of those feelings of being filled up," Clancy said softly, her voice burring into Abby's ear.

Abby slid her hand between Clancy's thighs and whispered, "So it's true what they say about lesbians? Do you have a nice big dildo just waiting for me?"

"I've got more than one," Clancy said, winking rakishly. "And I think you'd enjoy the experience."

"You know my motto," Abby reminded her. "Don't say no until you've at least tried it."

Clancy grinned toothily. "That's the best motto I think I've ever heard."

Chapter Sixteen

Abby's alarm went off at eight, and she lay in bed for a few minutes, stroking Clancy's back. She knew her lover was partially awake, but she'd learned that Clancy liked to wake up slowly, and she'd discovered that a soft, light touch helped her greet the day gently.

Leaning over to place a kiss on her shoulder, Abby slipped out of bed, earning twin grumpy looks from the pups. "You can stay right there," she told them, and as though they understood her words, they laid their heads back down and watched her leave the room. She was blow-drying her hair when Clancy came in with a cup of coffee for her. "How did I ever get by without you here?" Abby asked, cocking her head slightly.

"Search me." Clancy shrugged and sat on the edge of the tub. "We've got to use this whirlpool sometime. It looks like fun."

"It's a deal. I use it in the winter, but it never occurs to me to use it when it's warm out." She looked over at Clancy and changed the subject. "Do you want to go with me?"

"Uhm...where are you going?"

"Didn't I mention last night that I go to church on Sunday?"

"Noooo...you were begging some higher power for mercy at several points, but I don't recall any discussion of church."

"Funny," Abby said, reaching around to pinch her in a sensitive spot. "Well, I do go, and I'd love to have you go with me."

"Mmm...what kinda church do you go to?"

"Episcopal. What about you? I assume you're Catholic?"

"Ohh...going for the stereotype, huh? All Irish people are Catholic, blah, blah, blah."

"Oh, Lord, did I just say that? My apologies. I'll rephrase. Do you have a faith?"

"Uh-huh. Catholic," she teased, sticking her tongue out. Abby tried to grab it, but Clancy evaded her grasping fingers. "Actually," she said, "I haven't been to church, except for funerals, since I was in grade school. I think my parents had me baptized just in case."

"In case?"

"In case all the stuff they learned in school was true. They didn't want my little soul burning in hell because they couldn't take the time to drag me over to church and have the priest pour water over my head."

"Well, that was quite thoughtful of them," Abby said. She went into her closet and emerged with a muted, summery, plaid sundress. Clancy buttoned the dozens of small covered buttons and smoothed it out.

"Mmm…you look nice. I love the way you look in dresses."

"Thanks," Abby said, kissing her nose. "I like to wear dresses. Always have." She ran her hand down Clancy's bare body. "Sure you don't want to come? I don't have to leave for about ten minutes."

"Oh, I don't think so. I don't have anything nice to wear, and you'd look all out of place with my grubby little self next to you."

Abby placed her hands atop Clancy's shoulders. "You know me well in many ways, but there are some parts of me that you won't accept." Clancy gave her a puzzled glance, and Abby continued, "I'm not the kind of person who pays much attention to what others think about me or my choice of friends. Second, I wouldn't attend a church that wasn't filled with open-minded people. Last, I happen to think you look adorable in your normal attire, and I wouldn't dream of asking you to change one thing about it."

Clancy's cheeks flushed slightly, and she said, "I get a little insecure sometimes. Sorry."

"Don't be sorry. Just trust me. I know what's best for me, and I don't need for you to spend a moment trying to second-guess me."

Clancy wrapped her arms around her partner. "This is why I always wanted an older lover," she sighed. "Self-assured women are such a turn-on."

❧

Clancy was in her room, rooting through the velvet bag where she kept her jewelry, when Michael strolled in. He gave her a start, and she jumped noticeably when he asked, "Looking for something for a special occasion?"

"Very funny." She had placed each of her nipple rings and shields in a line on her dresser, and she shrugged and dumped everything else out of the bag. Slipping the rings back in, she sniffed and said, "Abby wants to see my collection."

"Ohh…I thought that you missed me so much, you just had to come see me. Little did I know you just missed your nipple rings."

"I miss you loads. As a matter of fact, Abby and I would love to have you come over. How about today? We could have brunch when she gets back from church."

"A churchgoer who doesn't like to talk about her feelings? I still don't see what you two have in common!"

"There's more to life than talkin', Mikey. Lots more!"

❧

Michael let himself be persuaded, and when Abby got home, he was frolicking in the pool with the dogs. Clancy had issued the challenge, and he was failing miserably in his quest to get each of them onto her own pool float while Clancy stood in the kitchen, laughing her ass off as she cleaned some strawberries.

"This is a happy little domestic scene," Abby said when she came up behind Clancy and wrapped her in her arms. "To the casual observer, this is the handsome young professional and his beautiful, sexy young wife, relaxing around the pool on a sunny summer day."

Clancy turned in her embrace and said, "The more interesting story is that the young wife is carrying on a steamy, torrid romance with the gorgeous, sexy, slightly older temptress who just sneaked in the back door. The hard part is going to be how the young wife manages to get her sexy mistress naked so she can have her way with her before the husband knows anything is up."

She bent and dipped her hand under the hem of Abby's dress, letting it slide up the cool expanse of bare thigh. When her fingers grazed silky panties, Abby purred softly and let her thighs drift apart. "Ooh…maybe she doesn't have to get her naked. The mistress can stand at the sink, acting like she's cleaning strawberries, while the wife sinks to her knees and pleasures her until her legs give out."

Clancy started to drop to her knees, but Abby grabbed her by the shoulders and tugged her back to her feet. "Don't even think about it, you little devil. I'm not going to have my first extended encounter with your best friend include a viewing of my private parts."

"He wouldn't mind. Nothing would make him happier! I think that's half of the reason he wanted to live with me. He thought he'd get a few peeks of girl-on-girl action."

"He hasn't, has he?" Abby asked, suddenly feeling a little jealous to think of Clancy with another woman.

"We've been over this, sweetheart. He's never seen me kiss another woman. I'm not that kinda girl."

Abby held her index finger and thumb an inch apart. "Tiny little bit of insecurity sneaked out. I'll behave." She gave Clancy a lingering kiss. "That's for going to the store. I appreciate it."

"I'll go every hour on the hour for a kiss like that."

After giving Michael a few tips that didn't help him in the least, Abby left him to his dog-wrangling and went to change into a swimsuit. She came back in casual shorts and a roomy tank top, and started to help Clancy.

"No, no," Clancy said. "I'm going to make brunch. I want you to go play with Michael and the dogs. I want you to get to know each other a little without my hovering over you."

Abby smiled and nodded, and just before she got to the door, she came back and put her hand on Clancy's cheek. "How should we act around him? Is it okay if we're just natural?"

"Within the limits of decency, yes. He's family. I have almost no secrets from Michael."

"Okay. I've got my marching orders." Another sweet kiss and she was off, leaving Clancy to gaze lovingly at her departing form.

❧

Late that night, while they lay in bed with a soft breeze floating into the room, Clancy reflected on their day. "I could spend every Sunday just like that."

"It was nice, wasn't it? I really like Michael. It's nice to see that you have someone you're that close to."

"We were both only children, and for some reason, we just adopted each other as family. I know we'll be friends for the rest of our lives."

"Oh, when you were outside, Maria called and asked if we'd like to go to her house for dinner on Wednesday. Any interest?"

"Our friends are coming out of the woodwork, aren't they? I assume Maria and Pam want to see if I pass inspection?"

"Maybe," Abby said. "Or they might just want to get a look at the kind of woman I'm attracted to. I'm sure they find this all quite puzzling."

"Sure. I'm happy to go if you want to."

"That wasn't a very enthusiastic response. Wanna skip it?"

"No. Not at all. They're your friends, and I want to meet them. I just have a feeling I'll be under a microscope, and that makes me a little uncomfortable. I mean, will I have anything in common with them?"

"One thing," she said, grinning. "They like chicks."

"That should carry us through five minutes of conversation. 'So you two eat pussy, huh? It's great, isn't it?'"

"Clancy! I'm certain that neither Pam nor Maria refers to it as 'eating pussy'!"

"See? We don't even have vulgarity in common."

"Oh, you'll like them just fine. They're actually two of my most interesting friends."

"What do they do?"

"Maria's a psychiatrist. She works in the chemical-dependency unit at Huntington Memorial. Pam's a techie. She works in the IT department at the Jet Propulsion Lab."

"Wow," Clancy said, her voice flat. "When do they have time to eat pussy?"

"Stop that! You'll like them. They're very down-to-earth."

"Do they have a garden? Houseplants?"

Abby took her question at face value, finally saying, "No. Neither is very domestic. They have a daughter, Alyssa, and they spend all of their spare time with her. They're really busy women. Not much time for hobbies." Furrowing her brow, she said, "Oh, they do really like the theater, and they go to the opera as often as they can."

"Opera, huh?" Clancy asked. "The only opera I've ever seen was when Bugs Bunny did The Barber of Seville. And I've never been to a play in my life. I don't know anything about jets...or propulsion...whatever that is, either."

"Oh, Clancy, that doesn't matter. They want to get to know you, not judge you."

"I know, I know. Uhm…how old is their daughter?"

"She just turned seven. She's a great kid. Extremely gifted, though. They have their hands full trying to keep her stimulated in school. She goes to a school for gifted children, and she's already reading at the fifth-grade level."

Oh, boy! Clancy groused to herself. *Maybe they'll have a mentally challenged dog I can bond with.*

♣

At six-thirty on Wednesday, Abby went downstairs to find Clancy touching up a pair of black crepe slacks with a cool iron. "Nice," she said, fingering the fabric. "I knew you had a few pieces of dress-up clothes hidden in your closet."

No, I don't, Clancy thought, *but the department store did. I just hope I got all the tags off.*

"Would you like to walk? It's barely a mile away."

"Sure. I'd really like to. When do we have to be there?"

"Seven o'clock. We can make it easily if you're ready soon."

"I'm almost done," Clancy said, grabbing her slacks and heading upstairs.

Mere moments later, she was back, looking very dapper in a pale-green print silk blouse, her tailored slacks, and a pair of very shiny black loafers. "You look luscious," Abby said, taking her in her arms. "I don't see it often, but that shade makes your eyes look green."

"They *were* green when I was younger," Clancy said. "They've slowly turned gray, but certain colors do bring a little color back to 'em."

"Such nice shiny shoes. You keep them well polished."

"Oh. They're pretty new," she said. *Three hours is pretty new, isn't it?*

"Well, you look lovely. Shall we?"

"Let's do it."

They walked down the tree-lined residential streets of Pasadena, a nice cool breeze blowing their hair around. "This is such a wonderful neighborhood," Clancy said. "The houses are fantastic, and the lots are all so big. That makes such a difference."

"It is nice. It's a fairly friendly place, too. You get to recognize people when you walk dogs."

"I'd guess that's so. Maybe we should take the girls out for walks in the evening. I know they're unhappy being cooped up in the house all day."

Abby impulsively leaned over and kissed her cheek. "I admire a lot of things about you, but one of the sweetest things about you is your thoughtfulness. You work hard all day, but you're still willing to walk the dogs because you think they might need it."

"Nobody likes to have her routine upset. Doggies have a schedule they try to keep, too."

Looking at the sweet, playful look on her face, Abby couldn't help but reach over and grasp Clancy's arm, placing both hands around her bicep and holding it close to her body. Clancy was pleased that Abby didn't have a problem with being affectionate in public, but a few minutes later, her whole body stiffened when an older couple, walking a dog, approached. She tried to telegraph Abby mentally to let go, because she didn't want her lover to experience the shock of getting a dirty look for their public display of affection. Much to her surprise, not only did they not get a dirty look, but the couple also practically beamed at them. *Damn, Abby lives in a very liberal neighborhood.*

Then reality hit her. *They thought she was my mother! That's the only reason for them to give us that encouraging look! They thought it was sweet that I was helping dear old Mom down the street!*

She cast a quick glance at Abby, who chatted away, oblivious to the thoughts running through Clancy's mind. *This is going to take some getting used to—but if it gets us a free pass for PDAs, I'm pumped!*

❧

They walked down Orange Grove Avenue, with Clancy waxing rhapsodic over the stately mansions and elegant apartment buildings. Abby took in the pleasant sound of Clancy's enthusiastic voice, not saying much herself—merely reveling in the state of deep satisfaction she felt from having someone she cared for holding her hand as they walked down the street. Pam and Maria lived in one of a series of townhomes tucked away down a long, mostly hidden drive. After they were buzzed in, Clancy noted with some displeasure that there was no chance for a garden, because all of the townhomes were connected—with no outdoor space for grass or flowers. Alyssa came to the door and threw her arms around Abby, hugging her soundly before she stepped back to greet Clancy. "Alyssa, this is my friend, Clancy O'Connor. Clancy, this little beauty is Alyssa."

"Good to meet you, Alyssa."

The young girl looked at her critically for a minute and furrowed her brow, her quick mind processing all of the information that her dark eyes took in. "Are you Abby's friend or Hayley's friend?"

Clancy smiled stiffly and said, "Abby's. Definitely Abby's. I don't know Hayley well at all."

The girl made a face and scrunched her eyes up, obviously not buying it. "You look like Hayley's friend, 'cause you look like a kid."

To Clancy's surprise, Abby seemed to find this funny, and she graciously agreed with the child. "She does look like someone Hayley would pal around with, doesn't she, Alyssa? But she's all mine. Hayley has to get her own friends."

More truth there than I'm comfortable admitting, Clancy decided.

Just then, one of the adults came out of the kitchen, and she stopped so abruptly upon seeing Clancy that when the other woman came out behind her, she plowed right into her. "This is Abby's friend," Alyssa announced. "She looks like Hayley's friend, but she's not."

Pam slapped her forehead, clearly embarrassed. Then she walked into the room and gave both women a seriously sheepish look. "I'm so sorry for the always pithy commentary that our beloved Alyssa provides. I'm Pam Swenson," she said, extending her hand, "and this is my partner, Maria Messina."

"Clancy O'Connor." She shook each hand while feeling more like a fish out of water than she could ever remember.

Abby hugged her friends and waved off Alyssa's comments good-naturedly. "Alyssa's good at keeping us all honest. I think it's refreshing." She turned to the child and said, "Clancy's younger than I am, but I really like her. We've been going out with each other, and I hope that you like her, too, because I want to keep her around for a while."

Dark eyes grew even darker, and her mouth curled into a pout. "You don't go out with girls. You like boys."

"Alyssa!" Maria whispered harshly. "Knock it off!"

"What?" she asked, perplexed. "Abby was married to Will! She likes boys!"

Abby crouched down so she was on the same plane as the child. "I do like boys, Alyssa, but I'm finding out that I like girls, too. I like Clancy a lot, and I think you will, too, when you get to know her." The child looked doubtful, but she smiled when Abby tickled under her chin. "Now, show me this big science project you're working on," she said, and the little girl took her hand, tugging her toward her room.

Clancy was rocking back and forth on her heels, wishing that her new pants had pockets so she'd have something to do with her hands.

Maria reached out, clasped her shoulder, and said, "I'm so sorry about that! She says whatever comes to mind."

"Ah, we're gonna get that a lot. And most people won't be so honest about it. We may as well get used to it."

"Come on in, and let me get you a drink," Pam offered. "Wine okay?"

I'd rather have a beer, Clancy thought, but decided to try to go with the flow. "Sure. Wine is fine."

They led her into the living room, and the three of them sat down and tried to make conversation. Clancy looked around, finding it hard to make and keep eye contact. The room was beautifully decorated—so beautifully laid out that Clancy was certain the women had hired someone to do it for them. It wasn't very kid-friendly, and she decided that Alyssa must not be allowed to use the place without supervision. "Abby tells us that you're working on that big project at her house," Pam began. "We haven't been over since you started. How's it coming?"

"Good," Clancy said. "It's a big job, but it's on track."

"It sounds really interesting," Maria said. "Abby's so complimentary about your skills...uhm...your talent. Have you always liked working with your hands?" She heard the words leave her mouth and cringed noticeably. Out of the corner of her eye, she saw her partner briefly cover her face with her hand.

Alyssa and Abby came back, saving Maria from further embarrassment, and she got up to get Abby a glass of wine. "You're a landscape architect, right?" Pam asked.

"Yeah, I am. I have my own business. I'm just starting out, but I love it."

"Will was a lawyer," Alyssa said, narrowing her eyes at Clancy yet again. "Isn't that better than being a land...whatever?"

"Alyssa!" This time it was Pam who tried to keep the child in line. "Honey, you don't even remember Will. You were just two when he died. Now, come on; you're making Clancy uncomfortable."

"That's okay," Clancy said, smiling at the mortified woman. She looked at the little girl and said, "You have to go to school longer to be a lawyer, and most people would say being a lawyer is better. But I like what I do. And I think that's important, too."

"My moms like what they do. Mom's a doctor," she said, raising a challenging eyebrow, "and Mama's a..." She looked at Pam, her face scrunched up in confusion. "Mama does computer something. It's hard," she added emphatically.

"I had a heck of a time getting through college," Clancy said. "I could never do well enough in school to be a doctor or a computer something." She looked at the child for a moment and said, "Some people do really well in school, and others don't. What's important is finding what you like and having the guts to stick with it—even if it's not what other people think is cool."

The child appeared to consider this for a minute and then looked at Clancy speculatively. "What's it called again? Land what?"

"Landscape architecture," she said. "I deal with everything outside of a house...like trees and plants and walls and putting in sprinkler systems."

Alyssa nodded quickly, urging Clancy to finish her description, and then asked, "Did you say plants?"

"Yeah. I know a lot about plants. Do you like plants?"

"No," she said immediately, making a face. "But I have a science project where I have to germinate seeds. Wanna see?"

"Yeah, I'd love to."

Alyssa walked over to Clancy and took her hand. "Let's go," she said, sounding like the conductor on a train. Clancy met Abby's encouraging look with an agreeable shrug; then she let the child drag her through the house.

"This is my room," she announced, walking over to a neatly laid-out worktable. "This is the project."

Clancy observed the well-marked terra cotta pots, showing every part of the life cycle of grass seed. "This is pretty cool."

The little girl was now sitting on her bed, staring at Clancy with those dark, penetrating eyes. "Abby likes boys. You're not a boy. Why is she going out with you?"

"Uhm...maybe you'd better ask her that," Clancy said, sitting down on the pint-size desk chair. "Does it bother you that she's dating me?"

"No," she said flatly, refusing to meet Clancy's eyes.

"Okay." She fidgeted for a moment, feeling the dark, beady eyes still glaring at her. Deciding not to let a seven-year-old get the better of her, Clancy said, "Hey, let's play a game where we pretend things, okay?"

"Okay," the child said warily.

"Let's pretend that it bothers you that Abby's dating me. If you had to make up a reason for why it upset you, what would that reason be?"

The little mouth scrunched up in a pout for just a minute before she said, "She likes boys."

"Uh-huh," Clancy said patiently. "She still likes boys. She just likes me, too."

"I like boys," she said quietly, and Clancy nodded in empathy.

"Do you think that means that you might like girls someday?"

"I don't," she said defiantly, her voice rising. "I like boys."

"That's cool," Clancy said. "I only like girls."

"Only girls?" The dark eyes narrowed.

"Yep. I only like girls. Ever since I was your age."

"My moms both liked boys when they were little," she said thoughtfully. "But they only like girls now."

"Everybody's different, Alyssa," Clancy said. "You can like whoever you like."

"Whomever," the child interrupted.

Clancy blinked, then blew out a breath. *Thank God this isn't Abby's kid. I don't think I could take it.* "Okay. You can like whomever you like. It doesn't matter what Abby does or what your moms did when they were little. It only matters that you do what you like."

"Kinda like you and land stuff, huh?"

"Yep. Kinda like me and land stuff."

Nodding, Alyssa got up and went to the door. "We're done." She turned and waited patiently for Clancy to join her; then she tucked her small hand into Clancy's and led her back to the party.

※

On the way home that night, Abby wrapped an arm around Clancy and said, "Alyssa's a little pistol, isn't she?"

Clancy chuckled evilly. "Little does she know that the trenches I've dug in your yard are exactly the right size for her. Her mothers would probably thank me if she mysteriously disappeared."

With an outraged squawk, Abby slapped at her sharply. "Don't even joke about that!"

Clancy grabbed her hands and playfully nuzzled into her neck. "You know I'm kidding. We got a few things ironed out when we were in her room."

"Such as?"

"It seems she was worried about your starting to like girls. You were the only person who was just like she was—and then you had to go screw it up."

Abby stopped dead in her tracks. "What?"

Clancy smiled and patted her affectionately. "No big deal. It sounds like she related to you because you liked boys—consistently. She says that her moms used to like boys, but they switched...and now you're switching..." Clancy said, twirling her finger to indicate a pattern.

"Oh, my God! She's worried that she might be gay, too!"

"Apparently," Clancy agreed.

"But that's odd. Very odd. She's been around gay people and straight people, and she's always acted like she thought nothing of it. I wonder why it bothers her now?"

"I don't think it was the gay thing. I think it was the consistency thing. She warmed up to me immediately when I convinced her that I've always been oriented in the same way. I think she had a moment of panic when she realized you and Pam and Maria had all changed at some point. She must have thought that might happen to her."

"Oh, I have to call Maria and tell her this," Abby sighed. "This isn't like Alyssa. But Pam said she's been having a hard time lately. It's really hitting her that she's different—because she has two moms. She's treated well at school and all, but it seems like she's struggling to work this all out in her head. She's also upset that she doesn't have a dad," Abby said. "They chose to have her via an anonymous donor, and that's a hard concept for a seven-year-old to grasp. I know they'll help her get comfortable with that over time, but she's having a tough time now." She grasped Clancy's arm tighter and said, "Thanks for helping with her. None of us got that out of her—but you did."

"I like kids," Clancy said agreeably. "Even when they don't like me."

"Oh, she liked you just fine. She didn't ask me to her room to listen to her new CD."

"Yeah. Lucky me," Clancy said. "I'm not even sure who the group was, but it's not on my list of 'must haves.'"

Abby released her arm and clasped her hand. "Thanks for putting up with so much tonight. I owe you."

"Nah. You suffered through my family's grilling. Let's call it even."

"It's a deal," Abby said, leaning over to place a soft kiss on Clancy's cheek. "I'm glad that I like girls," she whispered. "And I'm particularly glad that you're the girl I like."

❧

Once Alyssa was in bed, Pam and Maria could talk without fear of being overheard. Maria had organized and purchased dinner, so Pam was in charge of cleaning up. Maria jumped up to sit on the counter, swinging her legs. "The only landscape-architecture degree program around here is at Cal Poly. I looked it up when I put Alyssa to bed. Now, Clancy said she's only had her license for two years—"

Pam raised an eyebrow. "When did you question her, Detective?"

Maria stuck her tongue out. "I sneaked a question or two in every time I caught her attention. Abby hasn't told us shit! If she's not talking, I've got to figure things out for myself!"

"Well, we didn't ask her any direct questions, Maria. It's not like she pleaded the Fifth."

"You know Abby plays her cards close to the vest. She wouldn't like for us to ask questions. I don't have any choice!"

Pam smiled at her partner. "Okay. What did you deduce?"

"That kid can't be more than twenty-four! Trevor's gonna be twenty-four this year! What in the hell is Abby thinking?"

Pam's eyes had grown wide. "Are you sure she's that young? Jesus!"

"She looks younger than that! I'm giving her the benefit of the doubt!"

"Good Lord." Pam walked over to her lover and put her hands on her knees. "She must be...I don't have any idea what she must be doing! Women don't do this!"

"I know! Women don't get trophy wives! Especially when they have to switch sexual orientation to get one!"

"I'm completely dumbstruck," Pam said. "I would never have believed Abby would do something like this. She's the most reasonable, logical, steady, predictable person I've ever known."

Maria nodded her agreement. "But she does seem happy. Happier than she's been since Will died."

Pam laughed heartily. "I'd be happy if I had a twenty-four-year-old..." She stopped herself short, trying desperately to think of an acceptable ending for her sentence.

Maria reached around and slapped her on the butt. "I'm in a good mood. I'll let that one pass."

Dropping her head onto her lover's shoulder, Pam said, "I'd be happy if we had a twenty-four-year-old daughter. That would mean we'd been together all of our adult lives. Wouldn't that be wonderful?"

Maria wrapped her in a hug. "Given what you had to work with, that was excellent. Truly excellent!"

❦

On Saturday morning, Abby got out of bed reluctantly, gazing down at Clancy with palpable longing. *Why didn't I cancel the match for today? Hayley's coming home tomorrow, and this is our last morning to be able to lie in bed and play.* She sighed heavily and went into her room to get ready. Like clockwork, Clancy appeared, coffee in hand, moments after Abby emerged from the shower. "Hi," she yawned sleepily.

"Hi yourself." Abby pressed her damp body against Clancy and held her tight. She felt the emotion start to fill her chest and gave her a rough squeeze. "Don't want to get you all wet."

"I don't mind." She sat down on the edge of the tub. "Wish you could stay home this morning."

"I was just kicking myself for not canceling. I let the week get away from me."

"It's okay. We'll...have more time together...when Hayley goes back to school, if nothing else."

Trying to stop her stomach from doing flips at the thought of not being together for over a month, Abby patted her gently and said, "Sure we will. Now, I want you to go back to bed. You worked like a dog this week, and the weekend is the only time you have to recover."

"I did work hard. Getting those boulders in place was a bitch."

"Couldn't you have hired another man?"

"Sure." She grinned up at Abby and said, "But I desperately want this client to be satisfied. She's really special."

"So are you." Abby kissed her lightly and ordered, "Back to bed. And don't get up until you're well rested, okay?"

"No argument," Clancy said, shuffling back in the direction of the guest room.

"Clancy?" Abby said softly.

"Yeah?"

"I'll miss you." Clancy had a feeling she didn't mean just over the next few hours. She gave her a warm smile, her sadness bleeding through it, and went back to bed.

🐾

When Abby came home, Clancy was still dead to the world. The dogs barely looked up when she walked past, so Abby went into her room to drop off her things and change. When she was done, she stood in the doorway of the guest room, her heart feeling like it would explode from the feelings she was struggling with.

Clancy was lying on her back, one leg drawn up. Athena was lying between her legs, her dark head on Clancy's raised thigh. Artemis was plastered along Clancy's body, her head on a muscular shoulder, Clancy's hand resting on the dog's chest. They looked so content and peaceful that Abby was loath to join them and break the mood. But their time together was short, and she couldn't resist the pull of the always-welcoming body.

As she drew closer, Athena opened one dark chocolate eye and gave her the doggie version of a scowl. *God, she loves Clancy. I don't know how it happened so quickly, but she's solidly bonded with her.* She felt tears start to roll down her cheeks, and with a blinding flash of realization, she thought, *I love her, too. I don't know why it happened. I'm not sure how it happened. I don't know when it happened, but I love her with all my heart.*

With an unhappy grunt, Athena pulled away when Abby got into bed, and as soon as the dog hit the ground, Artemis was with her. They bracketed the bed and settled down for another nap.

Instinctively, Clancy wrapped her half-sleeping body around Abby, and Abby was struck by how much the sensation reminded her of cuddling Hayley when she was a young child. Clancy was very slow to wake, and her heavy limbs draped across Abby's body while she crawled toward sentience. The blonde head rested on her chest, and Abby gently stroked her, urging her back to sleep. She had learned exactly how much sensation woke her and how much calmed her, and she decided that she wanted to hold her in her sleep for a while. After a few minutes, Clancy's breathing evened out, and her body grew even heavier.

That was exactly the sensation that Abby sought—she wanted the full, heavy weight of Clancy's body atop hers. She desperately wanted to experience the very physicality of her—to feel her bones and muscles and flesh compressing her own. She had the irrational thought that as long as they stayed just like this, Clancy would never have to leave—that they could be together without interference from anyone on earth. But even as she had the thought, she knew it was folly. Hayley would be home the next day, and Clancy would go back to her apartment—for how long, neither knew.

"I love you," Abby whispered, her eyes closing to hold back the tears. "I love you," she whispered again, this time a little louder as she kissed the blonde head. "I love you." Louder still, lips pressing against warm skin. "Clancy, I love you." Tears were rolling down her face unabated as the words poured from her mouth. "I love you...I love you...I love you."

Suddenly, warm, moist lips were covering hers, and her tears were being kissed away. "I love you, Abby. I love you, too."

In moments, they were moving against each other, skin sliding against skin, aided by the wet, warm kisses that rained down from one woman to the other. "I don't want you to leave," Abby sobbed, her tears coming in waves.

"I don't want to leave," Clancy whispered fiercely. "But we'll work it out. We'll be together soon. As long as we love each other, we can get past anything or anyone in our way. I promise you."

"I can't lose you, Clancy. I can't!"

"Shh...shh..." Clancy soothed, kissing her face to whisk away the tears. "You won't lose me. I'm yours...forever, Abby. I'm yours forever."

It was after six when Clancy made her way down the stairs on rubbery legs, her body enervated by long hours of nearly ravenous lovemaking. She had never experienced anything that came close to the wild frenzy of sensation they had shared—the passionate joining of two women finally willing to declare their love for each other openly. But her body voiced its demands, and she decided that she needed a form of nourishment more substantial than kisses. She grabbed the box of granola, a bowl, a spoon, and a quart of milk, and climbed the stairs once again.

Abby was right where she had left her—nearly comatose and spread widthwise across the bed. "Come on, baby," Clancy urged, nudging her with her hip. "Move up so I can get in."

With a tortured groan, Abby moved, slowly drawing her body toward the head of the bed.

Clancy poured the cereal, doused it with milk, and alternated bites with Abby, seeing some signs of life come back to her lover when she got a few calories into her.

"Good," Abby said after they had cleaned the bowl twice.

"More?"

"No. That's enough for now." Abby was fully awake, and she leaned against Clancy. "We should do something with the puppies. They've been so patient today."

"It's nice to know they don't try to interrupt when we make love. Do you think they know that's why we close them out sometimes? I can just hear their little doggie conversation. 'We'd better keep our paws to ourselves when the humans start with all of that mouthing and licking. I don't know what they're doing, but I think it's keeping us on the other side of this door!'"

Abby laughed gently and agreed. "They're a pretty bright pair. I saw Athena's head come up to the edge of the bed once when you were howling so pitifully that I'm sure she thought you were breathing your last."

"I thought I was too, Athena," Clancy said to the dog. "Your mommy nearly killed me!"

"Let's take them out before they kill us both. We can only push them so far before they turn on us."

They walked up the arroyo, looking across the deep crevasse that cut along the edge of Pasadena. Neither spoke more than was necessary, concentrating on the dogs, trying to keep the leashes from tangling.

They'd gone about a mile when Clancy said, "I think we need to talk about what happened today."

Sparing a wry glance, Abby said, "I feel like I've said everything I have to say. I love you; I need you; I don't want you to leave; I don't know how I could go on if we weren't able to be together. What else can I add?"

"Come here." Clancy opened her arms, and Abby gladly fell into her embrace. "It's okay," she said, feeling like she was on the verge of tears again. "Everything that you said is a given. How do we do it?"

"I don't have a clue."

"Sure you do," Clancy insisted. "I'm sure you're going over scenarios in your mind."

"Yeah. And most of them involve Hayley storming out and vowing never to speak to me again."

"Look. That might happen," Clancy said, making Abby's eyes go wide. "But anything like that is temporary. She's seventeen, Abby, and you admit she's a drama queen. Her first reaction won't be her final reaction. You've got to trust that the love you've nurtured for all of these years will pull you through this."

"I'll try to remember that." She gave Clancy's hand a squeeze and said, "Maria said I should hide this from Hayley and Trevor until I was sure how I felt. But she also said that I should tell them once I'd made up my mind that this was right for me. I think she worries that they'll feel betrayed if the relationship goes on too long without their knowledge."

"That makes sense."

"I'm sure of how I feel. I love you, and I'm willing to risk a great deal to have you in my life. It won't be easy, but I'm going to tell Hayley as soon as possible. Clancy O'Connor is here to stay."

Chapter Seventeen

Clancy packed her clothes up and put them in the truck just after dawn on Monday. Then she took the vehicle out of the garage and parked it on the street. She sat in the truck, drinking a cup of coffee while she waited for her crew to arrive. Even though she was ten feet from Abby's gate, she felt disconnected and alone. She'd felt the same way when she'd awakened, and Abby had seemed distant also. She knew they were both trying to handle Hayley's return in their own ways, but she was troubled that they'd been unable to talk about it.

Abby left the house at ten, and Clancy spent a few minutes resting against the handle of her shovel. She was lost in her thoughts and didn't hear Armando ask her about the placement of one of the boulders. He finally touched her shoulder, making her jump. She forced herself to concentrate and finally managed to block the distractions from her mind.

The crew was sitting on the hill, eating lunch, when the back door opened, and Hayley came out with both dogs on leashes to let them have a bathroom break.

Clancy caught her eye. "Have a good trip?"

"Yeah. Thanks. I did. You've done a lot up there."

"Yep. We've had a good two weeks. The majority of the plumbing work is done."

"Well, it doesn't look very good, but I'm sure it will soon," she said, showing a smile that looked strained.

Clancy didn't reply, but she returned the smile.

The girl's blue eyes scanned the scene; then they stopped…and began to glitter with anger. "What happened to our tree?"

"Oh!" Clancy looked up at the gaping hole in the greenery, seeing only the huge, buff-colored scar from the massive branch she'd been forced to cut off. "I had to thin it to make sure it could withstand the storms."

Hayley glared at her. "You did this?"

"Yeah. I had to. The tree might have fallen if we have a series of bad storms."

"Might have fallen? You ruined a tree that Trevor and I picked out and planted with our father in case it *might* fall? Who the fuck are you to make that decision?"

"Your mom approved, Hayley—"

"It's not her decision either! That was our tree! Ours!" She turned and ran back into the house, with all of the other workers acting like they hadn't seen or heard a thing. Even Ramon kept his mouth shut, and that was a rarity. Clancy tried to concentrate, but she spent the rest of the afternoon trying to calm her roiling stomach.

Abby didn't come out when the crew finished for the day. Clancy stalled and poked around for five minutes after the others left; then she got in her truck and went home.

She made dinner and sat on the couch with the television on. She had no idea what program was playing, but the background noise was soothing. At seven, the phone rang, and she leaped for it. "Hello?"

"I miss you, and I love you, and I want you sitting right here in the kitchen."

"Sounds so good," Clancy said, hearing the longing in her own voice.

"We'll get there," Abby said, her tone confident enough to make Clancy perk up a little.

"I suppose you got an earful about the tree?"

"Yeah. That was odd, but I think she's over it."

"Really? She was so angry!"

"Oh, did she make a scene, honey? You should have told me."

"I can't come whining to you every time Hayley says something that upsets me. I have to learn how to deal with her myself."

"True, but you can't figure her out in a few weeks. She's a complex kid."

"So how did you calm her down?"

"We talked about the tree and how much fun it was to go to the nursery to pick it. Then I told her that it was important that it go on living…even if it was less attractive than it was before."

"That worked?"

"Well, she was angry that I hadn't called her to ask her opinion. And at first she said she'd rather have taken the risk to have it fall, but then she calmed down and agreed that we'd made the right choice."

"Huh. I would have thought she'd stay mad for weeks."

"She can…but only if she's really hurt. I think this surprised her more than anything. She's not crazy about change…if she's not the one making the change."

"Mmm. So what's going on over there?"

"We've spent the day talking. Once we got past the tree issue, she cheered right up. That awful mood she was in when she left seems to be over. She seems much more like my baby again."

"That must be a relief. A big relief."

"A little, but I wasn't worried. She has her roller-coaster periods, but she always comes back down to earth."

"So…can we see each other this week?"

"I'll try to figure out a way. I really will."

"You know, I've been thinking about the first time we made love. Hayley was at her friend's house, but it didn't seem to trouble you that she might come home. That puzzled me then, and I guess I'm wondering why you're more cautious about having me over now. That night was a hell of a lot riskier than just having me over for dinner like you used to."

"I…I guess you're right."

"So?"

"Uhm…I can't explain my actions very well. I guess I was so overcome with desire that I didn't show very good judgment. I'm more rational now."

"I guess that's good."

"It is," Abby said. "It's better to do this in a well-thought-out fashion."

"Got any idea what that is?"

"Yeah. I decided I should call my parents. They're both level-headed, and my mom is very good at helping me come up with long-term plans." She laughed. "At least she was the last time I asked."

"How long ago was that?"

"Mmm…I think the last time was when I asked for her advice about whether I should get my master's degree right after I graduated from UCLA or wait a few years."

"Great," Clancy said, laughing. "Maybe she's been honing her skills since then."

"Well, no matter what, I'm not going to let much time pass. I need to tell the kids so we have time to work through things before Hayley leaves for school."

"That's the best news I've heard all day," Clancy said. "The sooner we start, the sooner we'll be finished."

❦

On Tuesday, Clancy spent much of the afternoon bidding on a job in Monrovia. She arrived at Abby's just before the end of the work day and walked to the back door to see her lover. She paused at the door, smiling when she looked inside. Abby was sitting at the built-in desk that was part of the kitchen counter. She'd rolled her chair back and was resting her head on her crossed arms, looking like a very bored child who couldn't go out and play until her homework was finished. Both dogs lay at her feet, obviously so used to Clancy that they didn't call out the alarm when she approached. The landscaper knocked softly, and the dogs merely lifted their heads while their tails thumped furiously. Abby swiveled around, and the smile that came to her lips made Clancy parrot one of equal warmth.

Walking into the house, Clancy asked, "What are you working on? You don't look like you're having fun."

"I'm a big chicken," Abby said, sticking her lip out in an adorable pout. "I don't have the guts to call my parents and tell them about us."

"Oh, you poor baby." Clancy started to hug her and then asked, "Are we alone?"

"Nobody here but us chickens."

They hugged, with Clancy holding on until Abby released her. "So…you're what…writing to them?"

"Trying to. Not having much luck."

"Want me to help?"

Abby pushed the computer toward her lover. "Do it. Don't even show it to me. Say whatever you want."

Laughing, Clancy stood behind her and massaged her neck. "You can do this. Just tell the truth. Tell them everything that happened. How we met…how we grew to be friends…how we grew more and more attracted to each other until we…well, don't tell 'em that part. They'll be able to figure that out for themselves."

Abby nodded and then rested her cheek on Clancy's hand. "If you stand behind me and rub my neck and shoulders, I bet I could have this finished in ten minutes. You calm me down so well."

"Happy to." Clancy started to slide a kitchen chair over, but Abby stopped her.

"No, baby, I won't have you catering to my needs while I do this. Besides, Hayley's supposed to be home for dinner. Just give me a kiss that'll last me all night, and leave me to my misery."

Clancy pulled the chair around and straddled Abby's lap. She didn't let much of her weight settle, but she wrapped her arms around her tightly. "I never want you to be miserable. But I'll do my best to give you a long-lasting kiss." She leaned into her and felt the hairs on the back of her neck stand up when their lips met. In a moment, they were kissing deeply, nipping on each other's lips, tongues sliding against each other. Fortunately, the dogs jumped to their feet and scampered for the door a second before Hayley burst in.

Clancy managed to be on her feet, and the girl didn't seem to notice a thing. "Hi, Mom. Clancy." She dropped her bag and petted each dog. "The beach was awesome today. I'm gonna shower down here so I don't track sand upstairs. Back in a few."

Abby smiled and made a gesture that looked a little like a wave. Hayley went into the bathroom and closed the door. As soon as Abby heard the door click, she looked like she'd had her bones removed and started to slide down the seat of the chair.

Clancy grabbed her under the arms and held her up. "It's okay, babe. She didn't notice a thing."

"I'm too old for this," Abby moaned. "I could have a stroke!"

"You'll be fine," Clancy soothed. "Now get to work and write your letter. I'll see you tomorrow." She kissed Abby on the top of the head, lingering a few moments to smell her hair. "I love you." She kissed Abby once more, on the cheek; then she squeezed Abby's shoulder and left for the day.

The next day, Abby appeared the minute the crew started to pack up for the day. When Clancy finished chatting with Ramon, Abby walked over and joined her under the pergola.

"Hi," Clancy said, feeling a little uncomfortable.

"Hi. All finished?"

"Yeah."

"Everyone gone?"

"I think so."

"Wanna neck?" Abby's eyes were giving off an impish twinkle, and Clancy felt her unease vanish into thin air.

Letting out a relieved laugh, Clancy reached down and grasped her hand. "Is that a good idea?"

"No, of course not. But that doesn't stop me from wanting to." Leaning over just a few inches, Abby pressed her body against Clancy's shoulder and captured her earlobe in her teeth. "You have the cutest ears I think I've ever seen."

Clancy stiffened slightly and pulled away. "Abby, I don't want to chance having Hayley come home and catching us. Last night was bad enough."

Resting her head on her shoulder, Abby sighed and said, "I know. But the dogs proved how adept they are at being early-warning devices."

"Still…" Clancy murmured.

"No, you're right. Stranger things have happened. I'll do my best to behave until it's all out in the open."

Clancy asked the question that had been nagging at her all day. "Got any idea when that might happen?"

Abby let out a wry laugh and said, "It almost happened last night. We sat up and talked for hours, and when we went upstairs, the dogs ran for the guest room and curled up at the end of the bed, thumping their tails ferociously."

"Oh-oh."

"Yeah. Hayley noticed, of course, since they've never done that before, but I tried to slough it off as odd canine behavior." She laughed. "Luckily, they act odd enough on a consistent basis to make that excuse quite believable."

"So was that the end of it?"

"No. I went to my room, but they didn't follow. After a while, I came out, and they were still on the guest bed, looking quite depressed. They missed you," she said, a sad smile settling on her face. "I did too."

"I missed you. I woke up twenty times during the night, trying to find you."

"None of us slept well, either. Artemis went in with Hayley, but Athena wouldn't give up the watch. Every time I woke, her head was up. It looked like she was unable to relax until you came to bed."

"So what do you think? Do you want to wait for a while to let Hayley settle in? Or is it best to just tell her and let her have some time to deal with it?"

"I don't want to do it today," Abby said. "I wrote my letter yesterday and mailed it this morning. Now I want to talk to a couple of my good friends to get some opinions. Ellen has known Hayley since she was born, and she's my closest friend. So…I have to come out to Ellen to get her advice."

"The look on your face says that you're not happy about that."

Abby made a dismissive gesture. "No, that's not what the look says." She moved around a little, trying to face Clancy more directly. "I think better when I can look into your eyes."

Clancy dipped her head and kissed her, the kiss short but heartfelt. "The little things you say make me fall more in love with you every day. God, I hope this feeling never stops, 'cause I'm addicted to it."

Abby ran her finger over her lover's lips, loving their form and the way they felt under her fingertip. "Things will calm down," she said. "But even though it won't feel as exciting, the feelings get so much deeper and stronger. It's a damn good trade-off for the unbridled joy of falling in love."

Nuzzling at her partner's neck, Clancy said, "Let's have both. Joy and depth."

"It's a deal."

They sat quietly for a few minutes; then Abby reached over and held her lover's hand. Neither woman spoke, and the minutes ticked by until it was fully dark.

The phone rang, and Abby jumped noticeably, their reverie shattered. The dogs started to bark, sensing that they should be on guard because their mistress had been startled. Shushing them, she went into the house and answered, her voice just soft enough for Clancy not to be able to hear.

After a few minutes, Abby returned. She sat down with less grace than she usually exhibited and said, "I'm meeting Ellen for breakfast." She didn't say another word, and Clancy sensed that her partner didn't want to talk. So they held hands again and leaned gently against each other until Clancy had to leave.

Kissing Abby tenderly, she said, "You'll do fine tomorrow. It went great with Pam and Maria, didn't it?"

Abby nodded, looking young and frightened.

"I know it's hard. I really do, babe, but you'll get through it. Ellen's a good friend, right?"

"Yeah. Very good."

"Good friends support you. That's what makes them friends. Try not to worry, okay?"

Abby nuzzled her face into her lover's neck, desperately seeking comfort. "I'm just not used to this kinda thing. I've never had to reveal anything like this. It scares me to death."

"I know, I know." She held Abby tightly, trying to transfuse some of her confidence into her partner. "Just get it over with. It'll get easier with each person."

Abby picked up her head, looking into Clancy's soft gray eyes. "Are you sure?"

"It was for me," Clancy said. "Much easier."

They held each other for a few more minutes. Then Clancy kissed Abby one more time, patted the dogs on the head, and left her to dwell in her own troubled thoughts.

❧

The old friends met at one of their favorite haunts on Greene Street. It was early, so parking wasn't a problem, and they saw each other heading to the restaurant from opposite ends of the block. Abby's palms were damp, and the butterflies were dive-bombing her stomach walls, but she tried to compose her expression into a semblance of normalcy.

"Hi!" Ellen called when they were still twenty feet apart. "It seems like it's been months since we've been alone together. Where has the summer gone?"

They hugged each other, and the familiar exchange helped calm Abby down a tiny bit. "This summer has gone by faster than any I can recall," Abby said. "It seems like Hayley got home yesterday."

"I know things have been crazy for you, with all of the work at your house. But we both have to make time for each other. That's the only way to stay close."

Abby winced when she heard those words. She felt guilty enough about keeping her friend entirely in the dark about her new relationship, but having Ellen remind her that they were drifting apart really struck home. "I'm at fault," she admitted. "My friends are more important than my house. I'm going to concentrate on being more connected."

Ellen looked at her for a moment, obviously puzzled. "I'm not angry, Abby. Don't take me too seriously."

Abby slipped her arm under her friend's and led her into the restaurant. "I know you're not angry. I'm just reminding myself of what's important." While they waited to be seated, it dawned on Abby that she hadn't seen Neil, Ellen's husband, all summer. It took her by surprise to realize that Neil had fallen out of the relationship since Will had died. She saw the Chenoweth family once or twice a year, but her real connection was now just with Ellen.

She pondered that for a moment and then realized that every one of her important relationships had changed after Will's death. Some had become closer, like hers with Ellen, and some had become more distant. Nothing had stayed exactly the same.

A few minutes later, they were sipping cups of coffee while they waited for their order. Ellen put her forearms on the table, her usual posture when she wanted to dish. "So what's going on? Tell me everything."

Abby laughed, but to her own ears, it sounded like she'd been pinched. "Actually, a lot has been going on. A whole lot." She slipped her hand through her hair, needlessly straightening it. Then she had to fix her watch so that it sat precisely in the middle of her wrist. Those essentials taken care of, she had nothing to do but look at her friend.

Ellen inclined her head, silently encouraging her to continue.

"Remember I mentioned a few weeks ago that I had been seeing someone?"

"Sure, I remember. Are you ready to unveil this mystery man? It's not one of the gubernatorial candidates, is it?"

With another yelplike laugh, Abby shook her head. "No. No. No politicians." She nodded to the server when he placed their meals in front of them and then decided she had to have a bite of her omelet before she spoke again. After chewing the small bite over fifty times, she peeked up to see Ellen giving her a very concerned look. "I'm worried about your reaction to the person I'm dating," she said, drawing a little closer to the point.

"My reaction?" Ellen put her fork down and reached across the table to touch Abby's hand. "Is he married?"

"Oh! God, no!" Now her laugh was genuine. "It's nothing like that. I'd never go out with a married man. That would go against every principle I have."

"Then what?"

"I'm making myself crazy with this cat-and-mouse game." She took in a deep breath and spat it out. "Here's the truth. I'm seeing a woman."

"You're seeing a woman...what do you mean?"

Abby blinked at her, not expecting that particular response. "I'm dating a woman. Rather than a man...I'm dating a woman."

Her friend's fork dropped from her nerveless hand and clattered noisily against her plate. "I...I...Abby...how...?"

"It caught me by surprise, too. Actually, no one can be as surprised as I was; it just happened."

"Did Maria and Pam...set you up?"

"No, no, not at all," Abby said, swiftly shaking her head. "I think they're still a little bit in shock as well."

"Then how...where do you go to meet a lesbian? Is it someone from church?"

"No. That's another slightly funny angle," she said. "She's the landscape architect that I hired to work on my yard."

"But that can't...I distinctly remember your telling me about her. You described her as a girl. Surely you..." Ellen looked like she was about to faint, but Abby knew she didn't have any power to make this easier.

"She's not a girl. She's lucky to look very young for her age. Once I got to know her, I saw how mature and generous and kind she was, and I just...I fell in love with her."

"You're in *love* with her?" Ellen's voice was really too loud for the setting, but Abby didn't ask her to keep it down.

"Yes," she said firmly, her eyes locked with Ellen's. "I'm in love with her."

"Jesus, Abby! I can't believe that Maria hasn't sat you down and given you a good talking-to! Can't you see what's happening here?"

"Uhm...I think I know what's happening—" she began, but her friend cut her off.

"You *don't* know what's happening if you think you're in love! For God's sake! There *is* a man out there for you! Just because you haven't met him yet is no reason to go off the deep end!"

"Ellen," she said, her voice calm and soft, "this has nothing to do with my ability to attract men. I'll admit that I was demoralized about the whole dating thing—but Clancy would have appealed to me if my phone were ringing off the hook. We just clicked."

"Clancy? How old *is* this woman? That sounds like a kid's name."

Abby was beginning to take umbrage at the tone that Ellen was using, but she decided to keep calm and reply to her question. "She's twenty-nine," she said, staring her right in the eye.

"Twenty-nine! Twenty-nine! Trevor's almost twenty-nine! Have you completely lost your mind? You're dating the gardener, for God's sake, and she's young enough to be your child...your daughter, no less! Abby, I love you enough to tell you this to your face. You need help!"

"Help?"

"Yes! You need professional help! I know how much you've grieved for Will, but that doesn't give you the right to do something so against your nature!"

"This isn't against my nature," she said, no longer feeling nervous. "It feels entirely natural. Completely and totally natural."

"There's nothing natural about seeking out a girl your son's age to have sex with! Nothing!"

"What are you upset about?" Abby asked. "Are you upset that I'm dating a woman, or that she's younger than I am, or that she's not a professional? Because none of those is a very good reason to be angry with me."

"Abby, what would you do if I left my husband to run off and join the circus?"

Making a face, Abby said, "That's hardly analogous."

"Yes, it is! You've never been a lesbian before, you've never been interested in younger men, and you've always been a member of the decidedly upper class! I've never seen you searching for hole-in-the-wall Vietnamese restaurants in Hollywood or selling your old clothes at the flea market at the Rose Bowl. You're a wealthy woman, and you like being a wealthy woman! I guarantee you that you wouldn't date one of the boys from the supermarket! Why is it all right just because she's a woman?"

Her head was beginning to throb, and she found that she could hardly keep track of the conversation. All she wanted to do was go home and have Clancy hold her. "Why is *what* right? What rule am I breaking?"

Ellen pursed her lips. Her forehead was wrinkled in a deep frown, and her cheeks were drawn tightly against her teeth. "You're a forty-five-year-old widow. You have grown children. You have a name in this community. You don't ignore your husband's memory and your children's feelings and the respect of your peers to do what feels right at any given moment! Hell, I want to have the pool boy come in and show me what it's like to make love to a twenty-year-old, but I don't do it! It would hurt too many people! I care more about other people than I do myself!"

Abby spent a moment composing herself. Her face was flushed with anger, and she knew she was on the verge of unloading on Ellen. But she also knew that she could easily destroy their friendship with a few harsh words, and she was determined not to. "I can only assume that you think you're telling me all of this for my own good. But I know what's right for me. Loving Clancy is what's right, and the fact that some people won't be happy about it can't stop me. Love is too precious to throw away."

"Are two of those people Trevor and Hayley? How do they feel about Clancy?"

"I haven't told them yet," she said. "I thought it would be easier to talk to my friends first." With hurt coloring her voice, she added, "I thought my friends would be supportive."

"You thought wrong," Ellen said flatly. "If you don't care about your kids' feelings, then I'm doubly sure that you're doing this out of some temporary bout of insanity."

Abby was unable to hold it in for another moment. Her anger began to spill out of her like a pot boiling over. "I don't care about my children? How can you have the nerve…the gall…to say that to me! I've given up more than you know to be there for my kids…every time they need me. And that won't change because of Clancy. She knows the kids have to come first…but not because they don't approve of this. They're adults now, and they can make their own decisions—and so can I!"

"So if Trevor and Hayley decide they can't tolerate this, you'll let them walk away from you? Is that what you're saying?" Ellen's face was nearly purple with anger, and she was clutching her fork like a weapon.

"That won't happen. My children will never abandon me. Never!"

"What…if…they…do?" Ellen asked, spitting each word out.

"Then I'll wait for them to come around." The words were out before Abby had a moment to consider them. But once she said them, she knew they were the absolute truth. No one—not her kids, not her friends, not her parents—could persuade her to give Clancy up. She was desperately in love, and the rest of the world was going to have to learn to adapt.

❦

Clancy pulled into her parking spot only to see Abby's car in Michael's place. She ran up the path, finding her lover sitting on her steps, looking disconsolate. "Why didn't I go to work with you?" Abby asked.

"What happened?"

Abby didn't reply. She just got up and waited for Clancy to open the door. As soon as they entered, Abby closed her eyes and asked, "How about a hug?"

"Always." Clancy wrapped her strong, tanned arms tightly around Abby's body.

Placing a kiss on Clancy's neck, Abby sat down on the sofa. "I told her." She made a face as she said, "She wasn't supportive."

"Oh, damn…I'm sorry. I know she's a good friend—that must have hurt."

"Yes, it did. But it made me angry, too. I'm really disappointed in her. She said some things that make me wonder about her."

Clancy nodded and said, "Give her a little leeway. This had to be a massive shock to her."

"I know that," she said quietly, "but that's no reason to treat me like I'm out of my mind. She demanded—*demanded*—that I seek psychiatric help!"

"Ouch!" Clancy made a face and said, "Give her some time. She might come around."

With a heavy sigh, Abby said, "I hope so. We've been friends since before Will and I were married. Her husband, Neil, was one of Will's best friends. They were both so supportive after Will died. I can't stand the thought of losing them as friends."

"Give her time, and try again when she has time to cool off. If she's who you think she is, she'll be able to accept us."

"I hope so," Abby said. "I really hope so."

Michael wasn't due home until eight, so they went into Clancy's room, took off their clothes, and held each other for hours. Abby didn't talk much, sticking to her habit of processing her feelings before she could talk about them. At around seven, she asked whether she could use the phone.

"Of course you can." Clancy handed the receiver to her and then wrapped her body around Abby's naked form.

Smiling, Abby called Maria and found that Ellen had already called to tell her about Abby's revelation.

"Am I that wrong about her? I always thought she was so open-minded."

"I think she is," Maria ventured.

"How can you say that? This is nothing but antilesbian, anti-working-class prejudice!"

Maria chuckled softly and said, "Abby, I doubt that she'd call me to complain about your being a lesbian if her rationale was homophobic. Yes, she's upset that you're in a lesbian relationship—but not because of the lesbian angle per se."

"Then what is it?" Abby demanded irritably.

"I think that she's upset because of the sea change this is for you. I honestly don't think her reaction would be a bit different if Clancy were a thirty-year-old man. I think it's the age and the socioeconomic issues that have her most upset."

"Oh, so she's not homophobic. She's just ageist and classist."

"Okay, I'll grant that her position doesn't put her in the best light, but this *is* a big change for you. She's afraid that you're drawn to Clancy because other things haven't worked out well for you. I also think she's a little afraid that Clancy is taking advantage of you."

"Of course! Working-class people are always trying to pull one over on us!"

"I know this upsets you, and I understand why, but you go back a long way with Ellen. Don't take all of her words so seriously. She's concerned about you, and she's shooting her mouth off a little—but I'm certain that she means well."

Abby sighed and made a face. "You know I'll be more civil when this settles a bit. I'm just hurt. I expected more from one of my closest friends."

"I understand. I really do. If she was spouting off at me like she did at you, I'd be upset, too. But when someone gets this angry over something that really doesn't concern her, I always try to look behind the behavior and figure out why she reacted so strongly."

"Any ideas, Doc?"

"Yeah, a few, but I won't push them at you just yet. You and Ellen have known each other longer and better than I've known her. You'll figure out what's going on over time. I'm sure of it."

"You're an optimist," Abby said. "I don't know how you are, given what you see at work, but you are."

"You are too," Maria reminded her. "Only an optimist would do some of the things you've done this summer."

"An optimist or an idiot?" Abby asked, sensing that Maria wasn't saying everything that was on her mind.

"You're one of the brightest people I know," Maria said. "You've never done anything idiotic since I've known you...and I've been on the lookout."

Her cavalier reply reassured Abby, and she said, "I was really shaken today, Maria. It made me consider how much my friends mean to me. I'm more grateful than you'll ever know that you and Pam have been so understanding."

"We love you, Abby. We always will. Now go have Clancy wrap you up in her arms and give you some comfort. That always helps."

"That's one bit of advice I'll act on immediately," Abby said. "Give my love to Pam and Alyssa."

"I will. Call me if you need to talk anymore. I'm always available to you, sweetie."

"The same goes for me. Bye." As soon as she hung up, she tucked her head against Clancy's shoulder and let out a sigh. "Hayley should be home soon. I'd better go. But I need some hugs first."

"That's what I do best," Clancy said as she proceeded to hug her partner with all of her might.

Chapter Eighteen

Clancy knocked at the back door on Thursday evening, making a silly face that had Abby laughing. "Bring that cute mug in here, and let me kiss it."

Clancy opened the door and looked around stealthily. "Are we alone?"

"Yeah. Hayley went to Santa Barbara to surf. She won't be home until late."

"How late?" Clancy asked, her hungry look giving Abby a good idea of the reason for her interest in Hayley's schedule.

The brunette walked over to Clancy and slipped her arms around her. "They usually go out for dinner at a taco place they love. She probably won't be home until eleven or midnight. Why? Got something on your mind?" She nuzzled at Clancy's neck and then nipped her sensitive earlobe.

"Uh-huh. Your body." Strong arms enveloped Abby, squeezing her hard enough to force the air from her lungs. "I've been thinking about you all day. The way you feel in my arms; the way you always smell like flowers and fresh air." Her hands slipped down and cupped Abby's cheeks. "But most of all, I've been thinking about your ass. You have the most delightful ass I've ever laid eyes or hands on, and there's nothing I'd like more than to study it up close for a couple of hours."

"Clancy!" Abby blushed, enormously pleased by her lover's interest. "You sure do know how to turn a girl's head!"

"Your head is wonderful, but I'd really like to see your ass." Clancy massaged the cheeks with fierce intensity. "See it…touch it…bite it…kiss it…"

"Whew!" Abby pulled back a little, fanning herself. "I've gotta call Maria and tell her I'm canceling!" She headed for the phone, but Clancy pulled her back.

"What are you canceling?"

Abby draped her arms around her lover's neck. "I think Maria's holding something back, and I arranged to go over and talk to her tonight. I thought you might want to go with me."

"We can go—"

Abby kissed Clancy's lips, stopping them as they were about to form another word. "Now that you've got me thinking about asses, I don't want to go out. I wanna stay in. Inside you," she added, looking a little embarrassed at using this sort of playful banter.

Clancy ran her hand through her partner's hair, looking into her eyes. "Have you been worrying about Maria?"

Abby nodded. "Yeah. Something doesn't seem right. It makes me wonder if she's holding out on me to avoid hurting my feelings or if I'm just projecting."

"This sounds important," Clancy said. "I think we should go. I'll still feel like having sex later."

"That goes without saying," Abby said, kissing Clancy until the blonde's knees began to shake. "I'm absolutely insatiable for you. Nothing makes me happier than touching you."

Clancy slipped her hand into Abby's shorts and then gently tickled between her legs. "Nothing?"

With a soft growl, Abby pushed her pelvis forward, pressing her mound into Clancy's hand. "Okay," she purred. "Nothing makes me happier than touching and being touched."

"That's more like it." Clancy pinched her lover's lips together and then gave them a tug, grinning when Abby's eyes closed and her nostrils flared. "You're so easy."

"Only for you, baby." They kissed for a few minutes, neither wanting to leave the house. Finally, Abby pulled away. "Stay or go?"

Lazily, Clancy replied. "Go. Damn it. Go."

"I was going to walk. Want to walk with me?"

"Uhm…sure. But I have to shower and change first. I can't go like this."

Abby smiled at her dirt-streaked face; sweat-stained, rumpled shirt; and mud-caked knees. "I think you look adorable. You remind me of Trevor when he was about four."

"I'll take that as a compliment. But I really do have to go shower."

"You could shower here—" Abby began, but Clancy was shaking her head before the sentence was finished.

"That's asking for trouble," she said. "I know Hayley won't come home this early, but it's not worth the risk. I'll go home and then come pick you up."

"No, I'm ready to get going now. I'll walk, and you can go home and take your time. Actually, would you stop at the store and pick up something from the deli for all of us? Pam and Maria despise cooking, and they jump at the chance to avoid it."

"Sure. Any preferences?"

"For the adults, anything that strikes your fancy. But make sure you get some of their macaroni and cheese for Alyssa. She's addicted to the stuff."

"Will do. See you in a bit." She leaned in for a quick kiss and a squeeze of Abby's butt. "I couldn't resist," she said, a mischievous twinkle in her eyes.

❦

After leaving a note for Hayley, Abby started off on her walk, reaching her friends' home a short while later. She made idle conversation with the whole family for a bit, dropping in the news that Clancy would be joining them. Eventually, she turned to Maria and said, "Could we go to your office for a few minutes? I have some things to talk to you about."

Maria looked a little surprised, but she got up and said, "Why don't you see if your mom can help you with your math homework, Alyssa? Then you'll be finished by the time we're ready for dinner."

The child gave her mother a fairly unhappy look, but she got up and took Pam's hand, compliantly heading for her bedroom.

Abby watched the pair leave, saying, "I miss the days when I could tell Hayley what to do. It feels like she's in charge of the house now."

Maria put her arm around her friend's shoulders while they walked down the hall. "It's always hard when a kid's on the verge of adulthood. And Hayley was never a pushover, Abby. Let's be honest."

Abby laughed, nodding in agreement. "You're right. She's always had a lot of spirit."

They entered the office, and they both sat on the modern leather sofa. "What's up?" Maria asked.

Abby was suddenly shy and spent a moment playing with the seam on the back of the sofa. "I…uhm…I've been getting some vibes…"

After waiting for her friend to speak again, Maria said, "Come on, Abby, this is me. What's bothering you?"

Their eyes met, and Abby forced herself to spit it out. "You and Pam both say you're supportive of me, but I've had a funny feeling that you don't think this is a great idea."

"What isn't…you and Clancy?"

"Yeah. And it seems odd to me that you and Pam would be uncomfortable with my being in a lesbian relationship."

Maria reached out and put her hand on her friend's knee. "Oh, Abby, that's not it," she said, her expression filled with empathy.

"Then what is it?"

Maria stood and walked to the window, looking out at the traffic gliding down the wide expanse of Orange Grove Boulevard. Abby waited impatiently, her heart hammering in her chest.

"I haven't been entirely honest with you," Maria admitted.

Hurt, Abby blinked her eyes, trying not to cry. "Why? Don't you trust me?"

Maria went back to the sofa and sat next to her friend. She draped an arm around her back and was surprised to have Abby snuggle up next to her and rest her head on her shoulder. "Of course I trust you. I just didn't want to offer an opinion that you hadn't asked for."

"But I asked for your opinion."

"No, you didn't, honey. The first time we talked about this, I told you to tell them when you were sure about Clancy. I haven't said anything since."

"So you don't think I should tell them?"

"It's not that. It's just…it's just that I think you should wait and see where this winds up."

"Where *what* winds up?"

"Where you and Clancy wind up. What if this doesn't work out? Is it worth it to go through the whole thing if you decide you're not comfortable in this relationship?"

Abby stood up and walked around the room slowly, trying to expend some energy. Finally, she stopped and perched on the edge of Maria's desk. "Say what you're thinking, Maria. Just say it."

The doctor let out a sigh, regretting that she'd opened her mouth in the first place. "I'm afraid that you and Clancy aren't going to last. And I'd hate to see you upset Trevor and Hayley for nothing."

Abby's eyebrows arched up, and she stared at her friend before she could speak. "Well, I asked for it, so I can't fault you for being blunt."

"Oh, Abby, I would never have said anything. It's not my business! But I care about you and the kids so much that I'm willing to risk hurting you now to help you avoid more hurt later."

Walking back to the sofa, Abby sat down and patted her friend on the leg. "I know you love me and the kids. That's without question." She sat there quietly for a few moments and then asked, "Why do you think we won't make it?"

"I…I'm sorry to say I feel a little like Ellen does," Maria admitted. "This is such a radical move for you—it just doesn't seem like something you'd do! You're the most stable, rational, conservative person I know, and I mean that in the best possible way. You're not someone to make a huge change that will affect every part of your life! I worry that you either haven't thought it through or you're not letting the repercussions sink in. Either way, I'm very worried for you. I love you, and I want you to be happy, but I'm afraid this isn't what will make you happy."

Once more, Abby got up. She wrapped her arms around herself and leaned against the window, looking out but not seeing. "I haven't been this happy since before Will died," she said softly. "Do I have to put other people first all of the time? Haven't I done enough of that?" She turned to Maria, tears sliding down her cheeks. "I was the perfect daughter, then the perfect girlfriend, then the perfect wife and the perfect mother. I haven't done anything for myself—only myself—since I was a teenager! When will I get my turn?"

Maria got up and went to her, holding Abby in her arms while the taller woman cried. "Oh, Abby, I'm sorry for hurting you. I'm so sorry."

"I've sacrificed willingly," Abby sniffed. "I went to college even though I wanted to travel for a year first. But my parents didn't want me to lose focus on my degree…so I went. I got married long before I had planned, but it made sense, and it was what Will wanted. I had Trevor when I was barely twenty years old! I didn't get my Ph.D. because it would have been too hard to juggle my work with the kids. I didn't teach because I wanted to be home for them. I didn't work because I wanted to be able to go on trips with Will or attend conferences with him." She let out a big breath, looking tired and defeated. "I did everything because it made sense. It's what worked out. It made the people I loved happy. But I'm forty-five years old, and I want to live a little! I want to be carefree for the first time in my adult life. I want to swim naked in my pool and make love on the patio. I want to spend the whole day in bed with Clancy, eating pizza out of the box and drinking warm beer because we're too exhausted to go downstairs. I want all of that, and I can have it. I can have what I want. Finally, I can have it and think only of myself. Me! Just me!"

"Oh, Abby, you deserve that," Maria whispered. "You deserve it."

"Do I?" she asked tiredly. "Do I? What if you're right? What if it doesn't work out? What if my kids can't accept it?" She put her head down and cried again, her sobs breaking Maria's heart. "Will I ever come first?"

Clancy arrived while Abby was in Maria's office, her arms laden with cartons filled with delicious-smelling items. She was a little uncomfortable to be alone with Pam and Alyssa, so she volunteered to arrange the food. "Okay," Pam agreed. "I don't imagine they'll be long. I'll just finish up with Alyssa—"

The phone rang, and Pam smiled and threw up her hands when she heard rapid, determined little footsteps heading for the phone in the hallway. After a few moments, Pam gave Clancy a smirk and said, "No one calls us anymore. Since Alyssa declared herself our receptionist, people don't call, because she bends their ear for an hour. It works great on sales calls, though." Raising her voice, she called, "Honey, who is it?"

"Hayley," came the reply, and both Clancy and Pam froze in place for just a moment before they both ran to the child to stare at her in horror as they heard her say, "Clancy just got here. She brought me macaroni." Her face scrunched up, and she nodded her head. "Sure, I know her. She's your mom's girlfriend." She looked into Clancy's terror-struck face and asked, "Don't you know your mom likes girls now?"

Clancy leaped for the receiver, ripping it from Alyssa's hands. She fell to her knees and tucked an arm around the startled child to reassure her while she said, "Hayley!"

A small, thin voice gasped, "Is that true?"

"Hayley, it's…it's…uhm…your mom and I…"

"It's true!" she cried. "It's true!"

"Hayley, come on, calm down. Let us come home, and we'll all talk it out."

"Fuck you! Go fuck yourself, Clancy!" She slammed the phone down violently, and before the sound had finished reverberating in her ears, Clancy was running for the door.

"I'll be back. Tell Abby to wait for me." She wasn't even sure why she was certain that time was absolutely critical, but Clancy knew that she couldn't wait to explain to Abby what had happened. She had to stop Hayley before the girl could leave the house, and every second was precious.

Her truck was right outside, and she peeled out while still struggling with her seat belt. She raced down the streets of the quiet neighborhood, her heart thudding loudly in her chest. The only thought that kept going through her mind was that she had to stop Hayley from driving off when she was irrational. They could work through any problem with enough time and effort, but if Hayley drove off and hurt herself, Clancy was sure that was one thing Abby could never get over.

While Clancy was streaking down the street, Hayley was ripping off her sandy swimsuit and throwing on a clean pair of shorts and a T-shirt. She grabbed the keys to the Lexus and started to pull out just as Clancy reached the drive.

The yellow truck straddled the macadam, blocking the exit as Hayley cleared the garage. "Get the fuck out of my way!" she screamed, appearing hysterical.

Leaving the engine running, Clancy got out and approached the convertible. "Hayley, please get out and hear what I have to say."

"Are you fucking my mother?" she screamed, tears running down her face.

Clancy took a breath and said, "We're in love with each other," her eyes never leaving Hayley's.

The dark head bowed, and Hayley started slamming her head against the steering wheel, sobbing pitifully.

Going around to the side of the car, Clancy got in. Noticing that Hayley's foot was pressing the brake down, she slid the car into park and leaned over to kill the engine, tucking the keys into her shirt pocket.

"Why you? Of all people—why you?"

"I don't know," Clancy said quietly. "It just happened. All I know is that I love her. And she loves me."

"She does not!" A tear-streaked, outraged face glared at Clancy. "She does not love you!" Hayley fumbled with and finally yanked the door handle; the door opened, and she started running for the street. Clancy paused a moment and then took off after her, gaining on her easily because Hayley was barefoot.

"Hayley, wait!" She grabbed Hayley by the arm of her T-shirt, and the younger woman wrenched away from her so violently that the sleeve ripped half off.

She turned and swung hard, her fist catching Clancy right on the bone under her eye. Gasping in pain, the blonde doubled over, only to have Hayley kick her hard on the shoulder, knocking her to the ground.

Stunned, Clancy watched as Hayley ran for the truck. Clancy got to her feet and ran as fast as she could, grabbing the passenger-door handle and pulling it open just as Hayley threw the truck into gear. Holding onto the handle over the seat and the rail of the bed, Clancy powered herself into the seat, settled her weight, and jammed her foot onto the brake, banging her head into the windshield hard enough to see stars. She wrestled with Hayley for a second, but her superior strength and bulk allowed her to overpower the girl and get the truck into park. Jerking the key from the ignition, she glared at the girl and said, "This isn't the fucking end of the world! Now stop being such a big goddamned baby, and calm fucking down!"

Hayley reared back to slap her again, but Clancy reached out and roughly grabbed her hands. She shook her hard, giving her a lethal glare and saying, "I told you to calm down! I meant it!"

Hayley slumped against the door, tears flowing freely down her cheeks. Clancy's cell phone chirped, and she got out of the truck to answer, casting a worried glance at Hayley while she punched the answer button. "Hi," she said quietly.

"Where are you?"

It sounded like Abby had been crying. Clancy turned her back to the truck and said, "I'm at your house. Hayley's really upset, but I don't think you should come back quite yet. Give me a few more minutes with her, okay?"

"But—!"

"Abby, she's really angry. Let her vent some of her anger before you try to talk to her."

"But she's venting at you—"

"I can handle it. She's not my child. Trust me on this…please?"

"Do you have the number here?" Abby asked after a moment.

"No. Page me and leave the number. I'll call you soon."

Walking back to the driver's door, Clancy knocked lightly and then swung the heavy door open. "Come on. Let's go inside."

Wordlessly, the young woman got out and stood by the truck while Clancy parked it. Once in the kitchen, they spent a few minutes calming the dogs down, both animals agitated from hearing raised voices.

Hayley went to the freezer and took out a few ice cubes; then she wrapped them in a kitchen towel and handed it to Clancy. "Put that on your eye," she said, going to sit on one of the kitchen stools.

Puzzled, Clancy touched her eye, noticing for the first time that it was swollen and painful to the touch. She placed the cloth on it, flinching a bit when the cold hit her skin. "Can I have another one for my head? I banged it pretty hard."

Getting up to fetch another, Hayley brought it over. Then she gently ran her fingers through Clancy's hair, wincing when she felt the knot that was already forming. Pressing the cloth against the spot, she said, "I'm sorry I hit you. I've…never hit anyone in my whole life."

"It's okay. I've had worse."

"Bar fight?" Hayley asked, the ghost of a smile on her lips.

"Tree limb." Clancy returned her smile and asked, "What's going on? I thought this would bother you, but you act like this is the worst thing in the world. Where does that come from?"

"How would you like it if your father died and your mom fell in love with a chick?"

Clancy made a face, annoyed with herself for having such a visceral reaction to the mere thought. "Okay. It would be weird," she admitted. "I don't know what it's like to be in your shoes. Neither does your mom. But she loves you very much, and she doesn't want to hurt you. Neither do I."

Tears started to roll down the young woman's cheeks, and she muttered, "I don't want you to be with her."

"I can see that. But I am. It's what we both want."

"So I don't even get a vote?"

"I can't speak for your mom. You'll have to ask her that. But even if you get a vote, it's still two to one."

"She'd choose you over me," Hayley sobbed, dropping the cloth and distancing herself from Clancy. She walked to the other end of the kitchen, clutching her belly with her arms.

"That's not true. Your relationship with your mom is precious! There's no outsider who can ever mess with that. And as much as I love your mother, I'm an outsider. I'll always be an outsider. You're her flesh and her blood; you're her child. No matter how old you get, no matter how many fights you have—she's your mom."

Hayley dropped her head and then wiped her eyes with the hem of her T-shirt. "I hate this," she whispered.

"I know." Clancy walked over and stood next to her. "I know how upset you are, but I also know that your mom is worried sick. I want to go pick her up now. Will you at least try to be civil to her?"

"Yes."

Clancy had both sets of keys, but just to be sure, she decided to take Abby's car. There could be another set of keys that she didn't know about. When she reached the door, Hayley's soft voice floated over to her. "You're not going to come back with her, are you?"

"No. This is between the two of you. I'm going home."

"Good."

❧

When Clancy turned into the entrance to Pam and Maria's complex, she saw Abby standing on the front steps with Maria. As soon as Abby spotted the car, she patted Maria and ran toward Clancy. She flung the door open while the car was still moving. "Why did you leave me?" she asked, jumping into the car. It was clear that she'd been crying, and her voice was shaking with what Clancy guessed was a mix of anger and agitation.

"I don't know why I knew it was so important," Clancy said, "but I knew she was going to get in that car and take off. I couldn't risk her doing that and hurting herself. It's a good thing I left when I did. I barely stopped her from taking off in your car."

Abby's head dropped back against the headrest. She took in and let out several long, deep breaths. Finally, she patted Clancy absently and said, "Thank you for following your instincts. I never would have forgiven myself if she'd gotten hurt."

As soon as they pulled into the garage, Abby jumped out, but Clancy stopped her. "Abby, uhm…we talked a little, but I think it's best if I don't repeat anything she said. I'm gonna leave now."

"Oh. Right. Uhm…" She looked toward the door, her face contorted with anxiety, and Clancy waved her off.

"Go ahead. Just close the door after me, okay?"

Abby looked at the lost, lonely expression on her lover's face and ran around the car to hug her fiercely. "We'll get through this." A kiss on the temple, and she was gone, leaving Clancy alone in the dark garage, the quiet whir of a fan in the car the only sound.

Abby walked into the house tentatively, expecting the worst, but Hayley didn't answer when she called. The dogs were missing, too, but the open back door led her to the pool, where the lithe young woman was churning out laps. Abby watched her for a moment; then she went back into the house and put on her own suit. A few minutes later, she joined Hayley in the pool, quietly watching her work out her frustrations. A very long time passed, and Hayley finally drew to a stop, her muscles obviously giving out.

Hayley draped her arms on the pool deck, looked at her mother, and asked, "Are you mad at me?"

"Mad at you? Why on earth would I be mad at you?"

"'Cause I hit Clancy," she said quietly.

"You hit…?"

She nodded. "Didn't you see her eye? It was all swollen. And she hit her head on the windshield. Uhm…you'd better make sure she's okay."

"Shit!" Abby jumped out of the pool and raced for the kitchen, her hands shaking while she dialed Clancy's cell, which was answered on the second ring. "Are you all right? Hayley told me she hit you and that you hit your head on the windshield!"

"Yeah, I'm fine," Clancy said. "Just a headache. Don't worry about me."

"I am worried about you," Abby said, her voice shaking. "You might have a concussion."

"I don't think so. How are things there?"

"Clancy, listen to me. Go to the emergency room right now, or I'll come over there and take you."

Sighing, Clancy said, "I don't want to spend the whole night in the ER. I have to work in the morning."

"Then go back to Maria's. She'll know if you're hurt badly enough to need a CAT scan."

"Abby—"

"Clancy, I'm just about to rip my hair out. I can't take much more stress today. Now, please, if you love me, go see Maria!"

Clancy had never heard her lover sound so thoroughly agitated. "Fine. Give me her number so I can tell her I'm coming."

"I'll call her for you. And her number's on your pager, too. Call me as soon as she looks at you, okay?"

"I promise. I love you."

"I love you, too. I swear I do."

Clancy closed her cell phone, a little puzzled by the emphatic way that Abby had professed her love. There was something about her tone that sounded desperate, and a gnawing worry worked at her stomach all the way to Pam and Maria's home.

After calling Maria, Abby walked back to the pool and slipped in, wishing she could submerge herself for a few hours until things calmed down.

Hayley was squatting in the corner of the pool, crying. "I've never hit anybody in my life. I was just so mad…"

"I'm sure Clancy will be fine. Don't worry about her right now. She's going to go get her head checked to make sure she doesn't have a concussion."

"Jesus." Hayley covered her face with her hands. "I didn't know what I was doing. I had to get away from her…but she wouldn't let me go."

"She'll be fine. Now tell me what's going on in your head."

Hayley looked at her mother, unblinking. "Are you in love with her?"

Without hesitation, Abby nodded. "Yes, I am."

The narrow shoulders slumped, and Hayley turned away from the level gaze that her mother fixed her with. "I guess I'll go back up to Santa Cruz. I have some friends who rented an apartment. I can live with them until school starts."

"Hayley, there's no reason for you to leave! How can we work this out if you're gone?"

"I can't stay," she said quietly. "I just can't."

"But why?"

"You made your decision. Clancy's the one who matters."

"Of course Clancy matters to me, but you're my child! You're not in competition!"

"Yes, we are. You let me tell you about my crush on her…let me look like a fool…and never said a word. That's when you chose her." She walked over to the edge of the pool and pushed herself up, getting to her feet. "Don't start acting like you care now." Shaking her head to get the hair from her eyes, she wrapped a towel around herself and went inside.

Abby knew she should go after her, but she didn't have the strength. She went over to the hot tub and turned on the jets, trying to center herself before she had to face her daughter once again.

She'd just settled into the warm water when the doorbell rang. The dogs barked like mad, and Abby felt like joining them as she got out and wrapped a towel around herself.

Looking out the peephole, she spotted her neighbor, Marjorie. She would have rather opened the door to a proselytizing Jehovah's Witness selling insurance, magazines, and Amway products, but she knew she couldn't ignore her. Opening the door a crack, she said, "Hi, Marjorie. Something wrong? It's a little late for a social call."

Marjorie actually tried to push on the door, doing her best to get her head inside to see what was going on. "What happened tonight? I heard cars flying around, and Steve said he thought he saw your daughter and that contractor having a fight of some sort."

"A fight?" Abby did her best to look perplexed. "I'm sure Hayley's not the type to fight in the street, Marjorie. And my contractor's not here. You'd better check your sources." Abby didn't usually like to lie, but in Marjorie's case, she actually felt good about it.

The woman looked at her carefully. "Are you sure everything's all right?"

"Of course. Hayley and I were just in the spa; then she went up to bed. But I'll let you know if we're going to start sparring in the street. Maybe we can do that at our next block party."

"All...right," Marjorie said, looking unconvinced. "Something happened tonight. But maybe it was the O'Reillys. They've never seemed that happy to me. I'll keep an eye out."

"You do that. And be careful walking alone at this time of night. Someone might jump out of the bushes and hit you!" *I wish it could be me!*

❧

Steeling her nerves, Clancy rang the doorbell, wondering how the night had gone so wrong so quickly. Maria answered, looking as uncomfortable as Clancy felt. "I hear you accept house calls," Clancy said.

Maria put her hand on her shoulder and urged her into the house. "After the night you've had, waiting in the emergency room would be cruel and unusual punishment. Come into the kitchen where the light is good."

Walking down the hallway, Clancy asked, "Is Alyssa okay? I've been worried about her."

Maria glanced at her, surprised and pleased that Clancy would think of the girl during the turbulent night. "Yeah, she'll be fine. But she's pretty upset. She thinks she caused trouble for Abby...which she did," she added in a whisper.

"Would you like me to talk to her? I think I freaked her out by yanking the phone out of her hand and then running out of the house. She might feel better if she saw me acting normally."

Maria pursed her lips and then shook her head. "You haven't looked at yourself in a mirror, have you?"

Her hand flew to her cheek. "That bad?"

"Yeah. I don't think Alyssa would feel better to know that Hayley belted you."

Making a sheepish gesture, Clancy said, "I don't have much experience with kids, but that probably wouldn't be the best idea."

Maria pointed at a chair, and Clancy sat down. The doctor took a penlight from one of the kitchen drawers and turned it on. She touched Clancy's chin and said, "Look straight ahead." She spent a few moments looking at each eye, watching it dilate. "Your eyes look fine," she said. "The pupils are the same size, and they dilate at the same rate."

She sat down next to Clancy and touched the bruise under her eye. Clancy winced but didn't move, allowing Maria to feel the bone around her eye. "Okay. Now let me ask you a few questions."

"Questions?" Clancy asked weakly. "Don't make 'em too hard. I'm wiped."

Maria smiled at her. "Simple ones. Don't worry." She felt the knot that had formed right at Clancy's hairline. "Do you remember coming over with dinner?"

"Sure. I went home, showered, and went to the store. Then I drove over here."

"What were you doing when you hit your head?"

"Wrestling with Hayley and hitting the brakes too hard. I learned that seat belts are a good idea when you're fighting to take control of a truck."

Patting her on the shoulder, Maria said, "Does anything seem fuzzy or unclear?"

"Yeah, but not because of being hit in the head." Clancy smiled at her, and the doctor found herself returning the grin. "I'm not used to a lot of dyke drama."

Maria got up and went to the freezer, pulling out a pair of cold packs. She handed one to Clancy for her eye and held the other to her forehead. "Since both of your bumps are on the same side of your head, you need a little help."

"You've helped a lot," Clancy said. "I really appreciate your taking a look at me. I don't want to cause Abby any more worry." She thought for a moment and then asked, "How did she seem when you talked to her?"

"Not great. She was very worried about you. Frantic, actually."

"Oh, this is nothing," Clancy said, waving her free hand dismissively. "She's the one with problems. I just hope Hayley isn't as irrational with her as she was with me." She took in a deep breath and looked at Maria, her gray eyes filled with concern. "I hate for her to go through this alone, but I know it'd be worse if I were there."

Maria smiled at her, saying, "You really care about her, don't you?"

"God, yes! I'd do anything to help her!"

"I hope it all works out for you. I really do."

Abby knocked on Hayley's door, but the young woman didn't ask her to enter. "I don't want to talk now, Mom."

"Come on, honey, don't shut me out."

"I'm sorry. But I want to be alone. I don't feel like talking tonight. Just let me calm down."

"All right," Abby said, feeling her eyes fill with tears. Lonely and depressed, she walked down the hall to the guest room, grateful when the dogs jumped onto the bed, waiting for her. She cuddled them for a few minutes, relishing their simple, unquestioning devotion. "You don't even get mad at me when I take you to the groomer," she sighed into Athena's curly coat.

She lay down and dialed Clancy, not surprised in the least when she answered on the first ring. "Hi."

"Are you all right?" Clancy asked quickly.

"Yes. I'm so sorry that Hayley hit you. Are you all right?"

"I'm fine. Maria checked me out. But I'm worried sick about you."

"It sounds like it went better for me than it did with you. She didn't try to hit me."

"She was angry," Clancy reminded her. "It was no big deal."

"Yes, it is. It's a very big deal, and I'm sorry you had to suffer because of Hayley's temper."

"Forget about it. Now, how are you?"

Abby sighed heavily and said, "Well, other than her telling me that she thinks I've chosen you over her, she didn't talk much. She's worse than I am about talking when something's upset her."

"Ouch! No wonder you don't have many fights."

"Yeah, that's part of it. She's angry and hurt, but I'm sure she'll get over it. I just…I think that we should back off a little—just until she's more comfortable with this."

"Back off?"

Abby cleared her throat, trying to keep her gathering emotions at bay. "Clancy, I love you. That's not going to change. But I need to spend some time with Hayley. I have to give her some space so that she feels like she can express herself. Is that okay?"

"Sure. You do what you think is best." She paused a second and asked, "Can you come to my house?"

"Let's see how it goes. I want to make sure we handle this properly so that we can move forward."

Clancy did her best to still the doubts and the worries threatening to overwhelm her. She forced herself to take a leap of faith. "Okay. I'll let you decide how to handle this. I trust you."

"I love you, Clancy. And I'm so happy to know that you trust my judgment. I'm sorry for how badly this all went, but we can get through it. We *will* get through it."

"I know we will. I love you with all my heart. G'night."

"Try to sleep, honey. You have a big day tomorrow."

"I will. You, too."

Chapter Nineteen

Clancy got to work early and pulled up in front of Abby's house before her crew arrived. Her cell phone rang before she could turn the truck off, and she raised the device to her ear to hear Abby say, "Meet me out back. I have to see you."

After jumping out of the truck, the blonde headed for the yard. Abby grasped her when she reached the corner of the house and wrapped her in a nearly desperate hug. "How are you?" she whispered, pulling away to run her fingers gently over Clancy's bruised face.

"I'm fine, really," she said, flinching a bit when Abby's cool fingers touched the bump on her head.

"I'm so, so sorry," Abby said, pulling her into another hug and squeezing her hard. "I can't believe how badly everything turned out."

Clancy drew back and looked into Abby's eyes. "Nothing has turned out yet, babe. We had a bad night. That's all. Things will get better as long as we're patient."

Both heads turned at the sound of a heavy truck pulling up in front of the house. "Oh, damn," Abby sighed.

Clancy patted her and gave her a hearty hug. "Don't worry so much. We'll be fine…eventually."

Abby kissed her tenderly, barely brushing lips. "I won't be able to come out today, honey. I don't want to make things worse."

"That's fine," Clancy said, trying to convey her confidence. "Call me tonight. Just try to get through the day, and realize that things might be bad now, but they'll get better."

"Promise?" Abby asked, searching Clancy's gray eyes for the slightest sign of doubt.

Clancy put her hands on her shoulders and held her at arm's length. "I promise."

Abby gave her another quick kiss and dashed away just before Ramon and the rest of the crew entered the yard.

❧

After an exhausting day of helping the crew with the planting design, Clancy was almost relieved to be able to leave at the end of the day. Abby stuck her head out a few times, but they didn't converse at any length, and Clancy left with a vague feeling of uneasiness despite her assurances to Abby.

Hayley pulled into the driveway just as she was leaving, and Clancy turned her head and drove off, her heart thudding heavily in her chest.

❦

When Pam got home from work, Maria was in the kitchen making sandwiches for dinner. "Oh, you're cooking!" she said, a pleased smile on her face.

"We're in trouble when this constitutes cooking," Maria said. She wiped her hands on a towel and gave her lover a kiss. "Good day?"

"Yeah. Fine. How about you?"

"Not bad. I was distracted all day, though. I couldn't stop thinking about Abby."

Pam snatched a piece of turkey and stuffed it into her mouth before Maria could stop her. "Good," she said, smiling impishly. "I spent a lot of time thinking about her, too. And about Hayley. Did you hear from her?"

"Huh-uh. I'm afraid to call."

Pam kicked off her shoes and hoisted herself up onto the counter. "I'm feeling a little chicken myself. Maybe we should have Alyssa call."

Maria laughed wryly. "I think we should revisit having Alyssa answer the phone. If she even wants to after last night."

"She'll be fine. She seemed all right before she went to bed." She leaned over, grabbed a few carrot wedges, and started to munch on them. "We didn't get to talk much last night, since you collapsed as soon as you came to bed. How was Clancy?"

Maria took a carrot from her lover and took a bite. She looked pensive for a moment and then said, "Nothing serious. I'm sure she has a headache today, and she probably has a pretty good shiner, but she'll be fine. You know," she said, taking another bite, "she's a lot more mature than I thought. She doesn't seem as young as she did when we met her."

"It's only been a week, honey. I don't think you can mature much in seven days."

"You're too funny," Maria said, her expression completely deadpan. "I know, but I don't think she was comfortable with us the night we met her. I'm not sure we saw the real Clancy. Last night she seemed…I don't know. She seemed like a woman who knew what she wanted and would do what it took to get it. I…I'm feeling better about the whole thing."

"Really? She seemed like a kid to me last night. She acted really uncomfortable being alone with me and Alyssa."

"Well, she is from a different generation…and she's a gardener…and she doesn't act like she comes from one of the old Pasadena families. Maybe she feels intimidated by us."

"Hey! I almost forgot to tell you this. I was talking with someone at work who's having her landscape redone. She said she couldn't afford a landscape architect. Said most of 'em don't do residential work. She was really surprised when I told her that we have a friend whose architect is at her house all the time."

Maria gave her partner a concerned look. "Really? Fuck! Maybe she's not really an architect. Or maybe she's not a very good one. I don't know anything about the field. Maybe we should do some research."

Pam laughed. "Why? So we can tell Abby we checked her lover out, and she's a fraud? Don't you think we did enough damage to her family yesterday?"

"We wouldn't have to tell her."

"Yeah." Pam leaned back on her hands and smirked at her lover. "You're the type to learn something bad and keep it to yourself. I think we'd better stay out of it."

Letting out a breath that made her lips flap, Maria agreed. "Okay. I won't play private detective. But if she fleeces Abby for all she's worth, you're responsible!"

"Maybe Clancy's intimidated by Abby, too. Abby's at least as imposing as we are."

Maria tapped her lover's head. "I think the intimidation factor goes down when you're physically attracted to each other. When you're in love, nothing matters."

"Huh. I've never been in love with a younger woman"

"You'd better not start!" Maria said, giving her lover a hearty, possessive squeeze.

❧

At eleven o'clock, the phone rang, and Clancy reached across her futon to pick up. "Hi," she said.

"Do you miss me as much as I miss you?"

"Probably," Clancy said, feeling better just to hear Abby's voice. "I'm pretty competitive."

"Are you all right? I know this isn't what you hoped for when you fantasized about being with an older woman."

Clancy laughed. "No, I'd have to admit I never got off on thinking about jealous daughters. Luckily, you're worth it."

She said this with a great deal of confidence, and Abby sighed aloud. "Oh, I feel better just hearing you say that. I've been worried sick that this would all be too much for you."

"Damn, you don't know me very well if you think that. Hayley'd have to put a contract out on me to get rid of me. It's your opinion of me that matters. Not Hayley's."

"That's good. 'Cause Hayley's not happy with either of us right now."

"Is she jealous? I got a little vibe from her that led me to think that."

"I think she's a little jealous," Abby agreed. "But she seems to feel betrayed. At least that's what I'm guessing."

"She didn't say?"

"No. I chased her around the house all day long, but all she did was lie on various pieces of furniture, listening to her iPod. She didn't say two words all day."

That would have worked for about five minutes at my house, Clancy thought, but she knew that Abby and Hayley had a different relationship than she had with her parents, and she tried not to judge Abby's style. "So what do we do? Wait until she's ready to talk?"

"I…I guess so," Abby said, sounding very unsure of herself. "I haven't thought that far ahead. I have plans to have lunch with my friend Spencer tomorrow—"

"No tennis?"

"No. Ellen and Neil are out of town. Or at least that's what she told Maria. Other than seeing Spencer, I was just gonna hang around the house and hope my mere presence annoys Hayley enough to get her to talk."

"Can't make her, huh?" Clancy asked, grimacing when she heard the question come out of her mouth.

"Make her? How can you make someone talk about her feelings?"

Abby sounded truly puzzled, and Clancy knew it was pointless to go down this path. "Just wishful thinking."

"I hate to be apart, but I think I need to stay home until Hayley opens up. You *do* understand, don't you?"

"Yeah. Sure I do. You have to do what you think is right. And no matter what, she's gotta go back to school soon."

"Not for a month," Abby said. "Damn, now I'm upset that she's gonna be home for another month. I never thought I'd feel that way! I couldn't wait for her to come home."

"This is temporary, Abby. You're going through a rough patch. Don't stress about it too much."

"I don't know if that's possible. Stress is one of the cornerstones of motherhood."

The next morning, Abby was lying in bed, unable to sleep and unwilling to get up. She'd gotten so delightfully used to having Clancy in bed with her that now she had a hard time falling asleep, and she woke before dawn, feeling cranky and depressed.

The phone rang, and she reached out to grab it, wondering who had the nerve to call at six. "Hello?"

Abby heard her mother's voice and felt her mood lighten as if by magic. "I know it's too early to call, but I figured you're not sleeping well anyway."

"Damn, you know me too well," Abby said, turning onto her back with a smile on her face. "You aren't calling to disown me, are you?"

"No, falling in love isn't going to do it. You're going to have to try harder if you want to be disowned."

"I knew you'd understand, Mom," Abby said, feeling her mother's love and warmth even at a distance of three thousand miles.

"I didn't say that, honey," Elizabeth Tudor said, laughing. "I know it's not physically possible, but it felt like my jaw hit the floor when I read your letter. Aren't you supposed to figure out if you like men or women when you're a heck of a lot younger?"

"That's what they say. I guess I'm a late bloomer." She waited for a second and then asked, "Is Dad as nonchalant about this as you are?"

"You *have* met your father, haven't you? He's never been nonchalant in his life."

"You know what I mean. How's he taking it?"

"Well…he loves you, honey, and he wants you to be happy. But he's not sure this is the right choice for you. It'll take him a while."

"Is he angry? Upset? What's going on, Mom?"

"No, he's not angry, but he is upset. I didn't tell him I was calling you because I didn't want him to get on the phone and start lecturing you. I know you hate that."

"Hate's not a strong enough word. And I wouldn't take a lecture very well right now."

"That's what I figured. We'll just let him stew about this for a while, and you can talk to him when he's ready to listen. I told him to write to you, and I think he's going to. But don't read the letter if you don't want to have him tell you all the reasons you shouldn't do this."

"We've got a deal. You do realize he'd kill both of us if he knew you warned me when to throw his letters away."

"Oh, he doesn't have a mean bone in his body," Elizabeth said. "He just forgets that he can't talk to you like you're one of his students. He was a professor for far too long."

"But you're okay with this, Mom? Really okay with it?"

"Well…if I had my choice, I suppose I'd rather you found another man. I think that would be easier for you and for the kids. But I can't make your decisions, honey. And I know you wouldn't fall for someone who wasn't absolutely wonderful. So I'm confident this will all work out."

"Have I told you what a wonderful mother you are?" Abby asked, her voice breaking a little.

"Yes, honey, you have. But it's easy to be your mother. You've always been a great kid." Elizabeth cleared her throat dramatically. "Speaking of kids, how are you going to tell yours?"

With a sound between a gurgle and a groan, Abby said, "Hayley knows. Alyssa told her."

"Alyssa?"

"Yeah. Hard to believe that such a little girl could stir up such a mess. The poor thing was entirely innocent, of course, but having Hayley find out that way has made this hellish."

"Oh, Abby, how horrible for you!"

"It's been bad. I wanted to have this all planned out, with all sorts of contingencies factored in. You know how I am, Mom."

"I do. Maybe it wasn't wise for math and engineering nerds to have a child. You never stood a chance of being madcap."

"Well, lesbian love at forty-five is pretty madcap," Abby reminded her. "But Hayley's very, very hurt, or angry, or confused, or disappointed."

"Up to her old tricks, eh?"

"Yeah. She won't say a word. She just walks around the house and sighs dramatically every once in a while. I don't mean to make light of her feelings, but she's playing this like *Camille*."

"She has a flair for the dramatic, but she's the quietest diva in the world."

Abby laughed. "That sums her up. So I don't know what to do but wait her out." She took in a heavy breath and asked, "How did I get old enough to have problems like this?"

"Don't ask me. I refuse to believe I'm seventy years old. It's just not possible!" She laughed at her own incredulity and said, "I suppose we have to face reality, but I'm happier being in denial."

"I wish I could be in denial about this, but I have to tell Trevor now. I'm hoping he'll be more understanding than Hayley, but you never know."

"Oh, I'm sure Trevor will be all right. He'll be surprised, but he's always been a level-headed boy. He's so much like you, it isn't funny."

"That's true, Mom, but I don't know how I would have liked it if Dad had died when I was young and you showed up with a woman on your arm."

"A young woman," Elizabeth said, tactfully getting to the point, "only five years older than you."

"Don't remind me," Abby moaned. "It's not gonna be fun." She thought for a second and then said, "I'm surprised you don't have more questions for me. Are you really as matter-of-fact as you seem?"

"No, of course not," Elizabeth said, "but I'm not going to grill you over the phone. I want to talk about this in person. I can't get a good read on you unless I can see your eyes."

"When are you coming home? I'd love to get some advice on all of this, and it is hard when we can't see each other."

"Advice? My little girl wants advice?" Elizabeth laughed. "When was the last time you asked for that?"

"Honestly? I think it was when I asked you whether you thought I should go for my Ph.D. or settle for a master's."

"Hmm...that has been a while. What did you think of my advice?"

"It was great. It helped me make up my mind."

"Wanna know a secret?"

"Sure."

"I thought you should have gone for your Ph.D."

"Mom! You told me to stop at a master's!"

"I know I did, honey. That's what you wanted me to say. I supported you."

"Sheesh! You think your mom will tell the truth!" Abby was laughing, and Elizabeth joined her.

"The truth isn't always the best thing. You had a baby, and you wanted to have another one or two. Going for a doctorate would have been stressful for all of you. I could tell you wanted support for your decision, so that's what I did."

"Thanks, Mom. That's a good reminder. You've got to know your audience."

"True. And you know yours. So tell Trevor and get it over with. By the time he gets home, Hayley should be speaking again, and you can get things settled before she goes back to school."

"Good idea. I'll write to him today."

"Don't they have telephones in Italy?"

"No, I don't think so," Abby said. "That's my story, and I'm sticking to it!"

🌿

Abby got up and didn't even bother to take a shower. Five minutes later, she was sitting in the kitchen, starting to compose her letter. She wasn't sure what to say, but she knew that the only way to reach Trevor was to tell him the complete, unvarnished truth. Surprisingly, as soon as she began, the words flowed from her in a stream.

Dear Trevor,

> *I have some good, but possibly upsetting, news to share with you. Much to my surprise, I've fallen in love. I'm sure that you will have mixed feelings about my entering into a relationship with anyone, but this person might be harder than most to accept. I've fallen in love with Clancy...*

🌿

At around six, Abby answered the phone, pleased to hear Pam's voice. "Hi. Can I drop by on my way home from work?"

"Work on Saturday?"

"Yeah. We're putting in a new system. I had to check some things out."

"Of course you can come by. Am I making you dinner?"

Laughing, Pam said, "I wish you were. But I have to get home. I'll only impose on you for a few minutes."

"You can stay all night if you want to."

"I'll be there in about...oh...four minutes," she said, hanging up with a laugh.

Abby walked outside and let the dogs accompany her for a change. Pam parked on the street and entered the pedestrian gate when Abby managed to get the dogs out of the way to open it. "Athena, Artemis. Paws!" The dogs looked at her as though she were the most heartless creature on earth. But they did as they were told and let Pam enter unmolested.

Pam squatted down and let them lick her face, with Abby giving the threesome a resigned smirk. "You don't have to let them do that, you know."

Pam looked up at her while successfully avoiding having Athena stick her tongue in her mouth. "I know, but they act so disappointed when I don't let them kiss me."

"You've made your choice," Abby said. She hugged her friend when she stood but refused to kiss her. "I won't kiss dog lips."

"I know, I know. But I can talk to you, and they only seem to understand physical affection."

Abby gave her a sad smile and put her arm around her waist. "I could use some physical affection, too. It's been a tough week."

Pam squeezed her waist, surprised as always by how small Abby felt when she hugged her. She was a tall, fit, broad-shouldered woman, but she felt very lanky and slight when Pam put her arms around her. "I came by to apologize for the other night. We all feel so bad about what happened."

"Pam, you know I don't blame Alyssa. She didn't know she wasn't supposed to say anything. A little girl doesn't understand the meaning of the word 'discretion.'"

"No, but her mothers should. We shouldn't have let her start answering the phone. I'm sure no one but Alyssa enjoys it, and it was stupid of us to let her do it just so we didn't have to listen to sales calls and charity pitches."

"You're being silly," Abby said. "If I could train the dogs to answer the phone, I'd do it in a minute. Now come sit on the porch with me. Maybe you have the secret to solving my problems."

They walked up to the porch and sat down, both of them gazing at the lawn and flowers for a few minutes. "Wanna tell me what's been going on? Last I knew, Clancy and Hayley had a fight."

Abby nodded. "That's about the last thing that happened. Since then, no real change."

"Uhm…it's been two days. Something has to have happened since then."

"No, not really. Hayley's ignoring me but torturing me by staying home almost every minute."

"What have you done to make her talk?"

"Make her?" Abby asked, looking a little blank. "Clancy asked the same thing, but I don't know—"

"Yes, make her! You can't walk around on pins and needles waiting for her to bring it up!"

"But that's not…I don't usually…"

Pam put her hand on her friend's arm. "Abby, I know you like to let the kids think things through in their own way, but this is different! She's holding you hostage!"

Abby sat for a minute, seeing the situation through Pam's eyes. "I guess you're right. She's holding both Clancy and me hostage. We're not seeing each other while Hayley's upset, and I know it's driving Clancy crazy."

"It'd drive me crazy," Pam said. "To be honest, I wouldn't let you get away with it. Clancy must be a lot more patient than I am."

Abby looked at her, considering her comment. "I don't…I don't think she *is* very patient, to tell the truth." She put her head into her hands. "Damn, I'm so afraid I'm gonna screw this up!"

"There's no reason to screw it up," Pam insisted. "But I think you're making a mistake in not seeing Clancy. Why let Hayley dictate how you live your life? You're the adult."

"I don't feel like one right now. I'm so anxious that I jump at the slightest noise. The dogs are a mess because I'm so hyper."

Pam looked down at the pair, both heads up, ears alert, their dark brown eyes scanning the neighborhood. "They do look...concerned. I never thought about how attuned they must be to you."

"They're like emotional barometers."

Pam reached down and petted Artemis, smiling when Athena got up and tried to push her sister away. "You don't have many choices, Abby. You can either break it off with Clancy and chalk it up to a bout of temporary insanity or tell Hayley that she needs to learn how to deal with it. There really isn't a middle ground."

Not saying a word for over a minute, Abby said, "You're right. There is no middle ground." With a little of the normal spark in her eyes, Abby looked at Pam and said, "I'm gonna go into that house and break the ice. Hayley's not going to make me feel like a prisoner in my own home!"

❦

Abby went inside and found her daughter lying on the sofa in the den, watching some pseudoreality show on MTV. When she walked by the set, she turned off the TV and sat down, forcing Hayley to pull her feet up to avoid having them sat on. "We have to talk about what happened. You haven't said ten words to me since you found out about Clancy and me."

The girl looked at her for a long time, her clear blue eyes assessing Abby in a way that made her feel like she was under a microscope. "I don't have anything to say."

Abby let out a sigh and just managed to keep her eyes from rolling. "Yes, you do. You're obviously angry or upset or revolted or something!"

"I have feelings. But that doesn't mean I have anything to say. I don't want to talk about it."

"Why not?" Abby's voice grew a little louder, and she leaned closer to her child.

"Because we had an agreement," Hayley said, leaving her mother to grind her teeth in frustration.

"What agreement?"

"A couple of years ago, we had a big fight, and I said something that made you mad. You made me promise never to talk to you that way again. So...since I can't guarantee I'll be nice, I'm not gonna talk about it until I'm calm."

She looked a little too pleased with herself, which irritated Abby no end. "Fine. Since you won't talk, I'm going to live my life." She stood up and said, "I'm going to call Clancy and ask her to come over."

Before she took a step, Hayley called out, "Mom! Please don't!"

Abby turned and saw not the smug young woman who was driving her mad, but a frightened girl on the verge of panic. Abby sank back down onto the couch and opened her arms. Hayley scrambled into her embrace and cried, sounding like her heart had been broken. "Please don't, don't make me, please, Momma," she mumbled, crying hard.

Stroking her hair and rubbing her back, Abby asked. "Don't what, honey? Tell me what's upsetting you."

"Don't have Clancy come over. Please, please don't. I can't stand to see you two together."

Abby lifted Hayley's chin, gazing into her red-rimmed eyes. "Tell me why. Tell me how you feel."

"I can't," she gasped, struggling for air. "I can't."

"Yes, you can. You can tell me anything."

Hayley wriggled out of her mother's embrace. "I'm too mad!" she said, angry tears continuing to fall. "I'm furious with you and with her!"

"Tell me," Abby said, her own voice starting to rise.

"No!" She scrambled to her feet and stood there, her balance a little off because of the emotions running through her body.

"You have to tell me! Is it just because I've fallen in love? When I started dating, you didn't have any reaction at all. You barely acted interested."

"I was interested! I just didn't want to know too much."

"What's too much?"

"I just didn't wanna hear about it," Hayley said, dropping onto the sofa. "I thought it was…I don't know…something you did on your own time."

"So you thought I was just…what? Having a date to fill up my time when you were at school? Didn't it occur to you that I was starting to look for a partner?"

"No. I didn't think about that. You didn't seem like you were even having fun!"

Abby stared at her, seeing that Hayley looked truly terrified. "Is that it? Is it that I'm having fun now?"

The frightened look switched to anger in such a flash that Abby wasn't sure she'd seen it.

"Are you stupid?"

"No, I'm not stupid. I just don't know what to think…and you're not helping."

"I can't. I won't." Her bright blue eyes were blazing, and Abby knew they weren't going to get anywhere. But she wasn't ready to admit defeat.

"You're making things harder for both of us, Hayley. We can't get past this unless we talk."

"I don't want to talk! I'm so mad, I wanna hit you! I wanna grab you and shake you until you stop being so fucking stupid!" She spit the last words out, yelling so loudly that the dogs ran into the room, and each crawled under a table, seeking safety.

"Tell me how I'm being stupid!" Abby demanded, leaping to her feet. "Say anything you want! Call me names! Just talk!"

Hayley's body swayed a bit, her cheeks blazing red. "I could call you names for a week, and you'd still be stupid! You don't love her! She doesn't love you! You're breaking up our family for her, and you don't even care! Is sex the only thing you care about?"

Abby was stunned. She blinked her eyes, absolutely nonplussed by Hayley's question. "Sex? You think this is about sex?"

"What else could it be? The men you *should* be with obviously can't do it like a thirty-year-old can. You've lied to me my whole life! Love isn't what's important. Sex is! Fucking is all that matters!" And with that, she ran from the room, crying so hard that she stumbled on the steps and wound up crawling up the last few to get to her room and slam the door.

Abby flopped back onto the sofa, ridiculously happy when Artemis and Athena carefully stuck their heads out of their hiding places and, bodies low, stealthily climbed onto the sofa with her, licking the tears that continued to flow down her cheeks.

❦

Hayley didn't come down for dinner, and after a tearful late-night conversation with Clancy, Abby tried to sleep. She tossed and turned for what seemed like hours, waking fully when she heard a noise at her door. She flipped on the light and saw a piece of paper lying on the floor. Getting up, she picked it up and read.

Dear Mom,

> *I'm very sorry for the way I yelled at you today. I don't ever want to talk to you that way again, and I really wish you would have let me keep my feelings to myself.*
>
> *If you want me to leave, I will. I can stay with Gretchen if you want me out of your hair. But if I stay till school starts, I have to work things out for myself. I can't talk about this until I'm ready. Like I said, I'll leave if that drives you nuts, but I won't get into another fight about this. It hurts me too much, and I'm sure it hurts you, too.*
>
> *I love you even when I'm mad at you, and I hope you still love me.*

Hayley

Abby considered her words for a few minutes. Then she went to Hayley's room, knocked softly, and turned the knob. Hayley was sitting on her bed, dozens and dozens of spent tissues surrounding her. Her eyes were red-rimmed and puffy, and she looked young—very young—and confused and lonely. Without speaking, Abby sat by her and smiled when Hayley clutched her desperately and began to cry again.

"Shhh...don't cry, sweetheart. Don't cry." Abby ran her hand over Hayley's damp T-shirt, feeling the heat pouring from her body.

"Don't hate me, Mom. *Please* don't hate me."

"I don't hate you. I could never hate you. Love isn't like that, honey. I get angry with you, I get frustrated with you, but I never have hated you, and I never will." She ran her fingers through Hayley's dark hair and asked, "Do you hate me?"

Hayley looked up at her, and Abby's heart clutched in pain for her child. She looked so lost...so very, very lost. "I don't...I don't have names for the way I feel

275

sometimes," she whimpered. "I get so mad. It…it feels like I *do* hate you, and that scares me so much. It's so much worse when you make me talk before I'm ready."

Sighing, Abby hugged her tightly. "We're in a fix, aren't we? I need for you to talk, but it doesn't seem like you can. What do we do?"

"I don't know. You're the adult."

"Yeah…I guess I am, but I can't divine what's in your head. God knows I wish I could, but only you can know that. I can guess all day, but that won't do me much good."

"I'm not trying to be mean, Mom. I swear I'm not. I think I should leave. I just don't know what else to do."

Abby cupped her child's cheek and leaned over to kiss her forehead. "I don't want you to leave unless you want to. This is your house. I'd much rather you stay until you have to leave for school. But I need for you to try to talk to me…or your grandmother…or Maria…anyone you can open up to."

"Gramma knows?"

"Uh-huh."

"Is she mad?"

"No." Abby considered her options and decided to tell Hayley the whole truth. "Her only concern was that this would be hard for you and Trevor. She assumed you'd both be happier if I'd fallen in love with a man."

"Mmm."

"Do you think she's right?"

"I don't know," Hayley said, offering nothing. "All I know is that I'm not happy."

"That's clear. Now you have to decide if you want to stay and try to work this out or go. I desperately want you to stay…but I'll understand if you can't."

"You will?" Hayley's eyes were filled with hope. "You really will?"

"Yes. I really will. You have to do what you can. But if you stay, you have to try to talk about this."

"Okay. I'll see how I feel in a day or two." She looked at Abby with wide eyes. "Is that okay?"

"Of course it is."

"Does Trevor know?"

"I just wrote to him. It took me a while to get around to it."

"Scared, huh?" A flicker of a smile played across her mouth.

"After what happened with you? Terrified!"

❦

The next day, Hayley decided that she'd stay home until school started. Abby was pleased and got on the phone to tell Clancy. "Hi," she said when Clancy answered her cell phone.

"Hi. What's up?"

"Good news. Hayley's decided to stay home and try to work through her feelings."

Clancy tried to sound enthusiastic. "Good. That's...good."

"It *is* good," Abby said, obviously hearing the apathetic tone in Clancy's voice. "If she can open up, we can start to make some long-term plans. You *do* want to do that, don't you?"

"Plans? Like...?"

"Like for us," Abby said, her tone sharper than normal. "You do want to live together, don't you? Have people recognize us as a couple?"

"Of course! I guess I didn't realize Hayley was stopping us."

Seconds ticked by. Clancy realized she'd said something wrong but wasn't sure what it was.

"You don't know what it's like to be a parent," Abby said, a little frostily. "And even if you did, you wouldn't know what it's like to be Hayley's parent. If my kids are supportive, this will be a very easy transition for us. If they aren't...it's going to be tough. Don't you think it's wise to try to make things as easy as we can?"

"Of course! I didn't...I don't...uhm...did I do something wrong? Are you mad at me?"

Clancy could hear her lover blow out a breath. "No. I'm just on edge. I'm thinking about the letter making its way to Trevor. I was stupid not to call him. It makes me much more tense to wonder when he's going to get it and how long it will take him to respond. And even though Hayley has promised to try, I don't know how to help her through this. She's always been so bottled up."

"Wanna go out tonight? Or come over to my house?"

"I...don't think I'd better," Abby said, sounding a little down. "Hayley's staying home, and I feel like I should be here to maximize our opportunities to talk."

"Okay. Uhm...call me when you want to get together...or just talk."

"I will. And I'm sorry if I was curt before."

"'S okay. This is a hard time for all of us."

"It is. But we'll get there, Clancy. We will."

🌿

Clancy was sure that only three days had passed, but it felt so much like three weeks that she actually checked her calendar. By Thursday, she was feeling anxious and irritable. On a whim, she called her parents, and they insisted that she come up for dinner. Without even bothering to go home and change, she headed up to Sierra Madre, hoping that an evening with her family might brighten her mood.

She'd previously apprised her parents of the recent developments, but this was the first time they'd seen her, and they were all dismayed at how down she was, as well as by the black-and-blue smudge under her eye.

Her father took his usual turn at the grill, cooking some salmon steaks. Clancy sat in a chair and watched him work, allowing the familiar sights and sounds to soothe her. "Does this kid usually run the house?" John asked in his usual direct style.

Clancy sipped her beer and shook her head. "I don't think so, Dad, but I've gotta admit, I've only seen the whole group together a few times. I've gotten the impression that Abby and Hayley have always gotten along really well. Abby assures me that Hayley isn't a spoiled brat—even though she sure seems like one to me. I don't know either of them well enough to know if Abby doesn't know the kid's spoiled or if Hayley's really acting out of character."

"How old's the kid?"

"She's gonna be eighteen this weekend."

"Mmm…tough age. Still a kid, but feels like an adult."

"Yeah." Clancy picked at some dried bits of mortar that still clung to her shins. "I guess I've got to just keep my mouth shut and hope that Abby can work this out."

"Have you seen her at all?"

She shook her head. "Just when she brings water out. I talk to her on the phone every night, though. That helps a little."

"Darned little," he grumbled.

She got up and gave him a hug, surprising him a little with her enthusiasm. "You know, I came up here because I thought you could cheer me up. But seeing that you're pissed off, too, actually helps even more. Thanks for understanding, Dad."

"Any time, baby. I'm good at pissed."

After dinner, Clancy went into her grandmother's room to play a little gin rummy. The older woman always beat her granddaughter like a drum, but the game allowed them to have a little diversion while they talked, so the normally competitive Clancy didn't mind that she would, inevitably, lose.

"So, Bitsy," Eileen said, "do ya feel as bad as ya look?"

Clancy nodded, concentrating on her cards for a moment. "Yeah, I guess I do. Being in love can be hard, Gramma."

Eileen chuckled softly and said, "Hell, yeah, it can be hard. That's why God invented sex! If it wasn't for that, nobody would fall in love."

"I never looked at it that way," Clancy said, smirking at her grandmother's unique perspective.

"You *do* have sex with the woman, don't ya, peanut?"

"Gramma!"

"All I'm saying is that if you're not seeing her much, ya better be makin' use of the time ya do have. Makin' her want ya bad ain't a bad strategy."

Thoroughly embarrassed, the young woman said, "I think she misses me plenty, Gramma. We get along very well."

"I still can't figure out what the hell two girls can do in bed, but as long as you're happy, that's all that matters."

Patting her hand, Clancy said, "I'll give you a book if you really want to know— but what Abby and I do in bed is one thing you and I are *never* going to discuss."

"Be that way," Eileen said, wrinkling up her nose. "Keep an old woman in the dark." A tiny smile crept onto her face as she slapped her cards down and cried, "Gin!"

"I can't catch a break," Clancy grumbled, dropping her cards onto the pile and starting to deal again.

"So if you don't want to talk about sex, there's just one piece of advice I can give ya, Bitsy."

"What's that, Gramma?"

"You're gonna have to be more patient with this woman than you've ever been before. Don't push her, baby, or she'll be gone faster than you can blink."

"I have been patient. I've been very patient. I haven't even complained that we only see each other for five minutes a day—though I'm in her back yard."

"I mean more than that. I'm talking about the long haul. You don't know what it's like to be a mother, Clancy, and no matter how much you try to understand, you'll never know if you don't have kids of your own."

"So I've heard. But what's that mean? That I can't even have opinions?"

"Hell, no! I'm just saying that you'd better never...ever...try to get between a mother bear and her cubs."

"I have no intention of—"

"Now, don't get your dander up. I'm just trying to give you a little piece of advice; you can ignore me if you want to. I just don't want you to have this get ruined because you didn't know any better."

"What if this goes on until Hayley goes back to school?"

"Look, honey, the only point I'm trying to make is that you have to let Abby make the choices here. If she and her girl have a serious falling-out, you don't want it to be because of your buttin' in. She'll blame you for that, no matter how much she loves you."

"I guess you're right," Clancy said, looking more depressed by the minute.

"Now, I'm not saying that you have to keep your mouth shut; I know you can't do that," Eileen said fondly. "Just try to give her as much time as you can to make her own decisions. She's riskin' a hell of a lot more here than you are. Don't make her regret it."

The young woman nodded, her attention only peripherally on her cards. "I...I haven't spent much time thinking of what Abby's risking here. When I look at it, though, it's pretty scary."

"Sure is," Eileen said. "She's got kids and parents and friends and relatives who are all used to her being a certain way. That's a lot of people to disappoint, Bitsy. Have a little sympathy for her."

"I do, Gramma. And no matter how frustrated I get, I'll do my best to give her time. She's worth all of the time in the world."

"You really love her, don't ya, honey?"

Clancy nodded. "I do. She means the world to me, Gramma. I'll sacrifice whatever I have to in order to make her happy."

"That's my girl," Eileen said, smiling at her granddaughter. "Gin!" she added, laughing heartily.

Chapter Twenty

Abby answered the phone on Friday morning to hear Margaret O'Connor's voice. "Well, hello, Margaret. I'm pleased to hear from you."

"Did Clancy tell you she had dinner with us last night?"

"She did. She said she felt much better after seeing you all, as a matter of fact."

"Oh, that's good to know. It's obvious she's having a tough time with this, but I started thinking this morning, and I realized that this has to be even harder for you. Do you have people to talk to?"

Abby felt a few tears sting her eyes, and she took in a deep breath. "I think I see where Clancy gets her good-heartedness from. Yes, I told my parents, and I have friends who know the whole story. They're good listeners, too."

"Why don't you and I meet for lunch today?" Margaret offered. "I'm worried about you."

"All right. Hayley's taking my car this afternoon, but I'm free until about one or so. Let me come up there; I know you can't get away for long."

"Great. Come to my shop, and we'll walk down the street to grab a bite."

Abby parked her car right in front of O'Connor's Floral Creations and smiled when she saw Margaret behind the counter. "Oh, good, you're here," she said when Abby poked her head in. She turned and called to the back, "Angela, I'm leaving now. Be back in an hour." Then she grabbed her bag and stepped around the counter to join Abby.

"So, this is where young Clancy spent her Saturdays," Abby said, a fond smile on her face.

"This is it. She was either here or putting in a pool someplace." She shook her head and said, "Most kids would call the authorities to complain about the child-labor laws, but she liked to be with us."

"I know. She speaks fondly of those times." They left the shop and walked down the street, stopping at a small, authentic-looking '50s diner.

"Is this okay?" Margaret asked. "It's not fancy, but the chocolate malts are lethally good."

"Looks great."

"Does Clancy know you're here?" Margaret asked when they stepped inside the cool, cozy space.

"No. I…uhm…didn't have time to tell her."

"Well, she'll be jealous. She loves the malts here more than…more than trees, and that's saying something!"

Abby smiled and pulled her cell phone from her purse, quickly dialing a number. "Don't eat lunch," she said, smiling at Margaret. "I'm bringing you a surprise. Bye, now." She clicked off and said, "Thanks. I've been neglecting her horribly. Maybe this will let her know I'm thinking of her."

"She knows you love her, Abby," Margaret said. "I was pleased that you've told each other that, by the way. It was pretty obvious when you were at our house."

"I'm always the last to know," Abby said. "Sometimes my own feelings are very well hidden from me."

Their server came, and after ordering, Margaret leaned back in the booth and asked, "Are you making any progress with your daughter?"

"Not much," Abby said, shaking her head. "She's worse than I am when it comes to talking about personal things. We had one big blowup, but that's about it. She's not rude, and she talks about things in general—but she has a very hard time talking about things that are currently bothering her. She's promised to try…but I can't put her on a schedule."

"Mmm…well, she'll broach the subject at some point, won't she?"

Abby played with the salt and pepper shakers, shifting them back and forth across the Formica nervously. "I suppose so. I hope so. But we might not resolve anything before she goes back to school."

Margaret looked at her for a moment, seeing the lines of worry etched into her forehead. "Abby, what do you see happening here?"

"What do you mean?"

"What's your wish for how this will play out? What would you like to have happen?"

"Oh." She looked up at her and cocked her head in thought. "I'm hoping that Hayley comes to accept Clancy and that we can get on with our lives."

"What about your son?"

"Oh. Well, Trevor is in Europe for the rest of the summer. I wrote to him, but I haven't heard back." She sucked at her cheek, and Margaret could see her working the skin between her teeth. "I hope he takes it better than Hayley did."

Margaret shot her a worried glance and followed up. "What if he doesn't? Your friends and neighbors will all learn about this, too, and the rest of your family. Haven't you given any thought to how you'll handle all of that?"

"No," she mumbled. "This is all so new to me, Margaret. Clancy and I just said we loved each other the day before Hayley came back. I'm…I'm doing the best I can."

Margaret reached across the table and grasped her hand, giving it a squeeze. "I'm not criticizing you. I just don't want my little girl to get hurt if you decide you can't be with her—for whatever reason. It worries me that you haven't given much thought to the long term."

"We haven't made many plans," she said quietly. "I suppose I thought things would just work out as we encountered problems."

"I hope you know that I'm on your side. I want this to work out—because it's what Clancy wants. But there are things you two have to agree upon if you're going to be successful."

"Like what?" Abby asked, looking up at her through a lock of hair that had fallen in her face. She looked like a teenager who was being scolded for not having her homework done, and Margaret suddenly felt thirty years older than her companion.

"Do you want to live together? Are you ready to welcome Clancy into your social circle? Do you feel comfortable with her friends? And what about children? Clancy loves kids. Are you ready to start over and have another baby in the house?"

The questions were making Abby's head hurt, and she cursed at herself for having agreed to this lunch at all. "We haven't discussed any of that in any depth. I just know that I love her, and I'll do anything to make her happy."

"No, you won't." Margaret leveled her gaze and said, "You're a mother. I can see how much you love your children. If the decision comes down to Clancy or your kids, I think we both know that Clancy's going to lose."

"It won't come to that," Abby said firmly. "My kids love me, and once they see that this makes me happy, they won't stand in the way."

"I hope your kids are extraordinary," she said softly, "because most kids think of themselves first—and their parents last."

🌿

Abby walked into the house at one o'clock, and Hayley jumped to her feet. "Where've you been? I'm gonna be late!"

Feeling perturbed in general, Abby just placed her keys on the counter and said, "Then get going." She walked out to the patio and called, "Clancy! I brought you lunch!"

When she turned back around, Hayley was looking at her, a contrite smile on her face. "Sorry, Mom. I didn't mean to snap at you."

"That's all right. My nerves are a little on edge, too. Will I see you later?"

"Mmm…not sure. Do you need a definite answer?"

"No. I can make something simple for dinner. I'll see you when I see you."

Clancy came stomping across the patio just then, trying to knock some mud off her boots. She looked up and nodded to Hayley, who nodded back and then gave her mother a quick kiss and took off. "Well, that was progress," Clancy said. "She didn't belt me."

Abby smiled but otherwise ignored the comment. "I brought you a little treat," she said, extending the malt and a white bag.

Ripping off her gloves, Clancy took a long sip, rolling her eyes in pleasure. "Where did you get this?"

"Sierra Madre. Your mother invited me to lunch."

"This'd better be a double cheeseburger," she said, eyes sparkling as she hefted the bag.

"It is. Want me to put the fries in the broiler to crisp them up?"

"No, thanks. My stomach's not at all picky." She started to wolf down the meal, eating faster than Abby had ever seen her.

"Were you really starving?"

"Hell, yes! I normally eat at eleven or eleven-thirty, but we were trying to use up this batch of mortar before lunch. Then you called, so I'm two hours overdue!" Swallowing a bit of the thick malt, she asked, "So what's up with you and my mom? Are you conspiring against me?"

"Hardly. She's just concerned for us and for me. She's a very caring woman."

"She is. I see that much more now that I'm out of the house. It's hard to view your mom objectively when you live together." Clancy put her head down and paired bites of her burger with sips of her malt, finishing both before Abby could believe her eyes. She stood, stretched, and burped noisily. "Good meal," she said, patting her stomach. "Thanks for taking care of the laborer. I've got to get back to work— the guys took their lunch at the normal time, and I'm in charge of setting the stones."

"Hey, Clancy?" Abby asked quietly.

"Yeah?"

"Do you have any plans for the weekend? I…uhm…I'd really like to see you."

Looking at her curiously, Clancy said, "You can see me any time you want. Don't you know that?"

"I suppose I do," she said tentatively. "It's…you haven't…well, you haven't brought it up…"

Clancy stepped closer and said, "Look, I'm not the kind of woman who's gonna beg you to spend time with me. You're the one with the issue here. I'd be with you every moment if you wanted me to be."

"I'm sorry," she said, biting her lower lip to keep her emotions in check. "I just miss you."

Running her callused hand along Abby's arm, Clancy met her eyes and said softly, "I miss you, too. When do you want to get together?"

"Uhm…if her schedule holds, Hayley's going to invite some of her high school friends over for a barbecue tomorrow night. Are you free in the afternoon?"

"No, but I can get free."

"What did you have planned?"

"Oh, it's a friend's birthday party. A bunch of people I know are having a big bash for her. It won't kill me to miss it."

"No, you should go. You've already accepted the invitation, right?"

"Yeah." She looked down at her boots and said, "You could go with me."

Abby smiled and nodded. "It's a date."

Abby stuck her head out the back door just as the crew was finishing up that night. "Clancy? Got a minute?"

The landscaper nodded, waved goodbye to her men, and then walked over to the house. She kicked off the dirt caked onto her boots and then removed them before she went inside. As always, she was greeted by a pair of joyous pups, and she looked up from their adulation to ask, "Hayley gone?"

"Yeah. She called to say she's going to Old Pasadena for dinner and a movie. Are you busy tonight?"

"No," Clancy said, feeling a little resentful that Abby would see her only if Hayley was out of the house.

"I'm going over to Pam and Maria's, and I thought you might like to go with me."

Raising an eyebrow, Clancy asked, "Can I get the first lick in?"

"Lick?"

"We're going over to beat the snot out of Alyssa, right?" She broke into laughter as soon as she said it, making Abby laugh as well.

"No. Apparently she's feeling bad enough without being beaten. She thinks she's made Hayley hate me. Maria says she asks about me every day, and she prays for Hayley and me at night."

"Not me, huh?"

Abby helplessly shrugged her shoulders. "You know how kids are. She relates to the mother/child thing."

"Are you sure you want me to go?"

Looking at her for a moment, Abby said, "I wouldn't have asked you if I didn't." She reached out and touched Clancy's shoulder. "Are you all right?"

"Yeah, yeah." The architect squatted down to play with the dogs again. "I'll go home and shower; then I'll swing by to get you."

"I could walk."

"No way. That's what you did last time; I don't wanna jinx this visit."

❧

Clancy returned about an hour later, and Abby still felt that her partner was acting a little strangely. But Clancy wasn't very chatty, and Abby didn't think it wise to press the issue. She knew that Clancy was pretty direct and assumed she'd talk about what was bothering her eventually—if anything was. The short drive to her friends' home passed in awkward silence.

The adults were all a little uncomfortable with one another, given the way their last gathering had ended, but Alyssa acted sad and withdrawn for a good long time. Abby tried to draw her out, to no end, but Clancy eventually persuaded her to show her some of her toys. They were gone for a while, and Abby and Pam finally went down the hall to peek in. Clancy was sitting on the floor, and Alyssa was taking her temperature while listening to her heartbeat with a real stethoscope.

"I hope Maria never brings home scalpels," Pam whispered, making Abby suppress a giggle. They tiptoed away, speaking in their normal voices when they got to the living room. "Clancy's really good with her," Pam said.

"Well, she's the closest in age," Abby said, smirking. "No, that wasn't a jibe," she insisted when Maria gave her a look. "I meant that in the best way. There's a lot of kid left in Clancy, and I hope it stays there for a very long time."

"She's helping bring out the kid in you again," Pam said. "It's been gone for quite a while."

"Since Will died," she said quietly. "It's funny," she added after a moment of reflection, "I knew that I wasn't enjoying life like I used to, but things just didn't seem fun to me anymore. I couldn't understand how the world kept turning and how people continued to go on with their lives like nothing had happened. I couldn't see what was so damned entertaining."

Abby gazed towards Alyssa's room, a gentle smile blooming on her mouth. "When I'm with her, I see the humor in things again. Everything is brighter and more colorful when we're together." She looked thoughtful as she added, "I never thought I'd say this, but she's worth every bit of the trouble I'm having with Hayley. I feel centered, and desired, and vibrant again. Getting that is worth risking everything."

"You deserve that," Pam agreed. "Everyone does."

Clancy and Alyssa finally returned, and Abby noticed that Clancy now sported plastic bandages on both of her hands. "We missed you two," she said. She gestured to Alyssa, and with a bit of hesitation, the girl walked over to her and allowed Abby to pull her onto her lap. "Your moms bought all of the things we need to make steak enchiladas," she said, "but they don't know how to make them. Wanna help me?"

"What do I have to do?" the girl asked. "I don't know much."

"I need someone to make the tortillas. You know—Hayley's job."

The little girl gave her a puzzled look and then shot a glance at her moms. When they gave her encouraging nods, she got up and took Abby's hand. "Will you show me how?"

"Of course I will," Abby assured her, draping an arm across her narrow shoulders. They went into the kitchen, leaving Clancy to wish she could tag along. When they got there, Abby commented, "You know, I think Hayley was about your age when she started being a big help in the kitchen. Making tortillas was one of her first accomplishments."

"Do you really think I can?" Allysa asked, eyes wide.

"Yep. I know you love 'em, so why not learn how to make 'em?"

The delight in the little girl's eyes was almost too much for Abby to witness, recalling how proud Hayley was of herself the first time she perfected the technique. Will had made such a fuss over the child—promising to substitute tortillas for bread from that moment on—that Hayley willingly helped in the kitchen on every occasion.

Abby explained and demonstrated the technique to Alyssa, smiling when the child studied her with her usual laserlike focus and then tried her own hand. The small hands kneaded the dough into suppleness and then formed irregular, rough rounds. She watched, fascinated, while Abby put them in a tortilla press and cooked them briefly on a hot, dry griddle, and she swooned when Abby spooned a dollop of guacamole onto a still-warm tortilla and fed her a bite. "That's the best thing I ever ate!" she cried excitedly. "Can I give some to my moms?"

"Sure, honey. I'll cook the rest while you're gone."

"No! Don't do another one until I get back!" she ordered, scampering to the living room to deliver her creation. She was back in a flash, beaming proudly. "They loved 'em!"

"Of course they did," Abby said, giving her a warm hug. "The next time I want tortillas, I'm calling you!"

The glee vanished immediately from Alyssa's features. "Won't Hayley ever do it again?"

Abby sat on a step stool to equalize their heights and then placed her hands on Alyssa's shoulders. "Of course she will. She's just unhappy right now."

"'Cause of Clancy," she said quietly. "And 'cause I told her you like girls."

"Hey, sweetie," Abby said, lifting her chin to force eye contact, "I don't know where you got that idea, but it's not true. Hayley and I are just having a fight. This is about us—Hayley and me. It has nothing to do with you. I promise you."

"But I told...she wouldn't know..."

"Also not true. I was going to tell her that night or the next night, Alyssa. She would have been mad whether I told her or you did. I mean that."

"Why is she mad?" Alyssa asked, staring at Abby guilelessly. "Is it because you like girls now? My moms like girls...does she still like them?"

Abby wrapped her in a hug, closing her eyes tightly to avoid crying. She rocked her gently, cooing into her ear, "Of course she likes your moms, honey. She's...she's just having a hard time."

Reflecting her current fascination with fathers and her lack of one, Alyssa said quietly, "Maybe she misses her daddy."

Patting her gently, Abby nodded. "I'm sure she does, honey. I miss him, too."

"But you have Clancy now, huh?"

"I do," Abby said. "Clancy makes me happy—very happy."

"Maybe Hayley needs a Clancy, too," the little girl said thoughtfully.

That's part of the problem, I think!

🌱

After exhausting their knowledge of current events and the never-changing weather, Maria tried to keep the conversation flowing in the living room. She tossed off what sounded like a casual comment when it was, in fact, anything but casual. Nonetheless, she thought she could pull it off, given the dearth of topics to broach. "Clancy, I feel totally ignorant about your profession. We'd love to know more about what you do."

"Sure," the young woman said, still sitting on the chair like her underwear was too tight. "What do you want to know?"

"Well...do you have a postgraduate degree of some sort?"

"No. I went to Cal-Poly Pomona. It's a four-year degree program. You *can* get a master's degree, but I don't have one."

"Do you have a license?" Maria asked.

"Yeah," Clancy said, looking wary. "Why?"

"Oh! Well, I was talking to someone, and she...well...uhm...she said that most landscape architects don't..." She trailed off, feeling Clancy's gray eyes boring into her.

"Why don't you ask me what you really wanna know?" she asked, suddenly looking completely comfortable. She leaned forward and put her forearms on her knees. "Come on, ask."

Maria felt like she was being interrogated for a murder she didn't commit. A quick glance at Pam didn't help, because her partner was investigating the stucco ceiling with great interest. "I...uhm...looked on the Internet...just because I wanted to know more about what you do—"

"Don't bullshit me, Maria," Clancy said flatly. "I hate bullshit."

The doctor knew she was caught, so she gathered her courage and told the truth. "Fine. We don't know anything about you, and we asked around a little bit. I talked to a guy who's a pretty well-known landscape architect, and he said he'd never heard of you. He also said you sounded more like a garden designer than an architect. I thought...well, I thought you might have been lying to Abby. I wanted to check to make sure you are who you said you were."

The blonde leaned back in her chair. "Thanks for being honest." She crossed an ankle over her knee and stared at Maria again. "I am a landscape architect, but I'm not a typical one."

"What...what does that mean?"

"That means," Clancy said, "that I wanted to be trained and qualified to do the kinds of projects that interest me. My dad's company does water features, and I like to do them, too. But I didn't want some asshole with manicured fingernails and an L.L. Bean briefcase to tell me how he wanted me to do it. I wanted to be able to do the design, make sure the drainage was correct, and make sure the soil was stable. That's what an architect does."

"But...Abby says you're out in her yard digging and working harder than your staff."

Clancy sat up a little taller and said, "That's because I like to do that kind of work. I like to get my hands dirty. I like to plant, not just tell someone else what to plant. I like to sweat and have big muscles and callused hands. I don't have to; I want to. I could work for a well-known firm and just sit in front of a computer all day, doing the designing." She made a face, showing her distaste for such a job, "But I'd rather work on a chain gang. I like being outside every single day. I like being my own boss. I like lying under a shade tree with my crew while we eat lunch. That's who I am."

"I wasn't implying—"

"Yes, you were," Clancy said, interrupting her. "You don't want Abby to be with some grimy kid who plays in the dirt. You don't mind if she eats pussy; you just want her to eat the proper pussy." She stood up, looking much taller than her height. "Well, I might not be from an old Pasadena family, but Abby loves me. And if you want her to be happy, you'll get over yourselves and try to get to know me—'cause I'm not going anywhere!"

With that, she went into the bathroom, leaving Pam and Maria to stare at each other.

"I told you not to meddle," Pam said slowly.

"Fuck!" Maria slapped herself in the head. "Abby's gonna kill me!"

Pam walked over and put her arm around her lover. "No, she won't. I don't think Clancy'll tell her."

"What?"

"You heard me. I think she'll keep this among us. There's something about that kid that makes me think she won't want Abby to know about this."

"Why?" Maria asked, looking at Pam like she was delusional. "You saw how mad she was!"

"Yeah, she's mad, all right, but telling Abby would only make Abby mad, too. I don't think Clancy would do that." She extended a hand and helped Maria to her feet. "You were right about Clancy. She's a lot more mature than she looks." She kissed her lover on the cheek. "You should have remembered that before you tried to trap her. Now go catch her, and apologize when she comes out of the bathroom. I'll go into the kitchen and make sure no one interrupts."

"I screwed up, didn't I?" Maria asked.

"Yeah, you did, but I think we learned a lot about Clancy tonight. Not the way I would have liked to learn that she can take care of herself, but..."

"I just hope to God that she doesn't tell Abby," Maria said. "'Cause she'd kick my ass if she found out!"

Chapter Twenty-One

The phone rang early on Saturday morning. Abby lunged to catch it so the sound wouldn't wake Hayley. "Hello?"

"Hi. Pam here. I...uhm...was just calling to make sure you wanted to play today."

Waiting a beat, considering whether she was missing something, Abby asked, "Why wouldn't I?"

"Uhm...I didn't know if you wanted to see Ellen. I know you're—"

"Pam, if I were going to cancel, I would have called. And for the record, I'm not going to stop doing something I enjoy just because I'm upset with Ellen. If she wants to quit, that's her choice, but we've all been playing for ten years, and I'm not going to stop until my knees give out."

Laughing, Pam said, "I don't know why I bothered to call. If I had thought about it for two minutes, I would have known that you wouldn't quit over this."

"Tell Maria she owes you one for making you call," Abby said, laughing evilly.

❦

Ellen flinched noticeably when Abby came up behind her in the locker room and asked, "Ready to go?"

Turning, Ellen tried to keep the surprise from showing. "Yeah," she said, sounding excessively enthusiastic. "The usual, or should we flip a coin for teams?"

"Let's flip," Abby said, hoping she'd be paired with either Pam or Maria.

❦

She got her wish and was paired with Maria. Among the four of them, Abby was at the top of the depth chart, with Ellen and Pam a step below her. But Maria was a little heavy and a little slow, and had neither finesse nor strength. She played mostly to get some form of regular exercise and to take off the weight she had gained with Alyssa—a goal she predicted would take her until Alyssa was in college.

But Abby didn't mind being paired with Maria. It allowed her to really let loose and show her stuff—something she didn't do very often. She covered the court like a blanket, sliding over into Maria's territory time and again to whip the ball back over the net with her slicing backhand. She called out "Mine!" so many times that Maria started to get out of the way whenever she would have had to run to hit a return shot.

By the end of the match, Abby and Maria had trounced their opponents, and Maria had barely broken a sweat. Walking off the court, Maria put her hand on Abby's sweaty shoulder and said, "Can I be your partner forever? I think that was the most fun I've ever had on a tennis court."

"I was a little afraid I was insulting you, but when you started to call 'Yours!' I figured you didn't mind."

"Mind? Are you kidding? I would've been happy to hand you my racket so you could have covered the whole court!"

❦

The foursome almost always ate lunch at the club, but Abby approached Ellen on the way to the clubhouse and asked, "Would you be willing to have lunch with me—alone?"

Ellen looked at her watch, and Abby could tell that she was trying to fabricate an excuse to decline.

Staring at her, her blue eyes intent, Abby said, "We've been friends for twenty-six years, Ellen. That's gotta be worth something."

Ellen let out a breath and then nodded. "You're right. Do you wanna eat here or go somewhere else?"

"I'd just as soon stay. Is that all right?"

"Sure. Let's tell the girls."

❦

They were more than a little awkward with each other, trying to smile and banter a little about the match. But they both knew there was only one topic on the table, and Abby finally broached it. "We need to talk about our future—as friends."

"I know. I haven't wanted to, but you're right. We need to." She folded her hands on the table and waited for Abby to begin.

Their server walked by and indicated he'd be with them in a moment. Ellen spoke to him and then put her napkin on her lap. Abby watched her, noticing that her friend needed to have her hair touched up. *Direct sunlight is no friend to dark hair dye,* she thought, struck with the fleeting desire to tell her friend that her hair looked awful, just to hurt her. But she shook off the urge, knowing that was not only beneath her, but also counterproductive.

Abby focused her thoughts and said, "I've thought a lot about our argument, and I still can't understand why you were so angry with me. Then I thought that I might just have caught you off guard. So…I wanted to see where things stand now."

Ellen looked down and then leaned back when their server arrived with water and menus. She gave him a glance and said, "I'd like a Cobb salad and an iced tea. Abby?"

"That's fine," she said.

He nodded, jotted down their order, and walked away, leaving Ellen with no more excuses to delay. She looked at Abby, but her gaze didn't bear its usual openness. "I'm not angry anymore." Her fingers moved nervously on the tablecloth, brushing off specks of dust. "I can't say why I was angry in the first place, to be honest. I suppose I was so shocked that I let my mouth get away from me."

Abby smiled at her, unsuccessfully trying to hold her gaze. "You've had a little while to digest the news. What do you think now?"

"I…I have to say that I hoped you'd have come to your senses by now." Her posture started to indicate a combative attitude. "Have you told the kids?"

Abby nodded, choosing to ignore the initial insult. "Hayley knows, and I wrote to Trevor. I haven't heard back from him."

With a smile that looked far too much like a gloat, Ellen asked, "How did Hayley take it?"

"Not very well," Abby said, deciding to be honest. "She's not ready to talk about it much, but it's still very early. I'm confident we'll work things out."

"What if you don't?" Ellen asked, her face obscured by the waiter's white shirt as he placed their drinks on the table.

Abby picked up her tea and took a sip, looking over the rim of the glass. "We have to. We're family."

Frustrated, Ellen leaned back in her chair, blowing out a deep breath. "Why *do* this?" she asked, looking tired and every day of her fifty-three years. "Why put your kids through any more than they've already been through?"

With a smile that bridged curiosity and annoyance, Abby asked, "Why is my love life dependent on the approval of my kids?"

"Because this isn't a *normal* way to express your love," Ellen said, clearly exasperated.

Abby looked at her friend for nearly a minute before she managed to speak. "How dare you," she said quietly. "How can you say you're Pam and Maria's friend?"

"This isn't because of the gay thing," Ellen hissed. "There's nothing wrong with being gay—if you're gay! But you're not!"

"Do you hear yourself?" Abby asked. "You're sitting here telling me what my sexual orientation is. Where do you get off?"

"Look," Ellen said, leaning across the table so she could talk quietly. "I've known you for twenty-six years. I knew you before you were married to Will. If you were faking it, you were the best damned actress of the '80s *and* the '90s!"

"Faking what? Faking my love?"

"Yes!"

"Jesus Christ, Ellen! Don't you know anything about sexuality?"

"Of course I do," she replied, clearly angry. "And you're heterosexual!"

"You know me well," Abby said, "but you don't know my sexual self. I had a real sex life before I met Will, and I've had a fantasy life before, during, and after my marriage."

"What are you saying?" Ellen asked, her mouth dropping open.

"I'm saying that Clancy isn't the first woman I've kissed."

"So you kissed a girl! Big deal!"

"I did more than kiss her," Abby said, eyes blazing. "We kissed—passionately, not for a lark. I touched her breasts, and she touched mine. I was in the middle of unzipping her pants when my roommate walked in."

Ellen stared at her, looking suspicious. "So why didn't you do it the next time you and this other woman saw each other?"

"Because I met Will shortly after that happened." Her expression gentled, and her gaze shifted to look at the beauty of the San Gabriel Mountains in the distance. "I fell in love with him, and once I did, I didn't want anyone else—man or woman."

"So you could have been a lesbian…if your roommate hadn't walked in." Ellen was clearly not buying it, her skepticism serving to annoy Abby more by the minute.

"I guess I could have been. If I'd been sleeping with the girl I'm talking about, I suppose I wouldn't have accepted a date from Will."

"Your whole sexual identity is based on a cosmic accident? There's no way for me to understand that."

"You have *heard* of bisexuality, haven't you?" Abby asked unkindly.

"Yes, I've heard of it." The server arrived with their salads, deposited them, and departed, but neither woman took a bite.

"I didn't have the need or the opportunity to explore it, but falling in love with Clancy has let me see that I'm bisexual. It's not that big a deal."

"It is to Hayley," she snapped.

"Why don't you let me worry about my kids, and you can worry about yours. Okay?"

Ellen took a deep breath, obviously trying to calm herself. "Look, I knew Will before he met you. I was at the hospital when both of your kids were born. I've been at every birthday party, every graduation, every significant event in your family's life. Don't expect me to just fall in line when I know you're doing something that will forever damage that bond! I love you too much to let this pass!"

"What am I supposed to do? Have the kids screen my dates? What if they like someone at first but get angry with him or her a year later? Do I have to break up with the person?" She paused and cocked her head. "Do you hear how ridiculous this sounds?"

"Hayley's a good kid, and she loves you to death. She's also very comfortable around gay people. If she thought Clancy was a decent person, she wouldn't have a problem with this."

"You don't know what you're talking about," Abby said. "And I'm not going to betray Hayley's confidence by telling you what she's upset about. Suffice it to say that it's not because of Clancy's character."

"Speaking of character, what do you even know about this woman?"

"I know her very, very well," Abby said. "Better than I knew Will when I slept with him the first time."

"And you love her," Ellen said pugnaciously.

"I do."

"Tell me why. Tell me why you love her."

Abby reminded herself that she and Ellen really did have a long friendship and that her friend had been unflagging in her support after Will's death. "Okay," she said, "I will." She took another sip of her tea, thinking about her feelings for Clancy. "Here goes. I love her because she's kind and generous and funny and smart. Not in a bookish way, but she knows about life, and she knows people. She's very intuitive about people. And I love the way she gets pleasure from simple things. She's a lot like me in that way. She's happy to sit outside and enjoy nature."

Abby looked up at the clear, dry blue sky, thinking. "I love her because she's honest about her feelings and about her work. She works hard—harder than she has to—but she enjoys it. She likes to *earn* her living, not just wait for the day to be over. I also love the fact that she's a loving daughter and granddaughter. She's proud of her family, and that's a very endearing trait." Abby looked right into her friend's eyes and added, "And I think she's just about the prettiest woman I've ever seen. When I look at her, sometimes she takes my breath away." Her cheeks flushed when she admitted this, but she wanted Ellen to know—to really know—how she felt.

Her friend looked at her for a moment, and Abby was completely unable to read her expression. With her voice calm and interested, she asked, "How does she make you feel?"

"Feel?"

"Yeah. How do you feel when you're together?"

"Oh. Well, I…" Abby laughed and shook her head a little bit. "I've never thought about it like that." She grew pensive and then said, "She makes me feel lovable again. I was so down," she said, her face filled with pain from merely recalling that time. "I thought I'd never feel loved again, but in a very short time, I started looking forward to seeing her. Then I started to miss her when I didn't see her. Then…then she became all I thought about." She smiled, looking young and vibrant. "That's where I still am."

"But how do you *feel*?"

"I feel wonderful," Abby said. "Like I'm starting my life over again, in a way. But in another way, I feel like we've been together forever. We fit so well." Looking at Ellen, she realized she wasn't answering the question. "I…guess I don't know how to explain how it feels to be in love again. All I know is that she smiles when she sees me, and it makes my heart race. When we're out together, she'll barely touch me, and I feel tingly all over." She shrugged, looking helpless. "I don't know what else to say, Ellen. She makes me feel loved and cared for and pretty and sexy and desirable. Just like every woman should feel when she falls in love."

Ellen had been watching Abby carefully while she spoke, and her expression hadn't changed much from the beginning of the explanation to the end of it. It was still hard for Abby to tell what she was thinking, but she soon found out.

"What's in this for *her*?"

"For her?" Abby looked at her companion like she was speaking another language.

"Yes. For her. How would you feel if Trevor started dating a forty-year-old woman? Wouldn't you wonder why?"

Nonplussed, Abby sat quietly for a few moments. "I suppose I would." She looked at her friend. "But I trust my son. I trust his judgment. If he were to fall in love with an older woman, I'd assume he was getting what he needed from her. What else can you do?"

"Well, you don't treat your kids like I treat mine. I'd make sure he knew what he was losing by being with someone so much older. We're not talking a few years here, Abby; we're talking a generation!"

"I know I'm just a few years younger than Clancy's mother," Abby admitted, "but I can't let that bother me. I have to let my heart tell me what's right for me."

"And Clancy?"

"Her heart has to guide her. And I believe that she knows the downside of being with me."

Ellen leaned forward, looking empathetic. "Are you sure she's not using you? I mean…please, please don't take this the wrong way, but why would she want someone your age if she could have a young woman? I don't know what you see when you look in the mirror, but I don't recognize myself anymore!"

Abby looked at her friend, wondering where to start. She was insulted for herself and also on Clancy's behalf, but it was clear that Ellen's concern was genuine. "I don't know why she desires me. I don't have the body I had when I was her age, but she's very attracted to me. I know that she's sincere."

"I know you believe that, Abby. I can see that," Ellen said. She reached across the table and took her friend's hand. "But she can't be sincere. She can't have thought this through. She just can't." She sat up and said, "Or she wants your money or your prestige or to be invited into your social circle. There's just no other explanation."

Abby glared at her, wounded to the core. "Have you always known what's in everyone's heart? You know about my sexuality…about Clancy's motives…about Hayley's feelings! How dare you question Clancy's honesty and sincerity!"

"Abby! Women our age don't attract young people! They're either looking for a mother substitute or a meal ticket!"

"Clancy has a lovely mother of her own, and she makes a good living. All she wants from me is my love!"

"How do I reach you?" Ellen asked, frustrated and angry.

"You don't," Abby said. "Just like I haven't reached you. You haven't really heard me, and I think your arguments are ridiculous. I suppose we just have to go on as best we can and simply avoid the topic until it becomes clear that our love will last."

Ellen gazed at her old friend, pursing her lips, looking like she was about to cry. "I can't do that. I can't be your friend if you insist on continuing with this."

"What?"

"You heard me," Ellen said, tears rolling down her cheeks. "You're doing something that I think is harmful for you and the kids…as well as Clancy. I can't condone it, and I can't keep my mouth shut and let you do it."

Abby's hand went to her head, rubbing the spot over her eye that was throbbing in pain. "You won't be my friend because you don't approve of my lover?"

"No, that's not it. I can't be your friend when you're acting so selfishly. The Abby I love wouldn't do something that would upset her kids and her friends. That Abby cared more about the people around her than you do."

Abby stood up, pulled a twenty from her tennis skirt, and tossed the bill onto the table. "You're right. I'm never going to be that woman again. I've changed, and I'm putting myself first." She leaned over and stared at Ellen, her eyes flickering with passion. "I deserve it!"

🌿

Clancy arrived just after two, and Abby buzzed her in. An earlier phone call let her know that Hayley was gone, so she availed herself of the opportunity to play with the dogs without worrying about running into the girl.

Looking up at Abby as she entered, Clancy whistled, and her eyes widened. "Damn, you look good." Giving her a brief kiss, she said, "But I've gotta be honest—you're way too dressed up for this crowd."

"You said casual." Abby blinked. "Isn't this casual?"

Clancy eyed the linen campshirt that made Abby's eyes look like the bluest sky she'd ever seen and the pure-white, slim-fitting cotton slacks. "In your circle, yes, that would be casual. In my circle, you look like you're dressed to meet the queen." She pointed to her own snug, cropped red tank top, oversize red-and-white print shirt, and navy-blue board shorts. Then she asked, "Can you get closer to this?"

"Uhm…yeah, if I wear the clothes I normally put over my swimsuit."

"Perfect," Clancy said. "Either that or those adorable boxers you had on the first night we made love."

"Clancy! I'm not going to a party in my underwear!"

"You wouldn't be the first," Clancy insisted.

🌿

The party was being held at a house in Altadena, and when they were two blocks away, Clancy predicted, "This is gonna be a big one. There's already no place to park."

"Are you sure we shouldn't have brought gifts? Or at least a bottle of wine?"

"No. We don't do gifts. We just have a contest for who brings the dirtiest card."

"This should prove enlightening," Abby said, smiling nervously.

They had to go almost three blocks to find a spot for the car, and as they drew closer to the party, the music got louder and louder. By the time they reached the small frame house, they had to raise their voices just to hear each other speak.

Abby's eyes grew wide as they walked around the side of the house and took in the mass of bodies jammed into the small yard. "I have a lot of friends," Clancy commented. She scanned the crowd and found the birthday girl, tugging Abby with her to make the introductions. "Hey, Sabrina!" she shouted. "Happy birthday!"

"Clancy! Where've you been, babe? I haven't seen you all summer."

"I've been keeping busy." She slung her arm around Abby and pulled her close. "This is Abby," she said, smiling widely. "We've been keeping busy together."

"Hey, good to meet you, Abby. Uhm…the keg's over there," she said, pointing to a knot of people, "and we're gonna start cooking soon. Oh, Sheila's new baby is here. You gotta check him out!"

When they broke through the throng, it became clear why everyone was clustered together. A pool took up four-fifths of the yard, forcing the guests to surround it. A dozen women and a man were playing in the cool water, and Clancy inclined her head toward an attractive young woman who appeared to have been thrown in fully clothed. "That's my ex—Julie," she said.

Abby took a good look at the young woman, her eyes widening when she saw two substantial rings outlined by her snug tank top. "She's very nice looking," Abby said. The woman looked to be about Clancy's age, and her spiky black hair stuck up all over her head. The effect was achieved through ample use of some hair-care product, though, because she dunked her head, and her short black locks immediately conformed to her skull. She had dark, expressive eyes and skin turned a warm, dark gold by the sun. Julie gave off an energetic, bubbly vibe, and when she made eye contact with Clancy, she immediately swam over to the edge of the pool.

"Hey, you," she said, batting her eyes in a way that made Abby's hackles rise.

"Hi, Julie," Clancy said. Julie stuck her hand out, and when Clancy grasped it, Julie gave it a yank and pulled her into the pool headfirst. Luckily, the depth was sufficient to keep her from being killed or maimed, but Clancy wasn't especially grateful for the dunking. "God damn it!" she sputtered when her head broke through the water. "Will I never learn?" She fumbled in her pants and dug her wallet out; then she kicked off her sandals and handed them to Abby. "She's done that to me at least five times!" Clancy said, shooting her ex a wry grin.

Abby stood there, holding the dripping nylon wallet with two fingers, and Clancy said, "Julie, this is Abby. Abby, Julie."

"Good to meet you," Abby said, pulling her hand back when Julie started to reach for it. "I'd rather not go swimming," she added.

"Two minutes, and she's learned a lesson I haven't figured out in five years," Clancy grumbled.

"You always were a little slow," Julie said. She tried to dunk Clancy again and somehow wound up hanging off her back. Clancy tried to pull away, but Julie hung on tight. "Gimme a ride," she demanded, her throaty voice purring right into Clancy's ear.

Shrugging out of her hold, Clancy gave her a pointed look and said, "No, thanks. Abby rides me these days." Pressing her hands on the deck, she hoisted herself up and over the edge of the pool. "Have fun," she said, adding a small smile. Grasping Abby's hand, Clancy asked, "Care for a beer?"

"Uhm…love one," she said, giving the very perturbed-looking Julie a furtive glance. When they were out of earshot Abby asked, "What was that all about? She acted like she wanted to scent-mark you!"

"That's her usual style. She didn't like the fact that I brought a date, and she had to throw herself all over me to let you know she and I used to be an item. She makes it a point to let everyone know she was there first." She gave Abby a wry look and said, "She's never been able to let go."

"I don't blame her a bit," Abby sighed, wrapping her hands around Clancy's dripping wet arm. "I know that I couldn't let go, either."

"You don't have to let go," Clancy promised, turning her gaze to meet Abby's. A wicked smile crept onto her face, and she said, "I have a very strong desire to make you wet."

"Pardon?" Abby blinked.

Clancy laughed evilly and grasped her lover's hips, moving her backward until she had her pressed up against the house. "I want to get you wet," she repeated, "the hard way." She wrapped her arms around Abby and kissed her hard, grinding her pelvis roughly against her.

"My God, Clancy," she gasped when she could come up for air. "There are people everywhere."

"Nothing they haven't seen before," she murmured. "I can't kiss you at your house, and you won't come to my house. There's gotta be some place that I can kiss you, or I'm gonna explode!"

She could feel the moisture seeping through her clothing and Abby decided to release her inhibitions—for the afternoon, at least. "You *are* making me wet," she purred sexily.

Clancy's hand sneaked between their bodies, and she nodded. "Yep. You're drenched."

"That's not what I meant," Abby growled, latching onto the tip of Clancy's ear. "Your kisses make me wet…and hot…and I'd like nothing more than to make love to you all night long."

Clancy locked eyes with her, her entire body shivering with arousal. "Can you come to my house?"

Eyes filled with regret, Abby said, "No. It's Hayley's party, remember?"

Clancy nodded. Then grabbed Abby and thrust her hips a few times while she straddled a thigh. "My brain knows you have your reasons, but my body's starting to get pissed at me. She just wants to hump you."

"You're becoming more like the dogs every day." Abby said, smiling fondly at her partner and giving her a few light kisses, trying to ease the sexual tension.

"I've been compared to worse," Clancy admitted, giving Abby a firm swat on the butt.

Clancy had been to the house many times, and she knew her way around it quite well. "Come with me," she urged after they had secured plastic cups of beer. She led Abby to the far side of the house, where a quiet little alcove yielded two slightly bedraggled, but usable, lawn chairs. They sat down at the edge of the crowd, and after just a moment, Abby couldn't suppress her curiosity any longer. "So tell me about Julie."

"Sure, what do you want to know?"

"Well, I can certainly see why you'd be physically attracted to her, but what was the real attraction?"

"Mmm…I think at that point in my life, I just wanted someone who really wanted me," Clancy said thoughtfully. "You know how it is when you're young and inexperienced. You meet someone you're attracted to—you hit it off—and before you know it, you're exclusive with each other. I didn't realize that I had a list of requirements that any lover had to meet before I should spend my time with any one person."

"Makes sense," Abby nodded. She took a sip of her beer and grinned at her partner. "I haven't had beer from a keg since I was in college. It's really tasty, isn't it?"

"Yep. Don't know why, but it tastes fresher this way."

"Why didn't you two make it?" Abby asked. "I know you fought a lot; was that the problem?"

"No." Clancy shook her head briskly. "We didn't fight about day-to-day things. We only fought about her possessiveness." She smiled and said, "The thing I was attracted to is the thing that drove me crazy in the end."

"You couldn't work through it?"

"No. We tried to, but I don't think you can change your personality just to please a lover. She was needy and jealous of everything that took me away from her—including my family. Like she didn't understand that I wanted to spend my Sundays with them. She thought that since I lived with them, I didn't need to see them on the weekends."

"Did you ever try living together?"

"Not really. I slept at her apartment two or three nights a week, but we were never stable enough for me to want to make that commitment. I liked Julie, Abby, but I didn't love her. If I'd loved her, I'm sure I would have tried a lot harder to make it work."

"I'm sure you would have. You're quite determined when something is important to you."

"You're important to me," Clancy whispered, leaning over to kiss a moist path along Abby's jaw. "Very important."

After they had finished their beers, they mingled for a while, moving through the crowd to greet one person after another. Abby was amazed to find that Clancy actually knew the vast majority of people at the party, and her head was buzzing with names that she knew she'd never be able to recall. She was also surprised to see a number of men and women who looked at least as old as she was, and she commented on that to Clancy, "I thought I'd be the oldest one here. I was afraid people would think I was your aunt or some other relative you had to entertain."

Laughing, Clancy said, "I love my family, but I've never backed any of them up against a house to grind against. I think my friends know me well enough to know I'm not into that."

"You know what I mean," Abby said, squeezing Clancy's hand. "I'm really surprised to see middle-aged women."

"Huh. That's not odd with my friends."

"It is among mine."

"Your group of friends is all around the same age?"

"Well…yes, within five years or so. When a couple divorces, and the man marries a much younger woman, people stop inviting them to things."

Clancy gave her a crooked grin. "Open-minded group."

Abby looked at her for a moment and then nodded slowly. "I…I thought they were." She looked away, obviously thinking something over as they continued to wind their way through the crowd.

After they'd made the rounds, they finally encountered the new baby that Sabrina had mentioned. "Sheila!" Clancy cried. "Congratulations on the new member of the family." She pulled Abby close and said, "This is Abby. Abby, this is Sheila and her new son. Jacob, isn't it?" she asked.

"It is," the new mom smiled. "He's just been fed, so he's ready for a nice long nap."

"Mind if we rock him to sleep?"

"Be my guest." Sheila handed him off, giving him a kiss on the forehead. "I'll go check on my wife."

"We'll take him over to the side of the house." Clancy indicated with a nod. "It's quieter over there."

They went back to their little alcove. Clancy sat down and then placed the baby on her thighs. "Isn't he a doll?" she asked, playing with his perfect little feet.

"Mmm-hmm," Abby purred, stroking the baby's delightfully soft skin. "My friends have been out of the baby business for years now. I haven't been around one this tiny since Alyssa."

"I'm wild for babies," Clancy sighed. "I should have been a pediatric nurse, just so I could get my fill."

"You'd have been good at it," Abby decided, "but I think you'd have a very hard time with the fact that many of them would be desperately ill."

"Yeah. I think I do better with plants. As it is, I can have my day ruined by a transplanted tree that doesn't take."

Abby was trailing her fingers down the dozing baby's dark shock of hair. "You'd be a good mom," she said softly.

"I like to think I would be. I had some pretty good role models." She gazed at the baby for a few minutes and said, "Isn't it amazing to think that there's a whole adult human in this little body—just waiting to grow up. Everything he needs is right in this easy-to-carry package."

"Yes, as long as he gets some good parenting, he's good to go."

"Oh, he'll get that," Clancy said. "He has two very good moms." Two little eyelids popped open, and Jacob looked around, trying to figure out where he was and who was holding him. "What a beautiful boy you are," Clancy cooed, petting him softly.

Abby watched her interact with the tiny child, and Margaret's words kept coming back to her. *I don't know if I can give you this, sweetheart. God, I hope we know what we're doing. I don't want you to miss out on the things that I've already experienced, but I don't think I have the strength to start all over again. Thinking of having to deal with Hayley's drama when I'm sixty-five makes me sick to my stomach!*

Just before they reached Abby's street, Clancy turned onto a quiet block and turned off the engine. Shifting around, she gazed at her lover and asked, "Now what?"

Abby sneaked a look at her watch. "I have to get home. Hayley's friends are gonna come over at around seven, and I have to get dinner ready."

"I know," Clancy said. She stared out of the window, her gaze just over Abby's left shoulder. "Did you have a good time? You seemed…distracted or something."

Abby spent a moment debating whether she wanted to talk about what was bothering her. Deciding she had to, she said, "I had a tough morning. Ellen and I had another…discussion, for want of a better word, and it didn't go well."

Clancy's head snapped toward her partner. "Why didn't you tell me that?"

A little taken aback, Abby said, "Well, it wasn't that big a deal. I don't tell you about every discussion I have with my friends."

Narrowing her eyes, Clancy said, "An argument with Ellen is a big deal. I'd like it if you kept me up to date, okay?"

She said it with a tone so sharp it made Abby flinch. Wary, she nodded. "Of course. I'll try to remember to tell you things like this."

Still miffed, Clancy asked, "What was the argument about?"

Abby made a face. "It was about the same as last time, but she had the nerve to tell me I couldn't possibly be a lesbian."

Clancy managed a wry, short laugh. "Well, you're not. You have a long, happy marriage to show you're bisexual."

"You know what I mean," Abby said. "She doesn't think I'm attracted to women."

Finally smiling, Clancy said, "Interesting. She should see you in action."

Abby laughed. "That's what I said! I told her about making out with Katie in college just to let her know I've always been open-minded about sex."

"Huh. Did that help?"

"Not as much as it should have!" Abby laughed harder. "I had to add the fact that it wasn't just a few friendly kisses. I think she started to understand when I told her about feeling Katie up and starting to take her pants off before we were interrupted."

Clancy's smile vanished. "Whadda ya mean, feeling her up? You didn't tell me that!"

Surprised by her partner's reaction, Abby tried to backpedal a little. "It wasn't a big deal. I didn't think it was worth mentioning."

"Worth mentioning!" Her cheeks were flushed pink, and her gray eyes were wide. "I had to pull every bit of that story out of you! You knew I wanted to know everything that happened!"

Abby touched her partner's arm, wounded when Clancy pulled it back and glared at her. "I'm…I'm sorry," she said. "I knew you were interested, but I didn't *want* to tell you everything."

"Why? You hide things from me that you're willing to tell Ellen? Jesus Christ, Abby, what the fuck is going on?"

Clearly confused and agitated, Abby fidgeted in her seat. "I…I don't know," she said. "I told you everything I wanted to tell right then. I…can't explain why."

"You can't, or you won't?" Clancy was staring hard, her own eyes as dark as anthracite.

"I can't," Abby said, on the verge of tears. "I've told you a dozen times that I don't think quickly when things are emotional."

Clancy's head dropped back against the window. "Fine. Think about it and tell me—'cause that's fucked up."

Abby tried to reach out and touch her lover, but she was afraid. "I'll try to figure it out," she said. "I swear I didn't mean to hurt you."

Waving her hand, Clancy nodded. "I know." She let out a weary sigh. "So…that's it? Nothing tomorrow?"

"Well, I don't know what Hayley's planned. If she's gonna be gone, we could get together." She wrapped her arms around her own waist and hugged herself, her voice thin and shaking. "I don't like this either. It's not nearly enough for me."

"Yeah. I know," Clancy said, still not making eye contact.

"I love you," Abby said softly. "I love you, and I miss you, and I can't wait until we're able to be together all of the time."

"When will that be?" Clancy asked, her head snapping to face her lover and search her blue eyes.

Abby's uncertainly showed in her expression. "I don't know, sweetheart. I honestly don't know."

"I guess Hayley will tell us when we can get on with our lives, huh?"

The tone in her voice was so distant, so icy, that Abby couldn't form a reply. She sat quietly, knowing that Clancy would reach out to her as soon as she'd had a moment to replay her words. But Clancy didn't move. Once again she stared out her window, her jaw working soundlessly, a wall of frustration and anger keeping Abby from even thinking about touching her.

The seconds ticked away, with Abby's own swallowing sounding like a rifle shot in the otherwise silent car. Finally, she cleared her throat and said, "I've got to get home."

Clancy didn't say a word. She was so obviously angry that Abby could feel the heat radiating from her. But she didn't move, didn't turn the key, didn't respond in any way.

With shaking hands, Abby opened the door and started to get out. After she did, she leaned in, her hands on the doorframe. "Don't give up on me," she said, unable to stop the tears. "Please don't give up."

Once again, Clancy didn't look at her. Her voice was low and hard, and her features were stony. "I won't. I just need...I just need to know that I matter, too."

"You do, sweetheart. You matter more than I can say!"

"Time will tell," Clancy said flatly.

Abby stared at her for another few moments; then she sighed heavily and closed the door. She started to walk, sneaking a look back at the truck just before she turned the corner for her own street.

Her lover was just where she'd left her, not having moved an inch.

Chapter Twenty-Two

Abby walked into the kitchen the next morning and gave her daughter a bright smile, trying to hide her dark mood. She hated that she was so staged around the girl, but she didn't feel safe around her anymore. Technically, it wasn't Hayley's fault that she and Clancy were testy with each other, but it was hard not to blame her. "Want to go to church with me?"

Hayley looked up from her cereal, "Wish I could, but Lori invited me to go to Magic Mountain. She's gonna come pick me up."

"Oh...well, maybe next week. Everyone has been asking about you."

"I don't feel very religious, Mom, but I'll try to go with you before I leave."

"Only if you want to," Abby said. "Your spiritual life is your own. I was just making an offer."

Hayley looked at her for a second, her expressive eyes showing some wariness. As it seemed she often did when she felt her mother pull away, she tried to move closer. "I should be home by late afternoon. Wanna hang out in the pool and barbecue or something?"

"Okay. That would be fun. We only have a couple more weekends before you have to go back to school."

The girl looked at her again and gave her such a warm, loving smile that Abby felt her own lips parrot the expression. She bent, kissed Hayley's cheek, and then headed for the car, happy that her daughter had rebuffed the offer to accompany her. When she turned the engine over the little red convertible balked at going to church. With hardly any help, it drove straight to Clancy's.

Michael answered the door, giving Abby a warm, albeit curious, smile. "Is Clancy expecting you? 'Cause she's still zonked."

"No, she's not expecting me," Abby said. "I thought she might like to go to church with me...or spend the morning together."

"My guess is that she'd rather spend the morning with you than with Jesus. Want me to call her?"

"Mmm, no thanks. I know how to wake her."

"I bet she likes your way better than mine. I tend to stand at her door and holler at her."

"Feel free to keep doing it the way you've always done," Abby said, her hand on the door handle. She gave Michael an impish smile and added, "I'd prefer to be the only one who wakes her my way."

Soundlessly entering the room, Abby closed the door and leaned against it for a moment, taking in the sleeping form of her lover. She wasn't sure exactly what the pull was, but she found that she was inexorably drawn to her when the blonde was unaware she was being watched. There was a childlike innocence about Clancy that made Abby's heart ache, but the round, womanly curves made other, more southerly parts ache as well, and it was those parts that urged her to strip off her clothes and join Clancy in bed.

Even though they'd parted on bad terms, Abby trusted her partner enough to know that she wouldn't be turned away. She expected they'd have a serious discussion or even an argument, but she felt they were on surprisingly solid ground, given the lack of support they'd gotten so far. She wasn't sure why she was so confident, other than for the fact that Clancy was so mature—so stable.

Abby stepped out of her skirt and then pulled off her shell, leaving a silk camisole and matching bikinis. After a moment's thought, she decided to leave the garments on to give Clancy a nice, smooth surface to nestle against. Silently, stealthily, she slipped under the comforter. With a tiny, muted whimper, Clancy's body curled against hers, her breathing evening out immediately. *I was more anxious than tired two minutes ago, but now I feel safe and sleepy.* Rather than fight the urge, she allowed herself to drift into a contented doze, savoring the wish that someday they'd sleep in each other's arms every night.

When she woke a short while later, Abby started to nuzzle the back of Clancy's neck while her hand made gentle, soothing circles on Clancy's bare body.

"Damn, how baked was I last night?" the fuzzy voice mumbled. "I wake up with a gorgeous woman wrapped around me, and I have no recollection whatsoever of how she got here."

Abby's hand stopped stroking, and she tried to keep the surprise and jealousy from her voice. "Did you get high after you came home last night? You were perfectly sober when you dropped me off."

"I went back to the party," Clancy mumbled. "Stayed 'til the cops showed up after the neighbors complained. Then we went to an all-night diner until I was sober enough to drive home."

"We?" Abby reminded herself to work on delivering lines like this with no affect.

"Yeah. Some of my friends. Jacey drove my truck; then she went home with her girlfriend when I convinced 'em I was sober."

Trying to keep her tone light and cheerful, Abby said, "My, what a wild life you lead. Am I going to have to try to keep pace with you?"

"It won't be hard. That's the first time I've been out past midnight all year." She rolled over and wrapped her arms around Abby, smiling up at her. "I was so pissed off at you last night that I couldn't stand the thought of going home alone. Being around my friends and smoking a little dope cheered me up."

"I'm so sorry I made you angry," Abby whispered. "I've really screwed things up."

Clancy put a hand on the back of her head and pulled her close. A long, loving hug made both of them feel better immediately. "It's not a big deal. I'm just easy to annoy lately. Sorry I was so...whatever I was."

"No, it is a big deal. I spent most of the night thinking about it, and I think I know why I didn't tell you everything about my college experimentation."

Clancy lay on her back, looking at her partner with a calm, interested expression. "Tell me if you want, but you don't have to. I know you don't like to spill your guts. I'll just have to get used to it."

"No, no," Abby said. "I shouldn't be so bottled up." She dropped a kiss onto Clancy's cheek and said, "I think it's because I'm not used to sharing feelings. I have to practice."

Nodding her understanding, Clancy said, "I guess you haven't had much practice since Will's been gone."

"No, this isn't new. I've always been like this."

Rising up onto an elbow, Clancy gazed at her quizzically. "What do you mean? I thought you and Will were really close."

"We were. We were very close. But it's...different with a woman. Damn, Clancy, I don't think there were five times in over twenty years that Will asked me about my feelings. We just...didn't do that."

A few seconds passed before Clancy blinked slowly and asked, "Huh? How could you not do that?"

Abby laughed. "He was a man. I'm sure some men like to talk about feelings, but I never went out with one. Will used to say that men think the four scariest words are 'We have to talk.'"

Clancy looked at her suspiciously. "Are you serious? I mean, I hear jokes about that all of the time, but I thought it was pretty exaggerated."

"Not in my experience. My inner life was fully my own. Will didn't want to know what I was thinking or feeling. It's not that he didn't care about me—he did. But he assumed I'd tell him if something interested or bothered me. If I didn't bring something up, we didn't discuss it."

"Even if you acted like you were angry or upset?"

"Especially then!" Abby laughed, thinking back to the ways she'd tried to get her husband's attention. "If he could ignore it, he did! Actually, if I acted like I was upset, he was always extra nice—joking and trying to make me laugh. He'd do anything to try to divert me." She was smiling, thinking of the way they'd interacted.

"Didn't that drive you nuts?"

"No. Not at all. That's just how things were between us. I...honestly liked the way he and I interacted. It makes me uncomfortable when you try to make me tell you what's going on in my head. It...doesn't come easily for me."

Clancy scratched her head, looking completely flummoxed. "I've never known a woman who didn't like to talk about her feelings."

"You do now," Abby said. "I talk about them when I'm resolved…not when I'm thinking or processing them."

Collapsing back on the mattress, Clancy said, "I thought you'd talk more when you trusted me more. I'm…I'm not sure how things will work if that's not true."

With her eyes searching Clancy's calm face for clues, Abby tried to figure out whether or not her lover was upset. "Are you angry?" she asked, feeling very much out of her depth.

Clancy sat up and then wrapped her arms around her knees. "No, I'm not angry." Her face bore an expression that Abby had never seen on her before, and she had a very hard time deciphering it. "I'm worried."

Abby reached out to touch Clancy's face, but the blonde moved back just enough to elude the attempt. "I don't feel like touching right now," she said. "I thought we'd just had a misunderstanding. But I'm starting to feel like we might never be as close as I want to be." She leveled her gaze and stared at Abby for a moment. "As close as I need to be."

Abby's heart started to beat so quickly that she felt the pounding in her chest. "What are you saying?" she asked, her voice higher and thinner than normal. "Are you giving up?"

She reached out one more time, but Clancy rolled away and stood. She pulled on her shorts and tank top from the night before and sat back down on the edge of the futon, looking serious and thoughtful. "I don't want to give up," she said softly. "But I'd rather break up now than a year from now." She looked at Abby again and said, "I need a partner who shares things with me. Not little, ordinary things. I don't want to know everything that's on your mind. But I have to know how you're feeling about things. I have to. I can't compromise on this."

Abby scooted across the bed, her knees almost, but not quite, touching her partner's thigh. "I don't want you to compromise." She was so frightened that her voice was shaking noticeably, and she had to keep blinking hard to hold back the tears. "I want to change. I swear I do!"

Giving her a sad, resigned look, Clancy asked, "How do you do that? How do you change your personality to please me?"

"I work at it! I make myself go out of my comfort zone." She thought she saw Clancy's posture soften a little, so she put a hand on her shoulder. Exerting a little pressure, she pushed until Clancy was facing her. Their eyes met, her own reflecting near-panic. "I can't lose you, Clancy. I'll do whatever I have to do to change. I…swear…it."

Their gaze stayed locked, and Clancy's expression began to soften. "I don't wanna give up," she said, tears trickling down her cheeks. "I love you so much."

Before she finished the sentence, Abby was in her arms, both of them crying so hard that their bodies shook. "Please don't leave me," Abby begged, her voice hoarse and ragged. "Please, please, please!"

"I love you," Clancy said again. "But I can't be with you for the rest of my life if I'm gonna have to drag everything out of you. You're gonna have to learn how to share your feelings with me…when you're having them. You have to tell me when you're upset or anxious or worried. That's the whole point of being lovers."

"I swear I'll try harder," Abby said. "I'll practice…every day!"

Clancy looked at the earnest expression on Abby's face and tightened her hold. "I just want you to try. I need for you to make an effort and acknowledge that you understand why I want to know what's on your mind."

"I think I do," Abby said. "I think you want to know because my mood affects us. Sometimes you might be able to help me through something, rather than my struggling alone."

"Yeah, yeah," Clancy said. "That's it exactly. If we're gonna be lovers, there's an us. It's not just you and me. You have to take care of yourself, but you have to take care of us, too."

"I think I understand," Abby said. "But can you be patient with me while I try to change? I know I'll mess things up sometimes."

Clancy pulled away and looked deep into her eyes. "Of course I can be patient. I just haven't felt that you've been trying at all. And I can't live with a woman who tries to keep her life separate from mine. I just can't do it."

"I understand." Abby let out a big breath and sat up straight. "I feel very confused and conflicted. I'm going through so much with Hayley that it's about to drive me mad. Sometimes I don't even want her in my house, and that's never happened before. I wish I knew how to fix everything, but I don't," she said, tears starting to fall again.

Clancy put her arms around her and urged her stiff body to relax. "It's okay," she said quietly into Abby's ear. "You don't have to have all of the answers today. Just tell me what goes through your mind. What worries you. Those kinds of things."

Looking at Clancy through her tears, she said, "What worries me is losing you. I never thought things were that bad. I…I…I was sure you'd welcome me into your bed this morning. I've been so confident about us."

"Shhh," Clancy whispered, "I'm confident, too. I am, baby. It just threw me for a loop when you said you and Will didn't share feelings, and you liked it that way. That had never occurred to me."

"If something's bothering you, you have to tell me before you get to the point where you're ready to break up with me," Abby said, her voice still shaking. "It's cruel to spring something like that on me."

"I'm sorry," Clancy said. "I'm really sorry. I never should have said that."

"Promise you won't do it again," Abby said. "Please promise me."

Clancy nodded emphatically. "I do. I promise I won't ever threaten to give up on us unless we both agree that we can't get past something. If I ever say it again, it won't be a surprise."

"I promise, too," Abby said. "I want you beside me for the rest of my life. We can work through anything, baby. Anything."

Clancy put her arms around Abby's neck, letting her hands dangle down her back. "Let's lie down and start this day over again."

Letting herself be moved, she lay together with Clancy on the futon, her head resting just above Clancy's heart. "This is my favorite place in the world," she murmured. "I don't know how I'd go on without you."

Clancy kissed the top of her head. "I must still be stoned to have said what I did. I'd rather cut off an arm than lose you. You mean everything to me, sweetheart. You're my heart."

They lay quietly for a while, both of them lost in their thoughts. Even though they were physically close, there was a distance that didn't close until Clancy turned on her side and started to kiss her partner—long, soft, slow, gentle kisses that helped tumble the walls each had put up during the fight. Slowly, Clancy began to turn up the heat, smiling to herself when Abby started to move under her. "How long can you stay?" Clancy asked.

"All afternoon. I told Hayley that we could have dinner together tonight, but I'm free until then."

Clancy pushed up onto an arm, staying so close that her breath warmed Abby's lips. "I want to make love. Lots of love. But first, I have to get up and take a shower and brush my teeth. Any chance of your making me a little breakfast? Just toast and juice, is plenty."

"Sure. Can I put on some of your shorts and a shirt? I don't want to have to get dressed again."

"Michael would love to see you in that camisole," Clancy assured her.

"Maybe so, but it's not his day I'm trying to perk up."

❧

Abby curled up between Clancy's legs and rested her head on a muscled thigh. "I can see why Athena likes it here," she murmured. "I feel snug as a bug in a rug."

"I miss the girls," Clancy said, sounding a little wistful. "We couldn't have a dog when I was growing up, since no one was home much of the time, and I've never been in a position to have one."

"They miss you, too," Abby said. "Athena lies by the back door and moans when she sees you out on the hill."

After taking a noisy bite of her toast, Clancy said, "That's one worry you won't have for long. We're putting in the sod tomorrow. I'll put a plastic fence around the lawn to keep the pups off, but they can have the rest of the yard back tomorrow."

"Mmm…I'm so excited I could burst," Abby said, her eyes animated.

"We tested everything on Friday while you were playing golf. Everything works perfectly."

"I'm not surprised," Abby said. "Although I can't believe you haven't let me see the waterfall running. You're very secretive, Ms. O'Connor."

"No, I'm not really, I just want you to get the full impact. It loses its spark when you see it before it's complete."

"We've got to think of a way to celebrate."

"I've got a few ideas. We'll just have to make sure your neighbors are out of town."

Abby looked at her for a second, her eyes blinking slowly. "I'll buy their houses to get rid of them. I'd do anything to make you happy. Anything."

"Get me another glass of juice, and you've made some progress," Clancy said, smiling as she watched Abby slip back into her clothes from the night before. She looked silly in Clancy's clothes, but the fact that she didn't mind looking silly even in front of Michael gave Clancy more hope about their future than words alone could do.

※

"What took you so long?" Clancy asked in her sexiest voice. She was lying on her side, head braced on her hand, when Abby returned with the juice.

"I was only gone a minute. Michael was leaving, and I took a moment to say goodbye."

"Mmm ... glad he's gone. I have a surprise for you," she said seductively. As she rolled onto her back, the sheet tented up over her pelvis. Her hand slid under the crisp blue cotton and started to stroke up and down, her bicep twitching with each motion. Her eyes were locked on Abby's, and the taller woman gulped in surprise.

"What have you got under there? You don't have a pet snake, do you?"

"Come over here and see for yourself. You're gonna be intimately familiar with it in a few minutes."

Eyes wide, Abby asked, "I am?"

"Uh-huh. Very intimate. Very familiar."

Abby placed the juice on the bedside table; then she tossed off the clothes and slipped under the sheet, cuddling up against Clancy's chest. "Wanna introduce me to your friend?"

Clancy grabbed her in a tight hug. "I wanna blow some steam off. Sometimes I feel like making soft, sweet love, but today I wanna rock." She pulled back enough to look into Abby's eyes. "Are you okay with that?"

"Yeah," she said, her voice sexy and low. "There's nothing better than makeup sex. Really helps clean out the emotional leftovers."

Clancy lay down and put both hands behind her head. Twitching her hips, she asked, "Sure you don't mind getting a little wild?"

"Mind? You don't know me very well." Abby leaned in and kissed her, running her cool hand down her lover's belly, pausing to tickle the defined abs that always caught her attention. Her hand paused when she reached the top of Clancy's pelvis and encountered supple, smooth leather. As her tongue entered Clancy's warm mouth, her fingers dipped lower and touched a cool, pliable phallus of some girth. With a final heated kiss, she pulled the sheet back and slid down, her hot breath against Clancy's stomach as she said, "My, my, my, what a well-endowed woman you are." She grasped the tip and brought it to her mouth, giving it a kiss. "Flexible, too." With a thoroughly fascinated look on her face, Abby twisted the toy into a few extreme positions. "Looks like one of my lovemaking skills is gonna be wasted here. If this doesn't hurt, you won't be able to appreciate my genius."

"Well, I'll admit that I can't feel the same things that a guy can, but I get quite a buzz when it presses against me in just the right spot."

Eyes glimmering with excitement, Abby said, "I wanna give you a buzz. Show me how."

"I thought this was one of *your* lovemaking skills," Clancy said, giving her partner a mock scowl. "Now you want instruction?"

"I have plenty of experience," Abby said, smiling seductively as she moved her hand gently up and down the shaft. "But with a man, the sensation is *in* the penis. I don't think that's what'll work for you, big girl."

Clancy gave her an inquisitive look, a little surprised by Abby's interest. "You sure you wanna do this?"

"Yeah, I really am." She scooted down and kissed all across Clancy's belly, finally peering up at her with half-hooded eyes. "It turns me on to think about grinding this against you." She started to dip her head, but stopped herself abruptly. "Uhm…is this too…heterosexual for you? I don't want to talk you into…"

Clancy put her hand on the side of Abby's face, urging her to meet her eyes. "If you're involved…it's sexy. Period."

A shy but pleased smile lit Abby's face. "Really?"

"Really. Let's rock." Clancy hopped out of bed before Abby could blink, put one foot on the low futon, and grinned wickedly at her partner. "Work your magic."

"I've been in this position before," Abby said, chuckling mildly as she dropped to her knees. Giving Clancy a stupendously sexy look, Abby opened her mouth and began to delicately lick the silicone, keeping her eyes locked on her lover as she moved from base to tip. Pulling back, she held the toy in her hand and licked her lips, gazing at the object with a salacious smile. Shifting her eyes back to her partner, Abby sucked her in and started to slide up and down the length, a tiny grin pulling at the corners of her mouth. She had obviously done this many times, and it was clear that she was enjoying herself as much as her partner.

The dildo wasn't even pressing against Clancy yet, but the landscaper began to grow tremendously aroused just from the look on her lover's face. Clancy let her mind drift to thoughts of Abby performing this act on a man, a fantasy she'd used many times. She was particular about it, preferring to think of Abby in college, blowing one of the UCLA boys who couldn't break a pencil in half—but it always worked, and she began to moan softly. Swiveling her hips in a slow circle, she started to play with her nipples, grinding her teeth at the pulsing she felt in her groin.

When Abby heard the first signs of her partner's arousal, she pulled all the way back; flicked the tip of the toy with her tongue; and then delivered several wet, noisy kisses. With a sexy pout, she placed her elegant fingers along the shaft and swallowed Clancy in one stroke, pressing her lips against the base to push it firmly against the groaning woman. Staying right where she was, Abby nuzzled her entire face into Clancy while she grabbed her ass—hard, making Clancy shiver all over. "My God," Clancy moaned, running her hand through Abby's hair. "If this thing had sensation, I'd be done!"

Abby started to move her head, sliding up and down on the dildo, grinding it into the blonde on each downward stroke. Grasping Clancy's ass, Abby pressed hard against her partner, making the blonde gasp.

Looking up, Abby caught sight of Clancy—eyes closed tightly, tugging and pinching her nipples, her chest heaving. Seeing the familiar signs of her impending climax, Abby pushed her partner onto the futon and shoved the dildo aside, going down on her in a frenzy. Clancy's feet immediately settled onto Abby's shoulders, and her agile body began to twist and jerk in response to the stimulation. "Gentle, gentle, baby," Clancy groaned while writhing and shaking. "Kiss me. Just kiss me."

Reining in the passion that was on the verge of exploding, Abby forced herself to follow instructions, barely letting her tongue and lips caress the soft skin. As soon as she lightened up to a whisper-soft touch, Clancy cried out and climaxed noisily, her body shaking so hard that the futon rocked.

Clancy groaned throatily, pulling Abby to her chest. "Jesus!" she cried, panting raggedly for several moments. "I have never, ever been blown like that!"

"That's what you get for never giving a straight girl a chance," Abby murmured, cradling Clancy in her arms. "You have to learn to exploit our talents."

Her voice a burr, Clancy said, "If every straight woman gave head like that, there'd be no such thing as divorce."

Abby looked at the totally sated look on her partner's face, Clancy's small smile almost narcotized. Pleased by the sincere compliment, Abby leaned over and kissed her, chuckling. "I told you that I wanted to make sure Will never had the energy to even think about straying. If a man knows he'll always have his needs met, he can't wait to come home at night."

Clancy cuddled her lover tight and said, "God knows I can't wait to get home to be with you. I can only imagine how he felt." She kissed Abby's head and asked, "Did you really like giving head? I've never talked to a woman who does."

"Really?" Abby sat up a little and gazed at Clancy with a puzzled look. "How large is your sample size?"

"Well, not very big, and every one of them was a lesbian at the time we talked about it. Maybe that's part of the reason."

"Mmm…might be. I really enjoyed it once I got used to it. When I saw how much Will enjoyed it, I decided to learn how to do it as well as possible." She laughed softly and recalled, "Stephen lent me some gay videos so I could learn a few tricks. They were really helpful, to tell you the truth. Shocked the hell out of Will the first time I stopped him from coming by pressing hard against the base of his…"

Suddenly, Clancy's hand was covering her mouth. The blonde kissed her partner's forehead, chuckling. "I have a feeling you were just about to jump into TMI." At Abby's questioning look, she explained, "Too much information. I like to fantasize about you with a man, but I never, ever think about you with Will. You're always with a skinny college boy in my fantasies, and I'd like to keep it there."

Her brow furrowed, Abby said, "But I thought that you liked—"

"I do, baby," Clancy said. "I love hearing about how you felt about Will and how much you loved each other. I love to hear about the things you did together and all of the important events of your lives. But a little sexual detail goes a long, long way."

Abby nodded and said, "That makes sense. If I thought about you with Julie, it'd ruin the mood."

"You never think about me with another woman?"

"No. I don't like to think of that—at all. I like to believe that you're mine alone."

"I am," Clancy said, giving her partner a warm, wet kiss.

"But it doesn't bother you to think about me with men in general?"

"Huh-uh. I think it's hot. Guys are almost always pretty sexual, and I like to think of you giving as much as you got."

Abby smiled at her, then gave her a sexy kiss. "I love to hear about your fantasies. But what d'ya say we take our minds off our pasts and get busy with the present? I've got a clit that just won't quit!" She tugged on the dildo, eyes bright with desire. "What do you say we take this thing for a spin?"

Without a verbal response, Clancy pounced on Abby and tossed her onto her back. Abby's legs opened immediately, and Clancy's toy slipped between them, making her purr. Reaching down, Abby tried to manipulate the toy into herself, but Clancy shook her head and kissed her gently. "Not so fast, speedy. Let's take our time. I want you nice and wet."

Her voice heavy with desire, Abby said, "I'm as wet as I've ever been in my life." She took her lover's hand and slid it down her body, pressing callused fingers between her legs. "Yeah, come on in, baby. I'm ready for you."

"Almost ready," Clancy murmured. "But I think I can make you even hotter." They started to kiss and caress each other, their exploration building to fever pitch in a matter of minutes. It wasn't the dildo that made Abby's pulse quicken; it was that Clancy was wearing it—trying to entice and excite her, the pure sexiness of the act— and it was working perfectly.

"Come on—come inside me," Abby growled after a particularly fierce bite on the neck.

Clancy shifted her hips and wound up on her back once again. Looking up at Abby with a wicked gleam in her eye, she said, "I think you're ready now, hot stuff." Cocking her head, her eyes slightly narrowed, the blonde said, "You look like the kinda woman who likes to be on top. Come on," she taunted, wrapping her hand around the base of the dildo and wiggling it provocatively. "I wanna watch you ride me."

A jolt of white-hot desire hit Abby right between the legs at the incendiary words. She covered Clancy's mouth and kissed her voraciously, biting and sucking at her lips and tongue while she pinned her to the mattress by the shoulders. "Oh, I'm gonna ride you like you've never been ridden."

Getting to her knees astride Clancy's hips, Abby grasped the phallus and worked the tip of it against herself for a few moments. Clancy's heart almost stopped at the wantonly sexy look on her lover's face as Abby's eyelids grew heavy and finally closed. Her hips were shifting slowly back and forth, forcing her wetness against the slick knob. She reached out and grabbed Clancy's shoulder hard with one hand while the other pressed just the tip of the phallus between her lips. "Ooo," she gasped, shivering roughly when the firm object began to enter her. "Damn! You're a big girl!"

"Too big? I can go down a step."

"No, no," Abby said, her eyes squeezed shut. "I want you to stretch me wide open."

"Mmm, that's what I want, too," Clancy purred. She placed two fingers astride Abby's opening, a shiver chasing down her spine when she felt the flesh stretched tight. "Come on, you can do it. Take it slow…that's it…take your time…ease it in, baby. Don't force it."

Abby let out a deep breath, her eyes still shuttered tightly, fingers clenched around Clancy's muscular shoulder. Her flesh pulsed lightly against the silicone, and she felt her muscles slowly begin to stretch and loosen to allow her to accommodate the intrusion. Clancy's fingers continued to rub the distended tissues gently, simultaneously coating the phallus with the juices that flowed abundantly from her partner. A deep, throaty moan slipped from Abby's lips as she eased more and more of the hefty toy into herself. Her body was stiff—not a muscle moving except for her thighs, which slowly lowered her until the last inch disappeared. Her eyes opened and then immediately rolled back in her head and she lowered herself onto Clancy's chest, murmuring, "I did the hard work. Now let's see if you know how to use it."

"Oh, baby, I know how to use it. You just lie back and enjoy the ride." Using her powerful thighs and torso, Clancy rolled over, taking Abby with her. She hovered over her lover for a moment and said, "Talk to me, sweetheart. Tell me how it feels."

"I'm not sure I can speak," Abby said, letting out a gentle laugh. "But I'll try."

With a wicked grin, Clancy started to move, pressing into Abby with short, quick thrusts. When she was sure the dildo was well coated, she slowed down, compressing the base against her lover's vulva on every deliberate stroke. As soon as Abby started to pant, Clancy slowed down until she was barely moving and then spent a long, leisurely time kissing her partner with all of the love she felt in her heart. "How ya doin', baby?" Clancy asked, lifting her head a few inches.

"Mmm…I'm in heaven."

"Hitting all of your favorite spots?" Clancy asked, nuzzling against Abby's neck.

"Well, not all of 'em, but the ones you're getting to are very, very happy. No complaints, love."

"Hang in there, babe, I'll get to every spot—guaranteed."

Giving her partner a puzzled look, Abby began to ask, "How…?"

"Trust me, lover. I know what I'm doing." With that, Clancy began to move her, turning Abby onto her side, the dildo still wedged deep inside of her. Pushing Abby's leg up to her chest, the smaller woman instructed, "Grab your knee, and get ready. I'm gonna rock you." This angle let Clancy push hard, and in moments Abby was grunting with each thrust, unable to form words.

Slowing her pace, Clancy wiped the sweat from her eyes and slipped out of her partner, kissing Abby's cheek when she let out a small whimper. "I'll be right back," Clancy purred, pushing Abby onto her belly.

The taller woman stretched out, her muscles slightly fatigued from exertion. "I need a little rest," she sighed. "Lie on me, Clance. Let me feel your body." Clancy immediately fulfilled her request, letting the dildo slide between Abby's cheeks. "Uh-unh...not there," Abby said, chuckling. "That monster's way too big."

"I've got one no bigger than my finger. I think you might like it."

The brunette sneaked a glance over her shoulder, a wicked smile on her face.

With a quick bite to her partner's neck, Clancy said, "I love a woman who's willing to try everything." She rubbed her body against Abby, purring contentedly as their moist skin created just the right amount of friction. Sliding down just a bit, Clancy started to suck and bite her way down Abby's body, making her squirm under her assault. By the time she reached her smooth cheeks, Abby was growling—her low, sexy voice making Clancy's clit throb.

"Fill me up again," the taller woman begged. "I need you inside me."

Pushing one of Abby's legs up, Clancy entered her again, and began to thrust—first deeply, then shallowly, never staying with any one movement for too long, always keeping Abby slightly off balance. Clancy was clearly running the show, and Abby surrendered to her completely, knowing that the more experienced woman would take her just where she needed to go.

Clancy began to thrust harder and faster, the soft silicone rubbing against her own vulva. Spreading her hands across Abby's ass, she lifted up just enough to be able to pump into her with all of her might, getting such a perfect rhythm going that before she knew it, she was crying out in a loud voice—her own climax catching her completely off guard. "Oh, God," she moaned, having collapsed heavily against her partner. "God damn, that felt good!"

"Ooo, I was close," Abby groaned, her fists pounding against the mattress. "So close."

"Oh, damn, baby, I'm sorry. I got carried away."

"No, no," Abby soothed. "I'm not ready to come—but I almost couldn't stop myself. Take a minute and rest, sweetheart, and let me get my bearings." She reached behind herself and patted Clancy's wet ass. "You're working so hard—you deserve a nice rest."

Clancy obviously had more stamina than Abby would have guessed, because without even knowing how she got there, Abby found herself stretched out on her belly on the edge of the futon, her feet barely touching the floor. "And you need a nice, big orgasm," Clancy growled, nipping at the soft skin on Abby's back.

Clancy stood and pressed into her until Abby saw stars; then the landscaper pulled back until she was barely inside. Adjusting her angle, she gently pumped her hips back and forth, only just managing to stay inside. With a deep groan, Abby started to pant and then let out some of the most tortured sounds that Clancy had ever heard. Abby's clit had been pulsing painfully for untold minutes, but she didn't want this delicious ride to come to an end. "Give me a minute," she panted, holding onto Clancy's hip. "I'm close, but it feels sooooo good. I don't want it to stop—ever."

"I've got all day," Clancy soothed, lovingly brushing the damp strands of hair from Abby's face. She withdrew once again and helped her partner lie down on her back; then she climbed on top of Abby again. She dipped her head, kissing Abby slowly, letting her tongue explore the heated depths of her mouth. "I'm not too heavy for you, am I?"

Abby wrapped her arms around her lover, holding on so tightly that she nearly bruised her. "No, no, I want you as close as you can get. I love to feel you pressing me into the mattress just as hard as you can."

Clancy moved her hips just a few inches, gently sliding the dildo along Abby's swollen outer lips, making her grunt. "Ready for a little more?"

"Mmm...give me another minute," Abby murmured. "I'm still throbbing hard."

Trying to wedge her hand between their merged bodies, Clancy got an impish look on her face and asked, "Can I feel?"

"Huh-uh," Abby said, shaking her head while she chuckled weakly. "One touch, and I'm gone."

"You're in charge. You decide when you want to come."

"Oh, Clancy," Abby sighed. "This feels so fantastic. To have you lying on top of me, working so hard to bring me pleasure. I love being able to kiss you and look into your eyes while you're inside me."

"I love being with you like this," Clancy said, dipping her head to kiss Abby again. "I feel so close to you. I can feel your heart beating against my chest."

Abby held her tightly and then began to return her kisses, the caress growing in intensity until she was holding Clancy's head with both hands and hungrily consuming her. Abby's legs suddenly wrapped around Clancy's hips, and she pulled away just enough to murmur, "A little more, baby."

"You want it—I've got it," the blonde growled as she glided into her, Abby's slickness easing the way. Clancy pushed up onto her hands and thrust firmly, making Abby moan throatily.

"Deeper," Abby panted, hitting the mattress with the flat of her hands. "I need you deep inside."

Immediately fulfilling her partner's need, Clancy pried Abby's legs from their crushing hold and maneuvered one of them onto her shoulder. Pushing deep inside, she felt Abby's hands move to her arms, gripping them with a power that surprised her. The growl that sprang from Abby's throat was deeply thrilling for Clancy, and she tried to make her partner do it again. She slung Abby's other leg up and held on to her thighs, lifting her hips off the bed. Bracing herself firmly, she thrust hard and deep, watching Abby's eyes and mouth open wide—unable to emit a single sound.

Clancy gave her everything she had, sweat dripping down her chin to land on Abby's chest, her buttocks clenching with each powerful thrust. After just a few moments, Abby's expression grew pained, and Clancy could see that she was struggling.

Dipping her head until they were face to face, Clancy rasped, "You know you wanna come. Don't fight it. Come on, baby. Come for me." That simple command released Abby, and as soon as the base of the toy brushed against her clit she came explosively, grabbing everything her hands came in contact with—Clancy's hair, her skin, her sturdy biceps, the sweat-soaked sheet—her body jerking and spasming ceaselessly. Clancy slowed to a snail's pace, rocking gently while Abby's flesh pulsed and twitched.

Suddenly, Abby was kissing her—kissing every part that her lips could reach, lavishing kisses in her hair, on her damp face, all over her neck and shoulders. Wrapping her arms around Clancy, she grasped her in a bone-bruising embrace that seemed to grow tighter as the moments ticked by.

Slowly, Abby became aware of her surroundings again and loosened her fervid hold. "Jesus, you *do* know how to use that thing," she moaned. "But my legs were so fatigued that I had a hard time letting go enough to come."

"Mmm…simple solution," Clancy said, grinning wickedly. "Ankle restraints. I'll slap a pair on your ankles and clip them together. Then you can let your legs dangle around my shoulders without holding them up on your own."

"Damn, you *do* know what you're doing," Abby teased. Reaching down, she started to slide the phallus from herself but stopped abruptly. "Too soon," she murmured, patting Clancy's back. "Can you hold still for a minute, honey? I'm locked around this thing like a vise. Men get a little smaller when they're finished, but I don't think this thing has that ability."

"No rush; take all the time you need." Clancy was hovering over her, and she gently kissed her a few times. Slowly, Abby began to relax and get into the kisses, and after a few minutes, the dildo popped out all on its own, making Abby shiver roughly. "You must never, ever let men know how effective those are," she murmured. "They'll be outlawed before you can blink."

"It'll be our little secret," Clancy said, kissing a path down her throat and nipping at her still-thrumming pulse. She cuddled up against Abby, and they kissed gently, just exploring each other for long minutes, letting their kisses calm Abby's racing heart while they simultaneously managed to quicken Clancy's.

Slowly but surely, the passion started to grow, with Clancy eventually lying on her back, panting softly as Abby kissed her hungrily. The blonde was still wearing the dildo, and Abby stroked it with her fist, her hand sliding up and down the slick surface easily. "So do you…uhm…can I …?"

"You want me to flip for you?" Clancy asked, raising an eyebrow.

"Uhm…is that what it's called?"

"Yeah. That's what they call it. Some women won't flip for anyone." Clancy kissed her again and said, "I'm particular, but I'll gladly flip for you. I'll flip for any woman who can give me a good workout."

Eyes wide, Abby said, "Maybe we'd better wait until I have some more instruction. I'm sure I can't use it like you can."

"You can if you practice," Clancy said. "And there's no time like the present."

"Tell ya what," Abby said. "This time, why don't you use it on yourself while I do my favorite thing? I want to watch how you move it in yourself."

"Gladly," Clancy said, giving her lover a gentle smile. "We'll work up to the big show."

"How about we choose a day where I have some control of my muscles?" Abby suggested, laughing weakly. "You wore me out."

"That's my goal," Clancy said, beaming a grin at her. "I want you to be too tired to even think about ever leaving my bed."

"Mission accomplished," Abby assured her, sliding down Clancy's body to get to the business at hand.

❧

A half-hour later, Abby was jumping around the room, the silicone bouncing up to slap against her stomach. "Having one of these is fun!" she giggled, wiggling the well-used device at Clancy. "No wonder men are so fond of them."

"I think they're even more fun when you add a few million nerve cells and a nice blood supply."

"Yeah, yeah, of course that's true," Abby said, her voice bright and animated. "But that's not what I mean. I'm talking about the way it makes you feel to have one of these big things hanging between your legs."

Clancy reached over and wrapped her hand around the base of the toy. "There'd be fewer wars if everyone had one this big. What a wonderful world it would be if every one was exactly the same size. The 'Mine's bigger than yours' fights would be a thing of the past."

"Oh, if it wasn't that, it would be the size of their hands or their feet. Guys would be stuffing newspaper into their shoes to be able to wear a bigger size." Abby lifted her arms over her head and wiggled her hips to make the hefty appendage dance. "It just makes you feel powerful—like you rule the world!"

Clancy sat halfway up, an amused smile on her face. "You're really getting off on this, aren't you? I can't wait to see how you feel when you actually use it!"

"Yeah, I am." Abby grinned shyly and said, "I feel different about myself when I'm wearing this. I might wear it all the time!"

"People do," Clancy drawled, giggling at Abby's expression.

"You're kidding. Women do?"

"Yep. They call it 'packing.' They sell these cool little flesh-colored penises that I'm told feel like the real thing."

"To the wearer?" Abby asked, confusedly.

"Ahh…no," Clancy said, chuckling. "That would be a brisk seller, though, wouldn't it? No," she said still laughing. "They say it really feels like flesh—but there's no sensation, of course. Some women like to wear jockey shorts and put one of these little gizmos in the pouch. It's more of a mental thing than a physical thing, I'd think."

"I can see that," Abby said, unconsciously dropping her hand to stroke her faux phallus. "It really does give you a feeling of power—albeit temporarily. I mean, our culture is all about the power of sex…and this monster is the poster child for sex, isn't it?"

"Sure, I guess," Clancy said. Rolling onto her stomach, she crossed her legs at the ankle and lazily flexed her knees. "I've never seen anyone try on a simple sex toy and launch into a political analysis." Grinning wickedly, she asked, "Is this what those long nights in the dorm at UCLA were like?"

Abby climbed onto the futon and grabbed Clancy in a rough embrace. They wrestled playfully, with Clancy pinning her easily. Panting from exertion, the larger but weaker woman said, "When I was at UCLA, I opted out of the dildo demonstration, but the political elements were always present."

"Do you regret it?" Clancy asked, leaning over her from her victorious position.

"Not a bit," she said. "I'm sure I wouldn't have enjoyed it nearly as much as I did today. I enjoy sex much more now than I did then."

"I'll say it once again," Clancy said. "I'm a lucky, lucky woman."

Chapter Twenty-Three

C lancy was just getting out of the shower on Monday morning when her cell phone rang. Dashing for her room, still dripping, she picked up the little device, pleased and a little concerned to see Abby's name in the caller-identification window. "Hi," she said, slightly out of breath.

"Do you have plans for breakfast?"

"Uhm...no. Why?"

"I'd like to make you a nice meal and have a little time with you. Whadda ya say?"

"You're on," Clancy said, her smile blooming. "Be there in twenty."

🌿

Having breakfast with Abby cheered Clancy up dramatically. For the first time since she had been working on the landscape, she wished the day would go slower, because it was the last one at the Graham house. At three o'clock, she was rolling the new sod, taking her time to make sure it was done perfectly—as well as to waste enough time for Abby to get home from her afternoon meeting.

Her heart started to beat a little faster when she heard a quick horn honk and looked up to see Abby pulling into the driveway. She made it to the yard in record time, her ebullient smile warming Clancy's heart. "Today's the day!" she said, waving to all of the workmen.

"Sure is," Clancy said. "I was afraid we'd be gone by the time you got home, and we only like to do that when things don't work well." Abby walked over to her and put an arm around her, giving her a squeeze that looked far too friendly to be coming from a client.

The dogs had heard their owner drive up, and they began to bark their heads off once they saw her in the yard with Clancy. "Can I bring my entourage?" she asked.

"Yeah, but let us get rid of the last of our equipment first. I don't wanna risk having the gate left open."

"You're always so thoughtful," Abby said, making Clancy blush when every one of her men heard the compliment.

Ramon, always gallant, gave Abby one of his brilliant smiles. "Let me take the roller out, and you can show Mrs. Graham some of the details."

"I'll help you," Clancy said. She looked at Abby and held up a finger. "One minute." She pushed the roller while Ramon and the other men scrambled around making sure they'd taken everything to the truck.

Two of the men pushed the roller up the ramp and into the truck as Ramon walked over to Clancy. He leaned over and kissed her on the head, a rare but not unknown gesture. "I'm very happy for you, *jefa*," he said. "Mrs. Graham is a lovely woman, and it's easy to see how happy you make her."

Clancy flushed pink in a matter of seconds. "Thanks," she said. "I'm sorry I didn't come right out and tell you, but we're trying to take things slow."

"The daughter is a problem, no?"

"Yep. The daughter is a problem, but things will calm down…I hope."

"Things will be fine," Ramon said. "You are both very strong women. I have confidence in you."

Clancy gave him a hug, feeling a little awkward when she did. They had always been friendly and had often had barbecues together. She'd gone to watch soccer with the crew several times, and they'd all been to her parents' house for parties. But there had always been a bit of a barrier. She wasn't sure if it was cultural, because she was a woman, or because she was the boss, but she knew it was something. Nonetheless, she knew Ramon cared for her, and she felt the same about him. "Thanks," she said again, unable to think of anything more demonstrative. "Thanks a lot."

He pulled away and started to walk to the truck. "Enjoy the presentation," he said. "We'll leave you alone."

"You guys did most of the work," she complained. "Come take some of the praise!"

"No, no," he said. "This is for you alone. See you tomorrow." He ducked into the truck, turned on his banda music, and took off, leaving Clancy standing on the street, smiling at him.

When Clancy opened the gate, the dogs ran for her. After kissing her repeatedly, they ran around like they'd been captives for months—which, in a way, they had. Having the work crew in the yard all summer had really interfered with their usual routine of sunning themselves, taking frequent dips in the pool, and barking at the UPS truck, but the end was finally at hand.

Abby walked over to the gate and took Clancy's hand as she surveyed the entire picture. The finished product was more than she'd hoped for, with the wall and waterfall giving the impression that they'd been in place for years. The flow of the water had real force, which was exactly what Abby wanted to drown out the noise of the neighbors. "We can adjust the water pressure, if you want," Clancy said. "This is pretty loud, but it's a nice, calming noise, versus the shrieks of those kids."

"No," Abby said, shaking her head. "This is just what I wanted. Oh, the plants look wonderful, Clancy. You put in some very nice specimens. They really look healthy."

Clancy decided not to mention that her nurseryman was barely speaking to her after she'd made him reorder the plants three times when they didn't meet her exacting standards. "I left a little space on both sides of the stream for you to add things that strike your fancy," Clancy said. "Once you get used to it, I assume you'll want to tweak the design a bit. I know how you gardeners are."

"It's perfect," Abby said. "I couldn't be happier…with it or with you." She kissed her gently, running her hands up and down Clancy's shoulders and back.

"Isn't Hayley?"

"Yes, she's home, but she can't see us here. Besides, I don't care who sees us. I have to kiss you to thank you for this fantastic yard. I've never been happier." They stood there for a few minutes while Abby's sharp eyes took in every detail. "I just wish we could christen it," she said, her voice falling in disappointment.

"How do you want to christen it?"

"I wanna hop in the pool and sample the waterfall for a bit; then spread out a few cushions on the patio and see how much noise the water cancels out."

"What noise?"

"The moans and groans and whimpers that will come out of your mouth when I make love to you. That's what I've been dreaming of ever since I started to fall in love with you."

Clancy hugged her, holding on for a long time. "We'll do that as soon as Hayley leaves for school. We just have to wait."

"I hate to wait," Abby said, leaning her head against her lover's.

☙

The couple didn't see each other for the rest of the week. Clancy was roaming all over the San Gabriel Valley, and it was inconvenient for her to stop by Abby's at six just so they could have breakfast together. Abby still didn't feel comfortable going out at night if Hayley was going to be home, and the girl seemed to like nothing better than having a friend over for dinner—trapping her mother.

Hayley decided to have a big pool party on Sunday, and she and Abby were busy all weekend with preparations for the event. Clancy decided it was self-defeating to sit around and do nothing just because Abby wasn't available, so she invited Michael up to her parents' house for a barbecue of their own on Saturday.

Sunday morning was a reprise of the previous weekend, with Abby sneaking over to Clancy's for a sensual rather than spiritual communion. Clancy opened the door with a wide, sexy grin on her face. "I normally don't open the door to people trying to spread the Good Word, but you're too pretty to turn away. Come on in, and tell me all about Jesus." She reached out, sneaked her finger into the waistband of Abby's melon-colored linen skirt, and gave it a tug.

When Abby was standing on the threshold, Clancy let her hands wander over and under the wide straps of the square-cut, sleeveless white linen top. "Very pretty," she said. "It's a shame it has to come off." Before Abby could reply, the top was lying on the small wooden table by the door, and Clancy's mouth was nuzzling her breast through her camisole.

Strong hands went to Clancy's head and pulled her close, pressing her hard against the breast. "We've gotta work fast," the brunette got out, her words half-moaned. "I can only stay an hour."

Clancy's mouth stopped sucking; her grip eased and then released. She stood and looked at Abby with annoyance. "What?"

Immediately trying to placate her, Abby said, "Only two more weeks. Then Hayley's back at school."

Turning, the blonde walked into the kitchen and picked up her coffee cup. She hoisted herself onto the counter and assessed Abby with cool eyes. "Then Trevor gets home, and for all we know, he'll throw a bigger fit than Hayley has." Her mouth was working, and she looked like she wanted to say something more, but she put the big cup to her lips and sipped slowly, trying to control her temper.

Abby went to her and stood between her legs, gently stroking the skin that peeked out from her boxer shorts. "I know this is hard, honey, but we have so little time together..." She waited for an answer, and when she didn't receive one, she went on. "Let's not fight. We're wasting the only hour we've had alone this week."

"You wanted to make love?" Clancy asked, her tone even and calm.

With a nervous laugh, Abby nodded. "Yes, of course. I feel so close to you when we do." She trailed her fingers down Clancy's bare chest, feeling the soft skin where it covered bone, then muscle, then pliable flesh. Her hand covered the decorated breast; she squeezed it and then leaned in to kiss her partner.

Clancy kissed her but didn't try to escalate matters. She looked at Abby again and asked, "It doesn't bother you to fly over here, throw your clothes off, have sex, get dressed, and run home—all in an hour?"

"I'd rather we had all day. Hell, I'd rather we had all of our lives! But we don't right now. So I think about it like I did when I was in high school, and my boyfriend and I would park in front of my parents' house." She laughed, her lips parting as she recalled those days. "On the drive home, I'd think about what we'd do, and as soon as we parked, we'd be in this mad rush to touch each other. I knew we'd have a half-hour or so before my father turned the light on and off a couple of times, signaling me to come inside." She smiled at Clancy and said, "It wasn't what I wanted, but it was very exciting. Sometimes quick sex is a real turn-on."

Clancy put her cup on the counter and squirmed away from Abby. She slid from her perch and walked away, depositing herself on the sofa. "I like quick sex, too. But I like it because we're so hot for each other we can't wait, not because you lie to your child about going to church and show up unannounced."

Stung, Abby stayed right where she was. "I...I asked Hayley to go with me. I wasn't sure if she would or not until I was ready to leave the house."

Looking at the clock on her VCR, Clancy said, "It's 11:45. Is this the first service they have?"

"No," Abby said, confused. "But I always go to the 11:15 service. I always have."

"But you could go earlier?"

"Yes. There's a nine o'clock Mass."

"So you could have left before Hayley got up—like at seven—and have been gone for hours without her even noticing, right?"

Her voice had taken on a razor-sharp edge, and Abby knew she'd made a very serious error in judgment. She walked over to the sofa and sat down next to her partner. "Yes, I could have." She let out a heavy breath. "I don't know why I didn't."

Clancy pulled her legs up, planting both feet on the edge of the sofa. Her arms rested on her knees, hands dangling. "Maybe it's more exciting for you to make this like a game. Maybe the whole thing seems like a game."

Abby's voice grew sharp. "Don't put thoughts in my head. It might seem like I'm okay with how things are, but that's only because I'm trying my best to be upbeat. I hate this as much as you do."

Still not looking at her lover, Clancy said, "You don't know how much I hate this, so don't assume you know how I feel. You don't."

Angry and hurt, Abby got up and walked to the door. She slipped her top back on and said, "Call me when you feel like having a conversation. I don't have the strength to deal with both you and Hayley pouting." She waited a moment, hoping Clancy would ask her to stay, but the blonde head remained unmoved, staring at the blank television.

Clancy knew she should call and apologize, but she felt like sulking. Having little else to keep herself occupied, she went up to Sierra Madre, surprising her mother when she walked into the house in the late afternoon, sipping one of her favorite malts.

"Well, Clancy O'Connor, I think I've seen more of you in the last twenty-four hours than I have in the last three months!"

"Complaining?"

"Never!" Margaret kissed her and said, "You just missed your grandmother. Daddy just dropped her off at the church to play bingo."

Clancy found it funny that her grandmother had given up the religion long before but was completely unable to forsake her addiction to bingo—exclusively of the Catholic variety. "I'm gonna hang for a while, if that's okay. Want me to go to the store and buy something for dinner?"

"Are you quite all right?" Margaret asked, making a show of feeling her daughter's forehead.

"I owe you a few thousand meals, Mom. I'd be happy to pop for one."

Looking at her quizzically, Margaret said, "I'm serious. Is everything all right, honey?"

"No." She gave her mother a smile and said, "I've been thinking about how hard it is to be a parent. Watching Abby go through all of this crap with Hayley has given me a new perspective on how kids suck the life right out of you."

Margaret wrapped her daughter in a warm hug and said, "It was never hard being your mom." After placing a kiss on both cheeks, she released her child and said, "I really don't envy Abby, though. This has got to be hard on the whole family."

"Yeah, I'm sure it won't be a day at the beach with Trevor, either. Even though Abby thinks he'll be fine with it." Clancy had finished her malt, and she walked into the kitchen to throw the container away. She poked her head into the refrigerator and saw that the cupboard was pretty bare. "Let me go to the store and buy a nice roast. We can cook it outside on the rotisserie. You know how Dad loves that."

Margaret gave her daughter a kiss and patted her on the butt. "That would be lovely, honey. Buy whatever looks good."

❧

When Clancy returned, her father was already getting the rotisserie ready. "There's my best girl," he beamed when she went out back to say hello.

"Hi, Pop." She gave him a kiss and sat down to watch him putter with his toys.

Looking at her speculatively, he asked, "Fight?"

"Yeah."

"Talk about it?"

"Nah."

She watched him work and nodded when he offered a beer. He returned a few minutes later with the roast on the spit and two beers held by their necks in one large hand. She took hers and sipped it, not saying another word. John hummed a little while he worked; then he sat down and watched the roast begin to spin. They watched the meat as though it were a fascinating television show, neither speaking until it had begun to brown. "I'm so sick of Hayley that I'm thinking of going on vacation until she leaves for school," Clancy finally said.

"In August?" John's incredulity was loud and clear. "You can't pick up and leave during your busiest season!"

"It's my business," she grumbled, knowing she was acting childish.

"True. It's yours for as long as you don't piss off your clients or your crew." He took the bottle cap he'd removed earlier and flipped it at her, catching her on the shoulder. "What's really goin' on? The kid's gotta be leaving soon."

"Two weeks," Clancy said.

"Since when can't you wait two weeks for somethin' you really want? Jesus, you waited four years to go to college so you could go where you really wanted!"

"It's not the time," she said, feeling tired and cranky. "It's…it's that Hayley always comes first."

"You knew that going in," John said. "Little late to have circumstances change."

"I know that," she said, her voice testy and sharp. "I don't want circumstances to change. I just want Abby to spend a little time thinking of ways to see me more. We didn't have any time together this week, and it makes me nuts!"

"What does she say when you tell her that?"

Clancy leaned back in her chair and let her head loll back. "I just told her today. That's what we fought about."

"What did she say?" he asked again.

She gave him a vague shrug. "She didn't say much. She was mad at me for being mad at her."

John got up and put a thermometer in the roast, nodding when it registered just where he expected it to be. "So you told her you want her to keep you in the game, right?"

"Right."

"But this is the first time you've told her that, right?"

She shrugged again. "Not really. She knows I'm not happy with the way things are."

He put his hands on his hips, adopting the same stance he did when he chewed out one of his employees. "Have you specifically told her what you need her to do to make you happy?"

"No," she said, her voice barely audible.

"What the hell's wrong with you?" he asked, making her head snap up. "You don't take off from your job in August, and you don't get pissed because somebody isn't doing something if you didn't ask her to do it. Grow up!"

"I'm plenty grown up," she snapped.

"The hell you are! You knew this was gonna be hard, but you didn't want to quit. You've been stewing about this for a while, but you haven't told her how to fix it. That's not fair to her, and that's not mature! Now straighten out and fly right, or cut her loose. The last thing she needs is another kid!"

Clancy pressed her lips together, knowing she was on the verge of saying something very rude. Her father went into the house to get another beer, and she tried to calm her racing mind to let his words sink in. He was gone much longer than he needed to be, and when he came back, she took the offered beer and said, "Abby said the same thing to me today."

"What?"

"She said she didn't have the strength to have both Hayley and me acting like children."

"She's right," he said.

"I get it, Dad. I get it. You've made your point. I'll call her tonight and apologize."

"'Bout time," he mumbled, laughing softly to himself.

"Do you ever get tired of being right?"

"Not really. Comes naturally."

"Too bad I didn't get your hilarious sense of humor," she said, obviously teasing.

"I always thought so." He fussed with his roast for a moment and said, "To tell you the truth, I'm surprised it took you this long to snap. Not like you to be this patient with a woman."

She grinned wryly at him. "I've never been in love with one before, Dad. The rules change."

"They do indeed," he nodded, chuckling softly. "So is this kid always gonna be a problem?"

"Looks like it," she said. "But it's something I'm going to have to learn to deal with. I'd rather she was childless, but she's not. You've gotta take people like you find 'em."

"Too damned bad, ain't it?"

"Sure as hell is," she agreed, taking a long pull on her beer.

"So the kid's a real pain, huh?"

"She has been to me."

"Abby think so?"

"Yeah. She thinks Hayley's been pretty bad when it comes to me."

"But she doesn't think she's a snot in general? That's gonna be a problem, isn't it? How will you handle having a spoiled brat around?"

Clancy was working on removing the label from her beer bottle with her thumbnail. "Abby says she's not usually like this. I have my doubts."

"You worked with her for a few weeks. You were singing her praises then. What happened?"

"Huh." Clancy looked at her father. "I guess I was, wasn't I?"

"Yeah. And when I met her, she acted like a real polished young woman. She didn't seem like a jerk."

Dropping her head back against her chair, Clancy muttered, "I'm not even sure what's true anymore. Maybe it's me."

"You?"

"Yeah." She looked at her father and said, "I've run into more rich little bitches in Pasadena than I can count. Long time ago, I spent a few days flirting with a girl about my age. We were putting a pool in at a property up in La Canada. Stucco...cul-de-sac?"

"Yeah. I know the place." He laughed, shaking his head. "You were flirting with that cute girl who was lying in the sun the whole time we were there?"

"Yeah. She was hot, wasn't she?"

"It's been ten years, and I remember her," John said, grinning.

"Well, she slipped me her number on the day we finished. I was gonna call her, but I went up the next week to check the pool, and she had some friends over. She acted like she'd never seen me before. Just told me to turn the heat up a degree or two. Treated me like a stranger she could order around."

"I take it you never called her."

"Hell, no! I never flirted with one of those rich girls again, either. Girls like that always think they're too classy for working-class women."

"But Abby doesn't?"

"No! Abby's an adult. She knows who she is and what she wants. But I don't trust Hayley any farther than I can throw her. Never have. She made some crack about being richer than me when she was mad at me. She can be a real jerk."

John looked at his daughter with sympathetic eyes. "You'd better find a way to reach some kinda peace with this kid. 'Cause she's gonna be around a long, long time."

❧

Clancy went into the house and called Abby, feeling shitty about their fight. "Hi," she said when Abby picked up.

"Are we speaking?" Abby asked, a little archly.

"I am if you are. I called to apologize for being a baby. My dad agrees with you, by the way."

Abby laughed a little. "I always knew he was a smart guy."

"Yeah, he is. I know you're busy, but I just wanted to apologize and ask you to forgive me. I'm sorry I was so rude."

"It's okay. I should have never come over and expected you to jump to attention. That's not treating you with respect. I was going to call you to apologize as soon as I had a minute."

"Let's drop this one, okay? Chalk it up to frayed nerves."

"It's dropped. Call me later tonight, okay?"

"I will. I love you."

"Me, too. Give my love to your parents and your grandmother."

"'Kay. Later."

The next afternoon, Clancy was idling on the Pasadena freeway when she answered her cell phone.

"Where are you, honey?"

"Heading home. I'm almost at Fair Oaks."

"Did you have a good day?"

"Not bad. I spent too long at a client's house in Beverlywood, and now I'm stuck in traffic. I'm trying to get home to take a quick nap before dance class."

Abby pouted. "I wanna go."

"Michael's always happy to bow out. You know I'd rather take you."

With a tone filled with yearning, Abby said, "Hayley's gonna be home for dinner. I should stay."

"Whatever," the blonde said. She did her best not to let her annoyance show. Also, she was beginning to learn that Abby made a bigger effort to be with her when she acted more ambivalent. "I'll think of you when I'm leading Michael around the dance floor."

"You lead?"

"Yep. I told you before," Clancy said, her wicked grin managing to make it through the phone line. "I *always* lead."

Abby hung up, standing in place with her hand still on the phone, thinking of how wonderful it felt to have Clancy guide her around the dance floor. Hayley walked into the room and said, "That won't make it ring."

Shaking her head, Abby pulled her hand away and walked into the den, irritated by Hayley's mere presence.

On Tuesday morning, Hayley was up earlier than usual. She walked downstairs, wearing a mysterious smile. "Hey," she said when she spotted her mother. "Can I borrow the car this morning?"

"Sure. Going somewhere special?"

"Uh-huh."

Her smile grew, and she turned to go back upstairs, Abby following her with her eyes. *I think I could pin her. If I got her out the front door and called the locksmith…*

❦

Around noon, the dogs started to bark, and a moment later, Abby heard the garage door open. A loud clatter from the laundry room made her get up to see what was going on. She pushed open the door at the same time Trevor was pulling it from his side. Caught off balance, she fell into his arms, feeling his sturdy body hold her effortlessly. "You must've missed me," he said, laughing.

She had to scramble to get her feet set in the small space, because both dogs were jumping, barking, and doing their patented flips of joy at seeing Trevor. "God, yes!" she cried. She wrapped her arms around his neck, giving him a long, strong hug. "I missed you like crazy!"

"I missed you, too, Mom," he said softly. "Very much."

"Nice surprise, huh?" Hayley asked, giggling.

"The nicest," Abby agreed.

She backed up, giving the kids room to walk into the kitchen. She watched as Trevor hefted his bags into the room, marveling at how much his body looked like his father's. She gazed at him with a wistful smile, making him reach out and tweak her nose. "Don't tell me—I look older and better than when I left."

She hugged him again, letting her hand fall to give him a swat on the seat. "I know I'm predictable, but you should be used to that by now."

"You're not so predictable," Hayley said, her words teasing but her tone serious.

"Depends on the day," Abby said, refusing to let her daughter bait her into talking about Clancy at that moment. "Are you hungry, honey?" she asked her son.

"A little. I had lunch and dinner on the plane, but it wasn't very good."

"Oh, right, your body thinks it's nine, doesn't it?"

"Yeah. Maybe I'll just have some caffeine. I wanna stay up so I can go to bed around ten. I wanna get back on California time as soon as I can."

He walked over to the refrigerator and took out a can of Coke. While he poured it into a glass, Abby asked, "Did you leave early, honey, or did the program end sooner than it was supposed to?"

Trevor tilted his head back and nearly drained his glass. "A little of both," he said. "We were finished, but the other people in the program were dragging their feet in writing out the final report. They were working a couple of hours a day and hanging out until three or four a.m. I got sick of it and wanted to come home—so I left."

Abby stood next to him and put her hand on his waist. "Really?"

He avoided her eyes while filling his glass. "Yeah. I want to find a job, not sit around getting drunk in Venice. I mean, it was fun, but we'd been partying for over two weeks." He looked down and smiled at his mother. "Maybe I was just pissed that I hadn't hooked up with anyone."

"No one?"

"Nope. There were ten girls in the program, and the only decent ones were engaged. I didn't have a date the whole time I was gone."

"You should have been here," Hayley said. "Love was in the air." She was sitting on one of the tall chairs by Abby's counter-height desk. Her mother had grown tired of her lobbing innuendo-filled bombs into the conversation.

Staring at Hayley, Abby said, "I'm sure Trevor and I will discuss Clancy, but we'll do it alone."

The girl gulped noticeably, not used to having her mother be obviously upset with her. "I'm sorry," she said quietly. "I'll go swim for a while so you can talk."

"You don't need to leave, Hayley. You just need to stop being passive-aggressive."

Hayley nodded. "I think I'm better at leaving." With that, she went into the downstairs bathroom to put on her swimsuit.

As soon as she left, Trevor looked at his mother. "Has she been like this all summer?"

"Uh-huh. I almost put her in a FedEx box and sent her to you."

Trevor touched his mother's shoulder. "You should have, Mom. I'm serious. You shouldn't have to put up with her when she's being a jerk."

Abby laughed softly. "I think she acts like a jerk because I allow her to." She took her son's hand and led him into the living room so Hayley wouldn't hear them. They sat down on the sofa, just close enough to be able to touch once in a while. "I always encouraged you to say what was on your mind, Trevor, and you never abused that privilege. But Hayley's a very different kid. I think I should have set firmer limits with her. I thought the same techniques I used with you would work with her, but they haven't."

"She's not a bad kid, Mom. Believe me, I'd rather be with Hayley than most of the girls on my project. At least she's not obsessed with how she looks and whether someone else is getting attention."

"Really a bad bunch, huh?"

"Yeah," he said, his forehead wrinkled in thought. "The guys were good, but the girls really sucked. They were always pouting about something."

"Hayley's been doing her share of pouting."

"Yeah, but at least she's not usually like that. She...she's having a real hard time with this, Mom."

She put her hand on his knee, giving it a squeeze. "I know, honey." She took a deep breath. "How much do you know?"

"I know just about everything," he said. "I know what happened, and I know how it happened, and I know how Hayley feels about it." He shrugged. "It's more than a little weird, but I'm not mad at you or anything."

She gazed at him for a moment, feeling so much better to have him home again. "How do you feel, sweetheart?"

"I'm not sure," he admitted. "I guess it depends on the day. I want you to be happy, Mom, so that's what I focus on. If you're happy with Clancy...I want you to go for it."

"I think I already have," Abby said, her smile wry. "I've told your grandparents, Ellen, Pam, Maria, Spencer…I'm sure it won't be long before Marjorie is marching up and down the hill telling all of the neighbors."

He laughed at that, imagining the rotund older woman hefting herself up the steep hill to spread her juicy news. "How did everyone take it?"

"Ellen has been the worst," Abby said. "Well, your grandfather isn't very happy about it, but at least he hasn't insulted my intelligence."

Trevor's mouth dropped open. "Ellen did that?"

"Yep." Abby let her head drop back and felt the cushion press against the spot where she was getting a headache. "She told me she couldn't be friends with me anymore."

"No!" The look on his face showed that he assumed she was kidding, but her expression showed she was deadly serious. "But why…?"

"She thinks I'm being selfish," Abby said. "She thinks I'm putting my needs before yours and Hayley's."

His eyes narrowed, and he tilted his head. "We're adults now; you don't have to treat us like little kids anymore. It's not like being with a woman is such a big deal." He shoved some of his thick, dark hair from his eyes. "I mean, yeah, it's weird, and it's gonna take some getting used to, but it's not like you're going out with somebody who's mean or evil or something. Clancy's just a chick…right?"

"Pretty much," Abby agreed. "A young chick, but a chick."

"Yeah. That part's a little weird, too," he admitted. "I never thought my stepfather would be a girl just about my age, but…I guess you didn't either, right?"

His gaze had sharpened, and Abby had a feeling he wasn't asking his question. "What's on your mind, Trev? Come on, tell me."

He sat quietly for a moment and then asked, "You haven't been…uhm…wanting to be with women…before, right?"

She took a moment to consider his words. "Do you mean while your father was alive?"

"Yeah." He put his head down, unable to look at her.

She put her hand on his cheek, urging him to meet her eyes. "Honey, I loved your dad more than you'll ever know. He was my first love, and I wouldn't have traded him for all of the women in the world. I never, ever wished that I'd picked another man or a woman. He was the one. He'll always be the one."

She was crying now, and Trevor scooted over to hold her. "But you love Clancy, right?"

"Yes, of course I do. But it's not the same. It's hard to explain, but there's something unique about your first love. When you marry and have children together, there's…I don't even know how to put it into words. But it's different. Your father was the love of my life. That will never change, no matter how much I love Clancy. She'll be my partner, but with your dad…we were a family. Having you and Hayley made us into a unit. I know it'll never be like that with Clancy. And so does she," she added. "She wants to fit in, but she can't act like she's related to you and Hayley. She'll be your mother's partner."

"But…you'll want her to be at all of our family events, right?"

"Of course!"

"I'd like to have some kinda relationship with her," he said, looking a little confused. "But I don't know—"

"Honey. Just let things happen. If you like her, something will develop. If you don't like her…well, I guess you'll just have to have a few drinks to get through holiday dinners." She leaned over and tickled him on the ribs, making him giggle like a child.

"Stop!" he begged, squirming. "Please!"

"I'll be good," she promised, holding her hands up.

"Not fair," he insisted. "You know all of my weak spots."

She put her arm around him and hugged him tight. "I do. But you know most of mine, too. The blessing and the curse of family."

❦

Trevor went upstairs to unpack, but after just a few moments, he came racing down the stairs. "Mom! Why didn't you tell me you were done?"

"What?" she asked, meeting him at the stairs.

"The yard!" He trotted for the back door, both dogs following him. Abby was delighted by his glee, and she fell in line. They went outdoors, and Trevor stood with his hands on his hips, shaking his head in amazement. "I never would have believed this was our yard," he said. "This isn't just an improvement—it's a complete transformation." He turned and smiled at his mother. "Clancy's got a load of talent."

His smile was contagious, and she matched it immediately. "She does, Trev. Thanks for saying so."

"I've got to get into my suit and let that waterfall hit me," he said, grinning like a child. "Wanna join me?"

"Not right now, but I will soon."

He ran into the house, taking the stairs two at a time. "Hurry up, Mom. That pool looks too good!"

As soon as Trevor went outside, Abby reached Clancy on her cell phone. "Guess who's home," she said.

"Hmm…I'm gonna say Trevor, since he's the only one who's been gone. Isn't he home early?"

"Yeah. I think he's worried about his mom."

"Not angry with her?"

"Doesn't seem to be," Abby said. "We had a very nice chat, baby. And he positively loved the back yard. He wants to get to know you better, too. He seemed very accepting."

"Whew! Thank God someone's acting like he's supposed to."

"You can say that again! My boy came through for me!"

Chapter Twenty-Four

For a couple of days, Trevor did nothing but sleep and eat, but by Friday he was up in his room, making calls and trying to set up interviews. Abby was proud of how businesslike he was being about finding a job, even as she was disappointed by Hayley's lack of initiative. Her musings about finding a job when she returned from Maine had disappeared, and she seemed content to lie in the pool, listen to her music, and read popular novels.

On Friday afternoon, after having played golf with the women's league at her club, Abby returned to the house. Hayley was sitting on the desk chair in the kitchen, talking on the phone, but when Abby entered, she turned toward the wall and spoke more quietly. Trying to be respectful of the girl's privacy, Abby put a few things into the freezer and then went into the den, staying there until she heard Hayley hang up.

The girl walked into the den and dropped inelegantly into a chair, her ability to look almost boneless always amazing her mother. "Gramp's not very happy with you," she said with a careless air.

The short hairs on the back of Abby's neck rose. "What?"

"I was talking to Grampa. He thinks you're being selfish."

Abby got up and walked over to her daughter. The look she gave her made the girl sit up straight. "Listen. I'm sick and tired of your acting like a child! You're eighteen years old, and that's long past old enough to be respectful. No matter whom I'm involved with, I'm still your mother, and I'd advise you to remember that." She started to walk out of the room, but she was so angry she turned and added, "You're old enough to decide where to live, Hayley. If you feel closer to your grandparents, you might want to stay there when you're home from school."

The girl's mouth dropped as quickly as the tears started to flow. She got to her feet and ran by her mother, sobbing as she dashed to her room.

Abby stood right where she was, finally looking heavenward. *I'm so damned glad I didn't let you talk me into having another child, Will. God knows what the third one would have been like!*

🦋

Abby spent an hour trying to control her emotions, knowing she couldn't get away with yelling at her father—even though she was forty-five years old. When she felt calm enough to be rational, she called, partially relieved when her mother answered. "Where's your husband?" Abby said, laughing a little at her own tone.

"Oh, Lord, what did he do now?"

"He told Hayley I was being selfish! He's conspiring with my child!"

"Oh, crap!"

Profanity was very rare for Elizabeth, and even this mild curse made Abby laugh. "Can you rein him in, Mom? I don't wanna block his calls, but I will."

"I'll talk to him, honey. And I think we'd better come home. I think we all need to sit down and talk about this."

"Tell me when you're coming, and I'll be there to pick you up."

"I'll talk to your father and see what we can agree on. You know he hates to come back while his dahlias are in bloom."

Abby waited a second, trying to stop herself from telling her mother just where she thought her father could stick his dahlias.

"I know you're upset, Abby. We'll be home as soon as we can."

"Thanks, Mom. I could really use some support right now."

Abby called Clancy not long after the landscaper had returned home for the day. "Would you like to help me stay out of prison?"

"Ahh...yeah."

"I'm gonna kill my youngest if I have to see her again today. Can you help me out?"

"Sure," Clancy said, laughing. "I'll shower and change, and then come get you."

"Where do you want to go?"

"Does it matter?"

Abby laughed too. "Nope. I'll be waiting."

After listening to Abby rant about Hayley's behavior all the way to Sierra Madre, Clancy turned briefly and said, "I know you're upset, babe, but I can't tell you what to do. I'm too involved, and I don't think I can be objective."

"I don't normally seek advice about how to raise my kids," Abby insisted, "but I'm about ready to have someone step in and take over for me. I'm honestly at a loss."

"If you want someone to tell you what to do, Eileen Donovan is your woman. Whether you want her to or not, she'll tell you what you should do in any given situation. One really good thing about her, though—she doesn't mind if you ignore her advice; she just wants to offer it."

"I'm at her mercy," Abby moaned, resting her head back against the seat to try to stem the headache that was pounding behind her eyes.

They weren't at the house for more than two minutes when Eileen looked Abby up and down and asked, "That kid still giving you trouble?"

"She sure is," Abby said, nodding. "Worse now than ever."

Immediately, the other three members of the family disappeared, everyone recognizing when Eileen was about to deliver a lecture. "Tell me what's going on," she said, leaning back in her chair and gazing thoughtfully at Abby.

"Well, she's unhappy about Clancy and me being together. My father's not happy about it, either. She talked to him on the phone today, and he told her I was being selfish. It's not just that she told me that, but she acted so superior! I honestly wanted to slap her!"

"Did ya?"

"No, of course not! I've never hit the kids."

"Mmm...too late to start now, I guess," Eileen mused thoughtfully. "That how she normally is?"

"No, not really, Eileen. She's a lot like me in some ways. It's hard for her to talk about her feelings when she's upset, but she's usually respectful. Or at least she was before this started."

"What have you and Bitsy been doing to spend time together? Do you go to her place?"

Abby looked a little ashamed of herself when she said, "We haven't been seeing each other much. Clancy and I have had a couple of fights about it. I think she's running out of patience."

"She's never been very patient with girls. She knows what she wants, and she wants it right then."

"I know, but I just don't know what to do about my daughter. I'm...struggling."

"So instead of having a plan and sticking with it, you've given the kid what she wants—exactly what she wants," Eileen emphasized.

"I...I guess that's right. I thought that was the best way to handle it."

"Has it helped?" Eileen persisted. "At all?"

"Uhm...no."

"Look," Eileen said, grasping Abby's hand and holding it firmly. "The kid's manipulating the shit out of you. She's acting like a three-year-old, and you're letting her! Why should she change if she's getting what she wants?"

"What does she want?" Abby asked blankly.

"She doesn't want you and Clancy to be together!" Eileen cried. "Hell, you're the one who told me that in the first place!"

The expression on her face made Abby burst into laughter. "I hardly know my own name at this point."

"Look, Abby, I can tell that you love my little pip, but she's not the kind of kid who'll put up with your kid running her life. Matter of fact, I'm surprised she's hung in there for this long. She's a very independent little cuss, and letting someone else tell her what to do drives her stark raving mad! I hate to see you blow this with her, because I can see how much you care for her."

"But what should I do, Eileen?" she begged, panic starting to set in.

"Haven't you been listening?" Eileen cocked her head. "I'll tell you again—stop letting your girl run roughshod over you. You're the adult; remind her of that. It's your house; remind her of that, too. Don't let a three-year-old who's pitchin' a bitch run the damned house. It's not good for her, and it's not good for you."

"I'm normally a much better mom, Eileen, I swear it," Abby said earnestly. "I'm just having a hell of a time with this one. I can usually figure out how to help her choose the adult path—just not this time."

"When's the last time *you* were the issue?" Eileen asked. "It's easier when it's about curfews and boyfriends and jobs. This one hits too close to home."

Abby sat back in her chair and let out a relieved sigh. "I can't thank you enough, Eileen. I'm seeing this clearly for the first time. You're a life saver."

"Hope it helps. I wouldn't have an eighteen-year-old in my house again for all the tea in China!"

When Abby got home, there was a message from Maria on her machine. "Hi. Ellen called to say she won't be playing tennis with us anymore. I'm sorry, hon, but I couldn't talk any sense into her. Do you still wanna go tomorrow and look for a single?"

Abby leaned against the counter, trying to will herself not to cry. Hayley walked into the room and said, "Since you're not gonna play tennis tomorrow, can I have the car? I wanna go to Santa Barbara with Gretchen."

There was nothing snotty or rude about the question, but the fact that Hayley didn't show the slightest bit of sympathy for Abby's having lost her best friend struck her the wrong way. "No, you can't," she said. "Gretchen has a car. She can drive." She brushed past her daughter without even bothering to say goodnight.

Hayley didn't go to Santa Barbara on Saturday, but she did spend much of the day with Gretchen. She got home at around four p.m., finding the garage empty. "Where's Trevor?" she asked her mother.

"He and Sam took the car to go down to San Diego. They're staying overnight."

"Oh." She opened the refrigerator and took out a diet soda, nodding. "*That's* why I couldn't have the car."

Abby looked at her. "No, it's not. I didn't want you to have it because I was angry with you. I'm angry with you a lot these days," she said, her voice growing softer.

Tears were in Hayley's eyes before Abby could blink. "You've never gotten mad at me before this all started. Why are you being so mean?"

Abby walked over and put her arms around her. "I'm not trying to be mean, Hayley. But you've been rude and spiteful. You've gone behind my back to talk about me with your grandfather, and you haven't even tried to have any empathy for me. I don't expect this to be easy for you, but I do expect you to talk to me about it like an adult."

"I'm not an adult," the girl said, her tears making her hard to hear.

"Yes, you are," Abby said. "I know you don't always feel like one, but you are, honey. You're going to be a sophomore in college this year. You're old enough to vote, to get married, join the army—all sorts of things."

"But I don't *feel* like an adult," she said, nuzzling her face into her mother's shoulder. "I feel like a kid."

"I know it's hard," Abby said. "But you've got to try harder to be mature about this. I can't have this much tension in the house; it's not good for any of us."

"What do you want me to do?" Hayley asked, pulling away and wiping her eyes.

"I've given you a few weeks, honey, and you won't even have a civil discussion with me about Clancy. I can't wait any longer. I'm going to have her come here for dinner, and I'm going to sleep at her house sometimes. I need to see her."

Eyes wide and cheeks hot with anger, Hayley started to say, "You mean you need to fu—" She caught herself, and her jaw snapped shut. She stalked out of the room, went into the den, and put on her iPod headphones. A moment later, she was lying on the couch, her eyes closed as her music played.

"Are you sure this is a good idea?" Clancy asked when Abby let her in that evening.

"No. But your grandmother is right. I've given her enough time; now I have to live my life."

"Okay." Clancy stood in the entryway, looking around discreetly.

"She's in her room. Go on into the kitchen, and grab a drink. I'll tell her we're having dinner soon." Abby walked upstairs and knocked on Hayley's door, opening it even though she hadn't been invited in. "Clancy's here. We're going to have dinner in about fifteen minutes."

Hayley was sitting in front of her computer, IMing with someone. "Not hungry," she said.

"Suit yourself," Abby said, pursing her lips as she shut the door.

After dinner, Abby walked over to her partner and sat on her lap. Leaning close, she whispered, "I wanna make love. How about you?"

Laughing, Clancy nodded. "Yeah, I could get interested. Are we trying to force Hayley's hand?"

Abby kissed her lover on the nose. "I'm tempted, but I think we should go to your house."

Clancy's eyes lit up. "Really? You'll stay over?"

"Of course I will. I've told her that I've got to live my life, and that doesn't include any more drive-by sex."

Leaning her head back, Clancy blew a big air kiss into the sky. "I'm a happy, happy girl!"

The next morning, Abby woke and gingerly tried to get out of bed. She was expecting the worst but got up without much difficulty. On the way to the bathroom, she thought, *Either my back has acclimated, or I love sleeping with Clancy so much that I don't feel any pain. Oh, well, either way I'm thankful.*

Getting back onto the futon, Abby lay there quietly for a while and then decided that Clancy looked so delicious that she had to cuddle her. Within moments, she was sound asleep, the feel of her lover's body acting as a powerful sleep aid.

They spent the rest of the morning making love and napping. Abby hated to leave, but she was determined to make some headway with Hayley. When she returned home in the early afternoon, she went out onto the patio and saw Hayley floating in the pool. Kicking off her shoes, she padded over and sat on the deck, dangling her feet into the cool, clear water. "Feels good," she said.

That casual comment signaled no hard feelings from the night before, and Hayley sheepishly paddled over to her. "Sorry about last night, Mom. I just…I just can't stand to see her," she grumbled. "I feel like I have PMS all the damned time. I wish I could be more polite."

"This is a tough time for you, honey. I understand…really I do."

"Thanks," the girl said quietly.

Taking a breath, Abby said, "But even though I have empathy for you, Clancy and I are going to see more of each other. I've tried to give you time to get used to this, but I can't wait any longer."

The young woman gave her a look that was filled with sadness. She slid from the float and swam for the steps. Then she stood on the pool deck and said, "I think I need to leave."

"You can if you think it's best, but I wish you'd stay and try to work through your feelings."

"I can't, Mom. I just can't." She wrapped a towel around herself and started for the house, her slumped shoulders showing her defeat.

❧

Hayley got on the Internet and found that she could get a fare to San Francisco for the same price as her ticket to San Jose had cost. She sent an e-mail to Alexander and went next door to Trevor's room, finding him lying on his bed talking on the phone in his "adult" voice. He motioned for her to sit, so she plunked down onto his desk chair and spun around lazily while she waited.

When he hung up, he asked, "What's up?"

"Who were you talking to?" she asked. "You sounded so serious."

"Oh. I called one of my professors to ask if he had any leads on a job. He didn't," he said, getting up and stretching. "I think I might have to go back to being a lifeguard at the country club." He put his hands on his hips, trying to look impressive. "'No running, kids! I have a master's degree, and I'm not afraid to use it!'"

"Do your friends have jobs yet?"

He sat on the edge of his low dresser. "Some do; some don't. Seems like there are more jobs available on the East Coast. But I don't think I wanna leave California."

"Not even to get away from Mom and Clancy?" She said the name like she was on the verge of vomiting, and Trevor reached over and flicked her skull with his finger.

"Knock it off, will ya? Why does it matter who she's with? It's not like they're making out in the kitchen."

"That'll be next," Hayley said. "She was here for dinner last night, and Mom said that she's gonna eat here all the time."

Trevor sighed; then he got up and flopped back onto his bed, making the box springs cry out in protest. "So what are we supposed to do? I want Mom to be happy. I think this is weird, too, but...it's her life. We can't tell her what to do. Hell, we don't want her telling us what to do. It's the same thing, Hales."

"Sucks," she said, pouting.

"Yeah, well, a lot of life does. It sucked to lose Dad. I'm sure as hell not gonna lose Mom. If she wants to date an ax murderer, I'll just do my best not to piss him...or her...off."

"I can't stand to see them together."

Trevor sat up and looked at his sister for a moment. "I know you don't have any bad feelings about gay people. I know you love Mom. So something else is going on. Tell me what it is." He looked so serious, so adult that Hayley just stared at him for a moment.

"I...I don't know," she said, not able to meet his eyes.

"Yes, you do," he insisted. "You have to know."

Images of her mother and Clancy having sex filled her brain, and she shivered. They were very much like the fantasies she'd had about Clancy, and having her mother taking her place was making her feel sick. But even though she wanted to talk to her brother, she was ashamed and embarrassed to admit her jealousy— particularly because she was now completely focused on Alexander. "It's a lot of things," she said. "It's private."

He got up and went to stand by her. Looking into her eyes, he said, "You've got to get over this. Mom deserves better from you."

Bristling, the girl said, "She cares a lot more about what Clancy thinks than what I do. Once I'm gone, she'll be fine."

"What are you, stupid?" he asked, truly angry with her. "You and Mom have been so close! Do you think she's just gonna throw you aside?"

"That's what it seems like," Hayley said, sniffling away a few tears.

"Hayley," he said patiently, "I know you and Dad were really close, but after he died, you and Mom really bonded. You've been there for each other all through the really hard times. Don't let her down now."

"I...I don't know what to do," she said. "I think I'm gonna go to San Francisco until school starts."

"San Francisco?" He sat up and looked at his sister carefully. "You gonna stay with that guy?"

"Yeah," she said, swiveling in the chair. "I think."

"How old is he?"

"About your age. You'd like him. He's kinda like you."

Trevor scowled. "I don't trust an older guy who wants to date someone your age."

"What?" Hayley was clearly outraged.

"You heard me," he said. "A guy my age shouldn't be interested in a girl who's only eighteen. I'd never go out with someone who wasn't at least out of college. If you'd stayed with your class, you'd just be graduating from high school. There *should* be a big maturity gap."

"I'm mature," she insisted.

He smiled at his little sister. "You're pretty typical for an eighteen-year-old. But you change a lot in college. Things are different when you're working for a living."

"Like you know! You don't have a job!"

"I had a job this summer," he said, "and I interned every summer. It's different."

"Fine," she sniffed. "Maybe Alexander thinks I'm mature, even though you don't."

"Maybe," he said dubiously. "But I know one thing he's gonna expect if you stay with him. Are you ready for that?"

She laughed, seeing that Trevor was embarrassed. "Are you really asking me if I'm gonna have sex with him?"

"No. I'm *telling* you that he's gonna expect to have sex with you. If you don't wanna, you'd better not stay with him. There's a word for girls who lead a guy on."

She got up and started to walk out of the room, then turned. "It's two words," she said, sticking her tongue out at him. "Hyphenated."

❧

Alexander did want Hayley to stay with him, and he offered to pick her up at the airport. All she had to do was persuade her mother to pay for the ticket. She went downstairs and found her mother sitting under the pergola, reading a book. Hayley sat down on a chair and put her feet up on the seat of her mother's chair. "Whatcha reading?"

Abby held the large book up. "Robert Caro's biography of LBJ."

"Is it good?" the girl asked, clearly just trying to make conversation.

"Mmm…'good' isn't the right word. But it's very informative. I'm learning a lot about how Johnson's beliefs and policies helped create some of the social programs that people really thought would change America for the better."

"Did they?" Hayley asked.

"Well…no, for the most part, they didn't. The Voting Rights Act of 1964 had a decent impact, but I wouldn't say that most of the programs had the intended effect."

"Huh. That must be a bummer. He's not still alive, is he?"

"Gosh, no! He's been dead for a long time."

Hayley nodded. "You don't hear much about Johnson."

"You do if you're interested in American government," Abby said. "He was a very, very powerful president."

Looking puzzled, Hayley said, "I took American government this year. My professor just talked about what an asshole he was because of the Vietnam War."

Abby smiled at her. "You can't take everything your professors say at face value, honey. Teachers always have a point of view that isn't unbiased. If you care about a topic, you'd better do your own research."

"So…Johnson wasn't an asshole?"

"I didn't say that," Abby said, smiling. "When I was your age, I certainly thought he was. But he was in a difficult situation. Many people believed that losing Vietnam would spread Communism."

"But it didn't, did it?"

"No, it didn't."

"Why?" Hayley asked, looking truly interested.

"I think the best antidote for Communism is a free, functioning, capitalist state. Communism looks great on paper, but it hasn't worked. Once people in the Communist states began to understand how little they had compared to people in the capitalist countries, there was no way the governments could hold. Satellite TV did more to destroy Communism than war ever did."

"That's kinda cool," Hayley said. "And you lived through all of that, huh?"

"Yep. I saw it all. I was passionately opposed to the war, but I think that people who supported it had the best interests of the country at heart, too, even though I didn't think so at the time."

"I guess that's true," Hayley said. She put her feet on her mother's knees and rubbed them up and down. "It's cool that you know stuff. Most of my friends' moms are dolts."

"I don't know if that's true," Abby laughed. "But I appreciate the compliment."

"You think I'll like Clancy someday?" the girl asked, looking innocent and hopeful.

"I sure hope so. I'd like that more than you can imagine."

"Well, it's gonna take a while," Hayley said. "I really don't like her now, and I don't like you for being with her. So I'm gonna go visit Alexander for a week. I can take a nine o'clock flight tonight. Is that okay?"

"A week, huh?" Abby's mind was racing with the implications of what such a visit meant. "Are you sure you're ready for that?"

"Yes, Mother," Hayley said impatiently. "Trevor already asked me that."

"Can you change your ticket?"

"Not without a penalty, but since it's the same price as the ticket for San Jose, I thought you might pay for me to go to San Francisco now and let me use the ticket I already have to come home for Thanksgiving. It wouldn't cost you any more," she said quickly.

"That's fine," Abby said, making a dismissive gesture. "I'm really not cheap, honey. I just want you to make plans and stick with them."

"Okay. I understand."

Abby leaned forward and grasped both of Hayley's ankles, holding them tightly to get her attention. "I worry about you. Are you sure you're ready to spend a whole week with Alexander?"

"Yeah, I am," Hayley said, blushing.

"How will you protect yourself if you have sex with him?"

"If?" Hayley asked, laughing. "Trevor says I'm gonna have to do it just to get a ride from the airport."

A laugh burst from Abby. "Did he really say that?"

"No, but he said Alexander wouldn't want me to stay with him if I don't sleep with him."

"That's probably true," Abby said.

"I know what guys want, Mom. I'm not nine!"

"So…what will you use for birth control?"

Hayley pulled her feet away, stood up, and unbuttoned her shorts, pulling them and her underwear down a few inches in the back. "I'm on the birth-control patch," she said, showing it to her mother. "I went to Student Health before I left in May." She pulled her pants back up and sat down.

"Safer sex?" Abby asked.

"Yes," Hayley said dramatically. "I'll make him wear five or six condoms."

Abby leaned over and put her hands on Hayley's knees. "I don't want to lecture you, but I want you to make sure you don't get into a situation you're not ready for. You know that having sex is more of an emotional act than a physical one."

"I know that, Mom. Well, I think I do. And if I don't wanna do it, I won't. I don't care what I'm *supposed* to do."

"Fine," Abby said. "And you'd better have been kidding about extra condoms. You know that using another condom increases the risk of breakage."

Hayley's head dropped back, and she stuck out her tongue, acting like she'd been strangled. "You've been talking to me about safe sex since I was born!"

"Safer sex," Abby corrected. "The only safe sex is masturbation."

Hayley put her hands over her ears. "Enough! I know what to do, and I know what not to do!"

"I wouldn't torture you if I didn't love you," Abby said.

Hayley gave her a begrudging smile. "Can't you love me just a little less?"

Looking at her with complete seriousness, Abby said, "No, I can't. I love you with all of my heart, and I always will."

"Even if I don't like Clancy…ever?"

"Yes, Hayley, I'll still love you. That will never change."

The girl stared at her for a moment. "But you won't give Clancy up…no matter how much I don't like her, right?"

"Right," Abby said, staring at her. "Things have changed. I'm single now. I have to make decisions that work for me. I have to make my own life, Hayley."

"Even if it makes me uncomfortable being around you?"

Abby gazed at her daughter for a moment. "I've never met Alexander. He could be a royal pain. But I'm not giving you a hard time about going to stay with him. I've talked to you about love and commitment and sexuality for years, Hayley, but now it's time for you to make your own choices. Even if I don't like Alexander, I won't throw a fit every time you want to spend time with him. That's disrespectful of you…and your choices."

Tears coming to her eyes again, Hayley said, "And that's what I've done to you? I've disrespected you?"

"Yes. You have. You've hurt me and disappointed me this summer. You've been petulant and disrespectful and self-centered. You need to grow up, Hayley, and you'd better do it quickly if you want to have a relationship with a man—any man."

Hayley got up and stared at her mother for a few seconds. She was crying hard enough that she couldn't quite catch her breath. "I didn't want to hurt you. But you hurt me! You disrespected me! You broke promises to all of us!"

Abby stood and tried to grasp her shoulders, but Hayley slithered away. "What promises did I break? How did I hurt you?"

"It's too late," the girl cried. "It's too late now. Go be with Clancy. That's what really matters to you!" With that, she was gone, running into the house with the dogs barking wildly while they ran after her.

꽃

As soon as Trevor and Hayley left for the airport, Abby called Clancy. "Want to spend the evening with the world's worst mother?"

"I think she's in prison for killing her kids," Clancy said. "Got anything more interesting in mind?"

"Yeah," Abby said quietly. "I'm really down, and I'd love to curl up in your arms and have you tell me that everything will be all right."

"I'll be there in fifteen," Clancy replied, hanging up without waiting for a response.

True to her word, the yellow truck beeped once exactly fifteen minutes later. Abby stood on the porch and watched her drive in, immeasurably soothed by her mere presence. No sooner was Clancy out of her car than Abby was leaning heavily against her, murmuring, "I know I did the right thing, but my heart's about to break."

"It'll be all right," Clancy whispered into her ear. "Let's go sit down, and you can tell me all about it."

They did, sitting outdoors, Abby nestled against Clancy's side.

Abby told her tale, and Clancy said, "I'm sorry that's how it turned out. I kept hoping she'd rally and try to work this out."

"I did too," Abby said softly. "That's what I'm most upset about, to be honest. I'm very disappointed in her. She's…she's not the girl I thought she was." She looked up at her partner and said, "I've tried my damnedest to make sure she didn't turn out like so many girls of our social class do—those self-absorbed little monsters who don't care about anything but how they look and what they can buy."

"She's not like that," Clancy soothed. "Really, Abby, she's not. When we were working together, she was very down to earth. I'm around a lot of those kids, and I didn't get those rich-bitch vibes from her at all."

"I hope that's true," Abby sighed. She cocked her head and asked, "What do you think of her?"

"Ahh…I'd rather not say. I don't know her well enough to have a valid opinion."

"Come on," Abby said. "Don't be a chicken."

"I don't wanna insult her," Clancy said. "Especially since you say she hasn't acted like herself all summer."

"Okay. How was she just this summer? Give me an opinion of her based on your very limited experience."

Clancy rolled her eyes, knowing she wasn't going to get out of this one. "She doesn't act like a rich brat," she said again. "She acts like an average brat. Like she's used to being the center of attention. Like she always gets her way."

Abby nodded, not looking surprised by Clancy's opinion. "I swear she's changed so much since she went to school."

"I think that's true of most kids," Clancy assured her. "Give her a little time. I'm sure she'll snap out of it."

"Maybe," Abby said, obviously not so easily convinced.

They sat together in silence, the neighborhood beginning to quiet down. Traffic sounds decreased a little and children went indoors for dinner. The afternoon birds began to chatter, and a few hummingbirds hovered about, drinking their fill before the flowers began to close for the night.

The sun was bright, and the angle made both women squint. In a few seconds, they were both warm. "I'm gonna go get a drink," Clancy said. "Want anything?"

"Sure. I don't know what we have, but you know what I like. Surprise me."

Clancy kissed her, lingering just a moment before she got up. "I won't give you a mouthful of vodka like you did the last time I asked you to surprise me."

"Like that night turned out badly," Abby said, blinking her eyes slowly and sexily.

Looking thoughtful, Clancy said, "Good point. A little vodka never hurt anything."

After relaxing with a drink, they went into the house and made a simple dinner, both of them quietly reflective. After cleaning up, they went back outside to enjoy the quiet, warm evening. Abby settled back against Clancy and said, "I just can't relax, thinking about Hayley wandering around San Francisco with some man I've never met."

"What's the problem?" Clancy asked. "Are you worried about her having sex?"

"No, not really," Abby said. "I trust her to be careful. I mean…I don't think she's mature enough to be in a lasting relationship, but who is at first?"

Clancy gave her partner a light kiss on the cheek. "Good point. It's hard to know what you need from a relationship until you've been in a few sucky ones."

"Yeah. I know she's in for a lot of ups and downs before she'll settle down. I don't take most of that too seriously. What's really bothering me is the way that things are changing between us."

"Changing...how?"

"Our whole dynamic is getting out of whack. Even though she still acts like a kid most of the time, I felt a shift this afternoon. She's made it clear that she doesn't approve of something I'm doing—and that's never happened before. I felt our roles switch a little, and I hated it!"

"Ooh...that makes sense. That would be weird."

"Yeah, it was weird. I liked it better when she was the kid and I was the mom, and I could tell her what to do. I'm not sure I like her being an adult."

"Hard to stop her, though, isn't it?"

"Yeah." Abby laughed and snuggled up against Clancy's sturdy body. "It's funny," she said. "I like Trevor being an adult, but I don't feel like that with Hayley."

"Things will shift and shift again," Clancy said. "She still needs a lot of mothering."

"Oh, I know she does. I just worry that she won't let me give it to her." She made an unhappy little grunt and put her head on Clancy's shoulder, sitting quietly as they watched dusk settle onto the yard, the sound of the waterfall tranquilizing both of them.

❧

When it was dark, they went into the house and then decided to swim for a while. Trevor had said he'd be going to visit one of his friends on the west side after he took Hayley to the airport, so Abby wanted to make good use of their alone time.

They swam and played with the dogs for a long time, tossing the girls' favorite toy back and forth to wear them out. When the dogs were sufficiently winded, Clancy held onto the toy and swam over to her lover. She grasped her foot and kicked, dragging Abby with her while she moved toward the waterfall. "Where are we going?" Abby asked, trying to keep her head above water.

As soon as they were under the strong stream, Clancy pulled Abby into her arms. The sound of the water was so loud that it was hard to hear, but Abby stared at her lover, watching her lips. Clancy said, "I imagine we're on our own little island. Just us and this fantastic cool stream pouring over our heads. We're safe here, baby. No one can harm us."

"I always feel safe in your arms," Abby said, watching Clancy's smile bloom.

"Wanna sleep with me tonight?"

"I wanna sleep with you every night." She held on tight and started to kick, moving them away from the powerful water. "But I want to be here when Trevor gets home. I think he's a little upset about Hayley's leaving, too."

"Uhm...I guess I can't stay here, huh?"

"I don't think so. Not until I talk to Trev about it. I wouldn't like it if he started bringing a woman home without having asked if I minded."

Clancy let go and then spent a minute floating on her back. "Okay. Give me a few dozen kisses, and I'll be on my way."

Abby looked at the dogs and said, "Tell us if Trevor comes home, okay, girls? I'm gonna kiss Clancy until we're both deaf and blind."

❧

They were walking to the door when the phone rang, and Abby dashed inside to answer. To give her partner some privacy, Clancy stayed outside and threw a ball for the dogs. Neither dog was particularly obsessed with fetch on dry land, but they were competent at the game and willingly participated, because it seemed important to Clancy.

Abby appearing a few minutes later, wearing a big smile. "Hayley made it to Alexander's apartment, and she wanted me to know that he put her suitcase in the bedroom and told her he'd sleep on the sofa." She sat back down and let her head drop against the back of the chair. "I feel so much better."

"Because she might not have sex?"

"No, that's her business. I'm just glad she called. She wanted me to know she was all right and was taking care of herself."

"I'm glad she called, too," Clancy said. "That was pretty thoughtful of her—given that she's angry."

"Yes, it was," Abby said quietly. Glancing up at Clancy, she said, "That's why it's hard to stay mad at the little scamp! She's not consistently obnoxious!"

"I wouldn't go wishing for that," Clancy said. "She might go for that one just to spite you."

Chapter Twenty-Five

A bby was pleased to have Trevor come bounding down the stairs early the next morning, quietly singing a tune to himself. "Hi, Mom," he said, giving her a kiss. "Can I make you breakfast?"

Abby put her arms around him and hugged him close, the calming familiarity of his being home making her giddy with pleasure. "Let me cook for you. I've already eaten."

"You can if you want, but I'm able to take care of myself."

"That's clear, Trev, but I like to pamper you a little bit. I don't get to do it very often. How about some pancakes?"

His smile grew wider. "I haven't had pancakes in months! Let's do it!" He leaned against the counter, clad in a pair of jeans and a white T-shirt.

She patted him on the side, amazed as always that the little boy she could once effortlessly pick up was now so strong and solid. "Some young woman is going to be very, very lucky when she meets you."

He smiled his indulgent smile, the one he always gave his mother when she complimented him. "I'm still waiting."

Abby started to mix the batter for the pancakes, thinking that one of Trevor's most delightful qualities was that he never seemed to realize what a great catch he was. When he asked a girl out, he always acted like he was genuinely surprised that she would accept, even though Abby couldn't think of a girl who had ever turned him down.

He was a handsome young man and exuded a gentleness and sweetness that were obvious in even a casual interaction. He was very mature for his age and always had been. He'd really come through for Abby and Hayley after his father died, shouldering many responsibilities that most men his age would have run from. Abby often thought of how calm and businesslike he'd been when he went with her to make arrangements for his father's funeral. She couldn't have gotten through the day without him, and she knew from that day forward that her son had become a man.

Busying herself with mixing the proper proportions, she asked, "So how are you feeling, now that you've been home for a few days?"

"I feel fine," he said. "I'm a little worried about finding a job, but I know I just have to keep working at it."

Smiling, she clarified, "I meant about me…and Clancy."

"Oh!" He didn't respond for a few moments, and she was afraid to look at him, finding this level of intimate talk very discomfiting. "I guess I feel fine about it." He cleared his throat, and she could hear him shifting his weight. "I meant what I said, Mom. I want you to be happy. If Clancy's the person who makes you happy, that's all that matters."

Abby gathered the courage to face him, relieved to see his neutral smile. "But you have to have some feelings of your own, honey. This can't be what you expected to find when you left for Europe."

He put his arms around her and squeezed her tightly. His voice trembled when he said, "I expected to find you sitting on the porch, that sad look in your eyes that I'd do anything to help take away. I'm so happy that look isn't there anymore. I swear that's all that I want, Mom; I just want you to want to live again."

She held onto him while she cried, her tears sliding down her cheeks. "I love you, Trevor," she whispered. "Your father would be so proud of you."

"And he'd be happy for you. You know he would have been."

She nodded, pulling away to wipe her face. "I know, honey. That's never been an issue."

"But Hayley is," he said. "I wish we could have had more time together before she left. I really think I could have helped bring her around."

"It's hard," Abby said, trying to keep some of her sadness from showing. "I expected her to have a tough time, but this…" She reached over to take a tissue from a box and wiped her eyes. "I just hope she snaps out of it. It's breaking my heart to see her struggle like this."

He reached out and squeezed her shoulder. "That's just like you."

"What?"

"To be worried about how this is for her. If I were you, I'd be so pissed off, I wouldn't be able to see straight."

She smiled and gave him a tiny shake of her head. "I'm not angry," she said. "I know she's not a bad kid, and she wouldn't behave like she has if this weren't really driving her crazy." She stirred the batter, adding, "Of course, I wish she were more connected to her feelings. This would be a hell of a lot easier."

"You're gonna have to do most of the work there, Mom. She's hopeless."

"Oh, she's not so bad." Abby poured some of the batter onto a hot pan, listening to it sizzle for a moment. "How about you?" she asked. "Are you willing to share some of your feelings?"

He looked confused. "I already did."

"Not the big picture," she said. "I want to know how you feel about something specific."

"Sure. What is it?"

Without turning to look at him, she asked, "How would you feel if Clancy stayed overnight once in a while?" She sneaked a look at him, catching him frantically trying to compose his expression.

"Uhm…whatever, Mom. That's…fine."

He was trying so hard to look indifferent that she would have laughed if the topic weren't so serious. She didn't say anything for a moment, taking the time to flip his first pancake. When she was sure the temperature was right, she turned around and cupped his chin in her hand, studying him carefully. "You're a bad, bad liar, Trev. I don't think anyone would be ambivalent about that question. You should have at least acted like you'd thought about it before you tried to sell that one."

He put his hands in his pockets, pushing them out when he locked his elbows. "Aw, Mom, don't give me a hard time. I really want you to be happy. Can't we leave it at that?"

"No, baby, we can't." She slipped his pancake onto a plate and handed it to him. "Go sit down, and I'll bring you some syrup." He did as she asked and was studiously applying some butter when she sat down next to him. "We have to be honest—completely honest. That's the only way this will work."

"I am being honest," he said. "I honestly want you to do what makes you happy."

"I won't be happy if I think you're uncomfortable. Now tell me the truth. Is it a little soon for Clancy to be staying over?"

He ate a bite, smiling at her with approval. "Maybe a little," he said. "I'd like to spend more time with her, you know? Get to know her a little before she…moves in or whatever."

"Clancy and I need to spend time together, but we don't need to live together right now. I was just trying to get a feeling for how comfortable you are with the whole thing."

He took another bite, taking his time chewing while he thought about his answer. "I think I'm doing pretty well. I have to be around you two for a while to get used to this, but I don't lie awake at night worrying about it." He smiled, and his soft laugh made his mother smile in anticipation. "Good thing I'm used to you and Dad chasing each other around the house. At least I'm okay with your being affectionate."

She smiled fondly at her son. "We were affectionate."

He looked down at his empty plate, trying not to laugh. "You were more than that, Mom. You guys woke me up more times than I could count."

"We did not!" she shrieked, crimson with embarrassment.

"You did, too," he said, laughing at her discomfort. "Since you'd told me about making babies, I kept wondering why I didn't have more brothers and sisters; you didn't tell me about birth control."

"Did Hayley hear us, too?" she asked, looking ill.

"Not until she was older," he said. "When she was eleven or twelve, I caught her and Gretchen lurking outside your room one Sunday morning. They ran like rats when they saw me, giggling their asses off."

Abby's head dropped to the table. "Dear God," she moaned. "We always tried to be quiet."

He stared at her, eyebrows raised. "If you were trying to be quiet, you totally sucked!"

A couple of nights later, Clancy had the evening free, so Abby invited her over for dinner. Not seeing her lover every day was making Abby mad for her, and she showed Clancy just how much she'd missed her by voraciously devouring her lips. Clancy was pressed up against the counter, her feet spread shoulder width apart. Abby stood between her legs, kissing her ceaselessly. Her head was tilted, her tongue probing delicately along Clancy's palate, making her giggle. Clancy's hands were low on Abby's back, lightly squeezing her firm ass.

The soft click of nails on the tile floor didn't register with either woman, but the mumbled "Oh, shit" did. They broke apart, Abby's hand covering her mouth as she gasped, seeing Trevor standing in the doorway, both dogs sitting in front of him. The young man looked like he wished the floor would open up and swallow him, but the dogs seemed very happy to have a new playmate.

"Trevor, I'm sorry—" Abby started to say, but she stopped herself when she saw Clancy staring at her. Her gaze shifting between her lover and her son, she shut her mouth, waiting for someone else to speak.

Trying to act like nothing out of the ordinary had happened, Trevor walked into the kitchen and extended his hand. Clancy shook it, glad that the young man was doing his best to shrug off the embarrassing moment. "Hi," he said. "Haven't seen you since I got back."

"Good to see you, too, Trevor," she said. She decided to state the obvious, saying, "I'm sorry we were…you know. Kind of embarrassing…"

"No big deal," he said, smiling at his ashen mother. "Really. Don't worry about it. Hell, Mom's caught me doing worse."

"I have?" Abby asked weakly.

"Well, maybe not. But some of my girlfriends' mothers have."

"I'm sorry," Abby said again. She looked at Clancy quickly. "I know that we're not doing anything wrong, but it feels very odd to have you see us."

"I'm really sorry, Mom. I'll try not to sneak up on you."

"Don't be silly! This is your home, too. You shouldn't have to worry about wandering into the kitchen and finding us…"

He gave them both a stiff smile. "I just wanted a Coke." He walked over to the refrigerator and took out a soda, holding it up as evidence. Then he gave them a short wave and left the room, going back upstairs.

Abby blew out a breath that lasted as long as it took the young man to climb the stairs. "My whole life passed before my eyes," she moaned.

"He seemed fine," Clancy said. "It's over. We'll just make sure it doesn't happen again."

"Ever?" Abby asked, eyes wide. "We'll never be able to kiss when the kids are around?"

"Well…no, we have to be normal. But it won't be a big deal after a while. He'll get used to our being together."

Abby leaned on her partner heavily, not saying a word.

Clancy was in the middle of dicing some red pepper when Abby sat down next to her. "Are we doing the right thing?" she asked, pain and confusion filling her eyes.

"Pardon me?" Clancy blinked. "I don't know what you're talking about."

"Have we thought this through well enough? There are so many repercussions to our being together, and sometimes I feel like we're just stumbling blithely along, without any concern for the consequences."

Clancy placed her hands on Abby's shoulders, but Abby shook her head and stood, trying to distance herself from the embrace. With a flash of hurt crossing her features, Clancy said, "I know you're upset about Trevor, but it's not a big deal."

"It's not just him." Abby's arms were folded tightly across her stomach, and she looked like she was on the verge of panic. "There are so many things! We haven't even discussed where we think we're going. Is this permanent? Do you want us to live together?" Her eyes were wide as she said, "And I haven't even been able to work myself up to addressing the biggest issue!"

"What's that?" Clancy was so stunned by her lover's mood swing that she wasn't able to move a muscle.

"I know you want to have children," Abby said, her whole body shaking. "And I love you enough to do anything for you, but I don't think I can go through that again!"

Clancy climbed off her stool and approached her lover gingerly. "Where did this come from? Why are you so upset?" Reaching out with one hand, she placed it gently upon Abby's cheek, slightly heartened when she didn't flinch from the touch. "I want this to be permanent. I want to live with you…not now, but soon. As soon as Trevor's comfortable with it." Stroking trembling lips with her thumb, Clancy soothed, "Don't you want this to be permanent? Don't you love me enough to work things through?"

"That's the problem," Abby said, her voice choked with emotion. "I love you enough to let you go if I'm going to hold you back." She fell into Clancy's arms and let herself cry for a few minutes while the blonde tried to comfort her. "You're so much younger; you have your whole life ahead of you. You could find someone your own age who'd be able to raise a family with you…"

Clancy grasped her by the shoulders and held her at arm's length. "What's with this having-babies stuff? When have I ever said I wanted to have a baby?"

"At the party," she sobbed. "And your mom—"

"Oh, please!" Pulling her close, Clancy gave her a hearty squeeze and said, "I can see that I'm gonna have to debrief you when you spend time with my mom."

"You don't…?"

"No, I don't. I love babies, and I love to be around babies. But I pretty much decided a few years ago that I don't want to have a child. I don't want to give up what I'd have to give up to have one. My mom, however, desperately wants grandchildren, and she thinks that she can coerce me—or my lover—into giving her one."

"But you seemed so happy when you were holding little Jacob."

"I was. I truly love babies." She looked at Abby and asked, "Know what else I love?"

Abby's head shook, and she looked at Clancy curiously.

"Those cute little chimpanzees they have at the zoo. I've often spent the better part of an afternoon there—just looking at those little guys." She smoothed the lines on Abby's forehead and added, "If they were giving them out on the street corner, I wouldn't take one—but I love them. I feel the same about babies. I love them—I love to be around them—and at the end of the day, I want to go home without one." She placed a warm kiss on Abby's lips. "At the end of the day, I want to go home with you—just you."

"But—"

"But nothing," Clancy said, sounding confident and sure of herself. "Every couple has problems. Every couple has to make adjustments. We'll have to do that, too. But we can do it if we love each other enough."

"I do love you," Abby said. "I do! But you're so young…"

"So what? Why does it matter?"

"Our families…our friends…our interests…"

"Abby, we've been together for a while now, and I haven't seen our interests clash. And our families will be fine. What are you talking about?"

"You don't even know about LBJ!" Abby said, sounding a little frantic.

"LBJ?" Clancy stared at her, totally flummoxed.

"See?"

"No, I don't see," Clancy said. "You're nearly hysterical, baby. Now calm down, and let's talk about this rationally."

"I don't know if I can," Abby said, still shaking.

Trevor came back down the stairs, his feet hitting the treads so loudly that it sounded like he was trying to break them. When he got to the kitchen, he took one look at his mother and averted his eyes, quickly saying, "I'm gonna hang out at Sam's, okay?"

"No dinner?"

He still didn't look up. "We thought we'd go to In-N-Out," he said. "I haven't been since Easter."

"All right," Abby said, trying her best to sound like herself. "Have fun."

"Bye, Trevor," Clancy said.

"See ya," he said, exiting the room as quickly as he could.

As soon as he'd left, Abby leaned against her partner and started to cry, letting Clancy's comforting embrace keep her grounded.

꩜

They had dinner, neither speaking much while they ate. "Wanna watch TV?" Abby asked after they'd loaded the dishwasher.

"If you do."

"What do you like to watch?"

"Mmm…nothing in particular. If I want to veg, I watch HGTV. I like to see home remodeling."

"Nothing you watch regularly?"

"Nuh-uh. You?"

"No," Abby said. "I just thought that you might. I mean, the kids have a dozen shows they watch."

"I'm not a kid," Clancy said, smiling.

"No, but…there are so many things I don't know about you. I mean, how can we be as intimate as we are and not even know if we like the same TV shows?"

"Yeah," Clancy said, trying to sound upbeat. "That alone should doom us."

Giving her a pleading look, Abby said, "Don't tease. This worries me."

"Why?" Clancy asked. "We're getting to know each other. That's good. That'll keep us busy when we're not fucking each other stupid." She gave Abby an adorably goofy grin, and Abby was unable to stop herself from laughing at her.

"I've learned that I love you," Abby said, tugging her into a hug.

"I love you, too." They kissed a few times, but Clancy could tell that Abby wasn't fully relaxed. "Wanna talk some more?"

Abby looked sad and exhausted. She leaned against her partner and said, "Sometimes this seems so hard."

"It is hard," Clancy said. "But what do you do that's really worthwhile that isn't hard?"

Abby nodded slowly, but she didn't look convinced.

Clancy propped her partner up and slid to the floor. She knelt between Abby's legs, looking into her eyes. "Look, baby, we don't have a lot of choices at this point. We either break up or work through things. There is no middle ground."

The dull blue eyes brightened in fear. "I don't want to break up! I couldn't bear to lose you!"

"Then quit whining," Clancy said. Abby's eyes opened wider at the admonition. "That's right—you're whining. It's not productive. Hell, it's not attractive, either," she said, laughing. "I'm sorry, honey, but whining wasn't allowed at my house. I don't have a lot of tolerance for it."

"I hate it, too," Abby admitted sheepishly. "It drives me crazy when Hayley does it."

"Then stop." She grasped Abby by the shoulders and shook her gently. "Make a commitment to me and stick with it. No matter what happens, no matter who gives us a hard time—don't second-guess us. Don't ever do it again!"

Abby took a few deep breaths; she concentrated on Clancy's hands, finally calming down to the extent that she felt as though they were an extension of her own body. "I won't," she said, her voice strong and calm. "I won't."

❦

Trevor had to go to San Francisco on Friday to interview for a job, and he decided to go over to Santa Cruz to see Hayley for the weekend. Because he wouldn't be at the house, Clancy reverted to her favorite Saturday pastime of floating in the pool. While she was snoozing, Abby got out of the pool and called her mother to make arrangements to pick her parents up from the airport the next day.

When she went back outside, Clancy woke from her light slumber. "Where ya been?"

"Talking to my mom."

"Cool." The blonde closed her eyes again, settling her weight on the float.

"Wanna know what we were talking about?"

"Only if you wanna tell me," Clancy said, looking very nonchalant. "I don't wanna butt in."

"You know what?"

Always enjoying the playfulness and evident thought that Abby's expression conveyed, Clancy paddled over and gazed up at her. "What?"

"I really admire you."

"You do?" Clancy grinned, looking very pleased by the compliment. "What brought that on?"

"I was thinking about the fight we had when you were angry that I didn't tell you everything about my college flirtations."

"Not one of my finer moments," Clancy said. "That shouldn't make you admire me."

"But it does. You want to know what's going on in my head, but you've tried so hard to give me space. Like today," she said. "Most people would be on pins and needles about my family and their opinions, but I can tell you're really not worried about what I was talking to my mom about."

"I'm not. It's your family and your relationship; you'll handle it. If something upsets you, or if you have strong feelings about it, I know you'll try to talk to me about it. You promised, so I know you will. Other than that, I should just keep my nose out of it. I learned my lesson with the college thing. I can only be concerned with the things that happen between us. The rest of your life is your business."

"That's another thing I like," Abby said. "You're darned confident, Clancy O'Connor. You're not always worried that this isn't going to work out. Actually," she amended, "you're cocky."

"Why shouldn't I be?" she asked, flashing a convincingly cocky smile. "If I keep you happy and satisfied, you won't have any reason to leave. And if you do…you're obviously not a very bright woman. If that's true, why would I want *you*?"

"I just love self-confidence," Abby said. "It's *so* sexy."

"Gotta be honest," Clancy said. "I've had some very shaky days. In the beginning, I was sure you were gonna freak and not be able to hang in there." Abby nodded, having been worried about the same thing. "But once we got past the first couple of weeks, and you started telling people, I figured you probably wouldn't get cold feet." She grasped Abby's legs, which were dangling in the water, and kissed both of her knees. "That doesn't mean that I've been happy with the pace you've set, but I didn't think you'd break up with me. Once I was confident of that, I knew the only thing that would hold on to you, or make you leave, was me. And I'm very confident of me."

"You have every reason to be," Abby agreed, gazing at her lover with a look filled with admiration.

Clancy tugged at Abby's legs until they were wrapped around her waist and then kicked away from the side, nearly submerging herself. She had to work hard to stay above water, but her strong legs kept them afloat. "I'm having such a nice day," she said.

"Me, too," Abby said. "The only thing I'd add is a little loving. Up for it?" she asked, taking a nibble of Clancy's wet earlobe.

"Always," the blonde said, grinning sexily. "But only if we go to my house. I don't think I could relax here."

Abby started to protest that Trevor wouldn't return unexpectedly, but she knew that worrying about the smallest thing could ruin the mood. "Okay. Let's have dinner here and then go to your house for dessert."

"My favorite treat," Clancy said. "And it's never too filling."

Abby leaned back, floating while still encircling Clancy's waist. "Would you like to come out as a couple? In public, I mean."

"Uhm…sure, I guess. I mean, I'm out to everyone in the world, so it's not an issue for me. I'm a little surprised you're ready to do that, though."

"Why?" Abby started to slap at the water with her open hands. "Everyone I care about knows. Whether or not they're happy about it, they know."

"Good point," Clancy said. She removed Abby's legs from her waist and then moved around to tuck her hands under her lover's arms. "So tell me about our coming out. Is it some kinda party?"

"Yeah, it is." She settled against Clancy's body, letting the shorter woman carry her around the pool. "I love this," Abby said.

"What?"

"Playing like this. I never played in the pool before I met you."

"Really?" Clancy leaned forward so she could see Abby's eyes. "Why not?"

"Oh, I don't know. I guess Will and I tended to act like adults." She laughed a little; then she kissed Clancy on the neck and throat. "It's different when you have kids. You tend to forget your childlike traits. You're helping me rediscover them."

"Probably helps that Trevor and Hayley aren't sitting here watching us, too."

"That always helps me feel more uninhibited."

Clancy twirled in a circle while Abby leaned back and dropped the top of her head into the water, liking the sensation of the aquatic scalp massage.

"Are you gonna tell me about this party?" Clancy asked when Abby sat up and rested in her arms again.

"Oh! You make me forget my own name when you play with me like this." She recalled where she'd left off and asked, "Do you know about my involvement with the local battered women's shelter?"

"No, you've never told me about that. How'd you get involved?"

"Through my church. We're active in a lot of outreach programs, and that one appealed to me."

"I could get into helping a group like that," Clancy said. "My dad's brother and his wife are batterers, and it's really messed their kids up."

Abby gave her a puzzled look. "They batter their children?"

"No, no, not that I know of. They knock the stuffing out of each other."

Abby couldn't stop her eyes from widening, Clancy catching her look when she strained to see her face. "They fight each other?"

"Yeah. My Aunt Peggy has a killer right hook. She's broken my uncle's jaw and fractured his eye socket. But he's sent her to the hospital a time or two also."

"Wow," Abby said, not knowing how to respond.

With a grin, Clancy said, "People in your family don't beat each other up, do they?"

"Well," Abby said, trying to be diplomatic, "I don't have a very big family."

Clancy half-closed her eyes and nodded. "So tell me about this event."

"Okay. They have a big dinner dance—a fund-raiser, really—in late September. I'd like to take you if you're willing to get dressed up."

"How dressed?"

"It runs the gamut. Some of the older women will wear evening gowns; some of the men wear tuxedos, but there will be a smattering of men in sport coats and khakis."

"I could handle the sport coat," Clancy said, chuckling. She kissed the top of her partner's head. "I'd love to be your date—if you're ready to make a statement. We'll have to go shopping, but I'll make the supreme sacrifice for you and enter a store that doesn't sell fertilizer."

"Excellent! I know I'll be scared, but I'm ready." She smiled broadly and said, "When I'm with you…and my parents…I can face anything."

Clancy dropped her, laughing when Abby sputtered as her head broke the plane of the water. "Your parents? When did this come up?"

"That's one of the things I was talking to my mom about," Abby said. "That and the fact that they're coming home tomorrow."

Clancy stood next to her and grabbed her around the waist, tossing her around like a doll. "I changed my mind! I wanna know every word of every conversation you have!"

Abby grabbed her and held her close. "It'll be okay, honey. You'll like my parents. I thought you could go with me when I pick them up."

Clancy looked a little wide-eyed and said, "I don't even know what they do, or did, for a living. I don't know shit! I'm gonna look like a fool!"

"No, you won't," Abby said, reaching out to pat her. "I'll give you a little background."

"More than a little! Give me a lot."

Abby nodded and said, "Well, my father is an electrical engineer. He was a professor at Cal Tech when I was a child, but he and another friend started a business in…oh, 1962 or '63. They started out making specialized tubes for computers—back when a computer could fill a garage. They changed their product line little by little, finally coming up with a design to let computers share certain functions by moving information between multiple computers. In essence, they designed the precursor to the router," she said with a small smile.

"I don't know a lot about computers, but I know that's a big deal," Clancy said. "Does he still have the company?"

"No. They sold out about 1980. Luckily, he struck a wonderful deal with a much larger company that not only paid him quite a bit of money, but also gave him a small royalty for every router the company sold for a number of years. That was right before the big technology boom, and he did…quite well," Abby said, again giving Clancy an enigmatic smile.

"They're loaded, right?" Clancy asked, a similar smile on her face.

"Oh, yeah. Very much so."

"And you're their only heir, so that makes you…"

"Bad assumption," Abby said. "They believe that inherited wealth is a very bad thing. All of their estate will go to their favorite charities."

"Are you serious? They're not leaving their money to their only child?"

"Nope, and I agree with them completely. They're very generous with me, but their money isn't mine. I didn't earn it; they did."

"Isn't that weird?" Clancy asked, unable to get her mind around this one.

"No, not at all. I do just fine. Will left me well fixed, and I still receive his share of the profits from his law partnership. I have plenty of money to maintain my lifestyle without ever having to work. That's all that I need."

"Wow," Clancy said. "That's gonna take me a while to get used to." She thought about all of the information for a bit and then asked, "Are we talking a whole lot of money?"

Abby nodded. "A whole lot. Go-to-Paris-for-lunch kinda money."

"Wow. I've never known anyone that rich."

"You still don't," Abby teased. "You won't meet my parents until tomorrow."

"I'm being serious," Clancy said, seeing the teasing smile on her partner's face. "Hasn't it ever bothered you that you won't get their money?" She paused for a second and then added, "*You* don't have that kinda money, do you?"

"No, no, not at all. I have to spend almost all of my income, but I only touch my principal for things like home improvement. Like to have the landscaping done. I had to dip into my stash for that."

"But you have a pretty big stash, right?"

"Mmm…it's big for a woman who's never had a job, but I'm not in the position to donate a building to UCLA or anything like that." She cocked her head and asked, "Why? You've never been interested in my money before."

Clancy laughed. "I never knew how rich you are! I mean, how rich your parents are. It's kinda … weird."

"What's weird about it?"

"Uhm … I guess I thought you were upper middle-class. I'm gonna have to adjust my view."

Abby scowled. "Don't be silly. I'm no different than I was before you knew my parents were wealthy."

"I've got some ... issues with money. I already feel like I'm a dozen rungs below you on the social status ladder. Now I find out that you're up in the clouds on the money ladder too."

Abby looked at her carefully, waiting a few moments to speak. "Those things don't matter to me. If they matter to you ... we'd better work on it. I don't want you to feel beneath me ... in any way."

Clancy shook her head. "I don't usually. It just hits me once in a while and I let it get under my skin a little bit. Just one more item on the adjustment pile."

"The pile isn't too high, is it?" Abby asked, gazing at Clancy tentatively.

"Nah. I'm nothing if not persistent. We'll get to everything." Clancy continued to carry Abby around the pool, carefully dunking her periodically to cool her off. It was clear that she still had something on her mind, and she finally asked, "What do the kids think? Are they pissed they're not gonna inherit your money?"

"They might be, but they'd better get used to it. I'm leaving my money to you."

"To *me?*" Clancy almost dropped Abby, struggling to get her feet under her again. Abby disentangled her legs and floated a short distance away. "Are you crazy?"

"No," Abby calmly said, now floating on her back. "Will and I always told them they weren't getting money from us. After he died I rewrote my will to leave my money to various charities. But if we're going to be partners and live here together ... I'll leave the house and most of my money to you."

"Oh, great—another reason to hate me! And I wouldn't blame 'em! If some guy married my mom and she left him the house and everything in it ... I'd freak."

Clancy looked terribly aggrieved, and Abby stood and tried to soothe her. "I won't tell them right away." She put her arms around Clancy and kissed her. "But if it comes up, I'll tell the truth."

"Can we let this settle for a while? I'm not ready for this."

Her expression darkening, Abby asked, "What? The commitment or the inheritance?"

"The inheritance, of course! That's a huge decision, Abby, and I think you ought to think about it for a while. It was a different thing when you and Will were gonna leave everything to each other. There's no way they'll understand this."

"Fine." Abby pulled Clancy to her and held her until some of the tension went out of her body. "We'll talk about it some more. But if we live together and share our lives, I'm not going to have you thrown out of the house if I die."

"Later," Clancy said, closing her eyes momentarily. "We'll argue about this later."

Abby trailed her hand down Clancy's cheek, seeing how tense she was. "We'll talk about it later. I can see how upset this makes you."

"It's damned trippy! I just can't understand why you wouldn't leave your money to your kids."

"Why? You've always been self-supporting. Your parents didn't even pay for your college tuition."

"No, but they felt like shit about it. They really wanted to pay for me."

"Ahh…maybe that's the difference. Well, I've paid for their tuition and their room and board, and given them a generous allowance. I've told them I'll support them as long as they're in school. That includes postgraduate work. But once they're finished with school, they have to work. I might give them money to make a down payment on a house, but only if they've shown that they're mature enough to handle the mortgage."

"Damn, you're tough! I thought you'd be very…" She trailed off, not wanting to say what was really on her mind.

"Very what?"

"Uhm…different."

Seeing the evasive look on her face, Abby pinched her on the butt, laughing when Clancy squealed. "You thought I'd give them everything I had, even if I had to move into a transient hotel, didn't you?"

"Well, maybe not that bad. But I did think you'd baby them."

Abby kissed her again and said, "I baby them emotionally, but I'm trying to stop that."

"Is that how your parents were?"

"Not really. My parents are great, but they treated me like an adult from the time I was in high school. Luckily for them, I usually acted like one."

"Did your mom work with your dad?"

"No. She was a student of his at Cal Tech, and she went on to get her Ph.D. in computer science. She's been a professor at Cal Tech since I was about three. She should retire, but she loves it too much to even think of it."

"A student of your father's, huh?" Clancy asked. "Does that mean there's an—"

"Age difference? Yes, indeed. Ten years."

"Phew," Clancy said, wiping her brow. "That's one thing they won't be able to complain about. You're with a poor, relatively uneducated, blue-collar woman, but they can't bitch about the age difference!"

"You're not uneducated," Abby said and then stopped to listen to herself. "That's not what I meant!"

"I know what you meant," Clancy said. "And I'm only relatively uneducated. You've got a master's, and your mother has a Ph.D."

Abby wrinkled her nose. "My dad does, too."

"*Fuck* me," Clancy said, laughing good-naturedly. "I forgot you said he was a professor! Damn, this is a lot to take in. Why couldn't you just be rich? Rich *and* smart is overkill!" She lay on her back and kicked her way around a big circle. "I'm gonna have to practice being self-confident tonight 'cause I'm gonna need all of my goods tomorrow."

Chapter Twenty-Six

Abby spared a smile at Clancy on the way to the airport the next day. "You know, you didn't really have to wear long pants," she said.

"You've got on a dress, and I'm supposed to go in shorts?" Clancy asked. "Are you mad?"

"You're nervous, aren't you?" Abby asked sympathetically. "And come to think of it, where did you get those pants? Did you buy new clothes?"

"Yes," she said, grimacing. "I didn't want to wear those nice crepe ones I bought, and the only other long pants I have are jeans. I thought I could always use a nice pair of navy blue poplins."

Giving her another look, Abby asked, "That's a new blouse, too, isn't it?"

"Yes. I'm trying to at least look my age. Am I close?"

"You look wonderful. Really. My parents aren't into that dress-to-impress thing, anyway."

"You're wearing a dress," Clancy pointed out.

"Oh. Right." She grinned widely. "But it's a sundress. Practically a swimsuit cover-up."

"Uh-huh. I'd like to see the fool who wears a pink linen dress over a wet swimsuit." She took Abby's hand and gave it a kiss. "You look luscious, by the way. Very East Coast preppy. I like that about you."

"Well, Mom's a Mainer through and through. I guess I adopted the preppy look from her."

"I love the way you dress. Reminds me of the Kennedys, but sexy."

"Jackie or Rose?" Abby asked, winking at her.

"Who's Rose?" Clancy asked, looking blank for a moment before she chuckled evilly. "Gotcha!"

⁂

They waited at the baggage carousels for what seemed to Clancy like an eternity but was probably less than twenty minutes. She paced like a caged beast, with Abby watching her, a wry half-smile on her face.

"It'll be fine," she said for the fourth time.

"Easy for you to say—they have to like you!"

"Where's the confident Clancy O'Connor I find so sexy?"

"How can you talk about sex when your parents are going to be here at any minute?" Clancy whispered loudly.

"You're going to be pleasantly surprised. If they hated the ground you walked on, you'd never know. Trust me on this—if nothing else, they're amazingly polite."

"Well, that's something," Clancy allowed, making Abby smile at her grumpiness.

The plane was announced, and when the luggage started to careen down the chute, Clancy grabbed Abby and pressed a kiss to her mouth. "Just in case they ground you and won't let you go out with me again," she said dramatically.

Abby grasped her hand and tugged her over to the escalator that would admit the debarking passengers. She laced their fingers together and held on tight, despite Clancy's attempts to pull away. "Uhn-uh," she insisted, putting the linked hands to her lips and gently kissing Clancy's hand. "You're mine. I'm not letting you get away."

Clancy rolled her eyes but let herself be kept, finding herself reassured by the grasp of Abby's cool, dry hand.

Abby's eyes lit up with delight as a handsome older couple appeared at the top of the escalator. "Mom! Dad!" she called out to catch their attention.

Wide smiles graced both faces, and Clancy felt some of her unease dissipate when she saw nothing but warm affection from the pair. They approached, and each gave Abby a robust hug, allowing Clancy to spend a moment assessing them. Abby's mom was actually a little taller than her daughter and very impressive looking. She had very broad shoulders and a substantial chest, which narrowed to slim hips and remarkably long legs. Her hair was snow white, and her blue eyes were nearly identical to Abby's. Her jaw was even stronger, and her eyes were set deeper, giving her a very intent, focused look. There was no mistaking that this woman was Abby's mother, but there was also something very dissimilar about them.

Taking a long look at Abby's father, however, snapped the puzzle pieces into place. He was at least five inches shorter than his wife, and what little hair he had was cropped so short it looked like silver peach fuzz. His eyes were also blue but didn't have the vivid sparkle of his child's. The real similarity between him and his offspring was in their body styles. Abby looked like a slightly taller, distaff version of her father, with defined but not overly broad shoulders; a long, lean frame; and serviceable but not bulky musculature. He looked like an athlete—a swimmer, perhaps, like his daughter. Their skin tones were similar, too, with the man's skin bearing an even tan that made him appear healthy and vibrant.

"Mom, Dad," Abby said, "this is Clancy O'Connor...my..." She paused and gave Clancy an adorably puzzled look. "Girlfriend?" she finished tentatively.

"Not bad," Clancy said, returning the smile.

She extended her hand, and Abby's mother said, "Elizabeth Tudor. And this is my husband, Philip."

"It's good to meet you, Mr. and Mrs. Tudor," Clancy began, but Elizabeth waved off her attempt at formality.

"Elizabeth and Philip, please, Clancy."

"Will do," she said. "How was your flight?"

"The same as all of them," Elizabeth said. "Flying is the only time in my life that I hope to be bored."

"I'm glad you were bored," Abby said, giving her mother a warm hug. "I really missed you both this summer."

"You couldn't have been too lonely," Elizabeth said. "This is the only summer you haven't come to visit."

"Oh, I missed you. I just wanted you to come home sooner."

"Well, we're here now. You'll have to come for twice as long next summer. Have you ever been to Maine, Clancy?"

"No, I never have. I've always wanted to go, though."

"We're there from April to October. You and Abby are welcome at any time."

This is not going half bad, Clancy reassured herself as she smiled. *Not bad at all.*

❧

When they neared the car, Philip gave Abby a look and asked, "When did you get this, honey?"

"About an hour ago," she said, popping the locks on the Mercedes SUV. "It's Maria's. I got a new car, but it only seats two comfortably." At her father's raised eyebrow, she said, "Midlife crisis, Dad. A hot car and a younger woman."

"I haven't seen the car," he said, "but you did pretty well in the younger-woman department."

Clancy blushed under the weight of his teasing, making her all the more adorable.

"The car's not half as cute," Abby assured him, making even the tips of Clancy's ears color.

❧

When they arrived at their home, the Tudors let out twin sighs of relief. "I miss Pasadena when we're in Maine, and I miss Maine when we're in Pasadena," Elizabeth said. "My two favorite places on earth." A smiling, rotund black woman opened the front door, and both members of the older couple greeted her warmly. "Frances! Now I know I'm home!" Elizabeth cried as she wrapped her arms around the woman.

"As usual, Frances," Abby said dryly, "your greeting was more enthusiastic than mine."

"I cook better than you do," the woman said, giving Abby a hug.

"Clancy," Abby said, "this is Frances Adams, the only woman who can get away with slapping my butt."

Clancy knew that wasn't true, but she decided this wasn't the time to argue. "Hi," she said, extending her hand. "I'm Clancy O'Connor."

"Welcome," Frances said, giving her a friendly smile. She chuckled and said, "Listen to me! I sound like I live here!"

Deciding to inquire about the living arrangements at a later time, Clancy just returned her smile and walked into the entryway.

The house was a very large, Spanish-influenced, two-story stucco home, probably built in the 1920s, by Clancy's estimate. This section of Pasadena, close to the Cal Tech campus, was developed at around that time—when Pasadena was becoming the address for wealthy businessmen and attorneys who traveled into Los Angeles every day.

"Your home is fantastic," Clancy said, looking around at the large, airy, well-laid-out rooms. "Have you lived here long?"

"Not in the grand scheme of things," Philip said. "But probably a long time in your view. We moved here in 1978."

"Yeah, just when they got rid of me," Abby said. "They waited until I was engaged to get the cool house."

"Abby grew up in a perfectly decent house within walking distance of her school," Elizabeth informed Clancy. "Don't fall for that 'poor me' routine."

"That's true," Abby said, "but this place is a lot nicer than our old house."

"We had substantially more money when we bought this," Elizabeth said. "Those two things go hand in hand. Besides, you moved into a house that most people only dream about when you should have still been in college. Most girls aren't given a house like that, are they, Clancy?"

"I'm almost thirty and living in a small apartment in South Pas. My only real furniture is a futon. So I'd say Abby's experience isn't common."

"A futon?" Philip asked, cocking his head.

"Yes," Clancy said. "It's the world's most uncomfortable couch. Its best feature is that it folds out into the world's most uncomfortable bed. It gives you two pieces of furniture in one—but you don't want to use either one of 'em."

"It's not that bad," Abby said. "I was only in traction for a few days after I slept on it for the first time." Elizabeth raised an eyebrow in her daughter's direction, and Abby said, "Hey, I'm forty-five. My futon days are over."

"Your futon days never started," Clancy reminded her.

Impulsively, Elizabeth put her arm around Clancy's shoulders and gave her a squeeze. "I like you," she said, smiling warmly. "You don't let my girl get away with too much."

"She doesn't let me get away with anything," Abby corrected. "And that's just how I like it."

It turned out that Abby had inherited her rabid interest in gardening from her father, and after they all sat in the bright living room and enjoyed a glass of iced tea, he took Clancy on a tour.

The Tudor women remained in the light, airy living room, chatting about nothing in particular for a few minutes. After a while, Elizabeth looked at her daughter and said, "Are you sure she's telling the truth about her age? She looks like she's still in school!"

"Well, I haven't checked her license, but I think she's telling the truth," Abby said. "But she does look young, doesn't she?"

"Yes! She's going to love that in a few years, but she probably isn't very fond of it right now."

"Yeah, I think she'd like to look a little older than thirty. People probably think she's my daughter."

"You can't care what people think, honey. You have to live your life and do what you know is right." She cocked her head. "Is she right for you?"

"Yes," Abby said emphatically. "She's perfect for me. She's very childlike and playful, but in some ways she's more mature than I am. She hasn't had the pampered life I've had, Mom. She's had to work for everything she has, and that's made her strong and confident."

"She seems confident," Elizabeth agreed. "And she looks at you like she wants to put you in her pocket and carry you around."

Abby smiled. "She's protective of me, but she doesn't smother me. She really understands how to treat me. And I'm so crazy about her..." She shook her head. "It's actually embarrassing."

"I haven't seen that sparkle in your eyes in five years now. If that young woman is the one who put it back, I say good for you both."

Abby was sitting across the room, but she got up and joined her mother on the sofa. Grasping her hand, she stroked the soft, wrinkled skin and said, "She makes me incredibly happy, Mom. I thought...well, I thought that part of my life was over. I thought I'd have to live without what Will and I had. It's such a wonderful gift to feel that spark...that fire again."

Elizabeth wrapped Abby in her arms and whispered, "I'm happy for you, sweetheart. The last five years have been the hardest ones of my life." She pulled away and wiped at her eyes with the back of her hand. "It's horrible to see your child in so much pain, to see the joy you used to have for life just fade from your eyes." She shook her head roughly and said, "It's been horrid." Brushing the hair from Abby's forehead, she cocked her head and asked, "Has it been hard for you to...open yourself up again? I know how much you loved Will. Have you been able to love Clancy that way?"

Struggling with her own tears, Abby nodded. "I have." With a tender half-smile on her face, she said, "I don't know what it is about her, but we've been very open with each other from the start. It's so different. In a way, maybe that's why it's easier. It's nothing like it was with Will—this is a totally new experience."

"And you enjoy...what you do together?" Elizabeth asked, with only a tiny bit of hesitation in her voice.

"Yes," Abby said immediately. "Very much so. It's hard to describe, Mom. In a way, it's like it was with Will. I mean, I feel desired and loved and wanted with Clancy, and that's how I felt with Will. But the way we reach those feelings is totally different. I must be bisexual, because there's a whole new side of me that Clancy reaches. The part of me that Will touched is still his, and I really like the fact that it always will be. What I have with Clancy is hers alone. I wouldn't have explored this side of myself if Will hadn't died, but I'm glad that I'm exploring it now. And I'm very glad that Clancy's the one who's showing me how to express it. I love her, Mom, and I'm going to do my best to be with her the rest of my life."

"I hope that's true," Elizabeth sighed. "I hope you have a long, loving life together." She pulled away and placed gentle kisses upon each of her child's eyelids. "Forgive me for wishing this, but if this relationship is the right one for you, I hope that you die before she does. I never, ever want you to have to go through the pain of that loss again." She held her daughter tight, and soon both were crying softly, sharing once again the heartache that was still so raw, even after five long years.

They snuggled together for a few minutes, a rare but comforting occurrence. "How has my favorite grandson taken the news?" Elizabeth asked.

Abby blew out a breath. "He came through for me," she said. "Just like I'd hoped he would."

Elizabeth cocked her head. "Are you sure he isn't hiding his real feelings?"

Abby took the question at face value, knowing her mother didn't have a hidden agenda. "No, I can't be sure. You know how Trevor is," she admitted. "But he told me it was too soon to have Clancy move in or stay overnight, so I think I'm getting the truth out of him."

Elizabeth's eyes grew wide. "That must have been an interesting conversation."

Abby laughed. "I've had a lot of interesting conversations lately, and I think I'd rather have boring ones!"

"I guess I made a good choice in having just one child."

"Sometimes it would be nice to have only Trevor to deal with," Abby admitted, "but I love my girl with my whole heart. I just wish I understood her better."

"Trevor's like you," her mother said. "Hayley's like an emotional version of Will. And as much as you loved him, I know he still puzzled the heck out of you."

"True," Abby said, smiling in remembrance. "She's so much like him—plus the tears and the irrational behavior, of course."

"She's got a lot to cry about," Elizabeth said. "This has all been so hard for her."

"I know," Abby said, "but she'll get used to Clancy over time."

"Oh, honey," Elizabeth said. "Clancy's not the issue!"

"What is?"

"This whole year has been hard for her. You two had gotten to be so close—so much closer than you were when Will was alive. Leaving home was much harder than she's willing to admit."

"She adapted so well," Abby said.

"Yes, she did in some ways, but I think she thought things would go right back to how they'd been when she came home for the summer. But you weren't sitting on the porch just waiting for her—you were falling in love!"

With a woman she had a crush on, Abby thought, cringing.

"It's hard for a kid her age to get used to her mother dating again. No matter what she says, she's hurt and confused by it."

Abby nodded. "She kept telling me that I should go out and bed the first man I could get my hands on."

Elizabeth patted her daughter on the leg. "You and she have a strange intimacy. If you'd said something like that to me…" She trailed off, unable to even think of what her reaction would have been. "But no matter what she said, she didn't mean it. She wants stability, honey. She wants you and Trevor to stay just like you were when she left for school. She wants to grow up—but she doesn't want anyone else to grow. And you've changed immensely, Abby. I think your changes are all positive, but I can guarantee that Hayley doesn't."

Smirking, Abby said, "Maybe Hayley is Ellen's daughter. She hates change, too."

"I think the same dynamic is there," Elizabeth said. "Some of your loved ones don't want you to change—even if it's good for you. But you have to be tolerant, honey, even though it hurts."

"I'll hang in there as long as Hayley needs me to," Abby said, "but Ellen's an adult. She's gonna have to go to her own mother for advice on how to grow up!"

❧

Clancy was quickly at ease with Philip, and she was soon in her element, exclaiming over the seldom-seen plants with which he had dotted his yard. It became clear that Abby mirrored his style, with Clancy noting the judicious use of showy plants—shades of green and height variations being his main goal. She always felt that eye-popping plants should be highlighted, and she expressed her complete approval of Philip's choice of locations for some of the brightest ones.

"It's always amazed me how few people make use of our remarkable growing season and climate," he said thoughtfully. "Up in Maine, people slave over their land—working up until the snow is too high to wade through—just to have a show for four months or so."

"Are you from Maine, too?"

"Oh, no! I'm a third-generation Californian," he said proudly. "My grandfather moved here from Chicago, not long after they started settling the place. My grandmother suffered from asthma, and back then, everyone believed that the dry air would cure most anything." He smiled at Clancy and said, "This is one of the worst places in the country now for people with respiratory problems. Too much of a good thing, I guess." They walked along, Clancy making note of each item of interest. "What about you? Are you a local girl?"

"Pretty much," she said. "I grew up in Sierra Madre. My parents still live there. On my mom's side, her father came through California when he was in the war, and he vowed he'd move here. Went back to Michigan, married my grandmother, and took off. They settled in Sierra Madre, and he got a job at the quarry in Irwindale. Hard work," she said, shaking her head. "A few years ago, he died of a chronic respiratory disease. White lung. Too much dust."

"What about your father's people?" Philip asked, finding himself thoroughly charmed by the thoughtful young woman.

"The O'Connors have been in California for years and years. My grandfather moved down from San Francisco, also not long after the war. He was a police officer in the LAPD but was shot and sustained a permanent injury and had to retire. He and my grandmother moved up to Cucamonga, and he got a job as a security guard. They both died when I was small; I didn't know either of them well."

Philip looked at her sympathetically. "Was your grandfather shot in the line of duty?"

Her gray eyes danced merrily, and she lowered her voice, leaning in close. "This is a family secret, but I'll let you in on it. He and his partner were in a bar after work, and I'm guessing they were pretty well crocked. They got into a fight, which I'm told wasn't a rare occurrence," she said, "and his partner took out a stashed weapon and threatened my grandfather with it. They wound up out in the alley; they wrestled; and somehow, the gun went off and got my poor grampa right in the knee."

"Oh, my!" Philip gasped.

"Yeah," Clancy agreed shaking her head. "It was a pisser. But he wasn't the kind of guy to rat out a fellow cop, even though the other guy did shoot him. They made up some story about catching someone who was trying to break into the bar. It worked out all right," she shrugged. "My grampa got a small disability check from the department, and that plus his security-guard job paid him about the same. And my gramma liked it better because he didn't have to risk his life on a daily basis."

"Or work with a partner," Philip said, grinning.

"Or work with a partner," Clancy agreed, gracing him with one of her best smiles.

❧

After the tour, they switched off, with Elizabeth offering a flimsy excuse about giving Clancy a tour of the house. Both younger women knew it was so Philip could have some time alone with his daughter, but they played along without complaint.

Father and daughter sat out in the shady side yard, Abby enviously eyeing the small stand of lilacs nearby. "I just can't get lilacs to grow on my side of town. Your little microclimate is much more hospitable."

"One good reason to come visit," he said. Cocking his head, his smile growing wider, Philip said, "You know, Abby, if I were thirty years younger, that Clancy would be just my type."

She grinned at him and said, "You'd need to lose thirty years and some important equipment, Dad. She's not as open-minded as I am about going from one side to the other."

He patted her gently and chuckled, saying, "I think I'll stick with your mother, then."

"I'm glad you like her, Dad," she said, giving him a quick hug. "I knew you would."

"I do like her, and I hope you know that I don't have negative feelings about the gay lifestyle." He looked at her closely and said, "Having Stephen and Pam and Maria in our lives has really forced me to lose the silly little prejudices I had before I knew any gay people."

She looked at him, a frown settling on her forehead. "Where are you going with this, Dad? I sense a 'but' coming on."

"There is one," he said, dropping his head a little. "I just want you to know that I'm not saying this because of Clancy, or because she's a woman. And of course, I can hardly make a comment about the age difference."

"Uh-huh," she said. "Get on with it, Dad. You're not good at beating around the bush."

"I don't think you and Clancy should be together," he said. "Your mother and I don't agree about this, but I feel strongly about it."

"I heard that from Hayley," she said, narrowing her eyes at him.

"Right." He got up and shoved his hands into his pockets, standing up a little straighter. "That was a mistake," he admitted. "She was talking about how much she hated the arrangement, and I found myself agreeing with her. But I shouldn't have done that. I'm sorry."

"That's all right, Dad. I assume you didn't do it to undermine me. But it's been hard enough without her thinking she's got you on her side."

"She does," he said, holding up his hands to stop his daughter from commenting further. "I agree with her completely."

"But why?"

"The kids have been through enough," he said. "Losing their father at such a young age was enough trauma! You're making a huge mistake by doing something like this."

"Like what?" she asked, getting more frustrated by the moment.

"Like getting into a relationship with a woman! Not to mention how young she is! This is too far outside of the norm."

"But you're not antagonistic to gay people," she said flatly. "Just Clancy."

"Honey," he said, "you're not gay. Why would you choose to live this way when you can be happy with a man? It'd be so much easier for the kids."

"It would be easier for the kids if Will were still here," Abby said. "Nothing but losing me will ever be as traumatic for them."

"I know that, Abby, but you have to think about them first. You have to put your own needs aside and focus on them."

She stood abruptly and glared at him. "You're telling *me* this? After twenty-five years, you think you have to tell me that I have to make sacrifices for them? What do you think I've been doing all this time? Indulging myself?"

He looked up at her, his face pained. "Abby, please sit down. We can't discuss this if you're angry."

"Damned right I'm angry!" She stayed on her feet, unable to make herself let go of her indignation. "I've got an eighteen-year-old kid making demands on me, and now my eighty-year-old father is siding with her! Hell, yes, I'm angry!"

"I'm not siding with her."

"Of course you are! You're telling me to break up with Clancy, aren't you?"

He sighed and got to his feet. Placing his hands on her shoulders he gripped them lightly and said, "I don't want to side with her. I'm on both of your sides. I just…I just don't want to see this blow up in your face. She's your child, Abby, and losing the close relationship you have with her would be tantamount to losing Will again! I don't want to see you risk that."

She nodded, her anger dying down to a point where she was able to listen to him more attentively. "I don't want to risk that either, Dad, but letting her tell me how to live my life isn't the way to be close with her. I'm willing…hell, I'm eager to work to get past this, but she adamantly refuses. I can't give up something that's so important to me just because my kid is throwing a tantrum!"

"She *is* still a kid, Abby. I saw that so clearly when she was with us this summer. She looks like an adult, but there's still a young, struggling girl behind that façade."

"I know that, Dad, I really do." She let him wrap her in a hug, resting her head on his shoulder for comfort. "I love my children more than my own life, but I can't indulge her. She's welcome to express how she feels at any time, and I'll do my best to make this easier on her, but I'm not going to give Clancy up. Hayley's gone now; I'm sure she'll never live in my house again. I'm trying to let her live her life, and she's got to learn to do the same for me."

He pulled away and looked at her for a few moments. "I don't know why you're being so adamant about this, but it's not like you. I think you're letting your desire for Clancy get in the way of thinking straight."

Abby's chin jutted out and she narrowed her eyes. "This is like me, Dad. This is the part of me I've submerged for the last twenty-five years. Yes, I'm still a mom, but I don't have to give up the things that matter to me to keep my kids happy. They're adults now, and they have to learn to deal with disappointments and disagreements. Giving in now would just show Hayley that if she throws a big enough fit, she can get what she wants. I'm too good a mother to do that to her."

"I disagree, honey, but I can see that you're not going to listen to me. I just hope this doesn't blow up in your face. Or Hayley's."

꙳

True to Abby's prediction, Clancy had no idea that Philip was against their pairing, and when Abby revealed the content of their conversation on the drive home, Clancy was floored. "But he seemed so welcoming and friendly. Like he really liked me!"

"He does," Abby said. "He said if he were thirty years younger, he'd make a play for you himself."

Clancy gaped at that, the thought confusing her all the more. "Then why…?"

"He's worried about my relationship with Hayley. He seems to think that she's still an impressionable kid and that I have to give in to her demands just to make her happy." She shook her head and said, "I hate it when he gets involved in emotional issues. His engineering mind just wants to eliminate the static—fix the bug—whatever he needs to do to make things run smoothly again."

"So it's really not me?" she asked, her normal confidence entirely absent.

"No, of course not. He liked you a lot. And my mother is wild about you. She said she hopes we're together until death parts us."

"That follows along with my thinking," Clancy said softly, placing her hand on Abby's thigh. "I'm planning on celebrating at least a golden anniversary with you."

"That's a little optimistic," Abby said, smiling sadly.

"No, it's not," Clancy insisted. "I'll protect you and watch over you all the days of your long, long life, Abby. I promise that."

"I promise the same," Abby sighed, lifting Clancy's hand to kiss the smooth skin. "I look forward to having you right by my side, well into my dotage."

"I'll dote on you into your dotage," Clancy added, giving Abby a smile that conveyed every bit of her love.

Chapter Twenty-ðeven

After church on Sunday, Abby drove by to pick Clancy up for their planned shopping excursion. The gala wasn't for two more weeks, but Clancy wanted to buy something before she changed her mind about going. She was wearing cut-off jeans and a bright turquoise Hawaiian shirt, while Abby remained in her outfit from church—a simple, unstructured yellow dress and a straw hat with a pair of sunflowers tucked into the hatband. They looked more like mother and daughter than lovers, but Clancy didn't mind giving people the wrong idea in this instance. She needed all the help she could get when it came to picking out evening wear, and she wanted a compliant, friendly salesclerk.

They decided on the group of department stores and medium-size boutiques on Lake Street, and because Clancy had been shopping twice in the previous two months, she was starting to feel like an old hand.

Starting at the larger stores, they spent no more than five minutes in each, with Abby giving their collections a quick look before leading Clancy out once again. "What are you looking for that no one has?" Clancy asked as she tried to catch up to the longer stride of her partner.

"Those were too old for me," Abby scoffed. "You need something that makes you look like an elegant you, not like someone else."

Their next stop was a smaller store with a very helpful salesperson who seemed to understand the look they were going for. She actually produced a dress that would have looked fabulous on Clancy, but it would have revealed all of her back and most of her shoulders, and Abby discreetly reminded her of her multicolor tan. "This could work," she whispered, "but we'd have to put some self-tanning lotion on all of your pale spots."

"No, thanks. We'd never get it all to match, and I don't want to look like I just hopped off my tractor."

Thanking the woman for her time, they stopped at the next store, a medium-size boutique for young professionals. There was a small section of dressier attire, and in moments they found the perfect outfit—a long silk jacket with a Mandarin collar and matching slacks that fit like a glove, showing off Clancy's well-proportioned legs to perfection. The background color of the silk was nearly an exact match with Clancy's natural hair color, and there was a faint pattern to the fabric that revealed itself only under direct light. It was a complex, mature look, and Abby was effusive in her compliments. "It looks absolutely perfect on you," she gushed. "You look exactly your age and very sophisticated. I'm going to drive you up to your parents' house before we go to the dinner. Your mom has got to see this!"

"This is one time that I regret you're a mom," Clancy grumbled. "Why do all moms like to see people in dress-up clothes?"

"It's part of the genetic code," Abby decided. "You can't fight it."

Clancy glanced at the tag on the sleeve and made a face. "Well, this will set me back half a week's pay, but I think it's worth it."

Abby looked like she was hesitant to speak but did so anyway. "I…uhm…was going to offer to pay for your clothes. You're only going to this because of me. I hate to see you spend your hard-earned money on something you'll only wear once."

"Then I guess you'll just have to ask me out again," she said, patting Abby's cheek. She slipped out of the slacks and handed them to her partner to hold while she unbuttoned the jacket.

"I mean it," Abby said again. "I'd like to pay for this."

Clancy looked at her for a moment and then said, "I started to get paid to work in the flower shop when I was about twelve. I did the same work that an extra employee would have done, so my mom paid me the same wage. From that time on, I've paid for my own clothes, entertainment, and incidentals. I stopped feeling like a kid because I was responsible for myself. If I let you buy me clothes, it'll make me feel like a kid again, and I don't want that with you—ever. I don't notice our age difference very often, but if you start paying for things like this, I'm afraid I'm gonna feel it. Let's not risk that, okay?"

Abby looked at her for a long time, seeing the determined glint in the cool gray eyes. "You know what I love about you?" she finally asked, draping her arms around Clancy's neck.

"What?"

"I love that you know when to say no. You know yourself well enough to set limits about things and stick to them."

Clancy nodded and said, "I do know myself well. And if there's any chance of causing friction later on, I always choose not to take the risk. Our relationship is worth more than any minor thing we might fight over."

"No fighting," Abby sighed. "Just loving." She kissed her gently, sliding her hands inside the open jacket to tickle bare skin. "Only one thing I hate about going to church," she murmured. "No time for love in the morning."

Clancy grasped Abby's wrist and took a look at her watch. "It's not morning, but there's plenty of time for love. I don't have to be at work for eighteen hours." She was dropping soft, wet kisses all over Abby's face while she spoke, and the larger woman gave in willingly, surrendering to Clancy's desires and her proposal.

"Throw some money at someone near a cash register and take me home!"

They were both hot and ready for love by the time they burst through the front door of the apartment, giggling while they tried to undress each other. Their lips were merged while Abby's fingers worked at the button on Clancy's pants and then lowered the zipper. She pushed the pants down and slipped her hand into the bright pink bikinis, palming Clancy's ass. Once she had her hands on her skin, Clancy was hers for the taking. A sturdy thigh wrapped around Abby's legs, and the smaller woman ground her mound into her partner, all the while hungrily consuming her lips.

Abby had nearly lost all sense of decorum, but she retained enough to know they had to get into the bedroom. She had no idea what Michael's schedule was, but she knew she was not going to be the first woman he ever saw Clancy making love to.

Slowly, trying to remain entwined, she maneuvered Clancy out of her pants, across the living room, and into the bedroom. She wrapped her arms around the landscaper and spun, landing flat on her back with Clancy sprawled atop her. Now they both let go, kissing, sucking, biting each other in a frenzy, their lovemaking taking on an urgency and a forcefulness it had never had before.

Hands were everywhere at once, and pieces of clothing occasionally flew from the pile. Groans, moans, and the soft, wet slurp of rough kisses were the only sounds. Finally naked, they clung to one another and began to wrestle, each one trying to be on top. Clancy had never seen Abby behave with such abandon, and she absolutely loved it. Abby growled when she had her partner on her back and then scooted up so her knees were on Clancy's shoulders, pinning her.

The blonde panted, trying to catch her breath, and then stopped to survey the image that presented itself. Abby was wet with sweat, her chest heaving, eyes bright as she looked down at her lover. Clancy lowered her gaze and laughed, low and sexy. "Why in the hell am I fighting? I've never seen a better view." She narrowed her gaze and licked her lips. "Come here, baby, just a little closer. I'm gonna kiss you like you've never been kissed. Come on," she soothed. "Let me get my tongue on you."

Abby shook her head, put her hands on Clancy's shoulders, and scooted back. Lying down, nose to nose, she said, "I won. So I get to do what I want."

Clancy smiled at her and stuck her arms out, giving up without a fight. "Go, baby. Have at it."

The brunette got a devilish look in her eye and clambered off the futon. She spied two small tables flanking the bed and went to the one on the left. Giving her lover a wink, she said, "You don't mind if I snoop, do you?"

Clancy made a sweeping gesture with her hand. "Be my guest."

The first table yielded only a large supply of colored pencils, markers, and plastic templates. "You want to draw?" Clancy asked, rolling onto her tummy to watch.

"Keep your shirt on," Abby said, walking around the futon to check the other table. "Aha! Here's the stash!" She knelt down and started to root through the contents, with Clancy giggling in the background.

"Sure I can't help you find something in particular?"

"Nope. I know what I want, and I'm sure you have it." She sneaked a suspicious look back at Clancy. "Are you sure you've only had five lovers? There are enough things in here to supply an apartment building."

"Gotta be prepared. Never know when you're gonna meet a woman with special needs."

Abby stood up, her treasures hidden behind her back. "Close your eyes," she said. "I don't want to embarrass myself if I fumble around here."

Clancy put a hand over her eyes, but she was obviously peeking through her fingers.

"Come on," Abby pleaded. "Give me a minute to get prepared."

"Okay, okay. I just like messing with you."

Abby didn't say a word, but Clancy could hear a wide variety of noises coming from her side of the room, including a muttered curse word or two. But in a few minutes, she felt Abby's weight on the bed and knew the fun would soon begin. To her surprise, the first thing she experienced was a piece of cloth being placed over her eyes. "A blindfold? I had a blindfold in there?"

"Sure did," Abby said. "Do you mind wearing it?"

"No. I don't think you'll rob me when I'm not looking."

She'd barely uttered the last word when Abby started to kiss her again, starting out slow and tender and soft. These were the kisses that Clancy liked the best—the ones that promised a day full of pleasure. There was an unmistakable message to Abby's kisses when she planned on making love, and Clancy had never misread her lover's intent. As soon as she felt Abby's lips touch hers, she let out a long sigh and tried to open herself fully to the experience.

Abby sensed her receptivity and explored her body for a long time, lingering for a while at a few favorite spots but making sure that every part was lavished with affection. Time and again, she returned to Clancy's mouth, probing and teasing with her tongue until the blonde was humming with arousal.

The blindfold made the experience so much more intense for Clancy that she wondered why she hadn't pulled it out earlier. But then she remembered that she'd used it just once, with Julie, and she hadn't enjoyed it much at all. But she trusted Abby so completely that she was able to lie still and let the sensations wash over her like a gentle wave. Each kiss carried just a hint of surprise, heightening the pleasure and making Clancy feel like she had to savor each, because she didn't know if there would be another.

Abby worked her lover's body like a pro, caressing each delicate part with the skill and sureness of a master. After what seemed like hours, Abby rolled her partner onto her belly, finally urging her onto her hands and knees. Clancy's ass was twitching with anticipation, making Abby's mouth start to water. Clancy didn't have a shred of modesty when it came to expressing her sexuality, and Abby loved to watch her body demand what it needed. And there wasn't a doubt that Clancy needed her lover to enter her. She arched her back and spread her legs, presenting such a delightfully beautiful pose that Abby had to pause for a moment in sheer admiration. She ran her hand across Clancy's flank, murmuring, "You're such a beautiful woman. It makes me feel so special to have you be so open with me."

"That's because I love you. Only you."

Clancy felt her partner shift and sensed her warm breath on the back of her thigh. Then, just when she was ready to squirm out of her skin, she felt it—the first brush of sensation against her smaller opening. Her back arched even higher, and her legs spread impossibly wide as she pushed herself toward the touch. But Abby wouldn't give in to her desires immediately. She teased her lover for a long time until she was moaning in frustration. "Please," she begged. "Please."

Abby stroked her back, her mouth watering as she gazed at her Clancy's muscular ass. "Open up for me," she said, quietly but firmly.

"Unghhh!" Clancy reached behind herself, letting her head drop to the mattress. She grasped her cheeks and opened herself as wide as she could, emitting a contented purr when Abby began to tease her ass with the dildo. "Oh, yeah, I need it," she growled. "Put it in, baby. Put it in me."

Hands shaking, Abby bent over a little to make sure her aim was true. She held the petite silicone piece in her hand and slipped it into her partner, delightedly watching as goosebumps broke out all across Clancy's back.

"Yes!" she said, "that feels so damned good!" Abby delicately maneuvered the toy, slowly probing her lover with the well-lubricated object. Clancy had stopped speaking, her body coiled with tension. They settled into a slow, steady rhythm, with Clancy backing into Abby's hand, the wide base of the dildo tight against her cheeks on every stroke.

Eventually, Abby slowed down even further, and Clancy felt her move. Now Abby was pressing something against her cunt, and the blonde hoped she was finally going to get some relief. Arching her back again, she bore down, opening herself to what she hoped was something—anything to fill her up.

Abby didn't disappoint. She pressed a new, bigger toy firmly against Clancy; moved closer; and wrapped her arm around her lover's waist. Without a word, she probed at her opening and then slipped in all at once, stretching Clancy wide open with a smooth, steady pressure. "Oh, Jesus!" the blonde cried, grabbing handfuls of sheet to anchor herself.

Abby rested inside her, not moving for a good, long time, letting Clancy's body get used to the twin invasions. Finally, Abby grasped her partner's hips and started to move, going so slowly that it seemed like forever for her to nearly slip out.

Just as Clancy thought she'd lose her, Abby started to slide back in, going just as slowly and carefully as before. It was maddening, truly maddening, but Clancy had never felt so aroused in her life. Having Abby stretch her so fully and deny her the fucking she desperately craved was about to make her scream.

Clancy bore down again, trying to force her partner to move faster, harder, but all she managed was to make the smaller dildo almost pop out. Abby seemed to anticipate her action, and on the next maddeningly slow stroke, both dildos entered Clancy with the same, steady, unrelenting pressure. "God damn it, Abby, fuck me!"

"I am fucking you," she murmured, grasping Clancy tight around the waist and burying her teeth into her shoulder. "I'm fucking you slowly." She moved her hand along Clancy's thigh, then slid down between her legs. "And you're loving it," she growled. "You've never been wetter."

Clancy couldn't argue, mainly because she wasn't able to speak. She desperately wanted Abby to get wild, to start really grinding, but the fact that she refused made her crazy with desire. She didn't…couldn't just lose herself to the sensation of being pumped hard. Abby's deliberate style made her feel her flesh stretch bit by bit, feeling every inch of the dildos as they moved inside her. Her hunger grew with every stroke, needing Abby to plunge into her deeper, faster, harder. But her lover seemed to become even more purposeful, driving her mad. Clancy shoved her hips hard, groaning in frustration, but Abby never gave in. The blonde was covered in sweat, her skin glowing pink. The moment Abby saw that Clancy's frustration was beginning to equal her arousal she leaned over her, feeling the heat. "When you're ready, I want you to touch yourself and come for me."

As the words left her mouth, Clancy's hand flew between her legs, while Abby reached under her and pinched her nipples hard enough to make her groan. The nimble fingers gently massaged her clit for mere seconds before she came hard and loud, backing into Abby hard enough to stun the brunette. Clancy's knees, gave out and she fell to the bed, both dildos expelled at the same moment. "Oh…my…God," the blonde mumbled. "What in the hell did you do to me?"

Abby crawled up next to her, helped her onto her side, and cradled her in her arms until both of their heart rates slowed down. Clancy finally removed the blindfold and blinked a few times, the light in the room hurting her eyes at first. Giving Abby a doubtful look, she asked, "Where did you learn to fuck like that?"

Abby laughed. "I've been fucked a few times, remember? I just did what I like, and I hoped you'd like it, too."

Clancy sat up, resting her weight on her arm. "That's how you like it?"

"One of the ways. I like it a lot of ways, depending on the day."

"But I…I was really aggressive with you. Did you like that?"

"Honey, they heard me coming in the San Fernando Valley." She stroked Clancy's concerned face. "Of course I liked it."

"But you prefer it slow?"

Abby made a face. "I wouldn't put it that way. Sometimes I really like to go at it. But no matter how turned on I am at first, doing it slow and steady always makes me come. Always," she said.

Clancy lay back down, looking unhappy. "I always do it kinda the same way," she said. "It didn't occur to me that you wouldn't like it the same way Jul—" She stopped midword. "Sorry, I know you don't like to think about me with her."

Abby ran her fingers through her wet hair, catching beads of perspiration with her thumb. "It's okay. Did you use toys a lot with Julie?"

Clancy nodded. "Yeah. Pretty much exclusively."

"Well, honey, if you're used to one person, it makes sense that you'd develop a certain way of doing something. That's perfectly understandable."

The blonde's chuckle grew into a full-throated laugh. "Second time you've ever seen a dildo, and you teach me something new."

Abby leaned over her and kissed her soundly. "Who said it's the second time?" she asked. "I was straight, not unimaginative!"

🌱

Trevor and Hayley sat at a noisy breakfast place near the university on Sunday morning, both a little tired and slow from Saturday night. "It was kinda funny going to a bar with you," the young man said. "First time we've done that."

Hayley smiled at him. "Like we could have gotten away with it at home. You know Mom volunteers at the airport, sniffing for drugs."

Trevor laughed at his sister's penchant for exaggeration. "She's not that bad."

"Yes she is!" the girl insisted. "I couldn't eat rum-flavored candy when I was in high school."

"You did whatever you wanted when you stayed overnight at Gretchen's," Trevor reminded her.

"That's my point! I had to leave my own house to have a drink or smoke a joint!"

Trevor laughed again, finding his sister's histrionics amusing. "We both knew the rules. Mom told us both that she had a zero-tolerance policy, and she meant it."

"Yeah," she said, a pout on her pretty face. "We had to get the one mother in Pasadena who cared about us."

"I'm sure all of your friends felt sorry for you," Trevor said, trying to sound serious.

"Oh, yeah. That's why someone invited me for a sleepover just about every weekend. They knew I was in lockdown at home."

Trevor took a sip of his coffee, trying to hide the smirk that covered his face.

"It didn't bother you to have Mom keep an eye on you?"

"She didn't watch me as closely as she watched you," he said, smiling. "She had a reason to watch you."

"Oh, like you didn't do anything bad!"

"Didn't say that," he said. "But I never got caught."

Hayley's eyes lit up. "What's the best thing you ever got away with?"

"I'd never tell you. I don't do that."

"Why? You never tell me anything!"

"Not just you," he said. "I don't talk about my private life. That's why it's private."

"You are a weird guy," Hayley said, giving him a curious look. "I swear you were pretty normal until you went to college. What happened?"

"Nothing happened," he said, unruffled. "I just decided that I needed to keep my personal life personal."

Sensing something about his demeanor, she asked, "Because of Daddy?"

He nodded. "Yeah, I guess. It was really hard coming home and seeing how bad off you and Mom were. I would have stayed at school year-round, but I knew I couldn't do that."

"I bet it was," she said quietly, not making eye contact. "We were both a mess for a long time." She looked up at him. "But why did that make you start being secretive?"

"I wasn't secretive," he said. "I just didn't want Mom to worry about me. She had enough on her mind. So I told her the minimum. After a while, I realized I liked not having her ask questions."

"I can't imagine being like that."

"Yeah, I know," he replied, laughing. "I was surprised Alexander wasn't down here this weekend. I thought I'd have to watch you two going at it every two minutes."

"He's been down every other weekend. But I wanted to have some time alone with you."

"I'm glad. I didn't really want to spend the weekend with the two of you." He sat back in his chair. "How's it going with him, anyway?"

"Good," she said. "Really good. But I don't want to tell you everything. I know you hate to hear about personal lives." She added a smarmy smile, making him chuckle.

"I don't mind hearing about other people's lives. I just don't wanna talk about mine. Besides, one day I'll get married and have kids, and my secret life will be in the past. I'm enjoying it while I can."

"Well, things are great with Alexander. But you'll see for yourself. I'm gonna bring him home for Thanksgiving."

"See?" he smiled. "That's what happens when you have a public life. You've gotta bring the guy home for inspection."

"I don't mind. I wanna show him off."

His smile faded, and he said, "Mom's gonna show Clancy off in a couple of weeks."

"Huh?"

"She's taking her to a formal dinner dance." His expression was mostly neutral, but Hayley could see an unreadable emotion hidden behind his blue eyes.

Hayley made every other diner stare at them when she shouted, "A formal dance!"

"Yeah," he said quietly. "They were gonna go shopping this weekend. Clancy doesn't have any nice clothes."

Hayley's head dropped to the table, and she moaned, "She's lost her fucking mind."

Trevor patted her on the shoulder, partly to comfort her and partly to stop her from making a scene. "Come on, get up."

She lifted her head, looking disgusted. "How can you stand to be around them? They're like seventh-graders, making sure everybody knows that they're in loooove."

"It's not like that, Hayley. They really are in love. They're just living their lives"

She looked at him like he was mad. "So you're honestly gonna say that it doesn't bother you."

He sat quietly for a moment before saying, "Of course it bothers me. I saw that picture of Mom and Dad at that big anniversary party that Gran and Gramps threw for them." He paused and took in a breath, a fond smile on his face. "They always seemed happier when they were dressed up for a big party. Mom loved to get dressed up, and Dad loved looking at her." He looked at his sister and said, "He was so damned crazy about her."

A few tears shone in Hayley's bright eyes, and her voice was hoarse with emotion. "How can you watch them? How can you be there?"

"I'm not around them very much," he said. "I think about Dad all of the time and how different it was when he was alive." He looked out of the window of the restaurant, obviously thinking about something. "I know she loves Clancy, but it's different." He shook his head, looking like he was trying to dislodge a troubling thought. "Maybe it's because it's new. Maybe it's because they're both women. But it's so different."

"And you don't say anything to her?" Hayley asked, clearly frustrated. "She'd tone it down if you told her to. She listens to you."

"Why would I do that?" he asked. "There's nothing wrong with what they're doing. Just because it makes us uncomfortable doesn't make it wrong. Mom stays out of my personal life, and I'm gonna stay out of hers."

"I couldn't live with them," she said, a disdainful look on her face. "Not for all the money in the world."

His gaze landed on her and held. He didn't speak until she was becoming uncomfortable with his appraisal. "Maybe we don't feel the same about family."

"What? Our family?"

"Yeah, of course. Our family is one of the most important things in my life. I know how lucky we are to have such a great mom and grandparents. We're not children anymore. We can't just expect to be on the receiving end all of the time. We've had a sweet life so far with Mom and Dad supporting us in everything we've ever wanted to do. Well, it's time for a little payback. Mom needs our support, and I'm gonna give it to her. If it kills me," he said, his eyes flinty with determination.

❦

The following Friday night, Abby took Clancy out for a lovely dinner at one of Pasadena's finer restaurants. They went back to Clancy's apartment, and within minutes, Abby had begun seducing her partner. Clancy's blouse was partially unbuttoned, and Abby's hands were teasing the sensitive skin on the small of her back.

Clancy draped her arms around Abby's neck, closing her eyes as she kissed her, savoring the softness of her lips.

"Know what I wanna do?" Abby asked, her voice filled with innuendo.

"No, but I wanna do it, too," Clancy said, her breath catching as her zipper was lowered and Abby's inquisitive fingers slipped inside.

"Done," Abby said, capturing Clancy's pink earlobe between her teeth for a nibble. "You're gonna love it."

The next morning, Abby hopped out of bed and put on some of Clancy's clothes before heading for the shower. She was back in the room, rubbing her hair with a towel, when Clancy's eyes first opened. Gray eyes blinked slowly as Clancy stretched, smiling up at her lover. "Come back here and do me like you did me last night." She threw off the sheet and spread her arms and legs. "I'm all yours."

Abby sat on the edge of the futon and ran her hand across Clancy's belly. "Very tempting, but we'll be late."

"Late for what?"

"We're gonna play tennis with Pam and Maria this morning, remember?"

Clancy sat up quickly. "What? I don't play tennis!"

"But you told me last night that you'd love to play."

Clancy looked confused. "I said that? Me?"

"Yeah. I asked if you knew what I wanted to do, and you said you wanted to do it, too. You didn't ask what it was." She leaned over and kissed Clancy, her shower-fresh scent making the smaller woman smile.

"You tricked me," Clancy said. "You intentionally tricked me, and now you're just as happy as can be, aren't ya? You're actually proud of yourself!"

Giggling, Abby nodded. "I am, to tell you the truth. And if you hurry up and get ready, I'll bring you right back here and do you better than I did you last night."

Clancy was standing on the floor before Abby had managed to finish her sentence. "Give me five," she said, scampering off to the bathroom.

"I swear it was Pam's idea," Abby said a few minutes later while they drove to the club. "I told her that you didn't play, but she claims that she'd rather play with a rank beginner than with anyone else at the club. And I'd much rather be with you than with anyone else in the world, so it seemed like a great idea to me."

Clancy gave her a puzzled look; then recognition slowly dawned. "She wants me to play because I'll suck, right?"

"No, no, really," Abby said. "She's a pretty good player, but Maria's…well, Maria plays because it's an excuse to force herself to get some regular exercise. She's been playing for a few years now, but to be honest, she hasn't improved at all. It'll be like two beginners and two intermediate players. It should really work out." She put her hand on Clancy's thigh and said, "Besides, I think they both want to get to know you better. This could be fun."

"Or embarrassing," Clancy grumbled.

Clancy hadn't played tennis since she was forced to endure a semester's worth of group lessons in high school phys ed. She was obviously strong and well muscled, but she'd never been much for sports or organized exercise and had never been in a gym in her life. Still, she was in good shape from her job, and she did run a few miles in the morning if she hadn't done anything too physical for several days, giving her sufficient cardiovascular fitness to be able to stay on the court for an hour.

What she had in spades, though, was determination, and Abby couldn't help but smile at her furrowed brow as she tried to remind her body how to execute the required moves.

To Abby's surprise, Clancy had an absolutely lethal backhand—lethal mainly to the poor soul who got stung by it. Her strokes were wildly unpredictable, but each had enough mustard on it to raise a welt if her opponent got in the way.

They made it through two sets, both won by Abby and Clancy, and decided to have lunch together—winner buying, as usual. "Well, that was the most unusual set of tennis I've ever participated in," Abby said.

"We would have won that second set if Maria hadn't kept ducking," Pam insisted. "You can use your racquet to return the ball, honey."

"No way," Maria declared, her eyes wide. "I could lose an eye!"

"I've gotta say," Pam said, laughing, "you two will be unbeatable if Clancy can harness that power."

Abby reached over and playfully felt her lover's upper arm. "She is a powerful little thing, isn't she?"

"Little?" Maria gaped, eyeing Clancy, who bettered her by at least four inches and thirty pounds.

"Only Abby calls me little. Of course, that only refers to my height. She wasn't calling me little the other night when we were leg wrestling."

"Leg wrestling, eh?" Maria asked, seeing the blush that crawled up Abby's cheeks. "Isn't it amazing the creative ways you can manage to touch each other when you're first together?"

They chatted companionably and then tried to decide whether they would continue the tennis experiment. "It's up to you, Clancy," Pam said. "Ellen's definitely out, so we've got to find a fourth. I'd rather play with you, but we don't wanna push you."

"Sure, I'll give it a go. It'll be a nice way to spend a little time with my girl." She gave Abby a toothy grin, making her partner laugh at her antics.

"You know," Abby said, "you can only be my guest twice in a month. If you enjoy this, I'll have to add you as my spouse."

"Your spouse?" Clancy asked, her eyes widening.

"Yep. My spouse."

"Can I come to watch the membership director try not to act shocked?" Maria asked.

"How do we ahh…prove that we're spouses?" Clancy asked.

"When we did it, we had to show that we lived together and that we shared financial resources," Pam said.

"Well, we don't do that," Clancy said. "At least not yet."

"But we might…if I'm lucky, right?" Abby asked, her eyes dancing merrily.

"Yes," Clancy allowed. "If you're very, very lucky, I might let you move in with me. You can call dibs on which side of the futon you want."

"I'd be the happiest woman in town," Abby sighed, giving Clancy a look that didn't contain a shred of insincerity.

❦

Clancy got up to use the restroom, surprised to find Maria following her into the building. Maria touched her shoulder and pointed to a quiet spot near one of the event rooms. "Can we talk for a minute? I was going to follow you into the bathroom, but you never know who's gonna be in there."

"Uhm…sure." Clancy leaned against the wall and cocked her head. "What's up?"

"I wanted to apologize again for being so suspicious of you at first."

"At first? Does that mean you're not suspicious anymore?"

"Not at all," Maria said, her sincerity obvious. "I can see how much you two love each other. And if you wanted her money…well, you could have had it by now. She'd obviously give you everything she had if you asked for it."

Clancy's cheeks colored, realizing how true Maria's observation was. "I like that she has money," Clancy said. "I love her big house and that great yard and her pool. And her car is sizzling hot. But I'd feel just the same about her if she were unemployed and living with her parents."

"I can see that," Maria said. "It's obvious this isn't one-sided."

"Thanks," Clancy said. "I appreciate that."

Maria's head tilted, and she asked, "You never told her about my suspicions, did you?"

"No, of course not. You pissed me off, but telling her would have hurt her." Her gaze grew sharp, her gray eyes looking fierce. "I never want to hurt her if I can possibly avoid it."

"Thanks," Maria said. "It would have hurt her, and she'd been hurt enough by Ellen's stupidity. It would have been hard for her to know I was just as stupid."

Clancy clapped her on the shoulder. "You were looking out for her. That's not the worst thing you could have done."

"But she doesn't need me to do that," Maria said. "She's smarter than I am and more intuitive about people."

"I know that," Clancy said, her eyes twinkling. "But you weren't trying to be a jerk. That was just the result."

Maria bumped her with her shoulder. "I like you," she said, smiling. "You're gonna make Abby very happy."

"Just like she does for me," Clancy said, with a grin wide enough to light up the San Gabriel Valley. "And speaking of happy, you two should come by the house on your way home. Abby's disappointed that you haven't been by to see the yard yet."

Maria made a face. "We've wanted to, really, but we haven't had the whole day to spend over there."

Clancy cocked her head. "Then just stop by."

"You've never had a child," Maria said. "Alyssa was crazy about the pool before. Now that there's a waterfall…we'll have to stay until the moon rises."

"Come this afternoon," Clancy said. "Come close to dinner, and that'll make the day shorter."

"You'll feed us?" Maria asked, smiling so that her teeth showed.

"Yes, we'll feed you," Clancy said, laughing. She clapped the woman on the back and said, "I think I've figured out your hot button already."

☙

The charity dinner was scheduled for Friday night, and Clancy knocked off early to make sure she had time for a nap. Carrying her own evening wear in a garment bag, Abby arrived at the apartment an hour before they had to leave, mostly to ensure that her reluctant partner didn't try to escape. After Michael let her in, she stood in the doorway to Clancy's room and gazed at her lover, wishing fervently that they had an hour to play as Clancy's bare body started to work its magic on her libido. Instead, she gently woke her by rubbing her back, letting just the tips of her fingers play over the soft skin.

When she was coherent, Clancy mumbled, "Have I ever told you that was how my gramma woke me when I was little?"

Abby lay down and cuddled her close. "No, you haven't, but I assumed someone touched you that way when you were a child. The first morning I did that, you acted like you were in heaven."

"I didn't remember that sensation until you did it the first time. Maybe it's a mom thing."

"It doesn't bother you when I do things that remind you of your mom or your grandmother, does it?"

"No, not at all. You're all moms, and you just can't help being momlike sometimes. It only bothers me when I feel like you're trying to be *my* mom. That's a no-no."

"Got it," Abby said. "Now get your sweet little nondaughterly ass into the bathroom so we're on time."

☙

Clancy was dressed, observing herself in the full-length mirror while Abby was still in her slip. "You look wonderful," Abby said, slipping her arms around her partner.

Barely acknowledging the compliment, Clancy continued to poke at her hair. "Would you like it better all one color?"

"Huh? What brought that on?"

"It doesn't look very sophisticated," Clancy mused, getting to the heart of the matter. "I think it makes me look even younger."

Abby gazed at her thoughtfully and then nodded. "It probably does. But why does that matter?"

"I don't know," Clancy said, looking a trifle adolescent. "I guess I just want to look my age."

"You mean you want to look closer to my age."

Looking up at her with a question in her eyes, Clancy asked, "Is that such a bad thing?"

"No, not at all. But my hair shouldn't be this gray at forty-five. If you're going to get rid of your blonde to look older, I should get rid of my gray to look younger."

"But I like your gray."

Kissing her on the crown of the head, Abby reminded her, "And I like your blonde. Why don't we please ourselves and each other, huh? If other people don't like it, they can lump it."

"What does that expression even mean?" Clancy asked, grinning up at her partner.

"No idea. I just know that I love the way you look—it's the look I was first attracted to—and I don't want you to change it unless and until *you* don't like it any longer. Yours is the only opinion that matters."

❦

After an appropriate interlude to admire Abby's sexy black dress, which included an extended session of laying on of hands, they drove up to Sierra Madre to allow for a viewing. Margaret was beside herself, gushing over Clancy like she was wearing a wedding gown. "Abby, I don't know how you did it!" she cried. "She hasn't been this dressed up since her Confirmation into the church in seventh grade."

"Coincidentally, that's when I started buying my own clothes," Clancy said. "I decided I'd never be seen in a dress again, and I've stuck to my resolve."

"Well, you both look wonderful," Eileen said. "John, go get the camera."

He willingly did so, and after every permutation of mother/daughter, grandmother/daughter/daughter, et cetera, they were finally released. "I didn't ever go to a school dance," Clancy said. "Is that what it's like when your date shows up?"

"Pretty much," Abby said. "Darn! I should have bought you a corsage."

"I plant flowers. I don't wear 'em."

❦

Because the event was for one of the main charity outreaches for her church, Abby knew many of the people in attendance. Her parents were there, as were Maria and Pam, and several other sets of friends. As expected, Ellen and her husband, Neil, were there as well, but it soon became clear that neither of them was going to come by to say hello. They hadn't been there long when Abby leaned over to Clancy and said, "I'm not going to act like I don't recognize two of my oldest friends. I'll introduce you later—if they're civil." She got up, smoothed out her dress, held her head high, and strode over to the Chenoweths' table.

She knew every one of the eight people sitting around the table and gave each of them a friendly greeting. After a perfunctory hello, Ellen turned her attention back to the conversation she had been having with the woman to her right, leaving Abby to stand awkwardly behind her. Looking directly at Neil, Abby said, "I was going to bring Clancy over to meet you, but that doesn't seem like a good idea."

"I think you're right," Neil said, looking very uncomfortable. "I'm...uhm...sorry, Abby, but I don't think that would be wise."

"It doesn't have to be like this," she said quietly. Then she turned and went back to her table.

Everyone at her own table had been stealthily watching, but no one said anything when she returned. Clancy just gripped her hand under the table and gave it a squeeze.

Deciding not to let the slight ruin the evening, Abby stood and tugged Clancy up with her. "It's time to come out to a few people," she said. "Wanna mingle?"

"Love to," Clancy said, beaming up at her.

❦

"How many people have you two already told?" Abby asked Maria and Pam when they caught up to them near the dance floor.

"Told? You think we told?" Pam blinked ingenuously. "We're the souls of discretion!"

"I introduced Clancy as my partner to two dozen people, and we barely got a raised eyebrow," Abby said. "I know you two are behind that."

"Well," Maria said, "we wanted this to be as smooth as possible for you two. So we might have hinted at it at the last gay and lesbian outreach advisory board meeting."

"Just a hint, though," Pam said, nodding solemnly.

"News about sex travels fast, even at church," Abby said. "My mother said that three people called her this week to get her to deny the vicious rumor. We're semicelebrities, Clancy. Do you mind?"

"Not a bit. Maybe I'll get some business out of it," she said. "Landscaping isn't that exciting, but if people think I throw in a few orientation-turning lesbian sex acts, my phone might start ringing off the hook."

"You'd better not answer those calls," Abby said, brow furrowing.

"I have a very select list of clients," she said. "It's limited to you." Standing on her tiptoes to equalize for Abby's heels, Clancy placed a chaste kiss on her lips.

They were interrupted by someone standing right behind Abby, clearing his throat dramatically. She turned, smiled at an elegantly attired man, and allowed him to kiss her cheek. "Hello, Allan."

"And just what have you been up to, as if I didn't know?" he asked, eyeing Clancy showily.

With a small smile, Abby nodded, "Yes, the rumors are true. Allan Simpkins, this is my partner, Clancy O'Connor."

"Partner, huh?" he asked, nodding his approval. "You girls work fast, don't you?"

"No reason not to when you find the right one," Abby said, giving Clancy a wider smile.

"Well, everyone else was shocked, I tell you. Just shocked," he said dramatically. "But I didn't blink an eye. I always, and I do mean always, knew." He looked thoroughly pleased with himself, but Clancy saw a look in her lover's eyes that she knew meant trouble.

"What do you mean by that?" Abby asked sharply. Pam and Maria unconsciously backed up, their eyes going round, but Clancy leaned in closer and put her hand on Abby's back, which was tight with tension.

"I only meant that I knew you had some secret yearnings," he whispered loudly, for effect. "It's okay, Abby; the cat's out of the bag now."

She advanced on him, the toes of her shoes touching his. "Listen, Allan," she enunciated sharply, "I loved Will completely—totally—and fully. I never had another thought for another man, or another woman. I deeply resent your implication, and I demand an apology!"

"I only meant—" he said, backing up.

"I know what you meant," she rasped. "I was completely faithful to my husband until the day he died. Now I'm in love with Clancy, and I'll be the same with her! Two discrete events—neither of which has a God-damned thing to do with the other!"

"I didn't mean to imply anything different," he said, now backing away even quicker. "I wish you all the best." With that, he turned and practically ran back to his table, leaving three sets of wide eyes to stare at Abby.

"Pompous prick," she muttered.

Maria saw the stunned look on Clancy's face, and explained, "He's a big troublemaker at church. One of those guys who's always trying to create controversy where none exists. He's had that coming for years," she added, giving Abby an admiring look.

"Maybe coming tonight wasn't such a good idea," Abby sighed. "I feel like I've been beaten with clubs."

Clancy grasped her hand and said, "Let's go outside for a bit. A little fresh air will make you feel better."

Abby nodded and let herself be led outdoors. The night was chilly, but the brisk temperature was just the thing to cool her heated temper. "Why is it such a big deal to have labels for people?" she asked.

"It's only important to some. The people who matter don't see you as a thing or a stereotype; they see the real you. The you that I see."

"I suppose," Abby sighed, leaning against Clancy's body. "It's just tiring."

"It is. Let's just lie low a little bit and enjoy being with your parents, and Pam and Maria, and the other people who know how to behave."

Clancy started to walk back in, but Abby held her back. Searching her eyes, she asked, "You understand, don't you? I didn't want to be with women when I was with Will, and I don't want to be with anyone else now that I'm with you."

Brushing her mouth with a light kiss, Clancy said. "I do." She placed her hands on her lover's hips and pulled her close. "You're one of those rare people who falls in love with the soul, rather than the body."

"I love your soul, Clancy O'Connor," she sighed; then she bent to kiss her, lingering until the air began to chill. She ran her hands up and down her partner, feeling the soft flesh and firm muscles. "But I love your body, too. It's the nicest fringe benefit a woman could ever have."

At one point in the evening, Clancy found herself alone at the table with Philip. He got up, moved to be able to sit next to her, and said, "I assume that Abby told you I have reservations about your relationship."

"She did," Clancy said, "but I understood your reasons."

"I hope you understand my reservations have nothing to do with you."

She reached out and patted his hand, giving him a warm smile. "I can tell you like me, Philip. You don't look like the kind of guy who would be able to put on a front like that."

"No, no. I'm polite, but I don't go out of my way to make conversation with people I don't like."

"I know you're worried about Hayley. I just hope you know that Abby's devoted to those kids. She'd never do anything that she thought would permanently harm their relationship." She looked at him for a moment and said, "I honestly think she's doing what's best for Hayley by going through with this. She wants to show her that they can work things out by discussing them but not by making demands. I'm not a mom, Philip, but I am someone's child. If I'd thought I could have made my parents do things my way by pouting, God only knows how I would have turned out."

"I suppose we'll just have to see what happens," he said quietly. "I just wish I knew why Hayley was so antagonistic to the relationship."

Clancy wasn't about to tell him that one element was Hayley's crush on her, so she mentioned one of her other guesses. "I think she's having a hard time seeing Abby be with me because I'm a woman," Clancy said. "I know she's comfortable around gay people, but being comfortable with having your mom be in a gay relationship has to be a shock for a kid. It's probably also hard since I'm closer to her age than I am to Abby's."

"That makes sense," he said thoughtfully. "I just don't want to see any of you get hurt here, Clancy. Those women are my life."

"I know just what you mean, Philip," she said. "I feel the same way about Abby, and Abby won't be happy if Hayley doesn't eventually get comfortable with us. Besides wanting Abby to be happy, it's in my best interest to win Hayley over."

He gave her a look, lingering on her eyes. "You're very honest, aren't you? Most people wouldn't admit to having their own agenda."

She gave him a half-smile and said, "It's easier in the long run to be honest. I'm a very practical person."

"So am I," he said. "The problem is that Hayley isn't. She's still a flighty young woman."

"Yeah, she is," Clancy said. "But Abby thinks it's time for Hayley to learn how to be less self-centered. She's gotta learn sometime, Philip. Now's as good a time as any."

Chapter Twenty-Eight

For the next two weeks, Clancy went to the Graham house for dinner almost every night, but Trevor was rarely present. He always had an excuse, one just good enough to pass, but Abby knew he was avoiding them. She wasn't sure if she should confront him, reasoning that Trevor would bring it up when he was ready to talk. Even though Abby's style wouldn't have worked for Clancy, the blonde was happy that Abby didn't let Trevor's disappearing act change her behavior. Almost every night, they played with the dogs or took a long walk until it was nearly bedtime; then they both got into their cars and drove to Clancy's. Sleeping together every night made both of them content enough to give Trevor some time, but Abby finally decided that she had to broach the topic, even if her son wasn't ready.

On Clancy's bowling night, she invited him out to dinner, the invitation obviously taking him by surprise. But he put on a nice pair of slacks and a dress shirt, and escorted her to one of the family's favorite restaurants. After they'd ordered their food, Trevor gave his mother a curious look and asked, "So how are things going? Are you and Clancy doing okay?" He shook his head a little and said, "You and Clancy. That's hard to say—you know?"

Abby reached across the table and covered his large hand with her own. "No, I don't really know. I've never been in your position, Trevor, so I only know what you tell me." She paused until he met her eyes. "Which hasn't been much."

He looked down, studiously avoiding her gaze. "It feels…I don't know, kinda weird being at home. It feels better to go hang out with my old friends."

"I'm sure it does, honey, but you're not getting to know Clancy by doing that."

"I know," he said. His thick dark hair had fallen forward, making him look like a contrite little boy. "I'm doing my best, Mom, but I know I'm not making much progress."

When he looked up, she gazed into his eyes. "Do you think you'll ever get comfortable with Clancy sharing our home?"

"Ever?" he asked, shifting nervously in his chair. "Ever's a long time."

"I know it is," she said. "And I think you've answered my question." He looked at her, his expression so earnest that she felt sorry for him. "I know you're trying, honey, but I don't think this is gonna work out."

"No, no, it will!" His voice rose, and his cheeks were immediately flushed. "Don't give up, Mom, please!"

Startled, Abby stared at him. "Give up what?"

"Clancy!" He looked like he was on the verge of panic, and Abby was so surprised by his assumption that she was rendered speechless.

"It's been horrible to see what these last few years have done to you," he said, the words gushing out in a stream. "Even though you've always tried to put on a good front, I missed your sense of humor and your goofiness. It's so nice to see that come back, and I think Clancy is behind that. You can't give up on her just because of Hayley and me."

His sincerity and concern broke her heart, and she reached across the table again to grasp his hand. She gazed at him for a moment, her heart filled with love. "I'll never give her up. Never."

He cocked his head in confusion, waiting for her to continue.

"You're right. After your father died, I tried so hard to make it seem like I was okay, but I wasn't. Most days, it was hard for me to get up. If it hadn't been for you and Hayley..." She trailed off, leaving her thought unexpressed. She gave him a smile and said, "But now I feel vibrant and enthusiastic. Clancy taught me how to laugh again, how to look forward to waking up in the morning." She squeezed his hand hard, her words filled with passion. "She's given my life back to me, and I'll never, ever let her go."

"Then what...?"

She took a breath and gave him a somewhat nervous-looking smile. "Our living arrangement has to change."

He blinked; then his eyes grew wide. Abby saw how surprised he was, and for just a moment, she wavered. But then she steeled her nerves and spat it out. "I want you to be happy. God knows how much that means to me. But I don't think that's gonna happen with all of us living together. And I need to live with Clancy. I'm sorry, Trevor, but I need her."

His eyes closed, and he leaned his head back. "Thank God," he breathed.

"Thank God?"

Looking at her, he finally smiled, and she could see his whole body relax. "I've been racking my brain trying to think of a way to tell you I wanted to move out, but I didn't want you to think I was being a jerk. But you're right. It's just not gonna work out, Mom. It'd be the same if you wanted to have a man move in. I just have a hard time thinking about your being...you know...with anybody but Dad. Hell," he added, "I didn't really like to think about that, either, but at least I was used to him."

She threw her head back and laughed, and he joined her, mother and son laughing so hard that the diners at the surrounding tables shot glances at them. She covered her mouth with her napkin, trying to control herself. Finally, she wiped her eyes with the cloth and asked, "Now what do we do? How do we get from here to there? I know you don't have much money."

"Or a job," he said. "Although I've got a good lead. South Pas is supposed to get the money to hire an additional planner, and they want someone young…and cheap," he added, smiling. "I'm both!"

"I've always thought you were cheap," Abby said, smiling at him. "When is this supposed to happen?"

"They're on a calendar year–end, so they won't have the budget until January. But they're supposed to start interviewing in November."

"That's soon," she said, giving him an encouraging smile.

"Yeah, but I've already decided that I've been sitting around too long. I'm gonna start doing something. Make coffee, be a waiter, something! It's driving me nuts to just send out résumés and wait for the mail to come."

"You could always work with Clancy," Abby said, partially kidding.

His face lit up. "Really? Do you think she needs anyone? I'd love to work outside while I wait for my dream job."

"Ask her, honey. If she needs help, I'm sure she'd love to have you. She knows what a hard worker you are."

"That's one place I know I'd get a good recommendation," he agreed, smiling brightly.

"The best," she agreed. "I sing your praises to everyone who'll listen."

He smiled at her and said, "I don't doubt that a bit." Taking her hand, he said, "Don't worry. We'll get through this. If we could get through losing Dad, this'll be a snap."

❦

Clancy slept alone after bowling and was surprised to find Michael up and already working when she was ready to leave for work. "Well, if it isn't the Birdman of South Pasadena," she said when she entered the kitchen. He had newspapers spread over the kitchen table and a handmade birdhouse resting atop them.

"Hey, blondie!" He grinned back at her. "Alone today?"

"Yeah. I went bowling last night, and it didn't make sense for Abby to come over for just a few hours. Besides, she took her son out to dinner last night, and she wanted to stay home in case they got caught up in a discussion."

He raised an eyebrow. "How's that going? Is he any better than the daughter?"

"Yeah, yeah," she said. "He's a very nice kid."

"How old is this kid?" he asked, cocking his head.

"Uhm…twenty-five."

"Wow, he is a kid."

He was trying to look like he was being serious, and just to drive him crazy, she acted like she believed him. She took the paintbrush from his hand and spent a moment applying some hot-pink paint to the shutters on the birdhouse. "This one's nice," she said. "You guys selling many of them?"

"As many as my dad can make," he said. "We want to have at least two dozen of them for the craft fair in Arcadia in two weeks. You and Abby should come."

"We will," she said. "Actually, I bet she'd love one of these for the yard. She loves to sit out in the back and listen to the birds in the morning."

"You two seem awfully happy, Clance. Is the reality as true as the image?"

"Sure is," she said. "I didn't know it was possible to be this happy, Michael. She's the woman for me. No doubt."

"She must feel the same way," he said. "She looks at you like she thinks you walk on water."

"The feeling's mutual."

He gave her a long look and said, "You even look better, ya know? Heck, your clothes look better." He squinted in her direction and asked, "Creases?"

"Uhm...she does my laundry so I don't have to go to the laundromat. And she...irons my clothes."

He leaned back on the stool he was sitting on and shook his head. "She irons your clothes. You found a gorgeous, older, wealthy woman with the most beautiful house I've ever seen, and she not only loves you—she also irons your clothes."

Shrugging once again, she said, "She wants me to look nice."

He gave her a sober look and said, "If she's ironing your little dyke shorts, it must be true love. Are you ready to make this permanent?"

"Of course I am, and so is Abby, but we're kinda stuck until the kids are cool with it."

He scowled and then leaned forward to work on some of the intricate detail. "What if they never are?"

"Beats the hell out of me," Clancy said. "But they'd better come around, because I'm not letting her go. Ever." She kissed him on the head, grabbed her keys, and headed out to work.

Clancy had a very busy day and didn't have a moment to talk to Abby. On her drive back from Cucamonga, she made up for her oversight. "Hi. I know it's late, but I was swamped today. Want to go ahead and have dinner without me?"

"No, of course not! Come over right now, honey. We can eat as soon as you get here."

"Sure? I'm dirty."

"That's one of the reasons I love you," Abby said, smiling when she hung up.

Clancy was surprised to find Trevor sitting in the kitchen smiling at her when she walked into the room. "Hi," she said.

He stood up and shook her hand. "Hi. Can I get you a beer?"

"Sure," she said, puzzled but pleased to have him playing host.

He took two beers out and opened them both. "Glass?"

"Don't bother." She took the beer and sat down at the kitchen table, noting that Abby had disappeared.

Trevor sat opposite her and gave her a nervous smile. They sat there for a few moments, both uncomfortable. Finally, he spoke. "I…uhm…wanted to apologize for sneaking off nearly every time you've come over for dinner."

"That's all right," Clancy said. She took a drink and put her bottle down, the sound a little loud in the silent kitchen. "I know you've got your own life."

He made a face and took a drink. "It hasn't been that so much. It's been hard for me to be around you two."

She looked at him, a little taken aback by his candor.

"I'm gonna move out as soon as I get enough money saved up."

Her eyes shot open. "Trevor! This is your home! I don't wanna feel like I'm pushing you out!"

"No, no, really," he said. "I don't feel that way. I need to have my own place. I mean, I don't wanna see Mom with a girl, and I'm sure she feels the same about me." He laughed softly. "No guy wants to bring a girl home and have to introduce her to his mother in the morning."

Clancy laughed at his words and his expression. "Good point. I never thought of it from your point of view."

"It's time for me to get a job and an apartment. And it's time for you two to start your lives together. We'll all be happier."

She gave him a bright smile and clapped him on the shoulder. "You know, you're one of the nicest people I've ever met. Now I know why your mom's so proud of you."

He looked embarrassed and completely ignored her compliment. The door opened, and the dogs ran for Clancy. Abby came in, beaming at both of them, and Trevor sneaked a look in her direction. "Clancy and I have a lot in common, Mom. We both love the same woman."

Clancy laughed. "That's true. Sounds a little strange, but it's true."

"I think we're officially a nontraditional family," he said. "Strange is normal for us."

Abby walked over to him, and he got to his feet and hugged her, neither of them speaking. The connection between mother and son was so vibrant that Clancy could nearly feel it. Trevor sat back down, Abby standing behind him, her hand on his shoulder. Clancy gazed at them for a moment, thinking that things would be perfect if Abby and Will had wanted to have just one child.

❧

They'd nearly finished dinner when Trevor cleared his throat and said, "I'm not having much luck finding a job, Clancy. Could you use another hard-working guy?"

Clancy's eyes grew wide and darted between mother and son. "You're willing to do manual labor?"

"Sure! I'd love to work outside for a while. I've spent a lot of time sitting in classrooms. It'd be great to work with my hands before I have to spend the rest of my working life sitting in an office."

She leaned back in her chair, looking at him thoughtfully. "I don't have anything right now," she said. "But I'll see what I can dig up. How do you feel about heights?"

"Uhm…fine. Why?"

"I decorated a few houses for Christmas last year. I was thinking about doing a lot more this year. It's fairly easy work, and it helps fill out my schedule."

"Trevor's put up our lights for the last ten years," Abby said, smiling at her son. "He's a pro."

"Like I said, I'll check a few things out and get back to you," Clancy said. "I'm sure we can find something to keep you busy."

"That's what I need," he said. "I'm so sick of sitting around, I'm about to go nuts!"

"My kinda guy," Clancy said, giving him a grin.

❧

Later that night, lying next to Abby on the futon, Clancy said, "Trevor really surprised me when he asked for work. Was that his idea?"

"Well, I mentioned it, but he was very enthusiastic. He's always loved to work outside. He cut the grass from the time he was twelve until he went to college. He did a darned good job, too."

"And you're cool with that?"

"Sure," Abby said. "Why wouldn't I be?"

"Oh, I don't know. Spending a zillion dollars on his education…"

"That doesn't matter," Abby said. "All that matters is that he does something that he likes. I want him to do well at whatever it is he chooses. That's always been my fondest wish. But I don't have a doubt that my boy will be the best worker you've ever had. He's got a work ethic a mile wide."

Clancy thought for a moment, letting the words sink in. "Are you sure he and Hayley are related?"

"Funny," Abby said, pinching her partner. "One day my girl's gonna grow up, and you're gonna be amazed at what a good kid she is."

"I can't wait," Clancy said with utter sincerity.

❧

The next day, Clancy had been gone only about an hour when she called Abby from her cell phone. "Hi. Against my better judgment, I'm keeping a promise to call you."

"What? I don't have the faintest idea what you're talking about."

"I'm gonna trim a pretty big tree, and I'm following through like I said I would."

Abby gulped, her stomach doing a flip while she tried to get some moisture back into her mouth. "How big?" she finally got out.

Clancy paused and then quietly said, "It's really big, Abby. I'm not worried in the least, and I'm going to wear a safety belt, but it's big."

"Big like my live oak?" Abby asked, hoping against hope that Clancy was overstating the size.

"Uhm…no, it's twice that height. It's a really big, really old eucalyptus."

Trying to slow the rapid beating of her heart, Abby asked, "It's not a widowmaker, is it?"

"Well, I don't like to use that term, but it is a globulus."

"What are you going to do to it?" Abby asked, her voice shaking with fear. "Do you have to go all the way up?"

"Well, yeah," Clancy said, puzzled by her partner's demeanor. "People don't really want you to just trim the bottom."

"Can you wait until I get there?"

"What?"

"I want to be there," Abby said. "Please don't climb it alone."

"Honey, I'm not alone. My crew's with me."

"Why can't someone else do it?"

"Because I'm better trained," Clancy said. "This tree isn't called a widowmaker because it's big. It kills people because the branches get too heavy and break off during a good storm. I've been trimming this big girl for three years now, and it's in great shape. But the homeowner is waiting for me, and I've got to get to work. I can't wait for you, Abby, and given how you sound, it's not a good idea for you to watch me climb."

"I'm so worried about you, I'm sick to my stomach," Abby whispered. "Please don't do this."

"Baby, this is my job," Clancy soothed. "I don't know why you're so upset, but I have to do my job."

"Call me the second you get down. The very second."

"I promise. You can trust me."

"Okay." She swallowed and said, "I love you, Clancy. More than you'll ever know."

"Honey, calm down, and try to think about the facts. This is just another job for me. Don't make it sound like I'm jumping off a cliff. I'm careful—not just to make you feel better, but for myself. I like to climb, but I really hate to fall. The ground is remarkably hard."

"Please don't tease," Abby whispered. "There's nothing funny about this for me."

Grimacing, Clancy said, "I'm sorry, sweetheart. I'm not making light of this. I was just trying to…Oh, I don't know what I was trying to do, but it obviously didn't work."

"Go to work," Abby said. "Let's get it over with."

"Okay. I'll be careful."

"Call me," Abby said softly and then went outside to work in the yard, just to take her mind off her anxiety.

Working in the garden didn't help a bit. She did some heavy lifting, trying to stress her body to divert some of her emotional turmoil. Using all of her control, she stopped herself from calling Clancy, knowing that she wasn't in a position to answer her phone—if she even had it on her.

A half-hour passed, then an hour, each minute ticking by at an evolutionary pace. At an hour and twenty minutes, Abby was preparing herself for the worst, knowing that the next call would be from the hospital. Her mind raced, obsessing about the call, when she realized that Clancy probably didn't have her listed as a contact person on her health insurance. She was sitting by the phone in the kitchen, both dogs at her feet, knowing their owner was upset, when the phone finally rang over an hour and a half after they'd last spoken. "Hello?" she asked, her whole body trembling.

"Hi," Clancy said, slightly out of breath. "Sorry that took so long, but it was a monster." She paused, waited another beat, and then asked, "Abby?"

"This isn't working," she said, her emotions spurting out of her. "I have to go." She blindly jammed the phone onto the cradle and went up to her room, falling face first onto the bed. She cried until she had no more tears to shed, her body limp, her mind exhausted.

As soon as Clancy finished supervising the crew in removing and chipping up the detritus from the big tree, she shook hands with the hypervigilant homeowner and got into her truck. She dialed Abby immediately, and her lover picked it up only to say, "We can't talk about this on the phone. I'm having an emotional meltdown."

"I'll come home. Be there as soon as I can."

"*No!*" The sound of her own voice surprised her, but Abby insisted, "No, I don't want you to have to come home from work to take care of me. I know I'm being ridiculous. Don't give into my lunacy."

"Abby," she said softly, "I'd do anything to help you feel better. If I can help in any way, I'd really like to come over."

"No," she said. "That'll make me feel worse. I don't want to be a burden. I'll get over this."

Clancy sighed heavily and then said, "I love you. You know that, right?"

"I do. See you tonight." After she hung up, she stayed in bed, the dogs beside her, while she tried to collect her thoughts sufficiently to explain herself to her partner.

Clancy was sitting in her truck when Abby pulled into the driveway. She got out and walked through the open gate, going into the garage to meet Abby. "Where've you been? I've been worried about you. You didn't answer your cell."

"Oh, shit! I left it in the house when I was working in the yard. I obviously didn't put it into my purse when I went to my mom's."

"Did you just go to hang out?"

"Yeah. Sometimes I need my mom to kiss it and make it all better."

"Oh, Abby," Clancy murmured, taking her in her arms. "I'm so sorry you're having such a tough time with this."

"I am having a tough time today." She walked into the house and Clancy followed, both women being greeted by their canine companions. Abby went to the refrigerator and pulled out a bottle of wine. "Join me?"

"No, thanks," Clancy said. She sat down at the table and waited for Abby to sit. "Trevor around?"

"No. He's with Sam. They went down to Baja to surf. He won't be home until late tomorrow night."

"I've got an idea," Clancy said. "Why don't we see if we both fit in that nice spa tub you've got in your bathroom?"

"Really? I'd like that. It might help me relax a little."

"It's a deal. I'll call for some Chinese food. We can see if we can feed each other with chopsticks in the tub."

"Sounds great." She enveloped Clancy in a warm hug and held on for a long time. "I'll go fill the tub."

They were settled in the generously sized tub, with Clancy carefully feeding Abby pieces of spicy, garlicky shrimp. "That's truly delicious," Abby said, leaning forward to kiss her partner and suck some of the sauce from the corner of her mouth. "So are you."

They'd had about all they could manage, so Clancy got up, placed the tray on the vanity, and then settled back into the warm water. Abby turned on the jets, and she snuggled up between Clancy's spread legs and let the powerful pulse of the water soothe her. "I have to share something with you," she said.

Clancy felt her lover's body grow tense. "What is it, baby?"

"I haven't told you about the day Will died."

Her statement was so unexpected that Clancy almost asked her what she was talking about, but she moved her head just enough to see the soulless expression on her lover's face, and she realized this was vitally important to Abby. She didn't say a word; she just began to run her fingertips down Abby's arms in the most calming fashion she could manage.

"He'd been out of town for over a week," Abby said, her tone relatively unanimated. "He'd been in Australia on business, and he'd had very little sleep. His body clock was all messed up, and even though we'd been in bed together all night, I don't think he slept a wink. He was really agitated—way too much coffee on the plane, I think—and when I woke up, he was ready to burn off some energy." She sighed heavily, and just a hint of emotion started to return to her voice. "We made love for a very long time. We were more rambunctious than we'd been in a while— we'd missed each other—and like I said, he was very keyed up. When we finally collapsed, I felt like I'd run the marathon, but he was hopping out of bed, ready to go."

Clancy leaned forward, kissed her neck, and then tucked an arm under her breasts to hold her tightly, knowing what was to come.

"He wanted to go running, and even though I always went with him, I couldn't even think of it." She laughed softly and said, "He was pretty proud of himself when he left. He loved to drain every ounce of energy out of me."

Abby took in another deep breath and let it out slowly. "I got up and showered and then made breakfast for us. He had a set route, and it always took him forty-five minutes," she said. "You could set your watch by him. When he wasn't home after an hour, I started to worry, and after an hour and fifteen minutes, I knew something was wrong. I got in the car and started for the Rose Bowl, and about halfway there, I saw an ambulance pulled over to the curb. They were putting a body on a gurney, and I knew—somehow, I knew—that it was Will. I flew out of the car, and just as I got there, I saw that they'd pulled the sheet up over his face." She turned and curled into a fetal position, unable to speak, crying piteously while Clancy rocked her in her arms, her own tears falling onto the salt-and-pepper hair.

Abby finally collected herself enough to speak again, murmuring, "Today I felt like you might need me—like I could save you—if only I were with you."

"Oh, Abby," Clancy sobbed. "You poor, poor baby." She held her tenderly, caressing her with the gentlest touch. "Do you think that you could have saved him if you'd been with him?"

"I don't know," she said. "I truly don't know if I could have. One of the doctors said that CPR might have kept him alive; another said even the machine that shocks the heart into rhythm wouldn't have helped. All I know is that I wasn't there…and I should have been. At least I could have held him in my arms when he died."

"I understand," Clancy whispered. "I really understand."

Abby turned to make eye contact and said, "Do you understand why I was so frantic today? It felt like the whole nightmare was going to happen again."

"I do," she said. "I can see what happened." She wrapped Abby into an even tighter hug and quietly said, "That's why I'm not going to call you again when I climb."

"What?"

"You heard me. This is a setup. Doing it this way will make you crazy. I can't do that to you." She kissed her head and said, "I don't climb that often, and I'll ask Ramon to do more when he can, but I will occasionally have to trim a tree. I promise to be as careful as humanly possible; I'll wear a safety belt even for small trees; but I won't help you drive yourself nuts over it."

"That's what my mom said to do," Abby said quietly. "She says that what I don't know won't hurt me."

"Your mom is right. I plan on being by your side for at least fifty years, remember? There's no way I'm going to miss out on *that* party!"

Abby nodded slowly, turned, and gave Clancy a small kiss. "I remember. I'm holding you to that promise, you know."

"The same goes for me," Clancy said, placing a tender kiss on her lips and tucking her back into her arms. "Just for the record, it's getting too late in the year to trim most trees. So put it out of your mind until spring, okay?"

"Okay." Abby sighed. "Thanks. For everything—but mostly for understanding."

After their bath, they went into the guest bedroom and settled down between the cool, soft sheets. Clancy put her arm out, and Abby nestled up next to her, resting her head on her shoulder. "You've been quiet since I talked about Will. Everything okay?"

"Uh-huh," Clancy said. "Just thinking."

Abby tilted her head so she could see her face. "Thinking about what?"

"About you and Will. Your marriage."

"What?" Abby sat up, leaning on her elbow, looking puzzled. "What about my marriage?"

Clancy shrugged, obviously not in a hurry to talk. Abby lay back down, knowing how she hated to be pressed and thinking that Clancy might feel the same. She put her hand on her lover's belly and let it rest there.

It took a long time, the minutes passing in silence, but Clancy finally started to open up. "Sometimes it's hard to be second."

"Second? Second…how?"

Turning onto her side, dislodging Abby, Clancy looked at her for a moment. "Being your second love."

Abby didn't say a word, knowing that Clancy wasn't finished. She just looked into her eyes, trying to make her partner feel safe enough to share her thoughts.

"I'm so glad you loved Will. I hope you believe that."

"I do."

"But sometimes it's hard to be second when the first was so awesome. I mean…" She sat up and hugged her knees. "I don't really feel like I'm competing with Will, but sometimes it feels like there's a…I don't know…like a standard we have to meet. You know…like I'm being judged."

"Judged by whom?" Abby asked after Clancy grew silent again.

The blonde turned and looked at her. "By you. By Trevor and Hayley. By your parents. By your friends. By everyone who knew you as a couple." Her whole body shook, and she lay back down, looking tired.

Abby leaned over her, her face filled with concern. "Honey, I had no idea you felt like that."

"I don't," Clancy said. "I mean, I don't all of the time. Just when you talk about him and I can see how deeply you loved him. How perfect you were for each other."

Abby touched her cheek, moving her head a little so they were gazing into each other's eyes. "Is that what you think?"

"What?"

"That we were perfect for each other. That we had some sort of perfect relationship."

Clancy blinked slowly, then nodded. "Yeah. I do."

Abby dropped to the bed, her body making a loud thunk. "Oh, Clancy, I'm so sorry I've given you that impression. It's just not true, honey. Not true at all."

"What?" Now Clancy leaned over her lover, entirely puzzled. "What do you mean?"

"I mean that we were just a couple like any couple. We had as many problems as anyone else. Hell, there were times I wished I'd never met him!"

"What? Are you serious?"

"Of course I am." Abby pulled her down for a long kiss. "I'm sure there will be times I wish I'd never met you." She was smiling, but Clancy was at a complete loss.

"How can you say that?"

"I can say that because I've been deeply in love," Abby said. "The song is right, baby, it's a thin line between love and hate. There were plenty of times I wanted to hit him with a baseball bat and get as far away from him as possible!"

"But you've never, ever said anything like that."

Abby didn't say anything for a while, giving the issue the thought it deserved. Finally, she turned her head and gazed at her partner. "You don't think about the bad times when your lover dies. If he was a good man, and you had a good relationship, you just think about the good parts. You don't really do it on purpose. It just happens."

"You don't...you really don't compare us?"

"You and Will?" Abby laughed, "God, no! I told you before, you're not comparable. Being with him and being with you are two completely different experiences. I was looking for different things when I met him. I'm not sure I'd choose him if I met him today."

Dumbfounded, Clancy gasped, "You can't be serious!"

"I don't wanna go into everything that happened between us," Abby said. "It's too private. But he was a very good man for me when I was nineteen. He was a very good husband and a very good father. But if I had to start all over at forty-five, I don't think I would have picked someone like him."

Clancy sat up again and looked Abby right in the eye. "You've gotta give me something. I don't wanna pry, but you've gotta tell me at least one thing that would turn you off."

Abby reached up and brushed the hair from Clancy's forehead. Clancy looked so intent, so determined, that Abby knew she had to answer her. She took in a breath and chose the first thing that came to mind. "He had always been the boss," she said. "That was fine. I wanted someone to be in charge when I was a kid. But after being alone for five years, I've grown used to making my own decisions. I couldn't have picked someone who had to be the boss. And Will *had* to be the boss. I got to vote, but his vote counted more than mine did."

"Didn't that bother you when he was alive?" Clancy asked, unable to see Abby buckling under for anyone.

"Not a lot," she said airily. "No one gets everything she wants in a lover. I bet there were thirty things Will would have changed about me if he could have. We just made the best of each other's faults and limitations. That's what you do."

"Do I have faults and limitations?" Clancy asked, her sincerity making Abby hide a laugh.

"Yes, honey, you do."

"You don't have any," Clancy said. "I swear!"

Abby wrapped her arms around her and pulled her down. She kissed her soundly and then nibbled on her lips as she pulled away. "I guarantee that you won't say that if I ask you in a year. It takes a while to become a realist when you fall in love for the first time."

Clancy kissed her back, pressing her body into her partner's. "If we're together for a thousand years, I won't want to change one thing about you," she said with utter sincerity.

"I love you," Abby said, smiling at her lover's earnest face. "Every delusional part of you."

On the first of October, Clancy called the Graham household, pleased to have Trevor answer. "Hi," she said. "It's Clancy. I've got good news and bad news."

"For me?" Trevor asked, confused.

"Not really. Bad news about another guy, and good news for you."

"Hmm," he mused, laughing. "I guess I should be generous and ask about the bad news."

"Just like your mom," Clancy said. "A good-hearted soul."

"But not as patient."

"Gotcha. The bad news is that one of my dad's guys got his arm caught in the rigging when they were dropping a fiberglass pool into place. Broke it in two places."

"Ow! Is he gonna be all right?"

"Yeah. But he had to have surgery. He's gonna be out at least three months."

"I'm getting the impression that I'm gonna be installing pools for a while," Trevor said. "Does it matter that I don't know a darned thing about it?"

"Nope. To be honest, what my dad needs is a guy with a strong body and the ability to follow orders."

"I'm his man!" Trevor said, obviously delighted. "When do I start?"

"How about seven a.m.?"

"Great! I'm really excited, Clancy. And I can't thank you enough for thinking of me. Where do I go?"

"They're working in Altadena. Just south of the golf course. The house is on the corner of New York Avenue and Sierra Bonita."

There was a slight pause. Then Trevor said, "Got it. Give me your dad's number so I can call and see if I should bring any tools or gear."

"It's 818-555-1908. His name's John, in case you've forgotten."

"I'm good with names," Trevor said. "Your mom is Margaret, and your grandmother is Eileen."

"What's our dog's name?" she asked, laughing.

"Uhm…I don't think you have a dog."

"You *are* good."

"Thanks again, Clancy. And I'm gonna take you out to dinner as a finder's fee."

"It's a deal. Hey, don't you wanna know how much you'll be making?"

He laughed. "More than I'm making sitting on my ass."

"No, really, don't you want to know?"

"Nuh-uh. I wanna be surprised when I get my first paycheck. Kinda like Christmas."

She laughed, charmed by how like his mother Trevor was. "Okay. Well, I hope you have a merry Christmas, and I'll be waiting for that dinner."

"Depending on how much I make, it'll be somewhere between the Ritz and In-N-Out."

"I've never been to the Ritz, but I love a good double-double," she said. "So I'll be happy wherever we go."

"Thanks again. It's nice to have someone in the family who can get me a job where I can breathe fresh air."

"And plaster dust."

He laughed, a little nervous about what he was getting into. "And plaster dust."

❦

Clancy called Abby the next afternoon. "Hi. I'm finished for the day. Do you need me to pick anything up on my way over?"

"Yeah. How about my son?"

"Your son, huh? You didn't give the poor kid your car?"

"I played golf this morning, so I dropped him off. He looked so cute, Clancy, like a kid on his first day of school. I made lunch for him, and I nearly cried when he walked away from the car, his little lunchbox in his hand."

"He didn't have Harry Potter on his lunchbox, did he? 'Cause the other guys might have beaten him with it."

"No," Abby said, laughing. "It was a nice, plain, maroon, nylon insulated thing."

"I hope you made him a big lunch. I know he worked hard today. It was the first day on this job, and that's always a lot of manual labor."

"I made him three sandwiches and put in a couple of energy bars. That should hold him."

"No candy?"

"No, but I can stop at the store and get some. I didn't have time to prepare."

"I'll run by and get him. Need anything else?"

"No. I would go, but I'm making his favorite dish for dinner, and I can't leave in the middle of it."

"Okay. We'll be home soon."

"Give your dad a kiss for me," Abby said.

"He can kiss my mom," Clancy said, laughing.

❦

Trevor was such a dirty mess that he didn't even attempt to go into the house. He went into the back yard and stripped down to his boxer shorts and T-shirt; then he ran into the house, heading straight for the shower.

"My God, what happened to my baby?" Abby cried.

"He spent the whole day loading and dumping wheelbarrows full of dirt," Clancy said. "Or I guess I should say mud, since we've had so much rain lately. He's gonna be sore tomorrow."

"Oh, poor thing. He should sit in the spa for a while."

"You read my mind," Trevor said, giving his mother a kiss on the cheek. He had his swim trunks on and a towel over his shoulder. "I'm gonna soak until dinner." He opened the refrigerator and took out a beer. "Want one, Clancy?"

"Sure." She took the beer and clinked the neck of her bottle against Trevor's. "Blue-collar champagne."

He took a swig and let his head drop back. "Champagne never tasted this good."

"Did you have a good day, honey?" Abby asked.

"Yeah. It felt great to accomplish something. And when I get in, I'll tell you about the job. It's gonna be fantastic!" With a wide, satisfied smile he went outside, both dogs dutifully following him.

Abby shrugged her shoulders. "Well, it's not urban planning, but he seems happy."

"Yard planning, urban planning—same difference," Clancy said, sneaking a kiss.

🌿

That night in bed, Abby said, "Your birthday's in just a couple of weeks, Clancy. Are you ready to start planning the party to end all parties?"

The blonde smiled at her. "You remembered."

"Sure I remembered. It's one of the first personal things you ever told me. Shouldn't we start making up the guest list?"

Giving her a pleased smile, she asked, "Do you really wanna help?"

"Of course! I thought we'd have it here, since I have more room."

Another happy, yet bemused smile settled on the landscaper's face. "Are you serious?"

Abby took her hand and kissed it. "Of course I'm serious. How often does my partner turn thirty? We're gonna blow out all the stops!"

"Cool," Clancy said, looking like a kid who'd been given an unexpected present. "How many people should we invite?"

"As many as you want. They just have to fit in the house or the yard."

Clancy's eyes lit up. "Cool...really cool."

🌿

Much to Abby's surprise, Clancy wanted to invite Hayley. She didn't send invitations to her friends, preferring to invite everyone she ran into, but she bought some invitations for "the adults," as she called them. So Abby's parents, Pam and Maria, and Hayley all received proper invitations. A few days after they went out, Hayley called home, sounding chipper and unguarded. "Hi, Mom," she said. "I'm calling to respond to the birthday-party invite."

"Are you coming?" Abby asked, caught off guard.

"Yeah. Alexander thinks I should."

"Alexander?"

"Yeah. He thinks I should come home and try to be nice to Clancy. He doesn't understand why I'm not crazy about your relationship."

"Oh, really? Is he coming with you?"

"No. I wanted him to, but he thinks I should come alone."

"Sounds like he's in charge," Abby said, laughing.

"You know how guys are. He's...sure of himself."

"I'm glad he wants you to be close to your family."

"Oh, he's a typical Bay Area liberal," Hayley said dismissively. "He loves anybody who's different."

"Then he should love us," Abby said, containing a laugh. "We could be on a daytime talk show."

❧

Later that day, Abby called her mother. "Hi. Guess who's coming home for Clancy's birthday?"

"Really? That's quite a conciliatory move for our girl. She must be feeling better."

"She didn't sound much better. She's seeing that young man she met in Maine, and he thinks it's cool that I'm in a lesbian relationship. Hayley's coming because he wants her to."

"Well, that should prove interesting. At least she'll be motivated to be nice."

❧

The day before the party, the guest list had grown to just over a hundred, but Abby didn't mind a bit. She would have gladly hosted a party for all of Pasadena if it made Clancy happy, and it certainly did seem that her partner was enjoying the entire experience.

Clancy had a light day—just a client meeting in Monrovia and a trip to Pasadena City Hall to check on a building permit she was waiting on. She got to Abby's home a little after one, hoping to grab some lunch and then help with final preparations for the party.

The garage door opened, and Abby started to walk two men to a truck labeled Parsagian and Sons, Fine Rugs. She stopped to give Clancy a faux scowl. "I don't remember giving you permission to come over this early, sweetheart."

The men both gave Clancy a look and then shot another one at Abby, obviously trying to figure out why the young woman would need permission to enter the house. "Thanks so much for your help," Abby said, smiling at them. "I'm very happy with it."

"Any time," the driver said, pulling away.

Clancy tucked an arm around Abby's waist and asked, "So now I need permission to come home? What happened to the woman who used to count the hours until I was back in her arms again?"

"She's right here," Abby said. "I just have some things I'm working on that are...private."

"Private, huh?" Clancy asked, as two black-and-white fireballs launched themselves at her. Athena jumped so high that she landed in Clancy's arms—and at fifty pounds, it was all the muscular landscaper could do to keep her feet. "Good Lord!"

"They missed you," Abby said. "You don't normally come over this early, and they're quite excited about it."

"I should say so!"

When they entered the kitchen, Abby said, "Now you've got to make a decision. Your present is ready, but your birthday isn't until tomorrow. Do you want it now, or should I make you wait?"

Clancy fought her way past the giddy dogs and wrapped Abby in a tight hug, pressing her back against the counter. "Oh, you're not that cruel. Only an evil woman would tease me that way."

Smiling seductively, Abby said, "Maybe you could make it worth my while…"

"How would I do that?"

"Well, there's a part of your present that could…potentially…involve lying next to each other. And…clothing would be optional."

"Optional? No such thing. If you don't have to have clothes on, I want you naked."

"Hmm…good answer. I guess that would be some compensation for letting you peek a day early." She took Clancy's hand and said, "But you'd better not disappoint me."

Impulsively, Clancy wrapped a strong arm around Abby's waist and dipped her, leaning over her to kiss her enthusiastically. "Have I ever?"

"Never," Abby sighed. "And I doubt that you ever will."

"Then we're in agreement." Grinning rakishly, she settled Abby on her feet and asked, "I don't have any idea of what this present is, but I'm ready for it. Shall we?"

Abby grabbed a cloth napkin from the counter and twirled it until it was narrow and long. She placed it over Clancy's eyes and tied it loosely. "The last time I had on one of these, I had a very, very nice morning. Let's rock."

"This isn't necessarily that kind of event," Abby said. "But it could be."

"I'm stumped."

"Then let's get going." She stood in front of her partner with her back to her and put Clancy's hands on her waist. "Follow me, but be careful not to trip."

"Trip? Where are we going that I'd trip?" They walked through the kitchen and then started to climb the stairs. "Smells like paint."

"Yeah. There's paint involved." Finally, they reached Abby's bedroom, their furry escorts well behaved, seeming to know that Clancy couldn't avoid tripping over them. Abby removed the blindfold and said, "Surprise!"

Clancy blinked to find an enormous red ribbon that Abby had wrapped around the door, a big bow right in the center. "It's a…room!"

"Ready?" Abby asked, her excitement at the level of a four-year-old on Christmas morning.

"I'm always ready," Clancy reminded her playfully. Abby flung the door open, and Clancy took one step inside before she was struck mute. Her eyes were remarkably wide as they slowly shifted across the space, and she finally regained her ability to speak. "Holy crap!"

"Do you like it?" Abby was practically jumping up and down, but Clancy could only nod vacantly, still too stunned to speak in complete sentences.

"How…where…is…Jesus," she muttered, still staring open-mouthed. "What is it?"

"It's our new guest room and office!"

Clancy turned and stared at her, her mouth open wide enough to indicate a serious sinus problem. "Our?" she managed to get out.

The brunette grabbed her hand and jumped up and down a few times. "Yes! Ours! This is our guest room and our office!"

Clancy was so overwhelmed by the implications of that sentence that her practical mind took over. "There's no bed. Won't people mind sleeping on a drafting table?"

"Oh, ye of little faith," she scoffed. "Don't worry; it's a guest room. But before we get to that, I have to know what you think about the feel of the room. Will you be able to work here?"

"I think this is the most beautiful space I've ever been in," she said with utter sincerity. "But I don't know why it's mine…or ours…or whatever."

Abby took her hands and pressed them against her heart. "For your birthday, I wanted to give you an office where you could have lots of space and storage for all of your things. I've seen how you've got your drawing supplies all over your apartment, and you don't have any place to leave your work undisturbed. So…here it is!" They both looked into the room, Clancy still not able to get her bearings. "But that means you have to move in with me. Are you ready?"

"Hell, yes, I'm ready. But Trevor isn't."

"Now that he has a job, he is. He's ready to move out as soon as you move in."

"You're shitting me," Clancy said, stunned.

"Nope. I'm totally serious. Actually, half of your things are already here. Michael gave me the key to your apartment, and I had a moving company box up all of your drawing and drafting supplies this morning. Believe me, getting all of your stuff out of there and in here was no mean feat!"

"You did this all for me?" Clancy asked, amazed and dumbfounded.

"I'd do this for you twice a day if it would make you happy. Trevor's saved enough to move out, but he won't have a car. So I'm going to buy him a car or a small truck as a graduation present. He's set." She put her arms around Clancy and held her close. "And so are we."

Holding on for a long while, Clancy started to let everything sink in. "I can't believe this," she murmured, her warm breath caressing Abby's neck. "I can't believe how much work you went to for me."

"For us."

"You did this for me," Clancy insisted. "You could have done this years ago if you wanted an upstairs office. But you did this for me—so I'd feel like this was my home, too. You knew I'd never feel right sleeping in your old room." Tears formed in her eyes, and she rubbed her face against Abby's shoulder, a little embarrassed to show her how touched she was. "No one has ever loved me like this. And I don't mean the amount of money you spent—even though it had to have been a shitload!"

"Charming expression," Abby said, pinching her on the waist. "I don't know how you made it to thirty without dozens of women falling for you, but I'm glad I'm the first to ever make you feel really loved."

Clancy looked into her eyes, showing how deeply touched she was. She looked so vulnerable that Abby started to kiss and touch her gently, trying to make her feel safe again. "Now look around and check the place out," she said once she could tell her lover had her equilibrium back. Clancy walked over to the wall and touched the gorgeous wall covering, looking at Abby in amazement. "This feels like dried grass."

"It's grass cloth. I wanted it to remind you of your job." The grass cloth was the color of spring shoots on a ficus, and it had a sheen that made it appear to be raw silk rather than the harsh-feeling material that it really was. It covered every unbroken wall surface, and Clancy noted that one formerly unbroken wall now contained two sets of painted drawers, spaced about six feet apart.

"What's this?"

"Those are chests for the guests," Abby explained. She touched two panels that had been completely hidden by the expertly applied grass cloth, and two wide doors swung open. Smiling at her partner, Abby grasped a handle and pulled down a beautiful new queen-size bed. On either side of the bed were hanging rods for clothes, as well as the painted drawers.

"Amazing," Clancy murmured. The wall-to-wall carpet had been taken out and replaced by a wide-planked maple floor, and in the middle of the room lay a dark, leaf-green carpet. The border of the piece was, to Clancy's amazement, a stunningly accurate representation of her ivy tattoo, the intricate pattern curling all around the border. "Where did you ever find a carpet like this?"

"I had it made," Abby said. "It's really quite simple now that carpets like this are made with computers." She grasped Clancy's arm and pushed her sleeve up a little. "Not bad, if I do say so myself."

"Abby, I'm absolutely stunned. I'm truly speechless!"

"Do you like this space for your drawing table?" The table was resting on far edge of the carpet, allowing Clancy's tall chair to roll on the smooth wooden floor. It faced the center of the room with the big window behind it, securing plenty of natural light for the architect. Under the window, Abby had installed a wide window seat, flanked by deep bookshelves, one side filled with all of Clancy's books and magazines.

"Michael helped by telling me what was important and what was just clutter," Abby revealed when Clancy gave her another stunned look. The other side was filled with Abby's books, photos and family keepsakes, much as the room had been decorated when it was a bedroom.

Opposite Clancy's desk was a small writing table that now was the home of Abby's laptop, along with a comfortable, upholstered desk chair. "I love being officemates," Clancy said, looking up into Abby's eyes.

"I'm very quiet, and I don't chew gum or make any rude noises," Abby promised.

"I'm just not sure how much work we'll get done with that cushy-looking bed right there."

"Oh, the novelty will wear off...in ten years or so."

There were a number of beautifully framed botanical prints located at intervals throughout the room, and Clancy spent a moment reflecting on each one. "Damn, Abby, I'm just amazed at how much thought you put into this room. This is a plant lover's dream room."

"It does have a very tranquil feeling, doesn't it? But since I love plants, too, it was certainly no sacrifice on my part. This is the office I've always wanted. Now it's someplace for us to enjoy together."

"I like the sound of that. Everything is better when we do it together." She was tugging on Abby's hand, a sexy grin on her face, drawing her inexorably closer to the new bed. "There are a lot of things we do really, really well together," she purred, her voice filled with promise.

Abby placed a hand on her cheek and whispered, "Don't worry your pretty little head about that. We'll make that bed rock—as soon as you see the rest of your new room."

"There's more?" she asked blankly, her insistent libido hampering her ability to focus.

"Of course there's more. Do you see any place for your supplies?"

"Uhm...no, but I'm sure as hell not gonna complain. I'll keep everything in shoeboxes and stack 'em under my table."

"All of them are in the closet," Abby said. "And you're gonna be very impressed with the storage solutions Michael helped me think up."

Abby was tugging her by the hand, but the landscaper didn't move. "When do we have to pick Trevor up?"

Puzzled, Abby said, "Not until five at the earliest." She looked toward the closet. "Don't you wanna see the rest?"

"We don't have time. We're gonna have to rush as it is." Clancy grinned when Abby looked at her watch, seeing that it was barely 1:45.

Trailing her finger down the placket of Clancy's shirt, Abby gave her a sexy smile and asked, "Do you have...plans?"

"Sure do," Clancy said. "We're gonna christen that new bed."

Abby draped her arms around her lover's neck and leaned back, smiling at her. "Oh, are we?"

"Sure are." Without warning, Clancy swept her up in her arms, walking toward the new bed, Abby giggling as they went. She gently deposited her partner and then started to remove her clothes, her fingers nearly a blur as she worked at the buttons on her shirt.

"Slow down, sweetheart. We're not in a rush." Abby reached up and grasped Clancy's hands, stilling them.

"Maybe you're not," Clancy said, "but I've just discovered that huge presents make me hot."

Abby wrapped her arms around Clancy's waist, hugging her tight. "You're so damned adorable."

"And you're so damned dressed." Clancy wriggled out of the hug and started on Abby's clothing, her brows knit together in concentration.

Stroking her tanned arm, Abby asked, "Are you really in a huge hurry?"

Clancy nodded and then slipped Abby's shirt over her head. "I think I would have come over early even if I was busy. I've been thinking about you all day, and I'm ready to rock."

Her pupils were dilated, and Abby could see them get a little bigger when Clancy slipped her callused hands around and unhooked Abby's bra, cupping her breasts in her hands. "Mmm…just what I needed."

"Honey, slow down. Let me undress you."

Clancy looked down and saw that her shirt was half-unbuttoned, partially tucked into her pants, and that she was still wearing her boots. She made a silly face and said, "I'm out of my mind. Just the thought of making love to you makes me crazy."

"Stand still, sweetheart," Abby said. She methodically undressed Clancy and then stood up and took the rest of her own clothes off. Clancy was already lying on the new bed, looking like she'd been waiting for hours.

Abby settled in next to her, sliding across the crisp new sheets. "Now give me a nice, slow, sexy kiss," she said, pulling Clancy close.

The architect tried her best, but the kiss was hungry, filled with need, and a little rough. Abby felt like she was about to be eaten alive, and she tried to squirm away, only to have Clancy grasp both of her breasts and hang on tight.

Surprised, Abby broke the kiss. "Baby, I've been working on the room all day. I need a little romance. You've gotta give me a chance to catch up."

Clancy fell back onto the bed. "Shit! I'm sorry," she said. "I was fantasizing about you the whole way home, and I'm about to burst." She shook her head roughly. "I'll try to calm down and take it easy."

"No, no, I think we can work this out. Hmm…what can we do to satisfy you?" Tapping her lip with a finger, she mulled over the question for a moment. Then her eyes lit up as she said, "I know." She snuggled closer and whispered into Clancy's ear, "Since you can't wait another second, why don't you start, and I'll watch? Then I can jump in when I'm ready."

Gray eyes shifted to meet Abby's, seeing the playful grin and interested expression. "Would you like that?" she drawled sexily.

Abby nodded slowly, her grin growing brighter. "You've never shown me how you touch yourself. I want to know." Her smile faltered just a bit as she added, "That won't bother you, will it?"

"Heck, no," Clancy said, laughing. "One condition. I'll show you how I do it, but you have to come inside when I need it. You get to all sorts of interesting spots that I can't seem to reach."

"You're on," Abby said, her eyes filled with interest.

Clancy tossed a few pillows against the headboard and scooted up against them. Clearing her throat, she extended her hands and showily stretched her fingers, like a pianist warming up. "Okay," she began, "I'm gonna act like I'm starting from ground zero, even though I most definitely am not. But I want you to have the full experience of how I sweep myself off my feet."

Laughing at her display, Abby rolled onto her stomach, resting her chin on her braced hands. "This is fun."

"I should hope so. Sex has to be fun—even when you're just entertaining yourself." She stretched one more time, fluffed her pillows until they were just so, settled down, and took a few deep breaths to center herself. "I have to get into the right mood. Touching-myself mood is different from being-touched mood." She closed her eyes and let herself relax for a moment, trying to forget that Abby was watching her. Quickly realizing that wasn't going to work, Clancy decided to involve her partner by providing commentary.

Her eyes locked on Abby as she started to run her hands up and down her body, letting them lightly tickle across the expanse of pink and tanned flesh. "I usually touch myself all over. Just to sensitize my skin."

Even though the demonstration had only been going on for a few minutes, Abby could already feel the pulsing begin between her legs. She shifted slightly, trying to put a little pressure on her vulva, finally settling on just pressing her thighs together firmly.

Clancy didn't touch herself perfunctorily. Her hands continued to roam for many minutes, loving herself thoroughly, her eyes half-closed in pleasure. Abby's eyes were locked on her darting hands, watching the muscles and tendons flex under her tanned skin. "I always play with my breasts," she said, laughing softly. "No surprise there, huh?" Her agile fingers found her nipples, tweaking the firm points playfully; then she slipped her index finger into the ring and gave it a few strong tugs, growling when the pleasure-filled pain hit her. Then her hands cupped each breast in a surprisingly tender embrace, hefting them in her hands for a moment before she began to palpate the flesh. A low purr slid from her lips, and Abby's toes curled at the sound, the pounding between her legs growing stronger with each breath.

One of Clancy's hands insistently tugged at her nipple, and the other slid down her belly. Her smile grew sexier with each inch of her journey. Her fingers lightly brushed against her curls, her hips swaying in tandem with her hand. Suddenly, her fingers stilled, and she removed her hand from her breast and flung her arm up. Panting lightly, forearm draped languidly over her head, she gazed at Abby with a smolderingly hot look and whispered, "It makes me so hot to touch myself with you watching. I can feel how much you want to touch me, and knowing that you're struggling against the urge just makes it hotter."

Abby didn't—couldn't—say a word. She wanted to touch her partner so badly that she could taste it—could taste her—but she controlled herself, partly because it turned Clancy on to watch her resist. The thrumming between her legs had grown to a pounding need, and all she could do to satisfy it was rub her thighs together.

Seeing her partner struggle was driving Clancy's arousal, and she mercilessly tried to drive Abby to distraction. She lifted one leg, her heady scent wafting up to make Abby's mouth water. Lightly, she began running just the tips of her fingers along the back of her thigh, occasionally tickling just the edge of her dewy curls. "This is my favorite time," she murmured throatily. "Just before I slip my fingers into my wetness." Licking her lips, she once again met Abby's gaze and said, "I know it's gonna be great. It's gonna feel so damned hot…but I wait as long as I can stand it—just to make it last." Locking eyes, she pressed her fingers hard against the outside of her lips, starting at the crease of her thigh and working inward. "I've got to have some pressure against my clit, but I don't want to actually touch it yet. This helps take the edge off," she rasped, her voice sexy and raw.

Abby had no idea where her lover got the discipline to torture herself in this way—but she knew that she didn't have the same ability. Unable to hold off for another second, her hand slipped between her own legs, and she gasped as her fingers first touched the swollen folds. "Oh, yes," she hissed.

Clancy blinked at her, surprised that Abby succumbed so easily but more than willing to help her get where she needed to go. Because her teasing had gotten Abby this far, she decided to push her a little more. "Watch," she demanded, allowing her questing fingers to find their mark, growling softly as they nearly slipped from her abundant wetness. Abby groaned deeply as she watched Clancy's fingers gather and spread her moisture all around the bright pink flesh, her own hand frantically working at her thrumming need.

Taking her fingers from herself with a regret-filled sigh, Clancy rolled onto her side and slid the slickly-coated digits right into Abby, going in deep and stretching her to her capacity. Abby's free arm wrapped around Clancy's shoulders and pulled her in tight, their lips meeting in a searing kiss while Abby moaned insensibly. As soon as Clancy's fingers began to twitch inside of her, a powerful climax washed over her, her inner walls clamping down so hard on Clancy's fingers that she nearly cried out in pain. But soon the flesh began to pulse, and the contractions lessened with each beat until Clancy's fingers were gently expelled.

She gathered Abby into her arms and teased, "For a churchgoing woman, you sure do give into temptation easily."

"Easily!" Abby's voice was weak, but even in her debilitated state, she could summon up some amount of outrage. "You were torturing me!"

"That was the point," Clancy said, chuckling softly. "Where's the fun in it if I don't torture you?"

She held Abby in her arms, rocking her gently until she was mostly recovered. With some difficulty, the still-shaking woman sat up; then she pressed Clancy onto her back and hovered over her. "It's your turn to torture yourself, now. Ready?"

"I think it's a safe bet that I'm ready. I was ready an hour ago."

"Come on," Abby said, "we've got a deal here."

Never one to go back on her word, Clancy leaned back against her pillows and slipped her fingers between her lips. "Ooo…I didn't know it was possible to be this wet."

Unable to keep her hands to herself, Abby slipped a finger into her, just barely entering the incredibly slick orifice. "Remarkable," she breathed. "Simply remarkable."

"Uhm-hmm," Clancy agreed, her fingers starting to pick up the pace. Sliding down for a better view, Abby rested her head on a muscular thigh and settled down to see the show. In minutes, she was throbbing again, but this time she was able to resist her growing need, content to watch Clancy give herself pleasure.

The blonde was clearly enjoying herself, letting her pace pick up until her breathing grew erratic, then backing off until she was barely brushing the edge of her brown curls. She indulged herself lavishly, letting her body work itself up to a fever pitch, only to soothe it gently again and again.

As Clancy once again started to climb the slope, she grasped Abby's hand and guided her fingers inside, purring sexily when they hit their mark. "That's it," she panted, her legs spreading even wider. "Nice and steady, baby. Just…like…that," she moaned roughly, her fingers a blur as she felt the first signs of her building climax. She consciously lightened her touch, barely brushing the flats of her fingers over her tender flesh, the motion looking like someone stroking a skittish cat's back. Her teeth latched onto Abby's shoulder, somehow managing not to break the skin as the contractions raced through her body, finally rendering her completely spent and gasping for air.

Suddenly, Abby's warm, wet mouth was everywhere, kissing Clancy insistently, finally landing on her mouth as their breathing rapidly fell into sync. Clancy slid her hands across Abby's cheeks, cradling her head in her hands. Lifting her head just enough to be able to look into her eyes, she continued to kiss her lightly, covering her entire face with the gentle touches. Smiling up at her, Clancy murmured, "I have to be honest. It's not that good when I'm alone."

Abby kissed the curled up edges of her mouth and chuckled, "You'd be the last person in the world who needed a girlfriend if it were." She continued to drop soft kisses all across Clancy's face and neck, completely unable to stop touching and tasting her.

Clancy purred softly from the sensation of the warm, wet lips that moved across her body. She rolled over slowly, giving Abby new territory to claim, feeling like she was riding on a sensual cloud. "You're gonna have to stop that in the next month or two," she murmured.

"Mmm-mmm." Abby's head shook slowly, her soft hair brushing against Clancy's tender skin. "Tastes too good."

Clancy rolled over, letting Abby reach the sensitive skin around her waist. "It feels so good to be loved by you," she sighed. "I'm thoroughly addicted."

"No desire to kick the habit?" Abby asked softly, her lips still skimming across Clancy's sated body.

"None whatsoever." Clancy shifted under her and wrapped her arms around her waist, tugging Abby fully atop her body. "You're a very healthy addiction." She paused for a minute, then smiled brightly. "Not just healthy. Life-giving."

At four-thirty, they walked down the hall, showered and dressed once again. When they reached the guest room, Clancy poked her head inside, seeing the furniture that had formally been in the master bedroom. "Go on in," Abby said. "This is our new room." Clancy took her hand, looking around. All of Abby's things were in the closet, and she pointed out a dresser that was tucked away in a corner. "I thought we could put your shorts, socks, and underwear in there. I've ordered an armoire that'll look great with the rest of the furniture," Abby added. "That'll be for your hanging clothes."

"Are you really okay with this?" Clancy asked. "Is it gonna be hard to sleep in your old bed?"

Abby smiled at her concern and said, "I had them switch out the mattresses. This is the one we've been sleeping on." She pasted on a wan smile and admitted, "That would have been too much."

Clancy walked around the room and noted that Abby had not brought in any of the pictures of Will and the family. "Why'd you put all of the photos away?"

"Will's never far from my thoughts," Abby said softly. "I just don't want to be making love with you with pictures of my husband and kids in view. I know it's a little odd, but it feels like they're watching us," she said, her cheeks coloring.

Clancy hugged her tenderly, stroking her back in sympathy. "I understand that. I guess I just want there to be a place where you keep family memories."

"There are plenty of them in the office, and I put some of them in the kids' rooms. I'm not going to hide them away. Don't worry about that."

"Okay. I just want to make sure you know that it won't bother me to have them up. I like seeing pictures of your family. It reminds me of what a loving, devoted partner you are."

"I'm devoted to you now. Eternally."

Chapter Twenty-Nine

On Saturday morning, everyone was busy with preparation for the party. The doorbell rang, and Abby went to answer it, stunned to see Hayley standing there.

"Hi!" the girl said, perky and smiling. "Surprise!"

"How did you get here?"

"Gramma," Hayley said, turning to wave at the departing Mercedes.

Abby hugged her, giving her a good squeeze. "You don't ever have to ring the bell. This is your home."

"Good," Hayley said, smiling. "Where's Trev?"

"He's in the back yard. Waiting to hear from you so he can go pick you up."

"Cool! I'll go surprise him." Abby let her go alone, glad that she'd made that choice when the dogs nearly knocked the girl to the ground.

Clancy walked into the kitchen from the garage, asking, "What's going on? I heard some…" She looked outside and said, "Ahh, the prodigal daughter returns. Should I go say hello or wait a bit?"

"Actually, I was just going to ask you to go to the liquor store. The kegs are ready, and the store doesn't deliver, so you'll need the truck. Do you need Trevor to go with you?"

"Nah. It doesn't come naturally, but I can look helpless when I have to. I'll let the guys at the store load it all up."

"Good. I need to spend some time alone with Hayley today. I think I'll try to do that while you're gone. I'd like to make sure she's gonna do her best to be on her good behavior this weekend."

"No argument," Clancy said. "I'll be back in a while."

"Not before you kiss me goodbye," Abby said. She wrapped her arms around her partner and gave her a tender, lingering kiss.

Clancy stayed pressed against her, uttering a soft growl. "You always give me something to think about while I'm gone. Too bad we won't have time today."

"The birthday girl always gets her wish," Abby said. "It might be late, but you won't go to bed without as much love as you can handle."

"Like I said, you always give me something to think about." Clancy kissed her one more time and then took off on her errand.

Abby went to the door and called out, "Hayley, would you come in and help me for a while?"

The young woman jogged over to her mother. "Sure. What do you need?"

"We're gonna be swamped all day, and I thought we could spend a little time talking while I ice Clancy's cake."

Hayley went inside and sat down on a stool. "So…what's up?"

"Not much. I just wanted to see how things are going for you. You know…how you're feeling about me and Clancy."

"Okay. Hey, you don't mind if I go upstairs to change, do you? I don't want to get icing on my good sweater." She jumped off her chair and was racing up the stairs before Abby could say a word to stop her.

Abby heard the footsteps stop abruptly and then felt her heart start to race. Feeling sick to her stomach, she ran right up after her daughter, finding the girl standing in the doorway of the new office, a look of shocked outrage contorting her features. "Why don't you just fucking move?" she shouted when her mother approached. "You can get rid of everything that reminds you of him!" She pushed past Abby and ran to her room, slamming the door so hard that the whole house seemed to vibrate.

Abby went after her, breathing a silent prayer of thanks that the doors needed a key to lock them—and that the keys had been missing for years. A frighteningly loud crash rang out from Hayley's room, and then another, and Abby burst through the door to find Hayley huddled on the floor in the corner, two family pictures smashed against the opposite wall.

Ignoring the lethal look the young woman gave her, Abby sank to the floor next to her and wrapped her in her arms, holding on tight even when Hayley slapped at her ineffectually.

"Let me go!" she yelled, her hysterical tears almost obscuring her words. "Let me go!"

Abby would not, tightening her grip when Hayley tried to squirm away. "I will not let you go," she vowed. "You're my precious girl, and I'm not going to let you go until we have this out."

"I'm not precious," she sobbed. "Clancy is! She's the only thing that's precious to you anymore!"

"That's not true. Clancy's my partner, but she's an adult and can take care of herself. You're still my girl. You'll always be my girl—always!"

"There is no always!" Hayley cried. "You said you'd always love Daddy, and you don't! You've thrown him away, just like you're throwing me away!"

"Hayley! I am *not* throwing you away! Why would you even say that?"

"You're changing everything! Everything!"

"I changed my room, Hayley, not yours, not Trevor's. You're both welcome to visit or live here, and I'd love to have you here as much as you want to be here, but Clancy's going to be here, too."

"Clancy's taking his place! You're throwing away all of your memories!"

"Good God, Hayley, I'm not throwing his memory away! I love him as much today as I did when he was alive. There isn't a day that goes by that I don't think of him—or cry for him." She hooked her gold necklace with a finger and tugged it from her sweater. "I wear his wedding ring just so I have a little piece of him with me. He's a part of me, baby, and no matter how much I love Clancy, he always will be."

"You don't wear yours," she said, looking at Abby's bare ring finger.

"I tucked my ring into his hand on the day we buried him," she said quietly. "I needed him to have it with him forever—just like I'll always have his. Didn't you know that?"

"No," she sobbed. "You didn't tell me that."

"I was in such a state of shock, I don't know how I got through those first weeks, but I thought I'd told you that."

Hayley looked at her for a moment, then her expression hardened. "I'm surprised Clancy lets you wear his ring. She looks like the type who'd wanna protect her territory."

"That's a ridiculous thing to say. You don't know her well at all."

"I can still have an opinion."

"Of course you can. I'm just telling you you're wrong. Clancy doesn't tell me what to do. That's not the kind of woman she is. We have an equal partnership."

The girl was quiet for a while, but Abby could feel the tension running through her body. "Daddy was always in charge," she finally said. "I knew he could handle anything. I was never afraid of anything when he was home."

"I wasn't either," Abby said, choking up while she thought of how secure and safe the world had seemed while Will was alive.

The young woman looked at her mother for just a moment before the floodgates opened once again. "I want him back!" she cried piteously. "I want my daddy back!" She was crying so hard that Abby was sure she was going to be sick, but she kept her arms tight around her daughter's shaking body, providing as much comfort as she could.

"I want him back, too," Abby whispered. "I'd give anything to have him back."

"That's not true!" the young woman cried. "You can go be a lesbian now that he's gone. You probably would have left him—left us—for Clancy or some other woman!"

Abby gripped her shoulders and held her tight, keeping her face just inches from her own. "That's not true," she said evenly. "I would never—ever—have left your father. I loved him with all of my heart. We were very happily married. I would never have known about my ability to love a woman, and that would have been just fine with me. I love Clancy, baby, but I wish to God I had never had the opportunity to fall in love with her. I wish your daddy were downstairs right now, waiting for us to make the icing so he could keep sticking his finger in the bowl to test it."

Hayley's crying slowed noticeably, and she opened her eyes wide and looked at her mother. "How can you still love him and love her too?"

"It's easy," Abby said, a ghost of a smile on her lips. "It's just as easy as it was for your daddy and me to welcome Trevor and you into our family. I didn't love your dad any less when we had Trev, and I didn't love Trevor any less when we had you. I love you and Trevor equally. There's plenty of room in my heart for both of you, and for Daddy and for Clancy."

Her tears ebbing, Hayley's sad, resigned voice said, "It will never be the same. It will never be just us again."

Abby pressed her tightly against her chest and nodded her head. "You're right. It'll never be the same. Families change, and ours is changing now, just like it'll change when you and Trevor find someone you love and when you have children."

"I'm not going to have children," she said. "No way."

"Whatever you choose, you'll still find someone to love…maybe Alexander."

Immediately becoming guarded and defensive, Hayley snapped, "I don't love him!"

Surprised by the strength of her denial, Abby said, "You don't have to love him, honey. I just assumed that you were…close."

"We are," she said. "We're just as close as I want to be."

There was something about the way she said that that made Abby suspicious. "What do you mean by that? Is there something about Alexander that bothers you?"

"Yes!" Hayley said, speaking before she could censor herself. "He always wants more! He wants to spend more time together, see me more often, have more sex than I want to. He's been driving me crazy!"

Puzzled, Abby asked, "Then why are you still seeing him?"

Hayley dropped her head back, letting it bang against the wall. "Because I like him so much," she moaned. "He's exactly the kind of guy I've always wanted to meet."

"Hold on," Abby said, stretching her legs out to get comfortable. "You're not making sense. He drives you crazy, but he's just what you think you want?"

She ran her hands through her hair in an exasperated gesture. "Yes! We're close," she said. "We're plenty close. Why can't he be happy with that?"

"Honey, if he's pushing you to do things you're not ready for—"

"Not like that," Hayley said dismissively. She sighed heavily. "He says he loves me, and he wants to make love. Not just have sex."

Abby was stumped, and her expression reflected her puzzlement.

"He wants to have intercourse," she said, rolling her eyes. "I don't see why it isn't enough just to get off, but he wants more."

"Oh! I thought…I assumed…"

"Yeah, that's what everyone assumes," Hayley said. "But I don't want to be that close."

"Why? Why don't you want to be more intimate with him?"

"Because I'll fall in love with him!" she spat out. "And I don't want to!"

"Hayley, you're not making sense. What's so bad about falling in love?"

"You can't understand," the girl said. "You're the type who can get over someone. I can't! It's been over five years since Daddy died, and I miss him as much today as I did when I lost him! If I lose Alexander…" She started to cry, curling up in a ball just like she did when she was small. "Shit, who am I kidding? I *am* in love with him! I just knew this was gonna happen!"

"Hayley, falling in love isn't something to worry about or fear! I promise you that! Yes, it's a little frightening at first, but there aren't many things on this earth that can match the feeling of being in love. Don't try to close yourself off to it!"

"That's easy for you to say," she said. "You got over Daddy."

"You know," Abby said, calmly and evenly, "I'm sick of hearing you tell me what I feel. No one knows what's in another person's heart. Just because I've fallen in love again doesn't mean that I didn't love your father. He was my husband, and he was a terrific one. But I've let myself love again, just like he wanted me to."

"I'm sorry," Hayley said. "I know you hate it when I try to read your mind."

"That's all right. I know you're frustrated, but I think part of what's driving you crazy is that you seem to be confused about the different types of love there are. Your dad was the only father you'll ever have. No matter what happens to you in life, you've lost the man who raised you, and you can't replace him. The love you have for your parents is primal, baby. We were the people who gave you life, who protected you when you couldn't protect yourself. The bond you have with us is unbreakable."

"It feels broken," Hayley said, crying softly. "I feel so lost without him."

Feeling a deep wave of sympathy for her, Abby said, "I don't think I can ever really understand what it's like for you. I'm more than thirty years older than you were when you lost your dad, and I still have mine. It's not fair that you lost him when you were so young. But you did, and trying to keep Alexander at a distance isn't gonna bring your father back. Yes, losing someone you love is devastating, but you can go on. You have gone on. And if you're in love with Alexander, you've got to let yourself enjoy it—celebrate it! It's a gift that can't be replaced, baby, and you can't afford to shrug it off."

Hayley looked up at her mother, her expression so childlike that Abby wanted to take her in her arms and hold her. She didn't resist the impulse. Tucking her arms around her, she smiled when Hayley cuddled up even closer. The girl's breath was warm on Abby's neck, and she asked, "Do you really think it's different?"

"What, honey?"

"How I feel about losing Daddy and how you feel?"

"Of course it is. I was a young woman when I met your father. I changed and grew with him, but he wasn't the guiding force in my life; my parents were. Your father was a man I chose to love. But you carry half of his genes, Hayley. You have his ears and his hands and his laugh and his bad sense of direction and knobby knees."

The girl laughed, and gave her mother a scowl. "I do not have knobby knees!"

"They're adorable knees," Abby said, "but they're knobby!"

Hayley nuzzled her head against her mother's neck. "I love you, Mom. I'm sorry I'm so impossible sometimes."

Abby ran her hand through her daughter's long, black hair. "You know that bond you have with your parents? Well, I have an amazingly strong bond with you.

No matter how much you frustrate me at times, I love you with all my heart, and I wouldn't trade you for any other daughter in the world."

"I have a tough time believing that," Hayley said. "I'm sure you wish Trevor had been twins."

"Not true. But you won't believe me until you have children of your own. If you do, that is."

"One step at a time, okay, Mom? I'll never have the opportunity to have kids if I don't ever have intercourse."

"Good point," Abby said. "I guess you *were* listening to our talks about sex."

"It's not funny," Hayley said. "Do you think I should have sex with Alex?"

Abby held up a hand. "I will never, ever tell you whether or not to have sex with anyone, Hayley. You're an adult, and you have to make those decisions for yourself. I will tell you one thing, though. If you have to ask someone else…that's not a good sign."

"I don't have to ask anyone else when we're together," she said. "I want to be with him, and I want to love him. But I'm so afraid, Mom. I wanna know that it's gonna work out *before* I fall in love with him."

"God, wouldn't that be nice," Abby said wistfully. "But you have to risk to love, baby. It's the only way."

"Why does this have to be so hard?" Hayley asked. She leaned her head on her mother's shoulder and sighed heavily.

"You're making it harder than it has to be. You have to open yourself up and let your heart tell you what's right."

Hayley thought for a moment, then looked at her mother. "Is that what you did with Clancy?"

"Yes!" Abby said, laughing. "Do you think I would have fallen in love with her if I'd let my brain tell me what to do? Loving a younger *woman* wasn't on my to-do list, honey. Clancy captured my heart, and I'm damned glad she did."

"Are you really happy, Mom?"

"Yes. I am. I'm very, very happy. The only thing that would make me happier is if you could grow to accept Clancy into our family."

"I don't want another mother." She made a face and added, "Especially one I wanted to sleep with."

Abby chuckled softly and said, "Then you're in luck, because Clancy doesn't want to have a child. Especially an eighteen-year-old. And she really does prefer older women." She kissed her daughter on the top of her head. "She'd like to be your friend. That's all. She doesn't ever want to interfere with our relationship."

Hayley nodded and nuzzled her head against her mother's body, letting her embrace soothe her. "I'll try harder," she promised. "And Mom? I'm really sorry I broke our pictures."

"That's all right. We'll just reframe them. Don't worry about it."

"Let me clean up the mess," Hayley said, struggling to get up. "Then we can get started. What kind of cake did you make?"

"White cake. And she likes white icing, too."

"Just like Daddy," Hayley said, misting up again. She got to her feet and offered a hand to her mother. They went out into the hall and Hayley asked, "Is your furniture in the guest room now?"

"Yes. I wanted a new room to start my new relationship."

The young woman nodded briefly, then wet her lips and said, "I wish it were the same. But I guess what I really wish is that Daddy was still with us. I know that's impossible, so it makes sense that you want to change the room, Mom. It's just a little hard for me to see it. I just…I just think of being little and going into your room on Sunday mornings to get in bed with you. All four of us would snuggle together. I felt so safe and happy then." A few hot tears escaped, and she wiped at them roughly. "Do you and Clancy sleep on the bed now?"

"No, we don't. We never have. That's where you and Trevor were both conceived. I couldn't…I couldn't share it with anyone else." She ran her fingers through her daughter's dark hair and then bent to kiss her forehead. "I had the mattresses sealed in plastic and put in the garage. I doubt that I'll ever use them again—but I couldn't bear to give them away."

They held each other tightly, both crying for a few minutes.

"I hardly ever cry at school," Hayley muttered. "I just feel so emotional when I'm home."

"I understand," Abby said, hugging her close. "I feel more emotional when you're home, too. It's so close," she whispered, "so close to how it used to be."

Hayley nodded, her dark hair rubbing against Abby's sweater. "It doesn't feel close for me anymore. Having Clancy around changes everything."

"I understand that, honey," Abby sighed. "I really do."

The young woman looked up at her mother with watery blue eyes and asked, "It doesn't make you mad when I say things like that, does it?"

Abby's head shook decisively. "Not at all. I want you to tell me how you feel. It's the only way we'll get through this."

"Okay," she murmured. "I promise I'll try." She kissed her mother on the cheek and said, "I love you, Mom. I want you to be happy—so I promise I'll try."

"Thank you, Hayley," Abby whispered, squeezing her tight. "That's all I ask."

❦

Hayley was inside, cleaning up the shards of glass from the picture frames, when Abby went outside to see Clancy chatting with Trevor. "Hi," Abby said, putting her hand on Clancy's back. "How's everything going?"

"Great," Trevor said. "We got the tables set up, and I'm gonna take Clancy's truck to pick up the gas-powered heat lamps. I think we might need them tonight. It feels like it's getting a little colder."

"Thanks, honey. Would you mind taking Hayley with you? She's having a tough day."

"Okay, Mom. Maybe we'll stop somewhere and talk."

"You're my guy," Abby said, smiling at her son when he blushed just the tiniest bit.

❧

Clancy, Trevor, and Hayley had the kegs set up and had filled and tested the space heaters by four o'clock. It was getting a little chilly but was still warm enough to be outside. Clancy went in to get a sweatshirt, stopping to place a kiss on Abby's neck. "Ooh! Cold lips! Has the temperature dropped that much?"

"No, it's not too bad. I was sitting with the kids, and the wind has picked up a little."

"You and the kids, huh?" Abby asked. "What are you young folks doing?"

"Just talking. It's fun listening to them talk about their plans for saving the world." She popped a cherry tomato into her mouth and twitched her head at the platters of vegetables Abby was preparing. "Can I help?"

"No, I'd rather you spent some time with the kids. How's Hayley?"

"Fine," Clancy said. "She's not talking much, but I think that's because Trevor's been talking about some of the projects he's been working on. Why?"

"Oh, we had a long talk, and I thought she might still be upset."

"No, she's just quiet." Clancy reached around her lover and took a few carrot sticks. "Wanna talk about it?"

"Mmm…maybe later. I'm not sure we got anywhere, but she was a little more open than usual." She smiled at Clancy and shrugged. "You can never tell with Hayley, though. Her emotions are like the tides. You need a chart to figure her out."

"Well, I'll try not to incite her. I really want to have a nice, calm party."

"So do I, sweetheart. I wanna be the only person who gets under your skin tonight."

❧

Abby was amazed at the collection of friends that Clancy had amassed over the years—a few from high school, many from college, still more from her years in the lesbian social scene in the San Gabriel Valley. She had also invited at least a dozen people with whom she worked professionally, as well as her usual crew and their families. It was a very eclectic crowd, but Abby was reveling in the energy that pulsed through the house.

From Abby's side of the ledger, Pam, Maria, Alyssa, and Abby's parents were the only representatives, but she didn't mind that she knew so few of the people filling her house. These were Clancy's friends, and she was bound and determined to get to know each and every one of them—either this night or in the future.

Luckily, the night was warm enough to allow a large number of guests to remain outside. Clancy was a very capable hostess, meandering through the house and patio frequently to make sure they all were enjoying themselves.

Looking through the open French doors, Clancy scanned the crowd, her eyes landing on Abby no matter how many people surrounded her. She caught Abby's eye and inclined her head, and Abby excused herself from the conversation she was having. Just watching her walk across the room made Clancy's eyes light up, and when she reached her, Abby gave her a questioning smile.

"Did you want something?"

"Uh-huh. I needed you beside me."

"My favorite place," Abby said, putting her arm around Clancy's shoulders.

"One more thing. I want to take you out to a nice, quiet corner and kiss you senseless."

Abby laughed and said, "Well, we should stay inside and be good hostesses, but you know I can't refuse a birthday wish." Taking Clancy by the hand, she led her across the yard to stand behind the mammoth live oak. "Having a nice party?" she asked once her arms were wrapped around her lover.

"The nicest ever. Of course, it would have been nice to split a cupcake, too. All that matters is that we're together."

"I'm having a marvelous time," Abby said. "I really do like your friends."

"They're a good group. I think they're all a little stunned by your house, but they'll get over it eventually." From their position, they could see the dozen or so guests standing and sitting close to the space heaters.

"Our house," Abby said. "And we should get back in. But first, I want those kisses you promised. I need my fix!"

Abby spent a long time tucked in a quiet corner of the living room, speaking with John, Margaret, and Eileen. Clancy had been looking for her, and when she spied her, she went over and perched on the arm of Abby's chair, draping an arm around her shoulders. "Nice party, huh?" she asked, wrinkling her nose at her parents.

"A far sight better than your usual birthday party," John joked. "I never thought I'd see the day when my little girl graduated from her keg-of-beer-and-bowl-of-potato-chips days."

"I turned thirty," she reminded him. "That's the dividing line between keggers and serious parties."

Eileen patted Abby's leg and said, "This here's the dividing line, and you know it, Bitsy. Abby's gonna make an adult out of you yet. She's even got you in long pants!"

Clancy nodded and started to agree, but Abby interrupted to say, "I think the key for us is to meet in the middle. I could use a little loosening up, and Clancy could use a little...just a little, mind you...formalizing."

"Isn't she sweet?" Clancy sighed, giving Abby her best lovesick look.

"You both are," Eileen said, patting them both. "You're damned lucky to have found one another."

"I'll drink to that," Clancy said, clinking her beer bottle against Abby's wine glass.

The patio eventually became the dance floor, and when one of Clancy's favorite songs came on, she signaled to Abby, who joined her at the door. "I don't want to make you uncomfortable," she said quietly, "but I'd really love to dance with you. Do you think that would be okay?"

Through prior agreement, they had decided to try to keep their physical affection to a minimum when the kids were around, but Abby quickly reassured her partner. "Of course," she said. "I just wanted both of us to be conscious of how intimately we touched each other. We have a tendency to forget we're around company. Dancing is perfectly acceptable." She leaned over and whispered into Clancy's ear, "Just try to keep your hands around my waist. They tend to stray a little low."

"Don't blame me," Clancy said. "You're the one with the perfect ass. I truly can't help myself."

"I'll remind you if you get too frisky," Abby said, taking Clancy's hand to lead her outdoors.

The dance floor was crowded, and Clancy noticed that Trevor and Hayley were sitting outside, entertaining Alyssa. She felt a little uncomfortable dancing in front of them, but she reasoned that a slow exposure to their physical affection was probably the right way to go. Reminding herself to keep her hands around Abby's waist, she wrapped her in her arms and held her close, their bodies gently swaying to the music. "Now my birthday is complete," Clancy sighed heavily, her warm breath sending a shiver up Abby's spine when it tickled against her neck.

"Oh, no, it's not," Abby said. "We have plenty of games to play once we get rid of all of these people."

"Ooh, like Pin the Tail on the Donkey?" Clancy asked, grinning up at her lover impishly.

"Something like that," Abby said. "It does involve blindfolds and groping in the dark and…"

"Shh!" Clancy whispered. "Hayley might hear you!"

"She's busy with Alyssa."

Pressing Abby closer, Clancy whispered, "It turns me on so much to dance with you. It feels like we're making love standing up."

"That can be fun," Abby said, chuckling softly. "Tiring, but fun."

"I'll put that on my to-do list," Clancy said and then reminded herself that she was trying to keep it clean. "Just holding you makes me think sexy thoughts. How do you do it?"

"Magic," Abby whispered, placing a delicate kiss on her ear.

"Mmm…we've got to get rid of these people. Can you set off the smoke alarms or something?"

"It's your birthday," Abby said. "Say the word, and I'll send 'em packing."

Clancy didn't doubt her one bit, but she decided that they should stay on the polite path. "I can hold out. They'll leave soon enough."

"I don't know about that," Abby said, "but I agree that they'll leave eventually. Maybe we should close the bar."

"You *are* getting to know my friends," Clancy said, laughing heartily. "You've discovered the key to their collective happiness—an open bar."

An hour later, Clancy wandered through the still-filled house, looking for her partner. Figuring she must be upstairs showing off the new office, she went outside, taking a break from the noise and heat. She'd been outdoors for just a few minutes when Hayley joined her, sitting in a chair facing Clancy's. "Did Mom tell you about our talk?"

"Yeah, she told me that you'd talked and that you'd promised to try harder to accept us as a couple."

The girl looked suspicious. "She didn't tell you about my meltdown?"

Surprised, Clancy blinked; then a scowl settled on her face. "No. Why? You didn't hurt her, did you?"

"No! I just…I just assumed she told you everything," Hayley said.

"No, she doesn't. She keeps your confidences. The only time she tells me private things is when she needs advice. Other than that, it's none of my business."

"Oh. Well, I didn't know how you two handled things," she said.

Clancy looked at her for a moment, her gaze unwavering. "You don't know anything about us. But that was your choice. We could have all worked through our issues this summer, but you wouldn't do it."

"I know, I know," she said, seemingly contrite. "I…I want to apologize for being an asshole to you. I know it's inexcusable, but I really am sorry."

"I don't know you, Hayley. Having you angry with me hasn't bothered me much at all. It's your mother you've hurt."

The girl nodded. "I think I see that now. I can't really explain why this has been so hard for me, but I really am gonna try to be better."

"I hope so, for your mom's sake." Clancy wrapped her hands around her knee and rocked in her chair. "You know, I've never lost anyone as important as your father was to you. I can't imagine how it must have turned your world upside down—especially since you were so young. Your mom realizes that, too, and that's part of the reason she's been so patient with you." She smiled, an evil twinkle in her eyes. "I would have sent you packing after about a week, but your mom is a lot more patient and forgiving than I am."

"I know she is," Hayley said quietly. "Talking to my friends at school makes me see how good a mom she really is."

"She's better than you've deserved, to be honest." Clancy leaned forward and gazed directly into Hayley's eyes. "I know how much you miss your dad. Try to remember that your mom won't be here forever, either. You should thank God for every day you have with her."

"I'm gonna try," she insisted. "I know I've acted like a big baby, and I really am sorry."

"It's forgotten," Clancy said. "Now you and I have to work on figuring out how to be…" She paused, thinking of the fight they'd had earlier in the summer. "Whatever it is we wind up being."

Hayley gave her a half-smile. "That's covering all of the bases."

Clancy nodded. "Who knows what'll happen between us? All I know is that relationships change over time. I'd like to have the best relationship possible with you."

"For my mom?" The girl was staring at her, her blue eyes and frank gaze so much like Abby's that Clancy got a little chill from it.

"No. Your relationship with your mom will always be separate from how you and I feel about each other. We can't put on some act just to make her happy. We have to like or dislike each other because of who we are."

"Trevor likes you already," Hayley said, looking at Clancy through half-closed lids.

"I'm glad," Clancy said. "I like him, too."

"He's usually right about people."

"Well, that remains to be seen, huh?"

Hayley smiled. "It does. But I think absence does make the heart grow fonder. I like you better than I did when I was at home this summer."

"Same goes for me," Clancy said, laughing softly, thinking of how low a bar had been set.

"A whole day and no fights," the girl said. "That's a start!"

Abby went outdoors to cool down after being in the overly warm living room, and that was where her father found her. "You know," he said thoughtfully, "I was thinking about putting in a nice, big koi pond in the back yard. Do you think that's something Clancy could do?"

"Absolutely. She uses her father for the plumbing work, but she could design it and get it installed." She looked at him, a smile lighting up her face. "She does nice work, doesn't she?"

"She does," he said. "I was afraid this was going to look a little like a theme park—you know, where the boulders look fake and out of scale. But I'm very impressed with this. It looks amazingly natural."

"She's a pro, Dad. She really knows her stuff."

"That's always been my motto," he said. "Find an expert, and let her do her job without interference."

"You didn't follow your motto when you tried to tell me how to deal with Hayley."

She could see him bristle, but he didn't say anything for a few moments. "I'm a parent, too, Abby, and I think I did a good job of raising you."

"I do, too, Dad. But don't you think we'd both be better off if we stuck with our fields of expertise? You're an expert on raising me, but Hayley's my responsibility."

"I just want her to be happy. She's lost so much."

"I know that," Abby said. "So have I."

He looked at her, studying her features. "You're not the woman you were when Will was alive," he said, the realization just dawning on him. "You've changed."

"Yeah, I have," she said. "I had to, Dad. I had to get stronger and learn how to make my own decisions to deal with my life. I didn't have anyone to rely on to help me."

He nodded. "We tried to help, honey, but there was only so much we could do."

"I know that," she said. "You helped me a lot. But you wanted to step in and take Will's place every once in a while, and that's not what I needed."

He was obviously hurt. She could see that in his clear blue eyes. "I did my best," he said, his tone curt.

She sighed, feeling like this could last all night. "Dad, I'm not complaining. I'm trying to explain myself. I had to change after Will died, and I'm not ever going to be the way I was before. You've got to let go…just like I've got to let go of Hayley a little bit."

He frowned. "She's far too young to be on her own."

"Fine," she said, conceding the point for the moment. "I'm not."

He stretched and then rubbed his nose, both nervous habits. Then he turned toward her. "Point taken."

"Dad, I don't want you to stop caring. I just want you to stop trying to tell me what to do. I know you do it because you love me, but I'd really like it if you could find another way to show your love."

He let out a short laugh and smiled. "Like?"

"Honoring my wishes. Letting me deal with Hayley."

"I'll try," he said, obviously uncomfortable. "We'd better go in. Looks like Clancy's mom and grandmother have washed the glasses, so it's safe to go into the kitchen."

She chuckled softly, knowing they hadn't settled anything but feeling like they'd made a little progress. "So did I get my hatred of doing dishes from you?"

"You don't see your mother in there either, do you, honey?" he asked, slipping his arm around her shoulders to lead her back inside.

✿

When Clancy went back into the house, she couldn't find her partner. She went upstairs on the off chance she was up there but found only Trevor, packing a duffle bag. "Hi," she said, standing in his doorway.

He smiled brightly. "Hi! I was just gonna come downstairs to look for you."

"Beat you to it," she said. "What's up?"

"I have a present for you." He reached into his pocket, took out a small box, and handed it to her. "It's kind of a trade, but I think you'll like it."

She gave him a puzzled look and then opened the box, taking out a nice silver keychain engraved with her initials. "This is very nice, Trevor. But why are there keys on it?"

"Oh." He stood next to her. "This one is for the gate, and this one is for all of the entry doors." He held his hand out. "Now give me yours."

"What?"

"We're trading," he said. "I'm taking your apartment, and you're moving in here."

"Are you fucking kidding me?" she cried and then slapped her hand over her mouth. "Sorry about that."

"I'm twenty-five, Clancy. I've heard the word before." He poked her shoulder with his own. "You don't have to treat me like my mom does. I think we'll get along better if we act like peers."

"We are," she said, slipping her arm around him. "And we're gonna be friends, too."

"I think we already are," he said, smiling. "You got me a great job and a great apartment. And as soon as I get my next paycheck, I'll give you back your security deposit."

"Does Michael know about this?" she asked, laughing. "Or did you and your mom just dream this all up?"

"No, he knows," he said. "He said he was lonely without you, and once he learned that I can cook, he was really excited."

"He would be," she said, laughing. "Make a deal with him that he gives you free haircuts if you cook."

"Good idea," he said. "Any other tips?"

"You're welcome to my futon and the rest of my furniture if you want it. If not, just call a charity and have them pick it up."

"I like sleeping on a futon," he said. "I had one in my apartment, and I really got used to it."

"Your mom isn't a fan, but she's a good sport about it."

"She's always a good sport," Trevor said. "She's always been the kind of mom who'll try anything, ya know? Roller coasters, water slides…if we wanted to do it, she'd do it with us."

"You're a lucky guy, Trevor. And the best thing is that you know it."

"I do," he said. He looked around and said, "I guess I'm set." He hoisted his duffle bag and put a hand on her back, guiding her from the room. "Enjoy your new home, Clancy. I know you'll love living here."

She stopped and gave him another hug, feeling like she might cry. "This is still your home, Trevor. I want you over here as often as you want. And both you and Michael had better start coming over on weekends to hang out, especially when we can use the pool again."

"We will," he said, giving her a squeeze. "It'll be nice to float in one after installing them all week."

"Oh, you'll be working in an office by then."

"Hey, you never know. I like my job—a lot. I might stick with it."

"As long as your mother doesn't blame me, go for it!" she said, laughing as they walked back downstairs together. "Now I have to go find Michael and knock him silly for keeping me in the dark about all of this!"

Trevor spotted Michael by the keg, and he walked over to him. "Hi. Did Clancy find you?"

"Yeah," Michael said, laughing. "She thunked me on the head for not telling her about your moving in."

Trevor poured a beer for himself and took a few sips. He and Michael stood together for a little while, watching the party. "Clancy's gonna be good for my mom, isn't she?" Trevor asked, catching Michael by surprise.

"Yeah, yeah, she is," Michael said. "I mean, I don't know your mom well, but Clancy's the best. Really, Trevor. She's the best."

"I just wanna make sure she's not gonna get tired of her and dump her," he said. "I know my mom's really hooked."

"She's not like that," Michael said. "If there's one thing I'm sure of, it's how serious Clance is about love. She loves your mom, Trevor. She really loves her."

"She seems like she does," Trevor agreed. "But I...I worry about the whole thing."

"Well, it's gotta be weird for you," Michael said. "I couldn't handle it if my mom fell in love with a woman."

Trevor shrugged. "You might feel different if your mom had been depressed for five years. Seeing her happy again is worth a lot to me. A whole lot."

Michael clapped him on the shoulder. "You're a good guy. I think we're gonna get along great."

Trevor smiled at him. "I know we will. And I'm really ready to be able to start dating again. Having my own place is gonna be sweet."

"Let me know if you need anything or if I can help you move some stuff over."

"I'm fine," Trevor said. "I have to buy a futon, but other than that, I don't have much to do."

Michael gave him a quizzical look. "Is Clance taking hers?"

"No," Trevor said. "But if you think I'm gonna sleep on a bed where Clancy and my mom..." He trailed off, shaking his head quickly while making a face. "You're nuts!"

Chapter Thirty

After turning off the lights downstairs, Abby slipped into the bedroom and walked into the bath, smiling at Clancy when their eyes met in the mirror. Clancy finished brushing her teeth and stretched her body a little. Unable to resist the play of muscles that danced across Clancy's back, Abby gave her a gentle scratch. Then Clancy turned to pull her into a tight hug. "I had the nicest birthday in the history of birthdays."

"It's not over," Abby said. She leaned back in the hug, letting Clancy support her weight. They swayed together for a moment, smiling at each other. "Birthdays last until you go to sleep—and I have big plans for you."

"Plans? You have plans…for me?" Clancy batted her eyes ingenuously, and Abby leaned forward and nibbled on her ear.

"Big plans. Any complaints?"

"Not a one." Clancy walked over to the stereo and put in a rather vigorous orchestral CD. She took Abby's hand and started to tug her towards the bed. "Mmm," she sighed when she slid between in. "Fresh sheets. Yet another present."

"You deserve to have everything be perfect on your birthday," Abby insisted. "I'm gonna do my best to make sure that holds true for the rest of the night."

"Oh, it will. It's always perfect when we're together."

Abby smiled at her and ran her fingers through her hair, pushing the strands from her forehead. "I love you, Clancy," she whispered, hovering above the pink lips for a moment.

Clancy felt her heart rate start to pick up as she looked up into the depths of Abby's vivid blue eyes. She could feel the emotion surging between them, and her lips hungered for contact. "Kiss me," she whispered, unable to wait another second.

With her smile growing, Abby responded, pressing her lips gently to Clancy's. They kissed tenderly, unhurriedly, letting their bodies find a comfortable pace, and allowing the pressure to build slowly. "Mmm," Clancy sighed, "I think I could live on your kisses."

Abby lifted her head and smiled at her lover. "You are honestly the most talented kisser I've ever met. You know just how to turn me on—like you're slowly cranking up the heat under a simmering kettle. You could teach a master class."

"Uhn-uh," Clancy demurred gracefully. "You're the only one who inspires me."

"We make a good pair," Abby said, planting row after row of kisses along Clancy's brow and across her jaw line. She propped herself up on an elbow and regarded her lover for a moment, a contemplative look on her face. "You make me feel confident of myself. I feel safe to ask for what I need and what I want. I'm never embarrassed with you. That's been a real gift."

"I feel the same about you," Clancy said. "I have since the first night." She shook her head and let the intensity of her smile build. "I've never felt that with anyone else. There was always some awkwardness involved. But not with you. I felt understood from the start."

Abby started to kiss a path down her body, stopping whenever a particular spot caught her attention. "You're understood...you're desired...you're loved," she murmured against her damp skin. "You're very, very loved."

Clancy arched her back, letting out a pleasured gasp when Abby's hungry mouth suckled against her breast. "Oh, yeah, that's it," she urged, gently holding the back of Abby's head. "Come on, just a little harder." Her legs shot straight out in reaction when Abby gladly complied. "Oh, so good," she purred, increasing the pressure against Abby's head. "You're making me throb, baby."

Sliding down the bed, Abby urged Clancy's legs apart and nuzzled her cheek against her. "I can feel you," she whispered. "I can feel your pulse beating."

Shifting her hips while guiding Abby's head, Clancy tried to obtain the relief she desperately needed. "Come on," she gently cajoled. "Just turn your head and let me feel that sweet tongue."

The soft cheek moved lightly against her, causing Clancy to pump her hips in frustration. "It's your birthday," Abby murmured, shifting up to her elbow. "We can't let you finish so quickly."

"We can't?" Clancy asked weakly. "Are you sure?"

With a warm smile, Abby nodded her head. "I'm positive. You need a nice, long, slow simmer on your birthday. Don't you want that?" She gazed up at Clancy, and the blonde realized just how powerless she was against this lovely woman.

"I want whatever you want," Clancy sighed and then flopped down against the mattress. "It may kill me, but I want it."

"No, it won't kill you. You'll love it."

"God knows I'm not complaining," Clancy murmured. "It's just that your touch is so overwhelming. I lose all control."

Crawling back up to lie next to Clancy, Abby put on a contemplative look and asked, "How can we slow you down?"

"Fire hose? Mace?"

Abby gazed into the eyes that she loved, realizing how silly it was to set artificial rules for their lovemaking. She rolled Clancy onto her back and kissed her, breathing in her scent, feeling the softness of her lips. She was lost in the kisses, not another sensation penetrating her sensual fog. They moved slowly against each other, lips together, until Abby looked into the gray eyes and said, "I love you so much." Her warm breath tickled Clancy's sensitized lips. "I want to spend the rest of my life loving you."

"Are you proposing?" Clancy smiled up at her with such a warm, love-filled smile that Abby found herself nodding her assent.

"I am." She kissed her again, somehow managing to fill the lingering kiss with even more emotion. "I want to see your sweet face every morning for all of the days of my life."

"I want that too," Clancy whispered, surprised when a tear slipped past her temple.

Abby lifted her body up a little so that she could gaze into Clancy's eyes. "When I married Will, I knew that I loved him and that I wanted to build a life with him—but I didn't really know what it meant to give myself to another person." She reached up and unclasped her gold chain, letting the chain and Will's ring pool in her hand. She stared at the items for a moment and then placed them on her bedside table.

Clancy was completely shocked. "What are you doing?"

"I can't wear it anymore," she said, her eyes filling with tears. "I realized something when I was talking to Hayley yesterday. I can't be married to two people. Will's gone, and I have to concentrate on making a life with you."

"But...but..."

"No buts. I'll always love him." She took in a deep breath and said, "I don't know if I've ever said this to you, but there's a big part of me that wishes he were lying beside me right now." She was afraid to look, but she made herself meet Clancy's eyes. The gray depths were untroubled, surprising Abby. "Are you...okay with that?"

"Yeah, I am," Clancy said softly. "I love you so much that I'd gladly give you up to bring him back. I'd do anything to take away the pain you all have gone through."

Abby kissed her, gently brushing lips again and again. "You're the most generous person I've ever known."

Clancy laughed a little. "It's easy to be generous with wishes that can't come true." She hugged Abby tightly. "But I'm serious. You'd be crazy to be glad he died. I understand completely."

Abby smiled at her and then touched her face, letting her fingers brush across the symmetrical features. "I'm not glad he died, but I'm so happy to have found you." She nodded toward the ring. "Will is a wonderful part of my past." She kissed Clancy soundly. "You're my future."

"Are you positive?" Clancy asked. "It doesn't bother me to have you wear it."

"I'm positive," Abby said. "It would bother me. This is something that I need to do. I want to marry you. I want to merge our lives—in every way. I want to take our differences and let them come together to create a new, even stronger whole."

"Like a grafted tree," Clancy said, her eyes taking on a sparkle that always seemed to radiate from her when she spoke of her abiding passion.

Abby nodded tentatively, not really sure where Clancy was going with this but eager to hear her thoughts. "One of the first times I came over to have lunch, I was listening to you talk, and I started to think of you as a tree."

"As a tree," Abby parroted, not understanding the analogy.

"Yeah," the architect said. "I do that a lot. I think of what a certain person would look like as a tree."

"Like…"

"Oh, like I think of my gramma as a Dutch elm. Sturdy, stately, old, and tough. A little thing like Dutch elm disease wouldn't dare try to infect her."

Abby laughed, thinking of the flinty older woman covered with green leaves. "Okay. Tell me about my tree."

"Well," Clancy said thoughtfully. "You were talking about Will and how hard it was to have to raise the kids all alone. There was such an…almost tangible sadness about you that I started thinking of how that would look on a tree."

"Mmm…you've lost me."

Surprisingly, Clancy got out of bed and went to her briefcase, pulling out a sketchpad and a few pencils. Coming back to bed, she propped herself up with a few pillows, placed the pad on her thighs, and began to draw. "I started thinking of how your family depended on you and of how great your loss was. I thought of this cool citrus tree I saw once. I've gotta draw it to show you."

Abby lay on her side, her head propped up on her hand, and observed Clancy, delighting in watching the intent look in Clancy's gray eyes. Just the tip of her tongue poked out occasionally, and Abby had to force herself not to scoot up the bed and kiss it.

Slowly, the drawing took shape, turning into a beautifully rendered re-creation of a robust orange tree. "This is how I think of you," Clancy explained, shading in the trunk of the mature tree. "You're the sturdy, hearty host—the rootstock." She pointed to a gnarled, healed-over wound about halfway up the large trunk. "This represents Will," she said softly. "He was a nice, sweet tangerine that was grafted to you when you were just a sapling, and together you grew to make a beautiful, healthy tree." She pointed to two sturdy, but young, branches near the wound. "This particular rootstock naturally hybridized and created a new variety of citrus. That's Trevor and Hayley," she indicated. "A little bit of orange and a little bit of tangerine. Let's call them orangerines. Both of them are healthy young stock that are almost ready to start bearing fruit on their own."

She cast a quick glance at Abby and bent to brush her tears from her cheeks. With a warm kiss, she sat up again and pointed at the wound. "When this branch died, the whole tree was in shock, and it could have died. But it didn't. It took years for the wound to heal, but it kept on going." Bending for another kiss, she whispered, "The host had to keep going, and she did, Abby. She kept going to ensure the survival of the whole system." Clancy tapped her pencil on the bark of the trunk. "She's a survivor." She met Abby's eyes again and said, "The wound is still visible—and it always will be. But the trunk is ready to grow again. She's ready to take on another challenge."

Pointing out a large, weight-bearing branch near the healed wound, she said, "This scaffold is going to have to go." She looked at Abby and said, "That branch is filled with years of sorrow and pain and longing. All of the things that you have to let go of to be able to love again. We're gonna have to cut it away to let the scion—that's me—have a good growing medium."

She took an eraser and removed the weighty, gnarled branch, exposing a clean, pale surface. "Now we put a notch in the tree, here." She did so, using her eraser and her pencil. "Then we put another one in the scion and match up their cadmium layers so the scion can receive nourishment."

Quickly but surely, she sketched a branch that was perfectly attached to the tree, smaller and shorter than the two offshoots she had earlier pointed out. "This is me," she said. "I think I'll be a kumquat. Now, this is a risky thing; this branch is a little big to be a scion, and it has some special needs and requirements." She grinned at Abby and said, "But this big, healthy rootstock can handle them."

"Are you sure?" Abby asked, looking up at her with hope-filled eyes.

"Positive. But there will be problems." She tapped each of the smaller branches and said, "These two are going to have a period of shock. They're going to get a little less nurturing from the trunk, since the trunk has to parse out her nutrients to make sure this big graft takes. One of the branches in particular is gonna take a very long while to adjust. But the cool thing," she said, her eyes dancing, "the really cool thing is that once the graft takes, the whole system will be stronger. The stress and the increased demands make the trunk stronger; they make the roots stronger; they increase the available nutrients to all of the branches—not just the new graft."

Clancy was bubbling with excitement as she continued to sketch in dozens of perfectly drawn leaves. "Someday—and it'll take years—this tree will be a magnificent specimen. With oranges and orangerines and kumquats just dripping from its branches." She leaned in and kissed Abby gently, whispering, "We'll load our families and our friends down with all of this sweet, delicious fruit."

Abby took the sketchbook from her hands and placed a gentle kiss on the drawing. "I'm gonna frame this and put this on my dresser so I can see it every morning." She wrapped Clancy in her arms and kissed her tenderly, letting her lips convey what her heart was too overwhelmed to express. "I'll do my very best to make this graft take."

"All that matters is that you're right where you belong—right next to me."

"I'll do my best, Clancy." She kissed her lover gently, running her fingers through her hair. "You made me jump the gun on asking you to marry me, you know. I was going to do that on Christmas."

Clancy blinked at her, a curious grin turning up the corners of her mouth. "Were you really? You want to have a ceremony and everything?"

"Of course I do!" Abby pulled back, her disappointment obvious. "Don't you?"

"Well, sure. I think that would be fantastic. I just didn't think you'd want to do something so public. I mean, I'm sure it would be hard for the kids…"

"Clancy, I know it'll be difficult for them, but that's no reason not to do it. I know you don't have much of a relationship with organized religion—but I do. I want to give my kids the clear message that when you really love someone, you should be sure enough about him or her to commit yourself to that person—and ask for God's blessing. I don't just want to live with you; I want to show everyone how much you mean to me—how committed I am to you."

"I will," Clancy whispered. "I'll marry you, Abby. In front of God and our families and our friends. I will."

Abby kissed her fiercely. Then, surprisingly, she started to get out of bed, with Clancy still seeking her lips. "Be right back," Abby said, putting on her robe and leaving the room.

She was gone for only a few minutes, and when she returned, she was holding something behind her back. Clancy gave her a very curious look, her eyes wide with anticipation. "Whatcha got there, good-lookin'?"

"Your Christmas present. Well…one of them. But I think this is the right time to give it to you."

"Cool! Christmas and birthday rolled into one."

"Mmm…more like birthday and engagement rolled into one," Abby said, giving her partner a very satisfied-looking smile.

"Gimme!"

"So anxious," Abby said, grinning at her exuberant lover. She sat cross-legged on the bed facing Clancy.

Abby brought her hand around to rest in her lap, and Clancy saw the navy blue jewelry box resting there. The landscaper briefly allowed herself to worry. *Oh, God, please don't look disappointed. She doesn't know that it's dangerous to wear a ring when you're working. You can just put it on a necklace like she did. Smile, and make it look sincere!*

"This is a little…okay, very…untraditional, but so are we," Abby said, smiling warmly. "I really hope you like it, Clance, but if you don't, I hope you feel comfortable telling me so. I want this to be right."

Okay, okay, you can be honest. Tell her that you can't wear it during the day but that you'll put it on as soon as you put the tools away. She'll be fine with that. Now reassured, Clancy held her hand out and allowed Abby to place the box there. "I love it," she said, smiling sweetly.

"You haven't opened it," Abby helpfully pointed out.

"I don't have to open it to love it. The fact that you bought it for me is all that matters."

"C'mere, you romantic little devil." Abby rose to her knees and spent several moments kissing her partner. "Now, open it, for goodness' sake, or it *will* be your Christmas present."

Grinning, Clancy lifted the lid and stared at the gift for a moment, trying to comprehend exactly what it was. Inside the satin-lined box lay two fairly substantial gold hoops with a brilliant diamond floating at the base of each, seemingly immune from the laws of gravity.

"Do you like it?" Abby asked excitedly.

"Of course I do," Clancy said, a little furrow between her brows. "But…I'm not sure I understand…"

"It's a nipple ring," Abby said, giggling.

"Uhm…Abby…it's two nipple rings. That's a pretty expensive spare."

"Well," Abby said, "you told me that you wanted to have your other nipple pierced…"

"Oh! I get it! I can have a matching pair. Wow, Abby, these are phenomenal. I've never seen anything so beautiful."

"Wrong again," Abby said, shaking her head. "You're a little slow tonight. Must be old age." She took the box from her partner and pressed her fingernail into a tiny catch at the top of one of the rings; then she pulled the ring apart, the gold swinging away from the diamond. Holding it in her hand, she said, "It's your engagement ring. I talked to your parents, and your dad told me that you never wear a regular ring because of your job."

"Oh, Abby! That was so thoughtful of you!" She blinked, and asked, "But why two of them?"

"One for you and one for me."

"You're gonna get your nipple pierced?"

"Yep. It's traditional to wear your engagement ring on your left hand, so I thought we could both have our left nipples pierced. There's something so appealing about marking my body to show my love for you—and having you be the only one to see it."

"Oh, Abby." Clancy threw her arms around her partner. "You know me so well. This is exactly what I would have chosen—if I'd had the creativity to think of it."

"Well, you didn't know that I've been thinking about having my nipple pierced, so you were at a disadvantage. I see your face when I pull on your ring, and I need to experience it for myself."

After giving Abby a slow, probing kiss, the architect said, "You've made so many changes this year, Abby. Falling in love…with a woman. Having trouble with Hayley. Losing a close friend. Are you sure you want to make another change—especially one so permanent?"

"I'm absolutely sure. Our relationship is permanent, and I want a permanent sign on my body that signifies our bond." Stroking Clancy's face with her fingers, Abby said, "I told your family that one of our strengths is our willingness to extend ourselves—to try to see the world through each other's eyes. Piercing my nipple is my way of being more like you."

Clancy grinned at her and said, "And wearing a big diamond is my way of being more like you. Classy, elegant, and incredibly resilient."

Abby kissed her again and again, murmuring as she pressed her lips against her lover's neck, "A diamond isn't just resilient, Clance; it's impervious from harm—just like our love."

"Just like our love," Clancy sighed. "Always changing; always growing; always sustaining us through our long, long life together."

Giving her lover a wistful smile that spoke volumes, Abby said, "We can't guarantee how long we'll have, sweetheart. All we can do is try to treat every day like it's precious."

"Every day with you *is* precious," Clancy said. "And I'm going to spend the rest of my life showing you just how precious you are to me."

"What a wonderful goal," Abby sighed.

"Mmm…not a goal. That's a promise. A promise that I'm gonna have an absolutely fantastic time keeping." Giving Abby her cockiest grin, Clancy added, "And so are you."

Chapter Thirty-One

SIX MONTHS LATER

Abby turned the corner to enter the office, stopping abruptly as she caught sight of her partner. Clancy was at her drafting table, intently working on a set of plans that was spread out before her. Abby was well used to Clancy's work habits, but she was still greatly charmed every time she caught her with her tongue peeking out of her mouth, as though she could urge the plants she was drawing into the proper order by remote tongue control.

"Knock-knock," she said.

Clancy held up a finger, her eyes not moving. Abby noted that Clancy had immediately pulled her tongue back into her mouth, and she wondered if that was because her concentration had been broken or if Clancy became aware of it when she was interrupted. She knew she could ask her, but she found it too adorable to risk making Clancy self-conscious about it.

The finger went down as Clancy's chin tilted up. "Hi. Wassup?"

Abby walked over and took a quick look at the plans. "Oh, this is for Karen and Mike!"

"Yep. I've finally got time to really concentrate on it." She put her arm around Abby and gave her a quick hug. "I'm gonna have to hire another designer if you get me any more business."

"I told you when I met you that I'd keep you busy."

"I'm not complaining. I like everything you come up with to keep my hands busy."

Abby took the closest hand and brought it to her lips, kissing it. "Such nice hands."

"Who was on the phone earlier?"

"Oh, that's what I came up here for. You distracted me with your astonishing cuteness." She tickled her smiling partner under her chin. "I was having a discussion with my delightfully confounding daughter."

Clancy leaned back in her chair, cocking her head while she studied Abby's eyes. "If you're calling her delightful, you must have had a good chat."

"Not bad." Abby walked to her desk and sat down on her chair. She clasped her hands around a knee and leaned back, wearing a reflective expression. "I've become much more accepting of her. It took her longer than it normally would, but she's just trying to assert her independence. I think she finally feels like she can be herself and not be worried about me."

Clancy got up and walked over to Abby, standing behind her to gently rub her shoulders. "I'm glad she doesn't feel like she has to avoid upsetting you. And I'm even more glad that you're not taking it personally."

"I'm doing pretty well," Abby admitted. "Talking to her more often has helped. And going up there for a weekend was a wonderful idea." She let her head drop and bump against Clancy's stomach. "You had a very good idea."

"I didn't like having you gone, but I'll sacrifice a lot to make you happy." She bent and kissed the crown of Abby's head, pausing to sniff the delightful scent of her shampoo.

"That's because you love me," Abby confidently stated.

"Yup. No doubt."

"Her term is over in two weeks. She called to negotiate."

"Negotiate?"

"Uh-huh. She wants to bring Amber home for a couple of weeks."

Clancy's hands stopped kneading and rested lightly on Abby's shoulders. "Oh."

"Yeah," Abby said, chuckling softly. "They're in l-o-v-e, and they can't bear to separate."

Clancy kissed Abby's head again and walked over to the window seat and plopped down. "How do you feel about that?"

"I'm not surprised. They'd only been seeing each other for a couple of weeks when I visited, but it was pretty clear they were serious about each other. It would have taken an Act of Congress to drag me away from you after we'd been together for two months, so I can empathize."

"I can too. But...it's going to be...odd, isn't it?"

"Sure is." Abby moved to sit by Clancy and then scooted down so her head was in her partner's lap. "We had a little go-round on sleeping arrangements."

"Ugh. I'm gonna guess you want separate rooms."

"Yeah." Abby sighed, making a face. "I feel like I'm on shaky ground here."

"Why? I remember you telling her that she couldn't bring guys home to sleep."

"Yeah, I did, but my intent was to make it clear I wouldn't allow her to have casual sex here. That was when she was on her 'pick up a warm body' phase. This feels different."

"Because she says she's in love?"

"A bit. But also because she's trying to do just what I did with you. I know she and Amber have sex. I guess I feel a little silly saying they can't express their feelings when they're here. I want Hayley to think of this as her home. Do I have the right to tell her what she can do in her home?"

Clancy laughed, making Abby's head bounce a little. "Of course you do! I never took a woman to my parents' house. I lived there full time, and I was older than

Hayley. But they would have been uncomfortable, so I never even considered it. I had perfectly satisfying sex in the back of my mother's delivery van. I'll let 'em use my truck."

"That's a wonderful idea! They can keep all the neighbors up with their caterwauling!"

Clancy tickled Abby's ear, making her giggle. "You know what I mean. Everyone knows what's going on, but you don't make an issue of it. It's common politeness."

"Not something Hayley's filled with these days."

"But you have rules. You have standards. You don't have to compromise them for Hayley. As a matter of fact, you shouldn't."

Abby's eyes fixed on Clancy. "Shouldn't?"

"Shouldn't. She's pushing you. Seeing what she can get away with. I think you should decide what you're comfortable with and stick to it. Even if she pitches a bitch."

Abby blinked slowly, then revealed a warm, affectionate smile. "Know what I'm glad of?"

"That you have a sage, mature partner?"

"Yes…but also that you don't wanna have kids. I couldn't take another twenty years of this!"

❧

Several more phone calls led to an uneasy agreement between Hayley and Abby. On the day of their arrival, Trevor went to the airport to pick up his sister and Amber. He called his mother from the airport, catching her as she and Clancy were leaving the country club. "Hi, Mom. Just wanted to let you know the flight's gonna be an hour late. You don't have to rush home."

"Oh, thanks for calling, Trev. That'll give us time to have a little lunch."

"Do you need more time, Mom? I could take them to my apartment."

"Aww…you're a dear, but you've gone above and beyond the call of duty already. I'm not afraid of a couple of college girls."

He laughed softly. "That makes one of us. I'm a little nervous."

"Why, honey?"

"Nothing big. I'm just…it's gonna be weird to see her…"

He trailed off, leaving Abby to make a guess at his thought. "It's a little hard for me too, honey, and I'm…well, I'm in a similar position."

"Really?" he asked, sounding unsure of himself.

"Really. Change is hard, Trev. But we'll talk about it and try to keep up. That's all we can do."

"Well, I guess I should be used to this by now, huh?"

"And you did very well with your last experience with fledgling lesbianism. I'm sure this time will be easier."

"I guess you're right. Hayley's always doing something different. I should expect surprises by now."

"We'll be fine, Trev. Now go buy yourself a drink on me."

"Little early, Mom," he laughed.

"Extraordinary times call for extraordinary measures."

❧

Two hours later, Trevor pulled up in the driveway. The dogs' barking alerted Clancy. She checked her hair in the mirror, made a face, and messed it up just to spite herself. She trotted down the stairs, winking at Abby, who was coming out of the den. "Ready?"

"Yep. Just remember," she said, fluffing Clancy's hair into an even greater state of disarray, "they're girls. We're women."

"Gotcha, woman." Clancy snapped off a salute.

Abby opened the front door, and both dogs flew past her, practically doing cartwheels at Hayley's arrival. Clancy got her first glimpse of Amber and muttered, "Hottie!"

"Stop that!" Abby whispered. "That might be my new daughter-in-law."

Clancy grinned at her and took her hand, walking down the sidewalk to greet the girls.

Hayley gave her mother an enthusiastic hug, stepped back and said, "Hi, Clancy." She put her arm around her companion and said, "This is Amber. Amber, this is Clancy, my mom's partner."

Amber extended her hand and shook Clancy's. Then she looked at Abby and started to shake her hand but turned it into a hug when Abby leaned toward her.

"Good to see you again…Abby."

"It's good to see you, Amber. I'm glad you could visit." Abby turned her attention back to Hayley. "Are you bringing your things in?"

Hayley shook her head slightly and said, "We can do that later."

They all went into the house together, and Hayley said, "Let's go outside. I want to show Amber the new yard." She took Amber by the hand and started to tug her along while Amber tried to look around the house and compliment Abby.

"It looks like a nice house—"

"I did a little work on the yard," Hayley said, "but Clancy did the design and put it all together."

Clancy pulled Abby to a stop, letting the girls and the dogs go outdoors. Trevor stopped too. "I had a feeling Hayley would choose a wild-and-woolly dyke. Amber looks like she would fit in at the country club."

"I like her," Trevor said, "and they haven't been pawing each other." He laughed. "I had a feeling that Hayley might only be making a statement, but they seem comfortable together."

"I think so too," Abby said. "This might be a passing fancy, but I'm going to do my best to take Hayley at her word. If she says she's in love—she's in love. Now let's go be good hosts."

❧

The family spent the entire afternoon playing in the pool. In the late afternoon, Abby went inside to prepare some snacks, refusing Clancy's offer to help. As Abby expected, Hayley followed her in a few minutes later.

"Can I help?"

"Sure. I was going to make some guacamole. You can get out some chips and salsa."

Abby started to cut the avocados open, and before she'd split the second one, Hayley asked, "Doesn't this seem silly, Mom?"

"What's that, honey?"

"This charade. You know we're having sex. If we stay at Trevor's, we'll be having sex there. You can't stop us, so why does it matter where we are?"

Abby chuckled. "Honey, I have no desire to stop you from having sex. As a matter of fact, I'm happy that you seem to feel so comfortable with Amber. That's not the problem."

"Then what is?"

"I've told you before that I don't want you bringing people home to sleep with until you're fully committed. I don't think you're at that point with Amber."

Hayley stood next to her mother and looked right into her eyes. "Who makes that decision? You?"

"No. I'll trust you to be honest with me and tell me when you and Amber have made a commitment to each other."

"We're in love, Mom. Why isn't that enough?"

"You've only know each other for two months, honey. I'd like for you to express your sexuality with a person you're committed to. Someone you're making life plans with. You and Amber are just getting to know each other."

Hayley narrowed her eyes. "How long had you known Clancy when you were ready to destroy our family over your relationship?"

Abby gazed at her thoughtfully for a few moments. "I was never willing or ready to destroy our family. But I was ready to move on with my life. I trusted that you loved me enough to want me to be fulfilled and happy."

Hayley slapped her hand on the counter. "I do! And I think I've been pretty darned good with Clancy...recently."

"You've come a long way, and I hope you know that I'm very sincere in my desire to see *you* happy. But I'm not comfortable having you two share a room here."

"So if we sleep in separate rooms, you'll be satisfied?"

"Yes."

"Can we kiss?"

"Hayley, I'm not going to supervise you every minute. I want to treat you like an adult, and I trust you to behave like one. If you agree to my request, I know you'll honor it."

"So if we stay up late and roll around on the couch downstairs, that's okay? We just can't sleep in the same room?"

"I said what the rule is, Hayley. I want you to reserve your sexual expression for a person you're in love with and committed to. I know I can't make you do things my way when you're at school, but I can ask you to honor my wishes when you're at home. I'm not going to supervise you. I think you know what I want. You can try to find a loophole, but that's rather childish." She put her hands on Hayley's shoulders. "I know what it's like to be in a new relationship. I wouldn't have liked having to sleep apart from Clancy. Trevor was very generous in offering his apartment. You have options."

Hayley slipped away and went to the cabinets, finding the tortilla chips and the large serving bowl they used for pool parties. "I thought this was always going to be my home."

"It is your home, but you're still my child. I'll always be your mom and the one who's in charge of our home. When I'm ninety and move in with you, you can tell me what to do."

"Clancy'll only be seventy-five. She should be fine to take care of you."

"True," Abby said, chuckling. "Besides, you'll be sixty-three. You might not be *able* to take care of your old mother."

Hayley stopped, looking a little stunned, "Damn, that's old."

"All a matter of perspective."

Hayley opened the refrigerator and found a jar of salsa. "Peach?" she asked looking at the label.

"It's good," Abby said. "You'll like it."

Hayley arranged the salsa and chips in the bowl and then said, "I'm going out."

"Made up your mind?"

"I have to talk to Amber. This affects her too."

"Good move," Abby said. "That's a key element in a good relationship."

Hayley paused at the door, and Abby readied herself for a smart comeback. She was surprised and pleased when Hayley said, "I could do worse than have relationships like you've had, Mom. You know what you're doing."

When Hayley went back outside, Clancy spent a few moments making small talk; then she went inside. "Reach an agreement?"

"No, but I restated the rules and told her that I trusted her to follow them."

"Ooo," Clancy said, "I always hated being rational. It's so much easier having your parents tell you what to do rather than having to police yourself."

Abby pulled Clancy behind a cabinet so that no one outdoors could see them. She kissed her and said, "I'm an evil, evil mother."

Clancy ran her hands up and down her back. "You are evil! No matter what they decide, *we* can't have sex while they're visiting."

"Whaaa…but they might be staying at Trevor's."

"Then Trevor will be staying here," Clancy said, giving her a benign smile. "His room is right next to ours. I won't be able to relax enough to enjoy myself."

"I think I'm going to go tell Hayley that two months is plenty long to be committed." She started for the door while Clancy giggled and pulled on her swimsuit.

"Get back here, you. I'll sneak home at lunchtime if I have to, and if we don't get any time alone, we'll rent a motel room. I can't go two weeks without you."

Abby draped her arms around Clancy's neck and gazed into her eyes for a full minute. "I love you," she said, "and not many days will go by that I don't show you how much. Now let's go see what our guests have decided."

They walked outside with the food, and Hayley got out of the pool, walking over to them.

"Okay if we stay here tonight and move over to Trevor's tomorrow night, Mom? I don't feel like going over there now."

"Sure. Any way you want to structure it is fine with us."

Hayley grabbed a chip and went back toward the pool.

"That was painless," Clancy whispered.

"Thanks to you. You really helped me with this, baby."

"I think it's easier sometimes to have perspective when you don't have your own children. I can identify with Hayley and guess how she'll react to things."

"You're closer to her age." Abby snaked her arm around Clancy's waist and kissed her head.

"Youth has its advantages."

Keeping Clancy close, Abby murmured, "Stamina, drive, enthusiasm…did I mention stamina?"

"Look who's talking! I could hardly get out of bed this morning! You had me up half the night!"

"Storing up energy," Abby said, laughing. "Loving you recharges me."

Clancy gave her a quick hug. "My own little Energizer Bunny of love. She keeps going…and going…and going…"

※

FIVE YEARS LATER

Clancy maneuvered her large, spruce-green truck onto the concrete pad on the side of the garage. When she hopped out, she noticed a matchstick-size streak of mud on the gold letters on the door. Dutifully, she tugged the hem of her shirt out of her shorts and removed the offending streak. She heard a whine and then a laugh, and turned her head to see her partner and both dogs standing at the gate.

"So that's how you get dirt *inside* your shirts."

"Hey, it was on your name. 'O'Connor' was clean as a whistle."

"My name's lower," Abby said. "You got the prime spot."

"I like to be on top." Clancy leaned over the fence and gave her lover a long, slow kiss. "Miss me?"

"Always. But especially today."

"I hate to doubt your motives, but does that have anything to do with the fact that we're expecting a hundred people here later?"

With mock outrage, Abby's mouth dropped open. "I'm shocked! Every moment away from you seems like an hour!"

Clancy kissed her again. "Then why didn't you come with me to pick up the booze?"

Abby pulled Clancy's lower lip into her mouth and sucked on it gently. "I had to shave my legs," she whispered. "I know how you like them to be silky-smooth."

"Very good reason," Clancy said, grinning toothily. "You have your priorities right. Gonna help me unload?"

"My second reason for not going is that I didn't want to get dirty. If I help, that whole excuse goes down the drain."

"Such a girl."

Abby tapped her on the nose. "I'm absolutely certain you like girls. I don't want to screw up my status."

"I wouldn't let you get away with that if we weren't celebrating your birthday today."

"My real birthday isn't for another week, so I appreciate your indulgence."

"You're fun to indulge. Now go open the garage door so *I* can get dirty."

Abby stood in front of the mirror in the bedroom, trying to free the zipper on her dress. "Honey?"

Clancy was at her side before Abby had finished the word. "Hmm?"

"Zipper?"

Clancy's hands settled on Abby's hips and then investigated the dress, and the womanly curves it covered, with deep concentration. "Pretty. Very pretty." She worked on the zipper for a little while, her brow furrowed. "You should have called me before you forced it. There." She looked up to see a slight frown on Abby's face. "What's wrong, babe?"

A smile replaced the frown, and Abby shook her head. "I'm having second thoughts about today. It might have been a better idea to have two parties. Or just one...for Hayley."

"It was her idea to do it this way!"

"I know, I know. But we haven't been very successful with joint parties."

"We haven't had any...have we?"

"How could you forget the New Year's party? I still get hives when I think about it."

"That was years ago! And it wasn't the guests that made it bad; it was Trevor!"

Abby started to chuckle. "He didn't know Hayley was interested in that girl. And if it was that easy for him to get her into that dark corner, she probably wouldn't have been a very good match for Hayley anyway."

"Yeah," Clancy said, laughing. "But it was hard to convince her of that. I think she was a little alcohol-impaired that night too."

"I know I was! I think I had six drinks to calm down."

"I don't think anything like that will happen tonight. Trevor's fiancé doesn't leave him alone long enough for him to get into trouble."

"She loves him," Abby said. "I think it's cute."

"I do too. It reminds me of us, back in the old days."

Abby tugged on her nose. "We're still doing all right."

"We're doing more than all right," Clancy said. "I love you more every day. And I know today's going to be fun for everyone. I'd be totally shocked if she slapped Trevor and called him a...what was it?"

A sour expression covered Abby's face. "Pussy-hound. She called her dear brother a pussy-hound." She wrapped her arms around Clancy and nibbled fiendishly on her neck, making Clancy shriek with laughter. "And I don't for one moment believe you forgot that! You just like to make me say disgusting things!"

"I can't help it! You look so adorable when you say things like that. Those words look like they just don't wanna come out of your sweet mouth."

Abby released her hold and blinked her eyes coquettishly. "You think my mouth is sweet?"

"Every part of you is sweet." Clancy pulled Abby to herself and kissed her gently. Teasing her lips open with her tongue, she lost herself in the kiss, perfectly content to let the minutes tick away as she showed Abby how immensely happy she was to celebrate her birth.

🌱

Hayley and her date arrived an hour before the guests were scheduled. She wandered into the kitchen and gave Clancy a one-armed hug. "Hey," she said.

Clancy turned and gave her a kiss on the cheek. "I didn't hear you come in."

"Mom was outside cutting some roses, so the door was open."

Clancy dried her hands and put her shears down. "I've been arranging flowers as fast as she can cut 'em." She gave Hayley a quick once-over. "You look cute. I like that blouse."

"Thanks. I didn't want to get too dressed up, but I have to look like a lawyer now."

"Is Jeff with you?"

"Yeah. He's outside talking to Mom."

"Are his parents still in town?"

"No, they went home last night after the ceremony. We tried to talk them into staying for the party, but they were in a hurry to get back."

"That reminds me," Clancy said. "I have to go plug in my digital camera. Your mom drained it yesterday. There's a picture that commemorates every minute that passed from the time you put your cap and gown on until you went home."

"Well, unless I lose my mind, this is the last graduation for the Graham family. Last chance for cap-and-gown pictures."

"Trevor might go back," Clancy said, laughing.

"He's got two degrees he doesn't use now!"

Clancy grinned at her, making Hayley smile in reaction. "He uses his degrees. Urban planning, pool planning—it's all the same thing."

Hayley chuckled. "You wouldn't say that if you'd paid for his degrees."

"If *I'd* paid, he'd be an urban planner."

Giving Clancy a playful swat on the arm, Hayley asked, "Where is my overeducated brother? I thought he'd be here by now."

"They'll be here soon. They're stopping to pick up the cakes."

"Cakes?"

"Yeah. We thought it would look a little cheesy to have 'Happy Birthday, Abby' and 'Happy Graduation, Hayley,' crammed onto one. Besides, we had to get your favorite strawberry filling."

"Excellent! I bet Mom got chocolate. Can I do anything to help?"

"Nope, the caterers are going to take care of everything, and yes, your mom got chocolate. I didn't want her cooking at her own birthday party, and I knew she wouldn't let me do it without interfering."

"She'll probably interfere with the caterer."

"True," Clancy said. "But the caterer won't get in trouble if he tells her to get out of the kitchen."

🦢

Clancy sat by the pool chatting with Abby's parents. "Are you looking forward to getting back to Maine?"

"I am," Philip said. "I love my summer garden. I hope you and Abby can steal away for a visit again this year. I know you enjoyed puttering around in my authentic English garden."

"I sure did. I loved getting up early and seeing the dew on your hollyhocks and iris. We were actually thinking about coming out to pick Hayley up."

Elizabeth smiled. "That would be wonderful. I'm so looking forward to having my granddaughter with us until the middle of July. But I have a feeling this might be her last extended visit." She gave Clancy a smile tinged with sadness. "She's an adult now."

"I think she showed a lot of maturity by deciding to study for the bar exam up in Maine," Clancy said. "I think she'll be able to concentrate better. I don't think Jeff's very happy about it, though."

"I could be wrong," Elizabeth said, "but I don't think Jeff is ever going to be a member of the family."

Clancy chuckled. "I think it's going to take Hayley a long time to settle down. She might beat my record."

"How old were you, Clancy?" Philip asked.

"Thirty."

"So she's got six years." He paused and then smiled, his bright blue eyes twinkling merrily. "I think she'll beat your record easily!"

"She's an experimental girl," Elizabeth said.

Nodding, Clancy smiled. "I still can't see her as a lawyer."

"She loves to argue," Elizabeth said.

"I didn't think of it that way," Clancy said. "I guess it's not a bad idea to get paid to do what you love."

🦢

Clancy spotted Michael standing by the beer keg, and she made a beeline for him while he was alone. "Where's Becca?"

"Bathroom. Why?"

"I just wanted to have a second alone with you. It feels like forever since we hung out."

"It has been," Michael said. "But you know how it is when you get serious about a girl. She hates to have me go anywhere without her."

Clancy rolled her eyes. "You're worse than she is!"

"I am not!" He looked terribly insulted. "I'm just considerate. I know she doesn't like to be left out, so I try to include her in stuff."

"Then why were you the only guy who wanted to go to Jen's bridal shower?"

His face grew flushed. "I'm telling you for the last time! I thought Trevor was gonna have to be there, and I wanted to support my buddy!"

"Try to sell that to someone who hasn't been there," Clancy said, chuckling.

Becca came up behind Michael and put her arm around his waist. "Miss me?" she asked.

Clancy nearly choked at the lovesick expression on her friend's face. "Of course I did."

"I'm gonna go find my woman," Clancy said. "I haven't seen her in a while."

Becca reached over and kissed Michael's cheek. "Clancy's just as sweet as you are." She turned to Clancy and grinned. "He's so attentive! I can hardly get any work done at home. He's my favorite little distraction."

Michael's flush grew, making Clancy almost feel sorry for him. "He was just like that when we lived together," she lied, making Michael's eyes pop with outrage. "Always underfoot."

"Oh, I'm not complaining. I love knowing he wants to be with me. Not many men are into being together all the time."

"Not many can give their girlfriend an awesome haircut, either," Clancy said, wrinkling her nose and waving as she walked away, chuckling to herself.

Clancy noted that Philip's glass was empty, so she delivered some sangria on her way to find Abby. "Drink delivery," she said.

"You're a darned fine hostess," Philip said. "Say, could you clue us in on a few people?"

"Sure. I think I know everyone, except for Hayley's law-school friends."

"I was wondering about that girl your friend Michael is with. Don't I know her?"

"Probably. That's Becca Williams. She's an old friend of Trevor's and Sam and Nick and Daisy and…" She scanned the crowd. "I think that's the group."

"Oh! And she dates Michael now?"

"How'd you guess?" Clancy asked, smiling as she watched Becca sit on Michael's lap.

"So Trevor introduced Michael to his friend, and Michael introduced Trevor to Jennifer?"

"Yep. Rooming together paid off for both of them."

Elizabeth had been chatting with a friend from church, and she patted her husband's knee when her friend left them alone. "I'm sure I told you about Michael, honey."

"Must not have made an impression," he said. "My memory is more visual than aural."

"Becca leaves a nice visual, that's for sure," Clancy said, popping her eyebrows to underscore her point.

"You are such a devil," Elizabeth said, laughing.

"She only has eyes for our girl," Philip said, giving Clancy an affectionate smile.

"Wed but not dead. Right, Philip?"

"Don't try to get me into trouble. I admit to nothing!"

"I think it's nice that you and Abby aren't jealous of a little harmless awareness of other people," Elizabeth said.

"Abby's only worry about me is that I'll clock people who aren't nice to her." She cast a glance around and lowered her voice. "I hate to admit this, but I still have a hard time being nice to Sam, and his only sin is that his mom's an ass…jerk," she corrected.

"Ellen's a lot harder-headed than I ever would have guessed," Elizabeth said. "She hurt herself so much worse than Abby. And for what?"

"I think she just couldn't bear to be wrong," Clancy said. "I hope it was worth it."

"She lost dozens of friends when she quit the church. People there don't have much patience for intolerance. And no one could understand her opposition to you…absent being anti-gay."

"My gramma never met Ellen, but that hasn't stopped her from having an opinion," Clancy said. "She's certain that Ellen was just jealous of me. She thinks that Ellen wanted Abby to marry a professional, high-achieving guy who'd be gone much of the time. Leaving Ellen to continue as best friend and confidant."

"Hmm…Eileen might have a point," Elizabeth said. "Ellen did lose her place as Abby's best friend. And now that you're working together, Abby wouldn't have time for the things she and Ellen used to do together. Perhaps she just couldn't bear to have Abby pull away."

"That's Doctor Donovan's diagnosis. She believes a lot of people would rather hurt themselves than let someone else do it."

"So sad," Elizabeth said. "Abby would never have cut Ellen out of her life. She always manages to make time for everyone."

"You're right, and as long as I come first, she's allowed to continue to do that."

Clancy jumped up and danced away just as Elizabeth reached out to pinch her.

John O'Connor waved his daughter over to the sun-dappled chairs he'd claimed under the shade of a Chinese elm. Margaret, Eileen, Trevor, and Jennifer were all seated in a loose circle. "I say your hair looks just like your grandmother's," John said. "But Jennifer swears it's different."

"It's totally different, John," Jennifer said. "Clancy has highlights." She stood up and reached for a few strands of Clancy's hair. "See? This is her natural color. But this…" She held up another sample. "Is a couple of shades lighter." She started to grasp another hank of hair, but Clancy grasped her hand.

"You could send him to beauty school, and he'd never get it, Jen. He thinks there are four colors of hair."

"Four?" she asked, her eyes wide. "Clancy has four colors!"

"Blonde, blonde, blonde, and blonde," John declared. "And Eileen has the same one."

"I'd be out of a job if everyone thought like you did," Jennifer said.

"Don't you listen to him," Eileen said. "This is the best dye job I've ever had. I knew I was meant to be a blonde."

"Oh, you and Clancy both have spring coloring," Jennifer said. "You both look great blonde." She sat down and took Trevor's hand. "I'm a spring, too, but I think our kids will be winters, just like my guy here."

"I'm a winter," Trevor said, smiling goofily. "Chilly."

"You're as warm as a cup of cocoa," Jennifer said, giving him a dreamy smile.

"Anyone seen my winter girl?" Clancy asked.

"Not for a while," John said. "Maybe she's ordering the caterer around again."

"Then I'd better hang out here." Clancy sat on the arm of her father's chair. "Having fun?"

"Sure am," John said. "Lots of people I don't know, though. I don't see any of your friends here. What's up with that?"

"Nothin'. I still see my old buddies. I play softball with 'em and go bowling. But they're not really Abby's friends."

"Is that…okay?" Margaret asked, a worried look crossing her face.

"Yes, Mom. We each have our separate friends. Nothing to worry about."

"Worried? Who says I'm worried?"

"You've got the look you get whenever I tell you anything that makes you think there could possibly be a hint of a problem with me and Abby." Trevor and Jennifer chuckled, watching the interplay.

"I just don't want you two to…drift apart."

"Mom, we're together almost twenty-four hours a day! We need a little space once in a while. It's healthy to have separate interests."

"Just don't have too many," Margaret said.

"I'm never gonna want to go to church with Abby. She's never gonna want to play softball. But I don't think those little differences are gonna hurt us. I'm always ready to get home to her, Mom. That's what matters." She looked around. "As a matter of fact, it's been too long since I've seen her. I'm gonna find my girl…even if she's wrestling with the caterer."

It took longer than Clancy thought it would, and she was nearly ready to ask for help when she finally found her partner in the front yard. Clancy stood with her arms crossed over her chest, watching as Abby escorted a couple around the space, pointing out various plants as they walked. She knew the people were friends from Abby's church, but she couldn't recall their names. In just a few seconds, Abby looked up and saw Clancy standing in the doorway. A bright smile settled on her face, and she waved, signaling Clancy to join her.

When Clancy ambled over, Abby extended her hand, and Clancy took it. "Derek, Marsha, this is my spouse, Clancy O'Connor." She pulled Clancy toward her and said, "Derek and Marsha just renovated a house in Bungalow Heaven. They'd like their front yard to reflect the style of the house. Maybe make it look like it might have in 1915."

"You know when your house was built?" Clancy asked.

"We know a lot about our place," Marsha said. "We bought it from the daughter of the original owner." She laughed wryly. "They bought a kit from the Ready-Cut Bungalow Company for $650. Then they spent another $100 for plumbing…and that was the extent of their outlay. Remarkable, huh?"

"I'll say. I bet that was the best investment that family ever made."

"I hope the same holds true for us," Derek said. "It seemed like we'd never stop writing checks."

Clancy chuckled. "Don't stop now. A good landscape plan can make a house a home."

"We don't have this kind of space, of course, but I'd love just a few of the things you two have done here."

"You're talking to the right woman," Clancy said, draping her arm around Abby's shoulders. "Abby did the front all on her own. And that was before she got her landscape designer's training. She's got a real gift for horticulture."

"I love it," Abby said, blushing under Clancy's praise.

"If you want a testament for what a landscape can do for your home, just look across the street." All heads turned. "That house is approximately the same size and has a bigger lawn. But they've just planted a lawn and put a few pittisporum tobiras near the porch."

"It looks…" Marsha's eyebrows scrunched together. "You hardly notice the house. I wouldn't have noticed it was a Craftsman."

"Exactly!" Abby said. "A good design guides the eye. It should capture your attention at the property line and not let you look away until you're compelled to look at the house."

"We've been thinking we could do it ourselves, but we don't really know the first thing about gardening. I just hate to have gone this far and then drop the ball."

"We don't have to do everything at once," Abby said. "We can meet and discuss your vision. Then I can design a plan and give you fully detailed planting directions.

We'll be happy to pick out the plants and get them in the ground, but it's a good way to save money if you don't mind doing the labor yourselves."

"How much would the plan cost?" Derek asked.

"Less than the original house," Clancy teased. "Not bad for almost a hundred years of inflation."

"Okay. Let's do it," Derek said. "We can't scrimp now. We're gonna live in that house a long time. Heck, I'd like one of our kids to be living there a hundred years from now."

"That's the ideal view for landscaping," Clancy said. "It's a long-term project."

"I'll call you to set up a time to come by your house," Abby said. "I think I'm free near the end of the week, or I can always come by on the weekend, if that's better for you."

"Great!" Marsha said. "I'm really looking forward to this!"

"Me, too," Abby said.

"I could use some of that delicious lemonade," Marsha said.

"Don't have much if you're driving," Clancy said, earning an elbow from Abby.

"Family joke," Abby said. "We'll be right in."

As soon as the couple was out of earshot, Clancy said, "You don't even take your birthday off? You're a workaholic!"

"Oh, I am not. You know this is more like fun than a job for me."

"You bring in a lot of business for a hobbyist, sweetie."

"You know I don't fool around when I put my heart into something."

Clancy put her arms around Abby, giving her a love-filled hug. "Why don't we get rid of these people so you can put your heart into fooling around with me?" She rocked gently back and forth, smiling sexily at her partner.

"We could sneak upstairs for an hour. No one would miss us."

"I need more than an hour." She kissed Abby gently, smiling when she felt her partner flinch and sneak a look over her shoulder. "Still worried about the neighbors, baby?"

Abby dropped her head, letting it rest against Clancy's sternum. "Caught again."

Clancy tenderly lifted her chin, looking into her eyes with affection. "There's nothing wrong with wanting to keep our private life private. I never mean to make you uncomfortable."

"You don't—"

Clancy cut her off by pressing a finger against her lips. "It does make you uncomfortable to have your neighbors see me kissing you. I know you're fine with being affectionate, but I shouldn't take it too far." She slid her finger across Abby's soft lips, her gaze heating up. "You're just so luscious that I forget where we are."

Turning, Clancy took Abby's hand and led her up to the porch. It was deep and cool and shaded. The trees and plants left the east side of the space well hidden from the street, and that's where they'd moved the loveseat after they'd become intimate.

They sat down, and Abby immediately swung her legs over Clancy's, a pose she'd adopted soon after their relationship had begun. Whenever they were alone, Clancy knew she could count on at least one leg resting over hers. It was sometimes seductive, sometimes playful, and always soothing. She ran her hand up Abby's bare thigh, forcing herself to stay within a few inches of the hem of her dress. "Happy?" she asked.

"Very." Abby kissed her, breathing in slowly while their lips met. "I'm having a very nice birthday."

Clancy touched the corner of one of Abby's eyes. "Got a little something going on in those eyes. Sadness...melancholy...something."

With a crooked grin, Abby said, "I can't keep anything from you! It's still a little hard to get used to...even after all these years."

"Does it bother you, baby?"

Abby rested her cheek on Clancy's shoulder. "No, no, it doesn't bother me. It's just...not something I had to worry about with Will. I could hide anything I wanted from him."

With gentle fingers Clancy stroked Abby's face. "What do you want to hide?"

"Kinda defeats the purpose, doesn't it?" Abby asked wryly. "If I tell you, it's not hidden."

"True. But once you share it, you only have to keep half."

Abby lifted her head and kissed her partner's cheek. "I'm still not sure I buy that." She looked into Clancy's eyes and was quiet for a few seconds. Her features softened, and she said, "I'm a little depressed. It's...hard for me to have a birthday now."

"Now?"

"Since we've been together. Hitting 50 was a tough one, and it still rankles me to be in my 50s and have you be in your 30s. Two decades seems so...vast."

Clancy gazed at her partner for a bit and then surprised herself by saying. "I...I don't like it either."

A flash of pain streaked across Abby's features. "You...?"

"I wish I were in my 50s or that you were in your 30s. I wish...I wish we were the same age...which age doesn't matter."

Searching her eyes, Abby said, "You've never, ever said anything like that before. You always say it doesn't matter or shrug it off."

"I know I have. But lately, I've wanted to pull you back. To keep you from getting older. I want you to stay the same and let me catch up with you." Tears started to streak down her face, and Clancy rubbed at her eyes with her fists. "Damn it!"

"Tell me," Abby murmured, kissing Clancy's cheeks. "Tell me what's on your mind."

"It's...it's silly, really. You've got better genes than I have. You'll probably easily outlive me." She looked into Abby's eyes, trying to hide her fears but knowing she couldn't. "I can't bear the thought of being without you. The odds...they're not great. If we were the same age, we'd have a better chance of—"

"What?" Abby asked, a very thin laugh escaping. "Dying on the same day?" She took Clancy's chin in her fingers and placed soft kisses on every feature. "You could fall out of a tree tomorrow, sweetheart, or you could live for 40 years after I'm gone. No guarantees—for any of us."

"I know that. I really do know that. But being with you and seeing what losing Will did to your heart…" She closed her eyes as more tears leaked out. "I can't stand to think about it."

Abby was quiet for a minute, gently catching the tears that fell from Clancy's eyes with her fingers and sliding them from her cheeks. "Do you ever regret—"

"No!" Clancy could feel her heart racing. "Never! If I knew that we'd only have a year together, I wouldn't have hesitated to love you." She slid her arm down and around Abby's back, holding her close. "I could no more have stopped myself from loving you than I could flap my arms and fly. You're the one…the only woman I've ever truly loved." She kissed Abby, trying to convey in a kiss the love that surged through her body. "I will love you until the day I die," she whispered fervently.

They held each other for a long time, with Clancy holding on so tightly that Abby was eventually sitting completely on her lap. Their heads were side by side, with just a gentle caress of cheek moving against cheek, nuzzling each other while their emotions settled. "I'm sorry," Clancy finally said. "I shouldn't have said something like that on your birthday."

"My birthday's next week," Abby reminded her. "Today's just a party. We can get all of our dark feelings out of the way so we can enjoy the actual day." She kissed Clancy's damp cheek. "Can you do that, baby?"

Clancy nodded. "This doesn't happen to me very often. I don't…allow myself to think about the future too much. It doesn't…it's not how I like to live. Being in the moment works so much better for me."

"Then let's get back there," Abby said, her eyes brightening. "Let's be completely and totally in the moment."

"Mmm." Clancy rested her head on Abby's shoulder. "I wanna be in your arms…in our bed…making sweet, sweet love to you in this moment. We're gonna have to put the moment on hold."

"Ha!" Abby slid off Clancy's lap, giggling when Clancy slipped her hand up her dress and scratched her thighs. "You call yourself extemporaneous!"

"Huh-uh," Clancy said. "I'm pretty sure I've never used that word."

"Well, I'm using it now," Abby said. They walked into the house together, Clancy repeatedly giving Abby a puzzled look as they walked around the entire party, saying hello to everyone and refilling drinks. When they'd spoken to everyone, Abby approached Pam, who was in the kitchen talking with the caterer about her and Maria's upcoming anniversary party. Abby twitched her head, calling her aside. "Do me a favor?"

"Sure." Pam looked at Clancy, who looked puzzled. "What is it?"

"If anyone asks, say we went to buy more wine."

Pam pointedly looked at the case of white wine on the counter.

"Two favors," Abby said. "Have the caterer put that wine in the garage."

"What's going on?"

"I have to go live in the moment," Abby said, grinning lasciviously at Clancy. "But I don't want everyone to know what a terrible hostess I am."

Seeing the women eyeing each other like decadent desserts in a bakery window, Pam got the message. "Go for it, girls. I'll cover for you…just don't fall asleep like we do."

Clancy was already backing up, holding Abby's hand as she tugged her toward the staircase. "No sleeping," she said, her eyes boring into Abby. "Not a chance."

Abby waved goodbye and then turned and chased Clancy up the stairs. "I can still catch you, you little scamp!"

As soon as they reached their room, both of them panting, Clancy stopped and wrapped her arms around her lover and asked in a husky voice. "You've got me. What are you gonna do with me?"

"I," Abby said, latching her mouth onto Clancy's neck and biting it while she blindly kicked the door closed with her foot, "am going to make you moan, pant, gasp, groan, cry, plead, and howl. And you're going to love every minute of it." She leaned over and let their noses touch. "That's a promise."

Clancy slipped her hand up Abby's body, grasping the ring that marked her breast and signified the permanence of their love. Her heart was beating heavily, and she felt the humid, warm bit of air they shared on her lips. "What am I gonna do with you?"

"Whatever you want. Anything…everything you want."

"That's a dangerous offer." Clancy's voice was low and soft, and her whole body tingled with promise.

Abby's hands went to her shoulders and gently pushed against her so she could see her eyes. "I know," she whispered solemnly. "I trust you. With my heart…with my life…with my soul. I gave myself to you for the first time six years ago, and I give myself to you every time we make love. I'm yours."

She kissed Clancy so fiercely that a jolt of desire hit Clancy so hard that she stumbled backward. After collecting her wits, Clancy said, "And I'm yours, baby. Forever."

"Forever can't start fast enough!" Abby kicked off her shoes, and Clancy did the same. Then they started to race to undress, both of them laughing as clothes flew around the room. Abby finished just behind Clancy, so she made up time by leaping onto the bed from five feet away. Clancy jumped onto the bed just after she did, and they grasped each other and started to wrestle, giggling with delight as they grappled.

Abby maneuvered Clancy onto her back, grinning at her with lust in her eyes. "Submit," she growled.

Clancy's muscles relaxed, and she smiled when Abby lowered herself onto her body. "Always. I'll never refuse you, Abby. Never."

"Live in the moment," Abby whispered. "Be with me…right here…right now. Let the future go."

Blinking slowly, Clancy focused on her lover. She wiped all stray thoughts from her mind and concentrated on the delightful, wonderful woman whose beautiful body lay upon hers. "I'm yours now, and now is a very, very wondrous time."

The End